D0295232

Michael Crichton

Michael Crichton

Rising Sun

The Andromeda Strain

Binary

This edition first published by Cresset Editions in 1994
an imprint of the Random House Group
20 Vauxhall Bridge Road
London SW1V 2SA

ISBN 0 09 178585 5

Typeset in Baskerville 10/11.5 by
Pure Tech Corporation, Pondicherry, India
Printed and bound by
Mackays of Chatham PLC, Chatham, Kent

CONTENTS

ACKNOWLEDGEMENTS

For advice and assistance during my research, I am grateful to Nina Easton, James Flanigan, Ken Reich, and David Shaw, all of the *Los Angeles Times*; Steve Clemons of the Japan America Society of Southern California; Senator Al Gore; Jim Wilson of the Jet Propulsion Laboratory; Kevin O'Connor of Hewlett-Packard; Lieutenant Fred Nixon of the Los Angeles Police Department; Ron Insana of CNBC/FNN; and Keith Manasco. For suggestions and corrections of the manuscript at various points, I am indebted to Mike Backes, Douglas Crichton, James Fallows, Karel van Wolferen, and Sonny Mehta. Valery Wright shepherded the manuscript through seemingly endless revisions, Shinoi Osuka and later Sumi Adachi Sovak assisted ably with the Japanese text, and Roger McPeek gave me his understanding of video technology and future security systems.

The subject of Japanese-American relations is highly controversial. I wish to state clearly that the views expressed in this novel are my own, and are not to be attributed to any of the individuals listed above.

Rising Sun

To my mother,
Zula Miller Crichton

We are entering a world where the old rules no longer apply

— Phillip Sanders

Business is war

— Japanese motto

LOS ANGELES POLICE DEPARTMENT
CONFIDENTIAL TRANSCRIPT
OF INTERNAL RECORDS

Contents: Transcript of Video Interrogation
Detective Peter J. Smith
March 13-15

re: 'Nakamoto Murder' (A8895-404)

This transcript is the property of the Los Angeles Police Department and is for internal use only. Permission to copy, quote from, or otherwise reproduce or reveal the contents of this document is limited by law. Unauthorized use carries severe penalties.

Direct all inquiries to:

Commanding Officer
Internal Affairs Division
Los Angeles Police Department
PO Box 2029
Los Angeles, CA 92038-2029
Telephone: (213) 555-7600
Telefax: (213) 555-7812

Video Interrogation: Det. P.J. Smith
3/13-3/15

Case: 'Nakamoto Murder'

Description of interrogation: Subject (Lt. Smith) was interrogated for 22 hours over 3 days from Monday, March 13 to Wednesday, March 15. Interview was recorded on S-VHS/SD videotape.
Description of image: Subject (Smith) seated at desk in Video Room #4, LAPD HQ. Clock visible on the wall behind subject. Image includes surface of desk, coffee cup, and subject from the waist up. Subject wears coat and tie (day 1); shirt and tie (day 2); and shirt-sleeves only (day 3). Video timecode in lower right corner.

Purpose of interrogation: Clarification of subject role in 'Nakamoto Murder.' (A8895-404) Officers in charge of the interrogation were Det. T. Conway and Det. P. Hammond. Subject waived his right to an attorney.

Disposition of case: Filed as 'case unsolved.'

Transcript of: March 13 (1)

INT: Okay. The tape is running. State your name for the record, please.

SUBJ: Peter James Smith.

INT: State your age and rank.

SUBJ: I'm thirty-four years old. Lieutenant, Special Services Division. Los Angeles Police Department.

INT: Lieutenant Smith, as you know, you are not being charged with a crime at this time.

SUBJ: I know.

INT: Nevertheless you have a right to be represented here by an attorney.

SUBJ: I waive that right.

INT: Okay. And have you been coerced to come here in any way?

SUBJ: (long pause) No. I have not been coerced in any way.

INT: Okay. Now we want to talk to you about the Nakamoto Murder. When did you first become involved in that case?

SUBJ: On Thursday night, February 9, about nine o'clock.

INT: What happened at that time?

SUBJ: I was at home. I got a phone call.

INT: And what were you doing at the time you got the call?

First Night

Actually, I was sitting on my bed in my apartment in Culver City, watching the Lakers game with the sound turned off, while I tried to study vocabulary for my introductory Japanese class.

It was a quiet evening; I had gotten my daughter to sleep about eight. Now I had the cassette player on the bed, and the cheerful woman's voice was saying things like, 'Hello, I am a police officer. Can I be of assistance?' and 'Please show me the menu.' After each sentence, she paused for me to repeat it back, in Japanese. I stumbled along as best I could. Then she would say, 'The vegetable store is closed. Where is the post office?' Things like that. Sometimes it was hard to concentrate, but I was trying. 'Mr Hayashi has two children.'

I tried to answer. '*Hayashi-san wa kodomo ga fur . . . futur . . .*' I swore. But by then the woman was talking again.

'This drink is not very good at all.'

I had my textbook open on the bed, alongside a Mr Potato Head I'd put back together for my daughter. Next to that, a photo album, and the pictures from her second birthday party. It was four months after Michelle's party, but I still put the pictures in the album. You have to try and keep up with that stuff.

'There will be a meeting at two o'clock.'

The pictures on my bed didn't reflect reality any more. Four months later, Michelle looked completely different. She was taller; she'd outgrown the expensive party dress my ex-wife had bought for her: black velvet with a white lace collar.

In the photos, my ex-wife plays a prominent role – holding the cake as Michelle blows out the candles, helping her unwrap the presents. She looks like a dedicated mom. Actually, my daughter lives with me, and my ex-wife doesn't see much of her. She doesn't show up for weekend visitation half the time, and she misses child-support payments.

But you'd never know from the birthday photos.

'Where is the toilet?'

'I have a car. We can go together.'

I continued studying. Of course, officially I was on duty that night: I was a Special Services officer on call for division headquarters downtown.

But February ninth was a quiet Thursday, and I didn't expect much action. Until nine o'clock, I only had three calls.

Special Services includes the diplomatic section of the police department; we handle problems with diplomats and celebrities, and provide translators and liaison for foreign nationals who come into contact with the police for one reason or another. It's varied work, but not stressful: when I'm on call I can expect a half-dozen requests for help, none of them emergencies. I hardly ever have to roll out. It's much less demanding than being a police press liaison, which is what I did before Special Services.

Anyway, on the night of February ninth, the first call I got concerned Fernando Conseca, the Chilean vice-consul. A patrol car had pulled him over, Ferny was too drunk to drive, but he was claiming diplomatic immunity. I told the patrolmen to drive him home, and I made a note to complain to the consulate again in the morning.

Then an hour later, I got a call from detectives in Gardena. They'd arrested a suspect in a restaurant shooting who spoke only Samoan, and they wanted a translator. I said I could get one, but that Samoans invariably spoke English; the country had been an American trust territory for years. The detectives said they'd handle it. Then I got a call that mobile television vans were blocking fire lanes at the Aerosmith concert; I told the officers to give it to the fire department. And it was quiet for the next hour. I went back to my textbook and my sing-song woman saying things like, 'Yesterday's weather was rainy.'

Then Tom Graham called.

'It's the fucking Japs,' Graham said. 'I can't believe they're pulling this shit. Better get over here, Petey-san. Eleven hundred Figueroa, corner of Seventh. It's the new Nakamoto building.'

'What is the problem?' I had to ask. Graham is a good detective but he has a bad temper, and he tends to blow things out of proportion.

'The problem,' Graham said, 'is that the fucking Japs are demanding to see the fucking Special Services liaison. Which is you, buddy. They're saying the police can't proceed until the liaison gets here.'

'Can't proceed? Why? What have you got?'

'Homicide,' Graham said. 'Caucasian female approximately twenty-five years old, apparent six-oh-one. Lying flat on her back, right in their damn boardroom. Quite a sight. You better get down here as soon as you can.'

I said, 'Is that music in the background?'

'Hell, yes,' Graham said. 'There's a big party going on. Tonight is the grand opening of the Nakamoto Tower, and they're having a reception. Just get down here, will you?'

I said I would. I called Mrs Ascenio next door, and asked her if she would watch the baby while I was gone; she always needed extra money. While I waited for her to arrive I changed my shirt and put on my good suit. Then Fred Hoffmann called. He was watch commander at DHD downtown; a short, tough guy with gray hair. 'Listen, Pete. I think you might want help on this one.'

I said, 'Why is that?'

'Sounds like we got a homicide involving Japanese nationals. It may be sticky. How long have you been a liaison?'

'About six months,' I said.

'If I was you, I'd get some experienced help. Pick up Connor and take him downtown with you.'

'Who?'

'John Connor. Ever heard of him?'

'Sure,' I said. Everyone in the division had heard of Connor. He was a legend, the most knowledgeable of the Special Services officers. 'But isn't he retired?'

'He's on indefinite leave, but he still works cases involving the Japanese. I think he could be helpful to you. Tell you what. I'll call him for you. You just go down and pick him up.' Hoffman gave me his address.

'Okay, fine. Thanks.'

'And one other thing. Land lines on this one, okay, Pete?'

'Okay,' I said. 'Who requested that?'

'It's just better.'

'Whatever you say, Fred.'

Land lines meant to stay off the radios, so our transmissions wouldn't be picked up by the media monitoring police frequencies. It was standard procedure in certain situations. Whenever Elizabeth Taylor went to the hospital, we went to land lines. Or if the teenage son of somebody famous died in a car crash, we'd go to land lines to make sure the parents got the news before the TV crews started banging on their door. We used land lines for that kind of thing. I'd never heard it invoked in a homicide before.

But driving downtown, I stayed off the car phone, and listened to the radio. There was a report of a shooting of a three-year-old boy who was now paralyzed from the waist down. The child was a bystander during a 7-Eleven robbery. A stray bullet hit him in the spine and he was –

I switched to another station, got a talk show. Ahead, I could see the lights of the downtown skyscrapers, rising into mist. I got off the freeway at San Pedro, Connor's exit.

What I knew about John Connor was that he had lived for a time in Japan, where he acquired his knowledge of Japanese language and culture. At one point, back in the 1960s, he was the only officer who spoke fluent Japanese, even though Los Angeles then had the largest Japanese population outside the home islands.

Now, of course, the department has more then eighty officers who speak Japanese – and more, like me, who are trying to learn. Connor had retired several years before. But the liaison officers who worked with him agreed he was the best. He was said to work very fast, often solving cases in a few hours. He had a reputation as a skilled detective and an extraordinary interviewer, able to get information from witnesses like nobody else. But most of all, the other liaisons praised his even-handed approach. One said to me, 'Working with the Japanese is like balancing on a tightrope. Sooner or later, everybody falls off on one side or the other. Some people decide the Japanese are fabulous and can do no wrong. Some people decide they're vicious pricks. But Connor always keeps his balance. He stays in the middle. He always knows exactly what he is doing.'

John Connor lived in the industrial area off Seventh Street, in a large brick warehouse alongside a diesel truck depot. The freight elevator in the building was broken. I walked upstairs to the third floor and knocked on his door.

'It's open,' a voice said.

I entered a small apartment. The living room was empty, and furnished in the Japanese style: tatami mats, shoji screens, and wood-paneled walls. A calligraphy scroll, a black lacquer table, a vase with a single splash of white orchid.

I saw two pairs of shoes set out beside the door. One was a man's brogues. The other was a pair of women's high heels.

I said, 'Captain Connor?'

'Just a minute.'

A shoji screen slid back and Connor appeared. He was surprisingly tall, maybe a hundred and ninety centimeters, well over six feet. He wore a *yukata,* a light Japanese robe of blue cotton. I estimated he was fifty-five years old. Broad-shouldered, balding, with a trim moustache, sharp features, piercing eyes. Deep voice. Calm.

'Good evening, Lieutenant.'

We shook hands. Connor looked me up and down, and nodded approvingly. 'Good. Very presentable.'

I said, 'I used to work press. You never knew when you might have to appear in front of cameras.'

He nodded. 'And now you're the SSO on call?'

'That's right.'

'How long have you been a liaison?'

'Six months.'

'You speak Japanese?'

'A little. I'm taking lessons.'

'Give me a few minutes to change.' He turned and disappeared behind the shoji screen. 'This is a homicide?'

'Yes.'

'Who notified you?'

'Tom Graham. He's the OIC at the crime scene. He said the Japanese were insisting on a liaison officer being present.'

'I see.' There was a pause. I heard running water. 'Is that a common request?'

'No. In fact, I've never heard of it happening. Usually, officers call for a liaison because they have a language problem. I've never heard of the Japanese asking for a liaison.'

'Neither have I,' Connor said. 'Did Graham ask you to bring me? Because Tom Graham and I don't always admire each other.'

'No,' I said. 'Fred Hoffmann suggested I bring you in. He felt I didn't have enough experience. He said he was going to call you for me.'

'Then you were called at home twice?' Connor said.

'Yes.'

'I see.' He reappeared, wearing a dark blue suit, knotting his tie. 'It seems that time is critical.' He glanced at his watch. 'When did Graham call you?'

'About nine.'

'Then forty minutes have already passed. Let's go, Lieutenant. Where's your car?'

We hurried downstairs.

I drove up San Pedro and turned left onto Second, heading toward the Nakamoto building. There was a light mist at street level. Connor stared out the window. He said, 'How good is your memory?'

'Pretty good, I guess.'

'I wonder if you could repeat for me the telephone conversations you had tonight,' he said. 'Give them to me in as much detail as possible. Word for word, if you can.'

'I'll try.'

I recounted my phone calls. Connor listened without interruption or comment. I didn't know why he was so interested, and he didn't tell me. When I finished, he said, 'Hoffmann didn't tell you who called for land lines?'

'No.'

'Well, it's a good idea in any case. I never use a car phone if I can help it. These days, too many people listen in.'

I turned onto Figueroa. Up ahead I saw searchlights shining in front of the new Nakamoto Tower. The building itself was gray granite, rising up into the night. I got into the right lane and flipped open the glove box to grab a handful of business cards.

The cards said Detective Lieutenant Peter J. Smith, Special Services Liaison Officer, Los Angeles Police Department. Printed in English on one side, in Japanese on the back.

Connor looked at the cards. 'How do you want to handle this situation, Lieutenant? Have you negotiated with the Japanese before?'

I said, 'Not really, no. Couple of drunk driving arrests.'

Connor said politely, 'Then perhaps I can suggest a strategy for us to follow.'

'That's fine with me,' I said. 'I'd be grateful for your help.'

'All right. Since you're the liaison, it's probably best if you take charge of the scene when we arrive.'

'Okay.'

'Don't bother to introduce me, or refer to me in any way. Don't even look in my direction.'

'Okay.'

'I am a nonentity. You alone are in charge.'

'Okay, fine.'

'It'll help to be formal. Stand straight, and keep your suit jacket buttoned at all times. If they bow to you, don't bow back – just give a little head nod. A foreigner will never master the etiquette of bowing. Don't even try.'

'Okay,' I said.

'When you start to deal with the Japanese, remember that they don't like to negotiate. They find it too confrontational. In their own society they avoid it whenever possible.'

'Okay.'

'Control your gestures. Keep your hands at your sides. The Japanese find big arm movements threatening. Speak slowly. Keep your voice calm and even.'

'Okay.'

'If you can.'

'Okay.'

'It may be difficult to do. The Japanese can be irritating. You'll probably find them irritating tonight. Handle it as best you can. But whatever happens, don't lose your temper.'

'All right.'

'That's extremely bad form.'

'All right,' I said.

Connor smiled. 'I'm sure you'll do well,' he said. 'You probably won't need my help at all. But if you get stuck, you'll hear me say 'Perhaps I can be of assistance.' That will be the signal that I'm taking over. From that point on, let me do the talking. I'd prefer you not speak again, even if you are spoken to directly by them. Okay?'

'Okay.'

'You may want to speak, but don't be drawn out.'

'I understand.'

'Furthermore, whatever I do, show no surprise. *Whatever* I do.'

'Okay.'

'Once I take over, move so that you're standing slightly behind me and to my right. Never sit. Never look around. Never appear distracted. Remember that although you come from an MTV video culture, they do not. They are Japanese. Everything you do will have meaning to them. Every aspect of your appearance and behavior will reflect on you, on the police department, and on me as your superior and *sempai*.'

'Okay, Captain.'

'Any questions?'

'What's a *sempai*?'

Connor smiled.

We drove past the searchlights, down the ramp into the underground garage.

'In Japan,' he said, 'a *sempai* is a senior man who guides a junior man, known as a *kōhai*. The *sempai-kōhai* relationship is quite common. It's often assumed to exist whenever a younger man and an older man are working together. They will probably assume it of us.'

I said, 'Sort of a mentor and apprentice?'

'Not exactly,' Connor said. 'In Japan, *sempai-kōhai* has a different quality. More like a fond parent: the *sempai* is expected to indulge his *kōhai*, and put up with all sorts of youthful excesses and errors from the junior man.' He smiled. 'But I'm sure you won't do that to me.'

We came to the bottom of the ramp, and saw the flat expanse of the parking garage ahead of us. Connor stared out of the window and frowned. 'Where is everybody?'

The garage of the Nakamoto Tower was full of limousines, the drivers leaning against their cars, talking and smoking. But I saw no police cars. Ordinarily, when there's a homicide, the place is lit up like Christmas, with lights flashing from a half-dozen black and whites, the medical examiner, paramedics, and all the rest.

But there was nothing tonight. It just looked like a garage where somebody was having a party: elegant people standing in clusters, waiting for their cars.

'Interesting,' I said.

We came to a stop. The parking attendants opened the doors, and I stepped out onto plush carpet, and heard soft music. I walked with Connor toward the elevator. Welldressed people were coming the other way: men in tuxedos, women in expensive gowns. And standing by the elevator, wearing a stained corduroy coat and furiously smoking a cigarette, was Tom Graham.

When Graham played halfback at U.S.C. he never made first string. That bit of history stuck like a character trait: all his life he seemed to miss the crucial promotion, the next step up a detective's career. He had transferred from one division to another, never finding a precinct that suited him, or a partner that worked well with him. Always too outspoken, Graham had made enemies in the chief's office, and at thirty-nine, further advancement was unlikely. Now he was bitter, gruff, and putting on weight – a big man who had become ponderous, and a pain in the ass: he just rubbed people the wrong way. His idea of personal integrity was to be a failure, and he was sarcastic about anybody who didn't share his views.

'Nice suit,' he said to me, as I walked up. 'You look fucking beautiful, Peter.' He flicked imaginary dust off my lapel.

I ignored it. 'How's it going, Tom?'

'You guys should be attending this party, not working it.' He turned to Connor and shook his head. 'Hello, John. Whose idea was it to get you out of bed?'

'I'm just observing,' Connor said mildly.

I said, 'Fred Hoffmann asked me to bring him down.'

'Hell,' Graham said. 'It's okay with me that you're here. I can use some help. It's pretty tense up there.'

We followed him toward the elevator. I still saw no other police officers. I said, 'Where is everybody?'

'Good question,' Graham said. 'They've managed to keep all of our people around back at the freight entrance. They claim the service elevator gives fastest access. And they keep talking about the importance of their grand opening, and how nothing must disrupt it.'

By the elevators, a uniformed Japanese private security guard looked us over carefully. 'These two are with me,' Graham said. The security man nodded, but squinted at us suspiciously.

We got on the elevator.

'Fucking Japanese,' Graham said, as the doors closed. 'This is still our country. We're still the fucking police in our own country.'

The elevator was glass walled and we looked out on downtown Los Angeles as it went up into the light mist. Directly across was the Arco building. All lit up at night.

'You know these elevators are illegal,' Graham said. 'According to code, no glass elevators past ninety floors, and this building is ninety-seven floors, the highest building in L.A. But then this whole building is one big special case. And they got it up in six months. You know how? They brought in prefab units from Nagasaki, and slapped them together here. Didn't use American construction workers. Got a special permit to bypass our unions because of a so-called technical problem that only Japanese workers could handle. You believe that shit?'

I shrugged. 'They got it past the American unions.'

'Hell, they got it past the *city council*,' Graham said. 'But of course that's just money. And if there's one thing we know, the Japanese have money. So they got variances on the zoning restrictions, the earthquake ordinances. They got everything they wanted.'

I shrugged. 'Politics.'

'My ass. You know they don't even pay tax? That's right: they got an eight-year break on property taxes from the city. Shit: we're *giving* this country away.'

We rode for a moment in silence. Graham stared out the windows. The elevators were high-speed Hitachis, using the latest technology. The fastest and smoothest elevators in the world. We moved higher into the mist.

I said to Graham, 'You want to tell us about this homicide, or do you want it to be a surprise?'

'Fuck,' Graham said. He flipped open his notebook. 'Here you go. The original call was at eight thirty-two. Somebody saying there is a 'problem of disposition of a body.' Male with a thick Asian accent, doesn't speak good English. The operator couldn't get much out of him, except an address. The Nakamoto Tower. Black and white goes over, arrives at eight thirty-nine p.m., finds it's a homicide. Forty-sixth floor, which is an office floor in this building. Victim is Caucasian female, approximately twenty-five years old. Hell of a good-looking girl. You'll see.

'The blue suits stretch the tape and call the division. I go over with Merino, arriving at eight fifty-three. Crime scene IU and SID show up about the same time for PE, prints, and pics. Okay so far?'

'Yes,' Connor said, nodding.

Graham said, 'We're just getting started when some Jap from the Nakamoto Corporation comes up in a thousand-dollar blue suit and announces that he is entitled to a fucking conversation with the L.A.P.D. liaison officer before anything is done in their fucking building. And he's saying things like we got no probable cause.

'I go, what the fuck is this. We got an obvious homicide here. I think this guy should get back. But this Jap speaks excellent fucking English and he seems to know a lot of law. And everybody at the scene becomes, you know, concerned. I mean, there's no point in pushing to start an investigation if it's going to invalidate due process, right? And this Jap fucker is insisting the liaison must be present before we do anything. Since he speaks such fucking good English I don't know what the problem is. I thought the whole idea of a liaison was for people who don't speak the language and this fucking guy has Stanford law school written all over him. But anyway.' He sighed.

'You called me,' I said.

'Yeah.'

I said, 'Who is the man from Nakamoto?'

'Shit.' Graham scowled at his notes. 'Ishihara. Ishiguri. Something like that.'

'You have his card? He must have given you his card.'

'Yeah, he did. I gave it to Merino.'

I said, 'Any other Japanese there?'

'What are you, kidding?' Graham laughed. 'The place is swarming with them. Fucking Disneyland up there.'

'I mean the crime scene.'

'So do I,' Graham said. 'We can't keep 'em out. They say it's their building, they have a right to be there. Tonight is the grand opening of the Nakamoto Tower. They have a right to be there. On and on.'

I said, 'Where is the opening taking place?'

'One floor below the murder, on the forty-fifth floor. They're having one hell of a bash. Must be eight hundred people there. Movie stars, senators, congressmen, you name it. I hear Madonna is there, and Tom Cruise. Senator Hammond. Senator Kennedy. Elton John. Senator Morton. Mayor Thomas's there. District Attorney Wyland's there. Hey, maybe your ex-wife is there, too, Pete. She still works for Wyland, doesn't she?'

'Last I heard.'

Graham sighed. 'Must be great to fuck a lawyer, instead of getting fucked by them. Must make for a nice change.'

I didn't want to talk about my ex-wife. 'We don't have a lot of contact any more,' I said.

A little bell rang, then the elevator said, '*Yonjūsan-kai.*'

Graham glanced at the glowing numbers above the door. 'Can you believe that shit?'

'*Yonjūyon-kai,*' the elevator said. '*Mōsugu de gozaimasu.*'

'What'd it say?'

'We're almost at the floor.'

'Fuck,' Graham said. 'If an elevator's going to talk, it should be English. This is still America.'

'Just barely,' Connor said, staring out at the view.

'*Yonjūgo-kai,*' the elevator said.

The door opened.

Graham was right: it was a hell of a party. The whole floor had been made into a replica forties ballroom. Men in suits. Women in cocktail dresses. The band playing Glenn Miller swing music. Standing near the elevator door was a gray-haired, suntanned man who looked vaguely familiar. He had the broad shoulders of an athlete. He stepped onto the elevator and turned to me. 'Ground floor, please.' I smelled whiskey.

A second, younger man in a suit instantly appeared by his side. 'This elevator is going up, Senator.'

'What's that?' the gray-haired man said, turning to his aide.

'This elevator's going up, sir.'

'Well. I *want* to go *down.*' He was speaking with the careful, over-articulated speech of the drunk.

'Yes, sir. I know that, sir,' the aide replied cheerfully. 'Let's take the next elevator, Senator.' He gripped the gray-haired man firmly by the elbow and led him off the elevator.

The doors closed. The elevator continued up.

'Your tax dollars at work,' Graham said. 'Recognize him? Senator Stephen Rowe. Nice to find him partying here, considering he's on the Senate Finance Committee, which sets all Japanese import regulations. But like his pal Senator Kennedy, Rowe is one of the great pussy patrollers.'

'Oh, yeah?'

'They say he can drink pretty good, too.'

'I noticed that.'

'That's why he's got that kid with him. To keep him out of trouble.'

The elevator stopped at the forty-sixth floor. There was a soft electronic ping. '*Yonjūrkou-kai. Goriyou arigatō gozaimashita.*'

'Finally,' Graham said. 'Now maybe we can get to work.'

The doors opened. We faced a solid wall of blue business suits, backs turned to us. There must have been twenty men jammed in the area just beyond the elevator. The air was thick with cigarette smoke.

'Coming through, coming through,' Graham said, pushing his way roughly past the men. I followed, Connor behind me, silent and inconspicuous.

The forty-sixth floor had been designed to house the chief executive offices of Nakamoto Industries, and it was impressive. Standing in the carpeted reception area just beyond the elevators, I could see the entire floor – it was a gigantic open space. It was about sixty by forty meters, half the size of a football field. Everything added to the sense of spaciousness and elegance. The ceilings were high, paneled in wood. The furnishings were all wood and fabric, black and gray, and the carpet was thick. Sound was muted and lights were low, adding to the soft, rich quality. It looked more like a bank than a business office.

The richest bank you ever saw.

And it made you stop and look. I stood by the yellow crime-scene tape, which blocked access to the floor itself, and got my bearings. Directly ahead was the large atrium, a kind of open bullpen for secretaries and lower-level people. There were desks in clusters, and trees to break up the space. In the center of the atrium stood a large model of the Nakamoto Tower, and the complex of surrounding buildings still under construction. A spotlight shone on the model, but the rest of the atrium was relatively dark, with night lights.

Private offices for the executives were arranged around the perimeter of the atrium. The offices had glass walls facing the atrium, and glass walls on the outside wall as well, so that from where I was standing you could look straight out to the surrounding skyscrapers of Los Angeles. It made you think the floor was floating in midair.

There were two glass-walled conference rooms, on the left and right. The room on the right was smaller, and there I saw the body of the girl, lying on a long black table. She was wearing a black dress. One leg dangled down toward the floor. I didn't see any blood. But I was pretty far away from her, maybe sixty meters. It was hard to see much detail.

I heard the crackle of police radios, and I heard Graham saying,

'Here's your liaison, gentlemen. Now maybe we can get started on our investigation. Peter?'

I turned to the Japanese men by the elevator. I didn't know which I should talk to; there was an awkward moment until one of them stepped forward. He was about thirty-five and wore an expensive suit. The man gave a very slight bow, from the neck, just a hint. I bowed back. Then he spoke.

'*Konbanwa. Hajimemashite, Sumisu-san. Ishiguro desu. Dōzo yoroshiku.*' A formal greeting, although perfunctory. No wasted time. His name was Ishiguro. He already knew my name.

I said, '*Hajimemashite. Watashi wa Sumisu desu. Dōzo yoroshiku.*' How do you do. Glad to meet you. The usual.

'*Watashi no meishi desu. Dōzo.*' He gave me his business card. He was quick in his movements, brusque.

'*Dōmo arigatō gozaimasu.*' I accepted his card with both hands, which wasn't really necessary, but taking Connor's advice, I wanted to do the most formal thing. Next I gave him my card. The ritual required us both to look at each other's cards, and to make some minor comment, or to ask a question like 'Is this your office telephone number?'

Ishigura took my card with one hand and said, 'Is this your home phone, Detective?' I was surprised. He spoke the kind of unaccented English you can only learn by living here for a long time, starting when you're young. He must have gone to school here. One of the thousands of Japanese who studied in America in the seventies. When they were sending 150,000 students a year to America, to learn about our country. And we were sending 200 American students a year to Japan.

'That's my number at the bottom, yes,' I said.

Ishiguro slipped my card into his shirt pocket. I started to make a polite comment about his card but he interrupted me. 'Look, Detective. I think we can dispense with the formalities. The only reason there's a problem here tonight is that your colleague is unreasonable.'

'My colleague?'

Ishiguro gave a head jerk. 'The fat one there. Graham. His demands are unreasonable, and we strongly object to his intention to carry out an investigation tonight.'

I said, 'Why is that, Mr Ishiguro?'

'You have no probable cause to conduct one.'

'Why do you say that?'

Ishiguro snorted. 'I would think it's obvious, even to you.'

I stayed cool. Five years as a detective, and then a year in the press section had taught me to stay cool.

I said, 'No, sir, I'm afraid it's not obvious.'

He looked at me disdainfully. 'The fact is, Lieutenant, you have no reason to connect this girl's death to the party we're holding downstairs.'

'It looks like she's wearing a party dress –'

He interrupted me rudely. 'My guess is you'll probably discover that she has died of an accidental drug overdose. And therefore her death has nothing to do with our party. Wouldn't you agree?'

I took a deep breath. 'No, sir, I wouldn't agree. Not without an investigation.' I took another breath. 'Mr Ishiguro, I appreciate your concerns, but –'

'I wonder if you do,' Ishiguro said, interrupting me again. 'I insist that you appreciate the position of the Nakamoto company tonight. This is a very significant evening for us, a very *public* evening. We are naturally distressed by the prospect that our function might be marred by unfounded allegations of a woman's death, especially this, a woman of no importance . . .'

'A woman of no importance?'

Ishiguro made a dismissing wave. He seemed to be tired of talking to me. 'It's obvious, just look at her. She's no better than a common prostitute. I can't imagine how she came to be in this building at all. And for this reason, I strongly protest the intention of Detective Graham to interrogate the guests at the reception downstairs. That's entirely unreasonable. We have many senators, congressmen, and officials of Los Angeles among our guests. Surely you agree that such prominent people will find it awkward –'

I said, 'Just a minute. Detective Graham told you he was going to interrogate everybody at the reception?'

'That is what he said to me. Yes.'

Now, at last, I began to understand why I'd been called. Graham didn't like the Japanese and he had threatened to spoil their evening. Of course it was never going to happen. There was no way Graham was going to interrogate United States senators, let alone the district attorney or the mayor. Not if he expected to come to work tomorrow. But the Japanese annoyed him, and Graham had decided to annoy them back.

I said to Ishiguro, 'We can set up a registration desk downstairs, and your guests can sign as they leave.'

'I am afraid that will be difficult,' Ishigura began, 'because surely you will admit –'

'Mr Ishiguro, that's what we're going to do.'

'But what you ask is extremely difficult –'

'Mr Ishiguro.'

'You see, for us this is going to cause –'

'Mr Ishiguro, I'm sorry. I've just told you what police procedure is going to be.'

He stiffened. There was a pause. He wiped some sweat from his upper lip and said, 'I am disappointed, Lieutenant, not to have greater cooperation from you.'

'Cooperation?' That was when I started to get pissed off. 'Mr Ishiguro, you've got a dead woman in there, and it is our job to investigate what happened to –'

'But you must acknowledge our special circumstances –'

Then I heard Graham say, 'Aw, Christ, *what is this*?'

Looking over my shoulder, I saw a short, bookish Japanese man twenty meters beyond the yellow tape. He was taking pictures of the crime scene. The camera he held was so small it was nearly concealed in the palm of his hand. But he wasn't concealing the fact that he had crossed the tape barrier to take his pictures. As I watched, he moved slowly back toward us, raising his hands for a moment to snap a picture, then blinking behind his wireframe spectacles as he selected his next shot. He was deliberate in his movements.

Graham went up to the tape and said, 'For Christ's sake, get out of there. This is a crime scene. You can't take pictures in there.' The man didn't respond. He kept moving backward. Graham turned away. 'Who is this guy?'

Ishiguro said, 'This is our employee, Mr Tanaka. He works for Nakamoto Security.'

I couldn't believe what I was seeing. The Japanese had their own employee wandering around inside the yellow tapes, contaminating the crime scene. It was outrageous. 'Get him out of there,' I said.

'He is taking pictures.'

'He can't do that.'

Ishiguro said, 'But this is for our corporate use.'

I said, 'I don't care, Mr Ishiguro. He can't be inside the yellow tape, and he can't take pictures. Get him out of there. And I want his film, please.'

'Very well.' Ishiguro said something quickly in Japanese. I turned, just in time to see Tanaka slip under the yellow tape, and disappear among the blue-suited men clustered by the elevator. Behind their heads, I saw the elevator doors open and close.

Son of a bitch. I was getting angry. 'Mr Ishiguro, you are now obstructing an official police investigation.'

Ishiguro said calmly, 'You must try to understand our position, Detective Smith. Of course we have complete confidence in the Los Angeles Police Department, but we must be able to undertake our own private inquiry, and for that we must have –'

Their own private inquiry? The *son of a bitch.* I suddenly couldn't speak. I clenched my teeth, seeing red. I was furious. I wanted to arrest Ishiguro. I wanted to spin him around, shove him up against the wall, and snap the cuffs around his fucking wrists and –

'Perhaps I can be of assistance, Lieutenant,' a voice behind me said.

I turned. It was John Connor, smiling cheerfully.

I stepped aside.

Connor faced Ishiguro, bowed slightly, and presented his card. He spoke rapidly. '*Totsuzen shitsurei desuga, jikoshōkai shitemo yoroshii desuka. Watashi wa John Connor to mōshimasu. Meishi o dōzo. Dōzo yoroshiku.*'

'John Connor?' Ishiguro said. '*The* John Connor? *Omeni kakarete kōei desu. Watashi wa Ishiguro desu. Dōzo yoroshiku.' He was saying he was honoured to meet him.*

'*Watashi no meishi desu. Dōzo.*' A graceful thank you.

But once the formalities were completed, the conversation went so quickly I caught only an occasional word. I was obliged to appear interested, watching and nodding, when in fact I had no idea what they were talking about. Once I heard Connor refer to me as *wakaimono,* which I knew meant his protégé or apprentice. Several times, he looked at me severely, and shook his head like a regretful father. It seemed he was apologizing for me. I also heard him refer to Graham as *bushitsuki,* a disagreeable man.

But these apologies had their effect. Ishiguro calmed down, dropping his shoulders. He began to relax. He even smiled. Finally he said, 'Then you will not check identification of our guests?'

'Absolutely not,' Connor said. 'Your honored guests are free to come and go as they wish.'

I started to protest. Connor shot me a look.

'Identification is unnecessary,' Connor continued, speaking formally, 'because I am sure that no guests of the Nakamoto Corporation could ever be involved in such an unfortunate incident.'

'Fucking A,' Graham said, under his breath.

Ishiguro was beaming. But I was furious. Connor had contradicted me. He had made me look like a fool. And on top of that, he wasn't following police procedure – we could all be in trouble for that later on. Angrily, I shoved my hands in my pockets and looked away.

'I am grateful for your delicate handling of this situation, Captain Connor,' Ishiguro said.

'I have done nothing at all,' Connor replied, making another formal bow. 'But I hope you will now agree it is appropriate to clear the floor, so the police may begin their investigation.'

Ishiguro blinked. 'Clear the floor?'

'Yes,' Connor said, taking out a notebook. 'And please assist me to know the names of the gentlemen standing behind you, as you ask them to leave.'

'I am sorry?'

'The names of the gentlemen behind you, please?'

'May I ask why?'

Connor's face darkened, and he barked a short phrase in Japanese. I didn't catch the words, but Ishiguro turned bright red.

'Excuse me, Captain, but I see no reason for you to speak in this –'

And then, Connor lost his temper. Spectacularly and explosively. He moved close to Ishiguro, making sharp stabbing motions with his finger while he shouted: '*Iikagen ni shiro! Soko o doke! Kiiterunoka!*'

Ishiguro ducked and turned away, stunned by this verbal assault.

Connor leaned over him, his voice hard and sarcastic: '*Doke! Doke! Wakaranainoka?*' He turned, and pointed furiously toward the Japanese men by the elevator. Confronted with Connor's naked anger, the Japanese looked away, and puffed anxiously on their cigarettes. But they did not leave.

'Hey, Richie,' Connor said, calling to the crime unit photographer Richie Walters. 'Get me some IDs of these guys, will you?'

'Sure, Captain,' Richie said. He raised his camera and began moving down the line of men, firing his strobe in quick succession.

Ishiguro suddenly got excited, stepping in front of the camera, holding up his hands. 'Wait a minute, wait a minute, what is this?'

But the Japanese men were already leaving, wheeling away like a school of fish from the strobe flash. In a few seconds they were gone. We had the floor to ourselves. Alone, Ishiguro looked uncomfortable.

He said something in Japanese. Apparently it was the wrong thing.

'Oh?' Connor said. '*You* are to blame here,' he said to Ishiguro. '*You* are the cause of all these troubles. And *you* will see that my detectives get any assistance they need. I want to speak to the person who discovered the body, and the person who called in the original report. I want the name of every person who has been on this floor since the body was discovered. And I want the film from Tanaka's camera. *Ore wa honkida.* I will arrest you if you obstruct this investigation further.'

'But I must consult my superiors –'

'*Nameruna yo.*' Connor leaned close. 'Don't fuck with me, Ishiguro-san. Now leave, and let us work.'

'Of course, Captain,' he said. With a tight, brief bow he left, his face pinched and unhappy.

Graham chuckled. 'You told him off pretty good.'

Connor spun. 'What were you doing, telling him you were going to interrogate everybody at the party?'

'Aw, shit, I was just winding him up,' Graham said. 'There's no way I'm going to interrogate the mayor. Can I help it if these assholes have no sense of humor?'

'They have a sense of humor,' Connor said. 'And the joke is on you. Because Ishiguro had a problem, and he solved it with your help.'

'*My* help?' Graham was frowning. 'What're you talking about?'

'It's clear the Japanese wanted to delay the investigation,' Connor said. 'Your aggressive tactics gave them the perfect excuse – to call for the Special Services liaison.'

'Oh, come on,' Graham said. 'For all they know, the liaison could have been here in five minutes.'

Connor shook his head. 'Don't kid yourself: they knew exactly who was on call tonight. They knew exactly how far away Smith would be, and exactly how long it would take him to get here. And they managed to delay the investigation an hour and a half. Nice work, detective.'

Graham stared at Connor for a long moment. Then he turned away. 'Fuck,' he said. 'That's a load of bullshit, and you know it. Fellas, I'm going to work. Richie? Mount up. You got thirty seconds to document before my guys come in and step on your tail. Let's go, everybody. I want to get finished before she starts to smell too bad.'

And he lumbered off toward the crime scene.

With their suitcases and evidence carts, the SID team trailed after Graham. Richie Walters led the way, shooting left and right as he worked his way forward into the conference room. The walls of the conference room were smoked glass, which dimmed his flash. But I could see him inside, circling the body. He was shooting a lot: he knew this was a big case.

I stayed behind with Connor. I said, 'I thought you told me it was bad form to lose your temper with the Japanese.'

'It is,' Connor said.

'Then why did you lose yours?'

'Unfortunately,' he said, ' it was the only way to assist Ishiguro.'

'To *assist* Ishiguro?'

'Yes. I did all that for Ishiguro – because he had to save face in front of his boss. Ishiguro wasn't the most important man in the room. One of the Japanese standing by the elevator was the *jūyaku,* the real boss.'

'I didn't notice,' I said.

'It's common practice to put a lesser man in front, while the boss stays in the background, where he is free to observe progress. Just as I did with you, *kōhai.*'

'Ishiguro's boss was watching all the time?'

'Yes. And Ishiguro clearly had orders not to allow the investigation to begin. I needed to start the investigation. But I had to do it in such a way that he would not look incompetent. So I played the out-of-control *gaijin.* Now he owes me a favor. Which is good, because I may need his help later on.'

'He owes you a favor?' I said, having trouble with this idea. Connor had just screamed at Ishiguro – thoroughly humiliating him, as far as I was concerned.

Connor sighed. 'Even if you don't understand what happened, believe me: Ishiguro understands very well. He had a problem, and I helped him.'

I still didn't really understand, and I started to say more, but Connor held up his hand. 'I think we better take a look at the scene, before Graham and his men screw things up any more than they already have.'

It'd been almost two years since I worked the detective division, and it felt good to be around a homicide again. It brought back memories: the nighttime tension, the adrenaline rush of bad coffee in paper cups, and all the teams working around you – it's a kind of crazy energy, circling the center where somebody is lying, dead. Every homicide crime scene has that same energy, and that finality at the center. When you look at the dead person, there is a kind of obviousness, and at the same time there is an impossible mystery. Even in the simplest domestic brawl, where the woman finally decided to shoot the guy, you'd look at her, all covered in scars and cigarette burns, and you had to ask, why tonight? What was it about tonight? It's always clear what you are seeing, and there's always something that doesn't add up. Both things at once.

And at a homicide you have the sense of being right down to the basic truths of existence, the smells and the defecation and the bloating. Usually somebody's crying, so you're listening to that. And the usual bullshit stops, somebody died, and it's an unavoidable fact, like a rock in the road that makes all the traffic go around it. And in that grim and real setting, this camaraderie springs up, because you're working late with people you know, and actually know very well because you see them all the time. L.A. has four homicides a day; there's another one every six hours. And every detective at the crime scene already has ten homicides dragging on his backlog, which makes this new one an intolerable burden, so he and everybody else is hoping to solve it on the spot, to get it out of the way. There is that kind of finality and tension and energy all mixed together.

And after you do it for a few years, you get so you like it. And to my surprise, as I entered the conference room, I realized that I missed it.

The conference room was elegant: black table, high-backed leather chairs the lights of the nighttime skyscrapers beyond the glass walls. Inside the room, the technicians talked quietly, as they moved around the body of the dead girl.

She had blonde hair cut short. Blue eyes, full mouth. She looked about twenty-five. Tall, with a long-limbed, athletic look. Her dress was black and sheer.

Graham was well into his examination; he was down at the end of the table, squinting at the girl's black patent high heels, a penlight in one hand, his notebook in another.

Kelly, the coroner's assistant, was taping the girl's hands in paper bags to protect them. Connor stopped him. 'Just a minute.' Connor looked at one hand, inspecting the wrist, peering closely under the fingernails. He sniffed under one nail. Then he flicked the fingers rapidly, one after another.

'Don't bother,' Graham said laconically. 'There's no rigor mortis yet, and no detritus under the nails, no skin or cloth fibers. In fact, I'd say there aren't many signs of a struggle at all.'

Kelly slipped the bag over the hand. Connor said to him, 'You have a time of death?'

'I'm working on it.' Kelly lifted the girl's buttocks to place the rectal probe. 'The axillary thermocouples are already in place. We'll know in a minute.'

Connor touched the fabric of the black dress, checked the label. Helen, part of the SID team, said, 'It's a Yamamoto.'

'I see that,' Connor said.

'What's a Yamamoto?' I said.

Helen said, 'Very expensive Japanese designer. This little black nothing is at least five thousand dollars. That's assuming she bought it used. New, it's maybe fifteen thousand.'

'Is it traceable?' Connor asked her.

'Maybe. Depends on whether she bought it here, or in Europe, or Tokyo. It'll take a couple of days to check.'

Connor immediately lost interest. 'Never mind. That'll be too late.'

He produced a small, fiber-optic penlight, which he used to inspect the girl's scalp and hair. Then he looked quickly at each ear, giving a little murmur of surprise at the right ear. I peered over his shoulder, and saw a drop of dried blood at the pierced hole of her earring. I must have been crowding Connor, because he glanced up at me. 'Excuse me, *kōhai*.'

I stepped back. 'Sorry.'

Next, Connor sniffed the girl's lips, opened and closed her jaw rapidly, and poked around inside her mouth, using his penlight as a probe. Then he turned her head from side to side on the table, making her look left and right. He spent some time feeling gently along her neck, almost caressing it with his fingers.

And then, quite abruptly, he stepped away from the body and said, 'All right, I'm finished.'

And he walked out of the boardroom.

Graham looked up. 'He never was worth a damn at a crime scene.'

I said, 'Why do you say that? I hear he's a great detective.'

'Oh, hell,' Graham said. 'You can see for yourself. He doesn't even know what to do. Doesn't know procedure. Connor's no detective. Connor has *connections.* That's how he solved all those cases he's so famous for. You remember the Arakawa honeymoon shootings? No? I guess it was before your time, Petey-san. When was that Arakawa case, Kelly?'

'Seventy-six,' Kelly said.

'Right, seventy-six. Big fucking case that year. Mr. and Mrs. Arakawa, a young couple visiting Los Angeles on their honeymoon, are standing on the curb in East L.A. when they get gunned down from a passing car. Drive-by gang-style shooting. Worse, at autopsy it turns out Mrs Arakawa was pregnant. The press has a field day: L.A.P.D. can't handle gang violence, is the way the story goes. Letters and money come from all over the city. Everyone is upset about what happened to this fresh young couple. And of course the detectives assigned to the case don't discover shit. I mean, a case involving murdered Japanese nationals: they're getting *nowhere.*

'So, after a week, Connor is called in. And he solves it in one day. A fucking miracle of detection. I mean, it's a *week later.* The physical evidence is long gone, the bodies of the honeymooners are back in Osaka, the street corner where it happened is piled high in wilted flowers. But Connor is able to show that the youthful Mr Arakawa is actually quite a bad boy in Osaka. He shows that the street-corner gangland shooting is actually a *yakuza* killing contracted in Japan to take place in America. And he shows that the nasty husband is the innocent bystander: they were really gunning for the wife, knowing she was pregnant, because it's *her* father they wanted to teach a lesson. So. Connor turns it all around. Pretty fucking amazing, huh?'

'And you think he did it all with his Japanese connections?'

'You tell me,' Graham said. 'All I know is, pretty soon after that, he goes to Japan for a year.'

'Doing what?'

'I heard he worked as a security guy for a grateful Japanese company. They took care of him, is what it amounted to. He did a job for them, and they paid off. Anyway, that's the way I figure it. Nobody really knows. But the man is not a detective. Christ: just look at him now.'

Out in the atrium, Connor was staring up at the high ceiling in a dreamy, reflective way. He looked first in one direction, and then another. He seemed to be trying to make up his mind. Suddenly, he walked briskly toward the elevators, as if he were leaving. Then without warning, he turned on his heel, and walked back to the center of the room, and stopped. Next, he began to inspect the leaves on the potted palm trees scattered around the room.

Graham shook his head. 'What is this, gardening? I'm telling you, he's a strange guy. You know he's gone to Japan more than once. He always comes back. It never works out for him. Japan is like a woman that he can't live with, and can't live without, you know? Myself, I don't fucking get it. I like America. At least, what's left of it.'

He turned to the SID team, which was moving outward from the body. 'You guys find those panties for me yet?'

'Not yet, Tom.'

'We're looking, Tom.'

I said, 'What panties?'

Graham lifted the girl's skirt. 'Your friend John couldn't be bothered to finish his examination, but I'd say there's something significant here. I'd say that's seminal fluid oozing out of the vagina, she's not wearing panties, and there's a red line at the groin where they were ripped off. External genitals are red and raw. It's pretty clear she had forcible intercourse before she was killed. So I'm asking the boys to find the panties.'

One of the SID team said, 'Maybe she wasn't wearing any.'

Graham said, 'She was wearing them, all right.'

I turned back to Kelly. 'What about drugs?'

He shrugged. 'We'll get lab values on all fluids. But to the eye, she looks clean. Very clean.' I noticed that Kelly was distinctly uneasy, now.

Graham saw it, too. 'For Christ's sake, what are you hangdog about, Kelly? We keeping you from a late-night date, or what?'

'No,' Kelly said, 'but to tell you the truth, not only is there no evidence of a struggle, or of drugs – I don't see any evidence that she was murdered at all.'

Graham said, 'No evidence she was murdered? Are you kidding?'

Kelly said, 'The girl has throat injuries that suggest she may have been into one of the sexual bondage syndromes. She has signs beneath the makeup that she's been tied up before, repeatedly.'

'So?'

'So, technically speaking, maybe she wasn't murdered. Maybe she experienced sudden death from natural causes.'

'Aw, Christ. Come on.'

'It's quite possible this is a case of what we call death from inhibition. Instantaneous physiological death.'

'Meaning what?'

He shrugged. 'The person just dies.'

'For no reason at all?'

'Well, not exactly. There's usually minor trauma involving the heart or nerves. But the trauma isn't sufficient to cause death. I had one case where a ten-year-old kid got hit in the chest with a baseball – not very hard – and fell down dead in the school yard. Nobody within twenty meters of him. Another case, a woman had a minor car accident, banged into the steering wheel with her chest, not very hard, and while she was opening the car door to get out, she dropped dead. It seems to happen where there is neck or chest injury, which may irritate the nerves running to the heart. So, yeah, Tom. Technically, sudden death is a distinct possibility. And since having sex is not a felony, it wouldn't be murder.'

Graham squinted. 'So you're saying maybe *nobody* killed her?'

Kelly shrugged. He picked up his clipboard. 'I'm not putting any of this down. I'm listing the cause of death as asphyxiation secondary to manual strangulation. Because the odds are, she was strangled. But you should file it away in the back of your mind that maybe she wasn't. Maybe she just popped off.'

'Fine,' Graham said. 'We'll file it. Under medical examiner's fantasies. Meanwhile, any of you guys got an ID on her?'

The SID team, still searching the room, murmured no.

Kelly said, 'I think I got a time of death.' He checked his temperature probes and read off a chart. 'I register a core of ninety-six point nine. In this ambient room temperature, that's consistent with up to three hours postmortem.'

'Up to three hours? That's great. Listen Kelly, we already knew she died *sometime* tonight.'

'It's the best I can do.' Kelly shook his head. 'Unfortunately, the cooling curves don't discriminate well for under three hours. All I can say is death occurred sometime within three hours. But my impression is that this girl has been dead a while. Frankly, I would say it's close to three hours.'

Graham turned to the SID team. 'Anybody find the panties yet?'

'Not so far, Lieutenant.'

Graham looked around the room and said, 'No purse, no panties.'

I said, 'You think somebody cleaned up here?'

'I don't know,' he said. 'But doesn't a girl who's coming to a party in a thirty-thousand-dollar dress usually carry a purse?' Then Graham looked past my shoulder and smiled: 'Well, what do you know, Petey-san: One of your admirers to see you.'

Striding toward me was Ellen Farley, the mayor's press secretary. Farley was thirty-five, dark blonde hair cropped close to her head, perfectly groomed as always. She had been a newscaster when she was younger, but had worked for the mayor's office for many years. Ellen Farley was smart, fast on her feet, and she had one of the great bodies, which as far as anyone knew she retained for her own exclusive use.

I liked her enough to have done a couple of favors for her when I was in the L.A.P.D. press office. Since the mayor and the chief of police hated each other, requests from the mayor's office sometimes passed from Ellen to me, and I handled them. Mostly small things: delaying the release of a report until the weekend, so it'd run on Saturday. Or announcing that charges in a case hadn't been brought yet, even though they had. I did it because Farley was a straight shooter, who always spoke her mind. And it looked like she was going to speak her mind now.

'Listen, Pete,' she said. 'I don't know what's going on here, but the mayor's been hearing some pretty strong complaints from a Mr Ishiguro –'

'I can imagine –'

'And the mayor asked me to remind you that there is no excuse for officials of this city to be rude to foreign nationals.'

Graham said loudly, 'Especially when they make such large campaign contributions.'

'Foreign nationals can't contribute to American political campaigns,' Farley said. 'You know that.' She lowered her voice. 'This is a sensitive case, Pete. I want you to be careful. You know the Japanese have a special concern about how they are treated in America.'

'Okay, fine.'

She looked through the glass walls of the conference room, toward the atrium. 'Is that John Connor?'

'Yes.'

'I thought he was retired. What's he doing here?'

'Helping me on the case.'

Farley frowned. 'You know the Japanese have mixed feelings about him. They have a term for it. For somebody who is a Japan lover and goes to the other extreme, and turns into a basher.'

'Connor isn't a basher.'

'Ishiguro felt roughly treated.'

'Ishiguro was telling us what to do,' I said. 'And we have a murdered girl here, which everybody seems to be forgetting –'

'Come on, Pete,' she said, 'nobody's trying to tell you how to do your job. All I'm saying is you have to take into account the special –'

She stopped.

She was looking at the body.

'Ellen?' I said. 'Do you know her?'

'No.' She turned away.

'You sure?'

I could see she was rattled.

Graham said, 'You saw her downstairs earlier?'

'I don't – maybe. I think so. Listen, fellas, I've got to get back.'

'Ellen. Come on.'

'I don't know who she is Pete. You know I'd tell you if I did. Just keep it cordial with the Japanese. That's all the mayor wanted me to say. I've got to go now.'

She hurried back toward the elevators. I watched her leave, feeling uneasy.

Graham came over and stood beside me. 'She's got a great ass,' he said. 'But she ain't leveling, buddy, even with you.'

I said, 'What do you mean, even with me?'

'Everybody knows you and Farley were an item.'

'What are you talking about?'

Graham punched me on the shoulder. 'Come on. You're divorced now. Nobody gives a shit.'

I said, 'It's not true, Tom.'

'You can do what you want. Handsome guy like you.'

'I'm telling you, it's not true.'

'Okay, fine.' He held up his hands. 'My mistake.'

I watched Farley at the other end of the atrium, ducking under the tape. She pressed the elevator button, and waited for it to come, tapping her foot impatiently.

I said, 'You really think she knows who the girl is?'

'Damn right she does,' Graham said. 'You know why the mayor likes her. She stands by his side and whispers everybody's name to him. People she hasn't seen for years. Husbands, wives, children, everyone. Farley knows who this girl is.'

'Then why didn't she tell us?'

'Fuck,' Graham said. 'Must be important to somebody. She took off like a shot, didn't she? I tell you, we better figure out who this dead girl is. Because I fucking hate being the last one in town to know.'

Connor was across the room, waving to us.

'What does he want now?' Graham said. 'Waving like that. What's he got in his hand?'

'Looks like a purse,' I said.

'Cheryl Lynn Austin,' Connor said, reading. 'Born Midland, Texas, graduate of Texas State. Twenty-three years old. Got an apartment in Westwood, but hasn't been here long enough to change her Texas driver's license.'

The contents of the purse were spread out on a desk. We pushed them around with pencils.

'Where'd you find this purse?' I asked. It was a small, dark, beaded clutch with a pearl clasp. A vintage forties purse. Expensive.

'It was in the potted palm near the conference room.' Connor unzipped a tiny compartment. A tight roll of crisp hundred-dollar bills tumbled onto the table. 'Very nice. Miss Austin is well taken care of.'

I said, 'No car keys?'

'No.'

'So she came with somebody.'

'And evidently intended to leave with somebody, too. Taxis can't break a hundred-dollar bill.'

There was also a gold American Express Card. Lipstick and a compact. A pack of Mild Seven Menthol cigarettes, a Japanese brand. A card for the Daimatsu Night Club in Tokyo. Four small blue pills. That was about it.

Using his pencil, Connor upended the beaded purse. Small green flecks spilled out onto the table. 'Know what that is?'

'No,' I said. Graham looked at it with a magnifying glass.

Connor said, 'It's *wasabi*-covered peanuts.'

Wasabi is green horseradish served in Japanese restaurants. I had never heard of *wasabi*-covered peanuts.

'I don't know if they're sold outside Japan.'

Graham grunted. 'I've seen enough. So what do you think now, John? Is Ishiguro going to get those witnesses you asked for?'

'I wouldn't expect them soon,' Connor said.

'Fucking right,' Graham said. 'We won't see those witnesses until day after tomorrow, after their lawyers have briefed them on exactly what to say.' He stepped away from the table. 'You realize why they're delaying us. A Japanese killed this girl. That's what we're dealing with.'

'It's possible,' Connor said.

'Hey, buddy. More than possible. We're *here*. This is their building. And that girl is just the type they go for. The American beauty long-stemmed rose. You know all those little guys want to fuck a volleyball player.'

Connor shrugged. 'Possibly.'

'Come on,' Graham said. 'You know those guys eat shit all day long at home. Crammed into subways, working in big companies. Can't say what they think. Then they come over here, away from the constraints of home, and suddenly they're rich and free. They can do whatever they want. And sometimes one of them goes a little crazy. Tell me I'm wrong.'

Connor looked at Graham for a long time. Finally he said, 'So as you see it, Tom, a Japanese killer decided to dispatch this girl on the Nakamoto boardroom conference table?'

'Right.'

'As a symbolic act?'

Graham shrugged. 'Christ, who knows? We're not talking normality here. But I'll tell you one thing. I'm going to get the fucker who did this, if it's the last goddamned thing I do.'

The elevator descended rapidly. Connor leaned against the glass. 'There are many reasons to dislike the Japanese,' he said, 'but Graham knows none of them.' He sighed. 'You know what they say about us?'

'What?'

'They say Americans are too eager to make theories. They say we don't spend enough time observing the world, and so we don't know how things actually *are.*'

'Is that a Zen idea?'

'No,' he laughed. 'Just an observation. Ask a computer salesman what he thinks of his American counterparts, and he'll tell you that. Everyone in Japan who deals with Americans thinks it. And when you look at Graham, you realize they're right. Graham has no real knowledge, no first-hand experience. He just has a collection of prejudices and media fantasies. He doesn't know anything about the Japanese – and it never occurs to him to find out.'

I said, 'Then you think he's wrong? The girl wasn't killed by a Japanese?'

'I didn't say that, *kōhai,*' Connor replied. 'It's very possible Graham is right. But at the moment –'

The doors opened and we saw the party, heard the band playing 'Moonlight Serenade.' Two party-going couples stepped into the elevator. They looked like real estate people: the men silver-haired and distinguished looking, the women pretty and slightly tacky. One woman said, 'She's smaller than I thought.'

'Yes, tiny. And that . . . was that her boyfriend?'

'I guess. Wasn't he the one in the video with her?'

'I think that was him.'

One of the men said, 'You think she had her boobs done?'

'Hasn't everybody?'

The other woman giggled. 'Except me, of course.'

'Right, Christine.'

'But I'm thinking about it. Did you see Emily?'

'Oh, she did hers so *big.*'

'Well, Jane started it, blame her. Now everyone wants them big.'

The men turned and looked out the window. 'Hell of a building,' one said. 'Detailing is fantastic. Must have cost a fortune. You doing much with the Japanese now, Ron?'

'About twenty percent,' the other man said. 'That's way down from last year. It's made me work on my golf game, because they always want to play golf.'

'Twenty percent of your business?'

'Yeah. They're buying up Orange County now.'

'Of course. They already own Los Angeles,' one of the women said, laughing.

'Well, just about. They have the Arco building over there,' the man said, pointing out the window. 'I guess by now they have seventy, seventy-five percent of downtown Los Angeles.'

'And more in Hawaii.'

'Hell, they *own* Hawaii – ninety percent of Honolulu, a hundred percent of the Kona coast. Putting up golf courses like mad.'

One woman said, 'Will this party be on *ET* tomorrow? They had enough cameras here.'

'Let's remember to watch.'

The elevator said, '*Mōsugu de gozaimasu.*'

We came to the garage floor, and the people got off. Connor watched them go, and shook his head. 'In no other country in the world,' he said, 'would you hear people calmly discussing the fact that their cities and states were sold to foreigners.'

'Discussing?' I said. 'They're the ones doing the selling.'

'Yes. Americans are eager to sell. It amazes the Japanese. They think we're committing economic suicide. And of course they're right.' As he spoke, Connor pressed a button on the elevator panel marked EMERGENCY ONLY.

A soft pinging alarm sounded.

'What'd you do that for?'

Connor looked at a video camera mounted in the corner of the ceiling and waved cheerfully. A voice on the intercom said, 'Good evening, officers. Can I help you?'

'Yes,' Connor said. 'Am I speaking to building security?'

'That's right, sir. Is something wrong with your elevator?'

'Where are you located?'

'We're on the lobby level, southeast corner, behind the elevators.'

'Thank you very much,' Connor said. He pushed the button for the lobby.

The security office of the Nakamoto Tower was a small room, perhaps five meters by seven. It was dominated by three large, flat video panels, each divided into a dozen smaller monitor views. At the moment, most of these were black rectangles. But one row showed images from the lobby and the garage; another row showed the party in progress. And a third row showed the police teams up on the forty-sixth floor.

Jerome Phillips was the guard on duty. He was a black man in his midforties. His gray Nakamoto Security uniform was soaked around the collar, and dark under the armpits. He asked us to leave the door open as we entered. He appeared noticeably uneasy to have us there. I sensed he was hiding something, but Connor approached him in a friendly way. We showed our badges and shook hands. Connor managed to convey the idea that we were all security professionals, having a little chat together. 'Must be a busy night for you, Mr. Phillips.'

'Yeah, sure. The party and everything.'

'And crowded, in this little room.'

He wiped sweat from his forehead. 'Boy, you got that right. All of them packed in here. Jesus.'

I said, 'All of who?'

Connor looked at me and said, 'After the Japanese left the forty-sixth floor, they came down here and watched us on the monitors. Isn't that right, Mr. Phillips?'

Phillips nodded. 'Not all of 'em, but quite a few. Down here, smoking their damn cigarettes, staring and puffing and passing around faxes.'

'Faxes?'

'Oh, yeah, every few minutes, somebody'd bring in another fax. You know, in Japanese writing. They'd all pass it around, make comments. Then one of 'em would leave to send a fax back. And the rest would stay to watch you guys up on the floor.'

Connor said, 'And listen, too?'

Phillips shook his head. 'No. We don't have audio feeds.'

'I'm surprised,' Connor said. 'This equipment seems so up-to-date.'

'Up-to-date? Hell, it's the most advanced in the world. These people, I tell you one thing. These people do it right. They have the best fire alarm and fire prevention system. The best earthquake system. And of course the best electronic security system: best cameras, detectors, everything.'

'I can see that,' Connor said. 'That's why I was surprised they don't have audio.'

'No. No audio, and no color. They do high-resolution video only. Don't ask me why. Something to do with the cameras and how they're hooked up, is all I know.'

On the flat panels I saw five different views of the forty-sixth floor, as seen from different cameras. Apparently the Japanese had installed cameras all over the floor. I remembered how Connor had walked around the atrium, staring up at the ceiling. He must have spotted the cameras then.

Now I watched Graham in the conference room, directing the teams. He was smoking a cigarette, which was completely against regulations at a crime scene. I saw Helen stretch and yawn. Meanwhile, Kelly was getting ready to move the girl's body off the table onto a gurney, before zipping it into the bag, and he was –

Then it hit me.

They had cameras up there.

Five different cameras.

Covering every part of the floor.

I said, 'Oh my God' and I spun around, very excited. I was about to say something when Connor smiled at me in an easy way, and placed his hand on my shoulder. He squeezed my shoulder – hard.

'Lieutenant,' he said.

The pain was incredible. I tried not to wince. 'Yes, Captain?'

'I wonder if you'd mind if I asked Mr. Phillips one or two questions.'

'No, Captain. Go right ahead.'

'Perhaps you'd take notes.'

'Good idea, Captain.'

He released my shoulder. I got out my notepad.

Connor sat on the edge of the table and said, 'Have you been with Nakamoto Security long, Mr. Phillips?'

'Yes, sir. About six years now. I started over in their La Habra plant, and when I hurt my leg – in a car accident – and couldn't walk so good, they moved me to security. In the plant. Because I wouldn't have to walk around, you see. Then when they opened the Torrance plant, they moved me over there. My wife got a job in the Torrance plant, too. They do Toyota subassemblies. Then, when this building opened, they brought me here, to work nights.'

'I see. Six years altogether.'

'Yes, sir.'

'You must like it.'

'Well, I tell you, it's a secure job. That's something in America. I know they don't think much of black folks, but they always treated me okay. And hell, before this I worked for GM in Van Nuys, and that's . . . you know, that's *gone.*'

'Yes,' Connor said sympathetically.

'That place,' Phillips said, shaking his head at the memory. 'Christ. The management assholes they used to send down to the floor. You couldn't believe it. M.B. fucking A., out of Detroit, little weenies didn't know *shit.* They didn't know how the line worked. They didn't know a tool from a die. But they'd still order the foreman around. They're all pulling in two hundred fucking thousand a year and they didn't know shit. And nothing ever worked right. The cars were all a piece of shit. But here,' he said, tapping the counter. 'Here, I got a problem, or something doesn't work, I tell somebody. And they come right down, and they know the system – how it works – and we go over the problem together, and it gets *fixed.* Right away. Problems get fixed here. That's the difference. I tell you: these people *pay attention.*'

'So you like it here.'

'They always treated me okay,' Phillips said, nodding.

That didn't exactly strike me as a glowing endorsement. I had the feeling this guy wasn't committed to his employers and a few questions could drive the wedge. All we had to do was encourage the break.

'Loyalty is important,' Connor said, nodding sympathetically.

'It is to them,' he said. 'They expect you to show all this enthusiasm for the company. So you know, I always come in fifteen or twenty minutes early, and stay fifteen or twenty minutes after the shift is over. They like you to put in the extra time. I did the same at Van Nuys, but nobody ever noticed.'

'And when is your shift?'

'I work nine to seven.'

'And tonight? What time did you come on duty?'

'Quarter to nine. Like I said, I come in fifteen minutes early.'

The original call had been recorded about eight-thirty. So if this man came at a quarter to nine, he would have arrived almost fifteen minutes too late to see the murder. 'Who was on duty before you?'

'Well, usually it's Ted Cole. But I don't know if he worked tonight.'

'Why is that?'

The guard wiped his forehead with his sleeve, and looked away.

'Why is that, Mr. Phillips?' I said, with a little more force.

The guard blinked and frowned, saying nothing.

Connor said quietly, 'Because Ted Cole wasn't here when Mr. Phillips arrived tonight, was he, Mr. Phillips?'

The guard shook his head. 'No, he wasn't.'

I started to ask another question, but Connor raised his hand. 'I imagine, Mr. Phillips, you must have been pretty surprised when you came in this room, at a quarter to nine.'

'You damn right I was,' Phillips said.

'What did you do when you saw the situation?'

'Well. Right away, I said to the guy, "Can I help you?" Very polite but still firm. I mean, this is the security room. And I don't know who this guy is, I've never seen him before. And the guy is tense. *Very* tense. He says to me, "Get out of my way." Real pushy, like he owns the world. And he shoves past me, taking his briefcase with him.

'I say, "Excuse me, sir, I'll have to see some identification." He don't answer me, he just keeps going. Out the lobby and down the stairs.'

'You didn't try and stop him?'

'No, sir. I didn't.'

'Because he was Japanese?'

'You got that right. But I called up to central security – it's up on the ninth floor – to say I found a man in the room. And they say, "Don't worry, everything is fine." But I can hear they're tense, too. Everybody is tense. And then I see on the monitor . . . the dead girl. So that's the first I knew what it was about.'

Connor said, 'The man you saw. Can you describe him?'

The guard shrugged. 'Thirty, thirty-five. Medium height. Dark blue suit like they all wear. Actually he was more hip than most of them. He had this tie with triangles on it. Oh – and a scar on his hand, like a burn or something.'

'Which hand?'

'The left hand. I noticed it when he was closing the briefcase.'

'Could you see inside the briefcase?'

'No.'

'But he was closing it when you came in the room?'

'Yes.'

'Was it your impression he took something from this room?'

'I really couldn't say, sir.'

Phillips's evasiveness began to annoy me. I said, 'What do you think he took?'

Connor shot me a look.

The guard went bland: 'I really don't know, sir.'

Connor said, 'Of course you don't. There's no way you could know what was in somebody else's briefcase. By the way, do you make recordings from the security cameras here?'

'Yes, we do.'

'Could you show me how you do that?'

'Sure thing.' The guard got up from the desk and opened a door at the far end of the room. We followed him into a second small room, almost a closet, stacked floor to ceiling with small metal boxes, each with stenciled notations in Japanese *kanji* script, and numbers in English. Each with a glowing red light, and an LED counter, with numbers running forward.

Phillips said, 'These are our recorders. They lay down signals from all the cameras in the building. They're eight-millimeter, high-definition video.' He held up a small cassette, like an audio cassette. 'Each one of these records eight hours. We change over at nine p.m., so that's the first thing I do when I come on duty. I pop out the old ones, and switch over to the fresh ones.'

'And did you change cassettes tonight, at nine o'clock?'

'Yes, sir. Just like always.'

'And what do you do with the tapes you remove?'

'Keep 'em in the trays down here,' he said, bending to show us several long, thin drawers. 'We keep everything off the cameras for seventy-two hours. That's three days. So we keep nine sets of tapes all together. and we just rotate each set through, once every three days. Get me?'

Connor hesitated. 'Perhaps I'd better write this down.' He produced a small pad and a pen. 'Now, each tape lasts eight hours, so you have nine different sets . . .'

'Right, right.'

Connor wrote for a moment, then shook his pen irritably. 'This damn pen. It's out of ink. You have a wastebasket?'

Phillips pointed to the corner. 'Over there.'

'Thank you.'

Connor threw the pen away. I gave him mine. He resumed his notes. 'You were saying, Mr. Phillips, that you have nine sets . . .'

'Right. Each set is numbered with letters, from A to I. Now when I come in at nine, I eject the tapes and see whatever letter is already in there, and put in the next one. Like tonight, I took out set C, so I put in set D, which is what's recording now.'

'I see,' Connor said. 'And then you put tape set C in one of the drawers here?'

'Right.' He pulled open a drawer. 'This one here.'

Connor said, 'May I?' He glanced at the neatly labeled row of tapes. Then he quickly opened the other drawers, and looked at the other stacks of tapes. Except for the different letters, all the drawers looked identical.

'I think I understand now,' Connor said. 'What you actually do is use nine sets in rotation.'

'Exactly.'

'So each set gets used once every three days.'

'Right.'

'And how long has the security office been using this system?'

'The building's new, but we've been going, oh, maybe two months now.'

'I must say it's a very well-organized system,' Connor said appreciatively. 'Thank you for explaining it to us. I have only a couple of other questions.'

'Sure.'

'First of all, these counters here –' Connor said, pointing to the LED counters on the video recorders. 'They seem to show the elapsed times since the tapes began recording. Is that right? Because it's now almost eleven o'clock, and you put in the tapes at nine, and the top recorder says 1:55:30 and the next recorder says 1:55:10, and so on.'

'Yes, that right. I put the tapes in one right after another. It takes a few seconds between tapes.'

'I see. These all show almost two hours. But I notice that one recorder down here shows an elapsed time of only thirty minutes. Does that mean it's broken?'

'Huh,' Phillips said, frowning. 'I guess maybe it is. 'Cause I changed the tapes all one after another, like I said. But these recorders are the latest technology. Sometimes there are glitches. Or we had some power problems. Could be that.'

'Yes. Quite possibly,' Connor said. 'Can you tell me which camera is hooked to this recorder?'

'Yes, of course.' Phillips read the number off the recorder, and went out to the main room with the monitor screens. 'It's camera four-six slash six,' he said. 'This view here.' He tapped the screen.

It was an atrium camera, and it showed an overall view of the forty-sixth floor.

'But you see,' Phillips said, 'the beauty of the system is, even if one recorder screws up, there are still other cameras on that floor, and the video recorders on the others seem to be working okay.'

'Yes, they do,' Connor said. 'By the way, can you tell me why there are so many cameras on the forty-sixth floor?'

'You didn't hear it from me,' Phillips said. 'But you know how they like efficiency. The word is, they are going to *kaizen* the office workers.'

'So basically these cameras have been installed to observe workers during the day, and help them improve their efficiency?'

'That's what I heard.'

'Well, I think that's it,' Connor said. 'Oh, one more question. Do you have an address for Ted Cole?'

Phillips shook his head. 'No, I don't.'

'Have you ever been out with him, socialized with him?'

'I have, but not much. He's an odd guy.'

'Ever been to his apartment?'

'No. He's kind of secretive. I think he lives with his mother or something. We usually go to this bar, the Palomino, over by the airport. He likes it there.'

Connor nodded. 'And one last question: where is the nearest pay phone?'

'Out in the lobby, and around to your right, by the restrooms. But you're welcome to use the phone here.'

Connor shook the guard's hand warmly. 'Mr. Phillips, I appreciate your taking the time to talk to us.'

'No problem.'

I gave the guard my card. 'If you think of anything later that could help us, Mr. Phillips, don't hesitate to call me.' And I left.

Connor stood at the pay phone in the lobby. It was one of those new standing booths that has two receivers, one on either side, allowing two people to talk on the same line at once. These booths had been installed in Tokyo years ago, and now were starting to show up all over Los Angeles. Of course, Pacific Bell no longer was the principal provider of American public pay phones. Japanese manufacturers had penetrated that market, too. I watched Connor write down the phone number in his notebook.

'What are you doing?'

'We have two separate questions to answer tonight. One is how the girl came to be killed on an office floor. But we also need to find out who placed the original call, notifying us of the murder.'

'And you think the call might have been placed from this phone?'

'Possibly.'

He closed his notebook, and glanced at his watch. 'It's late. We better get going.'

'I think we're making a big mistake here.'

'Why is that?' Connor asked.

'I don't know if we should leave the tapes in that security room. What if somebody switches them while we're gone?'

'They've already been switched,' Connor said.

'How do you know?'

'I gave up a perfectly good pen to find out,' he said. 'Now come on.' He started walking toward the stairs leading down to the garage. I followed him.

'You see,' Connor said, 'when Phillips first explained that simple system of rotation, it was immediately clear to me that there might have been a switch. The question was how to prove it.'

His voice echoed in the concrete stairwell. Connor continued down, taking the steps two at a time. I hurried to keep up.

Connor said, 'If somebody switched the tapes, how would they go about it? They would be working hastily, under pressure. They'd be terrified of making a mistake. They certainly wouldn't want to leave any incriminating tapes behind. So probably they'd switch an entire set, and replace it. But replace it with what? They can't just put in the next set.

Since there are only nine sets of tapes all together, it would be too easy for someone to notice that one set was missing, and the total was now eight. There would be an obvious empty drawer. No, they would have to replace the set they were taking away with an entirely new set. Twenty brand-new tapes. And that meant I ought to check the trash.'

'That's why you threw your pen away?'

'Yes. I didn't want Phillips to know what I was doing.'

'And?'

'The trash was full of crumpled plastic wrappers. The kind that new video tapes come wrapped in.'

'I see.'

'Once I knew the tapes had been replaced, the only remaining question was, which set? So I played dumb, and looked in all the drawers. You probably noticed that set C, the set Phillips removed when he came on duty, had slightly whiter labels than the other sets. It was subtle, because the office has only been active two months, but you could tell.'

'I see.' Somebody had come into the security room, taken out twenty fresh tapes, unwrapped them, written new labels, and popped them into the video machines, replacing the original tapes that had recorded the murder.

I said, 'If you ask me, Phillips knows more about this than he was telling us.'

'Maybe,' Connor said, 'but we have more important things to do. Anyway, there's a limit to what he knows. The murder was phoned in about eight-thirty. Phillips arrived at quarter to nine. So he never saw the murder. We can assume the previous guard, Cole, did. But by a quarter of nine, Cole was gone, and an unknown Japanese man was in the security room, closing up a briefcase.'

'You think he's the one who switched the tapes?'

Connor nodded. 'Very possibly. In fact, I wouldn't be surprised if this man was the killer himself. I hope to find that out at Miss Austin's apartment.' He threw open the door, and we went into the garage.

A line of party guests waited for valets to bring their cars. I saw Ishiguro chatting up Mayor Thomas and his wife. Connor steered me toward them. Standing alongside the mayor, Ishiguro was so cordial he was almost obsequious. He gave us a big smile. 'Ah, gentlemen. Is your investigation proceeding satisfactorily? Is there anything more I can do to help?'

I didn't get really angry until that moment: until I saw the way he toadied up in front of the mayor. It made me so mad I began to turn red. But Connor took it in stride.

'Thank you, Ishiguro-san,' he said, with a slight bow. 'The investigation is going well.'

'You're receiving all the help you requested?' Ishiguro said.

'Oh, yes,' Connor said. 'Everyone has been very co-operative.'

'Good, good. I'm glad.' Ishiguro glanced at the mayor, and smiled at him, too. He was all smiles, it seemed.

'But,' Connor said, 'there is just one thing.'

'Just name it. If there is anything we can do . . .'

'The security tapes seem to have been removed.'

'Security tapes?' Ishiguro frowned, clearly caught off guard.

'Yes,' Connor said. 'Recordings from the security cameras.'

'I don't know anything about that,' Ishiguro said. 'But let me assure you, if any tapes exist, they are yours to examine.'

'Thank you,' Connor said. 'Unfortunately, it seems the crucial tapes have been removed from the Nakamoto security office.'

'Removed? Gentlemen, I believe there must be some mistake.'

The mayor was watching this exchange closely.

Connor said, 'Perhaps, but I don't think so. It would be reassuring, Mr. Ishiguro, if you were to look into this matter yourself.'

'I certainly will,' Ishiguro said. 'But I must say again. I can't imagine, Captain Connor, that any tapes are missing.'

'Thank you for checking, Mr. Ishiguro,' Connor said.

'Not at all, Captain,' he said, still smiling. 'It is my pleasure to assist you in whatever way I can.'

'The son of a bitch,' I said. We were driving west on the Santa Monica freeway. 'The little prick looked us right in the eye and *lied.*'

'It's annoying,' Connor said. 'But you see, Ishiguro takes a different view. Now that he is beside the mayor, he sees himself in another context, with another set of obligations and requirements for his behavior. Since he is sensitive to context, he's able to act differently, with no reference to his earlier behavior. To us, he seems like a different person. But Ishiguro feels he's just being appropriate.'

'What burns me is he acted so confident.'

'Of course he did,' Connor said. 'And he would be quite surprised to learn that you're angry with him. You consider him immoral. He considers you naive. Because for a Japanese, consistent behavior is not possible. A Japanese becomes a different person around people of different rank. He becomes a different person when he moves through different rooms of his own house.'

'Yeah,' I said. 'That's fine, but the fact is he's a lying son of a bitch.'

Connor looked at me. 'Would you talk that way to your mother?'

'Of course not.'

'So you change according to context, too,' Connor said. 'The fact is we all do. It's just that Americans believe there is some core of individuality that doesn't change from one moment to the next. And the Japanese believe context rules everything.'

'It sounds to me,' I said, 'like an excuse for lying.'

'He doesn't see it as lying.'

'But that's what it is.'

Connor shrugged. 'Only from your point of view, *kōhai*. Not from his.'

'The hell.'

'Look, it's your choice. You can understand the Japanese and deal with them as they are, or you can get pissed off. But our problem in this country is that we don't deal with the Japanese the way they really are.'

The car hit a deep pothole, bouncing so hard that the car phone fell off the receiver. Connor picked it up off the floor, and put it back on the hook.

Up ahead, I saw the exit for Bundy. I moved into the right lane. 'One thing I'm not clear about,' I said. 'Why do you think the man with the briefcase in the security room might be the killer?'

'It's because of the time sequence. You see, the murder was reported at eight thirty-two. Less than fifteen minutes later, at eight forty-five, a Japanese man was down there switching the tapes, arranging a cover-up. That's a very fast response. Much too fast for a Japanese company.'

'Why is that?'

'Japanese organizations are actually very slow to respond in a crisis. Their decision-making relies on precedents, and when a situation is unprecedented, people are uncertain how to behave. You remember the faxes? I am sure faxes have been flying back and forth to Nakamoto's Tokyo headquarters all night. Undoubtedly the company is still trying to decide what to do. A Japanese organization simply cannot move fast in a new situation.'

'But an individual acting alone can?'

'Yes. Exactly.'

I said, 'And that's why you think the man with the briefcase may be the killer.'

Connor nodded. 'Yes. Either the killer, or someone closely connected with the killer. But we should learn more at Miss Austin's apartment. I believe I see it up ahead, on the right.'

The Imperial Arms was an apartment building on a treelined street a kilometer from Westwood Village. Its fake Tudor beams needed a paint job, and the whole building had a run-down appearance. But that was not unusual in this middle-class section of apartments inhabited by graduate students and young families. In fact, the chief characteristic of the Imperial Arms seemed to be its anonymity: you could drive by the building every day and never notice it.

'Perfect,' Connor said, as we walked up the steps to the entrance. 'It's just what they like.'

'What who likes?'

We came into the lobby, which had been renovated in the most bland California style: pastel wallpaper with a flower print, overstuffed couches, cheap ceramic lamps, and a chrome coffee table. The only thing to distinguish it from a hundred other apartment lobbies was the security desk in the corner, where a heavyset Japanese doorman looked up from his comic book with a distinctly unfriendly manner. 'Help you?'

Connor showed his badge. He asked where Cheryl Austin's apartment was.

'I announce you,' the doorman said, reaching for the phone.

'Don't bother.'

'No. I announce. Maybe she have company now.'

'I'm sure she doesn't.' Connor said. '*Kore wa keisatsu no shigoto da.*' He was saying we were on official police business.

The doorman gave a tense bow. '*Kyugo shitu.*' He handed Connor a key.

We went through a second glass door, and down a carpeted corridor. There were small lacquer tables at each end of the corridor, and in its simplicity, the interior was surprisingly elegant.

'Typically Japanese,' Connor said, with a smile.

I thought: a run-down, fake Tudor apartment building in Westwood? Typically Japanese? From a room to the left, I heard faint rap music: the latest Hammer hit.

'It's because the outside gives no clue to the inside,' Connor explained. 'That's a fundamental principle of Japanese thinking. The public facade is unrevealing – in architecture, the human face, everything.

It's always been that way. You look at old samurai houses in Takayama or Kyoto. You can't tell anything from the outside.'

'This is a Japanese building?'

'Of course. Why else would a Japanese national who hardly speaks English be the doorman? And he is a *yakuza.* You probably noticed the tattoo.'

I hadn't. The *yakuza* were Japanese gangsters. I didn't know there were *yakuza* here in America, and said so.

'You must understand,' Connor said, 'there is a shadow world – here in Los Angeles, in Honolulu, in New York. Most of the time you're never aware of it. We live in our regular American world, walking on our American streets, and we never notice that right alongside our world is a second world. Very discreet, very private. Perhaps in New York you will see Japanese businessmen walking through an unmarked door, and catch a glimpse of a club behind. Perhaps you will hear of a small sushi bar in Los Angeles that charges twelve hundred dollars a person, Tokyo prices. But they are not listed in the guidebooks. They are not a part of our American world. They are part of the shadow world, available only to the Japanese.'

'And this place?'

'This is a *bettaku.* A love residence where mistresses are kept. And here is Miss Austin's apartment.'

Connor unlocked the door with the key the doorman had given him. We went inside.

It was a two-bedroom unit, furnished with expensive oversized rental pieces in pastel pink and green. The oil paintings on the walls had been rented, too; a label on the side of one frame said Breuner's Rents. The kitchen counter was bare, except for a bowl of fruit. The refrigerator contained only yogurt and cans of Diet Coke. The couches in the living room didn't look as if anybody had ever sat on them. On the coffee table was a picture book of Hollywood star portraits and a vase of dried flowers. Empty ashtrays scattered around.

One of the bedrooms had been converted to a den, with a couch and a television, and an exercise bike in the corner. Everything was brand new. The television still had a sticker that said DIGITAL TUNING FEATURE diagonally across one corner. The handlebars of the exercise bike were covered in plastic wrap.

In the master bedroom, I finally found some human clutter. One mirrored closet door stood open, and three expensive party dresses were thrown across the bed. Evidently she had been trying to decide what to wear. On the dresser top were bottles of perfume, a diamond necklace, a gold Rolex, framed photographs, and an ashtray with stubbed-out Mild Seven Menthol cigarettes. The top dresser drawer, containing panties and undergarments, was partially open. I saw her passport stuck in the corner, and thumbed through it. There was one visa for Saudi Arabia, one for Indonesia, and three entry stamps for Japan.

The stereo in the corner was still turned on, an ejected tape in the player. I pushed it in and Jerry Lee Lewis sang, 'You shake my nerves and you rattle my brain, too much love drives a man insane . . .' Texas music, too old for a young girl like this. But maybe she liked golden oldies.

I turned back to the dresser. Several framed color enlargements showed Cheryl Austin smiling in front of Asian backgrounds – the red gates of a shrine, a formal garden, a street with gray skyscrapers, a train station. The pictures seemed to be taken in Japan. In most of the pictures Cheryl was alone, but in a few she was accompanied by an older Japanese man with glasses and a receding hairline. A final shot showed her in what looked like the American West. Cheryl was standing near a dusty pickup truck, smiling beside a frail, grandmotherly woman in sunglasses. The older woman wasn't smiling and looked uncomfortable.

Tucked in beside the dresser were several large paper rolls, standing on end. I opened one. It was a poster showing Cheryl in a bikini, smiling and holding up a bottle of Asahi beer. All the writing on the poster was in Japanese.

I went into the bathroom.

I saw a pair of jeans kicked in the corner. A white sweater tossed on the countertop. A wet towel on a hook by the shower stall. Beads of water inside the stall. Electric hair-curlers unplugged by the counter. Stuck in the mirror frame, photos of Cheryl standing with another Japanese man on the Malibu pier. This man was in his midthirties, and handsome. In one photograph, he had draped his arm familiarly over her shoulder. I could clearly see the scar on his hand.

'Bingo,' I said.

Connor came into the room. 'Find something?'

'Our man with the scar.'

'Good.' Connor studied the picture carefully. I looked back at the clutter of the bathroom. The stuff around the sink. 'You know,' I said, 'something bothers me about this place.'

'What's that?'

'I know she hasn't lived here long. And I know everything is rented . . . but still . . . I can't get over the feeling that this place has a contrived look. I can't quite put my finger on why.'

Connor smiled. 'Very good, Lieutenant. It does have a contrived look. And there's a reason for it.'

He handed me a Polaroid photo. It showed the bathroom we were standing in. The jeans kicked in the corner. The towel hanging. The curlers on the counter. But it was taken with one of those ultra-wide-angle cameras that distort everything. The SID teams sometimes used them for evidence.

'Where did you get this?'

'From the trash bin in the hall, by the elevators.'

'So it must have been taken earlier tonight.'

'Yes. Notice anything different about the room?'

I examined the Polaroid carefully. 'No, it looks the same . . . wait a minute. Those pictures stuck in her mirror. They aren't in the Polaroid. Those pictures have been added.'

'Exactly.' Connor walked back into the bedroom. He picked up one of the framed pictures on the dresser. 'Now look at this one,' he said. 'Miss Austin and a Japanese friend in Shinjuku Station in Tokyo. She was probably drawn to the Kabukicho section – or perhaps she was just shopping. Notice the right-hand edge of the picture. See the narrow strip that's lighter in color?'

'Yes.' And I understood what that strip meant: there had been another picture on top of this one. The edge of this picture had stuck out, and was sun-faded. 'The overlying picture has been removed.'

'Yes,' Connor said.

'The apartment has been searched.'

'Yes,' Connor said. 'A very thorough job. They came in earlier tonight, took Polaroids, searched the rooms, and then put things back the way they were. But it's impossible to do that exactly. The Japanese say artlessness is the most difficult art. And these men can't help themselves, they're obsessive. So they leave the picture frames a little too squared-off on the counter, and the perfume bottles a little too carefully cluttered. Everything is a little forced. Your eye can see it even if your brain doesn't register it.'

I said, 'But why search the room? What pictures did they remove? Her with the killer?'

'That's not clear,' Connor said. 'Evidently her association with Japan, and with Japanese men, was not objectionable. But there was something they had to get right away, and it can only be –'

Then, from the living room, a tentative voice said, 'Lynn? Honey? You here?'

She was silhouetted in the doorway, looking in. Barefooted, wearing shorts and a tank top. I couldn't see her face well, but she was obviously what my old partner Anderson would call a snake charmer.

Connor showed his badge. She said her name was Julia Young. She had a Southern accent, and a slight slur to her speech. Connor turned on the light and we could see her better. She was a beautiful girl. She came into the room hesitantly.

'I heard the music – is she here? Is Cherylynn okay? I know she went to that party tonight.'

'I haven't heard anything,' Connor said, with a quick glance at me. 'Do you know Cherylynn?'

'Well, sure. I live right across the hall, in number eight. Why is everybody in her room?'

'Everybody?'

'Well, you two. And the two Japanese guys.'

'When were they here?'

'I don't know. Maybe half an hour ago. Is it something about Cherylynn?'

I said, 'Did you get a look at the men, Miss Young?' I was thinking she might have been looking out of the peephole of her door.

'Well, I *guess*. I said hello to them.'

'How's that?'

'I know one of them pretty well. Eddie.'

'Eddie?'

'Eddie Sakamura. We all know Eddie. Fast Eddie.'

I said, 'Can you describe him?'

She gave me a funny look. 'He's the guy in the pictures – the young guy with the scar on his hand. I thought everybody knew Eddie Sakamura. He's in the newspaper all the time. Charities and stuff. He's a big party guy.'

I said, 'Do you have any idea how I could find him?'

Connor said, 'Eddie Sakamura is part owner of a Polynesian restaurant in Beverly Hills called Bora Bora. He hangs out there.'

'That's him,' Julia said. 'That place is like his office. I can't stand it myself, it's too noisy. But Eddie's just running around, chasing those big blondes. He loves to look up to a girl.'

She leaned against a table, and pushed her full brown hair back from her face seductively. She looked at me and gave a little pout. 'You two guys partners?'

'Yes,' I said.

'He showed me his badge. But you didn't show me yours.'

I took out my wallet. She looked at it. 'Peter,' she said, reading. 'My very first boyfriend was named Peter. But he wasn't as handsome as you.' She smiled at me.

Connor cleared his throat and said, 'Have you been in Cherylynn's apartment before?'

'Well, I *guess*. I live right across the way. But she hasn't been in town much lately. Seems like she's always traveling.'

'Traveling where?'

'All over. New York, Washington, Seattle, Chicago . . . all over. She has this boyfriend who travels a lot. She meets him. Actually I think she just meets him when his wife isn't around.'

'This boyfriend is married?'

'Well, there's something in the way. You know. Obstructing.'

'Do you know who he is?'

'No. She once said he'd never come to her apartment. He's some big important guy. Real rich. They send the jet for her, and off she goes. Whoever he is, he drives Eddie crazy. But Eddie is the jealous type, you know. Got to be *iro otoko* to all the girls. The sexy lover.'

Connor said, 'Is Cheryl's relationship a secret? With this boyfriend?'

'I don't know. I never thought it was. It's just real intense. She's madly in love with the guy.'

'She's madly in love?'

'You can't imagine. I've seen her drop everything to run and meet him. One night she comes over, gives me two tickets to the Springsteen concert, but she's all excited because she's going to *Detroit.* She's got her little carry-on in her hand. She's got her little nice-girl dress on. Because he just called ten minutes ago and said, 'Meet me.' Her face all bright, she looks about five years old. I don't know why she can't figure it out.'

'Figure what out?'

'This guy is just using her.'

'Why do you say that?'

'Cherylynn is beautiful, and real sophisticated-looking. She's worked all over the world as a model, mostly in Asia. But deep down she's a small-town girl. I mean, Midland is an oil town, there's lots of money, but it's still a small town. And Cherylynn wants the ring on the finger and the kids and the dog in the yard. And this guy isn't going to do it. She hasn't figured it out.'

I said, 'But you don't know who this man is?'

'No, I don't.' A sly look crossed her face. She shifted her body, dropping one shoulder so her breasts thrust forward. 'But you're not really here because of some old boyfriend, are you?'

Connor nodded. 'Not really, no.'

Julia smiled in a knowing way. 'It's Eddie, isn't it?'

'Umm,' Connor said.

'I knew it,' she said. 'I knew he'd get in trouble sooner or later. We all talked about it, all the girls here in the Arms.' She made a vague gesture. 'Because he's just going too fast. Fast Eddie. You wouldn't think he was Japanese. He's so flashy.'

Connor said, 'He's from Osaka?'

'His father's a big industrialist there, with Daimatsu. He's a nice old guy. When he comes over to visit, sometimes he sees one of the girls on the second floor. And Eddie. Eddie was supposed to get educated here for a few years, then go home to work for the *kaisha,* the company. But he won't go home. He loves it here. Why not? He's got everything. He buys a new Ferrari every time he bangs up the old one. He's got more money than God. He's lived here long enough, he's just like an American. Handsome. Sexy. And with all the drugs. You know, real party animal. What's in Osaka for him?'

I said, 'But you said you always knew . . .'

'That he'd get in trouble? Sure. Because of that crazy side. That *edge.*' She shrugged. 'A lot of them have it. These guys come over from Tokyo, and even if they have a *shōkai,* an introduction, you still have to be careful. They think nothing of dropping ten or twenty thousand in a night. It's like a tip for them. Leave it on the dresser. But then, what they want to do – at least, some of them . . .'

She drifted into silence. Her eyes had a vacant, unfocused look. I didn't say anything, I just waited. Connor was looking at her, nodding sympathetically.

Abruptly, she began to speak again, as if unaware of the pause. 'And to them,' she said, 'their wishes, their desires, it's just as natural as leaving the tip. It's completely natural to them. I mean, I don't mind a little golden shower or whatever, handcuffs, you know. Maybe a little spanking if I like the guy. But I won't let anybody cut me. I don't care how much money. None of those things with knives or swords . . . But they can be . . . A lot of them, they are so polite, so correct, but then they get turned on, they have this . . . this *way* . . .' She broke off, shaking her head. 'They're strange people.'

Connor glanced at his watch. 'Miss Young, you've been very helpful. We may need to speak to you again. Lieutenant Smith will take your phone number –'

'Yes, of course.'

I flipped open my pad.

Connor said, 'I'm going to have a word with the doorman.'

'Shinichi,' she said.

Connor left. I took down Julia's number. She licked her lips as she watched me write. Then she said, 'You can tell me. Did he kill her?'

'Who?'

'Eddie. Did he kill Cherylynn?'

She was a pretty girl but I could see the excitement in her eyes. She was looking at me with a steady gaze. Her eyes were shining. It was creepy. I said, 'Why do you ask?'

'Because. He was always threatening to. Like this afternoon, he threatened her.'

I said, 'Eddie was here this afternoon?'

'Sure.' She shrugged. 'He's here all the time. He came to see her this afternoon, real worked up. They put extra soundproofing to the walls in this building when they took it over. But even so, you could hear them scream at each other in her apartment. Him and Cherylynn. She'd have on her Jerry Lee Lewis, the one she played day and night until you just about went crazy, and they'd be screaming and throwing things. He'd always say, "I'll kill you, I'll kill you, you bitch." So. Did he?'

'I don't know.'

'But she's dead?' Her eyes still shining.

'Yes.'

'It had to happen,' she said. She seemed completely calm. 'We all knew it. It was just a matter of time. If you want, call me. If you need more information.'

'Yes. I will.' I gave her my card. 'And if you think of anything else, you can call me at this number.'

She slipped it into the hip pocket of her shorts, twisting her body. 'I like talking to you, Peter.'

'Yes. Okay.'

I walked down the corridor. When I got to the end I looked back. She was standing in her doorway, waving good-bye.

Connor was using the phone in the lobby while the doorman stared sullenly at him, as if he wanted to stop him, but couldn't think of a reason why.

'That's right,' Connor was saying. 'All the outgoing calls from that phone between eight and ten p.m. That's right.' He listened for a moment. 'Well, I don't care if your data isn't organized that way, just get it for me. How long will it take? Tomorrow? Don't be ridiculous. What do you think this is? I need it within two hours. I'll call you back. Yes. Fuck you, too.' He hung up. 'Let's go, *kōhai*.'

We walked outside to the car.

I said, 'Checking your contacts?'

'Contacts?' He looked puzzled. 'Oh. Graham said something to you about my "contacts." I don't have any special informants. He just thinks I do.'

'He mentioned the Arakawa case.'

Connor sighed. 'That old thing.' We walked toward the car. 'You want to know that story? It's simple. Two Japanese nationals get killed. The department puts detectives on the case who can't speak Japanese. Finally, after a week, they give the case to me.'

'And what did you do?'

'The Arakawas were staying at the New Otani Hotel. I got the phone records of the calls they made to Japan. I called those numbers, and spoke to some people in Osaka. Then I called Osaka and talked to the police there. Again, in Japanese. They were surprised to hear we didn't know the whole story.'

'I see.'

'Not quite,' Connor said. 'Because the police department here was very embarrassed. The press had gone out on a limb, criticizing the department. All sorts of people had sent flowers. There had been a big show of sympathy for what turned out to be gangsters. A lot of people were embarrassed. So the whole thing became my fault. I had done something underhanded to solve the case. Pissed me off, I can tell you.'

'That's why you went to Japan?'

'No. That's another story.'

We came to the car. I looked back at the Imperial Arms, and saw

Julia Young standing at the window, staring down at us. 'She's seductive,' I said.

'The Japanese call women like that *shirigaru onna.* They say she has a light ass.' He opened the car door, and got in. 'But she's on drugs. We can't trust anything she told us. Even so, there's starting to be a pattern I don't like.' He glanced at his watch, and shook his head. 'Damn. We're taking too long. We'd better go to the Palomino, to see Mr. Cole.'

I started driving south, toward the airport. Connor sat back in his seat and folded his arms across his chest. He stared at his feet, looking unhappy.

'Why do you say there's a pattern you don't like?'

Connor said, 'The wrappers in the waste basket. The Polaroid in the trash. Those things shouldn't have been left behind.'

'You said yourself, they're in a hurry.'

'Maybe. But you know the Japanese think American police are incompetent. This sloppiness is a sign of their disdain.'

'Well, we're not incompetent.'

Connor shook his head. 'Compared to the Japanese, we *are* incompetent. In Japan, every criminal gets caught. For major crimes, convictions run ninety-nine percent. So any criminal in Japan knows from the outset he is going to get caught. But here, the conviction rate is more like seventeen percent. Not even one in five. So a criminal in the States knows he probably *isn't* going to get caught – and if he's caught, he won't be convicted, thanks to all his legal safeguards. And you know every study of police effectiveness shows that American detectives either solve the case in the first six hours, or they never solve it at all.'

'So what are you saying?'

'I'm saying that a crime occurred here with the expectation that it won't be solved. And I want to solve it, *kōhai.*'

Connor was silent for the next ten minutes. He sat very still, with his arms folded and his chin sunk on his chest. His breathing was deep and regular. I might have thought he had fallen asleep, except his eyes were open.

I just drove the car, and listened to him breathe.

Finally, he said: 'Ishiguro.'

'What about him?'

'If we knew what made Ishiguro behave as he did, we'd understand this case.'

'I don't understand.'

'It's hard for an American to see him clearly,' Connor said. 'Because in America, you think a certain amount of error is normal. You expect the plane to be late. You expect the mail to be undelivered. You expect the washing machine to break down. You expect things to go wrong all the time.

'But Japan is different. Everything *works* in Japan. In a Tokyo train station, you can stand at a marked spot on the platform and when the train stops, the doors will open right in front of you. Trains are on time. Bags are not lost. Connections are not missed. Deadlines are met. Things happen as planned. The Japanese are educated, prepared, and motivated. They get things done. There's no screwing around.'

'Uh-huh . . .'

'And tonight was a very big night for the Nakamoto Corporation. You can be sure they planned everything down to the smallest detail. They have the vegetarian hors d'oeuvres that Madonna likes and the photographer she prefers. Believe me: they're prepared. They have planned for every exigency. You know how they are: they sit around and discuss endless possibilities – what if there's a fire? What if there's an earthquake? A bomb scare? Power failure? Endlessly going over the most unlikely events. It's obsessive, but when the final night arrives, they've thought of everything and they're in complete control. It's very bad form not to be in control. Okay?'

'Okay.'

'But there is our friend Ishiguro, the official representative of Nakamoto, standing in front of a dead girl, and he's clearly not in control. He's *yōshiki nō,* doing Western-style confrontation, but he isn't comfortable – I'm sure you noticed the sweat on his lip. And his hand is damp; he keeps wiping it on his trousers. He is *rikutsuppoi,* too argumentative. He's talking too much.

'In short, he's behaving as if he doesn't even know who this girl is – which he certainly does, since he knows everybody invited to that party – and pretending he doesn't know who killed her. When he almost certainly knows that, too.'

The car bounced in a pothole, and jolted back up. 'Wait a minute. Ishiguro knows who killed the girl?'

'I'm sure of it. And he's not the only one. At least three people must know who killed her, at this point. Didn't you say you used to be in press relations?'

'Yes. Last year.'

'You keep any contacts in TV news?'

'A few,' I said. 'They might be rusty. Why?'

'I want to look at some tape that was shot tonight.'

'Just look? Not subpoena?'

'Right. Just look.'

'That shouldn't be a problem,' I said. I was thinking I could call Jennifer Lewis at KNBC, or Bob Arthur at KCBS. Probably Bob.

Connor said, 'It has to be somebody you can approach personally. Otherwise the stations won't help us. You noticed there were no TV crews at the crime scene tonight. At most crime scenes, you have to fight your way past the cameras just to get to the tape. But tonight, no TV crews, no reporters. Nothing.'

I shrugged. 'We were on land lines. The press couldn't monitor radio transmissions.'

'They were already there,' Connor said, 'covering the party with Tom Cruise and Madonna. And then a girl gets murdered on the floor above. So where were the TV crews?'

I said, 'Captain, I don't buy it.'

One of the things I learned as a press officer is that there aren't any conspiracies. The press is too diverse, and in a sense too disorganized. In fact, on the rare occasions when we needed an embargo – like a kidnapping with ransom negotiations in progress – we had a hell of a time getting cooperation. 'The paper closes early. The TV crews have to make the eleven o'clock news. They probably went back to edit their stories.'

'I disagree. I think the Japanese expressed concern about their *kigyou,* their company image, and the press cooperated with no coverage. Trust me, *kōhai*: the pressure is being applied.'

'I can't believe that.'

'Take my word for it,' Connor said. 'The pressure is on.'

Just then, the car phone rang.

'God damn it, Peter,' a familiar rough voice said. 'What the fuck's going on with that homicide investigation?' It was the chief. It sounded like he had been drinking.

'How do you mean, Chief?'

Connor looked at me, and punched the speaker phone button so he could hear.

The chief said: 'You guys harassing the Japanese? We going to have another set of racial allegations against the department here?'

'No, sir,' I said. 'Absolutely not. I don't know what you've heard –'

'I heard that dumb fuck Graham was making insults as usual,' the chief said.

'Well, I wouldn't exactly say insults, Chief –'

'Look, Peter. Don't shit me. I already reamed out Fred Hoffmann for sending Graham in the first place. I want that racist turd off the case. We've all got to get along with the Japanese from now on. It's the way the world is. You hearing me, Peter?'

'Yes, sir.'

'Now about John Connor. You got him with you, is that right?'

'Yes, sir.'

'Why did you bring him into this?'

I thought: why did *I* bring him in? Fred Hoffmann must have decided to say that Connor was my idea, and not his own.

'I'm sorry,' I said. 'But I –'

'I understand,' the chief said. 'You probably thought you couldn't handle the case yourself. Wanted some help. But I'm afraid you bought more trouble than help. Because the Japanese don't like Connor. And I got to tell you. I go way back with John. We entered the academy together back in fifty-nine. He's always been a loner and a troublemaker. You know, anybody who goes to live in some foreign country, it's because he can't fit in here at home. I don't want him screwing up this investigation now.'

'Chief –'

'This is how I see it, Peter. You got a homicide here, wrap it up and get it over with. Do it quick and do it neat. I'm looking to you and you alone. You hearing me?'

'Yes, sir.'

'The connection is good?'

'Yes, sir,' I said.

'Wrap it up, Pete,' the chief said. 'I don't want anybody else calling me on this.'

'Yes, sir.'

'Finish it by tomorrow latest. That's it.' And he hung up.

I put the phone back in the cradle.

'Yes,' Connor said. 'I'd say pressure is being applied.'

I drove south on the 405 freeway, toward the airport. It was foggier here. Connor stared out of the window.

'In a Japanese organization, you'd never get a call like that. The chief just hung you out to dry. He takes no responsibility – it's all your problem. And he's blaming you for things that have nothing to do with you, like Graham, and me.' Connor shook his head. 'The Japanese don't do that. The Japanese have a saying: fix the problem, not the blame. In American organizations it's all about *who* fucked up. Whose head will roll. In Japanese organizations it's about *what's* fucked up, and how to fix it. Nobody gets blamed. Their way is better.'

Connor was silent, staring out the window. We were driving past Slauson, the Marina freeway a dark curve arching above us in the fog.

I said, 'The chief was in the bag, that's all.'

'Yes. And uninformed, as usual. But even so, it sounds like we'd better have this case solved before he gets out of bed tomorrow.'

'Can we do that?'

'Yes. If Ishiguro delivers those tapes.'

The phone rang again. I answered it.

It was Ishiguro.

I handed the phone to Connor.

I could hear Ishiguro faintly through the receiver. He sounded tense, speaking rapidly. '*A, moshi moshi, Connor-san desuka. Keibi no heyani denwa shitandesugane. Daremo denaindesuyo.*'

Connor cupped his hand over the phone and translated. 'He called the security guard but no one was there.'

'*Sorede, chuōkeibishitsu ni renraku shite, hito wo okutte moraimasite, issho ni tēpu o kakunin shite kimashita.*'

'Then he called the main security office and asked them to come down with him to check the tapes.'

'*Tēpu wa subete rekōdā no naka ni arimasu. Nakunattemo torikaeraretemo imasen. Subete daijōbu desu.*'

'The tapes are all in the recorders. No tapes are missing or switched.' Connor frowned and replied. '*Iya, tēpu wa surikaerarete iru hazu nanda. Tēpu o sagase!*'

'*Dakara, daijōbu nandesu, Connor-san. Dōshiro to iun desu ka.*'

'He insists everything is in order.'

Connor said, '*Tēpu o sagase!*' To me, he said, 'I told him I wanted the damn tapes.'

'*Daijōbu da to itterudeshou. Dōshite sonnani tēpu ni kodawarundesuka.*'

'*Ore niwa wakatte irunda. Tēpu wa nakunatte iru.* I know more than you think, Mr. Ishiguro. *Mōichido iu, tēpu o sagasunda!*'

Connor banged the phone in the cradle, and sat back, snorting angrily. 'Bastards. They're taking the position that there are no missing tapes.'

'What does that mean?' I said.

'They've decided to play hardball.' Connor stared out the window at the traffic, and tapped his teeth with his finger. 'They'd never do it unless they felt they had a strong position. An unassailable position. Which means . . .'

Connor drifted off into his private thoughts. I saw his face intermittently reflected in the glass under passing street lamps. Finally he said, 'No, no, no,' as if he were talking to someone.

'No, what?'

'It can't be Graham.' He shook his head. 'Graham is too risky – too many ghosts from the past. And it's not me, either. I'm old news. So it must be you, Peter.'

I said, 'What are you talking about?'

'Something has happened,' Connor said, 'to make Ishigura think he has leverage. And I'd guess it's something to do with you.'

'Me?'

'Yeah. It's almost certainly something personal. You have any problems in your past?'

'Like what?'

'Any priors, arrests, internal affairs investigations, allegations of questionable conduct like drinking or homosexuality or chasing women? Any drug rehab program, problems with partners, problems with superiors. Anything personal or professional. Anything.'

I shrugged. 'Jeez, I don't think so.'

Connor just waited, looking at me. Finally he said, 'They think they have something, Peter.'

'I'm divorced. I'm a single parent. I have a daughter, Michelle. She's two years old.'

'Yes . . .'

'I lead a quiet life. I take care of my kid. I'm responsible.'

'And your wife?'

'My ex-wife is a lawyer in the D.A.'s office.'

'When did you get divorced?'

'Two years ago.'

'Before the child was born?'

'Just after.'

'Why did you get divorced?'

'Christ. Why does anybody get divorced.'

Connor said nothing.

'We were only married a year. She was young when we met. Twenty-four. She had these fantasies about things. We met in court. She thought I was a rough, tough detective facing danger every day. She liked that I had a gun. All that. So we had this affair. Then when she got pregnant she didn't want to have an abortion. She wanted to get married instead. It was some romantic idea she had. She didn't really think it through. But the pregnancy was hard, and it was too late to abort, and pretty soon she decided she didn't like living with me because my apartment was small, and I didn't make enough money, and I lived in Culver City instead of Brentwood. And by the time the baby was finally born, it was like she was completely disillusioned. She said she had made a mistake. She wanted her career. She didn't want to be married to a cop. She didn't want to raise a kid. She said she was sorry, but it was all a mistake. And she left.'

Connor was listening with his eyes closed. 'Yes . . .'

'I don't see why all this matters. She left two years ago. And after that, I couldn't – I didn't want to work detective hours any more, because now I had to raise the kid, so I took the tests and transferred to Special Services, and I worked the press office. No problems there. Everything went fine. Then last year this Asian liaison job came up, and it paid better. Another couple hundred a month. So I applied for that.'

'Uh-huh.'

'I mean, I can really use the money. I have extra expenses now, like Michelle's day care. You know what day care costs for two-year-olds? And I have full-time housekeeping, and Lauren doesn't make her child-support payments more than half the time. She says she can't manage on her salary, but she just bought a new BMW, so I don't know. I mean, what am I going to do, take her to court? She works for the fucking D.A.'

Connor was silent. Up ahead, I saw the airplanes coming down over the freeway. We were approaching the airport.

'Anyway,' I said. 'I was glad when the liaison job came along.

Because it works out better for the hours, and for the money. And that's how I got to be here. In this car with you. That's it.'

'*Kōhai,*' he said quietly. 'We're in this together. Just tell me. What is the problem?'

'There isn't any problem.'

'*Kōhai.*'

'There isn't.'

'*Kōhai* . . .'

'Hey, John,' I said, 'let me tell you something. When you apply for Special Services liaison, five different committees go over your record. To get a liaison job, you have to be *clean.* The committees went over my record. And they found nothing substantial.'

Connor nodded. 'But they found *something.*'

'Christ,' I said, 'I was a detective for five years. You can't work that long without a few complaints. You know that.'

'And what were the complaints against you?'

I shook my head. 'Nothing. Little stuff. I arrested a guy my first year, he accused me of undue force. That charge was dropped after inquiry. I arrested a woman for armed robbery, she claimed I planted a gram on her. Charge dropped; it was her gram. Murder suspect claimed I beat and kicked him during questioning. But other officers were present at all times. A drunken woman on a domestic violence call later claimed I molested her child. She dropped the charge. Teenage gang leader arrested for murder said I made a homosexual pass at him. Charge withdrawn. That's it.'

If you're a cop you know that complaints like these are background noise, like traffic on the street. There's nothing you can do about them. You're in an adversarial environment, accusing people of crimes all the time. They accuse you back. That's just the way it works. The department never pays any attention unless there's a pattern or repetition. If a guy has three or four complaints of undue force over a couple of years, then he gets an inquiry. Or a string of racial complaints, he gets an inquiry. But otherwise, as the assistant chief Jim Olson always says, being a cop is a job for the thick-skinned.

Connor didn't say anything for a long time. He frowned, thinking it over. Finally he said, 'What about the divorce? Problems there?'

'Nothing unusual.'

'You and your ex are on speaking terms?'

'Yes. We're okay. Not great. But okay.'

He was still frowning. Still looking for something. 'And you left the detective division two years ago?'

'Yes.'

'Why?'

'I already told you.'

'You said that you couldn't work the hours.'

'That was most of it, yeah.'

'That, and what else?'

I shrugged. 'After the divorce, I just didn't want to work homicide any more. I felt like – I don't know. Disillusioned. I had this little infant and my wife had moved out. She was going on with her life, dating some hotshot attorney. I was left holding the kid. I just felt flat. I didn't want to be a detective any more.'

'You seek counseling at that time? Therapy?'

'No.'

'Trouble with drugs or alcohol?'

'No.'

'Other women?'

'Some.'

'During the marriage?'

I hesitated.

'Farley? In the mayor's office?'

'No. That was later.'

'But there *was* somebody during the marriage.'

'Yes. But she lives in Phoenix now. Her husband got transferred.'

'She was in the department?'

I shrugged.

Connor sat back in his seat. 'Okay, *kōhai,*' he said. 'If this is all there is, you're fine.' He looked at me.

'That's all.'

'But I have to warn you,' he said. 'I've been through this kind of thing before, with the Japanese. When the Japanese play hardball, they can make things unpleasant. *Really* unpleasant.'

'You trying to scare me?'

'No. Just telling you the way things are.'

'Fuck the Japanese,' I said. 'I've got nothing to hide.'

'Fine. Now I think you better call your friends at the network, and tell them we'll be over, after our next stop.'

A 747 roared low overhead, its landing lights flaring in the fog. It passed the sputtering neon sign that read GIRLS! GIRLS! ALL NUDE! GIRLS! It was around eleven-thirty when we went inside.

To call the Club Palomino a strip joint was to flatter it. It was a converted bowling alley with cactus and horses painted on the walls. It seemed smaller inside than it appeared from the outside. A woman in a silver tassled G-string who looked close to forty danced listlessly in orange light. She seemed as bored as the customers hunched over tiny pink tables. Topless waitresses moved through the smoky air. The tape-recorded music had a loud hiss.

A guy just inside the door said, 'Twelve bucks. Two drink minimum.' Connor flipped his badge. The guy said, 'Okay, fine.'

Connor looked around and said, 'I didn't know Japanese came here.' I saw three businessmen in blue suits, sitting at a corner table.

'Hardly ever,' the bouncer said. 'They like the Star Strip downtown. More glitz, more tits. You ask me, those guys got lost from their tour.'

Connor nodded, 'I'm looking for Ted Cole.'

'At the bar. Guy with the glasses.'

Ted Cole was sitting at the bar. His windbreaker covered his Nakamoto Security uniform. He stared at us dully when we came up and sat beside him.

The bartender came over. Connor said, 'Two Buds.'

'No Bud. Asahi okay?'

'Okay.'

Connor flipped his badge. Cole shook his head and turned away from us. He looked studiously at the stripper.

'I don't know anything.'

Connor said, 'About what?'

'About anything. I'm just minding my own business. I'm off duty.' He was a little drunk.

Connor said, 'When did you get off duty?'

'I got off early tonight.'

'Why is that?'

'Stomach trouble. I got an ulcer, it acts up sometimes. So I got off early.'

'What time?'

'I got off at eight-fifteen at the latest.'

'Do you punch a time clock?'

'No. We don't do that. No time clock.'

'And who took over for you?'

'I got relieved.'

'By whom?'

'My supervisor.'

'Who is that?'

'I don't know him. Japanese guy. Never seen him before.'

'He's your supervisor, and you never saw him before?'

'New guy. Japanese. I don't know him. What do you want from me, anyway?'

'Just to ask a few questions,' Connor said.

'I got nothing to hide,' Cole said.

One of the Japanese men sitting at the table came up to the bar. He stood near us and said to the bartender, 'What kind of cigarettes you got?'

'Marlboro,' the bartender said.

'What else?'

'Maybe Kools. I have to check. But I know we got Marlboro. You want Marlboro?'

Ted Cole stared at the Japanese man. The Japanese seemed not to notice him as he stood at the bar. 'Kent?' the Japanese said. 'You got any Kent lights?'

'No. No Kent.'

'Okay then, Marlboro,' the Japanese man said. 'Marlboro is okay.' He turned and smiled at us. 'This is Marlboro country, right?'

'That's right,' Connor said.

Cole picked up his beer and sipped it. We were all silent. The Japanese man beat the bar with his hands, in time to the music. 'Great place,' he said. 'Lot of atmosphere.'

I wondered what he was talking about. This place was a dump.

The Japanese slid onto the bar stool next to us. Cole studied his beer bottle as if he'd never seen one before. He turned it in his hands, making rings on the bar top.

The bartender brought cigarettes, and the Japanese man tossed a five-dollar bill on the table. 'Keep the change.' He tore open the pack, and took out a cigarette. He smiled at us.

Connor took out his lighter to light the man's cigarette. As the man leaned over the flame, he said, '*Doko kaisha ittenno?*'

The man blinked. 'Sorry?'

'*Wakannē no?*' Connor said. '*Doko kaisha ittenno?*'

The man smiled, and slipped off the bar stool. '*Soro soro ikanakutewa. Shitsurei shimasu.*' He gave a little wave, and he went back to his friends across the room.

'*Dewa mata,*' Connor said. He moved around to sit on the stool where the Japanese man had been sitting.

Cole said, 'What was that all about?'

'I just asked him what company he worked for,' Connor said. 'But he didn't want to talk. I guess he wanted to get back to his friends.' Connor ran his hands under the bar, feeling. 'Feels clean.'

Connor turned back to Cole and said, 'Now then, Mr. Cole. You were telling me that a supervisor took over for you. At what time was that?'

'Eight-fifteen.'

'And you didn't know him?'

'No.'

'And before that time, while you were on duty, were you taping from the video cameras?'

'Sure. The security office always tapes from the cameras.'

'And did the supervisor remove the tapes?'

'Remove them? I don't think so. The tapes are still there, as far as I know.'

He looked at us in a puzzled way.

'You fellows are interested in the tapes?'

'Yes,' Connor said.

'Because I never paid much attention to the tapes. I was interested in the cameras.'

'How's that?'

'They were getting the building ready for the big party, and there were lots of last-minute details. But you still had to wonder why they pulled so many security cameras off other parts of the building and put them up on that floor.'

I said, 'They what?'

'Those cameras weren't on the forty-sixth floor yesterday morning,' Cole said. 'They were scattered all around the building. Somebody moved them during the day. They're easy to move, you know, because there's no wires attached.'

'The cameras have no wires?'

'No. It's all cellular transmission inside the building itself. Built that way. That's why they don't have audio: they can't transmit full bandwidth on cellular. So they just send an image. But they can move those cameras around to suit their purposes. See whatever they want to see. You didn't know that?'

'No,' I said.

'I'm surprised nobody told you. It's one of the features of the building they're most proud of.' Cole drank his beer. 'Only question I have is why somebody would take five cameras and install them on the floor *above* the party. 'Cause there's no security reason. You can lock off the elevators above a certain floor. So for security, you'd want your cameras on the floors below the party. Not above.'

'But the elevators weren't locked off.'

'No. I thought that was kind of unusual, myself.' He looked at the Japanese across the room. 'I got to be going soon,' he said.

'Well,' Connor said. 'You've been very helpful, Mr. Cole. We may want to question you again –'

'I'll write down my phone number for you,' Cole said, scribbling on a bar napkin.

'And your address?'

'Yeah, right. But actually, I'm going out of town for a few days. My mother's been feeling sick, and she asked me to take her down there to Mexico for a few days. Probably go this weekend.'

'Long trip?'

'Week or so. I got vacation days coming up, it seems like a good time to take it.'

'Sure,' Connor said. 'I can see how it would. Thanks again for your help.' He shook hands with Cole, and punched him lightly on the shoulder. 'And you take care of *your* health.'

'Oh, I will.'

'Stop drinking, and have a safe drive home.' He paused. 'Or wherever you may decide to go tonight, instead.'

Cole nodded. 'I think you're right. That's not a bad idea.'

'I know I'm right.'

Cole shook my hand. Connor was heading out the door. Cole said, 'I don't know why you guys are bothering.'

'With the tapes?'

'With the Japanese. What can you do? They're ahead of us every step of the way. And they have the big guys in their pocket. We can't beat 'em now. You two guys'll never beat 'em. They're just too good.'

Outside, beneath the crackling neon sign, Connor said, 'Come on, time is wasting.'

We got in the car. He handed me the bar napkin. On it was scrawled in block letters: THEY STOLE THE TAPES

'Let's get going,' Connor said.

I started the car.

The eleven o'clock news was finished for the night, and the newsroom was nearly deserted. Connor and I went down the hall to the sound stage where the *Action News* was still lit up.

On the set, the evening broadcast was being replayed with the sound off. The anchorman pointed to the monitor. 'I'm not stupid, Bobby. I watch these things. She did the lead-in and the wrap-up the last three nights.' He sat back in his chair and crossed his arms. 'I'm waiting to hear what you have to say, Bobby.'

My friend Bob Arthur, the heavyset, tired producer of the eleven o'clock news, sipped a tumbler of straight scotch as big as his fist. He said, 'Jim, it just worked out that way.'

'Worked out that way my ass,' the anchorman said.

The anchorwoman was a gorgeous redhead with a killer figure. She was taking a long time to shuffle through her notes, making sure she stayed to overhear the conversation between Bob and her coanchor.

'Look,' the anchorman said. 'It's in my contract. Half the lead-ins and half the wraps. It's contractual.'

'But Jim,' the producer said. 'The lead tonight was Paris fashions and the Nakamoto party. That's human interest stuff.'

'It should have been the serial killer.'

Bob sighed. 'His arraignment was postponed. Anyway, the public is tired of serial killers.'

The anchorman looked incredulous. 'The public is tired of serial killers? Now, where'd you get that?'

'You can read it yourself in the focus groups, Jim. Serial killers are overexposed. Our audience is worried about the economy. They don't want any more serial killers.'

'Our audience is worried about the economy so we lead off with Nakamoto and Paris fashions?'

'That's right, Jim,' Bob Arthur said. 'In hard times, you do star parties. That's what people want to see: fashion and fantasy.'

The anchor looked sullen. 'I'm a journalist, I'm here to do hard news, not fashion.'

'Right, Jim,' the producer said. 'That's why Liz did the intros tonight. We want to keep your image hard news.'

'When Teddy Roosevelt led this country out of the Great Depression, he didn't do it with fashion and fantasy.'

'Franklin Roosevelt.'

'Whatever. You know what I'm saying. If people are worried, let's *do* the economy. Let's *do* the balance of payments or whatever it is.'

'Right, Jim. But this is the eleven o'clock news in the local market, and people don't want to hear –'

'And that's what's wrong with America,' the anchorman pronounced, stabbing the air with his finger. 'People don't want to hear the real news.'

'Right, Jim. You're absolutely right.' He put his arm over the anchorman's shoulder. 'Get some rest, okay? We'll talk tomorrow.'

That seemed to be a signal of some kind, because the anchorwoman finished with her notes and strode off.

'I'm a journalist,' the anchor said. 'I just want to do the job I was trained for.'

'Right, Jim. More tomorrow. Have a good night.'

'Stupid dickhead,' Bob Arthur said, leading us down a corridor. 'Teddy Roosevelt. Jesus. They're not journalists. They're actors. And they count their lines, like all actors.' He sighed, and took another drink of scotch. 'Now tell me again, what do you guys want to see?'

'Tape from the Nakamoto opening.'

'You mean the air tapes? The story we ran tonight?'

'No, we want to see the original footage from the camera.'

The field tapes. Jeez. I hope we still have them. They may have been bulked.'

'Bulked?'

'Bulk degaussed. Erased. We shoot forty cassettes a day here. Most of them get erased right away. We used to save field tapes for a week, but we're cutting costs, you know.'

On one side of the newsroom were shelves of stacked Betamax cartridges. Bob ran his finger along the boxes. 'Nakamoto . . . Nakamoto . . . No, I don't see them.' A woman went past. 'Cindy, is Rick still here?'

'No, he's gone home. You need something?'

'The Nakamoto field tapes. They aren't on the shelf.'

'Check Don's room. He cut it.'

'Okay.' Bob led us across the newsroom to the editing bays on the far side. He opened a door, and we entered a small, messy room with two monitors, several tape decks, and an editing console. Tapes in boxes were scattered around the floor. Bob rummaged through them. 'Okay, you guys are in luck. Camera originals. There's a lot of it. I'll get Jenny to run you through them. She's our best spotter. She knows everybody.' He stuck his head out the door. 'Jenny? Jenny!'

'Okay, let's see,' Jenny Gonzales said, a few minutes later. She was a bespectacled, heavyset woman in her forties. She scanned the editor's notes and frowned. 'It doesn't matter how many times I tell them, they just will not put things in proper . . . Finally. Here we are. Four tapes. Two limo driveups. Two roving inside, at the party. What do you want to see?'

Connor said, 'Start with the driveups.' He glanced at his watch. 'Is there any way to do this fast? We're in a hurry.'

'Fast as you want. I'm used to it. Let's see it at high speed.'

She hit a button. At high speed, we saw the limousines pulling up, the doors jumping open, the people getting out, jerkily walking away.

'Looking for anyone in particular? Because I see somebody marked footages for celebrities during the edit.'

'We're not looking for a celebrity,' I said.

'Too bad. It's probably all we shot.' We watched the tape. Jenny said, 'There's Senator Kennedy. He's lost some weight, hasn't he. Oops, gone. And Senator Morton. Looking very fit. No surprise. That creepy assistant of his. He makes my teeth shiver. Senator Rowe, without his wife, as usual. There's Tom Hanks. I don't know this Japanese guy.'

Connor said, 'Hiroshi Masukawa, vice-president of Mitsui.'

'There you go. Senator Chalmers, hair transplant looking good. Congressman Levine. Congressman Daniels. Sober for a change. You know, I'm surprised Nakamoto got so many of these Washington people to attend.'

'Why do you say that?'

'Well, when you get down to it, it's just the opening of some new building. An ordinary corporate bash. It's on the West Coast. And Nakamoto is pretty controversial right at the moment. Barbra Streisand. I don't know who the guy is with her.'

'Nakamoto is controversial? Why?'

'Because of the MicroCon sale.'

I said, 'What's MicroCon?'

'MicroCon is an American company that makes computer equipment. A Japanese company named Akai Ceramics is trying to buy it. There's opposition to the sale in Congress, because of worries about America losing technology to Japan.'

I said, 'And what does this have to do with Nakamoto?'

'Nakamoto's the parent company of Akai.' The first tape finished, and popped out. 'Nothing there you wanted?'

'No. Let's go on.'

'Right.' She slid the second tape in. 'Anyway, I'm surprised how many of these senators and congressmen felt it was acceptable to show up here tonight. Okay, here we go. More driveups. Roger Hillerman, under secretary of state for Pacific affairs. That's his assistant with him. Kenichi Aikou, consul general of Japan here in L.A., Richard Meier, architect. Works for Getty. Don't know her. Some Japanese . . .'

Connor said, 'Hisashi Koyama, vice-president of Honda U.S.'

'Oh, yeah,' Jenny said. 'He's been here about three years now. Probably going home soon. That's Edna Morris, she heads the U.S. delegation to the GATT talks. You know, General Agreement on Tariffs and Trade. I can't believe she showed up here, it's an obvious conflict of interest. But there she is, all smiling and relaxed. Chuck Norris. Eddie Sakamura. Sort of a local playboy. Don't know the girl with him. Tom Cruise, with his Australian wife. And Madonna, of course.'

On the accelerated tape, the strobes flashed almost continuously as Madonna stepped from her limousine and preened. 'Want to slow it down? You interested in this?'

Connor said, 'Not tonight.'

'Well, we probably have a lot on her,' Jenny said. She pushed the very high-speed fast-forward and the image streaked gray. When she punched back, Madonna was wiggling toward the elevator, leaning on the arm of a slender Hispanic boy with a mustache. The image blurred as the camera swung back toward the street. Then it stabilized again.

'There's Daniel Okimoto. Expert on Japanese industrial policy. That's Arnold, with Maria. And behind them is Steve Martin, with Arata Isozaki, the architect who designed the Museum –'

Connor said, 'Wait.'

She punched the console button. The picture froze. Jenny seemed surprised. 'You're interested in Isozaki?'

'No. Back up, please.'

The tape ran backward, the frames flicking and blurring as the camera panned off Steve Martin, and went back to record the next arrival from the limousines. But for a moment in the pan, the camera swung past a group of people who had already gotten out of their limousines, and were walking up the carpeted sidewalk.

Connor said, 'There.'

The image froze. Slightly blurred, I saw a tall blonde in a black cocktail dress walking forward alongside a handsome man in a dark suit.

'Huh,' Jenny said. 'You interested in him, or her?'

'Her.'

'Let me think,' Jenny said, frowning. 'I've seen her at parties with the Washington types for about nine months now. She's this year's Kelly Emberg. The athletic modelly kind. But sophisticated, sort of a Tatiana look-alike. Her name is . . . Austin. Cindy Austin, Carrie Austin . . . Cheryl Austin. That's it.'

I said, 'You know anything else about her?'

Jenny shook her head. 'Listen, I think getting a name is pretty good. These girls show up all the time. You see a new one everywhere for six months, a year, and then they're gone. God knows where they go. Who can keep track of them?'

'And the man with her?'

'Richard Levitt. Plastic surgeon. Does a lot of big stars.'

'What's he doing here?'

She shrugged. 'He's around. Like a lot of these guys, he's a companion to the stars in their time of need. If his patients are getting divorced or whatever, he escorts the woman. When he's not taking out clients, he takes out models like her. They certainly look good together.'

On the monitor, Cheryl and her escort walked toward us in intermittent jerks: one frame every thirty seconds. Stepping slow. I noticed they never looked at each other. She seemed tense, expectant.

Jenny Gonzales said, 'So. Plastic surgeon and a model. Can I ask what's the big deal about these two? Because at an evening like this, they're just, you know, party favors.'

Connor said, 'She was killed tonight.'

'Oh, *she's* the one? Interesting.'

I said, 'You've heard about the murder?'

'Oh, sure.'

'Was it on the news?'

'No, didn't make the eleven o'clock,' Jenny said. 'And it probably won't be on tomorrow. I can't see it myself. It's not really a story.'

'Why is that?' I asked, glancing at Connor.

'Well, what's the peg?'

'I don't follow you.'

'Nakamoto would say, it's only news because it happened at their opening. They'd take the position that any reporting of it is a smear on them. But in a way they're right. I mean, if this girl got killed on the freeway, it wouldn't make the news. If she got killed in a convenience store robbery, it wouldn't make the news. We have two or three of those every night. So the fact that she gets killed at a party . . . who cares? It's still not news. She's young and pretty, but she's not special. It's not as if she has a series or anything.'

Connor glanced at his watch. 'Shall we look at the other tapes?'

'The footage from the party? Sure. You looking for this particular girl?'

'Right.'

'Okay, here we go.' Jenny put in the third tape.

We saw scenes from the party on the forty-fifth floor: the swing band, people dancing beneath the hanging decorations. We strained for a glimpse of the girl in the crowd. Jenny said, 'In Japan, we wouldn't have to do this by eye. The Japanese have pretty sophisticated video-recognition software now. They have a program where you identify an image, say a face, and it'll automatically search tape for you, and find every instance of that face. Find it in a crowd, or wherever it appears. Has the ability to see a single view of a three-dimensional object, and then to recognize the same object in other views. It's supposed to be pretty nifty. But slow.'

'I'm surprised the station hasn't got it.'

'Oh, it's not for sale here. The most advanced Japanese video equipment isn't available in this country. They keep us three to five years behind. Which is their privilege. It's their technology, they can do what they want. But it'd sure be useful in a case like this.'

The party images were streaming past, a frenetic blur.

Suddenly, she locked the image.

'There. Background camera left. Your Austin girl's talking to Eddie Sakamura. Of course he'd know her. Sakamura knows all the models. Normal speed here?'

'Please,' Connor said, staring at the screen.

The camera made a slow pan around the room. Cheryl Austin remained in view for most of the shot. Laughing with Eddie Sakamura, throwing her head back, resting her hand on his arm, happy to be with him. Eddie clowned for her, his face mobile. He seemed to enjoy making her laugh. But from time to time, her eyes flicked away, glancing around the room. As if she was waiting for something to happen. Or for someone to arrive.

At one point, Sakamura became aware he did not have her full attention. He grabbed her arm and pulled her roughly toward him. She turned her face away from him. He leaned close to her and said something angrily. Then a bald man stepped forward, very close to the camera. The light flared on his face, washing out his features, and his head blocked our view of Eddie and the girl. Then the camera panned left, and we lost them.

'Damn.'

'Again?' Jenny backed it up, and we ran it once more.

I said, 'Eddie's obviously not happy with her.'

'I'd say.'

Connor frowned. 'It's so difficult to know what we are seeing. Do you have sound for this?'

Jenny said, 'Sure, but it's probably walla.' She punched buttons and ran it again. The track was continuous cocktail party din. Only for brief moments did we hear an isolated phrase.

At one point, Cheryl Austin looked at Eddie Sakamura and said, '. . . can't help it if it's important to you I get . . .'

His reply to her was garbled, but later, he said clearly to her, 'Don't understand . . . all about the Saturday meeting . . .'

And in the last few seconds of the pan, when he pulled her to him, he snarled a phrase like '. . . be a fool . . . no cheapie . . .'

I said, 'Did he say "No cheapie"?'

'Something like that,' Connor said.

Jenny said, 'Want to run it again?'

'No,' Connor said. 'There's nothing more to be learned here. Go forward.'

'Right,' Jenny said.

The image accelerated, the party-goers becoming frenetic, laughing and raising glasses for quick sips. And then I said, 'Wait.'

Back to normal speed. A blonde woman in an Armani silk suit shaking hands with the bald-headed man we had seen a few moments before.

'What is it?' Jenny said, looking at me.

'That's his wife,' Connor said.

The woman leaned forward to kiss the bald man lightly on the mouth. Then she stepped back and made some comment about the suit he was wearing.

'She's a lawyer in the D.A.'s office,' Jenny said. 'Lauren Davis. She's assisted on a couple of big cases. The Sunset Strangler, the Kellerman shooting. She's very ambitious. Smart and well connected. They say she has a future if she stays in the office. It must be true, because Wyland doesn't ever let her get air time. As you see, she makes a good appearance, but he keeps her away from the microphones. The bald guy she's talking to is John McKenna, with Regis McKenna in San Francisco. The company that does the publicity for most high-tech firms.'

I said, 'We can go forward.'

Jenny pushed the button. 'She really your wife, or is your partner kidding?'

'No, she's really my wife. Was.'

'You're divorced now?'

'Yeah.'

Jenny looked at me, and started to say something. Then she decided not to, and looked back at the screen. On the monitor, the party continued at high speed.

I found myself thinking of Lauren. When I knew her, she was bright and ambitious, but she really didn't understand very much. She had grown up privileged, she had gone to Ivy League schools, and had the privileged person's deep belief that whatever she happened to think was probably true. Certainly good enough to live by. Nothing needed to be checked against reality.

She was young, that was part of it. She was still feeling the world, learning how it worked. She was enthusiastic, and she could be impassioned in expounding her beliefs. But of course her beliefs were always changing, depending on whom she had talked to last. She was very impressionable. She tried on ideas the way some women try on hats. She was always informed on the latest trend. I found it youthful and charming for a while, until it began to annoy me.

Because she didn't have any core, any real substance. She was like a television set: she just played the latest show. Whatever it was. She never questioned it.

In the end, Lauren's great talent was to conform. She was expert at watching the TV, the newspaper, the boss – whatever she saw as the source of authority – and figuring out what direction the winds were blowing. And positioning herself so she was where she ought to be. I wasn't surprised she was getting ahead. Her values, like her clothes, were always smart and up-to-date –

'. . . to you, Lieutenant, but it's getting late . . . Lieutenant?'

I blinked, and came back. Jenny was talking to me. She pointed to the screen, where a frozen image showed Cheryl Austin in her black dress, standing with two older men in suits.

I looked over at Connor, but he had turned away, and was talking on the telephone.

'Lieutenant? This of interest to you?'

'Yes, sure. Who are they?'

Jenny started the tape. It ran at normal speed.

'Senator John Morton and Senator Stephen Rowe. They're both on the Senate Finance Committee. The one that's been having hearings about this MicroCon sale.'

On the screen, Cheryl laughed and nodded. In motion, she was remarkably beautiful, an interesting mixture of innocence and sexuality. At moments, her face appeared knowing and almost hard. She appeared to know both men, but not well. She did not come close to either of them, or touch them except to shake hands. For their part, the senators seemed acutely aware of the camera, and maintained a friendly, if somewhat formal demeanor.

'Our country's going to hell, and on a Thursday night, United States senators are standing around chatting with models,' Jenny said. 'No wonder we're in trouble. And these are important guys. They're talking about Morton as a presidential candidate in the next election.'

I said, 'What do you know about them personally?'

'They're both married. Well. Rowe's semi-separated. His wife stays home in Virginia. He gets around. Tends to drink too much.'

I looked at Rowe on the monitor. He was the same man who had gotten on the elevator with us earlier in the evening. And he had been drunk then, almost falling down. But he wasn't drunk now.

'And Morton?'

'Supposedly he's Mr. Clean. Ex-athlete, fitness nut. Eats health food. Family man. Morton's big area is science and technology. The environment. American competitiveness, American values. All that. But he can't be that clean. I've heard he had a young girlfriend.'

'Is that right?'

She shrugged. 'The story is, his staffers are trying to break it off. But who knows what's true.'

The tape ejected and Jenny pushed in the next one. 'This is the last, fellas.'

Connor hung up the phone and said, 'Forget the tape.' He stood. 'We've got to go, *kōhai*.'

'Why?'

'I've been talking to the phone company about the calls made from the pay phone in the lobby of the Nakamoto building between eight and ten.'

'And?'

'No calls were made during those hours.'

I knew that Connor thought that someone had gone out of the security room and called from the pay phone – Cole, or one of the Japanese. Now his hopes of following a promising lead by tracing the call were dashed. 'That's too bad,' I said.

'Too bad?' Connor said, surprised. 'It's extremely helpful. It narrows things down considerably. Miss Gonzales, do you have any tapes of people leaving the party?'

'Leaving? No. Once the guests arrived, all the crews went upstairs to shoot the actual party. Then they brought the tape back here to make the deadline, while the party was still going on.'

'Fine. Then I believe we're finished here. Thanks for your help. Your knowledge is remarkable. *Kōhai*, let's go.'

Driving again. This time to an address in Beverly Hills. By now it was after one in the morning, and I was tired. I said, 'Why does the pay phone in the lobby matter so much?'

'Because,' Connor said, 'our whole conception of this case revolves around whether someone made a call from that phone, or not. The real question now is, which company in Japan has locked horns with Nakamoto?'

'Which company in Japan?' I said.

'Yes. It is clearly a corporation belonging to a different *keiretsu*,' Connor said.

I said, '*Keiretsu*?'

'The Japanese structure their businesses in large organizations they call *keiretsu*. There are six major ones in Japan, and they're huge. For example, the Mitsubishi *keiretsu* consists of seven hundred separate companies that work together, or have interrelated financing, or interrelated agreements of various sorts. Big structures like that don't exist in America because they violate our antitrust laws. But they are the norm in Japan. We tend to think of corporations as standing alone. To see it the Japanese way, you'd have to imagine, say, an association of IBM and Citibank and Ford and Exxon, all having secret agreements among themselves to cooperate, and to share financing or research. That means a Japanese corporation never stands alone – it's always acting in partnership with hundreds of other companies. And in competition with the companies of other *keiretsu*.

'So when you think about what Nakamoto Corporation is doing, you have to ask what the Nakamoto *keiretsu* is doing, back in Japan. And what companies in other *keiretsu* oppose it. Because this murder is embarrassing to Nakamoto. It could even be seen as an attack against Nakamoto.'

'An attack?'

'Think about it. Nakamoto plans a great, star-studded opening night for their building. They want it to go perfectly. For some reason, a guest at the party gets strangled. And the question is – who called it in?'

'Who reported the murder?'

'Right. Because after all, Nakamoto controls that environment completely: it's their party, their building. And it would be a simple matter for them to wait until eleven o'clock, after the party was over and the guests had left, to report the murder. If I were preoccupied with appearances, with the nuances of public face, that's the way I'd do it. Because anything else is potentially dangerous to the corporate image of Nakamoto.'

'Okay.'

'But the report wasn't delayed,' Connor said. 'On the contrary, somebody called it in at eight thirty-two, just as the party was getting under way. Thus putting the whole evening at risk. And our question has always been: who called it in?'

I said, 'You told Ishiguro to find the person who called. And he hasn't done it yet.'

'Correct. Because he can't.'

'He doesn't know who called it in?'

'Correct.'

'You don't think anybody from the Nakamoto Corporation made the call?'

'Correct.'

'An enemy of Nakamoto called?'

'Almost certainly.'

I said, 'So how do we find out who called the report in?'

Connor laughed. 'That's why I checked the lobby phone. It's crucial to that question.'

'Why is it crucial?'

'Suppose you work for a competing corporation, and you want to know what's going on inside Nakamoto. You can't find out, because Japanese corporations hire their executives for life. The executives feel they are part of a family. And they'd never betray their own family. So Nakamoto Corporation presents an impenetrable mask to the rest of the world, which makes even the smallest details meaningful: which executives are in town from Japan, who is meeting with whom, comings and goings, and so on. And you might be able to learn those details, if you strike up a relationship with an American security guard who sits in front of monitors all day. Particularly if that guard has been subjected to Japanese prejudice against blacks.'

'Go on,' I said.

'The Japanese often try to bribe local security officers from rival firms. The Japanese are honorable people, but their tradition allows such behavior. All's fair in love and war, and the Japanese see business as war. Bribery is fine, if you can manage it.'

'Okay.'

'Now, in the first few seconds after the murder, we can be certain of only two people who knew a girl had been killed. One is the killer himself. The other is the security guard, Ted Cole, who watched it on the monitors.'

'Wait a minute. Ted Cole watched it on the monitors? He knows who the killer is?'

'Obviously.'

'He said he left at eight-fifteen.'

'He was lying.'

'But if you knew that, then why didn't we –'

'He'll never tell *us,*' Connor said. 'The same way Phillips won't tell us. That's why I didn't arrest Cole, bring him down for questioning. In the end it would be a waste of time – and time is of the essence here. We know he won't tell us. My question is, *did he tell anyone else?*'

I began to see what he was driving at. 'You mean, did he walk out of the security office to the lobby pay phone, and call somebody to tell them that a murder had occurred?'

'Correct. Because he wouldn't use the phone in his office. He'd use the pay phone, and call somebody – an enemy of Nakamoto, a competing corporation. Somebody.'

I said, 'But now we know that no calls were made from that phone.'

'Correct,' Connor said.

'So your whole line of reasoning collapses.'

'Not at all. It is clarified. If Cole didn't notify anybody, then who phoned in the murder? Clearly, the source can only be the murderer himself.'

I felt a chill.

'He called it in to embarrass Nakamoto?'

'Presumably,' Connor said.

'Then where did he call from?'

'That's not clear yet. I assume from somewhere inside the building. And there are a few other confusing details that we have not begun to consider.'

'Such as?'

The car phone rang. Connor answered it, and handed the receiver to me. 'It's for you.'

'No, no,' Mrs Ascenio said. 'The baby is fine. I checked on her a few minutes ago. She is fine. Lieutenant, I wanted you to know Mrs Davis called.' That was how she referred to my ex-wife.

'When?'

'I think ten minutes ago.'

'Did she leave a number?'

'No. She say she can't be reached tonight. But she want you to know: something has come up, and maybe she go out of town. So she say maybe she don't take the baby this weekend.'

I sighed. 'Okay.'

'She say she call you tomorrow and let you know for sure.'

'Okay.'

I wasn't surprised. It was typical Lauren. Last-minute changes. You could never make plans involving Lauren because she was always changing her mind. Probably this latest change meant that she had a new boyfriend and she might go away with him. She wouldn't know until tomorrow.

I used to think all this unpredictability was bad for Michelle, that it would make her insecure. But kids are practical. Michelle seems to understand that's the way her mother is, and she doesn't get upset.

I'm the one who gets upset.

Mrs Ascenio said, 'You coming back soon, Lieutenant?'

'No. It looks like I'll be out all night. Can you stay?'

'Yes, but I have to leave by nine in the morning. You want I pull out the couch?'

I had a couch bed in the living room. She used it when she stayed over. 'Yes, sure.'

'Okay, good-bye, Lieutenant.'

'Good-bye, Mrs Ascenio.'

Connor said, 'Anything wrong?' I was surprised to hear tension in his voice.

'No. Just my ex pulling her usual shit. She's not sure she'll take the baby this weekend. Why?'

Connor shrugged. 'Just asking.'

I didn't think that was all there was to it. I said, 'What did you mean earlier, when you said that this case could turn ugly?'

'It may not,' Connor said. 'Our best solution is to wrap it up in the next few hours. And I think we can. Here's the restaurant up ahead on the left.'

I saw the neon sign. Bora Bora.

'This is the restaurant owned by Sakamura?'

'Yes. Actually he's just a part owner. Don't let the valet take the car. Park it in the red. We may need to leave quickly.'

The Bora Bora was this week's hot L.A. restaurant. The decor was a jumble of Polynesian masks and shields. Lime green wooden outriggers jutted out over the bar like teeth. Above the open kitchen, a Prince video played ghostlike on an enormous five-meter screen. The menu was Pacific Rim; the noise deafening; the clientele movie-industry hopeful. Everyone was dressed in black.

Connor smiled. 'It looks like Trader Vic's after a bomb went off, doesn't it? Stop staring. Don't they let you out enough?'

'No, they don't,' I said. Connor turned to speak to the Eurasian hostess. I looked at the bar, where two women kissed briefly on the lips. Farther down, a Japanese man in a leather bomber jacket had his arm around a huge blonde. They were both listening to a man with thinning hair and a pugnacious manner whom I recognized as the director of –

'Come on,' Connor said to me. 'Let's go.'

'What?'

'Eddie's not here.'

'Where is he?'

'At a party in the hills. Let's go.'

The address was on a winding road in the hills above Sunset Boulevard. We would have had a good view of the city up here, but the mist had closed in. As we approached, the street was lined on both sides with luxury cars: mostly Lexus sedans, with a few Mercedes convertibles and Bentleys. The parking attendants looked surprised as we pulled up in our Chevy sedan, and headed up to the house.

Like other residences on the street, the house was surrounded by a three-meter wall, the driveway closed off with a remote-controlled steel gate. There was a security camera mounted above the gate, and another at the path leading up to the house itself. A private security guard stood by the path and checked our badges.

I said, 'Whose house is this?'

Ten years ago, the only people in Los Angeles who maintained such elaborate security were either Mafioso, or stars like Stallone whose violent roles attracted violent attention. But lately it seemed everybody in wealthy residential areas had security. It was expected, almost fashionable. We walked up steps through a cactus garden toward the house, which was modern, concrete, and fortresslike. Loud music played.

'This house belongs to the man who owns Maxim Noir.' He must have seen my blank look. 'It's an expensive clothing store famous for its snotty salespeople. Jack Nicholson and Cher shop there.'

'Jack Nicholson and Cher,' I said, shaking my head. 'How do you know about it?'

'Many Japanese shop at Maxim Noir now. It's like most expensive American stores – it'd go out of business without visitors from Tokyo. It's dependent on the Japanese.'

As we approached the front door a large man in a sport coat appeared. He had a clipboard with names. 'I'm sorry. It's by invitation only, gentlemen.'

Connor flashed his badge. 'We'd like to speak to one of your guests,' he said.

'Which guest is that, sir?'

'Mr Sakamura.'

He didn't look happy. 'Wait here, please.'

From the entryway, we could see into the living room. It was crowded with party-goers, who at a quick glance seemed to be many of the same people who had been at the Nakamoto reception. As in the restaurant, almost everyone was wearing black. But the room itself caught my attention: it was stark white, entirely unadorned. No pictures on the wall. No furniture. Just bare white walls and a bare carpet. The guests looked uncomfortable. They were holding cocktail napkins and drinks, looking around for someplace to put them.

A couple passed us on their way to the dining room. 'Rod always knows what to do,' she said.

'Yes,' he said. 'So elegantly minimalist. The *detail* in executing that room. I don't know how he ever got that paint job. It's *absolutely* perfect. Not a brush stroke, not a blemish. A perfect surface.'

'Well, it has to be,' she said. 'It's integral to his whole conception.'

'It's really quite daring,' the man said.

'Daring?' I said. 'What are they talking about? It's just an empty room.'

Connor smiled. 'I call it *faux zen*. Style without substance.'

I scanned the crowd.

'Senator Morton's here.' He was standing in the corner, holding forth. Looking very much like a presidential candidate.

'So he is.'

The guard hadn't returned, so we stepped a few feet into the room. As I approached Senator Morton, I heard him say, 'Yes, I can tell you exactly why I'm disturbed about the extent of Japanese ownership of American industry. If we lose the ability to make our own products, we lose control over our destiny. It's that simple. For example, back in 1987 we learned that Toshiba sold the Russians critical technology that allowed the Soviets to silence their submarine propellers. Russian nuclear subs now sit right off the coast and we can't track them, because they got technology from Japan. Congress was furious, and the American people were up in arms. And rightly so, it was outrageous. Congress planned economic retaliation against Toshiba. But the lobbyists for American companies pleaded their case for them, because American companies like Hewlett-Packard and Compaq were dependent on Toshiba for computer parts. They couldn't stand a boycott because they had no other source of supply. The fact was, we couldn't afford to retaliate. They could sell vital technology to our enemy, and there wasn't a damned thing we could do about it. That's the problem. We're now dependent on Japan – and I believe America shouldn't be dependent on any nation.'

Somebody asked a question, and Morton nodded. 'Yes, it's true that our industry is not doing well. Real wages in this country are now at 1962 levels. The purchasing power of American workers is back where it was thirty-odd years ago. And that matters, even to the well-to-do folks that I see in this room, because it means American consumers don't have the money to see movies, or buy cars, or clothing, or whatever you people have to sell. The truth is, our nation is sliding badly.'

A woman asked another question I couldn't hear, and Morton said, 'Yes, I said 1962 levels. I know it's hard to believe, but think back to the fifties, when American workers could own a house, raise a family, and send the kids to college, all on a single paycheck. Now both parents work and most people still can't afford a house. The dollar buys less, everything is more expensive. People struggle just to hold on to what they have. They can't get ahead.'

I found myself nodding as I listened. About a month before, I had gone looking for a house, hoping to get a backyard for Michelle. But housing prices were just impossible in L.A. I was never going to be able to afford one, unless I remarried. Maybe not even then, considering –

I felt a sharp jab in the ribs. I turned around and saw the doorman. He jerked his head toward the front door. 'Back, fella.'

I was angry. I glanced at Connor, but he just quietly moved back to the entrance.

In the entryway, the doorman said, 'I checked. There's no Mr Sakamura here.'

'Mr Sakamura,' Connor said, 'is the Japanese gentleman standing at the back of the room, to your right. Talking to the redhead.'

The doorman shook his head. 'I'm sorry fellas. Unless you have a search warrant, I'll have to ask you to leave.'

'There isn't a problem here,' Connor said. 'Mr Sakamura is a friend of mine. I know he'd like to talk to me.'

'I'm sorry. Do you have a search warrant?'

'No,' Connor said.

'Then you're trespassing. And I'm asking you to leave.'

Connor just stood there.

The doorman stepped back and planted his feet wide. He said, 'I think you should know I'm a black belt.'

'Are you really?' Connor said.

'So is Jeff,' the doorman said, as a second man appeared.

'Jeff,' Connor said. 'Are you the one who'll be driving your friend here to the hospital?'

Jeff laughed meanly. 'Hey. You know, I like humor. It's funny. Okay,

Mr Wise Guy. You're in the wrong place. You've had it explained. Move out. *Now.*' He poked Connor in the chest with a stubby finger.

Connor said quietly. 'That's assault.'

Jeff said, 'Hey. Fuck you, buddy. I told you you're in the wrong place – .

Connor did something very fast, and Jeff was suddenly down on the floor, moaning in pain. Jeff rolled away, coming to rest against a pair of black trousers. Looking up, I saw that the man wearing the trousers was dressed entirely in black: black shirt, black tie, black satin jacket. He had white hair and a dramatic Hollywood manner. 'I'm Rod Dwyer. This is my home. What seems to be the problem?'

Connor introduced us politely and showed his badge. 'We're here on official business. We asked to speak to one of your guests, Mr Sakamura, who is the man standing over there in the corner.'

'And this man?' Dwyer asked, pointing to Jeff, who was gasping and coughing on the floor.

Connor said calmly, 'He assaulted me.'

'I didn't fucking assault him!' Jeff said, sitting up on his elbow, coughing.

Dwyer said, 'Did you *touch* him?'

Jeff was silent, glowering.

Dwyer turned back to us. 'I'm sorry this happened. These men are new. I don't know what they were thinking of. Can I get you a drink?'

'Thanks, we're on duty,' Connor said.

'Let me ask Mr Sakamura to come over and talk to you. Your name again?'

'Connor.'

Dwyer walked away. The first man helped Jeff to his feet. As Jeff limped away, he muttered, 'Fucking assholes.'

I said, 'Remember when police were respected?'

But Connor was shaking his head, looking down at the floor. 'I am very ashamed,' he said.

'Why?'

He wouldn't explain further.

'Hey, John! John Connor! *Hisashiburi dana!* Long time no see! How they hanging, guy? Hey!' He punched Connor in the shoulder.

Up close, Eddie Sakamura wasn't so handsome. His complexion was gray, with pock-marked skin, and he smelled like day-old scotch. His movements were edgy, hyperactive, and he spoke quickly. Fast Eddie was not a man at peace.

Connor said, 'I'm pretty good, Eddie. How about you? How you doing?'

'Hey, can't complain, Captain. One or two things only. Got a five-oh-one, drunk driving, try to beat that, but you know, with my record, it's getting hard. Hey! Life goes on! What're you doing here? Pretty wild place, huh? Latest thing: no furniture! Rod sets new style. Great! Nobody can sit down any more!' He laughed. 'New style! Great!'

I had the feeling he was on drugs. He was too manic. I got a good look at the scar on his left hand. It was purple-red, roughly four centimeters by three. It appeared to be an old burn.

Connor lowered his voice and said, 'Actually, Eddie, we're here about the *yakkaigoto* at Nakamoto tonight.'

'Ah, yes,' Eddie said, lowering his voice, too. 'No surprise she came to a bad end. That's one *henntai*.'

'She was perverted? Why do you say that?'

Eddie said, 'Want to step outside? Like to smoke cigarette and Rod doesn't allow smoking in the house.'

'Okay, Eddie.'

We went outside and stood by the edge of the cactus garden. Eddie lit a Mild Seven Menthol. 'Hey, Captain, I don't know what you heard already so far. But that girl. She fucked some of the people in there. She fucked Rod. Some of the other people. So. We can talk easier out here, okay with you?'

'Sure.'

'I know that girl real well. Real well. You know I'm *hipparidako*, hey? I can't help it. Popular guy! She's all over me. All the time.'

'I know that, Eddie. But you say she had problems?'

'Big problems, amigo. Grande problemos. I tell you. She was a sick girl, this girl. She got off on pain.'

'World's full of 'em, Eddie.'

He sucked on his cigarette. 'Hey, no,' he said. 'I'm talking something else. I'm talking, how she gets off. When you hurt her real bad she comes. She's always asking, more, more. Do it more. Squeeze harder.'

Connor said, 'Her neck?'

'Yeah. Her neck. Right. Squeeze her neck. Yeah. You heard? And sometimes a plastic bag. You know, dry-cleaning bag? Put it over her head and clamp it, hold it around her neck while you fuck her and she sucks the plastic against her mouth and turns blue in the face. Claws at your back. Gasp and wheeze. Christ Almighty. Don't care for that, myself. But I'm telling you, this girl has a pussy. I mean she gets off, it's wild ride. You remember afterwards. I'm telling you. But for me, too much. Always on the edge, you know? Always a risk. Always pushing the edge. Maybe this time. Maybe this is the last time. You know what I'm saying?' He flicked his cigarette away. It sputtered among the cactus thorns. 'Sometimes it's exciting. Like Russian roulette. Then I couldn't take it, Captain. Seriously. I couldn't. And you know me, I like a wild time.'

I decided that Eddie Sakamura gave me the creeps. I tried to make notes while he talked, but his words were tumbling out, and I couldn't keep up. He lit another cigarette, his hands shaking. He kept talking fast, swinging the glowing tip in the air for emphasis.

'And I mean, this girl, it's a *problem,*' Eddie said. 'Okay, pretty girl. She's pretty. But sometimes she can't go out, looks too bad. Sometimes, she needs a lot of makeup, because neck is sensitive skin, man. And hers is bruised. Ring around the collar. Bad. You saw that, maybe. You see her dead, Captain?'

'Yeah, I saw her.'

'So then . . .' he hesitated. He seemed to step back, reconsider something. He flicked ash from the cigarette. 'So. Was she strangled, or what?'

'Yes, Eddie. She was strangled.'

He inhaled. 'Yeah. Figures.'

'Did you see her, Eddie?'

'Me? No. What are you talking about? How could I see her, Captain?' He exhaled, blowing smoke into the night.

'Eddie. Look at me.'

Eddie turned toward Connor.

'Look in my eyes. Now tell me. Did you see the body?'

'No. Captain, come on.' Eddie gave a nervous little laugh, and looked away. He flicked the cigarette so it tumbled in the air, dripping sparks. 'What is this? Third degree? No. I didn't see the body.'

'Eddie.'

'I swear to you, Captain.'

'Eddie. How are you involved in this?'

'Me? Shit. Not me, Captain. I know the girl, sure. I see her sometimes. I fuck her, sure. What the hell. She's little weird, but she's fun. A fun girl. Great pussy. That's it, man. That's all of it.' He looked around, lit another cigarette. 'This's a nice cactus garden, huh? Xeriscape, they call it. It's the latest thing. Los Angeles goes back to desert life. It's *hayatterunosa*: very fashionable.'

'Eddie.'

'Come on, Captain. Give me break here. We know each other long time.'

'Sure, Eddie. But I have some problems. What about the security tapes?'

Eddie looked blank, innocent. 'Security tapes?'

'A man with a scar on his hand and a tie with triangles on it came into the Nakamoto security office and took the security videotapes.'

'*Fuck.* What security office? What're you doing, Captain?'

'Eddie.'

'Who said that to you? That's not *true*, man. Take the security tapes? I never did thing like that. What're you, crazy?' He twisted his tie, looked at the label. 'This is Polo tie, Captain. Ralph Lauren. Polo. Lot of these ties, bet you.'

'Eddie. What about the Imperial Arms?'

'What about it?'

'You go there tonight?'

'No.'

'You clean up Cheryl's room?'

'*What?*' Eddie appeared shocked. '*What?* No. Clean up her room? Where you getting all this shit, Captain?'

'The girl across the hall . . . Julia Young,' Connor said. 'She told us she saw you tonight, with another man. In Cheryl's room at the Imperial Arms.'

Eddie threw his arms in the air. 'Jesus. Captain. You listen. That girl wouldn't know, she saw me last night or last month, man. That girl is a fucking hophead. You look between her toes you find the marks. You look under her tongue. Look on her pussylips. You find 'em. That's a dream girl, man. She doesn't know when things happen. *Man.* You come here, give me this. I don't like this.' Eddie tossed his cigarette away, and immediately lit another. 'I don't like this one bit. You don't see what's going on?'

'No,' Connor said. 'Tell me, Eddie. What's going on?'

'This shit's not true, man. None of this true.' He puffed rapidly. 'You know what this is about? It's not about some fucking girl, man. It's about Saturday meetings. The *Doyou kai*, Connor-san. The secret meetings. That's what it's about.'

Connor snapped, '*Sonna bakana.*'

'No *bakana,* Connor-san. Not bullshit.'

'What does a girl from Texas know about *Doyou kai?*'

'She knows something. *Hontō nanda.* And she likes to cause trouble, this girl. She likes to make turmoil.'

'Eddie, I think maybe you better come in with us.'

'Fine. Perfect. You do their job for them. For the *kuromaku*.' He spun to Connor. 'Shit, Captain. Come on. You know how it works. This girl killed at Nakamoto. You know my family, my father, is Daimatsu. Now in Osaka they will read that a girl is killed at Nakamoto and I am arrested in connection. His son.'

'Detained.'

'Detained. Whatever. You know what that will mean. *Taihennakoto ni naru zo*. My father resign, his company must make apologies to Nakamoto. Perhaps reparations. Give some advantage in business. It is powerful *ōsawagi ni naruzo*. You will do this, if you take me into your custody.' He flicked his cigarette away. 'Hey. You think I did this murder, you arrest me. Fine. But you are just covering your ass, you maybe do a lot of damage to me. Captain: you know this.'

Connor said nothing for a long time. There was a long silence. They walked around the garden, in circles.

Finally, Eddie said, '*Connor-san. Matte kure yo . . .*' His voice sounded pleading. It seemed like he was asking for a break.

Connor sighed. 'You got your passport, Eddie?'

'Yeah, sure. Always.'

'Let's have it.'

'Yeah, sure. Okay, Captain. Here goes.'

Connor glanced at it, handed it to me. I slipped it in my pocket.

'Okay, Eddie. But this better not be *murina koto*. Or you'll be declared persona non grata, Eddie. And I will personally put you on the next plane for Osaka. *Wakattaka?*'

'Captain, you protect the honor of my family. *On ni kiru yo*.' And he bowed formally, both hands at his sides.

Connor bowed back.

I just stared. I couldn't believe what I was seeing. Connor was going to let him go. I thought he was crazy to allow it.

I handed Eddie my business card and gave my usual speech about how he could call me later if he thought of anything. Eddie shrugged and slipped the card into his shirt pocket, as he lit another cigarette. I didn't count: he was dealing with Connor.

Eddie started back toward the house, paused. 'I have this redhead here, very interesting,' he said. 'When I leave the party, I go to my house in the hills. You need me, I will be there. Good night, Captain. Good night, Lieutenant.'

'Good night, Eddie.'

We went back down the steps.

'I hope you know what you're doing,' I said.

'So do I,' Connor said.

' 'Cause he seems guilty as hell to me.'

'Maybe.'

'If you ask me, it'd be better to take him in. Safer.'

'Maybe.'

'Want to go back and get him?'

'No.' He shook his head. 'My *dai rokkan* says no.'

I knew that word: it meant sixth sense. The Japanese were big on intuition. I said, 'Yeah, well, I hope you're right.'

We continued down the steps in the darkness.

'Anyway,' Connor said. 'I owe him.'

'For what?'

'There was a time, a few years ago, when I needed some information. You remember the *fugu* poisoning business? No? Well anyway, no one in the community would tell me. They stonewalled me. And I needed to know. It was . . . it was important. Eddie told me. He was scared to do it, because he didn't want anyone to know. But he did it. I probably owe my life to him.'

We came to the bottom of the stairs.

'And did he remind you of that?'

'He would never remind me. It is my job to remember.'

I said, 'That's fine, Captain. All that obligation stuff is fine and noble. And I'm all for interracial harmony. But meanwhile, it's possible that he killed her, stole the tapes, and cleaned up the apartment. Eddie Sakamura looks like a blown-out speedball to me. He acts like a suspect. And we're just walking away. Letting him go.'

'Right.'

We kept walking. I thought it over and got more worried. I said, 'You know, officially this is my investigation.'

'Officially, it's Graham's investigation.'

'Yeah, okay. But we're going to look stupid if it turns out he did it.'

Connor sighed, as if he was losing patience. 'Okay. Let's go over it the way you think it might have happened. Eddie kills the girl, right?'

'Right.'

'He can see her any time but he decides to fuck her on the boardroom table, and he kills her. Then he goes down to the lobby, and pretends to be a Nakamoto executive – even though the last thing Eddie Sakamura looks like is an executive. But let's say he passes himself off.

He manages to dismiss the guard. He takes the tapes. He walks out just as Phillips comes in. Then he goes to Cheryl's apartment to clean that up, but somehow he adds a picture of himself, stuck in Cheryl's mirror. Next he stops by the Bora Bora and tells everybody he's going to a party in Hollywood. Where we find him, in a room without furniture, calmly chatting up a redhead. Is that how the evening lays out to you?'

I said nothing. It didn't make much sense, when he put it that way. On the other hand . . .

'I just hope he didn't do it.'

'So do I.'

We came down to the street level. The valet ran to get our car.

'You know,' I said, 'the blunt way he talks about things, like putting the bag over her head, it's creepy.'

'Oh, that doesn't mean anything,' Connor said. 'Remember, Japan has never accepted Freud or Christianity. They've never been guilty or embarrassed about sex. No problem with homosexuality, no problem with kinky sex. Just matter-of-fact. Some people like it a certain way, so some people do it that way, what the hell. The Japanese can't understand why we get so worked up about a straightforward bodily function. They think we're a little screwed up on the subject of sex. And they have a point.' Connor glanced at his watch.

A security car pulled up. The uniformed guard leaned out. 'Hey, is there a problem at the party up there?'

'Like what?'

'Couple of guys get in a fight? Some kind of fight? We had a report phoned in.'

'I don't know,' Connor said. 'Maybe you better go up and check.'

The guard climbed out of his car, hefted a big gut, and started up the stairs. Connor looked back at the high walls. 'You know we have more private security than police, now? Everyone's building walls and hiring guards. But in Japan, you can walk into a park at midnight and sit on a bench and nothing will happen to you. You're completely safe, day or night. You can go anywhere. You won't be robbed or beaten or killed. You're not always looking behind you, not always worrying. You don't need walls or bodyguards. Your safety is the safety of the whole society. You're free. It's a wonderful feeling. Here, everybody has to lock themselves up. Lock the door. Lock the car. People who spend their whole lives locked up are in prison. It's crazy. It kills the spirit. But it's been so long now that Americans have forgotten what it's like to really feel *safe*. Anyway. Here's our car. Let's get down to the division.'

We had started driving down the street when the DHD operator called. 'Lieutenant Smith,' she said, 'we have a request for Special Services.'

'I'm pretty busy,' I said. 'Can the backup take it?'

'Lieutenant Smith,' she said, 'we have patrol officers requesting Special Services for a vee dig in area nineteen.'

She was telling me there was a problem with a visiting dignitary. 'I understand,' I said, 'but I've already rolled out on a case. Give it to the backup.'

'But this is on Sunset Plaza Drive,' she said. 'Aren't you located –'

'Yes,' I said. Now I understood why she was insistent. The call was only a few blocks away. 'Okay,' I said. 'What's the problem?'

'It's a vee dig DUI. Reported in as G-level plus one. Last name is Rowe.'

'Okay,' I said. 'We're going.' I hung up the phone, and turned the car around.

'Interesting,' Connor said. 'G-level plus one is American government?'

'Yes,' I said.

'It's Senator Rowe?'

'Sounds like it,' I said. 'Driving under the influence.'

The black Lincoln sedan had come to a stop on the lawn of a house along the steep part of Sunset Plaza Drive. Two black and whites were pulled up at the curb, red lights flashing. Up on the lawn, a half-dozen people were standing beside the Lincoln. A man in his bathrobe, arms folded across his chest. A couple of girls in short glittery sequin dresses, a very handsome blond man about forty in a tuxedo, and a younger man in a blue suit, whom I recognized as the young man who had gotten on the elevator with Senator Rowe earlier.

The patrolmen had the video camera out, shining the bright light on Senator Rowe. He was propping himself up against the front fender of the Lincoln, holding his arm up to cover his face against the light. He was swearing loudly as Connor and I walked up.

The man in the bathrobe came toward us and said, 'I want to know who's going to pay for this.'

'Just a minute, sir.' I kept walking.

'He can't just ruin my lawn like this. It has to be paid for.'

'Just give me a minute, sir.'

'Scared the hell out of my wife, too, and she has cancer.'

I said, 'Sir, please give me a minute, and then I'll talk to you.'

'Cancer of the *ear*,' he said emphatically. 'The *ear*.'

'Yes, sir. All right, sir.' I continued toward the Lincoln, and the bright light.

As I passed the aide, he fell into step beside me and said, 'I can explain everything, Detective.' He was about thirty, with the bland good looks of a congressional staffer. 'I'm sure I can resolve everything.'

'Just a minute,' I said. 'Let me talk to the senator.'

'The senator's not feeling well,' the aide said. 'He's very tired.' He stepped in front of me. I just walked around him. He hurried to catch up. 'It's jet lag, that's the problem. The senator has jet lag.'

'I have to talk to him,' I said, stepping into the bright light. Rowe was still holding up his arm. I said, 'Senator Rowe?'

'Turn that fucking thing *off*, for fuck's sake,' Rowe said. He was heavily intoxicated; his speech so slurred it was difficult to understand him.

'Senator Rowe,' I said. 'I'm afraid I'll have to ask you to –'

'Fuck you and the horse you rode in on.'

'Senator Rowe,' I said.

'*Turn that fucking camera off.*'

I looked back to the patrolman and signaled to him. He reluctantly turned the camera off. The light went out.

'Jesus *Christ,*' Rowe said, finally dropping his arm. He looked at me with bleary eyes. 'What the fuck is going on here.'

I introduced myself.

'Then why don't you *do* something about this *fucking zoo,*' Rowe said. 'I'm just driving to my *fucking hotel.*'

'I understand that, Senator.'

'Don't know . . .' He waved his hand, a sloppy gesture. 'What the fucking *problem* is around here.'

'Senator, you were driving this car?'

'Fuck. Driving.' He turned away. 'Jerry? Explain it to them. Christ's sake.'

The aide came up immediately. 'I'm sorry about all this,' he said smoothly. 'The senator isn't feeling at all well. We just came back from Tokyo yesterday evening. Jet lag. He's not himself. He's tired.'

'Who was driving the car?' I said.

'I was,' the aide said. 'Absolutely.'

One of the girls giggled.

'No, he wasn't,' the man in the bathrobe shouted, from the other side of the car. '*He* was driving it. And he couldn't get out of the car without falling down.'

'Christ, fucking zoo,' Senator Rowe said, rubbing his head.

'Detective,' the aide said, 'I was driving the car and these two women here will testify that I was.' He gestured to the girls in party dresses. Giving them a look.

'That's a goddamn lie,' the man in the bathrobe said.

'No, that's correct,' the handsome man in the tuxedo said, speaking for the first time. He had a suntan and a relaxed manner, like he was used to having his orders obeyed. Probably a Wall Street guy. He didn't introduce himself.

'I was driving the car,' the aide said.

'All gone to shit,' Rowe muttered. 'Want to go to my hotel.'

'Was anyone hurt here?' I said.

'Nobody was hurt,' the aide said. 'Everybody is fine.'

I asked the patrolmen behind me. 'You got a one-ten to file?' That was the report of property damage for vehicular accident.

'We don't need to,' a patrolman said to me. 'Single car, and the amount doesn't qualify.' You only had to fill it out if the damage was more than two hundred dollars. 'All we got is a five-oh-one. If you want to run with that.'

I didn't. One of the things you learned about in Special Services was SAR, situational appropriate response. SAR meant that in the case of elected officials and celebrities, you let it go unless somebody was going to press charges. In practice, that meant that you didn't make an arrest short of a felony.

I said to the aide, 'You get the property owner's name and address, so you can deal with the damage to the lawn.'

'He already got my name and address,' the man in the bathrobe said. 'But I want to know what's going to be *done*.'

'I told him we'd repair any damage,' the aide said. 'I assured him we would. He seems to be –'

'Damn it, look: her planting is *ruined*. And she has *cancer* of the *ear*.'

'Just a minute, sir.' I said to the aide. 'Who's going to drive the car now?'

'I am,' the aide said.

'He is,' Senator Rowe said, nodding. 'Jerry. Drive the car.'

I said to the aide, 'All right. I want you to take a breatholyzer –'

'Sure yes –'

'And I want to see your driver's license.'

'Of course.'

The aide blew into the breatholyzer and handed me his driver's license. It was a Texas license. Gerrold D. Hardin, thirty-four years old. Address in Austin, Texas. I wrote down the details, and gave it back.

'All right, Mr. Hardin. I'm going to release the senator into your custody tonight.'

'Thank you, Lieutenant. I appreciate it.'

The man in the bathrobe said, 'You're going to *let him go*?'

'Just a minute, sir.' I said to Hardin, 'I want you to give this man your business card, and stay in contact with him. I expect the damage to his yard to be resolved to his satisfaction.'

'Absolutely. Of course. Yes.' Hardin reached into his pocket for a card. He brought out something white in his hand, like a handkerchief. He stuffed it hastily back in his pocket, and then walked over to give his card to the man in the bathrobe.

'You're going to have to replace all her begonias.'

'Fine, sir,' Hardin said.

'*All* of 'em.'

'Yes. That's fine, sir.'

Senator Rowe pushed off the front fender, standing unsteadily in the night. 'Fucking begonias,' he said. 'Christ, what a fucking night this is. You got a wife?'

'No,' I said.

'I do,' Rowe said. 'Fucking begonias. Fuck.'

'This way, Senator,' Hardin said. He helped Rowe into the passenger seat. The girls climbed into the back seat, on either side of the handsome Wall Street guy. Hardin got behind the wheel and asked Rowe for the keys. I looked away to watch the black and whites as they pulled away from the curb. When I turned back, Hardin rolled down the window and looked at me. 'Thank you for this.'

'Drive safely, Mr. Hardin,' I said.

He backed the car off the lawn, driving over a flower bed.

'*And* the irises,' the man in the bathrobe shouted, as the car pulled away down the road. He looked at me. 'I'm telling you, the other man was driving, and he was drunk.'

I said, 'Here's my card. If things don't turn out right, call me.'

He looked at the card, shaking his head, and went back into his house. Connor and I got back into the car. We drove down the hill.

Connor said, 'You got information on the aide?'

'Yes,' I said.

'What was in his pocket?'

'I'd say it was a pair of women's panties.'

'So would I,' Connor said.

Of course there was nothing we could do. Personally, I would have liked to spin the smug bastard around, push him up against the car and search him, right there. But we both knew our hands were tied: we had no probable cause to search Hardin, or to arrest him. He was a young man driving with two young women in the back seat, either of whom might be without her panties, and a drunken United States Senator in the front seat. The only sensible thing to do was to let them all go.

But it seemed like an evening of letting people go.

The phone rang. I pushed the speaker button. 'Lieutenant Smith.'

'Hey, buddy.' It was Graham. 'I'm over here at the morgue, and guess what? I have some Japanese bugging me to attend the autopsy. Wants to sit in and observe, it you can believe that shit. He's all bent out of shape because we started the autopsy without him. But the lab work is starting to come back. It is not looking good for Nippon Central. I'd say we have a Japanese perp. So: you coming here or what?'

I looked at Connor. He nodded.

'We're heading there now,' I said.

The fastest way to the morgue was through the emergency room at County General Hospital. As we went through, a black man covered in blood was sitting up on his gurney, screaming 'Kill the pope! Kill the pope! Fuck him!' in a drug-crazed frenzy. A half-dozen attendants were trying to push him down. He had gunshot wounds in his shoulder and hand. The floors and walls of the emergency room were spattered with blood. An orderly went down the hall, cleaning it up with a mop. The hallways were lined with black and Hispanic people. Some of them held children in their laps. Everyone looked away from the bloody mop. From somewhere down the corridor, we heard more screams.

We got onto the elevator. It was quiet.

Connor said, 'A homicide every twenty minutes. A rape every seven minutes. A child murdered every four hours. No other country tolerates these levels of violence.'

The doors opened. Compared to the emergency room, the basement corridors of the county morgue were positively tranquil. There was a strong odor of formaldehyde. We went to the desk, where the thin, angular deaner, Harry Landon, was bent over some papers, eating a ham sandwich. He didn't look up. 'Hey, guys.'

'Hey, Harry.'

'What you here for? Austin prep?'

'Yeah.'

'They started about half an hour ago. Guess there's a big rush on her, huh?'

'How's that?'

'The chief called Dr Tim out of bed and told him to do it pronto. Pissed him off pretty good. You know how particular Dr Tim is.' The deaner smiled. 'And they called in a lot of lab people, too. Who ever heard of pushing a full workup in the middle of the night? I mean, you know what this is going to cost in overtime?'

I said, 'And what about Graham?'

'He's around here someplace. He had some Japanese guy chasing after him. Dogging him like a shadow. Then every half hour, the Japanese asks me can he use the phone, and he makes a call. Speaks Japanese a while. Then he goes back to bothering Graham. He says he wants to see the autopsy, if you can believe that. Keeps pushing, pushing. But anyway, the Japanese makes his last call about ten minutes ago, and suddenly a big change comes over him. I was here at the desk. I saw it on his face. He goes *mojo mojo* like he can't believe his ears. And then he *runs* out of here. I mean it: *runs*.'

'And where's the autopsy?'

'Room two.'

'Thanks, Harry.'

'Close the *door*.'

'Hi, Tim,' I said as we came into the autopsy room. Tim Yoshimura, known to everyone as Dr. Tim, was leaning over the stainless-steel table. Even though it was one-forty in the morning, he was as usual immaculate. Everything was in place. His hair was neatly combed. His tie was perfectly knotted. The pens were lined up in the pocket of his starched lab coat.

'Did you *hear* me?'

'I'm closing it, Tim.' The door had a pneumatic self-closing mechanism, but apparently that wasn't fast enough for Dr Tim.

'It's only because I don't want that Japanese individual looking in.'

'He's gone, Tim.'

'Oh, is he? But he may be back. He's been unbelievably persistent and irritating. The Japanese can be a real pain in the arse.'

I said, 'Sounds funny coming from you, Tim.'

'Oh, I'm not Japanese,' he said seriously, 'I'm Japanese-American, which means in their eyes I'm *gaijin*. If I go to Japan, they treat me like any foreigner. It doesn't matter how I look, I was born in Torrance – and that's the end of it.' He glanced over his shoulder. 'Who's that with you? Not John Connor? Haven't seen you in ages, John.'

'Hi, Tim.' Connor and I approached the table. I could see the dissection was already well advanced, that the Y-shaped incision had been made, and the first organs removed and placed neatly on stainless steel trays.

'Now maybe *somebody* can tell me, what is the big deal about this case?' Tim said. 'Graham is so pissed off he won't say anything. He went next door to the lab to see the first of the results. But I still want to know why I got called out of bed to do this one. Mark's on duty, but he is apparently not senior enough to do it. And of course the M.E. is out of town at a conference in San Francisco. Now that he has that new girlfriend he is always out of town. So I get called. I can't remember the last time I got called out of bed.'

'You can't?' I said. Dr Tim was precise in all ways, including his memory.

'The last time was January three years ago. But that was to *cover.* Most of the staff was out with the flu, and the cases were backing up. Finally one night we ran out of lockers. They had these bodies lying around on the floor in bags. Stacked up in piles. Something had to be done. The smell was terrible. But no, I can't remember being called out just because a case was politically *tense.* Like this one.'

Connor said, 'We're not sure why it is tense, either.'

'Maybe you better find out. Because there's a lot of pressure here. The M.E. calls me from San Francisco, and he keeps saying, "Do it now, do it tonight, and get it done." I say, "Okay, Bill." Then he says, "Listen, Tim. Do this one right. Go slow, take lots of pictures and lots of notes. Document your ass off. Shoot with two cameras. Because I got a feeling that anybody who has anything to do with this case could get into deep shit." So. It's natural to wonder what the big deal is.'

Connor said, 'What time was that call to you?'

'About ten-thirty, eleven.'

'The M.E. say who called him?'

'No, But it's usually only one of two people: the chief of police or the mayor.'

Tim looked at the liver, pulling apart the lobes, then placed it on a steel tray. The assistant was taking flash pictures of each organ and then setting it aside.

'So? What've you found?'

'Frankly, the most interesting findings so far are external,' Dr Tim said. 'She had heavy makeup on her neck, to cover a pattern of multiple contusions. Bruises of different ages. Without a spectroscopic curve for the hemoglobin breakdown products at the bruise sites, I'd still say these bruises are of variable age, up to two weeks old. Perhaps older. Consistent with a pattern of repeated, chronic cervical trauma. I don't think there's any question: we're looking at a case of sexual asphyxia.'

'She's a gasper?'

'Yeah. She is.'

Kelly thought so. For once Kelly was right.

'It's more common in men, but it is certainly reported in women. The syndrome is the individual is sexually aroused only by the hypoxia of near-strangulation. These individuals ask their sexual partners to strangle them, or put a plastic bag over their head. When they're alone, they sometimes tie a cord around their neck, and hang themselves while they masturbate. Since the effect requires that they are strangled almost to the point of passing out, it's easy to make a mistake and go too far. They do, all the time.'

'And in this case?'

Tim shrugged. 'Well. She has physical findings consistent with a sexual asphyxia syndrome of long standing. And she has ejaculate in her vagina and abrasions on her external vaginal labia, consistent with a forced sexual episode on the same night of her death.'

Connor said, 'You're sure the vaginal abrasions occurred before death?'

'Oh, yes. They are definitely antemortem injuries. There's no question she had forced sex sometime before she died.'

'Are you saying she was raped?'

'No. I wouldn't go that far. As you see, the abrasions are not severe, and there are no associated injuries to other parts of her body. In fact, there are no signs of physical struggle at all. So I would consider the findings consistent with premature vaginal entry with insufficient lubrication of the external labia.'

I said, 'You're saying she wasn't wet.'

Tim looked pained. 'Well. In crude layman's terms.'

'How long before death did these abrasions occur?'

'It could be as much as an hour or two. It wasn't near the actual time of death. You can tell that from the extravasation and swelling of the affected areas. If death occurs soon after the injury, blood flow stops, and therefore the swelling is limited and absent. In this case, as you see, swelling is quite pronounced.'

'And the sperm?'

'Samples have gone to the lab. Along with all her usual fluids.' He shrugged. 'Have to wait and see. Now, are you two going to fill me in? Because it looks to me like this little girl was going to get into trouble, sooner or later. I mean, she's *cute*, but she's screwed up. So . . . what is the big deal? Why am I out of bed in the middle of the night to do a careful, documented post on some little gasper?'

I said, 'Beats me.'

'Come on. Fair is fair,' Dr. Tim said. 'I showed you mine, now you show me yours.'

'Why, Tim,' Connor said. 'You made a joke.'

'Fuck you,' Tim said. 'You guys owe me. Come on.'

'I'm afraid Peter is telling you the truth,' Connor said. 'All we know is that this murder occurred at the time of a big public Japanese reception, and they are eager to get it cleared up right away.'

'That makes sense,' Tim said. 'The last time the shit hit the fan around here, it was because of that thing involving the Japanese consulate. Remember, the Takashima kidnapping case? Maybe you don't remember: it never made the papers. The Japanese managed to keep it *very* quiet. But anyway, a guard was killed under odd circumstances, and for two days, they put a hell of a pressure on our office. I was amazed what they could do. We had Senator Rowe calling us in person, telling us what to do. The governor calling in person. Everybody calling us. You'd think it was the president's kid. I mean, these people have *influence.*'

'Of course they do. They've paid handsomely for it,' Graham said, coming into the room.

'Close the *door,*' Tim said.

'But this time, all their fucking influence won't help,' Graham said. 'Because this time, we have them by the short and curlies. We have a murder: and based on the lab results so far, we can say without question that the murderer was Japanese.'

The pathology lab next door was a large room lit by even banks of fluorescent lights. Rows of microscopes, neatly laid out. But late at night, only two technicians were working in the big space. And Graham was standing beside them, gloating.

'Look for yourself. Pubic hair comb-through reveals male pubic hair, moderate curl, ovoid cross section, almost certainly Asian in origin. The first semen analysis is blood type AB, relatively rare among Caucasians, but much more common among Asians. The first analysis of protein in the seminal fluid comes up negative for the genetic marker for . . . what's it called?'

'Ethanol dehydrogenase,' the technician said.

'Right. Ethanol dehydrogenase. It's an enzyme. Missing in Japanese. And missing in this seminal fluid. And there's the Diego factor, which is a blood-group protein. So. We have more tests coming, but it seems clear that this girl had forced sex with a Japanese man before she was killed by him.'

'It's clear you've found evidence of Japanese semen in her vagina,' Connor said. 'That's all.'

'Christ,' Graham said. 'Japanese semen, Japanese pubic hair, Japanese blood factors. We are talking a Japanese perp here.'

He had set out some pictures from the crime scene, showing Cheryl lying on the boardroom table. He started to pace back and forth in front of them.

'I know where you guys have been, and I know you've been wasting your time,' Graham said. 'You went for videotapes: but they're gone, right? Then you went to her apartment: but it was cleaned up before you ever got there. Which is exactly what you'd expect if the perp is Japanese. It lays right out, plain as can be.'

Graham pointed to the pictures. 'There's our girl. Cheryl Austin from Texas. She's cute. Fresh. Good figure. She's an actress, sort of. She does a few commercials. Maybe a Nissan commercial. Whatever. She meets some people. Makes some contacts. Gets on some lists. You with me?'

'Yes,' I said to Graham. Connor was staring intently at the pictures.

'One way or another, our Cheryl's doing well enough to be wearing a black Yamamoto gown when she gets invited to the grand opening of the Nakamoto Tower. She comes with some guy, maybe a friend or a hairdresser. A beard. Maybe she knows other people at the party, and maybe not. But in the course of the evening, somebody big and powerful suggests they slip away for a while. She agrees to go upstairs. Why not? This girl likes adventure. She likes danger. She's cruising for a bruising. So she goes upstairs – maybe with the other guy, maybe separately. But anyway, they meet upstairs, and they look around for a place to do it. A place that's exciting. And they decide – him, probably, *he* decides – to do it right on the fucking boardroom table. So they start doing it, they're whanging away but things get out of hand. Her loverboy gets a little too worked up, or else he's kinky, and . . . he squeezes her neck a little too hard. And she's dead. You with me so far?'

'Yes . . .'

'So now loverboy has a problem. He's come upstairs to fuck a girl, but unfortunately he's killed her. So what does he do? What *can* he do? He goes back down, rejoins the party, and since he is a big samurai cocksman, he tells one of his underlings that he has this little problem. He has unfortunately snuffed out the life of a local whore. Very inconvenient for his busy schedule. So the underlings run around and clean up the boss's mess. They clean up incriminating evidence from the floor upstairs. They remove the videotapes. They go to her apartment and remove evidence there. Which is all fine, except it takes time. So somebody has to stall the police. And that's where their smoothie suckass lawyer Ishiguro comes in. He delays us a good hour and a half. So. How does that sound?'

There was a silence when he had finished. I waited for Connor to speak.

'Well,' Connor said, at last. 'My hat is off to you, Tom. That sequence of events sounds correct in many respects.'

'You're damned right it does.' Graham puffed up.'Damn fucking right.'

The telephone rang. The lab technician said, 'Is there a Captain Connor here?'

Connor went to answer the phone. Graham said to me, 'I'm telling you. A jap killed this girl, and we are going to find him and fucking flay him. *Flay* him.'

I said, 'Why do you have it in for them, anyway?'

Graham gave me a sullen look. He said, 'What are you talking about?'

'I'm talking about how you hate the Japanese.'

'Hey, listen,' Graham said. 'Let's get something straight, Petey-san. I don't hate anybody. I do my job. Black man, white man, Japanese man, it makes no difference to me.'

'Okay, Tom.' It was late at night. I didn't want to argue.

'No, hell. You fucking think I'm prejudiced.'

'Let's just drop it, Tom.'

'No, hell. We're not going to drop it. Not now. Let me tell you something, Petey-san. You got yourself this fucking liaison job, isn't that right?'

'That's right, Tom.'

'And how come you applied for it? Because of your great love of Japanese culture?'

'Well, at the time, I was working in the press office –'

'No, no, cut the shit. You applied for it,' Graham said, 'because there was an extra stipend, isn't that right? Two, three thousand a year. An educational stipend. It comes into the department from the Japan-America Amity Foundation. And the department allows it as an educational stipend, paid to members of the force so that they can further their education in Japanese language and culture. So. How're those studies going, Petey-san.'

'I'm studying.'

'How often?'

'One night a week.'

'One night a week. And if you miss classes, do you lose your stipend?'

'No.'

'Fucking right you don't. In fact, it doesn't make any difference if you go to classes at all. The fact is, buddy, you got yourself a bribe. You got three thousand dollars in your pocket and it comes right from the land of the rising sun. Of course, it's not that much. Nobody can buy you for three grand, right? Of course not.'

'Hey, Tom –'

'But the thing is, they aren't buying you. They're just *influencing* you. They just want you to think twice. To tend to look favorably upon them. And why not? It's human nature. They've made your life a little better. They contribute to your well-being. Your family. Your little girl. They scratch your back, so why shouldn't you scratch theirs. Isn't that about it, Petey-san?'

'No, it isn't,' I said. I was getting angry.

'Yes, it is,' Graham said. 'Because that's how influence works. It's deniable. You say it isn't there. You tell yourself it isn't there – but it is. The only way you can be clean is to be *clean,* man. If you got no stake in it, if you got no income from it, then you can talk. Otherwise, man, they pay you and I say, they *own* you.'

'Just a fucking minute –'

'So don't you talk to me about *hating,* man. This country is in a war and some people understand it, and some other people are siding with the enemy. Just like in World War II, some people were paid by Germany to promote Nazi propaganda. New York newspapers published editorials right out of the mouth of Adolf Hitler. Sometimes the people didn't even know it. But they did it. That's how it is in a war, man. And *you* are a fucking collaborator.'

I was grateful when, at that moment, Connor came back to where we were standing. Graham and I were about to square off when Connor said calmly, 'Now, just so I understand, Tom. According to your scenario, after the girl was murdered, what happened to the tapes?'

'Oh, hell, those tapes are *gone,*' Graham said. 'You're never going to see those tapes again.'

'Well, it's interesting. Because that call was the division headquarters. It seems Mr Ishiguro is there. And he's brought a box of videotapes with him, for me to look at.'

Connor and I drove over. Graham took his own car. I said, 'Why did you say the Japanese would never touch Graham?'

'Graham's uncle,' Connor said. 'He was a prisoner of war during World War II. He was taken to Tokyo, where he disappeared. Graham's father went over after the war to find out what happened to him. There were unpleasant questions about what happened. You probably know that some American servicemen were killed in terminal medical experiments in Japan. There were stories about the Japanese feeding their livers to subordinates as a joke, things like that.'

'No, I didn't know,' I said.

'I think everybody would prefer to forget that time,' Connor said, 'and move on. And probably correctly. It's a different country now. What was Graham going on about?'

'My stipend as a liaison officer.'

Connor said, 'You told me it was fifty a week.'

'It's a little more than that.'

'How much more?'

'About a hundred dollars a week. Fifty-five hundred a year. But that's to cover classes, and books, and commuting expenses, baby-sitters, everything.'

'So you get five grand,' Connor said. 'So what?'

'Graham was saying I was influenced by it. That the Japanese had bought me.'

Connor said, 'Well, they certainly try to do that. And they're extremely subtle.'

'They tried it with you?'

'Oh, sure.' He paused. 'And often I accepted. Giving gifts to ensure that you will be seen favorably is something the Japanese do by instinct. And it's not so different from what we do, when we invite the boss over for dinner. Goodwill is goodwill. But we don't invite the boss over for dinner when we're up for a promotion. The proper thing to do is to invite the boss early in the relationship, when nothing is at stake. Then it's just goodwill. The same with the Japanese. They believe you should give the gift early, because then it is not a bribe. It is a gift. A way of making a relationship with you before there is any pressure on the relationship.'

'And you think that's okay?'

'I think it's the way the world works.'

'Do you think it's corrupting?'

Connor looked at me and said, 'Do you?'

I took a long time to answer. 'Yes. I think maybe so.'

He started to laugh. 'Well, that's a relief,' he said. 'Because otherwise, the Japanese would have wasted all their money on you.'

'What's so funny?'

'Your confusion, *kōhai*.'

'Graham thinks it's a war.'

Connor said, 'Well, that's true. We are definitely at war with Japan. But let's see what surprises Mr Ishiguro has for us in the latest skirmish.'

As usual, the fifth-floor anteroom of the downtown detective division was busy, even at two o'clock in the morning. Detectives moved among the beat-up prostitutes and twitching druggies brought in for questioning; in the corner a man in a checked sport coat was shouting, 'I said, shut the fuck *up*!' over and over to a female officer with a clipboard.

In all the swirl and noise, Masao Ishiguro looked distinctly out of place. Wearing his blue pinstripe suit, he sat in the corner with his head bowed and his knees pressed together. He had a cardboard box balanced on his knees.

When he saw us, he jumped to his feet. He bowed deeply, placing his hands flat on his thighs, a sign of additional respect. He held the bow for several seconds. Then he immediately bowed again, and this time he waited, bent over staring at the floor, until Connor spoke to him in Japanese. Ishiguro's reply, also in Japanese, was quiet and deferential. He kept looking at the floor.

Tom Graham pulled me over by the water cooler. 'Holy Christ,' he said. 'It looks like we got a fucking *confession* happening here.'

'Yeah, maybe,' I said. I wasn't convinced. I'd seen Ishiguro change his demeanour before.

I watched Connor as he talked to Ishiguro. The Japanese man remained hangdog. He kept looking at the floor.

'I never would have figured him,' Graham said. 'Not in a million years. Never him.'

'How is that?'

'Are you kidding? To kill the girl, and then to stay in the room, and order us around. What fucking nerves of steel. But look at him now: Christ, he's almost *crying*.'

It was true: tears seemed to be welling up in Ishiguro's eyes. Connor took the box and turned away, crossing the room to us. He gave me the box. 'Deal with this. I'm going to take a statement from Ishiguro.'

'So,' Graham said. 'Did he confess?'

'To what?'

'The murder.'

'Hell, no,' Connor said. 'What makes you think that?'

'Well, he's over there bowing and scraping –'

'That's just *sumimasen,*' Connor said. 'I wouldn't take it too seriously.'

'He's practically crying,' Graham said.

'Only because he thinks it'll help him.'

'He didn't confess?'

'No. But he discovered that the tapes had been removed, after all. That means he made a serious mistake, with his public blustering in front of the mayor. Now he could be accused of concealing evidence. He could be disbarred. His corporation could be disgraced. Ishiguro is in big trouble, and he knows it.'

I said, 'And that's why he's so humble?'

'Yes. In Japan, if you screw up, the best thing is to go to the authorities and make a big show of how sorry you are, and how bad you feel, and how you will never do it again. It's pro forma, but the authorities will be impressed by how you've learned your lesson. That's *sumimasen*: apology without end. It's the Japanese version of throwing yourself on the mercy of the court. It's understood to be the best way to get leniency. And that's all Ishiguro is doing.'

'You mean it's an act,' Graham said, his eyes hardening.

'Yes and no. It's difficult to explain. Look. Review the tapes. Ishiguro says he brought one of the VCRs, because the tapes are recorded in an unusual format, and he was afraid we wouldn't be able to play them. Okay?'

I opened the cardboard box. I saw twenty small eight-millimeter cartridges, like audio cassette cartridges. And I saw a small box, the size of a Walkman, which was the VCR. It had cables to hook to a TV.

'Okay,' I said. 'Let's have a look.'

The first of the tapes that showed the forty-sixth floor was a view from the atrium camera, high up, looking down. The tape showed people working on the floor, in what looked like an ordinary office day. We fast-forwarded through that. Shadows of sunlight coming through the windows swung in hot arcs across the floor, and then disappeared. Gradually, the light on the floor softened and dimmed, as daylight came to an end. One by one, desk lights came on. The workers moved more slowly now. Eventually they began to depart, leaving their desks one by one. As the population thinned, we noticed something else. Now the camera moved occasionally, panning one or another of the workers as they passed beneath. Yet at other times, the camera would not pan. Eventually we realized the camera must be equipped for automatic focusing and tracking. If there was a lot of movement in the frame – several people going in different directions – then the camera did not move. But if the frame was mostly empty, the camera would fix on a single person walking through, and track him.

'Funny system,' Graham said.

'It probably makes sense for a security camera,' I said. 'They'd be much more concerned about a single person on the floor than a crowd.'

As we watched, the night lights came on. The desks were all empty. Now the tape began to flicker rapidly, almost like a strobe.

'Something wrong with this tape?' Graham said, suspiciously. 'They fucked around with it?'

'I don't know. No, wait. It's not that. Look at the clock.'

On the far wall, we could see the office clock. The minute hands were sweeping smoothly from seven-thirty toward eight o'clock.

'It's time lapse,' I said.

'What is it, taking snapshots?'

I nodded. 'Probably, when the system doesn't detect anybody for a while, it begins to take single frames every ten or twenty seconds, until –'

'Hey. What's that?'

The flickering had stopped. The camera had begun to pan to the right, across the deserted floor. But there was nobody in the frame. Just empty desks, and occasional night lights, which flared in the video.

'Maybe they have a wide sensor,' I said. 'That looks beyond the borders of the image itself. Either that, or it's being moved manually. By a guard, somewhere. Maybe down in the security room.'

The panning image came to rest on the elevator doors. The doors were at the far right, in deep shadow, beneath a kind of ceiling overhang that blocked our view.

'Jeez, dark under there. Is someone there?'

'I can't see anything,' I said.

The image began to swim in and out of focus.

'What's happening now?' Graham said.

'Looks like the automatic focus is having trouble. Maybe it can't decide what to focus on. Maybe the overhang is bothering the logic circuits. My video camera at home does the same thing. The focus gets screwed up when it can't tell what I am shooting.'

'So is the camera trying to focus on something? Because I can't see anything. It just looks black under there.'

'No, look. There's someone there. You can see pale legs. Very faint.'

'Christ,' Graham said, 'that's our girl. Standing by the elevator. No, wait. Now she's moving.'

A moment later, Cheryl Austin stepped from beneath the ceiling overhang, and we saw her clearly for the first time.

She was beautiful and assured. She moved unhesitatingly into the room. She was direct, purposeful in her movements, with none of the awkward, shuffling sloppiness of the young.

'Jesus, she's good-looking,' Graham said.

Cheryl Austin was tall and slender; her short blonde hair made her seem even taller. Her carriage was erect. She turned slowly, surveying the room as if she owned it.

'I can't believe we're seeing this,' Graham said.

I knew what he meant. This was a girl who had been killed just a few hours before. Now we were seeing her on a videotape, walking around just minutes before her death.

On the monitor, Cheryl picked up a paperweight on one of the desks, turned it in her hand, put it back. She opened her purse, closed it again. She glanced at her watch.

'Starting to fidget.'

'She doesn't like to be kept waiting,' Graham said. 'And I bet she doesn't have much practice at it, either. Not a girl like that.'

She began to tap on the desk with her fingers in a distinct rhythm. It seemed familiar to me. She bobbed her head to the rhythm. Graham squinted at the screen, 'Is she talking? Is she saying something?'

'It looks like it,' I said. We could barely see her mouth moving. And then I suddenly put it together, her movements, everything. I realized I could sync her lips. 'I chew my nails and I twiddle my thumbs. I'm real nervous but it sure is fun. Oh baby, you drive me crazy . . .'

'Jesus,' Graham said. 'You're right. How'd you know that?'

'Goodness, gracious, great balls of –'

Cheryl stopped singing. She turned toward the elevators.

'Ah. Here we go.'

Cheryl walked toward the elevators. Just as she stepped beneath the overhang, she threw her arms around the man who had arrived. They embraced and kissed warmly. But the man remained beneath the overhang. We could see his arms around Cheryl, but we could not see his face.

'Shit,' Graham said.

'Don't worry,' I said. 'We'll see him in a minute. If not this camera, another camera. But I think we can say this is not somebody she just met. This is somebody she already knows.'

'Not unless she's *real* friendly. Yeah, look. This guy isn't wasting any time.'

The man's hands slid up the black dress, raising her skirt. He squeezed her buttocks. Cheryl Austin pressed against his body. Their clinch was intense, passionate. Together they moved deeper into the room, turning slowly. Now the man's back was to us. Her skirt was bunched around her waist. She reached down to rub his crotch. The couple half walked, half stumbled to the nearest desk. The man bent her back against the desk and suddenly she protested, pushing him away.

'Ah, ah. Not so fast,' Graham said. 'Our girl has standards, after all.'

I wondered if that was it. Cheryl seemed to have led him on, then changed her mind. I noticed that she had changed moods almost instantaneously. It made me wonder if she had been acting all along, if her passion was faked. Certainly the man did not seem particularly surprised by her sudden change. Sitting up on the desk, she kept pushing at him, almost angrily. The man stepped away. His back was still to us. We couldn't see his face. As soon as he had stepped back, she changed again: smiling, kittenish now. With slow movements, she got off the desk and adjusted her skirt, twisting her body provocatively as she looked around. We could see his ear and the side of his face, just enough to see that his jaw was moving. He was talking to her. She smiled at him, and came forward, slid her arms around his neck. Then they began kissing again, their hands moving over each other. Walking slowly through the office, toward the conference room.

'So. Did she choose the conference room?'

'Hard to say.'

'Shit, I still can't see his face.'

By now they were near the center of the room, and the camera was shooting almost directly down. All we saw was the top of his head.

I said, 'Does he look Japanese to you?'

'Fuck. Who can tell. How many other cameras were in that room?'

'Four others.'

'Well. His face can't be blocked in all four. We'll nail his ass.'

I said, 'You know, Tom, this guy looks pretty big. He looks taller than she is. And she was a tall girl.'

'Who can tell, in this angle? I can't tell anything except he has a suit on. Okay. There they go, toward the conference room.'

As they approached the room, she suddenly began to struggle.

'Oops,' Graham said. 'She's unhappy again. Moody young thing, isn't she?'

The man gripped her tightly and she spun, trying to twist free. He half carried her, half dragged her to the room. At the doorway, she spun a final time, grabbed the door frame, struggling.

'She lose the purse there?'

'Probably. I can't see clearly.'

The conference room was located directly opposite the camera, so we had a view of the entire room. But the interior of the conference room was very dark, so the two people were silhouetted against the lights of the skyscrapers through the outer glass windows. The man lifted her up in his arms and set her down on the table, rolled her onto her back. She became passive, liquid, as he slid her skirt up her hips. She seemed to be accepting, moving to meet him, and then he made a quick movement between their bodies, and suddenly something flew away.

'There go the panties.'

It looked as if they landed on the floor. But it was hard to tell for sure. If they were panties, they were black, or some other dark color. So much, I thought, for Senator Rowe.

'The panties were gone by the time we got there,' Graham said, staring at the monitor. 'Fucking withholding of evidence, pure and simple.' He rubbed his hands together. 'You got any Nakamoto stock, buddy, I'd sell it. 'Cause it isn't going to be worth shit by tomorrow afternoon.'

On the screen, she was still welcoming him, and he was fumbling with his zipper, when suddenly she tried to sit up, and slapped him hard on the face.

Graham said, 'There we go. A little *spice*.'

The man grabbed her hands, and tried to kiss her, but she resisted him, turning her face away. He pushed her back on the table. He leaned his weight on her body, holding her there. Her bare legs kicked and churned.

The two silhouettes merged and separated. It was difficult to determine exactly what was happening. It looked as if Cheryl kept trying to sit up, and the man kept shoving her back. He held her down, one hand on her upper chest, while her legs kicked at him, and her body twisted on the table. He still held her on the table, but the whole scene was more arduous than arousing. As it continued, I had trouble with the image I was seeing. Was this a genuine rape? Or was she play-acting? After all, she kept kicking and struggling, but she wasn't succeeding in pushing him away. The man might be stronger than she was, but I had the feeling that she could have kicked him back if she had really wanted to. And sometimes it looked as if her arms were locked around his neck, instead of trying to push him away. But it was difficult to know for sure when we were seeing –

'Uh-oh. Trouble.'

The man stopped his rhythmic pumping. Beneath him, Cheryl went limp. Her arms slid away from his shoulders, dropped back on the table. Her legs fell slack on either side of him.

Graham said, 'Is that it? Did it just happen?'

'I can't tell.'

The man patted her cheek, then shook her more vigorously. He seemed to be talking to her. He remained there for a while, maybe thirty seconds, and then he slipped away from her body. She stayed on the table. He walked around her. He was moving slowly, as if he could not believe it.

Then he looked off to the left, as if he had heard a sound. He stood frozen for a moment, and then he seemed to make up his mind. He went into action, moving around the room, looking in a methodical way. He picked up something from the floor.

'The panties.'

'He took 'em himself,' Graham said. 'Shit.'

Now the man moved around the girl, and bent briefly over her body on the far side.

'What's he doing there?'

'I don't know. I can't see.'

'Shit.'

The man straightened and moved away from the conference room, back into the atrium. He was no longer silhouetted. There was a chance we could identify him. But he was looking back into the conference room. Back at the dead girl.

'Hey, buddy,' Graham said, talking to the image on the monitor. 'Look over here, buddy. Come on. Just for a minute.'

On the screen, the man continued to look at the dead girl as he took several more steps into the atrium. Then he began to walk quickly away to the left.

'He's not going back to the elevators,' I said.

'No. But I can't see his *face.*'

'Where is he going?'

'There's a stairwell at the far end,' Graham said. 'Fire exit.'

'Why is he going there, instead of the elevator?'

'Who knows? I just want to see his face. Just once.'

But now the man was to the far left of our camera, and even though he was no longer turned away, we could see only his left ear and cheekbone. He walked quickly. Soon he would be gone from our view, beneath the ceiling overhang at the far end of the room.

'Ah, shit. This angle's no good. Let's look at another tape.'

'Just a minute,' I said.

Our man was moving toward a dark passageway that must lead to the staircase. But as he went, he passed a decorative gilt-frame mirror hanging on the wall, right by the passage. He passed it just as he went under the overhang, into final darkness.

'There!'

'How do you stop this thing?'

I was pressing buttons on the player frantically. I finally found the one that stopped it. We went back. Then forward again.

Again, the man moved purposefully toward the dark passage, with long, quick strides. He moved past the mirror, and for an instant – a single video frame – we could see his face reflected in the mirror – see it clearly – and I pressed the button to freeze the frame –

'Bingo,' I said.

'A fucking Jap,' Graham said. 'Just like I told you.'

Frozen in the mirror was the face of the killer as he strode toward the stairwell. I had no trouble recognizing the tense features of Eddie Sakamura.

'This one is mine,' Graham said. 'It's my case. I'm going to go bring the bastard in.'

'Sure,' Connor said.

'I mean,' Graham said, 'I'd rather go alone.'

'Of course,' Connor said. 'It's your case, Tom. Do whatever you think best.'

Connor wrote down Eddie Sakamura's address for him.

'It's not that I don't appreciate your help,' Graham said. 'But I'd rather handle it myself. Now, just so I have my facts straight: you guys talked to this guy earlier tonight, and you didn't bring him in?'

'That's right.'

'Well, don't worry about it,' Graham said. 'I'll bury that in the report. It won't come back to you, I promise you.' Graham was in a magnanimous mood, pleased at the prospect of arresting Sakamura. He glanced at his watch. 'Fucking A. Less than six hours since the original call, and we already have the murderer. Not bad.'

'We don't have the murderer quite yet,' Connor said. 'I'd bring him in right away, if I were you.'

'I'm leaving now,' Graham said.

'Oh, and Tom,' Connor said, as Graham headed toward the door. 'Eddie Sakamura is a strange guy, but he's not known to be violent. I doubt very much that he's armed. He probably doesn't even own a gun. He went home from the party with a redhead. He's probably in bed with her now. I think it would be advisable to bring him in alive.'

'Hey,' Graham said. 'What is it with you two?'

'Just a suggestion,' Connor said.

'You really think I'm going to shoot this little shithead?'

'You'll go out there with a couple of black and whites for backup, won't you?' Connor said. 'The patrolmen might be excitable. I'm just giving you the background.'

'Hey. Thanks for your fucking support,' Graham said, and he left. He was so broad, he had to turn slightly sideways to go through the door.

I watched him go. 'Why are you letting him do this alone?'

Connor shrugged. 'It's his case.'

'But you've been aggressive all night in pursuing his case. Why stop now?'

Connor said, 'Let Graham have the glory. After all, what has it got to do with us? I'm a cop on extended leave. And you're just a corrupt liaison officer.' He pointed to the videotape. 'You want to run that for me, before you give me a ride home?'

'Sure.' I rewound the tape.

'I was thinking we could get a cup of coffee, too,' Connor said. 'They make a good one in the SID labs. At least, they used to.'

I said, 'You want me to get coffee while you look at the tape?'

'That would be nice, *kōhai*,' Connor said.

'Sure.' I started the tape for him, and turned to leave.

'Oh, and *kōhai*. While you're down there, ask the night duty officer what facilities the department has for videotapes. Because all these need to be duplicated. And we may need hard copies of individual frames. Especially if there's trouble about Sakamura's arrest as Japan-bashing by the department. We may need to release a picture. To defend ourselves.'

It was a good point. 'Okay,' I said. 'I'll check.'

'And I take mine black with one sugar.' He turned to look at the monitor.

The scientific investigation division, or SID, was in the basement of Parker Center. It was after two in the morning when I got there, and most of the sections were closed down. SID was pretty much a nine-to-five operation. Of course, the teams worked at night collecting evidence from crime scenes, but the evidence was then stored in lockers, either down-town or at one of the divisions, until the next morning.

I went to the coffee machine, in the little cafeteria next to Latent Prints. All around the room were signs reading DID YOU WASH YOUR HANDS? THIS MEANS YOU and DON'T EXPOSE FELLOW OFFICERS TO RISK. WASH YOUR HANDS. The reason was that the SID teams used poisons, especially Criminalistics. There was so much mercury, arsenic, and chromium floating around that in the old days, officers had sometimes gotten sick by drinking from a Styrofoam cup that another lab worker had merely touched.

But these people were more careful; I got two cups of coffee and went back to the night-duty desk. Jackie Levine was on duty, with her feet up on the desk. She was a heavyset woman wearing toreador pants and an orange wig. Despite her bizarre appearance, she was widely acknowledged to be the best print lifter in the department. She was reading *Modern Bride* magazine. I said, 'You going to do it again, Jackie?'

'Hell, no,' she said. 'My daughter.'

'Who's she marrying?'

'Let's talk about something happy,' she said. 'One of those coffees for me?'

'Sorry,' I said. 'But I have a question for you. Who handles videotape evidence here?'

'Videotape evidence?'

'Like tape from surveillance cameras. Who analyzes it, makes hard copies, all that?'

'Well, we don't get much call for that,' Jackie said. 'Electronics used to do it here, but I think they gave it up. Nowadays, video either goes to Valley or Medlar Hall.' She sat forward, thumbed through a directory. 'If you want, you can talk to Bill Harrelson over at Medlar. But if it's anything special, I think we farm it out to JPL or the Advanced Imaging Lab at U.S.C. You want the contact numbers, or you want to go through Harrelson?'

Something in her tone told me what to do. 'Maybe I'll take the contact numbers.'

'Yeah, I would.'

I wrote the numbers down and went back up to the division. Connor had finished the tape and was running it back and forth at the point where Sakamura's face appeared in the mirror.

'Well?' I said.

'That's Eddie, all right.' He appeared calm, almost indifferent. He took the coffee from me and sipped it. 'Terrible.'

'Yeah, I know.'

'It used to be better.' Connor set the cup aside, turned off the video recorder, stood, and stretched. 'Well, I think we've done a good evening's work. What do you say we get some sleep? I have a big golf game in the morning at Sunset Hills.'

'Okay,' I said. I packed the tapes back in the cardboard box, and set the VCR carefully in the box, too.

Connor said, 'What're you going to do with those tapes?'

'I'll put 'em in the evidence locker.'

Connor said, 'These are the originals. And we don't have duplicates.'

'I know, but I can't get dupes until tomorrow.'

'Exactly my point. Why don't you keep them with you?'

'Take them home?' There were all sorts of departmental injunctions about taking evidence home. It was against the rules, to put it mildly.

He shrugged. 'I wouldn't leave this to chance. Take the tapes with you, and then you can arrange the duplication yourself, tomorrow.'

I stuck them under my arm. I said, 'You don't think anybody at the department would –'

'Of course not,' Connor said. 'But this evidence is crucial and we wouldn't want anybody to walk by the evidence locker with a big magnet while we were asleep, would we?'

So in the end I took the tapes. As we went out the door, we passed Ishiguro, still sitting there, contrite. Connor said something quickly to him in Japanese. Ishiguro jumped to his feet, bowed quickly, and scurried out of the office.

'Is he really so scared?'

'Yes,' Connor said.

Ishiguro moved quickly down the hall ahead of us, head bent low. He seemed almost a caricature of a mousy, frightened man.

'Why?' I said. 'He's lived here long enough to know that any case we might have against him for withholding evidence is not strong. And we have even less of a case against Nakamoto.'

'That's not the point,' Connor said. 'He's not worried about legalities. He's worried about scandal. Because that's what would happen if we were in Japan.'

We came around the corner. Ishiguro was standing by the banks of elevators, waiting. We waited, too. There was an awkward moment. The first elevator came, and Ishiguro stepped away for us to get on. The doors closed on him bowing to us in the lobby. The elevator started down.

Connor said, 'In Japan, he and his company could be finished forever.'

'Why?'

'Because in Japan, scandal is the most common way of revising the pecking order. Of getting rid of a powerful opponent. It's a routine procedure over there. You uncover a vulnerability, and you leak it to the press, or to the government investigators. A scandal inevitably follows, and the person or organization is ruined. That's how the Recruit scandal brought down Takeshita as prime minister. Or the financial scandals brought down Prime Minister Tanaka in the seventies. It's the same way the Japanese screwed General Electric a couple of years ago.'

'They screwed General Electric?'

'In the Yokogawa scandal. You heard of it? No? Well, it's classic Japanese maneuvering. A few years ago, General Electric made the best scanning equipment in the world for hospitals. GE formed a subsidiary,

Yokogawa Medical, to market this equipment in Japan. And GE did business the Japanese way: cutting costs below competitors to get market share, providing excellent service and support, entertaining customers – giving potential buyers air tickets and traveler's checks. We'd call it bribes, but it's standard procedure in Japan. Yokogawa quickly became the market leader, ahead of Japanese companies like Toshiba. The Japanese companies didn't like that and complained about unfairness. And one day government agents raided Yokogawa's offices and found evidence of the bribes. They arrested several Yokogawa employees, and blackened the company name in scandal. It didn't hurt GE sales in Japan very much. It didn't matter that other Japanese companies also offer bribes. For some reason, it was the non-Japanese company that got caught. Amazing, how that happens.'

I said, 'Is it really that bad?'

'The Japanese can be tough,' Connor said. 'They say "business is war," and they mean it. You know how Japan is always telling us that their markets are open. Well, in the old days, if a Japanese bought an American car, he got audited by the government. So pretty soon, nobody bought an American car. The officials shrug: what can they do? Their market is open: they can't help it if nobody wants an American car. The obstructions are endless. Every imported car has to be individually tested on the dock to make sure it complies with exhaust-emission laws. Foreign skis were once banned because Japanese snow was said to be wetter than European and American snow. That's the way they treat other countries, so it's not surprising they worry about getting a taste of their own medicine.'

'Then Ishiguro is waiting for some scandal? Because that's what would happen in Japan?'

'Yes. He's afraid that Nakamoto will be finished in a single stroke. But I doubt that it will. Chances are, it'll be business as usual in Los Angeles tomorrow.'

I drove Connor back to his apartment. As he climbed out of the car I said, 'Well, it's been interesting, Captain. Thanks for spending the time with me.'

'You're welcome,' Connor said. 'Call me any time, if you need help in the future.'

'I hope your golf game isn't too early tomorrow.'

'Actually, it's at seven, but at my age I don't need much sleep. I'll be playing at the Sunset Hills.'

'Isn't it a Japanese course?' The purchase of the Sunset Hills Country Club was one of the more recent outrages in L.A. The West Los Angeles golf course was bought for a huge cash price: two hundred million dollars in 1990. At the time, the new Japanese owners said no changes would be made. But now, the American membership was slowly being reduced by a simple procedure: whenever an American retired, his place was offered to a Japanese. Sunset Hills memberships were sold in Tokyo for a million dollars each, where they were considered a bargain; there was a long waiting list.

'Well,' Connor said, 'I'm playing with some Japanese.'

'You do that often?'

'The Japanese are avid golfers, as you know. I try to play twice a week. Sometimes you hear things of interest. Good night, *kōhai*.'

'Good night, Captain.'

I drove home.

I was pulling onto the Santa Monica freeway when the phone rang. It was the DHD operator. 'Lieutenant, we have a Special Services call. Officers in the field request assistance of the liaison.'

I sighed. 'Okay.' She gave me the mobile number.

'Hey, buddy.'

It was Graham. I said, 'Hi, Tom.'

'You alone yet?'

'Yeah. I'm heading home. Why?'

'I was thinking,' Graham said. 'Maybe we should have the Japanese liaison on hand for this bust.'

'I thought you wanted to do it alone.'

'Yeah, well, maybe you want to come over and help out with this bust. Just so everything is done by the book.'

I said, 'Is this a CYA?' I meant cover your ass.

'Hey. You going to help me out, or not?'

'Sure, Tom. I'm on my way.'

'We'll wait for you.'

Eddie Sakamura lived in a small house on one of those narrow twisting streets high in the Hollywood hills above the 101 freeway. It was 2:45 a.m. when I came around a curve and saw the two black and whites with their lights off, and Graham's tan sedan, parked to one side. Graham was standing with the patrolmen, smoking a cigarette. I had to go back a dozen meters to find a place to park. Then I walked over to them.

We looked up at Eddie's house, built over a garage at street level. It was one of those two-bedroom white stucco houses from the 1940s. The lights were on, and we heard Frank Sinatra singing. Graham said, 'He's not alone. He's got some broads up there.'

I said, 'How do you want to handle it?'

Graham said, 'We leave the boys here. I told 'em no shooting, don't worry. You and I go up and make the bust.'

Steep stairs ran up from the garage to the house.

'Okay. You take the front and I'll take the back?'

'Hell, no,' Graham said. 'I want you with me, buddy. He's not dangerous, right?'

I saw the silhouette of a woman pass one of the windows. She looked naked. 'Shouldn't be,' I said.

'Okay then, let's do it.'

We started up the stairs single file. Frank Sinatra was singing 'My Way.' We heard the laughter of women. It sounded like more than one. 'Christ, I hope they got some fucking drugs out.'

I thought the chances of that were pretty good. We reached the top of the stairs, ducking to avoid being seen through the windows.

The front door was Spanish, heavy and solid. Graham paused. I moved a few steps toward the back of the house, where I saw the greenish glow of pool lights. There was probably a back door going out to the pool. I was trying to see where it was.

Graham tapped my shoulder. I came back. He gently turned the handle of the front door. It was unlocked. Graham took out his revolver and looked at me. I took out my gun.

He paused, held up three fingers. Count of three.

Graham kicked the front door open and went in low, shouting 'Hold it, police! Hold it right there!' Before I got into the living room, I could hear the women screaming.

There were two of them, completely naked, running around the room and shrieking at the top of their lungs, 'Eddie! Eddie!' Eddie wasn't there. Graham was shouting, 'Where is he! Where is Eddie Sakamura?' The redhead grabbed a pillow from the couch to cover herself, and screamed, 'Get out of here, you fucker!' and then she threw the pillow at Graham. The other girl, a blonde, ran squealing into the bedroom. We followed her, and the redhead threw another pillow at us.

In the bedroom, the blonde fell on the floor and howled in pain. Graham leant over her with his gun. 'Don't shoot me!' she cried. 'I didn't do anything!'

Graham grabbed her by the ankle. There was all this twisting bare flesh. The girl was hysterical. 'Where is Eddie?' Graham said. 'Where is he?'

'*In a meeting!*' the girl squealed.

'Where?'

'*In a meeting!*' And flailing around, she kicked Graham in the nuts with her other leg.

'Aw, Christ,' Graham said, letting the girl go. He coughed and sat down hard. I went back to the living room. The redhead had her high heels on but nothing else.

I said, 'Where is he?'

'You bastards,' she said. 'You fucking bastards.'

I went past her toward a door at the far end of the room. It was locked. The redhead ran up and began to hit me on the back with her fists. 'Leave him alone! Leave him alone!' I was trying to open the locked door while she pounded on me. I thought I heard voices from the other side of the door.

In the next moment Graham's big bulk slammed into the door and the wood splintered. The door opened. I saw the kitchen, lit by the green light of the pool outside. The room was empty. The back door was open.

'*Shit.*'

By now the redhead had jumped on my back, and locked her legs around my waist. She was pulling my hair, screaming obscenities. I spun around in circles, trying to throw her off me. It was one of those strange moments where in the middle of all the chaos I was thinking, *be careful, don't hurt her,* because it would look bad for a pretty young girl to end up with a broken arm or cracked ribs, it would mean police brutality even though right now she was tearing my hair out by the roots. She bit my ear and I felt pain. I slammed myself back against the wall, and I heard her grunt as the breath was knocked out of her. She let go.

Out the window, I saw a dark figure running down the stairs. Graham saw it, too.

'Fuck,' he said. He ran, I ran, too. But the girl must have tripped me because I fell over, landing hard. When I got to my feet I heard the sirens of the black and whites and their engines starting up.

Then I was back outside, running down the steps. I was maybe ten meters behind Graham, about thirty feet, when Eddie's Ferrari backed out of the garage, ground the gears, and roared down the street.

The black and whites immediately took up pursuit. Graham ran for his sedan. He had pulled out to follow while I was still running for my own car, parked farther down the road. As his car flashed past me, I could see his face, grim and angry.

I got into my car and followed.

You can't drive fast in the hills and talk on the phone. I didn't even try. I estimated I was half a kilometer behind Graham, and he was some distance behind the two patrol cars. When I got to the bottom of the hill, the 101 overpass, I saw the flashing lights going down the freeway. I had to back up and pull around to the entrance below Mulholland, and then I joined traffic heading south.

When the traffic began to slow up, I stuck my flasher on the roof, and pulled into the right-hand breakdown lane.

I got to the concrete embankment about thirty seconds after the Ferrari hit it flat out at a hundred and sixty kilometers an hour. I guess the gas tank had exploded on impact, and the flames were jumping fifteen meters into the air. The heat was tremendous. It looked like the trees up on the hill might catch on fire. You couldn't get anywhere near the twisted wreck of the car.

The first of the fire trucks pulled up, with three more black and whites. There were sirens and flashing lights everywhere.

I backed up my car to make room for the trucks, then walked over to Graham. He smoked a cigarette as the firemen began to spray the wreck with foam.

'Christ,' Graham said. 'What a fucking cockup.'

'Why didn't the backup patrolmen stop him when he was in the garage?'

'Because,' Graham said, 'I told them not to shoot at him. And we weren't there. They were trying to decide what to do when the guy drove away.' He shook his head. 'This is going to look like shit in the report.'

I said, 'Still, it's probably better you didn't shoot him.'

'Maybe.' He ground out his cigarette.

By now, the firemen had gotten the fire out. The Ferrari was a smoking hulk crumbled against the concrete. There was a harsh smell in the air.

'Well,' Graham said. 'No point staying around here. I'll go back up to the house. See if those girls are still there.'

'You need me for anything else?'

'No. You might as well go. Tomorrow is another day. Shit, it'll be paperwork until we drop.' He looked at me. He hesitated. 'We in sync about this? About what happened?'

'Hell, yes,' I said.

'No way to handle it differently,' he said. 'Far as I can see.'

'No,' I said. 'Just one of those things.'

'Okay, buddy. See you tomorrow.'

'Good night, Tom.'

We got into our cars.

I drove home.

Mrs Ascenio was snoring loudly on the sofa. It was three forty-five in the morning. I tiptoed past her and looked in Michelle's room. My daughter lay on her back, her covers tossed aside, her arms flung over her head. Her feet stuck through the bars of the crib. I tucked the covers around her and went into my own room.

The television was still on. I turned it off. I pulled off my tie and sat down on the bed to remove my shoes. I suddenly realized how tired I was. I took off my coat and trousers and threw them onto the television set. I lay down on my back and thought I should take off my shirt. It felt sweaty and grimy on my body. I closed my eyes for a moment and let my head sink back into the pillow. Then I felt a pinching, and something tugging at my eyelids. I heard a chirping sound and thought in a moment of horror that birds were pecking at my eyes.

I heard a voice saying, 'Open your eyes, Daddy. Open your eyes.' And I realized that it was my daughter, trying to pull my eyelids open with small fingers.

'Yuuuh,' I said. I glimpsed daylight, rolled away, and buried my face in the pillow.

'Daddy? Open your eyes. Open your eyes, Daddy.'

I said, 'Daddy was out late last night. Daddy is tired.'

She paid no attention. 'Daddy, open your eyes. Open your eyes, Daddy? Open your eyes, Daddy.'

I knew that she would continue saying the same thing, over and over, until I lost my mind, or opened my eyes. I rolled onto my back and coughed. 'Daddy is still tired, Shelly. Go see what Mrs Ascenio is doing.'

'Daddy, open your eyes.'

'Can't you let Daddy sleep a while? Daddy wants to sleep a little longer this morning.'

'It's morning now, Daddy. Open your eyes. Open your eyes.'

I opened my eyes. She was right.

It was morning.

What the hell.

Second Day

'Eat your pancakes.'

'I don't want any more.'

'Just one more bite, Shelly.' Sunlight streamed through the kitchen window. I yawned. It was seven o'clock in the morning.

'Is Mommy coming today?'

'Don't change the subject. Come on, Shel. One more bite. Please?'

We were sitting at her kid-size table in the corner of the kitchen. Sometimes I can get her to eat at the little table when she won't eat at the big table. But I wasn't having much luck today. Michelle stared at me.

'Is Mommy coming?'

'I think so. I'm not sure.' I didn't want to disappoint her. 'We're waiting to hear.'

'Is Mommy going out of town again?'

I said, 'Maybe.' I wondered what 'going out of town' meant to a two-year-old, what sort of image she would have of it.

'Is she going with Uncle Rick?'

Who is Uncle Rick? I held the fork in front of her face. 'I don't know, Shel. Come on, open up. One more bite.'

'He has a new car,' Michelle said, nodding solemnly, the way she did whenever she was informing me of important news.

'Is that right?'

'Uh-huh. Black one.'

'I see. What kind of car is it?'

'Sades.'

'A Sades?'

'No. *Sades*.'

'You mean Mercedes?'

'Uh-huh. Black one.'

'That's nice,' I said.

'When is Mommy coming?'

'One more bite, Shel.'

She opened her mouth, and I moved the fork toward her. At the last moment she turned her head aside, pursing her lips. 'No, Daddy.'

'All right,' I said. 'I give up.'

'I'm not hungry, Daddy.'

'I can see that.'

Mrs Ascenio was cleaning up the kitchen before she went back to her own apartment. There was another fifteen minutes before my housekeeper Elaine came to take Michelle to day care. I still had to get her dressed. I was putting her pancakes in the sink when the phone rang. It was Ellen Farley, the mayor's press aide.

'Are you watching?'

'Watching what?'

'The news. Channel seven. They're doing the car crash right now.'

'They are?'

'Call me back,' she said.

I went into the bedroom and turned on the television. A voice was saying,'– reported a high-speed chase on the Hollywood freeway southbound, which ended when the suspect drove his Ferrari sportscar into the Vine Street overpass, not far from the Hollywood Bowl. Observers say the car hit the concrete embankment at more than a hundred miles an hour, instantly bursting into flames. Fire trucks were called to the scene but there were no survivors. The driver's body was so badly burned that his glasses melted. The officer in charge of the pursuit, Detective Thomas Graham, said that the driver, Mr Edward Sakamura, was wanted in connection with the alleged murder of a woman at a downtown location. But today, friends of Mr Sakamura expressed disbelief at this charge, and claimed that police strong-arm tactics panicked the suspect and caused him to flee. There are complaints that the incident was racially motivated. It is not clear whether police intended to charge Mr Sakamura with the murder, and observers noted that this was the third high-speed pursuit on the 101 freeway in the last two weeks. Questions of police judgement in these pursuits have arisen after a Compton woman was killed in a high-speed pursuit last January. Neither Detective Graham nor his assistant Lieutenant Peter Smith was available to be interviewed, and we are waiting to hear if the officers will be disciplined or suspended by the department.'

Jesus.

'Daddy . . .'

'Just a minute, Shel.'

The image showed the crumpled, smoking wreckage being loaded onto a flatbed truck for removal from the side of the highway. There was a black smear on the concrete where the car had struck the wall.

The station cut back to the studio, where the anchor-woman faced the camera and said, 'In other developments, KNBC has learned that two police officers interviewed Mr Sakamura earlier in the evening in connection with the case, but did not arrest him at that time. Captain John Connor and Lieutenant Smith may face disciplinary review by the department, with questions being raised of possible procedural violations. However, the good news is there are no longer delays for traffic moving southbound on the 101. Now over to you, Bob.'

I stared numbly at the TV. *Disciplinary review?*

The phone rang. It was Ellen Farley again. 'You get all that?'

'Yeah, I did. I can't believe it. What's it about, Ellen?'

'None of this is coming from the mayor's office, if that's what you're asking. But the Japanese community has been unhappy with Graham before. They think he's a racist. It looks like he played right into their hands.'

'I was there. Graham acted correctly.'

'Yeah, I know you were there, Pete. Frankly, it's unfortunate. I don't want to see you tarred by the same brush.'

I said, 'Graham acted correctly.'

'Are you listening, Pete?'

'What about this suspension and disciplinary review?'

'That's the first I heard of it,' Ellen said. 'But that would be internally generated. It's coming from your own department. By the way, is it true? Did you and Connor see Sakamura last night?'

'Yes.'

'And you didn't arrest him?'

'No. We didn't have probable cause to arrest him when we talked to him. Later on, we did.'

Ellen said, 'Do you really think he could have done this murder?'

'I know he did. We have it on tape.'

'On tape? Are you serious?'

'Yeah. We have the murder on a videotape from one of the Nakamoto security cameras.'

She was silent for a while. I said, 'Ellen?'

'Look,' Ellen said. 'Off the record, okay?'

'Sure.'

'I don't know what's going on here, Pete. There's more than I understand.'

'Why didn't you tell me who the girl was, last night?'

'I'm sorry about that. I had a lot to take care of.'

'Ellen.'

A silence. Then: 'Pete, this girl got around. She knew a lot of people.'

'Did she know the mayor?'

Silence.

'How well did she know him?'

'Listen,' Ellen said. 'Let's just say she was a pretty girl and she knew lots of people in this town. Personally, I thought she was unbalanced, but she was good-looking and she had a hell of an effect on men. You had to see it to believe it. Now there's a lot of irons in the fire. You saw the *Times* today?'

'No.'

'Take a look. If you ask me, you want to be very correct, the next couple of days. Dot your *i's* and cross your *t's*. Do everything by the book. And watch your back, okay?'

'Okay. Thanks, Ellen.'

'Don't thank me. I didn't call.' Then her voice got softer. 'Take care of yourself, Peter.'

I heard a dial tone.

'Daddy?'

'Just a minute, Shel.'

'Can I watch cartoons?'

'Sure, honey.'

I found her a station with some cartoons and walked into the living room. I opened the front door and picked up the *Times* from the mat. It took me a while to find the story on the last page of the Metro section.

CHARGES OF POLICE RACISM CLOUD JAPANESE FETE

I skimmed the first paragraph. Japanese officials of the Nakamoto corporation complained about 'callous and insensitive' police behavior, which they said detracted from a star-studded opening night at their new skyscraper on Figueroa. At least one Nakamoto official expressed the view that the police actions were 'racially motivated.' A spokesperson said: 'We do not believe the Los Angeles Police Department would behave in this fashion if a Japanese corporation were not involved. We feel strongly that the actions of the police reflect a double standard for treatment of Japanese at the hands of American officials.' Mr Hiroshi Ogura, chairman of the board of Nakamoto, was present at the party, which drew such celebrities as Madonna and Tom Cruise, but he could not be reached for comment on the incident. A spokesman said, 'Mr Ogura is deeply disturbed that official hostility should mar this gathering. He very much regrets the unpleasantness that occurred.'

According to observers, Mayor Thomas sent a staff member to deal with the police, but with little result. The police did not modify their behavior, despite the presence of the special Japanese liaison officer, Lieutenant Peter Smith, whose job is to defuse racially sensitive situations . . .

And so on.

You had to read four paragraphs before you discovered that a murder had occurred. That particular detail seemed to be almost irrelevant.

I looked back at the lead. The story was from the City News Service, which meant there was no byline.

I felt angry enough to call my old contact at the *Times,* Kenny Shubik. Ken was the leading Metro reporter. He had been at the paper forever, and he knew everything that was going on. Since it was still eight in the morning, I called him at home.

'Ken. Pete Smith.'

'Oh, hi,' he said. 'Glad you got my message.'

In the background, I heard what sounded like a teenage girl: 'Oh, *come on,* Dad. Why can't I go?'

Ken said, 'Jennifer, let me talk here for a minute.'

'What message?' I said.

Ken said, 'I called you last night, because I thought you ought to know right away. He's obviously working off a tip. But do you have any idea what's behind it?'

'Behind what?' I said. I didn't know what he was talking about. 'I'm sorry, Ken, I didn't get your message.'

'Really?' he said. 'I called you about eleven-thirty last night. The DHD dispatcher said you had rolled out on a case but you had a car phone. I told her it was important, and for you to call me at home if necessary. Because I felt sure you'd want to know.'

In the background, the girl said, 'Dad, *come on,* I have to decide what to *wear.*'

'Jennifer, damn it,' he said. 'Chill out.' To me he said, 'You have a daughter, don't you?'

'Yeah,' I said. 'But she's only two.'

'Just wait,' Ken said. 'Look, Pete. You really didn't get my message?'

'No,' I said. I'm calling about something else: the story in this morning's paper.'

'What story?'

'The Nakamoto coverage on page eight. The one about "callous and racist police" at the opening.'

'Jeez, I didn't think we had a Nakamoto story yesterday. I know Jodie was doing the party, but that won't run until tomorrow. You know, Japan draws the glitterati. Jeff didn't have anything on the scheds in Metro yesterday.'

Jeff was the Metro editor. I said, 'There's a story in the paper this morning about the murder.'

'What murder?' he said. His voice sounded odd.

'There was a murder at Nakamoto last night. About eight-thirty. One of the guests was killed.'

Ken was silent at the other end of the line. Putting things together. Finally he said, 'Were you involved?'

'Homicide called me in as Japanese liaison.'

'Hmmm,' Ken said. 'Listen. Let me get to my desk and see what I can find out. Let's talk in an hour. And give me your numbers so I can call you direct.'

'Okay.'

He cleared his throat. 'Listen, Pete,' he said. 'Just between us. Do you have any problems?'

'Like what?'

'Like a morals problem, or a problem with your bank account. Discrepancy about reported income . . . anything I should know about? As your friend?'

'No,' I said.

'I don't need the details. But if there's something that isn't quite right . . .'

'Nothing, Ken.'

' 'Cause if I have to go to bat for you, I don't want to discover I have stepped in shit.'

'Ken. What's going on?'

'I don't want to go into detail right now. But offhand I would say somebody is trying to fuck you in the ass,' Ken said.

The girl said, '*Dad*dy, that's dis*gus*ting.'

'Well, you're not supposed to be listening. Pete?'

'Yeah,' I said. 'I'm here.'

'Call me in an hour,' Ken said.

'You're a pal,' I said. 'I owe you.'

'Fucking right you do,' Ken said.

He hung up.

I looked around the apartment. Everything still looked the same. Morning sunlight was still streaming into the room. Michelle was sitting in her favorite chair, watching cartoons and sucking her thumb. But somehow everything felt different. It was creepy. It was like the world had tilted.

But I had things to do. It was also getting late; I had to get her dressed before Elaine came to take her to day care. I told her that. She started to cry. So I turned off the television set, and she threw herself on the floor and began to kick and scream. 'No, Daddy! *Cartoons,* Daddy!'

I picked her up and slung her underarm to the bedroom to get her changed. She was screaming at the top of her lungs. The phone rang again. This time it was the division dispatcher.

'Morning, Lieutenant. I have your uncleared messages.'

'Let me get a pencil,' I said. I put Michelle down. She cried even louder. I said, 'Can you pick out which shoes you want to wear today?'

'Sounds like you got a murder there,' the dispatcher said.

'She doesn't want to get dressed for school.'

Michelle was tugging at my leg. 'No, Daddy. No school, Daddy.'

'Yes, school,' I said firmly. She bawled. 'Go ahead,' I said to the dispatcher.

'Okay, eleven forty-one last night, you had a call from a Ken Subotik or Subotnick, *L.A. Times,* he said please call him. Message reads 'The Weasel is checking up on you.' He said you would know what that meant. You can call him at home. You have the number?'

'Yes.'

'Okay. One forty-two a.m. this morning, you had a call from a Mr Eddie Saka – looks like Sakamura. He said it's urgent, please call him at home, 555–8434. It's about the missing tape. Okay?'

Shit.

I said, 'What time was that call?'

'One forty-two a.m. The call was forwarded to County General and I guess their switchboard couldn't locate you. You were at the morgue or something?'

'Yeah.'

'Sorry, Lieutenant, but once you're out of your car, we have to go through intermediates.'

'Okay. Anything else?'

'Then at six forty-three a.m., Captain Connor left a beeper number for you to call. He said he's playing golf this morning.'

'Okay.'

'And at seven-ten, we had a call from Robert Woodson, who is with Senator Morton's office. Senator Morton wants to meet you and Captain

Connor at one o'clock today at the Los Angeles Country Club. He asked that you call and confirm that you will attend the meeting with the senator. I tried to reach you but your phone was busy. Will you call the senator?'

I said I would call the senator. I told the dispatcher to page Connor for me at the golf course, and have him call me in the car.

I heard the front door unlock. Elaine came in. 'Good morning,' she said.

'I'm afraid Shelly isn't dressed yet.'

'That's okay,' she said. 'I'll do it. What time is Mrs Davis coming to pick her up?'

'We're waiting to hear.'

Elaine had been through this routine many times before. 'Come on, Michelle. Let's pick your clothes for today. Time to get ready for school.'

I looked at my watch, and was on my way to get another cup of coffee when the phone rang. 'Lieutenant Peter Smith, please.'

It was the assistant chief, Jim Olsen.

'Hi, Jim.'

'Morning, Pete.' He sounded friendly. But Jim Olsen never called anybody before ten o'clock in the morning unless there was a big problem. Olsen said, 'Looks like we got ourselves a rattlesnake by the tail. You see the papers today?'

'Yeah, I did.'

'You happen to catch the morning news?'

'Some of it.'

'The chief's been calling me for damage control. I wanted to get where you stand before I make a recommendation. Okay?'

'Okay.'

'I just got off the phone with Tom Graham. He admits last night was a prime screwup. Nobody is covered in glory.'

'I'm afraid not.'

'Couple of naked broads impeded two able-bodied officers and prevented apprehension of the suspect? Is that about it?'

It sounded ridiculous. I said, 'You had to be there, Jim.'

'Uh-huh,' he said. 'Well, one good thing so far. I've been checking if correct pursuit procedures were followed. Apparently they were. We have recordings off the computers, and we have voice recordings off the radio, and it's all strictly by the book. Thank God. Nobody even swears. We can release those records to the media if this thing gets any worse. So we're covered there. But it's very unfortunate that Sakamura is dead.'

'Yes.'

'Graham went back to get the girls, but the house was deserted. The girls were gone.'

'I see.'

'In all the rush, nobody got the names of the girls?'

'No, I'm afraid not.'

'That means we have no witnesses to the events in the house. So we're a little vulnerable.'

'Uh-huh.'

'They're cutting Sakamura's body out of the wreck this morning to ship what's left to the morgue. Graham tells me as far as he's concerned, the case is wrapped up. I gather there are videotapes that show Sakamura killed the girl. Graham says he is ready to file his concluding five-seven-nine report. Is that how you see it? The case closed?'

'I guess so, Chief. Sure.'

'Then we can shut this fucker down,' the chief said. 'The Japanese community finds the Nakamoto inquiry irritating and offensive. They don't want it to continue any longer than necessary. So if we can call it a day, it would help.'

'It's okay with me,' I said. 'Let's call it a day.'

'Well that's good, Pete,' the chief said. 'I'm going to speak to the chief, see if we can head off any disciplinary action.'

'Thanks, Jim.'

'Try not to worry. Myself, I don't see a disciplinary issue. As long as we have videos that show Sakamura did it.'

'Yeah, we do.'

'About these videos,' he said. 'I've had Marty looking in the evidence locker. He can't seem to find 'em.'

I took a deep breath and said, 'No, I have them.'

'You didn't log them in the evidence locker last night?'

'No. I wanted to get copies made.'

He coughed. 'Pete. It'd be better if you had followed procedure on that.'

'I wanted to get copies made,' I said.

'Tell you what,' Jim said, 'get your copies made, and get the originals onto my desk by ten o'clock. Okay?'

'Okay.'

'It can take that long to locate the material from the evidence locker. You know how it is.'

He was saying he would cover for me. 'Thanks, Jim.'

'Don't thank me, because I didn't do anything,' he said. 'Far as I know, procedure has been followed.'

'Right.'

'But just between you and me: get it done right away. I can hold the fort for a couple of hours. But something's going on down here. I don't know exactly where it's coming from. So don't push it, okay?'

'Okay, Jim. I'm on my way now.'

I hung up the phone, and went to get copies made.

Pasadena looked like a city at the bottom of a glass of sour milk. The Jet Propulsion Laboratory, on the outskirts of town, was nestled in the foothills near the Rose Bowl. But even at eight-thirty in the morning, you couldn't see the mountains through the yellow-white haze.

I tucked the box of tapes under my arm, showed my badge, signed the guard's clipboard, and swore I was an American citizen. The guard sent me to the main building, across an inner courtyard.

For decades, the Jet Propulsion Laboratory had served as the command center for American spacecraft that photographed Jupiter and the rings of Saturn, and sent pictures back to earth as video images. JPL was the place where modern video-image processing had been invented. If anybody could copy these tapes, they could.

Mary Jane Kelleher, the press secretary, took me up to the third floor. We walked down a lime green corridor, past several doors that opened into empty offices. I mentioned it.

'It's true,' she said, nodding. 'We've been losing some good people, Peter.'

'Where are they going?' I said.

'Mostly to industry. We always lost a few to IBM in Armonk, or Bell Labs in New Jersey. But those labs don't have the best equipment or funding any more. Now it's the Japanese research labs like Hitachi in Long Beach, Sanyo in Torrance, Canon in Inglewood. They're hiring a lot of American researchers now.'

'Is JPL concerned about it?'

'Sure,' she said. 'Everybody knows the best way to transfer technology is inside somebody's head. But what can you do?' she shrugged. 'Researchers want to do research. And America doesn't do so much R and D any more. Budgets are tighter. So it's better to work for the Japanese. They pay well, and they genuinely respect research. If you need a piece of equipment, you get it. Anyway, that's what my friends tell me. Here we are.'

She took me into a laboratory crammed with video equipment. Black boxes stacked on metal shelves and on metal tables; cables snaking across the floor; a variety of monitors and display screens. In the center of all this was a bearded man in his midthirties named Kevin Howzer. He had an image on his monitor of a gear mechanism, in shifting rainbow colors. The desk was littered with Coke cans and candy wrappers; he had been up all night, working.

'Kevin, this is Lieutenant Smith from the L.A.P.D. He's got some unusual videotapes he needs copied.'

'Just copied?' Howzer sounded disappointed. 'You don't want anything *done* to them?'

'No, Kevin,' she said. 'He doesn't.'

'No problem.'

I showed Howzer one of the cassettes. He turned it over in his hand, and shrugged. 'Looks like a standard eight-millimeter cart. What's on it?'

'High-definition Japanese TV.'

'You mean it's an HD signal?'

'I guess so.'

'Shouldn't be a problem. You got a playback I can use?'

'Yes.' I took the playback machine out of the box and handed it to him.

'Jeez, they make these things nice, don't they? Beautiful unit.' Kevin examined the controls in front. 'Yeah, that's high-definition all right. I can handle it.' He turned the box around and peered at the plugs on the back. Then he frowned. He swung his desk light over and opened the plastic flap on the cassette, exposing the tape. It had a faint silver tinge. 'Huh. Do these tapes involve anything legal?'

'Actually, they do.'

He handed it back to me. 'Sorry. I can't copy it.'

'Why not?'

'See the silver color? That's evaporated metal tape. Very high density. I'll bet the format has real-time compression and decompression coming out of that box. I can't make you a copy, because I can't match the formats, which means I can't lay down a signal in an equivalent way that is guaranteed readable. I can make you a copy, but I can't be sure the copy is exact because I can't match formats. So if you have any legal issues – and I assume you do – you're going to have to take it somewhere else to get it copied.'

'Like where?'

'This could be the new proprietary D-four format. If it is, the only place that can copy it is Hamaguchi.'

'Hamaguchi?'

'The research lab in Glendale, owned by Kawakami Industries. They have every piece of video equipment known to man over there.'

I said, 'Do you think they'd help me?'

'To make copies? Sure. I know one of the lab directors, Jim Donaldson. I can call over there for you, if you like.'

'That would be great.'

'No problem.'

Hamaguchi Research Institute was a featureless, mirrored glass building in an industrial park in north Glendale. I carried my box into the lobby. Behind the sleek reception desk I could see an atrium in the center of the building, and smoked-glass-walled laboratories on all sides.

I asked for Dr Jim Donaldson and took a seat in the lobby. While I was waiting two men in suits came in, nodded familiarly to the receptionist, and sat on the couch near me. Ignoring me, they spread out glossy brochures on the coffee table.

'See here,' one of them said, 'this is what I was talking about. This is the shot we end with. This one closes.'

I glanced over, saw a view of wildflowers and snowcapped mountains. The first man tapped the photos.

'I mean, that's the Rockies, my friend. It's real Americana. Trust me, that's what sells them. And it's a hell of a parcel.'

'How big did you say it is?'

'It's a hundred and thirty thousand acres. The biggest remaining piece of Montana that's still available. Twenty by ten kilometers of prime ranch acreage fronting on the Rockies. It's the size of a national park. It's got grandeur. It's got dimension, scope. It's very high quality. Perfect for a Japanese consortium.'

'And they talked price?'

'Not yet. But the ranchers, you know, they're in a tough situation. It's legal now for foreigners to export beef to Tokyo, and beef in Japan is something like twenty, twenty-two dollars a kilo. But nobody in Japan will buy American beef. If Americans send beef, it will rot on the docks. But if they sell their ranch to the Japanese, then the beef can be exported. Because the Japanese will buy from a Japanese-owned ranch. The Japanese will do business with other Japanese. And ranches all around Montana and Wyoming have been sold. The remaining ranchers see Japanese cowboys riding on the range. They see the other ranches putting in improvements, rebuilding barns, adding modern equipment, all that. Because the other ranches can get high prices in Japan. So the American owners, they're not stupid. They see the writing on the wall. They know they can't compete. So they sell.'

'But then what do the Americans do?'

'Stay and work for the Japanese. It's not a problem. The Japanese need someone to teach them how to ranch. And everybody on the ranch gets a raise. The Japanese are sensitive to American feelings. They're sensitive people.'

The second man said, 'I know, but I don't like it. I don't like the whole thing.'

'That's fine, Ted. What do you want to do, write your congressman? They're all working for the Japanese, anyway. Hell, the Japanese are running these ranches with American government subsidies.' The first man twisted a gold chain at his wrist. He leaned close to his companion. 'Look, Ted. Let's not get all moral here. Because I can't afford it. And neither can you. We are talking a four-percent overall and a five-year payout on a seven hundred mil purchase. Let's make sure we keep that in sight, okay? You personally are looking at two point four million in the first year alone. And it's a five-year payout. Right?'

'I know. It just bothers me.'

'Well, Ted. I don't think you'll be bothered when this deal closes. But there's a couple of details we need to handle . . .' At that point, they seemed to realize I was listening. They stood up and moved out of earshot. I heard the first man say something about 'assurances that the State of Montana favors and approves . . .' and the second man was nodding, slowly. The first man punched him in the shoulder, cheering him up.

'Lieutenant Smith?'

A woman was standing beside my chair. 'Yes?'

'I'm Kristen, Dr Donaldson's assistant. Kevin over at JPL called about you. Something about tapes you need help with?'

'Yes. I need them copied.'

'I'm sorry I wasn't here to take Kevin's call. One of the secretaries took it, and she didn't really understand the situation.'

'How's that?'

'Unfortunately, Dr Donaldson isn't here right now. He's making a speech this morning.'

'I see.'

'And that makes it difficult for us. With him not in the lab.'

'I just want to copy some tapes. Perhaps someone else in the lab can help me,' I said.

'Ordinarily yes, but I'm afraid it's impossible today.'

It was the Japanese wall. Very polite, but a wall. I sighed. It was probably unrealistic to imagine a Japanese research company would help me. Even with something as neutral as copying tapes.

'I understand.'

'Nobody's in the lab this morning at all. They were all working late on a rush project last night, and I guess they were here to all hours. So everybody's late coming in today. That's what the other secretary didn't understand. People coming in late. So I don't know what to tell you.'

I made one last attempt. 'As you know, my boss is the chief of police. This is the second place I've stopped at already this morning. He's really riding me to get this duplicated right away.'

'I'd love to help you. I know Dr Donaldson would be happy to. We've done special work for the police before. And I'm sure we can duplicate whatever material you have. Maybe later today. Or if you care to leave it with us . . .'

'I'm afraid I can't do that.'

'Okay. Sure. I understand. Well, I'm sorry, Lieutenant. Perhaps you can come back later in the day?' She gave a little shrug.

I said, 'Probably not. I guess it's just my bad luck that everybody had to work last night.'

'Yes. It's a pretty unusual situation.'

'What was it, something came up? Research problem?'

'I really don't know. We have so much video capability on site, occasionally we get a rush request for something unusual. A TV commercial that needs a special effect, or something like that. We worked on that new Michael Jackson video for Sony. Or somebody needs to restore tape that has been ruined. You know, rebuild the signal. But I don't know what came up last night. Except that it must have been a lot of work. Something like twenty tapes to be worked on. And a real rush. I hear they didn't finish until after midnight.'

I thought: *It can't be.*

I was trying to think what Connor would do, how he would handle it. I decided it was worth a stab in the dark. I said, 'Well, I'm sure Nakamoto is grateful for all your hard work.'

'Oh, they are. Because it turned out real well for them. They were happy.'

I said, 'You mentioned that Mr Donaldson was giving a speech –'

'*Dr* Donaldson, yes –'

'Where is he doing that?'

'At a corporate-training seminar at the Bonaventure Hotel. Management techniques in research. He must be pretty tired this morning. But he's always a good speaker.'

'Thanks.' I gave her my card. 'You've been very helpful, and if there is ever anything you think of, or want to tell me, call me.'

'Okay.' She glanced at my card. 'Thank you.'

I turned to go. As I was leaving, an American in his late twenties, wearing an Armani suit and the smug look of an M.B.A. who reads the fashion magazines, came down and said to the other two men, 'Gentlemen? Mr Nakagawa will see you now.'

The men leapt up, grabbing their glossy brochures and pictures, and followed the assistant as he walked in calm measured strides toward the elevator.

I went back outside, into the smog.

The sign in the hallway read WORKING TOGETHER: JAPANESE AND AMERICAN MANAGEMENT STYLES. Inside the conference room, I saw one of those twilight business seminars where men and women sit at long tables covered in gray cloth, taking notes in semigloom as a lecturer drones on at the podium.

While I was standing there, in front of a table with the name tags of latecomers, a bespectacled woman came over to me and said, 'Have you registered? Did you get your packet?'

I turned slightly and flashed my badge. I said, 'I would like to speak to Dr Donaldson.'

'He's our next speaker. He's on in seven or eight minutes. Can someone else help you?'

'It'll just take a moment.'

She hesitated. 'But there's so little time before he speaks . . .'

'Then you better get going.'

She looked as if I had slapped her. I don't know what she expected. I was a police officer and I'd asked to speak to somebody. Did she think it was negotiable? I felt irritable, remembering the young fashion plate in the Armani suit. Walking in measured steps, like a person of weight and importance, as he led the real estate salesmen away. Why did that kid think he was important? He might have an M.B.A., but he was still just answering the door for his Japanese boss.

Now, I watched the woman circle the conference room, moving toward the dais where four men waited to speak. The business audience was still taking notes as the sandy-haired man at the podium said, 'There *is* a place for the foreigner in a Japanese corporation. Not at the top, of course, perhaps not even in the upper echelons. But there is certainly a place. You must realize that the place you hold as a foreigner in a Japanese corporation is an important one, that you are respected, and that you have a job to do. As a foreigner, you will have some special obstacles to overcome, but you can do that. You can succeed if you remember to *know your place.*'

I looked at the businessmen in their suits with their heads bowed, taking notes. I wondered what they were writing. Know your place?

The speaker continued: 'Many times you hear executives say, "I had no place in a Japanese corporation, and I had to quit." Or you will hear people say, "They didn't listen to me, I had no chance to get my ideas implemented, no chance for advancement." Those people didn't understand the role of a foreigner in Japanese society. They were not able to fit in, and so they had to leave. But that is *their* problem. The Japanese are perfectly ready to accept Americans and other foreigners in their companies. Indeed, they are eager to have them. And you will be accepted: so long as you remember your place.'

A woman raised her hand and said, 'What about prejudice against women in Japanese corporations?'

'There is no prejudice against women,' the speaker said.

'I've heard that women can't advance.'

'That is simply not true.'

'Then why all the lawsuits? Sumitomo Corporation just settled a big antidiscrimination suit. I read one-third of Japanese corporations have had suits brought by American employees. What about that?'

'It is perfectly understandable,' the speaker said. 'Any time a foreign corporation begins to do business in a new country, it is likely to make mistakes while it gets used to the habits and patterns of the country. When American corporations first went multinational in Europe in the fifties and sixties, they encountered difficulties in the countries they entered, and there were lawsuits then. So it is not remarkable that Japanese corporations also have some period of adjustment coming into America. It is necessary to be patient.'

A man said with a laugh, 'Is there ever a time when it's *not* necessary to be patient with Japan?' But he sounded rueful, not angry.

The others in the room continued to make notes.

'Officer? I'm Jim Donaldson. What is this about?'

I turned. Dr Donaldson was a tall, thin man with glasses and a precise, almost prissy air. He was dressed in collegiate style, a tweed sport coat and a red tie. But he had the nerd pack of pens peeking out of his shirt pocket. I guessed he was an engineer.

'I just had a couple of questions about the Nakamoto tapes.'

'The Nakamoto tapes?'

'The ones in your laboratory last night.'

'My laboratory? Mr, ah –'

'Smith, Lieutenant Smith.' I gave him my card.

'Lieutenant, I'm sorry, but I don't know what you're talking about. Tapes in my lab last night?'

'Kristen, your secretary, said everybody in the lab was working late on some tapes.'

'Yes. That's true. Most of my staff.'

'And the tapes came from Nakamoto.'

'From *Nakamoto*?' He shook his head. 'Who told you that?'

'She did.'

'I assure you, Lieutenant, the tapes were not from Nakamoto.'

'I heard there were twenty tapes.'

'Yes, at least twenty. I'm not sure of the exact number. But they were from McCann-Erickson. An ad campaign for Asahi beer. We had to do a logo transformation on every ad in the campaign. Now that Asahi beer is the number one beer in America.'

'But the question of Nakamoto –'

'Lieutenant,' he said impatiently, glancing at the podium, 'let me explain something. I work for Hamaguchi Research Labs. Hamaguchi is owned by Kawakami Industries. A competitor of Nakamoto. Competition among the Japanese corporations is very intense. *Very* intense. Take my word for it: my lab didn't do any work on any Nakamoto tapes last night. Such a thing would never happen, under any circumstances. If my secretary said it did, she's mistaken. It's absolutely out of the realm of possibility. Now, I have to give a speech. Is there anything else?'

'No,' I said. 'Thanks.'

There was scattered applause as the speaker on the podium finished. I turned and left the room.

I was driving away from the Bonaventure when Connor called in from the golf course. He sounded annoyed. 'I got your page. I had to interrupt my game. This better be good.'

I told him about the one o'clock appointment with Senator Morton.

'All right,' he said. 'Pick me up here at ten-thirty. Anything else?'

I told him about my trips to JPL and Hamaguchi, then my conversation with Donaldson.

Connor sighed. 'That was a waste of time.'

'Why?'

'Because Hamaguchi is funded by Kawakami, and they're in competition with Nakamoto. There is no way they would do anything to help Nakamoto.'

'That's what Donaldson told me,' I said.

'Where are you going now?'

'To the U.S.C. video labs. I'm still trying to get the tapes copied.'

Connor paused. 'Anything else I should know?'

'No.'

'Fine. See you at ten-thirty.'

'Why so early?'

'Ten-thirty,' he said, and hung up.

As soon as I hung up, the phone rang. 'You were supposed to call me.' It was Ken Shubik at the *Times*. He sounded sulky.

'Sorry. I got tied up. Can we talk now?'

'Sure.'

'You got information for me?'

'Listen.' He paused. 'Are you anywhere around here?'

'About five blocks from you.'

'Then come by for a cup of coffee.'

'You don't want to talk on the phone?'

'Well . . .'

'Come on, Ken. You always want to talk on the phone.' Shubik was like all the *Times* reporters, he sat at his desk in front of his computer and wore a headset and talked on the phone all day long. It was his preferred way of doing things. He had all his stuff in front of him, he could type his notes into the computer as he talked. When I was a press officer, my office had been at police headquarters in Parker Center, two blocks from the Times building. And still a reporter like Ken would rather talk to me on the phone than see me in person.

'Come on by, Pete.'

That was clear enough.

Ken didn't want to talk on the phone.

'Okay, fine,' I said. 'See you in ten minutes.'

The *Los Angeles Times* is the most profitable newspaper in America. The newsroom takes up one entire floor of the Times building, and thus is the area of a city block. The space has been skillfully subdivided, so you are never confronted by how large it actually is, and how many hundreds of people work there. But still it seems you walk for days past reporters sitting at clusters of modular workstations, with their glowing computer screens, their blinking telephones, and their tacked-up pictures of the kids.

Ken's workstation was in Metro, on the east side of the building. I found him standing by his desk, pacing. Waiting for me. He took me by the elbow.

'Coffee,' he said. 'Let's get coffee.'

'What is it?' I said. 'You don't want to be seen with me?'

'No. Shit. I want to avoid the Weasel. He's down hustling that new girl on Foreign. She doesn't know any better yet.' Ken nodded toward the far end of the newsroom. There, by the windows, I saw the familiar figure of Willy Wilhelm, known to everyone as Weasel Wilhelm. Willy's narrow, ferretlike face was at this moment composed into a mask of smiling attentiveness as he joked with a blonde girl sitting before a terminal.

'Very cute.'

'Yeah. A little big in the rear. She's Dutch,' Ken said. 'She's only been here a week. She hasn't heard about him.'

Most organizations had a person like the Weasel: somebody who is more ambitious than scrupulous, somebody who finds a way to make himself useful to the powers that be, while being roundly hated by everyone else. That was the case with Weasel Wilhelm.

Like most dishonest people, the Weasel believed the worst about everybody. He could always be counted on to portray events in their most unflattering light, insisting that anything less was a cover-up. He had a nose for human weakness and a taste for melodrama. He cared nothing for the truth of any situation, and he considered a balanced appraisal weak. As far as the Weasel was concerned, the underlying truth was always strong stuff. And that was what he dealt in.

The other reporters at the *Times* despised him.

Ken and I went into the central hallway. I followed him toward the coffee machines, but he led me into the library. In the middle of the floor, the *Times* had a library that was larger and better equipped than many college facilities.

'So, what is it about Wilhelm?' I said.

'He was in here last night,' Ken said. 'I came by after the theater to pick up some notes I needed for a morning interview I was doing from home. And I saw the Weasel in the library. Maybe eleven o'clock at night. You know how ambitious the little turd is. I could see it in his face. He had the scent of blood. So naturally, you want to know about what?'

'Naturally,' I said. The Weasel was an accomplished backstabber. A year earlier, he had managed to get the editor of the *Sunday Calendar* fired. Only at the last minute did he fail to land the job himself.

Ken said, 'So I whisper to Lilly, the night librarian. "What is it? What's the Weasel up to?" She says, "He's checking police reports on some cop." So that's a relief, I think. But then I begin to wonder. I mean, I'm still the senior Metro reporter. I still do a story out of Parker Center a couple of times a month. What does he know that I don't? For all I know, this should be my story. So I say to Lilly, what's the name of this cop?'

'Let me guess,' I said.

'That's right,' Ken said. 'Peter J. Smith.'

'What time was this?'

'About eleven.'

'Great,' I said.

'I thought you'd want to know,' Ken said.

'I do.'

'So I said to Lilly – this is last night – I said, "Lilly, what kind of stuff is he pulling?" And he's pulling everything, all the old clips from the morgue, and apparently he's got a source inside Parker who's going to leak him internal affairs records. Some kind of a hearing about child molestation. Charge brought a couple of years ago.'

'Ah, shit,' I said.

'That true?' Ken said.

'There was a hearing,' I said. 'But it was bullshit.'

Ken looked at me. 'Fill me in.'

'It was three years back,' I said. 'I was still a working detective. My partner and I answered a domestic violence call in Ladera Heights. Hispanic couple, fighting. Both very drunk. Woman wants me to arrest her husband, and when I refuse to, says he's sexually abusing her baby. I go look at the baby. The baby looks okay. I still refuse to arrest the husband. The woman is pissed. The next day she comes in and accuses *me* of sexual molestation. There's a preliminary hearing. Charges dismissed as without merit.'

'Okay,' Ken said. 'Now, you got any travel that's questionable?'

I frowned. 'Travel?'

'The Weasel was trying to locate travel records last night. Airplane trips, junkets, padded expenses . . .'

I shook my head. 'It doesn't ring a bell.'

'Yeah, I figured he must be wrong about that one. You're a single parent, you're not going on any junkets.'

'No way.'

'Good.'

We were walking deeper into the library. We came to a corner where we could see out to the Metro section of the newsroom through glass walls. I saw the Weasel still talking to the girl, chatting her up. I said, 'What I don't understand, Ken, is why me? I mean, I got no heat on me at all. No controversy. I haven't been a working detective for three years. I'm not even a press officer any more. I'm liaison. I mean, what I do is political. So why is a *Times* reporter gunning for me?'

'At eleven o'clock on a Thursday night, you mean?' Ken said. He was staring at me like I was an idiot. Like there was a drool coming down my chin.

I said, 'You think the Japanese are doing this?'

'I think the Weasel does jobs for people. He is a scumbag for hire. He does jobs for the studios, record companies, brokerage houses, even the realtors. He's a *consultant.* The Weasel now drives a Mercedes 500SL, you know.'

'Oh, yeah?'

'Pretty good on a reporter's salary, wouldn't you say?'

'Yeah, I would.'

'So. You got on the wrong side of somebody? You do that last night?'

'Maybe.'

'Because somebody called the Weasel to track you down.'

I said, 'I can't believe this.'

'Believe it,' Ken said. 'The only thing that worries me is the Weasel's source inside Parker Center. Somebody in the department's leaking him internal affairs stuff. You okay inside your own department?'

'As far as I know.'

'Good. Because the Weasel is up to his usual tricks. This morning I talked to Roger Bascomb, our in-house counsel.'

'And?'

'Guess who called him all hot and bothered with a question last night? The Weasel. And you want to guess what the question was?'

I said nothing.

'The question was, does serving as a police press officer make an individual a public personality? As in, a public personality who can't sue for libel?'

I said, 'Jesus.'

'Right.'

'And the answer?'

'Who cares about the answer? You know how this works. All the Weasel has to do is call a few people and say, "Hi, this is Bill Wilhelm over here at the *L.A. Times*. We're going with a story tomorrow that says Lieutenant Peter Smith is a child molester, do you have any comment on that?" A few well-placed calls, and the story doesn't even have to run. The editors can kill it but the damage is already done.'

I said nothing. I knew what Ken was telling me was true. I had seen it happen more than once.

I said, 'What can I do?'

Ken laughed. 'You could arrange one of your famous incidents of L.A. police brutality.'

'That's not funny.'

'Nobody at this paper would cover it, I can promise you that. You could fucking kill him. And if somebody made a home video? Hey, people here would *pay* to see it on video.'

'Ken.'

Ken sighed. 'I can dream. Okay. There's one thing. Last year, after Wilhelm was involved in the, ah, change of management over in *Calendar,* I got an anonymous package in the mail. So did a few other people. Nobody did anything about it at the time. It's pretty dirty pool. You interested?'

'Yeah.'

Ken took a small manila envelope from the inside pocket of his sport coat. It had one of those strings that you wrap back and forth to close it. Inside was a series of photos, printed in a strip. It showed Willy Wilhelm engaged in an intimate act with a dark-haired man. His head buried in his lap.

'You can't see the Weasel's face too well in all the angles,' Ken said.

'But it's him, all right. Action snap of the reporter entertaining his source. Having a drink with him, so to speak.'

'Who is the guy?'

'It took us a while. His name is Barry Borman. He's the regional head of sales for Kaisei Electronics in southern California.'

'What can I do with this?'

'Give me your card,' Ken said. 'I'll clip it to the envelope, and have it delivered to the Weasel.'

I shook my head. 'I don't think so.'

'It'd sure make him think twice.'

'No,' I said. 'It's not for me.'

Ken shrugged. 'Yeah. It might not work anyway. Even if we squeeze the Weasel's nuts, the Japanese probably have other ways. I still haven't been able to find out how that story ran last night. All I hear is, "Orders from the top, orders from the top." Whatever that means. It could mean anything.'

'Somebody must have written it.'

'I tell you, I can't find out. But you know, the Japanese have a powerful influence at the paper. It's more than just the ads they take. It's more than their relentless PR machine drumming out of Washington, or the local lobbying and the campaign contributions to political figures and the organizations. It's the sum of all those things and more. And it's starting to be insidious. I mean, you can be sitting around in a staff meeting discussing some article that we might run, and you suddenly realize nobody wants to *offend* them. It isn't a question of whether a story is right or wrong, news or not news. And it isn't a one-to-one equation, like 'We can't say that or they'll pull their ads.' It's more subtle than that. Sometimes I look at my editors, and I can tell they won't go with certain stories because they are afraid. They don't even know what they are afraid of. They're just afraid.'

'So much for a free press.'

'Hey,' Ken said. 'This is not the time for sophomore bullshit. You know how it works. The American press reports the prevailing opinion. The prevailing opinion is the opinion of the group in power. The Japanese are now in power. The press reports the prevailing opinion as usual. No surprises. Just take care.'

'I will.'

'And don't hesitate to call, if you decide you want to arrange mail service.'

I wanted to talk to Connor. I was beginning to understand why Connor had been worried, and why he had wanted to conclude the investigation quickly. Because a well-mounted campaign of innuendo is a fearsome thing. A skillful practitioner – and the Weasel was skillful – would arrange it so that a new story came out, day after day, even when nothing happened. You got headlines like GRAND JURY UNDECIDED ON POLICEMAN'S GUILT when in fact the grand jury hadn't met yet. But people saw the headlines, day after day, and drew their own conclusions.

The truth was, there was always a way to spin it. At the end of the innuendo campaign, if your subject was found blameless, you could still mount a headline like GRAND JURY FAILS TO FIND POLICEMAN GUILTY or DISTRICT ATTORNEY UNWILLING TO PROSECUTE ACCUSED COP. Headlines like that were as bad as a conviction.

And there was no way to bounce back from weeks of negative press. Everybody remembered the accusation. Nobody remembered the exoneration. That was human nature. Once you were accused, it was tough to get back to normal.

It was getting creepy, and I had a lot of bad feelings. I was a little preoccupied, pulling into the parking lot next to the physics department of U.S.C., when the phone rang again. It was assistant chief Olson.

'Peter.'

'Yes, sir.'

'It's almost ten o'clock. I thought you'd be down here putting the tapes on my desk. You promised them to me.'

'I've been having trouble getting the tapes copied.'

'Is that what you've been doing?'

'Sure. Why?'

'Because from the calls I get, it sounds like you aren't dropping this investigation,' Jim Olson said. 'In the last hour, you've been asking questions at a Japanese research institute. Then you've interrogated a scientist who works for a Japanese research institute. You're hanging around some Japanese seminar. Let's get it straight, Peter. Is the investigation over, or not?'

'It's over,' I said. 'I'm just trying to get the tapes copied.'

'Make sure that's all it is,' he said.

'Right, Jim.'

'For the good of the whole department – and the individuals in it – I want this thing behind us.'

'Right, Jim.'

'I don't want to lose control of this situation.'

'I understand.'

'I hope you do,' he said. 'Get the copies made, and get your ass down here.' And he hung up.

I parked the car, and went into the physics building.

I waited at the top of the lecture hall while Phillip Sanders finished his lecture. He stood in front of a blackboard covered with complex formulas. There were about thirty students in the room, most of them seated down near the front. I could see the backs of their heads.

Dr Sanders was about forty years old, one of those energetic types, in constant motion, pacing back and forth, tapping the equations on the blackboard in short emphatic jabs with his chalk as he pointed to the 'signal covariant ratio determination' and the 'factorial delta bandwidth noise.' I couldn't even guess what subject he was teaching. Finally, I concluded it must be electrical engineering.

When the bell rang on the hour, the class stood and packed up their bags. I was startled: nearly everyone in the class was Asian, both men and women. Those that weren't Oriental were Indian or Pakistani. Out of thirty students only three were white.

'That's right,' Sanders said to me later, as we walked down the hallway toward his laboratory. 'A class like Physics 101 doesn't attract Americans. It's been that way for years. Industry can't find them, either. We would be up shit creek if we didn't have the Orientals and Indians who come here to get doctorates in math and engineering, and then work for American companies.'

We continued down some stairs, and turned left. We were in a basement passageway. Sanders walked quickly.

'But the trouble is, it's changing,' he continued. 'My Asian students are starting to go home. Koreans are going back to Korea. Taiwanese the same. Even Indians are returning home. The standard of living is going up in their countries, and there's more opportunity back home now. Some of these foreign countries have large numbers of well-trained people.' He led me briskly down a flight of stairs. 'Do you know what city has the highest number of Ph.D.'s per capita in the world?'

'Boston?'

'Seoul, Korea. Think about *that* as we rocket into the twenty-first century.'

Now we were going down another corridor. Then briefly outside, into sunlight, down a covered walkway, and back into another building.

Sanders kept glancing back over his shoulder, as if he was afraid of losing me. But he never stopped talking.

'And with foreign students going home, we don't have enough engineers to do American research. Not enough trained people. Even big companies like IBM are starting to have trouble. Trained people simply don't exist. Watch the door.'

The door swung back toward me. I went through. I said, 'But if there are all these high-tech job opportunities, won't they begin to attract students?'

'Not like investment banking. Or law.' Sanders laughed. 'America may lack engineers and scientists, but we lead the world in the production of lawyers. America has half the lawyers in the entire world. Think of that.' He shook his head.

'We have four percent of the world population. We have eighteen percent of the world economy. But we have fifty percent of the lawyers. And thirty-five thousand more every year, pouring out of the schools. That's where our productivity's directed. That's where our national focus is. Half our TV shows are about lawyers. America has become Land of Lawyers. Everybody suing. Everybody disputing. Everybody in court. After all, three quarters of a million American lawyers have to do *something*. They have to make their three hundred thousand a year. Other countries think we're crazy.'

He unlocked a door. I saw a sign that said ADVANCED IMAGING LABORATORY in hand-painted lettering, and an arrow. Sanders led me down a long basement hallway.

'Even our brightest kids are badly educated. The best American kids now rank twelfth in the world, after the industrialized countries of Asia and Europe. And that's our top students. At the bottom, it's worse. One-third of high school graduates can't read a bus schedule. They're illiterate.'

We came to the end of the hallway, and turned right. 'And the kids I see are lazy. Nobody wants to work. I teach physics. It takes years to master. But all the kids want to dress like Charlie Sheen and make a million dollars before they're twenty-eight. The only way you can make that kind of money is in law, investment banking, Wall Street. Places where the game is paper profits, something for nothing. But that's what the kids want to do, these days.'

'Maybe at U.S.C.'

'Trust me. Everywhere. They all watch television.'

He swung another door open. Still another corridor. This one smelled moldy, damp.

'I know, I know. I'm old-fashioned,' Sanders said. 'I still believe that every human being stands for something. You stand for something. I stand for something. Just being on this planet, wearing the clothes we wear, doing the work we do, we each stand for something. And in this little corner of the world,' he said, 'we stand for cutting the crap. We analyze network news and see where they have been fucking around with the tape. We analyze TV commercials and show where the tricks are –'

Sanders suddenly stopped.

'What's the matter?'

'Wasn't there someone else?' he said. 'Didn't you come here with someone else?'

'No. Just me.'

'Oh, good.' Sanders continued on at his same breakneck pace. 'I always worry about losing people down here. Ah, okay. Here we are. The lab. Good. This door is just where I left it.'

With a flourish, he threw the door open. I stared at the room, shocked.

'I know it doesn't look like much,' Sanders said.

That, I thought, was a serious understatement.

I was looking at a basement space with rusty pipes and fittings hanging down from the ceiling. The green linoleum on the floor curled up in several places to expose concrete beneath. Arranged around the room were battered wooden tables, each heaped with equipment, and drooping wires down the sides. At each table, a student sat facing monitors. In several places, water plinked into buckets on the floor. Sanders said, 'The only space we could get was here in the basement, and we don't have the money to put in little amenities like a ceiling. Never mind, doesn't matter. Just watch your head.'

He moved forward into the room. I am about a hundred and eighty centimeters tall, not quite six feet, and I had to crouch to enter the room. From somewhere in the ceiling above, I heard a harsh rasping sizzle.

'Skaters,' Sanders explained.

'Sorry?'

'We're underneath the ice rink. You get used to it. Actually, it's not bad now. When they have hockey practice in the afternoon, then it's a bit noisy.'

We moved deeper into the room. I felt like I was in a submarine. I glanced at the students at their workstations. They were all intent on their work; nobody looked up as we passed. Sanders said, 'What kind of tape do you want to duplicate?'

'Eight-millimeter Japanese. Security tape. It might be difficult.'

'Difficult? I doubt that very much,' Sanders said. 'You know, back in my youth, I wrote most of the early video image-enhancement algorithms. You know, despeckling and inversion and edge tracing. That stuff. The Sanders algorithms were the ones everybody used. I was a graduate student at Cal Tech then. I worked at JPL in my spare time. No, no, we can do it.'

I handed him a tape. He looked at it. 'Cute little bugger.'

I said, 'What happened? To all your algorithms?'

'There was no commercial use for them,' he said. 'Back in the eighties, American companies like RCA and GE got out of commercial electronics entirely. My image enhancement programs didn't have much use in America.' He shrugged. 'So I tried to sell them to Sony, in Japan.'

'And?'

'The Japanese had already patented the products. In Japan.'

'You mean they already had the algorithms?'

'No. They just had patents. In Japan, patenting is a form of war. The Japanese patent like crazy. And they have a strange system. It takes eight years to get a patent in Japan, but your application is made public after eighteen months, after which royalties are moot. And of course Japan doesn't have reciprocal licensing agreements with America. It's one of the ways they keep their edge.

'Anyway, when I got to Japan I found Sony and Hitachi had some related patents and they had done what is called "patent flooding". Meaning they covered possible related uses. They didn't have the rights to use my algorithms – but I discovered I didn't have the rights, either. Because they had already patented the *use* of my invention.' He shrugged. 'It's complicated to explain. Anyway, that's ancient history. By now the Japanese have devised *much* more complicated video software, far surpassing anything we have. They're years ahead of us now. But we struggle along in this lab. Ah. Just the person we need. Dan. Are you busy?'

A young woman looked up from the computer console. Large eyes, horn-rim glasses, dark hair. Her face was partially blocked by the ceiling pipes.

'You're not Dan,' Sanders said, sounding surprised. 'Where's Dan, Theresa?'

'Picking up a midterm,' Theresa said. 'I'm just helping run the real-time progressions. They're finishing now.' I had the impression that she was older than the other students. It was hard to say why, exactly. It certainly wasn't her clothes: she wore a bright colored headband and a U2 T-shirt under a jeans jacket. But she had a calm quality that made her seem older.

'Can you switch to something else?' Sanders said, walking around the table to look at the monitor. 'Because we have a rush job here. We have to help out the police.' I followed Sanders, ducking pipes.

'Sure, I guess,' the woman said. She started to shut down units on the desk. Her back was turned to me, and then finally I could see her. She was dark, exotic-looking, almost Eurasian. In fact she was beautiful, drop-dead beautiful. She looked like one of those high cheek-boned models in magazines. And for a moment I was confused, because this woman was too beautiful to be working in some basement electronics laboratory. It didn't make sense.

'Say hello to Theresa Asakuma,' he said. 'The only Japanese graduate student working here.'

'Hi,' I said. I blushed. I felt stupid. I felt that information was coming at me too fast. And all things considered, I would rather not have a Japanese handling these tapes. But her first name wasn't Japanese, and she didn't look Japanese, she looked Eurasian or perhaps part Japanese, so exotic, maybe she was even –

'Good morning, Lieutenant,' she said. She extended her left hand, the wrong hand, for me to shake. She held it out to me sideways, the way someone does when their right hand is injured.

I shook hands with her. 'Hello, Miss Asakuma.'

'Theresa.'

'Okay.'

'Isn't she beautiful?' Sanders said, acting as if he took credit for it. 'Just beautiful.'

'Yes,' I said. 'Actually, I'm surprised you're not a model.'

There was an awkward moment. I couldn't tell why. She turned quickly away.

'It never interested me,' she said.

And Sanders immediately jumped in and said, 'Theresa, Lieutenant Smith needs us to copy some tapes. *These* tapes.'

Sanders held out one to her. She took it in her left hand and held it to the light. Her right hand remained bent at the elbow, pressed to her waist. Then I saw that her right arm was withered, ending in a fleshy stump protruding beyond the sleeve of her jeans jacket. It looked like the arm of a Thalidomide baby.

'Quite interesting,' she said, squinting at the tape. 'Eight-millimeter high density. Maybe it's the proprietary digital format we've been hearing about. The one that includes real-time image enhancement.'

'I'm sorry, I don't know,' I said. I was feeling foolish for having said anything about being a model. I dug into my box and brought out the playback machine.

Theresa immediately took a screwdriver and removed the top. She bent over the innards. I saw a green circuit board, a black motor, and three small crystal cylinders. 'Yes. It's the new setup. Very slick. Dr Sanders, look: they're doing it with just three heads. The board must generate component RGB, because over here – you think this is compression circuitry?'

'Probably digital to analog converter,' Sanders said. 'Very neat. So small.' He turned to me, holding up the box. 'You know how the Japanese can make things this way and we can't? They *kaizen* 'em. A process of deliberate, patient, continual refinements. Each year the products get a little better, a little smaller, a little cheaper. Americans don't think that way. Americans are always looking for the quantum leap, the big advance forward. Americans try to hit a home run – to knock it out of the park – and then sit back. The Japanese just hit singles all day long, and they never sit back. So with something like this, you're looking at an expression of philosophy as much as anything.'

He talked like this for a while, pivoting the cylinders, admiring it. Finally I said, 'Can you copy these tapes?'

'Sure,' Theresa said. 'From the converter, we can run a signal out of this machine and lay it down on whatever media you like. You want three-quarter? Optical master? VHS?'

'VHS,' I said.

'That's easy,' she said.

'But will it be an accurate copy? The people at JPL said they couldn't guarantee the copy would be accurate.'

'Oh, hell, JPL,' Sanders said. 'They just talk like that because they work for the government. We get things *done* here. Right Theresa?'

But Theresa wasn't listening. I watched her plugging cables and wires, moving swiftly with her good hand, using her stump to stabilize and hold the box. Like many disabled people, her movements were so fluid it was hardly noticeable that her right hand was missing. Soon she had the small playback machine hooked to a second recorder, and several different monitors.

'What're all these?'

'To check the signal.'

'You mean for playback?'

'No. The big monitor there will show the image. The others let me look at the signal characteristics, and the data map: how the image has been laid down on the tape.'

I said, 'You need to do that?'

'No. I just want to snoop. I'm curious about how they've set up this high-density format.'

Sanders said to me, 'What is the actual source material?'

'It's from an office security camera.'

'And this tape is original?'

'I think so. Why?'

'Well, if it's original material we want to be extra careful with it,' Sanders said. He was talking to Theresa, instructing her. 'We don't want to set up any feedback loops scrambling the media surface. Or signal leaks off the heads that will compromise the integrity of the data stream.'

'Don't worry,' she said. 'I got it handled.' She pointed to her setup. 'See that? It'll warn of an impedance shift. And I'm monitoring the central processor too.'

'Okay,' Sanders said. He was beaming like a proud parent.

'How long will this take?' I said.

'Not long. We can lay down the signal at very high speed. The rate limit is a function of the playback device, and it seems to have a fast-forward scan. So, maybe two or three minutes per tape.'

I glanced at my watch. 'I have a ten-thirty appointment I can't be late for, and I don't want to leave these . . .'

'You need all of them done?'

'Actually, just five are critical.'

'Then let's do those first.'

We ran the first few seconds of each tape, one after another, looking for the five that came from the cameras on the forty-sixth floor. As each tape started, I saw the camera image on the central monitor of Theresa's table. On the side monitors, signal traces bounced and jiggled like an intensive care unit. I mentioned it.

'That's just about right,' she said. 'Intensive care for video.' She ejected one tape, stuck in another, and started it up. 'Oops. Did you say this material was original? It's not. These tapes are copies.'

'How do you know?'

'Because we got a windup signature.' Theresa bent over the equipment, staring at the signal traces, making fine adjustments with her knobs and dials.

'I think that's what you got, yes,' Sanders said. He turned to me. 'You see, with video it's difficult to detect a copy in the image itself. The older analog video shows some degradation in successive generations, but in a digital system like this, there is no difference at all. Each copy is literally identical to the master.'

'Then how can you say the tapes are copies?'

'Theresa isn't looking at the picture,' Sanders said. 'She's looking at the signal. Even though we can't detect a copy from the image, sometimes we can determine the image came from another video playback, instead of a camera.'

I shook my head. 'How?'

Theresa said, 'It has to do with how the signal is laid down in the first half-second of taping. If the recording video is started before the playback video, there is sometimes a slight fluctuation in the signal output as the playback machine starts up. It's a mechanical function: the playback motors can't get up to speed instantaneously. There are electronic circuits in the playback machine to minimize the effect, but there's always an interval of getting up to speed.'

'And that's what you detected?'

She nodded. 'It's called a windup signature.'

Sanders said, 'And that never happens if the signal is coming direct from a camera, because a camera has no moving parts. A camera is instantaneously up to speed at all times.'

I frowned. 'So these tapes are copies.'

'Is that bad?' Sanders said.

'I don't know. If they were copied, they might also be changed, right?'

'In theory, yes,' Sanders said. 'In practice, we'd have to look carefully. And it would be very hard to know for certain. These tapes come from a Japanese company?'

'Yes.'

'Nakamoto?'

I nodded. 'Yes.'

'Frankly I'm not surprised they gave you copies,' Sanders said. 'The Japanese are extremely cautious. They're not very trusting of outsiders. And Japanese corporations in America feel the way we would feel doing business in Nigeria: they think they're surrounded by savages.'

'Hey,' Theresa said.

'Sorry,' Sanders said, 'but you know what I mean. The Japanese feel they have to put up with us. With our ineptitude, our slowness, our stupidity, our incompetence. That makes them self-protective. So if these tapes have any legal significance, the last thing they'd do is turn the originals over to a barbarian policeman like you. No, no, they'd give you a copy and keep the original in case they need it for their defense. Fully confident that with your inferior American video technology, you'd never be able to detect that it was a copy, anyway.'

I frowned. 'How long would it take to make copies?'

'Not long,' Sanders said, shaking his head. 'The way Theresa is scanning now, five minutes a tape. I imagine the Japanese can do it much faster. Say, two minutes a tape.'

'In that case, they had plenty of time to make copies last night.'

As we talked, Theresa was continuing to shuffle the tapes, looking at the first portions of each. As each image came up, she'd glance at me. I would shake my head. I was seeing all the different security cameras. Finally, the first of the tapes from the forty-sixth floor appeared, the familiar office image I had seen before.

'That's one.'

'Okay. Here we go. Laying it onto VHS.' Theresa started the first copy. She ran the tape forward at high speed, the images streaky and quick. On the side monitors, the signals bounced and jittered nervously. She said, 'Does this have something to do with the murder last night?'

'Yes. You know about that?'

She shrugged. 'I saw it on the news. The killer died in a car crash?'

'That's right,' I said.

She turned away. The three-quarter profile of her face was strikingly beautiful, the high curve of her cheekbone. I thought of what a playboy Eddie Sakamura was known to be. I said, 'Did you know him?'

'No,' she said. After a moment she added, 'He was Japanese.'

Another moment of awkwardness descended on our little group. There was something that both Theresa and Sanders seemed to know that I did not. But I didn't know how to ask. So I watched the video.

Once again, I saw the sunlight moving across the floor. Then the room lights came up as the office personnel thinned. Now the floor was empty. And then, at high speed, Cheryl Austin appeared, followed by the man. They kissed passionately.

'Ah ha,' Sanders said. 'Is this it?'

'Yes.'

He frowned as he watched the action progress. 'You mean the murder is *recorded*?'

'Yes,' I said. 'On multiple cameras.'

'You're kidding.'

Sanders fell silent, watching events proceed. With the streaky high-speed image, it was difficult to see more than the basic events. The two people moving to the conference room. The sudden struggle. Forcing her back on the table. Stepping away suddenly. Leaving the room in haste.

Nobody spoke. We all watched the tape.

I glanced at Theresa. Her face was blank. The image was reflected in her glasses.

Eddie passed the mirror, and went into the dark passageway. The tape ran on for a few more seconds, and then the cassette popped out.

'That's one. You say there are multiple cameras? How many all together?'

'Five, I think,' I said.

She marked the first cassette with a stick-on label. She started the second tape in the machine, and began another high-speed duplication.

I said, 'These copies are exact?'

'Oh, yes.'

'So they're legal?'

Sanders frowned. 'Legal in what sense?'

'Well, as evidence in a court of law –'

'Oh, no,' Sanders said. 'These tapes would never be admissible in a court of law.'

'But if they're exact copies –'

'It's nothing to do with that. All forms of photographic evidence, including video, are no longer admissible in court.'

'I haven't heard that,' I said.

'It hasn't happened yet,' Sanders said. 'The case law isn't entirely clear. But it's coming. All photographs are suspect these days. Because now, with digital systems, they can be changed perfectly. *Perfectly*. And that's something new. Remember years ago, how the Russians would remove politicians from photographs of their May Day line ups? It was always a crude cut-and-paste job – and you could always see that something had been done. There was a funny space between the shoulders of the remaining people. Or a discoloration on the back wall. Or you could see the brushstrokes of the retoucher who tried to smooth over the damage. But anyway, you could see it – fairly easily. You could *see* the picture had been altered. The whole business was laughable.'

'I remember,' I said.

'Photographs always had integrity precisely because they were impossible to change. So we considered photographs to represent reality.

But for several years now, computers have allowed us to make seamless alterations of photographic images. A few years back the *National Geographic* moved the Great Pyramid of Egypt on a cover photo. The editors didn't like where the pyramid was, and they thought it would compose better if it was moved. So they just altered the photograph and moved it. Nobody could tell. But if you go back to Egypt with a camera and try to duplicate that picture, you'll find you can't. Because there is no place in the real world where the pyramids line up that way. The photograph no longer represents reality. But you can't tell. Minor example.'

'And someone could do the same thing to this tape?'

'In theory, any video can be changed.'

On the monitor, I watched the murder occurring a second time. This camera was from the far end of the room. It didn't show the actual murder very well, but afterward, Sakamura was clearly visible as he walked toward the camera.

I said, 'The image could be changed how?'

Sanders laughed. 'These days, you can make any damn change you want.'

'Could you change the identity of the murderer?'

'Technically, yes,' Sanders said. 'Mapping a face onto a complex moving object is now possible. Technically possible. But as a practical matter, it'd be a bitch to do.'

I said nothing. But it was just as well. Sakamura was our leading suspect and he was dead; the chief wanted the case finished. So did I.

'Of course,' Sanders said, 'the Japanese have all sorts of fancy video algorithms for surface mapping and three-dimensional transformations. They can do things that we can't begin to imagine.' He drummed his fingers on the table again. 'What is the timetable of these tapes? What's their history?'

I said, 'The murder happened at eight-thirty last night, as shown on the clock. We were told the tapes were removed from the security office around eight forty-five p.m. We asked for them, and there was some back-and-forth with the Japanese.'

'As always. And when did you finally take possession?'

'They were delivered to division headquarters around one-thirty a.m.'

'Okay,' Sanders said. 'That means they had the tapes from eight forty-five to one-thirty.'

'Right. A little less than five hours.'

Sanders frowned. 'Five tapes, with five different camera angles, to change in five hours?' Sanders shook his head. 'No way. It just can't be done, Lieutenant.'

'Yeah,' Theresa said. 'It's impossible. Even for them. It's just too many pixels to change.'

I said, 'You're sure about that.'

'Well,' Theresa said, 'the only way it could be done that fast is with an automated program, and even the most sophisticated programs need you to polish the details by hand. Things like bad blur can give it all away.'

'Bad blur?' I said. I found I liked asking her questions. I liked looking at her face.

'Bad motion blur,' Sanders said. 'Video runs at thirty frames a second. You can think of each frame of video as a picture that's shot at a shutter speed of one-thirtieth of a second. Which is very slow – much slower than pocket cameras. If you film a runner at a thirtieth of a second, the legs are just streaks. Blurs.

'That's called motion blur. And if you alter it by a mechanical process, it starts to look wrong. The image appears too sharp, too crisp. Edges look odd. It's back to the Russians: you can see it's been changed. For realistic motion, you need the right amount of blur.'

'I see.'

Theresa said, 'And there's the color shift.'

'Right,' Sanders said. 'Inside the blur itself, there is a color shift. For example, look there on the monitor. The man is wearing a blue suit, and his coat is swinging out as he spins the girl around the room. Now. If you take a frame of that action, and blow it up to its pixels, you will find that the coat is navy but the blur is progressive shades of lighter blue, until at the edge it seems almost transparent – you can't tell from a single frame exactly where the coat ends and the background begins.'

I could vaguely imagine it. 'Okay . . .'

'If the edge colors don't blend smoothly, you will notice it immediately. It can take hours to clean up a few seconds of tape, as in a commercial. But if you don't do it, you will see it like *that*.' He snapped his fingers.

'So even though they duplicated the tapes, they couldn't have altered them?'

'Not in five hours,' Sanders said. 'They just didn't have time.'

'Then we are seeing what actually happened.'

'No doubt about it,' Sanders said. 'But we'll poke around with this image, anyway, after you go. Theresa wants to fiddle with it, I know she does. So do I. Check in with us later today. We'll tell you if there's anything funny. But basically, it can't be done. And it wasn't done here.'

As I pulled into the parking circle at the Sunset Hills Country Club, I saw Connor standing in front of the big stucco clubhouse. He bowed to the three Japanese golfers standing with him, and they bowed back. Then he shook hands with them all, tossed the clubs into the back seat, and got into my car.

'You're late, *kōhai*.'

'Sorry. It's only a few minutes. I was held up at U.S.C.'

'Your lateness inconvenienced everyone. As a matter of politeness, they felt obliged to keep me company in front of the club while I waited for you. Men of their position are not comfortable standing around. They are busy. But they felt obligated and could not leave me there. You embarrassed me very much. And you reflected poorly on the department.'

'I'm sorry. I didn't realize.'

'Start to realize, *kōhai*. You're not alone in the world.'

I put the car in gear, and drove out. I looked at the Japanese in the rearview mirror. They were waving as we left. They did not appear unhappy, or in a rush to leave. 'Who were you playing with?'

'Aoki-san is the head of Tokio Marine in Vancouver. Hanada-san is a vice-president of Mitsui Bank in London. And Kenichi Asaka runs all of Toyota's Southeast Asian plants from K.L. to Singapore. He's based in Bangkok.'

'What are they doing here?'

'They're on vacation,' Connor said. 'A short holiday in the States for golf. They find it pleasant to relax in a slower-paced country like ours.'

I drove up the winding drive to Sunset Boulevard, and stopped to wait for the light. 'Where to?'

'The Four Seasons Hotel.'

I turned right heading toward Beverly Hills. 'And why are these men playing golf with you?'

'Oh, we go way back,' he said. 'A few favors here and there, over the years. I'm nobody important. But relationships must be maintained. A phone call, a small gift, a game when you're in town. Because you never know when you will need your network. Relationships are your source of information, your safety valve, and your early warning system. In the Japanese way of seeing the world.'

'Who asked for this game?'

'Hanada-san was already intending to play. I just joined him. I'm quite a good golfer, you know.'

'Why did you want to play?'

'Because I wanted to know more about the Saturday meetings,' Connor said.

I remembered the Saturday meetings. On the video we had seen at the newsroom, Sakamura had grabbed Cheryl Austin and said: You don't understand, this is all about the Saturday meetings.

'And did they tell you?'

Connor nodded. 'Apparently they began a long time ago,' he said. 'Nineteen eighty or so. First they were held in the Century Plaza, and later in the Sheraton, and finally in the Biltmore.'

Connor stared out of the window. The car jounced over the potholes on Sunset Boulevard.

'For several years, the meetings were a regular event. Prominent Japanese industrialists who happened to be in town would attend an ongoing discussion of what should be done about America. Of how the American economy should be managed.'

'*What?*'

'Yes.'

'That's outrageous!'

'Why?' Connor said.

'*Why?* Because this is *our* country. You can't have a bunch of foreigners sitting around in secret meetings and deciding how to manage it!'

'The Japanese don't see it that way,' Connor said.

'I'm sure they don't! I'm sure they think they have a goddamn right!'

Connor shrugged. 'As a matter of fact, that's exactly what they think. And the Japanese believe they have earned the right to decide –'

'*Christ* –'

'Because they have invested heavily in our economy. They have lent us a lot of money, Peter: a *lot* of money. Hundreds of billions of dollars. For most of the last fifteen years, the United States has run a billion dollars of trade deficit a *week* with Japan. That's a billion dollars every week that they must do something with. A torrent of money roaring toward them. They don't especially want so many dollars. What can they do with all their excess billions?

'They decided to lend the money back to us. Our government was running a budget deficit, year after year. We weren't paying for our own programs. So the Japanese financed our budget deficit. They invested in us. And they lent their money, based on certain assurances from our government. Washington assured the Japanese that we would set our house in order. We would cut our deficit. We would improve education, rebuild our infrastructure, even raise taxes if necessary. In short, we would clean up our act. Because only then does an investment in America make sense.'

'Uh-huh,' I said.

'But we did none of those things. We let the deficit get worse, and we devalued the dollar. We cut its value in half in 1985. You know what that did to Japanese investments in America? It fucked them. Whatever they invested in 1984 now paid half its previous return.'

I vaguely remembered something about this. I said, 'I thought we did that to help our trade deficit, to boost exports.'

'We did, but it didn't work. Our trade balance with Japan got worse. Normally, if you devalue your currency by half, the cost of everything imported doubles. But the Japanese slashed prices on their VCRs and copiers, and held their market share. Remember, business is war.

'All we really accomplished was to make American land and American companies cheap for the Japanese to buy, because the yen was now twice as strong as it had been. We made the biggest banks in the world all Japanese. And we made America a poor country.'

'What does this have to do with the Saturday meetings?'

'Well,' Connor said, 'suppose you have an uncle who is drunk. He says if you lend him money he'll stop drinking. But he doesn't stop drinking. And you'd like to get your money. You want to salvage what you can from your bad investment. Also, you know that your uncle, being a drunk, is likely to get loaded and hurt somebody. Your uncle is out of control. So something has to be done. And the family sits down together to decide what to do about their problem uncle. That's what the Japanese decided to do.'

'Uh-huh.' Connor must have heard the skepticism in my voice.

'Look,' he said. 'Get this conspiracy stuff out of your head. Do you want to take over Japan? Do you want to run their country? Of course not. No sensible country wants to take over another country. Do business, yes. Have a relationship, yes. But not *take over*. Nobody wants the responsibility. Nobody wants to be bothered. Just like with the drunken uncle – you only have those meetings when you're forced to. It's a last resort.'

'So that's how the Japanese see it?'

'They see billions and billions of their dollars, *kōhai*. Invested in a country that's in deep trouble. That's filled with strange individualistic people who talk constantly. Who confront each other constantly. Who argue all the time. People who aren't well educated, who don't know much about the world, who get their information from television. People who don't work very hard, who tolerate violence and drug use, and who don't seem to object to it. The Japanese have billions of dollars in this peculiar land and they would like a decent return on their investment. And even though the American economy is collapsing – it will soon be third in the world after Japan and Europe – it's still important to try and hold it together. Which is all they're trying to do.'

'That's it?' I said. 'They're just doing the good work of saving America?'

'Somebody needs to do it,' Connor said. 'We can't go on this way.'

'We'll manage.'

'That's what the English always said.' He shook his head. 'But now England is poor. And America is becoming poor, too.'

'Why is it becoming poor?' I said, speaking louder than I intended.

'The Japanese say it's because America has become a land without substance. We let our manufacturing go. We don't make things anymore. When you manufacture products, you add value to raw materials, and you literally create wealth. But America has stopped doing that. Americans make money now by paper manipulation, which the Japanese say is bound to catch up to us because paper profits don't reflect real wealth. They think our fascination with Wall Street and junk bonds is crazy.'

'And therefore the Japanese ought to manage us?'

'They think *someone* ought to manage us. They'd prefer we do it ourselves.'

'Jesus.'

Connor shifted in his seat. 'Save your outrage, *kōhai*. Because according to Hanada-san, the Saturday meetings stopped in 1991.'

'Oh?'

'Yes. That was when the Japanese decided not to worry about whether America would clean up its act. They saw advantages in the present situation: America is asleep, and inexpensive to buy.'

'So there aren't Saturday meetings any more?'

'There are occasional ones. Because of *nichibei kankei:* the ongoing Japanese-American relationship. The economies of the two countries are interlocked by now. Neither country can pull out, even if they wanted to. But the meetings are no longer important. They are basically social functions. So what Sakamura said to Cheryl Austin is wrong. And her death had nothing to do with the Saturday meetings.'

'What does it have to do with?'

'My friends seemed to think it was personal. A *Chijou no motsure,* a crime of passion. Involving a beautiful, *irokichigai* woman and a jealous man.'

'And you believe them?'

'Well, the thing is, they were unanimous. All three of these businessmen. Of course Japanese are reluctant to express disagreement among themselves, even on the golf course of an underdeveloped peasant country. But I have learned that unanimity toward a *gaijin* may cover a multitude of sins.'

'You think they were lying?'

'Not exactly.' Connor shook his head. 'But I had the impression they were telling me something by not telling me. This morning was a game of *hara no saguriai.* My friends were not forthcoming.'

Connor described his golf game. There had been long silences all morning. Everyone in the foursome was polite and considerate, but spoken comments were rare and reserved. Most of the time, the men walked over the course in complete silence.

'And you had gone there for information?' I said. 'How could you stand it?'

'Oh, I was getting information.' But as he explained it, it was all unspoken. Basically, the Japanese have an understanding based on centuries of shared culture, and they are able to communicate feelings without words. It's the closeness that exists in America between a parent and child – a child often understands everything, just from a parent's glance. But Americans don't rely on unspoken communication as a general rule, and the Japanese do. It is as if all Japanese are members of the same family, and they can communicate without words. To a Japanese, silences have meaning.

'It's nothing mystical or wonderful,' Connor said. 'For the most part it is because the Japanese are so hemmed in by rules and conventions, they end up unable to say anything at all. For politeness, to save face, the other person is obliged to read the situation, the context, and the subtle signs of body posture and unstated feeling. Because the first person feels he can't actually put anything into words. Any speaking at all would be indelicate. So the point must be gotten across in other ways.'

I said, 'And that's how your morning was spent? Not talking?'

Connor shook his head. He felt he had quite clear communication with the Japanese golfers, and wasn't troubled by the silences at all.

'Because I was asking them to talk about other Japanese – members of their family – I had to frame my questions with great delicacy. Just as I would if I were asking whether your sister was in jail or any subject that was painful or awkward for you. I would be attentive to how long it took you to answer, and the pauses between your statements, the tone of your voice – all sorts of things. Beyond the literal communication. Okay?'

'Okay.'

'It means you get the feeling by an intuition.'

'And what was the intuition you got?'

'They said, "We are mindful that you have performed services for us in the past. We feel a desire to help you now. But this murder is a Japanese matter and thus we are unable to tell you everything that we might like to. From our reticence, you may draw useful conclusions about the underlying issue." That's what they said to me.'

'And what is the underlying issue?'

'Well,' Connor said. 'They mentioned MicroCon several times.'

'That high-tech company?'

'Yes. The one that's being sold. Apparently it's a small company in Silicon Valley that makes specialized computer machinery. And there are political problems about the sale. They referred to those problems several times.'

'So this murder has something to do with MicroCon?'

'I think so.' He shifted in his chair. 'By the way, what did you learn at U.S.C. about the tapes?'

'For one thing, that they were duplicated.'

Connor nodded. 'I assumed that,' he said.

'You did?'

'Ishiguro would never give us the originals. The Japanese think everybody who is not Japanese is a barbarian. They mean it, literally: *barbarian.* Stinking, vulgar, stupid barbarian. They're polite about it, because they know you can't help the misfortune of not being born Japanese. But they still think it.'

I nodded. That was more or less what Sanders had said, too.

'The other thing,' Connor said, 'is that the Japanese are extremely successful, but they are not daring. They are plotters and plodders. So they're not going to give us the originals because they don't want to take any chances. What else did you learn about the tapes?'

'What makes you think there was something else?' I said.

'When you looked at the tapes,' he said, 'I'm sure you noticed an important detail that –'

And then we were interrupted by the telephone.

'Captain Connor,' said a cheerful voice, over the speaker phone. 'This is Jerry Orr. Over at Sunset Hills Country Club? You left without taking the papers with you.'

'The papers?'

'The application,' Orr said. 'You need to fill it out, Captain. Of course it's just routine. I can assure you, there won't be any problem with it, considering who your sponsors are.'

'My sponsors,' Connor said.

'Yes, sir,' Orr said. 'And congratulations. As you know, it's almost impossible to obtain a membership at Sunset these days. But Mr Hanada's company had already bought a corporate membership some time ago, and they have decided to put it in your name. I must say, it's a very nice gesture from your friends.'

'Yes, it is,' Connor said, frowning.

I was looking at him.

'They know how fond you are of playing golf here,' Orr said. 'You know the terms, of course. Hanada will purchase the membership over five years, but after that time, it'll be transferred to your name. So when you retire from club membership, you're free to sell it. Now: will you be picking up the paperwork here, or should I send it to your home?'

Connor said, 'Mr Orr, please convey my heartfelt appreciation to Mr Hanada for his very great generosity. I hardly know what to say. But I will have to call you back about this.'

'That's fine. You just let us know where to send it.'

'I'll call you back,' Connor said.

He pushed the button to end the call, and stared forward, frowning. There was a long silence.

I said, 'How much is a membership at that club worth?'

'Seven fifty. Maybe a million.'

I said, 'Pretty nice gift from your friends.' I was thinking again of Graham, and the way Graham had always implied that Connor was in the pocket of the Japanese. There didn't seem to be much doubt of it now.'

Connor was shaking his head. 'I don't get it.'

'What's not to get?' I said. 'Jesus, Captain. Seems pretty straightforward to me.'

'No, I don't get it,' Connor said.

And then the phone rang again. This time, it was for me.

'Lieutenant Smith? It's Louise Gerber. I'm *so* glad I was able to reach you.'

I didn't recognize her name. I said, 'Yes?'

'Since tomorrow is Saturday, I was wondering if you had any time to look at a house.'

Then I remembered who she was. A month earlier I had gone out with a broker to look at houses. Michelle is getting older, and I wanted to get her out of an apartment. To get her a backyard if I could. It was pretty discouraging. Even with a real estate slump, the smallest houses were four and five hundred thousand. I couldn't possibly qualify for that, on my salary.

'This is a very special situation,' she said, 'and I thought of you and your little girl. It's a small house in Palms – very small – but it's a corner lot and it has a charming backyard. Flowers and a lovely lawn. The asking is three hundred. But the reason I thought of you is that the seller is willing to take back all the paper on it. I think you could get it for very little down. Do you want to see it?'

I said, 'Who is the seller?'

'I don't really know. It's a special situation. The house is owned by an elderly woman who has gone into a nursing home and her son who lives in Topeka intends to sell it, but he wants an income flow instead of an outright sale. The property's not formally listed yet, but I know the seller is motivated. If you could get in tomorrow, you might be able to do something. And the backyard is charming. I can just see your little girl there.'

Now Connor was looking at me. I said, 'Miss Gerber, I'd have to know more about it. Who the seller is, and so on.'

She sounded surprised. 'Gee, I thought you'd jump at it. A situation like this doesn't come along very often. Don't you want to look at it?'

Connor was looking at me, nodding. He mouthed, say yes.

'I'll have to get back to you about this,' I said.

'All right, Lieutenant,' she said. She sounded reluctant. 'Please let me know.'

'I will.'

I hung up.

'What the hell is going on?' I said. Because there wasn't any way to get around it. Between us, we had just been offered a lot of money. A *lot* of money.

Connor shook his head. 'I don't know.'

'Is it to do with MicroCon?'

'I don't know. I thought MicroCon was a small company. This doesn't make sense.' He looked very uneasy. 'What exactly *is* MicroCon?'

I said, 'I think I know who to ask.'

'MicroCon?' Ron Levine said, lighting a big cigar. 'Sure, I can tell you about MicroCon. It's an ugly story.'

We were sitting in the newsroom of American Financial Network, a cable news operation located near the airport. Through the window of Ron's office, I could see the white satellite dishes on the roof of the adjacent garage. Ron puffed on his cigar and grinned at us. He had been a financial reporter at the *Times* before taking an on-camera job here. AFN was one of the few television operations where the on-camera people weren't scripted; they had to know what they were talking about, and Ron did.

'MicroCon,' he said, 'was formed five years ago by a consortium of American computer manufacturers. The company was intended to develop the next generation of X-ray lithography machines for computer chips. At the time MicroCon started up, there were no American manufacturers of lithography machines – they'd all been put out of business in the eighties, under intense competition from the Japanese. MicroCon developed new technology, and has been building machines for American companies. Okay?'

'Okay,' I said.

'Two years ago, MicroCon was sold to Darley-Higgins, a management company in Georgia. Darley's other operations were foundering, the company decided to sell MicroCon to raise cash. They found a buyer in Akai Ceramics, an Osaka company that already made lithography machines in Japan. Akai had plenty of cash, and was willing to acquire the American company for a high price. Then Congress moved to stop the sale.'

'Why?'

'The decline of American business is starting to disturb even Congress. We've lost too many basic industries to Japan – Steel and shipbuilding in the sixties, television and computer chips in the seventies, machine tools in the eighties. One day somebody wakes up and realizes these industries are vital for American defense. We've lost the ability to make components essential to our national security. We're entirely dependent on Japan to supply them. So Congress starts to worry. But I hear the sale is going through, anyway. Why? Do you guys have something to do with the sale?'

'In a sense,' Connor said.

'Lucky you,' Ron said, puffing on his cigar. 'If you're involved in a sale to the Japanese, it's like striking oil. Everybody gets rich. You two are looking at some pretty big gifts, I imagine.'

Connor nodded. 'Very big.'

'I'm sure,' Ron said. 'They'll take care of you: buy you a house or a car, get you cheap financing, something like that.'

I said, 'Why would they do that?'

Ron laughed. 'Why would they eat sushi? It's the way they conduct business.'

Connor said, 'But isn't MicroCon a small sale?'

'Yeah, pretty small. The company's worth a hundred million. Akai's buying it for a hundred and fifty. On top of that, they probably have another twenty million in incentives to the current corporate officers, maybe ten million in legal, ten million in consultant fees spread around Washington, and ten million in miscellaneous gifts for people like you. So call it two hundred million, in total.'

I said, 'Two hundred million for a hundred-million company? Why are they paying more than it's worth?'

'They're not,' Ron said. 'As far as they're concerned, they're getting a bargain.'

'Why?'

'Because,' Ron said, 'if you own the machines that are used to make something, like computer chips, you own the downstream industries that depend on those machines. MicroCon will give them control over the American computer industry. And as usual, we're allowing it to happen. Just the way we lost our television industry, and our machine-tool industry.'

'What happened to the TV industry?' I said.

He glanced at his watch. 'After World War II, America was the world's leading manufacturer of televisions. Twenty-seven American companies like Zenith, RCA, GE, and Emerson had a solid technological lead over foreign manufacturers. American companies were successful around the world, except in Japan. They couldn't penetrate the closed Japanese market. They were told if they wanted to sell in Japan, they had to license their technology to Japanese companies. And they did, reluctantly, under pressure from the American government, which wanted to keep Japan as a friendly ally against Russia. Okay?'

'Okay . . .'

'Now, licensing is a bad idea. It means Japan gets our technology for their own use, and we lose Japan as an export market. Pretty soon Japan begins to make cheap black-and-white TVs and exports them to America – something we can't do in Japan, right? By 1972, sixty percent of American black-and-white sales are imports. By 1976, one hundred percent are imports. We've lost the black-and-white market. American workers don't make those sets any more. Those jobs are gone from America.

'We say it doesn't matter: our companies have moved on to color. But the Japanese government starts an intensive program to develop a color-television industry. Once again, Japan licenses American technology, refines it in their protected markets, and floods us with exports. Once again, exports drive out American companies. Exactly the same story. By 1980 only three American companies still make color TVs. By 1987, there's only one, Zenith.'

'But Japanese sets were better and cheaper,' I said.

'They may have been better,' Ron said, 'but they were only cheaper because they were sold below production cost, to wipe out American competitors. That's called dumping. It's illegal under both American and international law.'

'Then why didn't we stop it?'

'Good question. Especially since dumping was only one of many illegal Japanese marketing techniques. They also fixed prices: they had something called the Tenth-Day Group. Japanese managers met every ten days in a Tokyo hotel to set prices in America. We protested, but the meetings continued. They also pushed distribution of their products by collusive arrangements. The Japanese allegedly paid millions in kickbacks to American distributors like Sears. They engaged in massive customs fraud. And they destroyed the American industry, which could not compete.

'Of course, our companies protested, and sued for relief – there were dozens of cases of dumping, fraud, and antitrust brought against Japanese companies in federal court. Dumping cases are usually resolved within a year. But our government provided no help – and the Japanese are skilled foot-draggers. They paid American lobbyists millions to plead their case. By the time the suits came to trial twelve years later, the battle was over in the marketplace. And of course all during this time, American companies could never fight back in Japan. They couldn't even get a foot in the door in Japan.'

'You're saying the Japanese took over the television industry illegally?'

Ron shrugged. 'They couldn't have done it without our help,' he said. 'Our government was coddling Japan, which they saw as a tiny emerging country. And American industry was perceived as not needing government help. There's always been a strain of antibusiness sentiment in America. But our government never seemed to realize, it's just not the same here. When Sony develops the Walkman, we don't say, "Nice product. Now you have to license it to GE and sell it through an American company." If they seek distribution, we don't tell them, "I'm sorry, but American stores all have preexisting arrangements with American suppliers. You'll have to distribute through an American company here." If they seek patents, we don't say, "Patents take eight years to be awarded, during which time your application will be publicly available so that our companies can read what you've invented and copy it free of charge, so that by the time we issue a patent our companies will already have their own version of your technology."

'We don't do any of those things. Japan does all of them. Their markets are closed. Our markets are wide open. It's not a level playing field. In fact, it's not a playing field at all. It's a one-way street.

'And by now we have a defeatist business climate in this country. American companies got their asses handed to them in black-and-white television. They got their asses handed to them in color television. The U.S. government refused to help our companies fight illegal Japanese trade practices. So when Ampex invented the VCR, they didn't even try to make a commercial product. They just licensed the technology to Japan and moved on. And pretty soon you find that American companies don't do research. Why develop new technology if your own government is so hostile to your efforts that you won't be able to bring it to market?'

'But isn't American business weak and badly managed?'

'That's the standard line,' Ron said. 'As promoted by the Japanese and their American spokesmen. It's only with a few episodes that people ever glimpsed how outrageous the Japanese really were. Like the Houdaille case. You know that one? Houdaille was a machine-tool company that claimed its patents and licenses were being violated by companies in Japan. A federal judge sent Houdaille's lawyer to Japan to gather evidence. But the Japanese refused to issue him a visa.'

'You're kidding.'

'What do they care?' Ron said. 'They know we'll never retaliate. When the Houdaille case came before the Reagan administration, it did nothing. So Houdaille got out of machine tools. Because nobody can compete against dumped products – that's the whole point of doing it.'

'Don't you lose money if you dump?'

'For a while, yes. But you're selling millions of units, so you can refine your production lines, and get your costs down. A couple of years later, you really can make the products for a lower cost. Meanwhile you've wiped out the competition and you control the market. You see, the Japanese think strategically – they're in for the long haul, for how things will look fifty years from now. An American company has to show a profit every three months or the CEO and the officers will be out on the street. But the Japanese don't care about short-term profits at all. They want market share. Business is like warfare to them. Gaining ground. Wiping out the competition. Getting control of a market. That's what they've been doing for the last thirty years.

'So the Japanese dumped steel, televisions, consumer electronics, computer chips, machine tools – and nobody stopped them. And we lost those industries. Japanese companies and the Japanese government target specific industries, which they take over. Industry after industry, year after year. While we sit around and spout off about free trade. But free trade is meaningless unless there is also fair trade. And the Japanese don't believe in fair trade at all. You know, there's a reason the Japanese love Reagan. They cleaned up during his presidency. In the name of free trade, he spread our legs real wide.'

'Why don't Americans understand this?' I said.

Connor laughed. 'Why do they eat hamburgers? It's the way they are, *kōhai*.'

From the newsroom, a woman called, 'Somebody named Connor here? Call for you from the Four Seasons Hotel.'

Connor glanced at his watch and stood up. 'Excuse me.' He walked out into the newsroom. Through the glass I saw him talking on the phone, making notes.

'You realize,' Ron said, 'it's all still going on. Why is a Japanese camera cheaper in New York than in Tokyo? You ship it halfway around the world, pay import duty and distribution costs, and it's still cheaper? How is that possible? Japanese tourists buy their own products here because they're cheaper. Meanwhile, American products in Japan cost seventy percent more than here. Why doesn't the American government get tough? I don't know. Part of the answer is up there.'

He pointed to the monitor in his office; a distinguished-looking man was talking above a running tickertape. The sound was turned low. 'You see that guy? That's David Rawlings. Professor of business at Stanford. Specialist in the Pacific Rim. He's a typical – turn that up, will you? He might be talking about MicroCon.'

I turned the knob on the set. I heard Rawlings say: '. . . think American attitudes are completely irrational. After all, Japanese companies are providing jobs for Americans, while American companies are moving jobs for Americans, while American companies are moving jobs offshore, taking them away from their own people. The Japanese can't understand what the complaints are about.'

Ron sighed. 'Typical bullshit,' he said.

On the screen, Professor Rawlings was saying, 'I think the American people are rather ungrateful for the help our country is getting from foreign investors.'

Ron laughed. 'Rawlings is part of the group we call the Chrysanthemum Kissers. Academic experts who deliver the Japanese propaganda line. They don't really have a choice, because they need access to Japan to work, and if they start to sound critical, their contacts in Japan dry up. Doors are closed to them. And in America, the Japanese will whisper in certain ears that the offending person is not to be trusted, or that their views are "out of date." Or worse – that they're racist. Anybody who criticizes Japan is a racist. Pretty soon these academics begin to lose speaking engagements and consulting jobs. They know that's happened to their colleagues who step out of line. And they don't make the same mistake.'

Connor came back into the room. He said, 'Is there anything illegal about this MicroCon sale?'

'Sure,' Ron said. 'Depending on what Washington decides to do. Akai Ceramics already has sixty percent of the American market. MicroCon will give it a virtual monopoly. If Akai were an American company, the government would block the sale on antitrust grounds. But since Akai is not an American company, the sale isn't scrutinized closely. In the end, it'll probably be allowed.'

'You mean a Japanese company can have a monopoly in America but an American company can't?'

'That's the usual outcome these days,' Ron said. 'But American laws often promote the sale of our companies to foreigners. Like Matsushita buying Universal Studios. Universal's been for sale for years. Several American companies tried to buy it, but couldn't. Westinghouse tried in 1980. No deal: violates antitrust. RCA tried. No deal: violates conflict of interest. But when Matsushita came in, there were no laws against it at all. Recently our laws changed. Under present law, RCA could buy Universal. But back then, no. MicroCon is just the latest example of crazy American regulations.'

I said, 'But what do American computer companies say about the MicroCon sale?'

Ron said, 'American companies don't like the sale. But they don't oppose it, either.'

'Why not?'

'Because American companies feel over-regulated by the government already. Forty percent of all American exports are covered by security regulations. Our government doesn't allow our computer companies to sell to Eastern Europe. The cold war is over but the regulations still exist. Meanwhile the Japanese and Germans are selling products like mad. So the Americans want less regulation. And they see any attempt to block the MicroCon sale as government interference.'

I said, 'It still doesn't make sense to me.'

'I agree,' Ron said. 'The American companies are going to get killed in the next few years. Because if Japan is the sole source of chip-making machines, they're in a position to withhold the machines from American companies.'

'Would they do that?'

'They've done it before,' Ron said. 'Ion implanters and other machines. But the American companies can't get together. They squabble among themselves. And meanwhile the Japanese are buying high-tech companies at the rate of about one every ten days. For the last six years. We're being disemboweled. But our government doesn't pay attention, because we have something called CFIUS – the Committee on Foreign Investment in the United States – that monitors the sale of high-tech companies. Except CFIUS never does anything. Of the last five hundred sales, only one was blocked. Company after company gets sold, and nobody in Washington says boo. Finally, Senator Morton makes a stink, and says "Wait a minute here." But nobody's listening to him.'

'The sale is going through anyway?'

'That's what I heard today. The Japanese PR machine is hard at work, cranking out favourable publicity. And they are tenacious. They are on top of everything. I mean everything –'

There was a knock at the door, and a blonde woman stuck her head in. 'Sorry to disturb you, Ron,' she said, 'but Keith just got a call from the Los Angeles representative for NHK, Japanese national television. He wants to know why our reporter is bashing Japan.'

Ron frowned. 'Bashing Japan? What's he talking about?'

'He claims our reporter said on air, "The damn Japanese are taking over this country." '

'Come on,' Ron said. 'Nobody would say that – on air. Who's supposed to have said that?'

'Lenny. In New York. Over the backhaul,' the woman said.

Ron shifted in his chair. 'Uh – oh,' he said. 'Did you check the tapes?'

'Yeah,' she said. 'They're tracing the download now in the main control room. But I assume it's true.'

'Hell.'

I said, 'What's the backhaul?'

'Our satellite feed. We pick up segments from New York and Washington every day, and replay them. There's always about a minute before and after that isn't aired. We cut it out, but the raw transmission can be picked up by anybody with a private dish who wants to hunt for our signal. And people do. We warn the talent to be careful what they do in front of a camera. But last year, Louise unbuttoned her blouse and miked herself – and we got calls from all over the country.'

Ron's phone rang. He listened for a moment, and said, 'Okay. I understand,' and hung up. 'They checked the tape. Lenny was talking on camera before the feed, and he said to Louise, "The goddamn Japanese are going to own this country if we don't wise up." It wasn't on air, but he did say it.' He shook his head ruefully. 'The NHK guy knows we didn't run it?'

'Yeah. But he's saying it can be picked up and he's protesting on that basis.'

'Hell,' Ron said. 'So they even monitor our backhaul. Jesus. What does Keith want to do?'

'Keith says he's tired of warning New York talent. He wants you to handle it.'

'Does he want me to call the NHK guy?'

'He says use your judgment, but we have a deal with NHK for the half-hour show we send them every day and he doesn't want that risked. He thinks you should apologize.'

Ron sighed. 'Now I have to apologize for what wasn't even on air. God *damn* it.' He looked at us. 'Guys, I have to go. Was there anything else?'

'No,' I said. 'Good luck.'

'Listen,' Ron said. 'We all need good luck. You know NHK is starting Global News Network with a billion dollars in capitalization.

They're going to take on Ted Turner's CNN around the world. And if past history is any guide . . .' He shrugged. 'Kiss the American media goodbye.'

As we were leaving, I heard Ron say on the phone, 'Mr Akasaka? Ron Levine, over here at AFN. Yes, sir. Yes, Mr Akasaka. Sir, I wanted to express my concern and deep apologies about what our reporter said over the satellite –'

We closed the door, and left.

'Where now?' I said.

The Four Seasons Hotel is favored by stars and politicians, and it has a graceful entrance, but we were parked around the corner by the service entrance. A large dairy truck was pulled up to a loading dock, and kitchen staff were unloading cartons of milk. We had been waiting here for five minutes. Connor glanced at his watch.

I said, 'Why are we here?'

'We're complying with the Supreme Court, *kōhai*.'

At the loading dock, a woman in a business suit came out, looked around, and waved. Connor waved back. She disappeared again. Connor got out his billfold and took out a couple of twenties.

'One of the first things I learned as a detective,' Connor said, 'is that hotel staff can be extremely helpful. Particularly since the police have so many restrictions these days. We can't go into a hotel room without a warrant. If we did, whatever we found in a search would be inadmissible, right?'

'Right.'

'But the maids can go in. Valet and housekeeping and room service can go in.'

'Uh-huh.'

'So I've learned to maintain contacts at all the big hotels.' He opened the door. 'I'll only be a moment.'

He walked to the loading dock and waited. I tapped the steering wheel with my hands. The words came into my head:

> I changed my mind, this love is fine.
> Goodness, gracious, great balls of fire

On the loading dock, a maid in uniform came out, and talked to Connor briefly. He took notes. She held something golden in the palm of her hand. He didn't touch it, he just looked at it, and nodded. She slipped it back in her pocket. Then he gave her money. She went away.

> You shake my nerves and you rattle my brain.
> Too much love drives a man insane.
> You broke my will, but what a thrill –

A valet came out into the loading dock, carrying a man's blue suit on a hanger. Connor asked a question, and the valet looked at his watch before he answered. Then Connor crouched down and peered closely at the lower edges of the suit coat. He opened the jacket and examined the trousers on the hanger.

The valet took away the first suit, and brought a second one out onto the dock. This one was a blue pinstripe suit. Connor repeated his inspection. He seemed to find something on the coat, and scraped it carefully into a small glassine bag. Then he paid the valet and walked back to the car.

I said, 'Checking Senator Rowe?'

'Checking a number of things,' he said. 'But, yes, Senator Rowe.'

'Rowe's aide had white panties in his pocket last night. But Cheryl was wearing black panties.'

'That's true,' Connor said. 'But I think we are making progress.'

'What've you got in the bag?'

He took the little glassine bag out, and held it to the light. I saw small dark strands through the plastic. 'Carpet fibers, I think. Dark, like the carpet at the Nakamoto conference room. Have to check with the lab to be sure. Meanwhile, we have another problem to solve. Start the car.'

'Where are we going?'

'Darley-Higgins. The company that owns MicroCon.'

In the lobby beside the receptionist, a workman was mounting large gold letters on the wall: DARLEY-HIGGINS INC. Beneath that it read EXCELLENCE IN MANAGEMENT. More workmen were laying carpet in the hallway.

We showed our badges and asked to see the head of Darley-Higgins, Arthur Greiman.

The receptionist had a Southern accent and an upturned nose. 'Mr Greiman is in meetings all day. Is he expecting you?'

'We're here about the MicroCon sale'.

'Then you want Mr Enders, our vice-president for publicity. He speaks to people about MicroCon.'

'All right,' Connor said.

We sat down on a couch in the reception area. On a couch across the room sat a pretty woman in a tight skirt. She had a roll of blueprints under her arm. The workmen continued to hammer. I said, 'I thought the company was in financial trouble. Why're they redecorating?'

Connor shrugged.

The secretary answered the phone, routing the calls. 'Darley-Higgins, one moment, please. Darley-Higgins . . . Oh, please hold, Senator . . . Darley-Higgins, yes, thank you . . .'

I picked up a brochure from the coffee table. It was the annual report of Darley-Higgins Management Group, with offices in Atlanta, Dallas, Seattle, San Francisco, and Los Angeles. I found a picture of Arthur Greiman. He looked happy and self-satisfied. The report included an essay signed by him entitled, 'A Commitment to Excellence.'

The secretary said to us, 'Mr Enders will be right with you.'

'Thank you,' Connor said.

A moment later, two men in business suits walked out into the hallway. The woman with the blueprints stood. She said, 'Hello, Mr Greiman.'

'Hello, Beverly,' the older man said. 'I'll be with you in a minute.'

Connor stood up, too. The secretary immediately said, 'Mr Greiman, these men –'

'Just a minute,' Greiman said. He turned to the man with him, who was younger, in his early thirties. 'Just make sure you get it straight with Roger,' Greiman said.

The younger man was shaking his head. 'He won't like it.'

'I know he won't. But tell him anyway. Six million four in direct compensation for the CEO is the minimum.'

'But Arthur –'

'Just tell him.'

'I will, Arthur,' the younger man said, smoothing his tie. He lowered his voice. 'But the board may balk at raising you above six when company earnings are down so much –'

'We're not talking about *earnings,*' Greiman said. 'We're talking about compensation. It has nothing to do with earnings. The board has to match current compensation levels for chief executives. If Roger can't bring the board into line on this, I'm going to cancel the March meetings and ask for changes. You tell him *that.*'

'Okay, I will, Arthur, but –'

'Just do it. Call me tonight.'

'Right, Arthur.'

They shook hands. The young man walked off unhappily. The receptionist said, 'Mr Greiman, these gentlemen –'

Greiman turned to us. Connor said, 'Mr Greiman, we'd like to speak to you for a minute about MicroCon.' And he turned slightly aside, and showed his badge.

Greiman exploded in rage. 'Oh, for Christ's sake. Not *again.* This is goddamned *harassment.*'

'Harassment?'

'What would you call it? I've had senatorial staffers here, I've had the F.B.I. here. Now I have the L.A. police? We're not criminals. We own a company and we have the right to sell it. Where is Louis?'

The receptionist said, 'Mr Enders is coming.'

Connor said calmly, 'Mr Greiman, I'm sorry to disturb you. We have only one question. It'll just take a minute.'

Greiman glowered. 'What's your question?'

'How many bidders were there for MicroCon?'

'That's none of your business,' he said. 'Anyway, our agreement with Akai stipulates that we can't discuss the sale publicly in any way.'

Connor said, 'Was there more than one bidder?'

'Look, you have questions, you talk to Enders. I'm busy.' He turned to the woman with blueprints. 'Beverly? What have you got for me?'

'I have a revised layout for the boardroom, Mr Greiman, and tile samples for the washroom. A very nice gray I think you'll like.'

'Good, good.' He led her down the hallway away from us.

Connor watched them go, and then abruptly turned towards the elevator. 'Come on, *kōhai.* Let's get some fresh air.'

'Why does it matter if there were other bidders?' I said, when we were back in the car.

'It goes back to the original question we had,' Connor said. 'Who wants to embarrass Nakamoto? We know the sale of MicroCon has strategic significance. That's why Congress is upset. But that almost certainly means other parties are upset, too.'

'In Japan?'

'Exactly.'

'Who will know that?'

'Akai.'

The Japanese receptionist tittered when she saw Connor's badge. Connor said, 'We would like to see Mr Yoshida.' Yoshida was the head of the company.

'One moment, please.' She got up and hurried away, almost running.

Akai Ceramics was located on the fifth floor of a bland office-block in El Segundo. The decor was spare and industrial-looking. From the reception area, we could see into a large space, which was not partitioned: lots of metal desks and people at the phones. The soft click of word processors.

I looked at the office. 'Pretty bare.'

'All business,' Connor said, nodding. 'In Japan, ostentation is frowned on. It means you are not serious. When old Mr Matsushita was the head of the third biggest company in Japan, he still took the regular commercial jet between his head offices in Osaka and Tokyo. He was the head of a fifty-billion-dollar company. But no private jets for him.'

As we waited, I looked at the people working at the desks. A handful were Japanese. Most were Caucasian. Everyone wore blue suits. There were almost no women.

'In Japan,' Connor said, 'if a company is doing poorly, the first thing that happens is the executives cut their own salaries. They feel responsible for the success of the company, and they expect their own fortunes to rise and fall as the company succeeds or fails.'

The woman came back, and sat at her desk without speaking. Almost immediately, a Japanese man wearing a blue suit came toward us. He had gray hair, horn-rimmed glasses, and a solemn manner. He said, 'Good morning. I am Mr Yoshida.'

Connor made the introductions. We all bowed and exchanged business cards. Mr Yoshida took each card with both hands, bowing each time, formally. We did the same. I noticed that Connor did not speak Japanese to him.

Yoshida led us to his office. It had windows looking toward the airport. The furnishings were austere.

'Would you like coffee, or tea?'

'No thank you,' Connor said. 'We are here in an official capacity.'

'I understand.' He gestured for us to sit down.

'We would like to talk to you about the purchase of MicroCon.'

'Ah, yes. A troubling matter. But I am not aware that it should involve the police.'

'Perhaps it doesn't,' Connor said. 'Can you tell us about the sale, or is the agreement sealed?'

Mr Yoshida looked surprised. 'Sealed? Not at all. It is all very open, and has been from the beginning. We were approached by Mr Kobayashi, representing Darley-Higgins in Tokyo, in September of last year. That was the first we learned the company was for sale. Frankly, we were surprised that it would be offered. We began negotiations in early October. The negotiating teams had the basis of a rough agreement by mid-November. We proceeded to the final stage of negotiations. But then the Congress raised objections, on November sixteenth.'

Connor said, 'You said you were surprised that the company would be offered for sale?'

'Yes. Certainly.'

'Why is that?'

Mr Yoshida spread his hands on his desk and spoke slowly. 'We understood that MicroCon was a government-owned company. It had been financed in part by funds from the American government. Thirteen percent of capitalization, if I remember. In Japan, that would make it a government-owned company. So naturally we were cautious to enter into negotiations. We do not want to offend. But we received assurance from our representatives in Washington there would be no objection to the purchase.'

'I see.'

'But now there are difficulties, as we feared. I think now we make a cause for Americans. In Washington, some people are upset. We do not wish this.'

'You didn't expect Washington would make objections?'

Mr Yoshida gave a diffident shrug. 'The two countries are different. In Japan we know what to expect. Here, there is always an individual who may have another opinion, and speak it. But Akai Ceramics does not wish a high profile. It is awkward now.'

Connor nodded sympathetically. 'It sounds as if you want to withdraw.'

'Many in the home office criticize me, for not knowing what would happen. But I tell them, it is impossible to know. Washington has no firm policy. It changes every day, according to the politics.' He smiled and added, 'Or, I would say, that is how it seems to us.'

'But you expect the sale to go forward?'

'This I cannot say. Perhaps the criticism from Washington will be too much. And you know the Tokyo government wants to be friends with America. They give pressure on business, not to make purchases that will upset America. Rockefeller Center and Universal Studios, these purchases that make criticism for us. We are told to be *yōjinbukai*. It means . . .'

'Discreet,' Connor said.

'Careful. Yes. Wary.' He looked at Connor. 'You speak Japanese?'

'A little.'

Yoshida nodded. For a moment he seemed to consider switching to Japanese, but did not. 'We wish to have friendly relations,' he said. 'These criticisms of us, we feel they are not fair. The Darley-Higgins company has many financial difficulties. Perhaps bad management, perhaps some other reason. I cannot say. But that is not our fault. We are not responsible for that. And we did not seek MicroCon. It was offered to us. Now we are criticized for trying to help.' He sighed.

Outside, a big jet took off from the airport. The windows rattled.

Connor said, 'And the other bidders from MicroCon? When did they drop out?'

Mr Yoshida frowned. 'There were no other bidders. The company was privately offered. Darley-Higgins did not wish to make known their financial difficulties. So we cooperated with them. But now . . . the press makes many distortions about us. We feel very . . . *kizu tsuita*. Wounded?'

'Yes.'

He shrugged. 'That is how we feel. I hope you understand my poor English.'

There was a pause. In fact, for the next minute or so, nobody said anything. Connor sat facing Yoshida. I sat beside Connor. Another jet took off, and the windows vibrated again. Still nobody spoke. Yoshida gave a long sigh. Connor nodded. Yoshida shifted his chair, and folded his hands over his belly. Connor sighed, and grunted. Yoshida sighed. Both men seemed to be entirely focused. Something was taking place, but I was not clear what. I decided it must be this unspoken intuition.

Finally, Yoshida said, 'Captain, I wish no misunderstanding. Akai Ceramics is an honorable company. We have no part in any . . . complications that have occurred. Our position is difficult. But I will assist you in whatever way I can.'

Connor said, 'I am grateful.'

'Not at all.'

Then Yoshida stood up. Connor stood up. I stood up. We all bowed, and then we all shook hands.

'Please do not hesitate to contact me again, if I can be of assistance.'

'Thank you,' Connor said.

Yoshida led us to the door to his office. We bowed again, and he opened the door.

Outside was a fresh-faced American man in his forties. I recognized him at once. He was the blond man who had been in the car with Senator Rowe the night before. The man who hadn't introduced himself.

'Ah, Richmond-san,' Yoshida said. 'Very good luck you are here. These gentlemen are just asking about MicroCon *baishū*.' He turned to us. 'Perhaps you will like to talk to Mr Richmond. His English is much better than mine. He can give you many more details you may wish to know.'

'Bob Richmond. Myers, Lawson, and Richmond.' His handshake was firm. He was suntanned, and looked as though he played a lot of tennis. He smiled cheerfully. 'Small world, isn't it?'

Connor and I introduced ourselves. I said, 'Did Senator Rowe get back all right?'

'Oh yes,' Richmond said. 'Thanks for your help.' He smiled. 'I hate to think how he's feeling this morning. But I guess it's not the first time.' He shifted back and forth on the balls of his feet, like a tennis player waiting for a serve. He looked slightly concerned. 'I must say, you two are the last people I ever expected to see here. Is there anything I should know about? I represent Akai in the MicroCon negotiations.'

'No,' Connor said mildly. 'We're just getting general background.'

'Is this to do with what happened at Nakamoto last night?'

Connor said, 'Not really. Just background.'

'If you like, we can talk in the conference room.'

'Unfortunately,' Connor said, 'we're late for an appointment. But perhaps we can talk later.'

'You bet,' Richmond said. 'Happy to. I'll be back in my office in about an hour.' He gave us his card.

'That's fine,' Connor said.

But Richmond still seemed worried. He walked with us to the elevator. 'Mr Yoshida is from the old school,' he said. 'I'm sure he was polite. But I can tell you he is furious about what happened with this MicroCon thing. He's taking a lot of heat from Akai Tokyo. And it's very unfair. He really was sandbagged by Washington. He got assurances there would be no objection to the sale, and then Morton pulled the rug out from under him.'

Connor said, 'Is that what happened?'

'No question about it,' Richmond said. 'I don't know what Johnny Morton's problem is, but he came right out of left field on this. We made all the proper filings. CFIUS registered no objection until long after the negotiations were concluded. You can't do business like this. I just hope John sees the light, and lets this thing go through. Because at the moment it looks pretty racist.'

'Racist? Really?'

'Sure. It's exactly like the Fairchild case. Remember that one? Fujitsu tries to buy Fairchild Semiconductor in eighty-six, but Congress blocks the sale, saying it's against national security. Congress doesn't want Fairchild sold to a foreign company. Couple of years later Fairchild is going to be sold to a French company, and this time there's not a peep from Congress. Apparently, it's okay to sell to a foreign company – just not a *Japanese* company. I'd say that's racist policy, pure and simple.' We came to the elevator. 'Anyway, call me. I'll make myself available.'

'Thank you,' Connor said.

We got on the elevator. The doors closed.

'Asshole,' Connor said.

I was driving north toward the Wilshire exit, to meet Senator Morton. I said, 'Why is he an asshole?'

'Bob Richmond was the assistant trade negotiator for Japan under Amanda Marden until last year. He was privy to all the strategy meetings of the American government. One year later, he turns around and starts working for the Japanese. Who now pay him five hundred thousand a year plus bonuses to close this deal. And he's worth it, because he knows everything there is to know.'

'Is that legal?'

'Sure. It's standard procedure. They all do it. If Richmond worked for a high-tech company like Microsoft, he'd have to sign an agreement that he wouldn't work for a competing company for five years. Because you shouldn't be able to peddle trade secrets to the opposition. But our government has easier rules.'

'Why is he an asshole?'

'This racist stuff.' Connor snorted. 'He knows better. Richmond knows exactly what happened with the Fairchild sale. And it had nothing to do with racism.'

'No?'

'And there's another thing Richmond knows: the Japanese are the most racist people on earth.'

'They are?'

'Absolutely. In fact, when the Japanese diplomats –'

The car phone rang. I pushed the speaker button and said, 'Lieutenant Smith.'

Over the speaker a man said, 'Jesus, *finally*. Where the hell have you guys been? I want to get to sleep.'

I recognized the voice: Fred Hoffmann, the watch commander from the night before.

Connor said, 'Thanks for getting back to us, Fred.'

'What is it you wanted?'

'Well, I'm curious,' Connor said, 'about the Nakamoto calls you got last night.'

'You and everybody else in this town,' Hoffmann said. 'I got half the department on my ass about this. Jim Olson is practically camping on my desk, going through the paperwork. Even though it was all routine at the time.'

'If you'd just review what happened . . .'

'Sure. First thing, I got the transmittal from Metro. That was the original phone-in. Metro wasn't sure what it meant, because the caller had an Asian accent and sounded confused. Or maybe on drugs. He kept talking about 'problems with the disposition of the body.' They couldn't get it clear what he was talking about. Anyway, I dispatched a black and white about eight-thirty. Then when they confirmed a homicide, I assigned Tom Graham and Roddy Merino – for which I got all *kinds* of shit later.'

'Uh-huh.'

'But what the hell, they were up on the roster next. You know we're supposed to stay in strict rotation for detective assignments. To avoid the appearance of special treatment. That's policy. I was just following it.'

'Uh-huh.'

'Anyway. Then Graham calls in at nine o'clock, and reports there's trouble at the scene, and there is a request for the Special Services liaison. Again, I check the list. Pete Smith is the SSO on call. I give Graham his number at home. And I guess he called you, Pete.'

'Yes,' I said. 'He did.'

'All right,' Connor said. 'What happened after that?'

'About two minutes after Graham calls, maybe nine oh five, I get a call from somebody with an accent. I would say it sounds like an Asian accent, but I don't know for sure. And the guy says that on behalf of Nakamoto he is requesting Captain Connor be assigned to the case.'

'The caller didn't identify himself?'

'Sure he did. I made him identify himself. And I wrote down the name. Koichi Nishi.'

'And he was from Nakamoto?'

'That's what he said,' Hoffmann said. 'I'm just sitting there, working the phone, what the hell do I know. I mean, this morning Nakamoto is formally protesting the fact that Connor was assigned to the case and saying they have nobody named Koichi Nishi employed by them. They're claiming it's all a fabrication. But let me tell you, somebody called me. I'm not making it up.'

'I'm sure you're not,' Connor said. 'You say the caller had an accent?'

'Yeah. His English was pretty good, you know, almost hip, but there was a definite accent. The only thing I thought was funny was that he seemed to know a hell of a lot about you.'

'Oh?'

'Yeah. First thing he says to me, do I know your phone number or should he give it to me. I say I know the number. I'm thinking, I don't need some Japanese to tell me the phone numbers of people on the force. Then he says, you know, Captain Connor doesn't always answer his phone. Be sure to send somebody down there to pick him up.'

'Interesting,' Connor said.

'So I called Pete Smith, and told him to swing by and pick you up. And that's all I knew. I mean, this is all in the context of some political problem they're having at Nakamoto. I knew Graham was unhappy. I figured other people were unhappy, too. And everybody knows Connor has special relationships with the community, so I put it through. And now there is all this shit coming down. Fucking beats me.'

'Tell me about the shit,' Connor said.

'It starts maybe eleven o'clock last night, when the chief called me about Graham. Why did I assign Graham. I tell him why. But he's still not happy. Then right at the end of my watch, maybe five a.m., there is the business about how Connor got brought in. How did it happen, why did it happen. And now there's a story in the *Times* and this whole thing about racism by the police. I don't know which way to turn here. I keep explaining I did the routine thing. By the book. Nobody is buying that. But it's true.'

'I'm sure it is,' Connor said. 'Just one more thing, Fred. Did you ever listen to the original Metro call?'

'Damn right I did. I heard it about an hour ago. Why?'

'Did the voice that called in sound like Mr Nishi?'

Hoffmann laughed. 'Christ. Who knows, Captain. Maybe. You're asking me if one Asian voice sounds like another Asian voice I heard earlier. Honestly, I don't know. The original voice on the call sounded pretty confused. Maybe in shock. Maybe on drugs. I'm not sure. All I know is, whoever Mr Nishi actually was, he knew a hell of a lot about you.'

'Well, that's very helpful. Get some rest.' Connor thanked him, and hung up. I pulled off the freeway and headed down Wilshire, to our meeting with Senator Morton.

'Okay, Senator, now look this way, please . . . a little more . . . that's it, that's *very* strong, very *masculine,* I like it a lot. Yes, bloody good. Now I will need three minutes, please.' The director, a tense man wearing a bomber jacket and a baseball cap, climbed down off the camera and barked orders in a British accent. 'Jerry, get a scrim there, the sun is too bright. And can we do something about his eyes? I need a little fill in the eyes, please. Ellen? You see the shine on his right shoulder. Flag it, love. Pull the collar smooth. The microphone is visible on his tie. And I can't see the gray in his hair. Bring it up. And straighten out the carpeting on the ground so he doesn't trip when he walks, people. *Please.* Come on now. We're losing our lovely light.'

Connor and I were standing to one side, with a cute production assistant named Debbie who held a clipboard across her breasts and said meaningfully, 'The director is Edgar Lynn.'

'Should we recognize that name?' Connor said.

'He's the *most* expensive and *most* sought-after commercial director in the world. He is a *great* artist. Edgar did the *fantastic* Apple 1984 commercial, and . . . oh, lots of others. And he has directed famous movies, too. Edgar is *just* the *best.*' She paused. 'And not too crazy. Really.'

Across from the camera, Senator John Morton stood patiently while four people fussed with his tie, his jacket, his hair, his makeup. Morton was wearing a suit. He was standing under a tree with the rolling golf course and the skyscrapers of Beverly Hills in the background. The production crew had laid down a strip of carpet for him to walk on as he approached the camera.

I said, 'And how is the senator?'

Debbie nodded. 'Pretty good. I think he has a shot.'

Connor said, 'You mean a chance for the presidency?'

'Yeah. Especially if Edgar can do his magic. I mean, let's face it, Senator Morton is not exactly *Mel Gibson,* you know what I mean? He's got a big nose, and he's a little bald, and those freckles are a *problem* because they photograph so prominently. They distract you from his eyes. And the eyes are what sell a candidate.'

'The eyes,' Connor said.

'Oh, yeah. People get elected on their eyes.' She shrugged, as if it was common knowledge. 'But if the senator puts himself in Edgar's hands . . . Edgar is a great artist. He can make it happen.'

Edgar Lynn walked past us, huddled with the cameraman. 'Christ, clean up the luggage under his eyes,' Lynn said. 'And get the chin. Firm that chin with a hard inky low and up.'

'Okay,' the cameraman said.

The production assistant excused herself and we waited, watching. Senator Morton was still some distance away, being worked over by the makeup and wardrobe people.

'Mr Connor? Mr Smith?' I turned. A young man in a blue pinstripe suit was standing beside us. He looked like a Senate staffer: well turned-out, attentive, polite. 'I'm Bob Woodson. With the senator's office. Thank you for coming.'

'You're welcome,' Connor said.

'I know the senator is eager to talk to you,' Woodson said. 'I'm sorry, this seems to be running a little late. We were supposed to finish shooting by one.' He glanced at his watch. 'Now, I guess it may be quite a while. But I know the senator wants to talk to you.'

Connor said, 'Do you know what about?'

Someone shouted, 'Run-through! Run-through for sound and camera, please!'

The cluster around Senator Morton vanished, and Woodson turned his attention to the camera.

Edgar Lynn was back looking through the lens. 'There still isn't enough gray. Ellen? You will have to add gray to his hair. It isn't reading now.'

Woodson said, 'I hope he doesn't make him look too old.'

Debbie, the production assistant, said, 'It's just for the shot. It isn't reading for the shot, so we add some gray. See, Ellen is just putting it at the temples. It'll make him distinguished.'

'I don't want him old. Especially when he's tired, he sometimes looks old.'

'Don't worry,' the assistant said.

'All right now,' Lynn said. 'That's enough for now. Senator? Shall we try a run-through?'

Senator Morton said, 'Where does this begin?'

'Line?'

A script girl said, ' "Perhaps like me . . ." '

Morton said, 'Then we've already done the first part?'

Edgar Lynn said, 'That's right, love. We start here with your turn to the camera, and you give us a very strong, very direct *masculine* look, and begin "Perhaps like me." Right?'

'Okay,' Morton said.

'Remember. Think *masculine.* Think *strong.* Think *in control.*'

Morton said, 'Can we shoot it?'

Woodson said, 'Lynn's going to piss him off.'

Edgar Lynn said, 'All right. Shoot the rehearsal. Here we go.'

Senator Morton walked toward the camera. 'Perhaps like me,' he said, 'you're concerned about the erosion of our national position in recent years. America is still the greatest military power, but our security depends on our ability to defend ourselves militarily and economically. And it is economically that America has fallen behind. How far behind? Well, under the last two administrations, America has gone from the greatest creditor nation to the greatest debtor nation the world has ever seen. Our industries have fallen behind the rest of the world. Our workers are less educated than workers in other countries. Our investors demand short-term gain and cripple our industries' ability to plan for the future. And as a result, our standard of living is declining rapidly. The outlook for our children is bleak.'

Connor murmured, 'Somebody is actually saying it.'

'And in this time of national crisis,' Morton continued, 'many Americans have another concern, as well. As our economic power fades, we are vulnerable to a new kind of invasion. Many Americans fear that we may become an economic colony of Japan, or Europe. But especially Japan. Many Americans feel that the Japanese are taking over our industries, our recreation lands, and even our cities.' He gestured to the golf course with skyscrapers in the background.

'And in doing so, some fear that Japan now has the power to shape and determine the future of America.'

Morton paused, beneath the tree. He gave the appearance of thinking.

'How justified are these fears for the American future? How much should we be concerned? There are some who will tell you foreign investment is a blessing, that it helps our nation. Others take the opposite view, and feel we are selling our precious birthright. Which view is correct? Which should – which is – which – oh, *fuck*! What's the line again?'

'Cut, cut,' Edgar Lynn called. 'Take five, everybody. I need to clean up a few things, and then we can do it for real. Very good, Senator. I liked it.'

The script girl said, '"Which should we believe for the future of America", Senator.'

He repeated, 'Which should we believe for the future of . . .' He shook his head. 'No wonder I can't remember it. Let's change that line, Margie? Let's change that line, please. Never mind, bring me a script, I'll change it myself.'

And the crowd of makeup and wardrobe people descended on him again, touching him up and fluffing him down.

Woodson said, 'Wait here, I'll try and get you a few minutes with him.'

We stood beside a humming trailer, with power cables coming out of it. As soon as Morton approached us, two aides came running up, brandishing thick books of computer printout. 'John, you better look at this.'

'John, you better consider this.'

Morton said, 'What is it?'

'John, this is the latest Gallup and Fielding.'

'John, this is the cross-referenced analysis by voter age-brackets.'

'And?'

'Bottom line, John, the president is *right.*'

'Don't tell me that. I'm running *against* the president.'

'But John, he's right about the C-word. You can't say the C-word in your television ad.'

'I can't say "conservation"?'

'You can't say it, John.'

'It's death, John.'

'The figures show it.'

'You want us to run over the figures, John?'

'No,' Morton said. He glanced at Connor and me. 'I'll be right with you,' he said, with a smile.

'But look here, John.'

'It's very clear, John. Conservation means diminution of life-style. People are already experiencing diminution of life-style. They don't want any more of it.'

'But that's wrong,' Morton said. 'That's not how it works.'

'John, it's what the voters *think.*'

'But they're wrong about this.'

'John, you want to educate the voters, well and good.'

'Yes, I do want to educate the voters. Conservation is not synonymous with diminution of life-style. It is synonymous with more wealth, power, and freedom. The idea is not to make do with less. The idea is to do all the things you are doing now – heat your house, drive your car – using less gas and oil. Let's have more efficient heaters in our houses, more efficient cars on our streets. Let's have cleaner air, better health. It can be done. Other countries have done it. Japan has done it.'

'John, please.'

'Not Japan.'

'In the last twenty years,' Morton said. 'Japan cut the energy cost of finished goods by sixty percent. America has done nothing. Japan can now make goods cheaper than we can, because Japan has pushed investment in energy-efficient technology. Conservation is competitive. And we aren't being competitive –'

'Fine, John. Conservation *and* statistics. *Really* boring.'

'Nobody cares, John.'

'The American people care,' Morton said.

'John: they absolutely don't.'

'And they aren't going to listen. Look, John. We have age-regressions here, particularly among the over fifty-fives, which is the most solid voting block, and they are straight ahead on this issue. They want no decreases. No conservation. The old people of America don't want it.'

'But older people have children, and grandchildren. They must care about the future.'

'Older people don't give a flying fuck, John. It's right here in black and white. They think their kids don't care about them, and they're right. So they don't care about their kids. It's that simple.'

'But certainly the children –'

'Children don't vote, John.'

'Please, John. Listen to us.'

'No conservation, John. Competitiveness, yes. Look to the future, yes. Face our problems, yes. A new spirit, yes. But no conservation. Just look at the numbers. Don't do it.'

'Please.'

Morton said, 'I'll think about it, fellas.'

The two aides seemed to realize that that was all they were going to get. They closed their printouts with a snap.

'You want us to send Margie over to rewrite?'

'No. I'm thinking about it.'

'Maybe Margie should just rough out a few lines.'

'No.'

'Okay, John. Okay.'

'You know,' Morton said, as they were leaving, 'some day an American politician is going to do what he thinks is right, instead of what the polls tell him. And it's going to look revolutionary.'

The two aides turned back together. 'John, come on. You're tired.'

'It's been a long trip. We understand.'

'John. Trust us on this, we have the figures. We are telling you with ninety-five percent confidence intervals how the people feel.'

'I know damn well how they feel. They feel frustrated. And I know why. It's been fifteen years since they've had any *leadership*.'

'John. Let's not do this one again. This is the twentieth century. Leadership is the quality of telling people what they want to hear.'

They walked away.

Immediately, Woodson came up, carrying a portable phone. He started to speak, but Morton held up his hand. 'Not now, Bob.'

'Senator, I think you need to take this –'

'*Not now.*'

Woodson backed away. Morton glanced at his watch. 'You're Mr Connor and Mr Smith?'

'Yes,' Connor said.

'Let's walk,' Morton said. He started away from the film crew, toward a hill overlooking the rolling course. It was Friday. Not many people were playing. We stood about fifty meters from the crew.

'I asked you to come,' Morton said, 'because I understand you're the officers in charge of the Nakamoto business.'

I was about to protest that it wasn't true, that Graham was the officer in charge, when Connor said, 'That's true, we are.'

'I have some questions about that case. I gather it's been resolved now?'

'It seems to be.'

'Is your investigation finished?'

'For all practical purposes, yes,' Connor said. 'The investigation is concluded.'

Morton nodded. 'I'm told you officers are particularly knowledgeable about the Japanese community, is that right? One of you has even lived in Japan?'

Connor gave a slight bow.

'You were the one playing golf with Hanada and Asaka today?' Morton said.

'You're well informed.'

'I spoke with Mr Hanada this morning. We have had contact in the past, on other matters.' Morton turned abruptly and said, 'My question is this. Is the Nakamoto business related to MicroCon?'

'How do you mean?' Connor said.

'The sale of MicroCon to the Japanese has come before the Senate Finance Committee, which I chair. We've been asked for a recommendation by staff from the Committee on Science and Technology, which must actually authorize the sale. As you know, the sale is controversial. In the past I have gone on record as opposing the sale. For a variety of reasons. You're familiar with all this?'

'Yes,' Connor said.

'I still have problems about it,' Morton said. 'MicroCon's advanced technology was developed in part with American taxpayer money. I'm outraged that our taxpayers should pay for research that is being sold to the Japanese – who will then use it to compete against our own companies. I feel strongly we should be protecting American capacity in high-tech areas. I feel we should be protecting our intellectual resources. I feel we should be limiting foreign investment in our corporations and our universities. But I seem to be alone in this. I can't find support in the Senate or in industry. Commerce won't help me. The trade rep's worried it'll upset the rice negotiations. *Rice.* Even the Pentagon is against me on this. And I just wondered, since Nakamoto is the parent company of Akai Ceramics, whether the events of last night had any relationship to the proposed sale.'

He paused. He was looking at us in an intense way. It was almost as if he expected that we would know something.

Connor said, 'I'm not aware of any linkage.'

'Has Nakamoto done anything unfair or improper to promote the sale?'

'Not that I am aware, no.'

'And your investigation is formally concluded?'

'Yes.'

'I just want to be clear. Because if I back down on my opposition to this sale, I don't want to find that I've stuck my hand in a box of snakes. One could argue that the party at Nakamoto was an attempt to win over opponents to the sale. So a change of position can be worrisome. You know in Congress they can get you coming and going, with a thing like this.'

Connor said, 'Are you abandoning your opposition to the sale?'

From across the lawn, an aide said, 'Senator? They're ready for you, sir.'

'Well.' Morton shrugged. 'I'm out on a limb with this thing. Nobody agrees with my position on MicroCon. Personally, I think it's another Fairchild case. But if this battle can't be won, I say, let's not fight it.

Plenty of other battles to be fought, anyway.' He straightened, smoothed his suit.

'Senator? When you're ready, sir.' And he added. 'They're concerned about the light.'

'They're concerned about the light,' Morton said, shaking his head.

'Don't let us keep you,' Connor said.

'Anyway,' Morton said. 'I wanted your input. I understand you to say that last night had nothing to do with MicroCon. The people involved had nothing to do with MicroCon. The people involved had nothing to do with it. I'm not going to read next month that someone was working behind the scenes, trying to promote or block the sale. Nothing like that.'

'Not as far as I know,' Connor said.

'Gentlemen, thank you for coming,' he said. He shook both of our hands, and started away. Then he came back. 'I appreciate your treating this matter as confidential. Because, you know, we have to be careful. We are at war with Japan.' He smiled wryly. 'Loose lips sink ships.'

'Yes,' Connor said. 'And remember Pearl Harbor.'

'Christ, that too.' He shook his head. He dropped his voice, becoming one of the boys. 'You know, I have colleagues who say sooner or later we're going to have to drop another bomb. They think it'll come to that.' He smiled. 'But I don't feel that way. Usually.'

Still smiling, he headed back to the camera crew. As he walked, he collected people, first a woman with script changes, then a wardrobe man, then a sound man fiddling with his microphone and adjusting the battery pack at his waist, and the makeup woman, until finally the senator had disappeared from view, and there was just a cluster of people moving awkwardly across the lawn.

I said, 'I like him.'

I was driving back into Hollywood. The buildings were hazy in the smog.

'Why shouldn't you like him?' Connor said. 'He's a politician. It's his job to make you like him.'

'Then he's good at his job.'

'Very good, I think.'

Connor stared out the window silently. I had the sense that something was troubling him.

I said, 'Didn't you like what he was saying in the commercial? It sounded like all the things you say.'

'Yes. It did.'

'Then what's the matter?'

'Nothing,' Connor said. 'I was just thinking about what he actually *said.*'

'He mentioned Fairchild.'

'Of course,' Connor said. 'Morton knows the real story about Fairchild, very well.'

I started to ask him what it was, but he was already telling me.

'Have you ever heard of Seymour Cray? For years, he was the best designer of supercomputers in the world. Cray Research made the fastest computers in the world. The Japanese were trying to catch up with him, but they just couldn't do it. He was too brilliant. But by the mid-eighties, Japanese chip dumping had put most of Cray's domestic suppliers out of business. So Cray had to order his custom-designed chips from Japanese manufacturers. There was nobody in America to make them. And his Japanese suppliers experienced mysterious delays. At one point, it took them a *year* to deliver certain chips he had ordered – and during that time, his Japanese competitors made great strides forward. There was also a question of whether they had stolen his new technology. Cray was furious. He knew they were fucking with him. He decided that he had to form a liaison with an American manufacturer, and so he chose Fairchild Semiconductor, even though the company was financially weak, far from the best. But Cray couldn't trust the Japanese anymore. He had to make do with Fairchild. So now Fairchild was making his next generation of custom chips for him – and then he learned that Fairchild was going to be sold to Fujitsu. His big competitor. It was concern about situations like that, and the national security implications, that led Congress to block the sale to Fujitsu.'

'And then?'

'Well, blocking the sale didn't solve Fairchild's financial problems. The company was still in trouble. And it eventually had to be sold. There was a rumor it was going to be bought by Bull, a French company that didn't compete in supercomputers. That sale might have been permitted by Congress. But in the end, Fairchild was sold to an American company.'

'And MicroCon is another Fairchild?'

'Yes, in the sense that MicroCon will give the Japanese a monopoly on vital chip-making machinery. Once they have a monopoly, they can withhold the machines from American companies. But now I think –'

That was when the phone rang. I left it on the speakerphone.

It was Lauren. My ex-wife.

'Peter?'

I said, 'Hello, Lauren.'

'Peter, I am calling to inform you that I'm going to pick up Michelle early today.' Her voice sounded tense, formal.

'You are? I didn't know you were picking her up at all.'

'I never said that, Peter,' she answered quickly. 'Of course I'm picking her up.'

I said, 'Okay, fine. By the way, who's Rick?'

There was a pause. 'Really. That is beneath you, Peter.'

'Why?' I said. 'I'm just curious. Michelle mentioned it this morning. She said he has a black Mercedes. Is he the new boyfriend?'

'Peter. I hardly think that is on the same level.'

I said, 'The same level as what?'

'Let's not play games,' she said. 'This is difficult enough. I'm calling to tell you I have to pick up Michelle early because I'm taking her to the doctor.'

'Why? She's over her cold.'

'I'm taking her for an examination, Peter.'

'For what?'

'An *examination.*'

'I heard you,' I said, 'But –'

'The physician who will examine her is Robert Strauss. He is an expert, I'm told. I have been asking people in the office who is the best person. I don't know how this is going to turn out, Peter, but I want you to know I am concerned, particularly in the light of your history.'

'Lauren, what are you talking about?'

'I'm talking about child abuse,' she said. 'I'm talking about sexual molestation.'

'What?'

'There's no getting around it, at this point. You know you've been accused of it in the past.'

I felt churning nausea. Whenever a relationship goes sour, there's always some residue of resentment, some pockets of bitterness and anger – as well as lots of private things that you know about the other person, that you can use against them. If you choose to do that. Lauren never had.

'Lauren, you know that abuse charge was trumped up. You know everything about that. We were married at the time.'

'I only know what you told me.' Her voice sounded distant now, moralistic, a little sarcastic. Her prosecutor's voice.

'Lauren, for Christ's sake. This is ridiculous. What's going on?'

'It is not ridiculous. I have my responsibilities as a mother.'

'Well, for God's sake, you've never been particularly worried about your responsibilities as a mother before. And now you –'

'It's true that I have a demanding career,' she said, in an icy tone, 'but there has never been any question that my daughter comes first. And I deeply, *deeply* regret if my past behavior in any way contributed to this unpleasant circumstance now.' I had the feeling that she wasn't talking to me. She was rehearsing. Trying out the words to see how they would sound before a judge. 'Clearly, Peter, if there is child abuse, Michelle cannot continue to live with you. Or even to see you.'

I felt pain in my chest. A wrenching.

'What are you talking about? Who told you there was child abuse?'

'Peter, I don't think it's appropriate for me to comment at this point in time.'

'Was it Wilhelm? Who called you, Lauren?'

'Peter, there's no point in going into this. I'm officially notifying you that I'm going to pick Michelle up at four p.m. I want her ready to go at four this afternoon.'

'Lauren –'

'I have my secretary, Miss Wilson, listening on the line and making stenographic notes of our conversation. I'm giving you formal notice of my intention to pick up my daughter and take her for a physical examination. Do you have any questions about my decision?'

'No.'

'Four o'clock, then. Thank you for your cooperation. And let me add on a personal note, Peter, I'm truly sorry that it has come to this.'

And she hung up.

I had been involved in sex abuse cases when I was a detective. I knew how it worked. The fact is, you usually can't determine anything from a physical exam. It's always equivocal. And if a kid is questioned by a psychologist who hammers her with questions, the kid will eventually start to go along, and make up answers to please the psychologist. Normal procedure requires the psychologist to videotape the kids, to prove that the questioning wasn't leading. But the situation is almost always unclear when it finally comes before a judge. And the judge must therefore rule conservatively. Which means, if there is a possibility of abuse, to keep the child away from the accused parent. Or at least, not allow unsupervised visitation. No overnight visits. Or perhaps not even –

'That's enough,' Connor said, sitting beside me in the car. 'Come back now.'

'Sorry,' I said. 'But it's upsetting.'

'I'm sure. Now: what haven't you told me?'

'About what?'

'The molestation charge.'

'Nothing. There's nothing to it.'

'*Kōhai*,' he said quietly. 'I can't help you if you won't tell me.'

'It had nothing to do with sexual molestation,' I said. 'It was something else entirely. It was about money.'

Connor said nothing. He just waited. Looking at me.

'Ah, hell,' I said.

And I told him.

You have these times in your life when you believe you know what you're doing. Later on, you can look back, and you see you weren't acting right at all. You drifted into something, and you were completely screwed up. But at the time, you thought everything was fine.

What happened to me was, I was in love. Lauren was one of those patrician-acting girls, lean and graceful and understated. She looked like she grew up with horses. And she was younger than me, and beautiful.

I always knew it wouldn't work between us, but I was trying to make it work anyway. We had gotten married and had begun living together and she was starting to be dissatisfied. Dissatisfied with my apartment, where it was located, how much money we had. All of that. She was throwing up, which didn't help. She had crackers in the car, crackers by the bed, crackers everywhere. She was so miserable and so unhappy that I tried to please her in little ways. Get her things. Bring her things. Cook her meals. Do little domestic things. It wasn't my usual way, but I was in love. I was drifting into this habit of pleasing her. Trying to please her.

And there was constant pressure. More this, more that. More money. More, more.

We also had a specific problem. Her health insurance through the D.A.'s office didn't cover pregnancy and neither did mine. After we got married, we couldn't get coverage in time to pay for the baby. It was going to cost eight thousand dollars and we had to come up with it. Neither of us had the money. Lauren's father was a doctor in Virginia but she didn't want to ask him for the money because he disapproved of her marrying me in the first place. My family doesn't have any money. So. There wasn't any money. She worked for the D.A. I worked for the department. She had a lot of debts on her MasterCard and owed money on her car. We had to come up with eight thousand dollars. It's hanging over our heads. How we are going to do this. And it gets to be an unspoken thing, at least from her, that I should handle it.

So one night in August I'm out on a domestic violence call in Ladera Heights. Hispanic couple. They've been drinking and going at it pretty good, she's got a split lip and he's got a black eye, and their kid's screaming in the next room, but pretty soon we calm them down and we can see that nobody is seriously injured, so we're about to leave. And the wife sees we're about to leave. At that point she starts yelling that the husband has been fooling with the daughter. Physically abusing the daughter. When the husband hears this, he looks really pissed, and I think it's bullshit, the wife is just doing something to harass him. But the wife insists we check the daughter, so I go into the kid's room and the kid is about nine months old and screaming red in the face, and I pull the covers back to check for bruises and there I see a kilo of white brick. Under the covers with the kid.

So.

I don't know, it's one of those situations, they're married so she'd have to testify against her husband, there's no probable cause, the search is invalid, on and on. If he's got a halfway decent lawyer he can beat this, no problem. So I go out and call the guy in. I know I can't do anything. All I'm thinking is that if his kid ever got this brick in her mouth, chewed on it, it would kill her. I want to talk to him about that. I figure I'll fuck him over a little. Scare him a little.

So now it's him and me in the kid's room. The wife is still out in the living room with my partner, and suddenly the guy pulls out an envelope two centimeters thick. He cracks it open. I see hundred-dollar bills. An inch thick of hundred-dollar bills. And he says, 'Thanks for your help, officer.'

There's got to be ten thousand dollars in that envelope. Maybe more. I don't know. The guy holds out the envelope and looks at me. Expecting me to take it.

I say something lame about how it's dangerous to hide shit in a kid's bed. Right away, the guy picks up the brick, puts it on the floor, kicks it out of sight under the bed. Then he says, 'You are right. Thank you, officer. I would hate something happens to my daughter.' And he holds out the envelope.

So.

Everything is in turmoil. The wife is outside screaming at my partner. The kid is in here screaming at us. The guy is holding the envelope. He smiles and nods. Like, go ahead and take it. It's yours. And I think . . . I don't know what I thought.

Next thing I know, I'm out in the living room and I say everything is fine with the kid, and now the woman starts to scream in her drunken way that *I* abused her child – now it's me, not the husband – and that I am in a conspiracy with the husband, that we are both child abusers. My partner figures she's crazy drunk and we leave, and that's it. My partner says, 'You were in that room a while.' And I say, 'I had to check the kid.' And that's it. Except the next day she comes in and makes a formal complaint that I abused her child. She's hung over and she has a record, but even so it's a serious charge and it goes through the system as far as the preliminary, where it gets thrown out as entirely without merit.

That's it.

That's what happened.

That's the whole story.

'And the money?' Connor said.

'I went to Vegas for the weekend. I won big. I paid taxes on thirteen thousand in unearned income that year.'

'Whose idea was that?'

'Lauren. She told me how to handle it.'

'So she knows what happened?'

'Sure.'

'And the department investigation? Did the preliminary board issue a report?'

'I don't think it got that far. They just heard it orally and dismissed it. There's probably a notation in the file, but not an actual report.'

'All right,' Connor said. 'Now tell me the rest.'

So I told him about Ken Shubik, and the *Times*, and the Weasel. Connor listened silently, frowning. As I talked, he began to suck air through his teeth, which was the Japanese way of expressing disapproval.

'*Kōhai*,' he said, when I finished, 'you are making my life extremely difficult. And certainly you make me appear foolish when I should not. Why didn't you tell me this earlier?'

'Because it had nothing to do with you.'

'*Kōhai*.' He was shaking his head. '*Kōhai* . . .'

I was thinking about my daughter again. About the possibility – just the possibility – that I would not be able to see her – that I would not be able to –

'Look,' Connor said, 'I told you it could be unpleasant. Take my word for it. It can get much more unpleasant than this. This is only the beginning. It can get *nasty*. We must proceed quickly and try to wrap everything up.'

'I thought everything *was* wrapped up.'

Connor sighed, and shook his head. 'It's not,' he said. 'And now we must resolve everything before you meet your wife at four o'clock. So let's make sure we are done by then.'

'Christ, I'd say it's pretty fucking wrapped up,' Graham said. He was walking around Sakamura's house in the Hollywood hills. The last of the SID teams was packing up cases to leave.

'I don't know why the chief has such a bug up his ass on this,' Graham said. 'The SID boys have been doing most of their work right here, on the spot, because he's in such a rush. But thank God: everything ties up perfect. Sakamura is our boy. We combed his bed for pubic hair – it matches the pubic hair found on the girl. We got dried saliva off his toothbrush. It matches blood type and genetic markers for the sperm inside the dead girl. Matchup is ninety-seven percent sure. It's his come inside her, and his pubic hair on her body. He fucked her and then he killed her. And when we came to arrest him, he panicked, made a break for it, and died as a result. Where is Connor?'

'Outside,' I said.

Through the windows, I could see Connor standing down by the garage, talking to policemen in a black-and-white patrol car. Connor was pointing up and down the street; they were answering questions.

'What's he doing down there?' Graham said.

I said I didn't know.

'Damn, I don't understand him. You can tell him the answer to his question is no.'

'What question?'

'He called me an hour ago,' Graham said. 'Said he wanted to know how many pairs of reading glasses we found here. We checked. The answer is, no reading glasses. Lots of sunglasses. Couple of pairs of women's sunglasses. But that's it. I don't know why he cared. Strange man, isn't he? What the hell is he doing now?'

We watched as Connor paced back and forth around the squad car, then pointed up and down the road again. One man was in the car, talking on the radio. 'Do you understand him?' Graham said.

'No, I don't.'

'He's probably trying to track down the girls,' Graham said. 'Christ, I wish we had gotten the ID on that redhead. Especially now it's turned out this way. She must have fucked him, too. We could have gotten some sperm from her, and made an exact match with all the factors. And I look like a horse's ass, letting the girls get away. But shit, who knew it was going to go that way. It was all so fast. Naked girls up here, prancing around. A guy gets a little confused. It's natural. Shit, they were good looking, weren't they?'

I said they were.

'And there's nothing left of Sakamura,' Graham said. 'I talked to the PEO boys an hour ago. They're downtown, cutting the corpse out of the car, but I guess he's burned beyond identification. The M.E.'s office is going to try, but good luck.' He stared unhappily out the window. 'You know what? We did the best we could with this fucking case,' he said. 'And I think we did pretty good. We got the right guy. We did it fast, no fuss no muss. But all I hear now is a lot of Japan-bashing. Fuck. You can't win.'

'Uh-huh,' I said.

'And *Christ* they have juice now,' Graham said. 'The heat on my ass is terrific. I got the chief calling me, wanting this thing wrapped up. I got some reporter at the *Times* investigating me, hauling out some old shit about a questionable use of force on a Hispanic back in 1978. Nothing to it. But this reporter, he's trying to show I've always been a racist. And what is the background of his story? That last night was a 'racist' incident. So I am now an example of racism rearing its ugly head again. I tell you. The Japanese are masters of the smear job. It's fucking scary.'

'I know,' I said.

'They getting to you, too?'

I nodded.

'For what?'

'Child abuse.'

'Christ,' Graham said. 'And you got a daughter.'

'Yes.'

'Doesn't it piss you off? Innuendo and smear tactics, Petey-san. Nothing to do with reality. But try and tell that to a reporter.'

'Who is it?' I asked. 'The reporter talking to you.'

'Linda Jensen, I think she said.'

I nodded. Linda Jensen was the Weasel's protégé. Somebody once said that Linda didn't fuck her way to the top. She fucked other people's reputations to the top. She had been a gossip columnist in Washington before graduating to the big time in Los Angeles.

'I don't know,' Graham said, shifting his bulk. 'Personally, I think it's not worth it. They're turning this country into another Japan. You've already got people afraid to speak. Afraid to say anything against them. People just won't talk about what's happening.'

'It would help if the government passed a few laws.'

Graham laughed. 'The government. They *own* the government. You know what they spend in Washington every year? Four hundred million fucking dollars a year. That's enough to pay the campaign costs of everybody in the United States Senate *and* the House of Representatives. That is a lot of fucking money. Now you tell me. Would they spend all that money, year after year, if it wasn't paying off for them? Of course they wouldn't. Shit. The end of America, buddy. Hey. Looks like your boss wants you.'

I looked out the window. Connor was waving to me.

I said, 'I better go.'

'Good luck,' Graham said. 'Listen. I may take a couple of weeks off.'

'Yeah? When?'

'Maybe later today,' Graham said. 'The chief mentioned it. He said as long as the fucking *Times* is on my ass, maybe I should. I'm thinking of a week in Phoenix. I got family there. Anyway, I wanted you to know, I might be going.'

'Okay, sure,' I said.

Connor was still waving to me. He seemed impatient. I hurried down to see him. As I came down the steps, I saw a black Mercedes sedan pull up, and a familiar figure emerge.

It was Weasel Wilhelm.

By the time I got down there, the Weasel had his notepad and tape recorder out. A cigarette hung from the corner of his mouth. 'Lieutenant Smith,' he said. 'I wonder if I could talk to you.'

'I'm pretty busy,' I said.

'Come on,' Connor called to me. 'Time's a'wasting.' He was holding the door open for me.

I started toward Connor. The Weasel fell in step with me. He held a tiny black microphone toward my face. 'I'm taping, I hope you don't mind. After the Malcolm case, we have to be extra careful. I wonder if you would comment on racial slurs allegedly made by your associate Detective Graham during last night's Nakamoto investigation?'

'No,' I said. I kept walking.

'We've been told he referred to them as "fucking Japs".'

'I have no comment,' I said.

'He also called them "little Nips". Do you think that kind of talk is appropriate to an officer on duty?'

'Sorry. I don't have a comment, Willy.'

He held the microphone up to my face as we walked. It was annoying. I wanted to slap it away, but I didn't. 'Lieutenant Smith, we're preparing a story on you and we have some questions about the Martinez case. Do you remember that one? It was a couple of years back.'

I kept walking. 'I'm pretty busy now, Willy,' I said.

'The Martinez case resulted in accusations of child abuse brought by Sylvia Morelia, the mother of Maria Martinez. There was an internal affairs investigation. I wondered if you had any comment.'

'No comment.'

'I've already talked to your partner at that time, Ted Anderson. I wondered if you had any comment on that.'

'Sorry. I don't.'

'Then you aren't going to respond to these serious allegations against you?'

'The only one I know that's making allegations is you, Willy.'

'Actually, that's not entirely accurate,' he said, smiling at me. 'I'm told the D.A.'s office has started an investigation.'

I said nothing. I wondered if it was true.

'Under the circumstances, Lieutenant, do you think the court made a mistake in granting you custody of your young daughter?'

All I said was, 'Sorry. No comment, Willy.' I tried to sound confident. I was starting to sweat.

Connor said, 'Come on, come on. No time.' I got into the car. Connor said to Wilhelm, 'Son, I'm sorry, but we're busy. Got to go.' He slammed the car door. I started the engine. 'Let's go,' Connor said.

Willy stuck his head in the window. 'Do you think that Captain Connor's Japan-bashing represents another example of the department's lack of judgment in racially sensitive cases?'

'See you, Willy.' I rolled up the window, and started driving down the hill.

'A little faster wouldn't bother me,' Connor said.

'Sure,' I said. I stepped on the gas.

In the rearview mirror, I saw the Weasel running for his Mercedes. I took the turn faster, tires squealing. 'How did that lowlife know where to find us? He monitoring the radio?'

'We haven't been on the radio,' Connor said. 'You know I'm careful about the radio. But maybe the patrol car phoned in something when we arrived. Maybe we have a bug in this car. Maybe he just figured we'd turn up here. He's a scumbag. And he's connected to the Japanese. He's their plant at the *Times*. Usually the Japanese are a little more classy about who they associate with. But I guess he'll do everything they want done. Nice car, huh?'

'I notice it's not Japanese.'

'Can't be obvious,' Connor said. 'He following us?'

'No. I think we lost him. Where are we going now?'

'U.S.C. Sanders has had enough time screwing around by now.'

We drove down the street, down the hill, toward the 101 freeway. 'By the way,' I said. 'What was all that about the reading glasses?'

'Just a small point to be verified. No reading glasses were found, right?'

'Right. Just sunglasses.'

'That's what I thought,' Connor said.

'And Graham says he's leaving town. Today. He's going to Phoenix.'

'Uh-huh.' He looked at me. 'You want to leave town, too?'

'No,' I said.

'Okay,' Connor said.

I got down the hill and onto the 101 going south. In the old days it would be ten minutes to U.S.C. Now it was more like thirty minutes.

Especially now, right at midday. But there weren't any fast times, anymore. Traffic was always bad. The smog was always bad. I drove through haze.

'You think I'm being foolish?' I said. 'You think I should pick up my kid and run, too?'

'It's one way to handle it.' He sighed. 'The Japanese are masters of indirect action. It's their instinctual way to proceed. If someone in Japan is unhappy with you, they never tell you to your face. They tell your friend, your associate, your boss. In such a way that the word gets back. The Japanese have all these ways of indirect communication. That's why they socialize so much, play so much golf, go drinking in *karaoke* bars. They need these extra channels of communication because they can't come out and say what's on their minds. It's tremendously inefficient, when you think about it. Wasteful of time and energy and money. But since they cannot confront – because confrontation is almost like death, it makes them sweat and panic – they have no other choice. Japan is the land of the end run. They never go up the middle.'

'Yeah, but . . .'

'So behavior that seems sneaky and cowardly to Americans is just standard operating procedure to Japanese. It doesn't mean anything special. They're just letting you know that powerful people are displeased.'

'Letting me know? That I could end up in court over my daughter? My relationship with my kid could be ruined? My own reputation could be ruined?'

'Well, yes. Those are normal penalties. The threat of social disgrace is the usual way you're expected to know of displeasure.'

'Well, I think I know it, now,' I said. 'I think I get the fucking picture.'

'It's not personal,' Connor said. 'It's just the way they proceed.'

'Yeah, right. They're spreading a lie.'

'In a sense.'

'No, not in a sense. It's fucking lie.'

Connor sighed. 'It took me a long time to understand,' he said, 'that Japanese behavior is based on the values of a farm village. You hear a lot about samurai and feudalism, but deep down, the Japanese are farmers. And if you lived in a farm village and you displeased the other villagers, you were banished. And that meant you died, because no other village would take in a troublemaker. So. Displease the group and you die. That's the way they see it.

'It means the Japanese are exquisitely sensitive to the group. More than anything, they are attuned to getting along with the group. It means not standing out, not taking a chance, not being too individualistic. It also means not necessarily insisting on the truth. The Japanese have very little faith in truth. It strikes them as cold and abstract. It's like a mother whose son is accused of a crime. She doesn't care much about the truth. She cares more about her son. The same with the Japanese. To the Japanese, the important thing is relationships between people. That's the real truth. The factual truth is unimportant.'

'Yeah, fine,' I said. 'But why are they pushing now? What's the difference? This murder is solved, right?'

'No, it's not,' Connor said.

'It's not?'

'No. That's why we have all the pressure. Obviously, somebody badly *wants* it to be over. They want us to give it up.'

'If they are squeezing me and squeezing Graham – how come they're not squeezing you?'

'They are,' Connor said.

'How?'

'By making me responsible for what happens to you.'

'How are they making you responsible? I don't see that.'

'I know you don't. But they do. Believe me. They do.'

I looked at the line of cars creeping forward, blending into the haze of downtown. We passed electronic billboards for Hitachi (# 1 IN COMPUTERS IN AMERICA), for Canon (AMERICA'S COPY LEADER), and Honda (NUMBER ONE RATED CAR IN AMERICA!). Like most of the new Japanese ads, they were bright enough to run in the daytime. The billboards cost thirty thousand dollars a day to rent: most American companies couldn't afford them.

Connor said, 'The point is the Japanese know they can make it very uncomfortable. By raising the dust around you, they are telling me, "handle it". Because they think I can get this thing done. Finish it off.'

'Can you?'

'Sure. You want to finish off now? Then we can go have a beer, and enjoy some Japanese truth. Or do you want to get to the bottom of why Cheryl Austin was killed?'

'I want to get to the bottom.'

'Me, too,' Connor said. 'So let's do it, *kōhai*. I think Sanders's lab will have interesting information for us. The tapes are the key, now.'

Phillip Sanders was spinning like a top. 'The lab is shut down,' he said. He threw up his hands in frustration. 'And there's nothing I can do about it. *Nothing.*'

Connor said, 'When did it happen?'

'An hour ago. Buildings and Grounds came by and told everybody in the lab to leave, and they locked it up. Just like that. There's a big padlock on the front door, now.'

I said, 'And the reason was?'

'A report that structural weakness in the ceiling has made the basement unsafe and will invalidate the university's insurance if the skating rink comes crashing down on us. Some talk about how student safety comes first. Anyway, they closed the lab, pending an investigation and report by a structural engineer.'

'And when will that happen?'

He gestured to the phone. 'I'm waiting to hear. Maybe some time next week. Maybe not until next month.'

'Next *month*?'

'Yeah. Exactly.' Sanders ran his hand through his wild hair. 'I went all the way to the dean on this one. But the dean's office doesn't know. It's coming from high up in the university. Up where the board of governors knows rich donors who make contributions in multi-million-dollar chunks. The order came from the highest levels.' Sanders laughed. 'These days, it doesn't leave much mystery.'

I said, 'Meaning what?'

'You realize Japan is deeply into the structure of American universities, particularly in technical departments. It's happened everywhere. Japanese companies now endow twenty-five professorships at M.I.T., far more than any other nation. Because they know – after all the bullshit stops – that they can't innovate as well as we can. Since they need innovation, they do the obvious thing. They buy it.'

'From American universities.'

'Sure. Listen, at the University of California at Irvine, there's two floors of a research building that you can't get into unless you have a Japanese passport. They're doing research for Hitachi there. An American university closed to Americans.' Sanders swung around, waving his arms. 'And around here, if something happens that they don't like, it's just a phone call from somebody to the president of the university, and what can he do? He can't afford to piss the Japanese off. So whatever they want, they get. And if they want the lab closed, it's closed.'

I said, 'What about the tapes?'

'Everything is locked in there. They made us leave everything.'

'Really?'

'They were in a hell of a rush. It was gestapo stuff. Pushing and prodding us to get out. You can't imagine the panic at an American university if it thinks it may lose some funding.' He sighed. 'I don't know. Maybe Theresa managed to take some tapes with her. You could ask her.'

'Where is she?'

'I think she went ice skating.'

I frowned. 'Ice skating?'

'That's what she said she was going to do. So you could check over there.'

And he looked right at Connor. In a particularly meaningful way.

Theresa Asakuma wasn't ice skating. There were thirty little kids in the rink, with a young teacher trying in vain to control them. They looked like fourth graders. Their laughter and yells echoed in the high ceiling of the rink.

The building was almost deserted, the bleachers empty. A handful of fraternity boys sat up in one corner, looking down and punching each other on the shoulder. On our side, up high, near the ceiling, a janitor mopped. A couple of adults who looked like parents stood at the railing, down near the ice. Opposite us, a man was reading a newspaper.

I didn't see Theresa Asakuma anywhere.

Connor sighed. Wearily, he sat on the wooden bleachers and leaned back. He crossed his legs, taking his ease. I stood there, watching him. 'What are you doing? She's obviously not here.'

'Have a seat.'

'But you're always in such a rush.'

'Have a seat. Enjoy life.'

I sat down next to him. We watched the kids skating around the perimeter of the ice. The teacher was shouting, 'Alexander? Alexander! I've told you before. No hitting! Don't you hit her!'

I leaned back against the bleachers. I tried to relax. Connor watched the kids and chuckled. He appeared entirely at ease, without a care in the world.

I said, 'Do you think Sanders is right? The Japanese squeezed the university?'

'Sure,' Connor said.

'And all that business about Japan buying into American technology? Buying professorships at M.I.T.?'

'It's not illegal. They're supporting scholarship. A noble ideal.'

I frowned. 'So you think it's okay?'

'No,' he said. 'I don't think it's okay at all. If you give up control of your own institutions you give up everything. And generally, whoever pays for an institution controls it. If the Japanese are willing to put up the money – and if the American government and American industry aren't – then the Japanese will control American education. You know they already *own* ten American colleges. Own them outright. Bought them for the training of their young people. So that they can be assured of the ability to send young Japanese to America.'

'But they already can do that. Lots of Japanese go to American universities.'

'Yes. But as usual, the Japanese are planning ahead. They know in the future it may get tougher. They know that sooner or later, there will be a backlash. No matter how diplomatically they play it – and they are in the acquisition phase now, so they're playing it very diplomatically. Because the fact is, countries don't like to be dominated. They don't like to be occupied – economically or militarily. And the Japanese figure some day the Americans will wake up.'

I watched the kids skating in the rink. I listened to their laughter. I thought of my daughter. I thought of the four o'clock meeting.

I said, 'Why are we sitting here?'

'Because,' he said.

So we sat there. The teacher was rounding the kids up now, leading them off the ice. 'Skates off here. Skates off here, please. That means you too, Alexander! Alexander!'

'You know,' Connor said, 'if you wanted to buy a Japanese company, you couldn't do it. The people in the company would consider it shameful to be taken over by foreigners. It would be a disgrace. They would never allow it.'

'I thought you could. I thought the Japanese had liberalized their rules.'

Connor smiled. '*Technically*. Yes. Technically, you can buy a Japanese company. But as a practical matter, you can't. Because if you want to take over a company, you first have to approach its bank. And get the agreement of the bank. That's what is necessary, in order to proceed. And the bank doesn't agree.'

'I thought General Motors own Isuzu.'

'GM owns a third of Isuzu. Not a controlling interest. And yes, there are isolated instances. But overall, foreign investment in Japan has declined by half in the last ten years. One company after another finds the Japanese market just too tough. They get tired of the bullshit, the hassles, the collusion, the rigged markets, the *dangō*, the secret agreements to keep them out. They get tired of the government regulations. The run around. And eventually they give up. They just . . . give up. Most other countries have given up: Germans, Italians, French. Everybody's getting tired of trying to do business in Japan. Because no matter what they tell you, Japan is closed. A few years ago, T. Boone Pickens bought one-fourth of the stock of a Japanese company, but he couldn't get on the board of directors. Japan is *closed*.'

'So what are we supposed to do?'

'The same thing the Europeans are doing,' Connor said. 'Reciprocity. Tit for tat. One of yours for one of mine. Everybody in the world has the same problem with Japan. It's just a question of what solution works best. The European solution is pretty direct. Works well, at least so far.'

On the rink, some teenage girls began to do warmups and a few tentative leaps. Now the schoolteacher was leading her charges along the corridor past us. As she went by, she said, 'Is one of you Lieutenant Smith?'

'Yes, ma'am,' I said.

One kid said, 'Do you have a gun?'

The teacher said, 'That woman asked me to tell you that what you're looking for is in the men's locker room.'

'It is?' I said.

The kid said, 'Can I see it?'

The teacher said, 'You know, the Oriental woman? I think she was Oriental.'

'Yes,' Connor said. 'Thank you.'

'I want to see the gun.'

Another kid said, 'Quiet, stupid. Don't you know anything? They're *undercover*.'

'I want to see the gun.'

Connor and I started walking away. The kids trailed after us, still asking to see our guns. Across the rink, the man with the newspaper looked up curiously. He watched us leave.

'Nothing like an inconpicuous exit,' Connor said.

The men's locker room was deserted. I started going through the green metal lockers, one after another, looking for the tapes. Connor didn't bother. I heard him call to me, 'Back here.'

He was in the rear by the showers. 'You found the tapes?'

'No.'

He was holding open a door.

We went down a flight of concrete stairs to a landing. There were two doors. One opened onto a below-grade truck entrance. The other went into a dark hallway with wooden beams. 'This way,' Connor said.

We went down this hallway, crouched over. We were underneath the rink again. We passed throbbing stainless-steel machinery, and then came to a series of doors.

'Do you know where we're going?' I said.

One of the doors was ajar. He pushed it open. The room lights were out, but I could see that we were in a lab. Off in a corner, I saw a faint monitor glow.

We walked toward it.

Theresa Asakuma leaned back from the table, pushed her glasses up on her forehead, and rubbed her beautiful eyes. 'It's okay as long as we don't make much noise,' she said. 'They had a guard outside the main door earlier. I don't know if he's still there.'

'A guard?'

'Yeah. They were serious about shutting down the lab. It was spectacular, like a drug bust. It really surprised the Americans.'

'And you?'

'I don't have the same expectations about this country.'

Connor pointed to the monitor in front of her. It showed a freeze-frame image of the couple, embracing as they moved toward the conference room. The same image, seen from other camera angles, was reproduced on other monitors on the desk. Some of the monitors had superimposed red lines, radiating out from the night lights. 'What have you learned from the tapes?'

Theresa pointed to the main screen. 'I'm not certain,' she said. 'To be completely certain, I would have to run 3-D modeling sequences to match the dimensions of the room and keep track of all the light sources, and the shadows cast by all the sources. I haven't done that, and I probably can't with the equipment in this room. It would probably require an overnight run on a mini. Maybe I could get time next week from the astrophysics department. The way things are going, maybe not. But in the meantime, I have a strong feeling.'

'Which is?'

'The shadows don't match.'

In the darkness, Connor nodded slowly. As if that made sense to him.

I said, 'Which shadows don't match?'

She pointed to the screen. 'As these people move around the floor, the shadows they cast don't line up exactly. They're in the wrong place, or the wrong shape. Often it's subtle. But I think it is there.'

'And the fact that the shadows don't match means . . .'

She shrugged. 'I'd say the tapes have been altered, Lieutenant.'

There was a silence. 'Altered how?'

'I'm not sure how much has been done. But it seems clear that there was another person in that room, at least part of the time.'

'Another person? You mean a third person?'

'Yes. Someone watching. And that third person has been systematically erased.'

'No *shit,*' I said.

It was making my head spin. I looked at Connor. He was staring intently at the monitors. He seemed completely unsurprised. I said, 'Did you already know this?'

'I suspected something of the sort.'

'Why?' I said.

Connor smiled. 'Details, *kōhai.* Those little things we forget.' He glanced at Theresa, as if he was reluctant to talk too much in front of her.

I said, 'No, I want to hear this. When did you first know the tapes were altered?'

'In the Nakamoto security room.'

'Why?'

'Because of the missing tape.'

'What missing tape?' I said. He had mentioned it before.

'Think back,' Connor said. 'In the security room, the guard told us that he changed the tapes when he came on duty, around nine o'clock.'

'Yes . . .'

'And the tape recorders all had timers, showing an elapsed time of about two hours. Each recorder started about ten or fifteen seconds later than the previous one. Because that was the time interval it took him to change each tape.'

'Right . . .' I remembered all that.

'And I pointed out to him one tape recorder that didn't fit the sequence. Its tape was only running for half an hour. So I asked if it was broken.'

'And the guard seemed to think it was.'

'Yes. That's what he said. I was letting him off the hook. Actually, he knew perfectly well it was not broken.'

'It wasn't?'

'No. It was one of the few mistakes that the Japanese have made. But they only made it because they were stuck – they couldn't get around it. They couldn't beat their own technology.'

I leaned back against the wall. I looked apologetically at Theresa. She looked beautiful in the semidarkness of the monitors. 'I'm sorry. I'm lost.'

'That's because you are rejecting the obvious explanation, *kōhai.* Think back. If you saw a line of tape recorders, each one running a few seconds later than the one before, and you saw one recorder way out of sequence, what would you think?'

'That someone had changed the tape in that one recorder at a later time.'

'Yes. And that's exactly what happened.'

'One tape was switched later?'

'Yes.'

I frowned. 'But why? All of the tapes were replaced at nine o'clock. So none of the replacements showed the murder, anyway.'

'Correct,' Connor said.

'Then why switch one tape after that?'

'Good question. It's puzzling. I couldn't make sense of it for a long time. But now I know,' Connor said. 'You have to remember the timing. The tapes were all changed at nine. Then one tape was changed again at ten-fifteen. The obvious assumption was that something important happened between nine o'clock and ten-fifteen, that it was recorded on the tape, and the tape was therefore taken away for some reason. I asked myself: what could this important event be?'

I thought back. I frowned. I couldn't think of anything.

Theresa began to smile and nod, as if something had just amused her. I said, 'You know?'

'I can guess,' she said, smiling.

'Well,' I said. 'I'm glad everyone seems to know the answer except me. Because I can't think of anything important being recorded on that tape. By nine o'clock, the yellow barrier was up, isolating the crime scene. The girl's body was on the other side of the room. There were a lot of Japanese standing by the elevators, and Graham was calling me on the phone for help. But nobody actually began an investigation until I got there at about ten. Then we had a lot of back and forth with Ishiguro. I don't think anybody crossed the tape until almost ten-thirty. Say ten-fifteen at the earliest. So if somebody looked at a recording, all it would show is a deserted room, and a girl lying on the table. That's all.'

Connor said, 'Very good. Except you have forgotten something.'

Theresa said, 'Did anybody cross the room? Anybody at all?'

'No,' I said. 'We had the yellow barrier up. Nobody was allowed on the other side of the tape. In fact –'

And then I remembered. 'Wait a minute! There was somebody! That little guy with the camera,' I said. 'He was on the other side of the barrier, taking pictures.'

'That's right,' Connor said.

'What little guy?' she said.

'A Japanese guy. He was taking pictures. We asked Ishiguro about him. He said his name was, ah . . .'

'Mr Tanaka,' Connor said.

'That's right, Mr Tanaka. And you asked Ishiguro for the film from his camera.' I frowned. 'But we never got it.'

'No,' Connor said. 'And frankly, I never thought we would.'

Theresa said, 'This man was taking pictures?'

'I doubt that he was actually taking pictures,' Connor said. 'Perhaps he was, because he was using one of those little Canons –'

'The ones that shoot video stills, instead of film?'

'Right. Would there be any use for those, in retouching?'

'There might be,' she said. 'The images might be used for texture mapping. They'd go in fast, because they were already digitized.'

Connor nodded. 'Then perhaps he was taking pictures, after all. But it was clear to me that his picture-taking was just an excuse to allow him to walk on the other side of the yellow line.'

'Ah,' Theresa said, nodding.

I said, 'How do you know that?'

'Think back,' Connor said.

I had been standing facing Ishiguro when Graham yelled: Aw, Christ, what is this? And I looked back over my shoulder and saw a short Japanese man about ten meters beyond the yellow tape. The man's back was turned to me. He was taking pictures of the crime scene. The camera was very small. It fitted into the palm of his hand.

'Do you remember how he moved?' Connor said. 'He moved in a distinctive way.'

I tried to recall it. I couldn't.

Graham had gone forward to the tape, saying: For Christ's sake, you can't be in there. This is a goddamned crime scene. You can't take pictures! And there was a general uproar. Graham was yelling at Tanaka, but he continued to be entirely focused on his work, shooting the camera and backing toward us. Despite all the yelling, Tanaka didn't do what a normal person would do – turn around and walk toward the tape. Instead, he backed up to the yellow stripe and, still turned away, ducked his head and went under it.

I said, 'He never turned around. He backed up all the way.'

'Correct. That is the first mystery. Why would he back up? Now, I think, we know.'

'We do?'

Theresa said, 'He was repeating the walk of the girl and the killer in reverse, so it would be laid down on videotape and he would have a good record of where the shadows in the room were.'

'That's right,' Connor said.

I remembered that when I protested, Ishiguro had said to me: This is our employee. He works for Nakamoto Security.

And I had said: This is outrageous. He can't take pictures.

And Ishiguro had explained: But this is for our corporate use.

And meanwhile the man had disappeared in the crowd, slipping through the knot of men at the elevator.

But this is for our corporate use.

'Damn it!' I said. 'So Tanaka left us, went downstairs, and removed a single tape, because that tape had a record of his own walk across the room, and the shadows he cast?'

'Correct.'

'And he needed that tape to make changes in the original tapes?'

'Correct.'

I was finally beginning to understand. 'But now, even if we can figure out how the tapes were altered, they won't stand up in a court of law, is that right?'

'That's right,' Theresa said. 'Any good lawyer will make sure they're inadmissible.'

'So the only way to go forward is to get a witness who can testify to what was done. Sakamura might know, but he's dead. So we're stuck unless we can somehow get our hands on Mr Tanaka. I think we better get him in custody right away.'

'I doubt that will ever happen,' Connor said.

'Why not? You think they'll keep him from us?'

'No, I don't think they have to. It is very likely that Mr Tanaka is already dead.'

Connor immediately turned to Theresa. 'Are you good at your job?'

'Yes,' she said.

'Very good?'

'I think so.'

'We have little time left. Work with Peter. See what you can extract from the tape. *Gambatte:* try very hard. Trust me that your efforts will be rewarded. In the meantime, I have some calls to make.'

I said, 'You're leaving?'

'Yes. I'll need the car.'

I gave him the keys. 'Where are you going?'

'I'm not your *wife.*'

'I'm just asking,' I said.

'Don't worry about it. I need to see some people.' He turned to go.

'But why do you say Tanaka is dead?'

'Well, perhaps he's not. We'll discuss it when there is more time. Right now, we have a lot to finish before four o'clock. That is our true deadline. I think you have surprises in store for you, *kōhai.* Just call it my *chokkan,* my intuition. Okay? You have trouble, or something unexpected, call me on the car phone. Good luck. Now work with this lovely lady. *Urayamashii ne!*'

And he left. We heard the rear door close.

I said to Theresa, 'What did he say?'

'He said he envies you.' She smiled in the darkness. 'Let's begin.'

She pressed buttons on the equipment in rapid succession. The tape rolled back to the beginning of the sequence.

I said, 'How are we going to do this?'

'There are three basic approaches to learn how video has been doctored. The first is blur and color edges. The second is shadow lines. We can try to work with those elements, but I've been doing that for the last two hours, and I haven't gotten very far.'

'And the third method?'

'Reflected elements. I haven't looked at them yet.'

I shook my head.

'Basically, reflected elements – REs – are portions of the scene that are reflected within the image itself. Like when Sakamura walks out of the room, and his face is reflected in the mirror. There are almost certainly other reflections in that room. A desk lamp may be chrome, and it may show the people, distorted, as they pass. The walls of the conference room are glass. We may be able to pull a reflection off the glass. A silver paperweight on a desk, with a reflection in it. A glass vase of flowers. A plastic container. Anything shiny enough to make a reflection.'

I watched her reset the tapes, and prepare to run forward. Her one good hand moved quickly from one machine to the next as she talked. It was odd to stand next to a woman so beautiful, who was so unselfconscious of her beauty.

'In most images, there is something reflective,' Theresa said. 'Outside, there are car bumpers, wet streets, glass windowpanes. And inside a room there are picture frames, mirrors, silver candlesticks, chrome table-legs . . . There's always something.'

'But won't they fix the reflections, too?'

'If they have time, yes. Because now there are computer programs to map an image onto any shape. You can map a picture onto a complicated, twisted surface. But it takes time. So. Let's hope they had no time.'

She started the tapes forward. The first portion was dark, as Cheryl Austin first appeared by the elevators. I looked at Theresa. I said, 'How do you feel about this?'

'What do you mean?'

'Helping us. The police.'

'You mean, because I am Japanese?' She glanced at me, and smiled. It was an odd, crooked smile. 'I have no illusions about Japanese. Do you know where Sako is?'

'No.'

'It is a city – a town, really – in the north. In Hokkaido. A provincial place. There is an American airfield there. I was born in Sako. My father was a *kokujin* mechanic. You know that word, *kokujin*? *Niguro*. A black man. My mother worked in a noodle shop where the air force personnel went. They married, but my father died in an accident when I was two years old. There was a small pension for the widow. So we had some money. But my grandfather took most of it, because he insisted he had been disgraced by my birth. I was *ainoko* and *niguro*. They are not nice words, what he called me. But my mother wanted to stay there, to stay in Japan. So I grew up in Sako. In this . . . *place* . . .'

I heard the bitterness in her voice.

'You know what the *burakumin* are?' she said. 'No? I am not surprised. In Japan, the land where everyone is supposedly equal, no one speaks of *burakumin.* But before a marriage, a young man's family will check the family history of the bride, to be sure there are no *burakumin* in the past. The bride's family will do the same. And if there is any doubt, the marriage will not occur. The *burakumin* are the untouchables of Japan. The outcasts, the lowest of the low. They are the descendants of tanners and leather workers, which in Buddhism is unclean.'

'I see.'

'And I was lower than *burakumin* because I was deformed. To the Japanese, deformity is shameful. Not sad, or a burden. *Shameful.* It means you have done something wrong. Deformity shames you, and your family, and your community. The people around you wish you were dead. And if you are half black, the *ainoko* of an American big nose . . .' She shook her head. 'Children are cruel. And this was a provincial place, a country town.'

She watched the tape go forward.

'So I am glad to be here. You Americans do not know in what grace your land exists. What freedom you enjoy in your hearts. You cannot imagine the harshness of life in Japan, if you are excluded from the group. But I know it very well. And I do not mind if the Japanese suffer a little now, from my efforts with my *one good hand.*'

She glared at me. The intensity turned her face to a mask. 'Does that answer your question, Lieutenant?'

'Yes,' I said. 'It does.'

'When I come to America, I think the Americans are very foolish about the Japanese – but never mind. Here is the sequence now. You watch the top two monitors. I will watch the bottom three. Look carefully for objects that reflect. Look closely. Here it comes.'

I watched the monitors in the darkness.

Theresa Asakuma was feeling bitter about the Japanese, but so was I. The incident with Weasel Wilhelm had made me angry. Angry the way somebody who's scared can be angry. One sentence he had said kept coming back to my mind, again and again.

Under the circumstances, don't you think the court made a mistake in granting you custody of your young daughter?

I never wanted custody. In all the turmoil of the divorce, of Lauren moving out, packing up, this is yours, this is mine – in all that, the last thing I wanted was custody of a seven-month-old baby. Shelly was just starting to move around the living room, holding onto the furniture. She would say 'Mama'. Her first word. But Lauren didn't want the responsibility and kept saying, 'I can't handle it, Peter. I just can't handle it.' So I took custody. What else could I do?

But now it was almost two years later. I had changed my life. I had changed my job, my schedule. She was *my* daughter now. And the thought of giving her up was like twisting a knife in my stomach.

Under the circumstances, Lieutenant, don't you think . . .

On the monitor, I watched as Cheryl Austin waited in the darkness for the arrival of her lover. I watched the way she looked around the room.

The court made a mistake . . .

No, I thought, the court didn't make a mistake. Lauren couldn't handle it, and had never been able to handle it. Half the time, she skipped on her weekends. She was too busy to see her own daughter. Once after a weekend she returned Michelle to me. Michelle was crying. Lauren said, 'I just don't know what to do with her.' I checked. Her diapers were wet and she had a painful rash. Michelle always gets a rash when her diapers aren't changed promptly.

Lauren hadn't changed her diapers often enough during the weekend. So I changed her, and there were streaks of shit in Michelle's vagina. She hadn't cleaned her own daughter properly.

Don't you think the court made a mistake?

No, I didn't.

Under the circumstances, don't you think –

'Fuck it,' I said.

Theresa stabbed a button, stopped the tapes. The images froze on the monitors all around us. 'What is it?' she said. 'What did you see?'

'Nothing.'

She looked at me.

'I'm sorry. I was thinking of something else.'

'Don't.'

She started the tape again.

On multiple monitors, the man embraced Cheryl Austin. Images from the different cameras were co-ordinated in an eerie way. It was as if we could see all sides of the event – front and back, top and sides. It was like a moving architectural blueprint.

And it felt creepy, to watch.

My two monitors showed the view from the far end of the room, and from high above, looking straight down. Cheryl and her lover were small in one monitor, and in the other one, I saw only the tops of their heads. But I watched.

Standing alongside me, Theresa Asakuma breathed slowly, regularly. In and out. I glanced at her.

'Pay attention.'

I looked back.

The lovers were in a passionate embrace. The man pressed Cheryl back against a desk. In my top view, I could see her face, looking straight up as she lay back. Beside her, a framed picture on the desk fell over.

'There,' I said.

Theresa stopped the tape.

'What?' she said.

'There.' I pointed to the framed picture. It lay flat, facing upward. Reflected in the glass, we could see the outline of the man's head as he bent over Cheryl. It was very dark. Just a silhouette.

'Can you get an image from that?' I said.

'I don't know. Let's try.'

Her hand moved swiftly across the controls, touching them briefly. 'The video image is digital,' she said. 'It's in the computer now. We'll see what we can do with it.' The image began to jump, growing larger in increments as she zoomed in on the picture frame. The image moved past Cheryl's frozen, grainy face, her head thrown back in an instant of passion. Moved down from her shoulder, toward the frame.

As the picture enlarged, it became more grainy. It began to decompose into a pattern of dots, like a newspaper photo held too close to your face. Then the dots themselves enlarged, formed edges, turned into small blocks of gray. Pretty soon I couldn't tell what we were looking at.

'Is this going to work?'

'I doubt it. But there's the edge of the frame, and there's the face.'

I was glad she could see it. I couldn't.

'Let's sharpen.'

She pressed buttons. Computer menus dropped down, flashed back. The image became crisper. Grittier. But I could see the frame. And the outline of the head.

'Sharpen again.'

She did that.

'All right. Now we can adjust our grayscale . . .'

The face in the frame began to emerge from the gloom.

It was chilling.

Enlarged so much, the grain was severe – each pupil of the eyes was a single black spot – and we really couldn't see who it was. The man's eyes were open, and his mouth was twisted, distorted in passion, or arousal, or hate. But we couldn't really tell.

Not really.

'Is that a Japanese face?'

She shook her head. 'There's not enough detail in the original.'

'You can't bring it out?'

'I'll work on it later. But I think, no. It won't ever be there. Let's go on.'

The images snapped back into full movement. Cheryl suddenly shoved the man away, pushing his chest with the flat of her hand. The face disappeared from the picture frame.

We were back to the original five views.

The couple broke and she complained, pushing him repeatedly. Her face looked angry. Now that I had seen the man's face reflected in the frame, I wondered if she had become frightened of what she saw. But it was impossible to tell.

The lovers stood in the deserted room, discussed where to go. She was looking around. He nodded his head. She pointed toward the conference room. He seemed to agree or accept.

They kissed, clinched again. There was a familiarity in the way they joined and parted, joined again.

Theresa saw it, too. 'She knows him.'

'Yes. I'd say.'

Still kissing, the couple moved awkwardly toward the conference room. At this point my monitors were no longer very useful. The far camera showed the whole room, and the couple moving laterally across it, from right to left. But the figures were tiny, and difficult to see. They were moving between the desks, heading toward –

'Wait,' I said. 'What was that?'

She went back, frame by frame.

'There,' I said.

I pointed to the image. 'See that? What's that?'

As the couple moved across the room, the camera tracked past a large Japanese calligraphy scroll hanging on the wall near the elevator. The scroll was encased in glass. For a brief moment, there was a glint of light in the glass. That was what had caught my eye.

A glint of light.

Theresa frowned. 'It's not a reflection from the couple,' she said.

'No.'

'Let's look.'

She began zooming again. The image jumped toward the hanging scroll, growing grittier with each step. The glint enlarged, broke in two fragments. There was a fuzzy spot of light in one corner. And a vertical slit of light, running almost the length of the picture.

'Let's rock it,' she said.

She began to make the image go forward and back, one frame at a time. Flipping from one to the other. In one frame, the vertical slit was missing. In the next frame, it was there. The vertical bar lasted for the next ten frames. Then it was gone, never to reappear. But the fuzzy spot in the corner was always present.

'Hmmm.'

She pushed in on the spot. Under ever-increasing magnification, it disintegrated until it looked like a cluster of stars from an astronomy picture. But it seemed to have some kind of internal organization. I could almost imagine an X shape to it. I said so.

'Yes,' she said. 'Let's sharpen.'

She did that. The computers worked on the data. The fuzzy cluster resolved itself. Now it looked like Roman numerals.

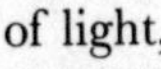

'What the hell is that?' I said.

She kept working. 'Edge trace,' she said. The outline of the Roman numerals appeared more clearly.

ΓIX:Ǝ

Theresa continued to try and resolve it. As she worked, in some ways the image seemed to get better, and in some ways, less clear. But eventually we could recognize it.

TIXƎ

'It's the reflection of an exit sign,' she said. 'There's an exit at the far end of the room opposite the elevators, is that right?'

'Yes,' I said.

'It's being reflected in the glass of the scroll. That's all it is.' She flipped to the next frame. 'But this vertical bar of light. That's interesting. See? It appears, and is gone.' She ran it back and forth several times.

And then I figured it out.

'There's a fire exit back there,' I said. 'And a staircase going downstairs. That must be the reflection of the light from the stairwell as someone opens the door and closes it again.'

'You mean someone came into the room,' she said. 'From the back stairs?'

'Yes.'

'Interesting. Let's try and see who it is.'

She ran the tapes forward. At this high magnification, the grainy image spattered and popped like fireworks on the screen. It was as if the smallest components of the image had a life of their own, their dance independent of the image they assembled to make. But it was exhausting to watch. I rubbed my eyes. 'Jesus.'

'Okay. *There.*'

I looked up. She had frozen the image. I couldn't see anything but erratic black-and-white dots. There seemed to be a pattern but I couldn't tell what it was. It reminded me of the sonograms when Lauren was pregnant. The doctor would say, The head is there, that's the baby's stomach there . . . But I couldn't see anything. It was just abstract. My daughter still in the womb.

The doctor had said, See? She wiggled her fingers. See? Her heart is beating.

I had seen that. I had seen the heart beating. The little heart and the little ribs.

Under the circumstances, Lieutenant, don't you think –

'See?' Theresa said. 'That's his shoulder. That's the outline of the head. Now he is moving forward – see him getting larger? – and now he is standing in that far passageway, looking around the corner. He is cautious. You can see the profile of his nose for a moment as he turns to look. See that? I know it's hard. Watch carefully. Now he is looking at them. He is watching them.'

And suddenly, I could see it. The spots seemed to fall into place. I saw a silhouetted man standing in the hallway by the far exit.

He was watching.

Across the room, the lovers were wrapped up in their kiss. They didn't notice the new arrival.

But someone was watching them. It gave me a chill.

'Can you see who he is?'

She shook her head. 'Impossible. We are at the limits of everything. I cannot even resolve eyes, a mouth. Nothing.'

'Then let's go on.'

The tapes snapped back, full speed. I was jarred by the sudden return to normal size and normal movement. I watched as the lovers, kissing passionately, continued to cross the room.

'So now they are being watched,' Theresa said. 'Interesting. What kind of a girl is this?'

I said, 'I believe the term is *torigaru onnai.*'

She said, 'She is light in her bird? *Tori* what?'

'Never mind. I mean she is a loose woman.'

Theresa shook her head. 'Men always say things like that. To me, it looks like she loves him, but she is troubled in her mind.'

The lovers were approaching the conference room, and Cheryl suddenly twisted away, attempting to break free from the man.

'If she loves him, she's got a strange way of showing it,' I said.

'She senses something is wrong.'

'Why?'

'I don't know. Perhaps she hears something. The other man. I don't know.'

Whatever the reason, Cheryl was struggling with the lover, who now had both arms around her waist and was almost dragging her into the conference room. Cheryl twisted once more at the door, as the man tried to pull her in.

'A good chance here,' Theresa said.

The tape froze again.

All the walls of the conference room were glass. Through the outer walls, the lights of the city were visible. But the inner walls, facing the atrium, were dark enough to act as a black mirror. Since Cheryl and her lover were near the inner glass walls, their images were reflected in the glass as they struggled.

Theresa ran the tape forward, frame by frame, looking for an image that might hold up. From time to time, she zoomed in, probed the pixels, zoomed back out. It was difficult. The two people were moving quickly, and they were often blurred. And the lights from the skyscrapers outside sometimes obscured otherwise good images.

It was frustrating.

It was slow.

Stop. Zoom in. Slide around in the image, trying to locate a section that had enough detail. Give up. Go forward again. Stop again.

Finally, Theresa sighed. 'It's not working. That glass is murder.'

'Then let's keep going.'

I saw Cheryl grab the door frame, trying to keep from being pulled into the conference room. The man finally pulled her free, she slid backward with a look of terror on her face, and then she swung her arms back to hit the man. Her purse went flying. Then they were both inside the room. Silhouettes moving quickly, turning.

The man shoved her back against the table, and Cheryl appeared in the camera that aimed straight down on the conference room. Her short blonde hair contrasted with the dark wood of the table. Her mood changed again, she stopped struggling for a minute. She had a look of expectation. Excitement. She licked her lips. Her eyes followed the man as he leaned over her. He slid her skirt up her hips.

She smiled, pouted, whispered in his ear.

He pulled her panties away, a quick jerk.

She smiled at him. It was a tense smile, half-aroused, half-pleading. She was excited by her own fear.

His hands caressed her throat.

Standing in the darkened laboratory, with the hiss of skaters on the ice above, we watched the final violent act, again and again. It played on five monitors, different angles, as her pale legs went up, onto his shoulders, and he crouched over her, hands fumbling at his trousers. With repetition, I noticed small things not seen before. The way she slid down the table to meet him, wiggling her hips. The way his back arched at the moment of penetration. The change in her smile, catlike, knowing. Calculating. How she urged him on, saying something. Her hands around his back, caressing. The sudden change in mood, the flash of anger in her eyes, the abrupt slap. The way she fought him, first to arouse him, and then later, struggling in a different way, because then something was wrong. The way her eyes bulged, and she had a look of real desperation. Her hands pushing his arms, shoving his coat sleeves up, revealing the tiny metallic sparkle of cuff links. The glint of her watch. Her arm falling back, palm open. Five fingers pale against the black of the table. Then a tremor, the fingers twitching, and stillness.

His slowness to understand something was wrong. The way he went rigid for a moment, then took her head in his hand, moved it back and forth, trying to arouse her, before he finally pulled away. Even looking at his back, you could almost feel his horror. He remained slow, as if in a trance. Pacing around the room in aimless half steps, first this way, then that. Trying to recover his wits, to decide what to do.

Each time I saw the sequence repeated, I felt a different way. The first few times, there was a tension, a voyeuristic sensation, itself almost sexual. And then later, I felt progressively more detached, more analytical. As if I was drifting away, moving back from the monitor. And finally, the entire sequence seemed to break down before my eyes, the bodies losing their human identities altogether, becoming abstractions, elements of design, shifting and moving in dark space.

Theresa said, 'This girl is sick.'

'It looks that way.'

'She is not a victim. Not this one.'

'Maybe not.'

We watched it again. But I no longer knew why we were watching. Finally I said, 'Let's go forward, Theresa.'

We had been running the sequence to a certain point on the tape counter, and then going back to run again. So we had seen a part of the tape again and again, but we hadn't gone farther. Almost immediately as we went forward, something remarkable happened. The man stopped pacing and looked sharply off to one side – as if he had seen something, or heard something.

'The other man?' I said.

'Perhaps.' She pointed to the monitors. 'This is the area in the tapes where the shadows do not seem to match up. Now, we know why.'

'Something was erased?'

She ran the tape backward. On the side monitor view, we could see the man look up, in the direction of the exit. He gave every appearance that he had seen someone. But he did not appear frightened or guilty.

She zoomed in. The man was just a silhouette. 'You can't see anything, can you?'

'Profile.'

'What about it?'

'I am looking at the jaw line. Yes. See? The jaw is moving. He is talking.'

'Talking to the other man?'

'Or to himself. But he is certainly looking off. And now see? He has sudden new energy.'

The man was moving around the conference room. His behavior purposeful. I remembered how confusing this part had been, when I saw it the night before at the police station. But with five cameras, it was clear. We could see exactly what he was doing. He picked up the panties from the floor.

And then he bent over the dead girl, and removed her watch.

'No kidding,' I said. 'He took her watch.'

I could only think of one reason why: the watch must have an inscription. The man put the panties and the watch in his pocket, and was turning to go, when the image froze again. Theresa had stopped it.

'What is it?' I said.

She pointed to one of the five monitors. 'There,' she said.

She was looking at the side view, from the overall camera. It showed the conference room as seen from the atrium. I saw the silhouette of the girl on the table, and the man inside the conference room.

'Yeah? So?'

'*There,*' she said, pointing. 'They forgot to erase that one.' In the corner of the screen, I saw a ghostly form. The angle and the lighting were just right to enable us to see him. It was a man.

The third man.

He had come forward, and now was standing in the middle of the atrium, looking toward the killer, inside the conference room. The image of the third man was complete, reflected in the glass. But it was faint.

'Can you get that? Can you make it out?'

'I can try,' she said.

The zooms began. She punched in, saw the image decompose. She sharpened it, heightened contrast. The image streaked, and went dull, flat. She coaxed it back, reconstituted it. She moved closer, enlarging it. It was tantalizing. We could almost make an identification.

Almost, but not quite.

'Frame advance,' she said.

Now, one by one, the frames clicked ahead. The image of the man was alternately sharper, blurred, sharp.

And then at last, we saw the waiting man clearly.

'No *shit,*' I said.

'You know who he is?'

'Yes,' I said. 'It's Eddie Sakamura.'

After that, we made swift progress. We knew, without a doubt, that the tapes had been altered and the identity of the killer had been changed. We watched as the killer came out of the room, and moved toward the exit, with a regretful look back at the dead girl.

I said, 'How could they change the killer's face in just a few hours?'

'They have very sophisticated mapping software,' she said. 'It's by far the most advanced in the world. The Japanese are becoming much better in software. Soon they will surpass the Americans in that, as they already have in computers.'

'So they did it with better software?'

'Even with the best software it would be daring to try it. And the Japanese are not daring. So I suspect this particular job was not so hard. Because the killer spends most of his time kissing the girl, or in shadow, so you can't see his face. I am guessing they had the idea very late, as an afterthought, to make a change of identity. Because they saw that they only had to change this part coming up . . . There, where he passes the mirror.'

In the mirror, I saw the face of Eddie Sakamura, clearly. His hand brushing the wall, showing the scar.

'You see,' she said, 'if they changed that, the rest of the tape could pass. In all the cameras. It was a golden opportunity, and they took it. That is what I think.'

On the monitors, Eddie Sakamura went past the mirror, into shadow. She ran it back. 'Let's look.'

She put up the reflection in the mirror, and step-zoomed into the face until it broke into blocks. 'Ah,' she said. 'You see the pixels. You see the regularity. Someone has done some retouching here. Here, on the cheekbone, where there is a shadow beneath his eye. Normally you get some irregularity at the edge between two gray scales. Here, the line is cleaned up. It has been repaired. And let me see –'

The image spun laterally.

'Yes. Here too.'

More blocks. I couldn't tell what she was looking at. 'What is it?'

'His right hand. Where the scar is. You see, the scar has been added, you can tell from the way the pixels configure.'

I couldn't see it, but I took her word for it. 'Then who was the actual killer?'

She shook her head. 'It will be difficult to determine. We have searched the reflections and we have not found it. There is a final procedure which I did not try, because it is the easiest of all, but it is also the easiest to change. That is to search the shadow detail.'

'Shadow detail?'

'Yes. We can try to do image intensification in the black areas of the picture, in the shadows and the silhouettes. There may be a place where there is enough ambient light to enable us to derive a recognizable face. We can try.'

She didn't sound enthusiastic about the prospects.

'You don't think it will work?'

She shrugged. 'No. But we might as well try. It is all that is left.'

'Okay,' I said. 'Let's do it.'

She started to run the tape in reverse, walking Eddie Sakamura backward from the mirror toward the conference room. 'Wait a minute,' I said. 'What happens after the mirror? We haven't looked at that part.'

'I looked earlier. He goes under an overhang, and moves away, toward the staircase.'

'Let's see it anyway.'

'All right.'

The tape ran forward. Quickly, Eddie Sakamura went toward the exit. His face flashed in the mirror as he went past it. The more often I saw it, the more fake that moment looked. It even seemed as if a small delay, a tiny pause, had been added to his movement. To help us make the identification.

Now the killer walked on, into a dark passage leading toward the staircase,which was somewhere around the corner, out of view. The far wall was light, so he was silhouetted. But there was no detail visible in the silhouette. He was entirely dark.

'No,' she said. 'I remember this part. Nothing here. Too dark. *Kuronbō*. What they used to call me. Black person.'

'I thought you said you could do shadow detail.'

'I can, but not here. Anyway, I am sure this part has been retouched. They know we will examine the section of tape on either side of the mirror. They know we will go in with pixel microscopes and scan every frame. So they will have fixed that area carefully. And they will blacken the shadows on this person.'

'Okay, but even so –'

'Hey!' she said suddenly. 'What was that?'

The image froze.

I saw the outline of the killer, walking away toward the white wall in the background, the exit sign above his head.

'Looks like a silhouette.'

'Yes, but something is wrong.'

She ran the tape backward, slowly.

As I watched, I said, '*Machigai no umi oshete kudasaii.*' It was a phrase I had learned from one of my early classes.

She smiled in the darkness. 'I must help you with your Japanese, Lieutenant. Are you asking me if there has been a mistake?'

'Yes.'

'The word is *umu,* not *umi. Umi* is ocean. *Umu* means you are asking yes or no about something. And yes, I believe there may have been a mistake.'

The tape continued backward, the silhouette of the killer coming back toward us. She sucked in her breath, in surprise.

'There *is* a mistake. I cannot believe it. Do you see it now?'

'No,' I said.

She ran the tape forward for me. I watched as the man walked away in silhouette.

'There, do you see it now?'

'No. I'm sorry.'

She was becoming irritable. 'Pay attention. Look at the shoulder. Watch the shoulder of the man. See how it rises and falls with each step, in a rhythmic way, and then suddenly . . . There! You see it?'

I did. Finally. 'The outline seemed to jump. To get bigger.'

'Yes. Exactly. To jump bigger.' She adjusted the controls. 'Quite a lot bigger, Lieutenant. They tried to blend the jump into the up-step, to make it less conspicuous. But they did not try very hard. It is clear anyway.'

'And what does that mean?'

'It means they are arrogant,' she said. She sounded angry. I couldn't tell why.

So I asked her.

'Yes. Now it pisses me off,' she said. She was zooming in on the image, her one hand moving quickly. 'It is because they have made an obvious mistake. They expect we will be sloppy. We will not be thorough. We will not be intelligent. We will not be *Japanese.*'

'But –'

'Oh, I *hate* them.' The image moved, shifted. She was concentrating on the outline of the head, now. 'You know Takeshita Noboru?'

I said, 'Is that a manufacturer?'

'No. Takeshita was prime minister. A few years ago, he made a joke about visiting American sailors on a Navy ship. He said America is now so poor, the Navy boys cannot afford to come ashore to enjoy Japan. Everything is too expensive for them. He said they could only remain on their ship and give each other AIDS. Big joke in Japan.'

'He said that?'

She nodded. 'If I was American, and someone said that to me, I would take this ship away, and tell Japan to go fuck itself, pay for its own defense. You didn't know Takeshita said this?'

'No . . .'

'American news.' She shook her head. 'Such nothing.'

She was furious, working quickly. Her fingers slipped on the controls, the image jumped back, lost definition. 'Shit fuck.'

'Take it easy, Theresa.'

'Fuck, take it easy. We're going to score now!'

She moved in on the silhouetted head, isolating it, then following it, frame by frame, I saw the image jump larger, distinctly.

'You see, that is the join,' she said. 'That is where the changed image goes back to the original. Here on, it's original material on the tape. This is the original man walking away from us, now.'

The silhouette moved toward the far wall. She proceeded frame by frame. Then the outline began to change shape.

'Ah. Okay. Good, what I hoped for . . .'

'What is it?'

'He is taking a last look. A look back at the room. See? The head is turning. There is his nose, and now, the nose is gone again, because he has turned completely. Now he is looking back at us.'

The silhouette was dense black.

'Lot of good it does us.'

'Watch.'

More controls.

'The detail is there,' she said. 'It is like dark exposure on film. The detail has been recorded, but we cannot see it yet. So . . . Now I have enhancement. And now I will get the shadow detail . . . Now!'

And in a sudden, shocking moment, the dark silhouette blossomed, the wall behind flaring white, making a kind of halo around the head.

The dark face became lighter, and we could see the face for the first time, distinctly and clearly.

'Huh, white man.' She sounded disappointed.

'My God,' I said.

'You know who he is?'

'Yes,' I said.

The features were twisted with tension, the lip turned up in a kind of snarl. But the identity was unmistakable.

I was looking at the face of Senator John Morton.

I sat back, staring at the frozen image. I heard the hum of the machinery. I heard water dripping into buckets, somewhere in the darkness of the laboratory. I heard Theresa breathing alongside me, panting like a runner who has finished a race.

I sat there and just stared at the screen. Everything fell into place, like a jigsaw puzzle that assembled itself before my eyes.

Julia Young: She has a boyfriend who travels a lot. She's always traveling. New York, Washington, Seattle . . . she meets him. She's madly in love with him.

Jenny, in the TV studio: Morton has a young girlfriend that's driving him crazy. Makes him jealous. Some young girl.

Eddie: She likes to cause trouble, this girl. She likes to make turmoil.

Jenny: I've seen this girl hanging around at parties with some of the Washington types for about six months now.

Eddie: She was a sick girl. She liked pain.

Jenny: Morton heads the Senate Finance Committee. The one that's been having hearings about this MicroCon sale.

Cole, the security guard, in the bar: They have the big guys in their pocket. They own 'em. We can't beat 'em now.

And Connor: Somebody wants this investigation to be over. They want us to give it up.

And Morton: So your investigation is formally concluded?

'Hell,' I said.

She said, 'Who is he?'

'He's a senator.'

'Oh.' She looked at the screen. 'And why do they care about him?'

'He has a powerful position in Washington. And I think he has something to do with the sale of a company. Maybe other reasons, too.'

She nodded.

I said, 'Can we print a picture of this?'

'No. We don't have equipment for hard copies. The lab can't afford it.'

'Then what can we do? I need something to take with me.'

'I can take a Polaroid for you,' she said. 'Not great, but okay for now.' She started poking around the lab, stumbling in the dark. Finally she came back with a camera. She moved close to the screen and shot several copies.

We waited for them to come out, standing in the blue light from the monitors.

'Thanks,' I said. 'For all your help.'

'You are welcome. And I'm sorry.'

'Why?'

'I know you expected it would be a Japanese man.'

I realized she was speaking for herself. I didn't answer her. The pictures darkened. They were good quality, the image clear. As I slipped them in my pocket, I felt something hard there. I brought it out.

'You have a Japanese passport?' she said.

'No. It's not mine. It's Eddie's. I put it back in my pocket. 'I have to go,' I said. 'I have to find Captain Connor.'

'All right,' She turned back to the monitors.

'What are you going to do?' I said.

'I will stay, and work more.'

I left her, went out the back door, and made my way down the dark passageway to the outside.

Blinking in the harsh daylight, I went to a pay phone and called Connor. He was in the car.

'Where are you?' I said.

'Back at the hotel.'

'What hotel?'

'The Four Seasons,' Connor said. 'It's Senator Morton's hotel.'

'What are you doing there?' 'I said. 'Do you know that –'

'*Kōhai*,' he said. 'Open line, remember? Call yourself a taxi and meet me at 1430 Westwood Boulevard. We will meet there in twenty minutes.'

'But how –'

'No more questions.' And he hung up.

I looked at the building at 1430 Westwood Boulevard. It had a plain brown facade, just a door with a painted number. On one side was a French bookstore. On the other side was a watch repair place.

I went up and knocked on the door. I noticed a small sign in Japanese characters beneath the numbers.

Nothing happened, so I opened the door. I found myself in an elegant, tiny sushi bar. It had only four seats for customers. Connor was alone there, sitting at the far end. He waved to me. 'Say hello to Imae. The best sushi chef in Los Angeles. Imae-san, Sumisu-san.'

The chef nodded and smiled. He put something on the shelf before my seat. '*Kore o dōzo, Sumisu-san.*'

I sat down. '*Dōmo, Imae-san.*'

'*Wakatta.*'

I looked at the sushi. It was some kind of pink fish eggs, with a raw yellow egg yolk sitting on top. I thought it looked revolting.

I turned to Connor.

He said, '*Kore o tabetakoto arukai?*'

I shook my head. 'Sorry. You lost me.'

'You'll have to work on your Japanese, for your new girlfriend.'

'What new girlfriend?'

Connor said, 'I thought you would thank me. I gave you all that time with her.'

'You mean Theresa?'

He smiled. 'You can do much worse, *kōhai*. And I gather you have, in the past. Anyway, I asked you if you knew what that was.' He pointed to the sushi.

'No, I don't.'

'Quail egg and salmon roe,' he said. 'Good protein. Energy. You need it.'

I said, 'Do I have to?'

Imae said, 'Make you strong for girlfriend.' And he laughed. He said something quickly in Japanese to Connor.

Connor replied, and the two had a good laugh.

'What's funny?' I said. But I wanted to change the subject, so I ate the first of the sushi. If you got past the slimy texture, it was actually very good.

Imae said, 'Good?'

'Very good,' I said. I ate the second one, and turned to Connor. 'You know what we found on those tapes? It's unbelievable.'

Connor held up his hand. 'Please. You must learn the Japanese way to have relaxation. Everything in its place. *Oaisō onegai shimasu.*'

'*Hai, Connor-san.*'

The sushi chef produced the bill, and Connor peeled off money. He bowed and there was a rapid exchange in Japanese.

'We're leaving now?'

'Yes,' Connor said. 'I've already eaten, and you, my friend, can't afford to be late.'

'For what?'

'For your ex-wife, remember? We'd better go to your apartment now, and meet her.'

I was driving again. Connor was staring out the window. 'How did you know it was Morton?'

'I didn't,' Connor said. 'At least, not until this morning. But it was clear to me last night that the tape had been altered.'

I thought of all the effort that Theresa and I had gone to, all the zooming and inspection and image manipulation. 'You're telling me you just looked at the tape, and you could tell?'

'Yes.'

'How?'

'There was one glaring error. Remember when you met Eddie at the party? He had a scar on his hand.'

'Yes. It looked like an old burn scar.'

'Which hand was it on?'

'Which hand?' I frowned. I thought back to the meeting. Eddie in the cactus garden at night, smoking cigarettes, flicking them away. Eddie turning, moving nervously. Holding the cigarettes. The scar had been on . . . 'His left hand,' I said.

'That's right,' Connor said.

'But the scar appears on the tape, too,' I said. 'You see it clearly when he walks past the mirror. His hand touches the wall for a moment –'

I stopped.

On the tape, his *right* hand had touched the wall.

'Jesus,' I said.

'Yes,' Connor said. 'They made a mistake. Maybe they got confused about what was a reflection and what wasn't. But I imagine they were working hastily, and they couldn't remember which hand it was, and they just added the scar anyway. Mistakes like that happen.'

'So last night, you saw the scar on the wrong hand . . .'

'Yes. And I knew at once that the tape was changed,' Connor said. 'I had to prepare you to analyze the tape in the morning. So I sent you to SID, to get names of places that would work on the tape. And then I went home to bed.'

'But you allowed us to arrest Eddie. Why? You must have known that Eddie wasn't the killer.'

'Sometimes, you have to let things play out,' Connor said. 'It was clear we were meant to think that Eddie killed the girl. So: play it out.'

'But an innocent man died,' I said.

'I wouldn't call Eddie innocent,' Connor said. 'Eddie was in this up to his neck.'

'And Senator Morton? How did you know it was Morton?'

'I didn't, until he called us in for that little meeting today. Then he gave himself away.'

'How?'

'He was smooth. You have to think about what he actually said,' Connor said. 'Wedged in between all the bullshit, he asked us three times if our investigation was finished. And he asked us if the murder had anything to do with MicroCon. When you think about it, that's a very peculiar question.'

'Why? He has contacts. Mr Hanada. Other people. He told us that.'

'No,' Connor said, shaking his head. 'If you take away all the bullshit, what Senator Morton told us was his train of thought: Is the investigation over? And can you connect it to MicroCon? Because I am now going to change my position on the MicroCon sale.'

'Okay . . .'

'But he never explained a crucial point. Why was he changing his position on the MicroCon sale?'

'He told us why,' I said. 'He had no support, nobody cares.'

Connor handed me a Xerox. I glanced at it. It was a page from a newspaper. I gave it back. 'I'm driving. Tell me.'

'This is an interview Senator Morton gave in *The Washington Post.* He repeats his stand on MicroCon. It's against the interest of national defense and American competitiveness to sell the company. Blah blah. Eroding our technology base and selling off our future to the Japanese. Blah blah. That was his position on Thursday morning. On Thursday night he attends a party in California. By Friday morning, he has a different view of MicroCon. The sale is fine with him. Now you tell me why.'

'Jesus,' I said. 'What are we going to do?'

Because there is a thing about being a policeman. Most of the time, you feel pretty good. But at certain points, it comes back to you that you are just a cop. The truth is, you're pretty far down the ladder. And you are reluctant to take on certain kinds of people, certain kinds of power. It gets messy. It gets out of control. You can have your ass handed to you.

'What do we do' I said again.

'One thing at a time,' Connor said. 'Is this your apartment building up here?'

The TV minivans were lined up along the street. There were several sedans with PRESS signs behind the windshield. A knot of reporters stood outside the front door to my apartment, and along the street. Among the reporters I saw Weasel Wilhelm, leaning against his car. I didn't see my ex-wife.

'Keep driving, *kōhai,*' Connor said. 'Go to the end of the block and turn right.'

'Why?'

'I took the liberty of calling the D.A.'s office a while ago. I arranged for you to meet your wife in the park down here.'

'You did?'

'I thought it would be better for everybody.'

I drove around the corner. Hampton Park was adjacent to the elementary school. At this hour of the afternoon, kids were outside, playing baseball. I drove slowly along the street, looking for a parking place. I passed a sedan with two people inside. There was a man in the passenger seat, smoking a cigarette. There was a woman behind the wheel, drumming her fingers on the dashboard. It was Lauren.

I parked the car.

'I'll wait here,' Connor said. 'Good luck.'

She always favored pale colors. She was wearing a beige suit and a cream silk blouse. Her blonde hair was pulled back. No jewelry. Sexy and businesslike at the same time, her particular talent.

We walked along the sidewalk on the edge of the park, looking at the kids playing ball. Neither of us said anything. The man who had come with her waited in the car. A block away, we could see the press clustered outside my apartment.

Lauren looked at them and said, 'Jesus *Christ,* Peter. I can't believe you, I really can't. This is very badly handled. This is very insensitive to my position.'

I said, 'Who told them?'

'Not me.'

'Someone did. Someone told them you were coming at four o'clock.'

'Well, it wasn't me.'

'You just happened to show up with full makeup on?'

'I was in court this morning.'

'Okay. Fine.'

'Fuck you, Peter.'

'I said, fine.'

'Such a fucking detective.'

She turned, and we walked back the way we had come. Moving away from the press.

She sighed. 'Look,' she said. 'Let's try and be civil about this.'

'Okay.'

'I don't know how you managed to get yourself into this mess, Peter. I'm sorry, but you're going to have to give up custody. I can't permit my daughter to be raised in a suspect environment. I can't allow that. I have my position to think of. My reputation in the office.'

Lauren was always preoccupied with appearances. 'Why is the environment suspect?'

'Why? Child abuse is an extremely serious allegation, Peter.'

'There's no child abuse.'

'The allegations from your past must be dealt with.'

'You know all about those allegations,' I said. 'You were married to me. You know everything about it.'

She said stubbornly, 'Michelle has to be tested.'

'Fine. The exam will be negative.'

'At this point, I don't really care what the exam shows. It's gone beyond that, Peter. I'm going to have to get custody. For my peace of mind.'

'Oh, for Christ's sake.'

'Yes, Peter?'

'You don't know what it's like to raise a child. It'll take too much time away from your career.'

'I have no choice, Peter. You have left me no choice.' Now she sounded long suffering. Martydom was always one of her strong suits.

I said, 'Lauren, you know the past accusations are false. You're just running with this thing because Wilhelm called you.'

'He didn't call *me*. He called the assistant D.A. He called my *boss*.'

'Lauren.'

'I'm sorry, Peter. But you brought it on yourself.'

'Lauren.'

'I mean it.'

'Lauren, this is very dangerous.'

She laughed harshly. 'Tell me. You think I don't know how dangerous this is, Peter? This could be my ass.'

'What are you talking about?'

'What do you *think* I'm talking about, you son of a bitch?' she said, furiously. 'I'm talking about Las Vegas.'

I was silent. I didn't follow her line of thought at all.

'Look,' she said. 'How many times have you been to Las Vegas?'

'Just once.'

'And the one time you went, you won big?'

'Lauren, you know all about that –'

'Yes, I do. Clearly I do. And what is the timing of your big winning trip to Las Vegas, and the accusations against you of child abuse? A week apart? Two weeks apart?'

So that was it. She was worried that somebody could put those two things together, that it could be traced back, somehow. And that it would implicate her.

'You should have made another trip, last year.'

'I was busy.'

'If you remember, Peter, I told you to go every year, for the next couple of years. Establish a pattern.'

'I was busy. I had a child to raise.'

'Well.' She shook her head. 'Now we're here.'

I said, 'What's the problem? They'll never figure it out.'

That was when she really exploded. 'Never figure it out? They've *already* figured it out. They already *know*, Peter. I'm sure they've already talked to Martinez or Hernandez or whoever that couple is.'

'But they can't possibly –'

'For Christ's *sake*. How do you think somebody gets a job as Japanese liaison? How did *you* get the job, Peter?'

I frowned, thinking back. It was more than a year ago. 'There was a posting of the job in the department. A list of candidates applied for it . . .'

'Yes. And then what?'

I hesitated. The truth was, I wasn't sure exactly what happened administratively. I had just applied for the job and had forgotten all about it, until it came through. I had been busy in those days. Working in the press section was a hectic job.

'I'll tell you what happens,' Lauren said. 'The chief of Special Services for the department makes a final determination of appropriate candidates, *in consultation with members of the Asian community*.'

'Well, that's probably true, but I don't see –'

'And do you know how long the members of the Asian community take to review the list of candidates? *Three months,* Peter. That's long enough to learn everything about the people on that list. *Everything*. They know everything from the size of your shirt collar to your financial status. And believe me, they know about the allegations of child abuse. And your trip to Las Vegas. And they can put it together. *Anybody* can put it together.'

I was going to protest, when I found myself remembering what Ron said earlier in the day: Now they watch the backhaul.

She said, 'You're going to stand there and tell me you don't know how all this works? That you weren't paying attention to the process? Christ, Peter, come on. You understood what was involved in that liaison job: *you wanted the money*. Just like everybody else who has anything to do with the Japanese. You know how they make their deals. There's something for everyone. You get something. The department gets something. The chief gets something. Everybody gets taken care of. And in return they get to pick exactly the kind of person they want as a liaison. They know they have a handle on you going in. And now they have a handle on me, too. All because you didn't take your goddamn trip to Las Vegas last year and establish a pattern, the way I told you to.'

'So now you think you have to get custody of Michelle?'

She sighed. 'At this point, we're just playing out our roles.'

She glanced at her watch, and looked toward the reporters. I saw that she was impatient to get on with it, to meet the press and make the speech she had already prepared for herself. Lauren had always had a strong sense of drama.

'Are you sure what your role is, Lauren? Because it's going to get very messy around here in the next few hours. You may not want to be involved.'

'I *am* involved.'

'No.' I took the Polaroid out of my pocket and showed it to her.

'What's this?'

'That's a video frame from the Nakamoto security tapes, taken last night. At the time of the murder of Cheryl Austin.'

She frowned at the picture. 'You're kidding.'

'No.'

'You're going with this?'

'We have to.'

'You're going to arrest Senator Morton? You're *out* of your *fucking* mind.'

'Maybe.'

'You'll never see daylight, Peter.'

'Maybe.'

'They'll bury you so fast and so deep you'll never know what hit you.'

'Maybe.'

'You can't make this work. You know you can't. In the end, it's only going to harm Michelle.'

I didn't say anything to that. I found I liked her less all the time. We walked along, her spike heels clicking on the sidewalk.

Finally she said, 'Peter, if you insist on following this reckless course of action, there's nothing I can do. As your friend, I advise you not to. But if you insist, there is nothing I can do to help you.'

I didn't answer. I waited and watched her. In the hard sunlight, I saw she was starting to get wrinkles. I saw the dark roots of her hair. The fleck of lipstick on her tooth. She took off her sunglasses and glanced at me, her eyes worried. Then she turned away, looking toward the press. She tapped the sunglasses in the palm of her hand.

'If this is really what's happening, Peter, I think maybe I had better hold off a day and let events take their course.'

'All right.'

'You understand: I'm not dropping my concerns, Peter.'

'I understand.'

'But I don't think the question of Michelle's custody should be mixed up in some other, crazy controversy.'

'Of course not.'

She put her glasses back on. 'I feel sorry for you, Peter. I really do. At one time you had a promising future in the department. I know you've been mentioned for a position under the chief. But nothing can save you if you do this.'

I smiled. 'Well.'

'You have anything besides photographic evidence?'

'I don't know if I should give you too many details.'

'Because if you only have photographic evidence, you have no case, Peter. The D.A. won't touch it. Photographic evidence doesn't fly anymore. It's too easily doctored. The courts know it. If all you have is a picture of this guy doing the crime, it won't wash.'

'We'll see.'

'Peter,' she said. 'You are going to lose everything. Your job, your career, your child, everything. Wake up. Don't do it.'

She started back toward the car. I walked with her. We didn't say anything. I waited for her to ask how Michelle was, but she never did. It wasn't surprising. She had other things to think about. Finally we arrived at her car, and she went around to the driver's side to get in.

'Lauren.'

She looked at me over the top of the car.

'Let's keep it clean for the next twenty-four hours, okay? No well-placed calls to anybody.'

'Don't worry,' she said. 'I never heard any of this. Frankly, I wish I never heard of *you*.'

And she got in the car and drove off. As I watched her go, I felt my shoulders drop, and a tension leave me. It was more than the fact that I'd done what I set out to do – I had talked her out of it, at least for a while. It was more than that. There was something else, finally gone.

Connor and I went up the rear stairs of my apartment building, avoiding the press. I told him what had happened. He shrugged.

'This was a surprise to you? How the liaisons are chosen?'

'Yeah. I guess I never paid attention.'

He nodded. 'That's how it happens. The Japanese are very skilled at providing what they call incentives. Originally, the department had qualms about letting outsiders say anything about which officers would be chosen. But the Japanese said they simply wanted to be consulted. Their recommendations wouldn't be binding. And they pointed out that it made sense for them to have some input in the choice of liaisons.'

'Uh-huh . . .'

'And just to show they were even-handed, they proposed a contribution to the officers' relief fund, to benefit the whole department.'

'How much was that?'

'I think half a million. And the chief was asked to come to Tokyo and consult on criminal record-keeping systems. Three-week trip. One-week stopover in Hawaii. All first class. And lots of publicity, which the chief loves.'

We got to the second-floor landing. Went up to the third.

'So,' Connor said, 'by the time it's all finished, it's rather difficult for the department to ignore the recommendations of the Asian community. Too much is at stake.'

'I feel like quitting,' I said.

'That's always an option,' he said. 'Anyway, you got your wife to back off?'

'My ex-wife. She got the point right away. She's a finely tuned political animal, Lauren is. But I had to tell her who the murderer was.'

He shrugged. 'There's not much she can do in the next couple of hours.'

I said, 'But what about these pictures? She says they won't stand up in court. And Sanders said the same thing: the day of photographic evidence is over. Do we have any other evidence?'

'I've been working on that,' Connor said. 'I think we're all right.'

'How.'

Connor shrugged.

We came to the back entrance to my apartment. I unlocked the door, and we went into the kitchen. It was empty. I went down the corridor to the front hall. My apartment was quiet. The doors to the living room were closed. But there was the distinct smell of cigarette smoke.

Elaine, my housekeeper, was standing in the front hall, looking out the window at the reporters on the street below. She turned when she heard us. She looked frightened.

I said, 'Is Michelle all right?'

'Yes.'

'Where is she?'

'Playing in the living room.'

'I want to see her.'

Elaine said, 'Lieutenant, there's something I have to tell you first.'

'Never mind,' Connor said. 'We already know.'

He threw open the door to the living room. And I had the biggest shock of my life.

John Morton sat in the makeup chair at the television studio, a Kleenex tucked around his collar, while the girl powdered his forehead. Standing at his side, his aide Woodson said, 'This is how they recommend you handle it.' He handed a fax to Morton.

'The basic through-line,' Woodson said, 's that foreign investment invigorates America. America is made stronger by the influx of foreign money. America has much to learn from Japan.

'And we aren't learning it,' Morton said gloomily.

'Well, the argument can be made,' Woodson said. 'It's a viable position and as you can see, the way Marjorie shaped it, it doesn't read as a change of position so much as a refinement of your previous view. You can skate on this one, John. I don't think it is going to be an issue.'

'Is the question even going to come up?'

'I think so. I've told the reporters you are prepared to discuss a modification of your position on MicroCon. How you now favor the sale.'

'Who'll ask it?'

'Probably Frank Pierce of the *Times*.'

Morton nodded. 'He's okay.'

'Yeah. Business orientation. Should be fine. You can talk about free markets, fair trade. Lack of national security issues on this sale. All that.'

The makeup girl finished, and Morton stood up from the chair.

'Senator, I'm sorry to bother you, but could I have your autograph?'

'Sure,' he said.

'It's for my son.'

'Sure,' he said.

Woodson said, 'John we have a rough assembly of the commercial if you want to see it. It's very rough, but you might like to give comments. I've set it up for you in the next room.'

'How much time have I got?'

'Nine minutes to airtime.'

'Fine.'

He started out the door and saw us. 'Good evening, gentlemen,' he said. 'You need me for anything?'

'Just a short conversation, Senator,' Connor said.

'I've got to look at a tape,' Morton said. 'Then can we talk. But I've only got a couple of minutes . . .'

'That's all right,' Connor said.

We followed him into another room, which overlooked the studio below. Down there, on a beige-colored set that said NEWSMAKERS reporters were shuffling through their notes and being fitted with microphones. Morton sat in front of a television set, and Woodson plugged in a cassette.

We saw the commercial that was shot earlier in the day. It had a timecode running at the bottom of the frame, and it opened with Senator Morton, looking determined, walking over the golf course.

The basic message was that America had lost its economic competitiveness, and that we had to get it back.

'It's time for all of us to pull together,' Morton said, on the monitor. 'Everyone from our politicians in Washington, to our leaders of business and labor, to our teachers and children, to all of us in our homes. We need to pay our bills as we go, and cut the government deficit. We need to increase savings. To improve our roads and education. We need a government policy of energy conservation – for our environment, for our children's lungs, and for our global competitiveness.'

The camera moved close to the senator's face, for his closing remarks.

'There are some who say that we are entering a new era of global business,' he said. 'They say it no longer matters where companies are located, or where things are made. That ideas of national economies are old-fashioned and out of date. To those people, I say – Japan doesn't think so. Germany doesn't think so. The most successful countries in the world today maintain strong national policies for energy conservation, for the control of imports, for promotion of exports. They nourish their industries, protecting them against unfair competition from abroad. Business and government work together to look after their own people and their jobs. And those countries are doing better than America, because those economic policies reflect the real world. Their policies work. Ours don't. We do not live in an ideal world, and until we do, America had better face the truth. We had better build our own brand of hard-nosed economic nationalism. We had better take care of Americans. Because nobody else will.

'I want to make it clear: the industrial giants of Japan and Germany are not the cause of our problems. Those countries are challenging America with new realities – and it is up to us to face those realities, and meet their economic challenge head on. If we do so, our great country will enter an era of unparalleled prosperity. But if we continue as we are, mouthing the ancient platitudes of a free market economy, disaster awaits us. The choice is ours. Join me in choosing to meet the new realities – and to make a better economic future for the American people.'

The screen went blank.

Morton sat back. 'When does this run?'

'It'll start in nine weeks. Test run in Chicago and the Twin Cities, associated focus groups, any modifications, then the national break in July.'

'Long after MicroCon . . .'

'Oh, yes.'

'Okay, good. Go with it.'

Woodson took the tape, and left the room. Morton turned to us. 'Well? What can I do for you?'

Connor waited until the door had closed. Then he said, 'Senator, you can tell us about Cheryl Austin.'

There was a pause. Morton looked at each of us. A blank expression came over his face. 'Cheryl Austin?'

'Yes, Senator.'

'I'm not sure that I know who –'

'Yes, Senator,' Connor said. And he handed Morton a watch. It was a woman's gold Rolex.

'Where did you get this?' Morton said. His voice was low now, icy.

A woman knocked on the door. 'Six minutes, Senator.' She closed the door.

'Where did you get this?' he repeated.

'Don't you know?' Connor said. 'You haven't even looked at the back. At the inscription.'

'*Where did you get this?*'

'Senator, we'd like you to talk to us about her.' He took a glassine bag from his pocket, and set it on the table next to Morton. It contained a pair of women's black panties.

'I have nothing to say to you gentlemen,' Morton said. 'Nothing at all.'

Connor took a videotape from his pocket, and set it next to the senator. 'This is a tape from one of five different cameras which recorded the incident on the forty-sixth floor. The tape has been altered, but it was still possible to extract an image that shows who the person with Cheryl Austin was.'

'I have nothing to say,' Morton said. 'Tapes can be edited and changed and then changed again. It doesn't mean anything. This is all lies and baseless allegation.'

'I'm sorry, Senator,' Connor said.

Morton stood up and began to pace. 'I want to impress upon you gentlemen the severity of the charges that you are considering. Tapes can be altered. These particular tapes have been in the custody of a Japanese corporation which, it could be argued, has a wish to exert influence over me. Whatever they may or may not show, I assure you they will not stand up to scrutiny. The public will clearly see this as an attempt to blacken the name of one of the few Americans willing to speak up against the Japanese threat. And as far as I am concerned, you two are pawns in the hands of foreign powers. You don't understand the consequences of your actions. You are making damaging allegations without proof. You have no witnesses to anything that may allegedly have happened. In fact, I would even say –'

'Senator.' Connor's voice was soft but insistent. 'Before you go any farther, and say anything you may regret, would you look down at the studio? There's somebody there you need to see.'

'What is the meaning of this?'

'Just look, Senator. If you would, please.'

Snorting angrily, Morton strode to the window and looked down at the studio. I looked too. I saw the reporters swiveling in their chairs, laughing and joking with each other as they waited to ask questions. I saw the moderator, adjusting his tie and clipping on his mike. I saw a workman wiping the shiny sign that said NEWSMAKERS. And in the corner, standing right where we had told him to stand, I saw a familiar figure with his hands in his pockets, looking up at us.

Eddie Sakamura.

Of course Connor had put it all together. When he opened the door to my living room and saw my daughter sitting on the floor, playing with her Tinkertoys with Eddie Sakamura, he hadn't even blinked. He just said, 'Hello, Eddie. I was wondering how long it'd take you to get here.'

'I've been here all day,' Eddie said. He sounded put out. 'You guys. Never come here. I wait and wait. Have a peanut butter jelly sandwich with Shelly. You have a nice girl, Lieutenant. Cute girl.'

'Eddie is funny,' my daughter said. 'He smokes, Daddy.'

'I see that,' I said. I felt slow and stupid. I was still trying to understand.

My daughter came over and held her arms up. 'Pick me up, Daddy.' I picked her up.

'Very nice girl,' Eddie said. 'We made a windmill. See?' He spun the spokes of the Tinkertoy. 'Works.'

I said, 'I thought you were dead.'

'Me?' he laughed. 'No. Never dead. Tanaka dead. Mess hell out of my car, too.' He shrugged. 'I have bad luck with Ferraris.'

'So does Tanaka,' Connor said.

I said, 'Tanaka?'

Michelle said, 'Daddy, can I watch Cinderella?'

'Not right now,' I said. 'Why was Tanaka in the car?'

'Panicky guy,' Eddie said. 'Very nervous guy. Maybe guilty, too. Must have got scared, I don't know for sure.'

Connor said, 'You and Tanaka took the tapes.'

'Yes. Sure. Right after. Ishiguro says to Tanaka: Get the tapes. So Tanaka gets them. Sure. But I know Tanaka, so I go along. Tanaka takes them to some lab.'

Connor nodded. 'And who went to the Imperial Arms?'

'I know Ishiguro sends some men, to clean up. I don't know who.'

'And you went to the restaurant.'

'Sure, yes. Then I went to the party. Rod's party. No problem.'

'And what about the tapes, Eddie?'

'I told you. Tanaka takes them. I don't know where. He's gone. He works for Ishiguro. For Nakamoto.'

'I understand,' Connor said. 'But he didn't take all the tapes, did he.'

Eddie gave a crooked grin. 'Hey.'

'You kept some?'

'No. Just one. Just a mistake, you know. In my pocket.' He smiled.

Michelle said, 'Daddy, can I watch Disney channel?'

'Sure,' I said. I put her down. 'Elaine will help you.'

My daughter went away. Connor kept talking to Eddie. Slowly the sequence of events came out. Tanaka had gone off with the tapes, and at some point in the evening, apparently realized that one was missing. He figured it out, Eddie said, and he came back to Eddie's house to collect the missing tape. He had interrupted Eddie with the girls. He had demanded the tape.

'I don't know for sure, but after I talk to you, I figure they set me up. We have a big argument.'

'And then the police came. Graham came.'

Eddie nodded slowly. 'Tanaka-san shit a brick. Hey! He's unhappy Japanese man.'

'So you made him tell you everything . . .'

'Oh yeah, Captain. He tells me very fast –'

'And in return you told him where the missing tape was.'

'Sure. In my car. I gave him the keys. So he can unlock it. He has the keys.'

Tanaka had gone into the garage to get the tape. The patrolmen downstairs ordered him to a halt. He started the car and drove off.

'I watch him go, John. Drives like shit.'

So it had been Tanaka who was driving the car when it hit the embankment. It was Tanaka who had burned to death. Eddie explained that he hid in the shrubbery behind the swimming pool and waited until everybody left.

'Cold as shit out there,' he said.

I said to Connor, 'You knew all this?'

'I suspected. The reports of the crash said that the body was badly burned, and that even the glasses had melted.'

Eddie said, 'Hey, I don't wear glasses.'

'Exactly,' Connor said. 'Even so, I asked Graham to check, the next day. He never found any glasses in Eddie's house. So it couldn't have been Eddie in the car. The next day, when we went to Eddie's house, I had the patrolman check the license plates on all the cars parked on the street. Sure enough: there was a yellow Toyota sedan, a short distance up the road, registered to Akira Tanaka.'

'Hey, pretty good,' Eddie said. 'Smart.'

I said, 'Where were you, all this time?'

'At Jasmine's house. Very nice house.'

'Who's Jasmine?'

'Redhead number. Very nice woman. Got a Jacuzzi, too.'

'But why did you come here?'

Connor said to me, 'He had to. You have his passport.'

'Right,' Eddie said. 'And me, I have your business card. You give me. Home address and phone. I need my passport, Lieutenant. I got to go now. So I come here, and wait. And holy shit, all the reporters. Cameras. Everything. So I stay low, play with Shelly.' He lit a cigarette, turned nervously. 'So. What do you say, Lieutenant? How about you give me my passport? *Netsutuku.* No harm done. I'm dead anyway. Okay?'

'Not just yet,' Connor said.

'Come on, John.'

'Eddie, you have to do a little job first.'

'Hey. What job? I got to go, Captain.'

'Just one job, Eddie.'

Morton took a deep breath, and turned away from the studio window. I had to admire his self-control. He seemed completely calm. 'It appears,' he said, 'that my options at this moment are somewhat reduced.'

'Yes, Senator,' Connor said.

He sighed. 'You know it was an accident. It really was.'

Connor nodded sympathetically.

'I don't know what it was about her,' Morton said. 'She was beautiful, of course, but it wasn't . . . it wasn't that. I only met her a short time ago. Four, five months ago. I thought she was a nice girl. Texas girl, sweet. But it was . . . one of those things. It just happened. She had this way of getting under your skin. It was crazy. Unexpected. I started to think about her all the time. I couldn't . . . she would call me, when I was on a trip. She would find out when I was on a trip, somehow. And pretty soon, I couldn't tell her to stay away. I couldn't. She always seemed to have money, always had a plane ticket. She was crazy. Sometimes, she would make me so *mad.* It was like my . . . I don't know. Demon. Everything changed when she was around. Crazy. I had to stop seeing her. And eventually I had the feeling she was paid for. Someone was paying her. Someone knew about her. And me. So I had to stop it. Bob told me. Hell, everybody in the office told me. I couldn't. Finally I did. It was over. But when I came to that reception, there she was. Shit.' He shook his head. 'It just happened. What a mess.'

The girl stuck her head in the door. 'Two minutes, Senator. They're asking for you downstairs if you're ready.'

Morton said to us, 'I'd like to do this first.'

'Of course,' Connor said.

His self-possession was extraordinary. Senator Morton conducted a televised interview with three reporters for half an hour, without a trace of tension or discomfort. He smiled, cracked jokes, bantered with the reporters. It was as if he had no problems at all.

At one point he said, 'Yes, it's true that the British and the Dutch both have larger investments in America than the Japanese. But we can't ignore the reality of targeted, adversarial trade as practiced by Japan – where business and government make a planned attack on some segment of the American economy. The British and Dutch don't operate that way. We haven't lost basic industries to those countries. But we've lost many to Japan. That is the real difference – and that's the reason for concern.'

He added, 'And, of course, if we want to buy a Dutch or English company, we can. But we can't buy a Japanese company.'

The interview continued, but nobody asked him about MicroCon. So he steered it: in reply to a question, he said, 'Americans should be able to criticize Japan without being called racists or bashers. Every country has conflicts with other countries. It's inevitable. Our conflicts with Japan should be freely discussed, without these ugly epithets. My opposition to the MicroCon sale has been termed racist, but it is nothing of the sort.'

Finally, one reporter asked him about the MicroCon sale. Morton hesitated, then he leaned forward across the table.

'As you know, George, I have opposed the MicroCon sale from the beginning. I still oppose it. It is time for Americans to take steps to preserve the assets of this nation. Its real assets, its financial assets, and its intellectual assets. The MicroCon sale is unwise. My opposition continues. Therefore, I am pleased to say that I have just learned Akai Ceramics has withdrawn its bid to purchase the MicroCon Corporation. It think this is the best solution all around. I applaud Akai for its sensitivity on this matter. The sale will not go forward. I am very pleased.'

I said, 'What? The bid was withdrawn?'

Connor said, 'I guess it is now.'

Morton was cheerful as the interview drew to a close. 'Since I've been characterized as so critical of Japan, perhaps you'll let me express my admiration for a moment. The Japanese have a wonderful lighthearted side, and it shows up in the most unlikely places.

'You probably know that their Zen monks are expected to write a poem close to the moment of death. It's a traditional art from, and the most famous poems are still quoted hundreds of years later. So you can imagine, there's a lot of pressure on a Zen *roshi* when he knows he's nearing death and everyone expects him to come up with a great poem. For months, it's all he can think about. But my favorite poem was written by one particular monk who got tired of all the pressure. It goes like this.'

And then he quoted this poem.

Birth is thus,
Death is thus,
Poem or no poem
What's the fuss?

All the reporters started laughing. 'So let's not take all this Japan business too seriously,' Morton said. 'That's another thing we can learn from the Japanese.'

At the end of the interview, Morton shook hands with the three reporters and stepped away from the set. I saw that Ishiguro had arrived in the studio, very red-faced. He was sucking air through his teeth in the Japanese manner.

Morton said cheerfully, 'Ah, Ishiguro-san. I see you have heard the news.' And he slapped him on the back. Hard.

Ishiguro glowered. 'I am extremely disappointed, Senator. It will not go well from this point.' He was clearly furious.

'Hey,' Morton said. 'You know what? Tough shit.'

'We had an *arrangement,*' Ishiguro hissed.

'Yes, we did,' Morton said. 'But you didn't keep your end of it, did you?'

The senator came over to us and said, 'I suppose you want me to make a statement. Let me get this makeup off, and we can go.'

'All right,' Connor said.

Morton walked away, toward the makeup room.

Ishiguro turned to Connor and said, '*Totemo taihenna koto ni narimashita ne.*'

Connor said, 'I agree. It is difficult.'

Ishiguro hissed through his teeth. 'Heads will roll.'

'Yours first,' Connor said. '*Sō omowa nakai.*'

The senator was walking toward the stairway going up to the second floor. Woodson came over to him, leaned close, and whispered something. The senator threw his arm around his shoulder. They walked arm in arm a moment. Then the senator went upstairs.

Ishiguro said bleakly, '*Konna hazuja nakatta no ni.*'

Connor shrugged. 'I am afraid I have little sympathy. You attempted to break the laws of this country and now there is going to be big trouble. *Eraikoto ni naruyo, Ishiguro-san.*'

'We will see, Captain.'

Ishiguro turned and gave Eddie a frosty look. Eddie shrugged and said, 'Hey, I got no problems! Know what I mean, compadre? You got all problems now.' And he laughed.

The floor manager, a heavyset guy wearing a headset, came over. 'Is one of you Lieutenant Smith?'

I said I was.

'A Miss Asakuma is calling you. You can take it over there.' He pointed to the living-room set. Couch and easy chairs, against a morning city skyline. I saw a blinking telephone by one chair.

I walked over and sat in the chair and picked up the phone. 'Lieutenant Smith.'

'Hi, it's Theresa,' she said. I liked the way she used her first name. 'Listen, I've been looking at the last part of the tape. The very end. And I think there may be a problem.'

'Oh? What kind of problem?' I didn't tell her Morton had already confessed. I looked across the stage. The senator had already gone upstairs; he was out of sight. Woodson, his aide, was pacing back and forth at the foot of the stairs, a pale, stricken look on his face. Nervously, he fingered his belt, feeling it through the suit coat.

Then I heard Connor say, 'Ah, *shit!*' and he broke into a run, sprinting across the studio toward the stairs. I stood up, surprised, dropped the phone, and followed him. As Connor passed Woodson, he said 'You *son of a bitch,*' and then he was taking the stairs two at a time, racing upward. I was right behind him. I heard Woodson say something like, '*I had* to.'

When we got to the second floor hallway Connor shouted 'Senator!' That was when we heard the single, cracking report. It wasn't loud: it sounded like a chair falling over.

But I knew it was a gunshot.

Second Night

The sun was setting on the *sekitei.* The shadows of the rocks rippled over the concentric circles of raked sand. I sat and stared at the patterns. Connor was somewhere inside, still watching television. I could faintly hear the newscast. Of course, a Zen temple would have a television set on the premises. I was starting to become accustomed to these contradictions.

But I didn't want to watch TV any more. I had seen enough, in the last hour, to know how the media was going to play it. Senator Morton had been under a great deal of stress lately. His family life was troubled; his teenage son had recently been arrested for drunk driving, after an accident in which another teenager had been seriously injured. The senator's daughter was rumored to have had an abortion. Mrs Morton was not available for comment, although reporters were standing outside the family town-house in Arlington.

The senator's staff all agreed that the senator had been under enormous pressure lately, trying to balance family life and his own impending candidacy. The senator had not been himself; he had been moody and withdrawn, and in the words of one staffer, 'He seemed to have been troubled by something personal.'

While no one questioned the senator's judgment, one colleague, Senator Dowling, said that Morton had 'become a bit of a fanatic about Japan lately, perhaps an indication of the strain he was under. John didn't seem to think accommodation with Japan was possible anymore, and of course we all know that we have to make an accommodation. Our two nations are now too closely bound together. Unfortunately, none of us could have known the strain he was really under. John Morton was a private man.'

I sat watching the rocks in the garden turn gold, then red. An American Zen monk named Bill Harris came out and asked me if I wanted tea, or perhaps a Coke. I said no. He went away. Looking back inside, I saw flickering blue light from the tube. I couldn't see Connor.

I looked back at the rocks in the garden.

The first gunshot had not killed Senator Morton. When we kicked open the bathroom door, he was bleeding from the neck, staggering to his feet. Connor shouted 'Don't!' just as Morton put the gun in his mouth and fired again. The second shot was fatal. The gun kicked out of his hands and went spinning across the tile floor of the bathroom. It came to rest near my shoes. There was a lot of blood on the walls.

Then people started screaming. I had turned back and I saw the makeup girl in the doorway, holding her hands to her face and screaming at the top of her lungs. Eventually, when the paramedics came, they sedated her.

Connor and I had stayed until the division sent Bob Kaplan and Tony Marsh. They were the detectives in charge, and we were free to go. I told Bob we'd give statements whenever he wanted them, and we left. I noticed that Ishiguro had already gone. So had Eddie Sakamura.

That had bothered Connor. 'That damn Eddie,' he said. 'Where is he?'

'Who cares?' I said.

'There's a problem with Eddie,' Connor said.

'What problem?'

'Didn't you notice how he acted around Ishiguro? He was too confident,' Connor said. '*Much* too confident. He should have been frightened and he wasn't.'

I shrugged. 'You said it yourself, Eddie's crazy. Who knows why he does what he does.' I was tired of the case, and tired of Connor's endless Japanese nuances. I said I thought Eddie had probably gone back to Japan. Or to Mexico, where he had said earlier that he wanted to go.

'I hope you're right,' Connor said.

He led me toward the rear entrance to the station. Connor said he wanted to leave before the press arrived. We got into our car and left. He directed me to the Zen center. We had been there ever since. I had called Lauren but she was out of the office. I called Theresa at the lab but her line was busy. I called home, and Elaine said that Michelle was fine, and the reporters had all gone. She asked if I wanted her to stay and give Michelle dinner. I said yes, that I might be home late.

And then for the next hour, I watched television. Until I didn't want to watch any more.

It was almost dark. The sand was purple-gray. My body was stiff from sitting, and it was growing chilly. My beeper went off. I was getting a call from the division. Or perhaps it was Theresa. I got up and went inside.

On the television set, Senator Stephen Rowe was expressing sympathy for the bereaved family, and talking about the fact that Senator Morton had been overstressed. Senator Rowe pointed out that the Akai offer had not been withdrawn. The sale was, so far as Rowe knew, still going through, and there would not now be any serious opposition.

'Hmmm,' Connor said.

'The sale is back on?' I said.

'It seems it was never off.' Connor was obviously worried.

'You don't approve of the sale?'

'I'm worried about Eddie. He was so cocky. It's a question of what Ishiguro will do now.'

'Who cares?' I was tired. The girl was dead, Morton was dead, and the sale was going forward.

Connor shook his head. 'Remember the stakes,' he said. 'The stakes are huge. Ishiguro isn't concerned about a sordid little murder, or even the strategic purchase of some high-tech company. Ishiguro is concerned about Nakamoto's reputation in America. Nakamoto has a large corporate presence in America, and it wants it to be larger. Eddie can damage that reputation.'

'How?'

He shook his head. 'I don't know, for sure.'

My beeper went off again. I called in. It was Frank Ellis, the watch officer at division headquarters for the evening.

'Hey, Pete,' he said. 'We got a call for Special Services. Sergeant Matlovsky, down at vehicle impound. He's asking for language assistance.'

'What is it?' I said.

'He says he's got five Japanese nationals down there, demanding to inspect the wrecked vehicle.'

I frowned. 'What wrecked vehicle?'

'That Ferrari. The one in the high-speed pursuit. Apparently it's pretty ragged: the impact crushed it, and there was a fire. And the body was cut out with torches by the VHDV teams this morning. But the Japanese insist on inspecting the vehicle anyway. Matlovsky can't tell from the paperwork whether it's okay to let somebody 'ook at it or not. You know, whether it's material to an ongoing investigation or not. And he can't speak the language to understand the Japanese. One of the Japanese claims to be related to the deceased. So, you want to go down there and handle it?'

I sighed. 'Am I on tonight? I was on last night.'

'Well, you're on the board. You traded nights with Allen, looks like.'

I dimly remembered. I had traded nights with Jim Allen so he could take his kid to the King's hockey game. I had agreed to it a week ago, but it seemed like something from my distant past.

'Okay,' I said. 'I'll handle it.'

I went back to tell Connor I had to leave. He listened to the story and suddenly jumped to his feet, 'Of course! Of *course!* What was I thinking of? Damn!' He pounded his hand in his fist. 'Let's go, *kōhai.*'

'We're going to the impound?'

'Impound? Absolutely not.'

'Then what are we doing?'

'Oh, damn it, I'm a fool!' he said. He was already heading for the car. I hurried after him.

As I pulled up in front of Eddie Sakamura's house, Connor leapt from the car, and raced up the steps. I parked and ran after him. The sky was deep blue. It was almost night.

Connor was taking the steps two at a time. 'I blame myself,' he said. 'I should have seen it earlier. I should have understood what it meant.'

'What *what* meant?' I said. I was panting a little, at the top of the steps.

Connor threw open the front door. We went inside. The living room was exactly as I had last seen it, earlier in the day, when I had stood there talking to Graham.

Connor went quickly from room to room. In the bedroom, a suitcase lay open. Armani and Byblos jackets lay on the bed, waiting to be packed. 'The little idiot,' Connor said. 'He should never have come back here.'

The pool lights were on outside. They cast a green rippling pattern on the ceiling. Connor went outside.

The body lay face down in the water, naked, floating in the center of the pool, a dark silhouette in the glowing green rectangle. Connor got a skimmer pole and pushed Eddie toward the far edge. We hauled him up onto the concrete lip.

The body was blue and cold, beginning to stiffen. He appeared unmarked.

'They would be careful about that,' Connor said.

'About what?'

'About not letting anything show. But I'm sure we can find the proof . . .' He got out his penlight and peered inside Eddie's mouth. He inspected the nipples, and the genitals. 'Yes. There. See the rows of red dots? On the scrotum. And there on the side of the thigh . . .'

'Alligator clips?'

'Yes. For the electric shock coil. *Damn!*' Connor said. 'Why didn't he tell me? All that time, when we were driving from your apartment to the television station to see the senator. He could have said something then. He could have told me the truth.'

'About what?'

Connor didn't answer me. He was lost in his own thoughts. He sighed. 'You know, in the end, we are just *gaijin*. Foreigners. Even in his desperation, we're excluded. And anyway, he probably wouldn't tell us because . . .'

He fell silent. He stared at the corpse. Finally, he slid the body back into the water. It floated out again.

'Let somebody else do the paperwork,' Connor said, standing up. 'We don't need to be the ones who found the body. It doesn't matter.' He watched Eddie drift back to the center of the pool. The head tilted down slightly. The heels bobbed on the surface.

'I liked him,' Connor said. 'He did favors for me. I even met his family in Japan. Some of his family. Not the father.' He watched the body rotate slowly. 'But Eddie was okay. And now, I want to *know*.'

I was lost. I had no idea what he was talking about, but I didn't think I should say anything. Connor looked angry.

'Come on,' he said finally. 'We have to move fast. There's only a couple of possibilities. And once again, we have fallen behind events. But if it's the last thing I do, I want to get that son of a bitch.'

'What son of a bitch?'

'Ishiguro.'

We were driving back to my apartment. 'You take the night off,' he said.

'I'm going with you,' I said.

'No. I'll do this alone, *kōhai*. It's better if you don't know.'

'Know what?' I said.

We went on like this for a while. He didn't want to tell me. Finally he said, 'Tanaka went to Eddie's house last night because Eddie had the tape. Presumably, the original.'

'Right . . .'

'And Tanaka wanted it back. That's why they had an argument. When you and Graham came, and all hell broke loose, Eddie told Tanaka the tape was in the Ferrari. So Tanaka went down there, panicked when he saw the police, and drove the car away.'

'Right.'

'I always assumed the tape was destroyed in the crash, and the fire.'

'Yes . . .'

'But obviously it wasn't. Because Eddie wouldn't dare to be so cocky around Ishiguro unless he still had the tape. The tape would be his ace in the hole. He knew it. But he obviously didn't understand how ruthless Ishiguro would be.'

'They tortured him for the tape?'

'Yes. But Eddie must have surprised them. He didn't tell them.'

'How do you know?'

'Because,' Connor said, 'otherwise, there wouldn't be five Japanese nationals asking to inspect the wreck of the Ferrari in the middle of the night.'

'So they're still looking for the tape?'

'Yes. Or evidence of the tape. They may not even know how many are missing, at this point.'

I thought it over.

'What are you going to do?' I said.

'Find the tape,' Connor said. 'Because it matters. People are dying for that tape. If we can find the original . . .' He shook his head. 'It'll put Ishiguro in deep shit. Which is just where he belongs.'

I pulled up in front of my apartment building. As Elaine had said, all the reporters were gone. The street was quiet. Dark.

'I still want to go with you,' I said again.

Connor shook his head. 'I'm on extended leave,' he said. 'You're not. You've got your pension to think of. And you don't want to know exactly what I am going to do tonight.'

'I can guess,' I said. 'You're going to retrace Eddie's steps from last night. Eddie left the house and went to stay with the redhead. Maybe he went somewhere else, too –'

'Look,' Connor said. 'Let's not waste more time, *kōhai*. I have some contacts and some people I can lean on. Leave it at that. If you need me, you can call me on the car phone. But don't call unless you have to. Because I'll be busy.'

'But –'

'Come on, *kōhai*. Out of the car. Spend a nice night with your kid. You did a good job, but your job is finished now.'

Finally, I got out of the car.

'*Sayonara*,' Connor said, with an ironic wave. And he drove off.

'Daddy! Daddy!' She ran toward me, arms outstretched. 'Pick me up, Daddy.'

I picked her up. 'Hi, Shelly.'

'Daddy, can I watch Sleeping Beauty?'

'I don't know. Have you had dinner yet?'

'She ate two hot dogs and an ice cream cone,' Elaine said. She was washing dishes in the kitchen.

'Jeez,' I said. 'I thought we were going to stop feeding her junk food.'

'Well, it's all she would eat,' Elaine said. She was irritable. It was the end of a long day with a two-year-old.

'Daddy, can I watch Sleeping Beauty?'

'Just a minute, Shelly, I'm talking to Elaine.'

'I tried that soup,' Elaine said, 'but she wouldn't touch it. She wanted a hot dog.'

'Daddy, can I watch Disney channel?'

'Michelle,' I said.

Elaine said, 'So I thought it was better that she eat something. I think she was thrown off. You know, the reporters and everything. All the excitement.'

'Daddy? Can I? Sleeping Beauty?' She was squirming in my arms. Patting my face to get attention.

'Okay, Shel.'

'Now, Daddy?'

'Okay.'

I put her down. She ran into the living room and turned on the TV, pushing the remote without hesitation. 'I think she watches too much television.'

'They all do,' Elaine said, shrugging.

'Daddy?'

I went into the living room and plugged in the cassette. I fast-forwarded to the credits, then let it run.

'Not this part,' she said impatiently.

So I fast-forwarded to the beginning of the action. Pages turning in a book.

'This part, this part,' she said, tugging at my hand.

I let the tape run at normal speed. Michelle sat in the chair and started sucking her thumb. She pulled her thumb out of her mouth and patted the seat beside her. 'Here, Daddy,' she said.

She wanted me to sit with her.

I sighed. I looked at the room. It was a mess. Her crayons and coloring books were scattered over the floor. And the large Tinkertoy windmill.

'Let me clean up,' I said. 'I'll be right here, with you.'

She popped her thumb back in her mouth, and turned to the screen. Her attention was total.

I cleaned up the crayons and put them back in the cardboard box. I folded up her coloring books and set them on the shelf. I was suddenly tired and sat down for a minute on the floor next to Michelle. On the screen, three fairies, red, green, and blue, were flying into the throne room of the castle.

'That's Merryweather,' Michelle said, pointing. 'She's the blue one.'

From the kitchen, Elaine said, 'Can I fix you a sandwich, Lieutenant?'

'That'd be great,' I said. I found I just wanted to sit there and be with my daughter. I wanted to forget everything, at least for a while. I was grateful that Connor had dropped me off. I sat and watched the TV dumbly.

Elaine brought in a salami sandwich with lettuce and mustard. I was hungry. Elaine looked at the TV, shook her head, and went back into the kitchen. I ate my sandwich, and Michelle insisted on a few bites. She likes salami. I worry about the additives in it, but I guess it's no worse than hot dogs.

After I had the sandwich, I felt a little better. I got up to finish cleaning up the room. I picked up the Tinkertoy windmill and started taking it apart, putting the sticks back into the cardboard tube. Michelle said, 'No this, no this!' in a pained voice. I thought she didn't want me to take apart the windmill, but that wasn't it at all. She was cupping her hands over her eyes. She didn't like to see Maleficent, the bad witch. I fast-forwarded past the witch, and she relaxed again.

I dismantled the Tinkertoy windmill and put everything back into the tube container. I put the metal cap on the tube and set it on the lowest shelf of the bookcase. That was where it always went. I like to keep the toys low, so Michelle can get to them herself.

The tube fell of the shelf, onto the carpet. I picked it up again. There was something on the shelf. A small rectangle. I knew at once what it was.

It was an eight-millimeter video cassette, with Japanese writing on the label.

Elaine said, 'Lieutenant? Do you need anything else?' She had her coat on; she was ready to go.

'Hang on a minute,' I said.

I went to the phone, and called the switchboard downtown. I asked them to connect me to Connor in my car. I waited impatiently. Elaine looked at me.

'Just another minute, Elaine,' I said.

On the TV, the prince was singing a duet with Sleeping Beauty while birds chirped. Michelle was sucking her thumb.

The operator said, 'I'm sorry, there is no answer from the car.'

'Okay,' I said. 'Do you have a forwarding number for Captain Connor?'

A pause. 'He's not on our active roster.'

'I know that. But did he leave a number?'

'I don't have anything, Lieutenant.'

'I'm trying to find him.'

'Wait a minute.' She put me on hold. I swore.

Elaine stood in the front hallway. She was waiting to go.

The operator came back on. 'Lieutenant? Captain Ellis says that Captain Connor has gone.'

'Gone?'

'He was here a while ago, but he's gone now.'

'You mean he was *downtown*?'

'Yes, but he's gone now. I don't have a number for him. I'm sorry.'

I hung up. What the hell was Connor doing downtown?

Elaine was still standing in the front hallway. 'Lieutenant?'

I said, 'Just a minute, Elaine.'

'Lieutenant, I have a –'

'I said, *just a minute.*'

I started pacing. I didn't know what to do. I was suddenly overwhelmed with fear. They had killed Eddie for the tape. They wouldn't hesitate to kill anybody else. I looked at my daughter, watching television with her thumb in her mouth. I said to Elaine, 'Where's your car?'

'In the garage.'

'Okay. Look. I want you to take Michelle and I want you to go –'

The phone rang. I grabbed it, hoping it was Connor. 'Hello.'

'*Moshi moshi. Connor-san desu ka?*'

'He's not here,' I said. As soon as the words were out of my mouth, I cursed myself. But it was too late, the damage was done.

'Very good, Lieutenant,' the voice said, heavily accented. 'You have what we want, don't you?'

I said, 'I don't know what you are talking about.'

'I think you do, Lieutenant.'

I could hear a faint hiss on the line. The call was coming from a car phone. They could be anywhere.

They could be right outside.

Damn!

I said, 'Who is this?'

But I heard only a dial tone.

Elaine said, 'What is it, Lieutenant?'

I was running to the window. I saw three cars double-parked in the street below. Five men getting out of them, dark silhouettes in the night.

I tried to stay calm. 'Elaine,' I said. 'I want you to take Michelle, and both of you go into my bedroom. Get under the bed. I want you to stay under there and be very quiet, no matter what happens. Do you understand?'

'No, Daddy!'

'Do it now, Elaine.'

'No, Daddy! I want to watch Sleeping Beauty.'

'You can watch it later.' I had taken out my gun and was checking the clip. Elaine's eyes were wide.

She took Michelle. 'Come on, honey.'

Michelle squirmed in her arms, protesting. 'No, Daddy!'

'*Michelle.*'

She went silent, shocked at my tone. Elaine carried her into the bedroom. I loaded another clip, and put it in my jacket pocket.

I turned off the lights in the bedroom, and in Michelle's room. I looked at her crib, and the covers with little elephants sewn onto it. I turned off the lights and went into the kitchen.

I went back into the living room. The TV was still playing. The wicked witch was instructing her raven to find Sleeping Beauty. 'You are my last hope, my pet, do not fail me,' she said to the bird. The bird flew away.

I stayed low. I moved toward the door. The phone rang again. I crawled back to answer it.

'Hello.'

'*Kōhai.*' It was Connor's voice. I heard the static hiss of the car phone.

I said, 'Where are you?'

'You have the tape?'

'Yes, I have the tape. Where are you?'

'At the airport.'

'Well, *get here.* Right away. And call for backup! Jesus!'

I heard a sound on the landing, outside my door. A soft sound, like footsteps.

I hung up the phone. I was sweating.

Christ.

If Connor was at the airport, he was twenty minutes away from me. Maybe more.

Maybe more.

I was going to have to handle this on my own.

I watched the door, listening intently. But I didn't hear anything else on the landing outside.

From the bedroom, I heard my daughter say, 'I want Sleeping Beauty. I want *Daddy*.' I heard Elaine whispering to her. Michelle whimpered.

Then it was quiet.

The phone rang again.

'Lieutenant,' the heavily accented voice said, 'there is no need for backups.'

Christ, they were listening to the car phone.

'We want no harm, Lieutenant. We want only one thing. Will you be so kind, to bring the tape out to us?'

'I have the tape,' I said.

'We know.'

I said, 'You can have it.'

'Good. It will be better.'

I knew I was on my own. I was thinking fast. My sole idea was: Get them away from here. Get them away from my daughter.

'But not here,' I said.

There was a knock on the front door. Quick, insistent rapping.

Damn!

I could feel events closing in around me. Things were happening too fast. I was crouched down on the floor, with the phone pulled down from the table above. Trying to stay below the windows.

The knock came again.

I said into the phone, 'You can have the tape. But first call off your boys.'

'Say again, please?'

Christ, a fucking language problem!

'Call your men away. Get them out in the street. I want to see.'

'Lieutenant, we must have tape!'

'I know that,' I said. 'I'll give it to you.' While I talked, I kept my eyes on the door. I saw the knob turning. Someone was trying to open the front door. Slowly, quietly. Then the knob was released. Something white slid under the door.

A business card.

'Lieutenant, please cooperate.'

I crawled forward and picked up the card. It said: Jonathan Connor, Captain, Los Angeles Police Department.

Then I heard a whisper from the other side.

'*Kōhai.*'

I knew it was a trick. Connor said he was at the airport, so it had to be a trick –

'Perhaps I can be of assistance, *kōhai.*'

Those were the words he had used before, at the start of the case. I was confused to hear them.

'Open the fucking door, *kōhai.*'

It was Connor. I reached up and opened the door. He slipped into the room, bent over. He was dragging something blue: a Kevlar vest. I said, 'I thought you were –'

He shook his head, and whispered, 'Knew they must be here. Had to be. I've been waiting in the car in the alley behind the house. How many are there in front?'

'I think, five. Maybe more.'

He nodded.

The accented voice on the phone said, 'Lieutenant? You are there? Lieutenant?'

I held the receiver away from my ear so Connor could listen while I talked. 'I'm here,' I said.

On the TV, there was a loud witch's cackle.

'Lieutenant, I hear something with you.'

'It's just Sleeping Beauty,' I said.

'What? Sreeping Booty?' the voice said, puzzled. 'What is this?'

'Television,' I said. 'It's the *television.*'

Now I heard whispers on the other end of the line. The rush of a car going by on the street. It reminded me that the men were in an exposed position outside. Standing there on a residential street lined with apartment buildings on both sides. Lots of windows. People that might look out at any time. Or people walking by. The men would have to move quickly.

Perhaps they already were.

Connor was tugging at my jacket. Signaling me to undress. I slid out of my coat as I spoke into the phone.

'All right,' I said. 'What do you want me to do?'

'You bring tape to us.'

I looked at Connor. He nodded. Yes.

'All right,' I said. 'But first get your people back.'

'I am sorry?'

Connor made a fist. His face turned to a snarl. He wanted me to be angry. He covered the phone and whispered in my ear. A Japanese phrase.

'Pay attention!' I said '*Yoku kike!*'

At the other end, there was a grunt. Surprise.

'*Hai*. The men come away. And now, you come, Lieutenant.'

'Okay,' I said. 'I'm coming.'

I hung up the phone.

Connor whispered, 'Thirty seconds,' and disappeared out the front door. I was still buttoning up my shirt around the vest. Kevlar is bulky and hot. Immediately I started to sweat.

I waited thirty seconds, staring into the face of my watch. Watching the hand go around. And then I went outside.

Someone had turned the lights out in the hallway. I tripped over a body. I got to my feet, and looked at a slender Asian face. It was just a kid, surprisingly young. A teenager. He was unconscious, breathing shallowly.

I moved slowly down the stairs.

There wasn't anybody on the second-floor landing. I kept going down. I heard canned laughter from a television, behind one of the doors on the second floor. A voice shouted, 'So tell us, where did you go on this first date?'

I continued down to the ground floor. The front door of the apartment building was glass. I looked out and saw only parked cars, and a hedge. A short section of lawn in front of the building. The men and the cars were somewhere off to the left.

I waited. I took a breath. My heart was pounding. I didn't want to go out there, but all I could think was to get them away from my daughter. To move the action away from my –

I stepped out into the night.

The air was cold on my sweating face and neck.

I took two steps forward.

Now I could see the men. They stood about ten meters away, beside their cars. I counted four men. One of them waved to me, beckoning me over. I hesitated.

Where were the others?

I couldn't see anybody except the men by the cars. They waved again, beckoning me. I started toward them when suddenly a heavy thumping blow from behind knocked me flat onto my face on the wet grass.

It was a moment before I realized what had happened.

I had been shot in the back.

And then the gunfire erupted all around me. Automatic weapons. The street was lit up like lightning from the gunfire. The sound echoed off the apartment buildings on both sides of the street. Glass was shattering. I heard people shouting all around me. More gunfire. I heard the sound of ignitions, cars roaring past me down the street. Almost immediately there was the sound of police sirens and tires squealing, and the glare of searchlights. I stayed where I was, face down on the grass. I felt like I was there for about an hour. Then I realized that the shouts now were all in English.

Finally someone came and crouched over me and said, 'Don't move, Lieutenant. Let me look first.' I recognized Connor's voice. His hand touched my back, probing. Then he said, 'Can you turn over, Lieutenant?'

I turned over.

Standing in the harsh light of the searchlights, Connor looked down at me. 'They didn't penetrate,' he said. 'But you're going to have a hell of a sore back tomorrow.'

He helped me to my feet.

I looked back to see the man who had shot me. But there was nobody there: just a few shell casings, glinting dull yellow in the green grass, by the front door.

Third Night

The headline read VIETNAMESE GANG VIOLENCE ERUPTS ON WESTSIDE. The story reported that Peter Smith, an L.A.P.D. Special Services officer, was the target of a vicious grudge attack by an Orange County gang known at the Bitch Killers. Lieutenant Smith had been shot twice before backup police units arrived on the scene to disperse the attacking youths. None of the suspects had been apprehended alive. But two had been killed in the shooting.

I read the papers in the bathtub, soaking my aching back. I had two large, ugly bruises on either side of my spine. It hurt to breathe.

I had sent Michelle to stay with my mother in San Diego for the weekend, until things were sorted out. Elaine had driven her down, late last night.

I continued reading.

According to the story, the Bitch Killers was thought to be the same gang that had walked up to a black two-year-old boy, Rodney Howard, and shot the child in the head while he was playing on his tricycle in the front yard of his Inglewood home a week earlier. That incident was rumored to be an initiation into the gang, and the viciousness of it had touched off a furor about whether the L.A.P.D. was able to handle gang violence in southern California.

There were a lot of reporters outside my door again, but I wasn't talking to any of them. The phone rang constantly, but I let the answering machine take it. I just sat in the tub, and tried to decide what to do.

In the middle of the morning I called Ken Shubik at the *Times*.

'I wondered when you'd check in,' he said. 'You must be pleased.'

'About what?'

'About being alive,' Ken said. 'These kids are murder.'

'You mean the Vietnamese kids last night?' I said. 'They spoke Japanese.'

'No.'

'Yes, Ken.'

'We didn't get that story right?'

'Not really.'

'That explains it,' he said.

'Explains what?'

'That was the Weasel's story. And the Weasel is in bad odor today. There's even talk of firing him. Nobody can figure it out, but something's happening around here,' he said. 'Somebody high in editorial all of a sudden has a bug up his ass about Japan. Anyway, we're starting a series investigating Japanese corporations in America.'

'Oh, yeah?'

'Of course you'd never know it from today's paper. You see the business section?'

'No, why?'

'Darley-Higgins announced the sale of MicroCon to Akai. It's on page four of the business section. Two-centimeter story.'

'That's it?'

'Not worth any more, I guess. Just another American company sold to the Japanese. I checked. Since 1987, there have been a hundred and eighty American high-tech and electronics companies bought by the Japanese. It's not news any more.'

'But the paper is starting to investigate?'

'That's the word. It won't be easy, because all the emotional indicators are down. The balance of payments with Japan is dropping. Of course it only looks better because they don't export so many cars to us now. They make them here. And they've farmed out production to the little dragons, so the deficits appear in their columns, not Japan's. They've stepped up purchases of oranges and timber, to make things look better. Basically, they treat us as an underdeveloped country. They import our raw materials. But they don't buy our finished goods. They say we don't make anything they want.'

'Maybe we don't, Ken.'

'Tell it to the judge.' He sighed. 'But I don't know if the public gives a damn. That's the question. Even about the taxes.'

I was feeling a little dull. 'Taxes?'

'We're doing a big series on taxes. The government is finally noticing that Japanese corporations do a lot of business here, but they don't pay much tax in America. Some of them pay none, which is ridiculous. They control their profits by overpricing the Japanese subcomponents that their American assembly plants import. It's outrageous, but of course, the American government has never been too swift about penalizing Japan before. And the Japanese spend half a billion a year in Washington, to keep everybody calmed down.'

'But you're going to do a tax story?'

'Yeah. And we're looking at Nakamoto. My sources keep telling me

Nakamoto's going to get hit with a price-fixing suit. Price-fixing is the name of the game for Japanese companies. I pulled a list of who's settled lawsuits. Nintendo in 1991, price-fixing games. Mitsubishi that year, price-fixing TVs. Panasonic in 1989. Minolta in 1987. And you know that's just the tip of the iceberg.'

'Then it's good you're doing the story,' I said.

He coughed. 'You want to go on record? About the Vietnamese who speak Japanese?'

'No,' I said.

'We're all in this together,' he said.

'I don't think it would do any good,' I said.

I had lunch with Connor at a sushi bar in Culver City. As we were pulling up, someone was placing a CLOSED sign in the window. He saw Connor, and flipped it to say OPEN.

'They know me here,' Connor said.

'You mean they like you?'

'It's hard to know about that.'

'They want your business?'

'No,' Connor said. 'Probably Hiroshi would prefer to close. It won't be profitable for him to keep his people on, just for two *gaijin* customers. But I come here often. He is honoring the relationship. It doesn't really have to do with business or liking.'

We got out of the car.

'Americans don't understand,' he said. 'Because the Japanese system is fundamentally different.'

'Yeah, well, I think they're starting to understand,' I said. I told him Ken Shubik's story about price fixing.

Connor sighed. 'It's a cheap shot to say that the Japanese are dishonest. They're not – but they play by different rules. Americans just don't get it.'

'That's fine,' I said. 'But price-fixing is illegal.'

'In America,' he said. 'Yes. But it's normal procedure in Japan. Remember, *kōhai*: fundamentally different. Collusive agreements are the way things are done. The Nomura stock scandal showed that. Americans get moralistic about collusion, instead of just seeing it as a different way of doing business. Which is all it is.'

We went into the sushi bar. There was a lot of bowing and greeting. Connor spoke Japanese and we sat at the bar. We didn't order.

I said, 'Aren't we going to order?'

'No,' Connor said. 'It would be offensive. Hiroshi will decide for us what we would like.'

So we sat at the bar and Hiroshi brought us dishes. I watched him cutting fish.

The phone rang. From the far end of the sushi bar, a man said, '*Connor-san, onna no hito ga matteru to ittemashita yo.*'

'*Dōmo,*' Connor said, nodding. He turned to me, and pushed back from the bar. 'Guess we won't eat, after all. Time for us to go to our next appointment. You brought the tape with you?'

'Yes.'

'Good.'

'Where are we going?'

'To see your friend,' he said. 'Miss Asakuma.'

We were bouncing along the potholes of the Santa Monica freeway, heading downtown. The afternoon sky was gray; it looked like rain. My back hurt. Connor was looking out the window, humming to himself.

In all the excitement, I had forgotten about Theresa's call the night before. She had said she was looking at the last part of the tape, and she thought there was a problem.

'Have you talked to her?'

'Theresa? Briefly. I gave her some advice.'

'Last night, she said there was a problem with the tape.'

'Oh? She didn't mention that to me.'

I had the feeling he wasn't telling me the truth, but my back was throbbing and I wasn't in the mood to press him. There were times when I thought Connor had become Japanese himself. He had that reserve, that secretive manner.

I said, 'You never told me why you left Japan.'

'Oh, that.' He sighed. 'I had a job, working for a corporation. Advising on security. But it didn't work out.'

'Why not?'

'Well, the job was all right. It was fine.'

'Then what was it?'

He shook his head. 'Most people who've lived in Japan come away with mixed feelings. In many ways, the Japanese are wonderful people. They're hardworking, intelligent, humorous. They had real integrity. They are also the most racist people on the planet. That's why they're always accusing everybody else of racism. They're so prejudiced, they assume everybody else must be, too. And living in Japan . . . I just got tired, after a while, of the way things worked. I got tired of seeing women move to the other side of the street when they saw me walking toward them at night. I got tired of noticing that the last two seats to be occupied on the subway were the ones on either side of me. I got tired of the airline stewardesses asking Japanese passengers if they minded sitting next to a *gaijin*, assuming that I couldn't understand what they were saying because they were speaking Japanese. I got tired of the exclusion, the subtle patronizing, the jokes behind my back. I got tired of being a nigger. I just . . . got tired. I gave up.'

'Sounds to me like you don't really like them.'

'No,' Connor said. 'I do. I like them very much. But I'm not Japanese, and they never let me forget it.' He sighed again. 'I have many Japanese friends who work in America, and it's hard for them, too. The differences cut both ways. They feel excluded. People don't sit next to them, either. But my friends always ask me to remember that they are human beings first, and Japanese second. Unfortunately, in my experience that is not always true.'

'You mean, they're Japanese first.'

He shrugged. 'Family is family.'

We drove the rest of the way in silence.

We were in a small room on the third floor of a boarding house for foreign students. Theresa Asakuma explained it was not her room; it belonged to a friend who was studying in Italy for a term. She had set up the small VCR and a small monitor on a table.

'I thought I should get out of the lab,' she said, running the machine fast forward. 'But I wanted you to see this. This is the end of one of the tapes you brought me. It begins right after the senator has left the room.'

She slowed the tape, and I saw the wide view of the forty-sixth floor of the Nakamoto building. The floor was deserted. The pale body of Cheryl Austin lay on the dark conference table.

The tape continued to roll.

Nothing happened. It was a static scene.

I said, 'What are we looking at?'

'Just wait.'

The tape continued. Still nothing happened.

And then I saw, clearly, the girl's leg twitch.

'What was *that*?'

'A spasm?'

'I'm not sure.'

Now the girl's arm, outlined against the dark wood, moved. There was no question about it. The fingers closed and opened.

'She's still alive!'

Theresa nodded. 'That's the way it looks. Now watch the clock.'

The clock on the wall said 8:36. I watched it. Nothing happened. The tape ran for two more minutes.

Connor sighed.

'The clock isn't moving.'

'No,' she said. 'I first noticed the grain pattern, on a close scan. The pixels were jumping back and forth.'

'Meaning what?'

'We call it rock and roll. It's the usual way to diguise a freeze-frame. A normal freeze is visible to the eye, because the smaller units of the image are suddenly static. Whereas in a regular picture, there's always some small movement, even if it's just random. So what you do is you rock and roll, cycling three seconds of image over and over. It gives a little movement, makes the freeze less obvious.'

'You're saying the tape was frozen at eight thirty-six?'

'Yes. And the girl was apparently alive at that time. I don't know for sure. But maybe.'

Connor nodded. 'So that's why the original tape is so important.'

'What original tape?' she said.

I produced the tape I had found in my apartment the night before.

'Run it,' Connor said.

In crisp color, we saw the forty-sixth floor. It was from the side camera, with a good view of the conference room. And it was one of the original tapes: we saw the murder, and we saw Morton leave the girl behind on the table.

The tape ran on. We watched the girl.

'Can you see the wall clock?'

'Not in this angle.'

'How much time do you think has gone by?'

Theresa shook her head. 'It's time lapse. I can't say. A few minutes.'

Then, the girl moved on the table. Her hand twitched, and then her head moved. She was alive. There was no question about it.

And in the glass of the conference room, we saw the shape of a man. He walked forward, appearing from the right. He entered the room, looking back once to make sure he was alone. It was Ishiguro. Very deliberately, he walked to the edge of the table, placed his hands on the girl's neck, and strangled her.

'Jesus.'

It seemed to take a long time. The girl struggled toward the end. Ishiguro held her down, long after she had stopped moving.

'He's not taking any chances.'

'No,' Connor said. 'He's not.'

Finally, Ishiguro stepped back from the body, shot his cuffs, straightened his suit jacket.

'All right,' Connor said. 'You can stop the tape now. I've seen enough.'

We were back outside. Weak sunlight filtered through the smoggy haze. Cars roared by, bouncing on the potholes. The houses along the street looked cheap to me, in disrepair.

We got in our car.

'What now?' I said.

He handed me the car phone. 'Call downtown,' he said, 'and tell them we have a tape that shows Ishiguro did the murder. Tell them we're going to Nakamoto now, to arrest Ishiguro.'

'I thought you didn't like car phones.'

'Just do it,' Connor said. 'We're about finished, anyway.'

So I did it. I told the dispatcher what our plan was, where we were going. They asked if we wanted backup. Connor shook his head, so I said we didn't need backup.

I hung up the phone.

'Now what?'

'Let's go to Nakamoto.'

After seeing the forty-sixth floor so many times on videotape, it was strange to find myself there again. Although it was Saturday, the office was busy and active, secretaries and executives were hurrying about. And the office looked different during the day; sunlight poured in through the large windows on all sides, and the surrounding skyscrapers looked close, even in the L.A. haze.

Looking up, I saw that the surveillance cameras had been removed from the walls. To the right, the conference room where Cheryl Austin had died was being remodeled. The black furniture was gone. Workmen were installing a blond wood table and new beige chairs. The room looked completely different.

On the other side of the atrium, a meeting was being held in the large conference room. Sunlight streamed in through the glass walls on forty people sitting on both sides of a long table covered in green felt. Japanese on one side, Americans on the other. Everyone had a neat stack of documents in front of them. Prominent among the Americans, I noticed the lawyer, Bob Richmond.

Standing beside me, Connor sighed.

'What is it?'

'The Saturday meeting, *kōhai.*'

'You mean *that's* the Saturday meeting Eddie was talking about?'

Connor nodded. 'The meeting to conclude the MicroCon sale.'

There was a receptionist seated near the elevators. She watched us staring for a moment, then said politely, 'Can I help you, gentlemen?'

'Thank you,' Connor said. 'But we're waiting for someone.'

I frowned. From where we were standing, I could clearly see Ishiguro inside the conference room, seated near the center of the table on the Japanese side, smoking a cigarette. The man to his right leaned over to whisper something to him; Ishiguro nodded and smiled.

I glanced over at Connor.

'Just wait,' Connor said.

Several minutes passed, and then a young Japanese aide hurried across to the atrium and entered the conference room. Once inside, he moved more slowly, circling the table unobtrusively until he was standing behind the chair of a distinguished, gray-haired man seated toward the far end of the table. The aide bent and whispered something to the older man.

'Iwabuchi,' Connor said.

'Who is he?'

'Head of Nakamoto America. Based in New York.'

Iwabuchi nodded to the young aide, and got up from the table. The aide pulled his chair out for him. Iwabuchi moved down the line of Japanese negotiators. As he passed one man, he brushed him lightly on the shoulder. Iwabuchi continued to the end of the table, then opened the glass doors and walked outside, onto a terrace beyond the conference room.

A moment later, the second man stood to leave.

'Moriyama,' Connor said. 'Head of the Los Angeles office.'

Moriyama also went outside onto the terrace. The two men stood in the sun and smoked cigarettes. The aide joined them, speaking quickly, his head bobbing. The senior men listened intently, then turned away. The aide remained standing there.

After a moment, Moriyama turned back to the aide and said something. The aide bowed quickly and returned to the conference room. He moved to the seat of another man, dark-haired with a moustache, and whispered in his ear.

'Shirai,' Connor said. 'Head of finance.'

Shirai stood up, but did not go onto the terrace. Instead, he opened the inner door, crossed the atrium, and disappeared into an office on the far side of the floor.

In the conference room, the aide went to still a fourth man, whom I recognized as Yoshida, the head of Akai Ceramics. Yoshida also slipped out of the room, going into the atrium.

'What's going on?' I said.

'They're distancing themselves,' Connor said. 'They don't want to be there when it happens.'

I looked back at the terrace, and saw the two Japanese men outside moving casually along the length of the terrace, toward a door at the far end.

I said, 'What are we waiting for?'

'Patience, *kōhai*.'

The young aide departed. The meeting in the conference room proceeded. But in the atrium, Yoshida pulled the young aide over and whispered something.

The aide returned to the conference room.

'Hmmm,' Connor said.

This time the aide went to the American side of the table, and whispered something to Richmond. I couldn't see Richmond's face, because his back was to us, but his body jerked. He twisted and leaned back to whisper something to the aide. The aide nodded and left.

Richmond remained seated at the table, shaking his head slowly. He bent over his notes.

And then he passed a slip of paper across the table to Ishiguro.

'That's our cue,' Connor said. He turned to the receptionist, showed her his badge, and we walked quickly across the atrium toward the conference room.

A young American in a pinstripe suit was standing in front of the table and saying, 'Now, if you will direct your attention to Rider C, the summary statement of assets and –'

Connor came into the room first. I was right after him.

Ishiguro looked up, showing no surprise. 'Good afternoon, gentlemen.' His face was a mask.

Richmond said smoothly, 'Gentlemen, if this can wait, we're in the middle of something rather complicated here –'

Connor interrupted him, 'Mr Ishiguro, you are under arrest for the murder of Cheryl Lynn Austin,' and then he read him his Miranda rights, while Ishiguro stared fixedly at him. The others in the room were entirely silent. Nobody moved at the long table. It was like a still life.

Ishiguro remained seated. 'This is an absurdity.'

'Mr Ishiguro,' Connor said, 'would you please stand?'

Richmond said softly, 'I hope you guys know what you are doing.'

Ishiguro said, 'I know my rights, gentlemen.'

Connor said, 'Mr Ishiguro, would you please stand?'

Ishiguro did not move. The smoke from his cigarette curled up in front of him.

There was a long silence.

Then Connor said to me, 'Show them the tape.'

One wall of the conference room consisted of video equipment. I found a playback machine like the one I had used, and plugged the tape in. But no image came up on the big central monitor. I tried pushing various buttons, but couldn't get a picture.

From a rear corner, a Japanese secretary who had been taking notes hurried up to help me. Bowing apologetically, she pushed the proper buttons, bowed again, and returned to her place.

'Thank you,' I said.

On the screen, the image came up. Even in the bright sunlight, it was clear. It was right at the moment we had seen in Theresa's room. The moment where Ishiguro approaches the girl and holds the struggling body down.

Richmond said, 'What is this?'

'It's a fake,' Ishiguro said. 'It's a fraud.'

Connor said, 'This is a tape taken by Nakamoto security cameras on the forty-sixth floor Thursday night.'

Ishiguro said, 'It's not legal. It's a fraud.'

But nobody was listening. Everybody was looking at the monitor. Richmond's mouth was open. 'Jesus,' he said.

On the tape, it seemed to take a long time for the girl to die.

Ishiguro was glaring at Connor. 'This is nothing but a sensational publicity stunt,' he said. 'It is a fabrication. It means *nothing*.'

'Jesus Christ,' Richmond said, staring at the screen.

Ishiguro said, 'It has no legal basis. It is not admissible. It will never stand up. This is just a disruption –'

He broke off. For the first time, he had looked down to the other end of the table. And he saw that Iwabuchi's chair was empty.

He looked the other way. His eyes darted around the room.

Moriyama's chair was empty.

Shirai's chair.

Yoshida's chair.

Ishiguro's eyes twitched. He looked at Connor in astonishment. Then he nodded, gave a guttural grunt, and stood. Everyone else was staring at the screen.

He walked up to Connor. 'I'm not going to watch this, Captain. When you are through with your charade, you will find me outside.' He lit a cigarette, squinting at Connor. 'Then we will talk. *Kicchiirito na*.' He opened the door and walked onto the terrace. He left the door open behind him.

I started to follow him out, but Connor caught my eye. He shook his head fractionally. I remained where I was.

I could see Ishiguro outside, standing at the railing. He smoked his cigarette and turned his face to the sun. Then he glanced back at us and shook his head pityingly. He leaned against the railing, and put his foot on it.

In the conference room, the tape continued. One of the American lawyers, a woman, stood up, snapped her briefcase shut, and walked out of the room. Nobody else moved.

And finally, the tape ended.

I popped it out of the machine.

There was silence in the room. A slight wind ruffled the papers of the people at the long table.

I looked out at the terrace.

It was empty.

By the time we got out to the railing, we could hear the sirens faintly, on the street below.

Down on ground level, the air was dusty and we heard the deafening sound of jackhammers. Nakamoto was building an annex next door, and construction was in full swing. A line of big cement trucks was pulled up along the curb. I pushed my way through the cluster of Japanese men in blue suits, and broke through to look down into the pit.

Ishiguro had landed in a wet concrete pouring. His body lay sideways, just the head and one arm sticking above the soft concrete surface. Blood ran in spreading fingers across the gray surface. Workmen in blue hard-hats were trying to fish him out, using bamboo poles and ropes. They weren't having much success. Finally a workman in thigh-high rubber boots waded in to pull the body out. But it proved more difficult than he expected. He had to call for help.

Our people were already there, Fred Perry and Bob Wolfe. Bob shouted over the din of jackhammers. 'You know anything about this, Pete?'

'Yeah,' I said.

'Got a name?'

'Masao Ishiguro.'

Wolfe squinted. 'Spell that?'

I started to try to spell it, talking over the sound of the construction. Finally I just reached in my pocket and fished out his card. I gave it to Wolfe.

'This is him?'

'Yeah.'

'Where'd you get it?'

'Long story,' I said. 'But he's wanted for murder.'

Wolfe nodded. 'Let me get the body out and we'll talk.'

'Fine.'

Eventually, they used the construction crane to pull him out. Ishiguro's body, sagging and heavy with concrete, was lifted into the air, and swung past me, over my head.

Bits of cement dripped down on me, and spattered on the sign at my feet. The sign was for the Nakamoto Construction Company, and it said in bold letters: BUILDING FOR A NEW TOMORROW. And underneath, PLEASE EXCUSE THE INCONVENIENCE.

It took another hour to get everything settled at the site. And the chief wanted our reports by the end of the day, so afterward we had to go down to Parker to do the paperwork.

It was four o'clock before we went across the street to the coffee shop next to Antonio's bail bond shop. Just to get away from the office. I said, 'Why did Ishiguro kill the girl in the first place?'

Connor sighed. 'It's not clear. The best I can understand it is this. Eddie was working for his father's *kaisha* all along. One of the things he did was supply girls for visiting dignitaries. He'd been doing that for years. It was easy – he was a party guy; he knew the girls; the congressmen wanted to meet the girls, and he got a chance to make friends with the congressmen. But in Cheryl he had a special opportunity, because Senator Morton, head of the Finance Committee, was attracted to her. Morton was smart enough to break off the affair, but Eddie kept sending her in private jets to meet him unexpectedly, keeping the thing alive. Eddie liked her, too: he had sex with her that afternoon. And it was Eddie who arranged for her to come to the party at Nakamoto, knowing that Morton would be there. Eddie was pushing Morton to block the sale, so Eddie was preoccupied with the Saturday meeting. By the way, on the news-station tape you thought he said "no cheapie" to Cheryl. He was saying *nichibei*. The Japanese-American relationship.

'But I think Eddie just intended for Cheryl to meet Morton. I doubt he had any idea about the forty-sixth floor. He certainly didn't expect her to go up there with Morton. The idea of going there must have been suggested during the party by someone from Nakamoto. The company left the floor accessible for a very simple reason: there's a bedroom suite up there that executives sometimes use. Somewhere in the back.'

I said, 'How did you know that?'

Connor smiled. 'Hanada-san mentioned he had once used it. Apparently it's quite luxurious.'

'So you *do* have contacts.'

'I have a few. I imagine Nakamoto was probably just being accommodating, too. They may have installed cameras up there with the idea of blackmail, but I'm told there were no cameras in the bedroom suite. And the fact that they had a camera right in the conference room suggests to me that Phillips was right – the cameras were placed to *kaizen* the office workers. Certainly they couldn't have expected the sexual encounter to occur where it did.

'Anyway, when Eddie saw Cheryl going off with Morton to another part of the Nakamoto building, it must have alarmed the hell out of him. So he followed them. He witnessed the murder, which I believe was probably accidental. And Eddie then helped out his friend Morton, calling him over, getting him out of there. Eddie went back to the party with Morton.'

'What about the tapes?'

'Ah. You remember we talked about bribery. One of Eddie's bribes was to a low-level security officer named Tanaka. I believe Eddie supplied him with drugs. Anyway, Eddie had known him for a couple of years. And when Ishiguro ordered Tanaka to pull the tapes, Tanaka told Eddie.'

'And Eddie went down and got the tapes himself.'

'Yes. Together with Tanaka.'

'But Phillips said Eddie was alone.'

'Phillips lied, because he knew Tanaka. That's also why he didn't make more of a fuss – Tanaka said it was all right. But when Phillips told us the story, he left Tanaka out.'

'And then?'

'Ishiguro sent a couple of guys to clean out Cheryl's apartment. Tanaka took the tapes someplace to get them copied. Eddie went to the party in the hills.'

'But Eddie kept one.'

'Yes.'

I thought it over. 'But when we talked to Eddie at the party, he told a completely different story.'

Connor nodded. 'He lied.'

'Even to you, his friend?'

Connor shrugged. 'He thought he could get away with it.'

'What about Ishiguro? Why did he kill the girl?'

'To get Morton in his pocket. And it worked – they got Morton to change his position on MicroCon. For a while there, Morton was going to allow the sale to go forward.'

'Ishiguro would kill her for that? For some corporate sale?'

'No, I don't think it was calculated at all. Ishiguro was high-strung, under great pressure. He felt he had to prove himself to his superiors. He had much at stake – so much, that he behaved differently from an ordinary Japanese under these circumstances. And in a moment of extreme pressure, he killed the girl, yes. As he said, she was a woman of no importance.'

'Jesus.'

'But I think there's more to it than that. Morton was very ambivalent about the Japanese. I had the sense there was a lot of resentment – those jokes about dropping the bomb, all that. And having sex on the boardroom table. It's . . . disrespectful, wouldn't you say? It must have infuriated Ishiguro.'

'And who called in the murder?'

'Eddie.'

'Why?'

'To embarrass Nakamoto. Eddie got Morton safely back to the party, and then called in. Probably from a phone somewhere at the party. When he called, he didn't know about the security cameras yet. Then Tanaka told him about them, and Eddie started to worry that Ishiguro might set him up. So he called back.'

'And he asked for his friend John Connor.'

'Yes.'

I said, 'So Eddie was Koichi Nishi?'

Connor nodded. 'His little joke. Koichi Nishi is the name of a character in a famous Japanese movie about corporate corruption.'

Connor finished his coffee and pushed away from the counter.

'And Ishiguro? Why did the Japanese abandon him?'

'Ishiguro had played it too fast and loose. He acted too independently Thursday night. They don't like that. Nakamoto would have sent him back pretty soon. He was destined to spend the rest of his life in Japan in a *madogiwa-zoku*. A window seat. Somebody who's bypassed by corporate decisions, and stares out the window all day. In a way, it's a life sentence.'

I thought it over. 'So when you used the car phone, calling the station, telling them what you planned . . . who was listening?'

'Hard to say.' Connor shrugged. 'But I liked Eddie. I owed him one. I didn't want to see Ishiguro go home.'

Back in the office there was an elderly woman waiting for me. She was dressed in black and she introduced herself as Cheryl Austin's grandmother. Cheryl's parents died in a car crash when she was four, and she had raised the little girl afterward. She wanted to thank me for my help in the investigation. She talked about what Cheryl had been like, as a little girl. How she had grown up in Texas.

'Of course, she was pretty,' she said, 'and the boys surely did like her.

Always a bunch of them hanging around, you couldn't shake them off with a stick.' She paused. 'Of course, I never thought she was entirely right in the head. But she wanted to keep those boys around. And she liked them to fight over her, too. I remember when she was seven or eight, she'd get those kids brawling in the dust, and she'd clap her hands and watch them go at it. By the time she was teenage, she was real good at it. Knew just what to do. It wasn't real nice to see. No, something was wrong in the head. She could be mean. And that song, she always played it, day and night. About lose my mind, I'd think.'

'Jerry Lee Lewis?'

'Of course, I knew why. That was her Daddy's favorite song. When she was just a little bit of a thing, he'd drive her to town in his convertible, with his arm around her, and the radio making that awful racket. She'd have her best sundress on. She was such a pretty thing when she was a child. The image of her mother.'

Then the woman started to cry, thinking about that. I got her a Kleenex. Tried to be sympathetic.

And pretty soon she wanted to know what had happened. How Cheryl had died.

I didn't know what to say to her.

As I was coming out of the ground-floor entrance to Parker Center, walking out by the fountains, a Japanese man in a suit stopped me. He was about forty, with dark hair and a moustache. He greeted me formally, and gave me his card. It took a moment to realize that this was Mr Shirai, the head of finance for Nakamoto.

'I wanted to see you in person, Sumisu-san, to express to you how much my company regrets the behavior of Mr Ishiguro. His actions were not proper and he acted without authority. Nakamoto is an honorable company and we do not violate the law. I want to assure you that he does not represent our company, or what we stand for in doing business. In this country, the work of Mr Ishiguro put him in contact with many investment bankers, and men who make leveraged buy-outs. Frankly, I believe he was too long in America. He adopted many bad habits here.'

So there it was, an apology and an insult in the same moment. I didn't know what to say to him, either.

Finally, I said, 'Mr Shirai, there was the offer of financing, for a small house . . .'

'Oh, yes?'

'Yes. Perhaps you didn't hear of it.'

'Actually, I believe I have heard something of that.'

I said, 'I was wondering what you intended to do about that offer now.'

There was a long silence.

Just the splash of the fountains off to my right.

Shirai squinted at me in the hazy afternoon light, trying to decide how to play it.

Finally he said, 'Sumisu-san, the offer is improper. It is of course withdrawn.'

'Thank you, Mr Shirai,' I said.

Connor and I drove back to my apartment. Neither of us talked. I was driving on the Santa Monica freeway. The signs overhead had been spray-painted by gangs. I was aware of how uneven and bumpy the roadway was. To the right, the skyscrapers around Westwood stood hazy in smog. The landscape looked poor and decrepit.

Finally I said, 'So is that all this was? Just competition between Nakamoto and some other Japanese company? Over MicroCon? Or what?'

Connor shrugged. 'Multiple purposes, probably. The Japanese think in those ways. And to them, America is now only an arena for their competition. That much is true. We're just not very important, in their eyes.'

We came to my street. There was a time when I thought it was pleasant, a little tree-lined street of apartments, with a playground at the end of the block for my daughter. Now I wasn't feeling that way. The air was bad, and the street seemed dirty, unpleasant.

I parked the car. Connor got out, shook my hand. 'Don't be discouraged.'

'I am.'

'Don't be. It's very serious. But it can all change. It's changed before. It can change again.'

'I guess.'

'What are you going to do now?' he asked.

'I don't know,' I said. 'I feel like going somewhere else. But there's nowhere to go.'

He nodded. 'Leave the department?'

'Probably. Certainly leave Special Services. It's too . . . unclear for me.'

He nodded. 'Take care, *kōhai.* Thanks for your help.'

'You, too, *sempai.*'

I was tired. I climbed the stairs to my apartment and went inside. It was quiet, with my daughter gone. I got a can of Coke from the refrigerator and walked into the living room, but my back hurt when I sat in the chair. I got up again, and turned on the television. I couldn't watch it. I thought of how Connor said everybody in America focused on the unimportant things. It was like the situation with Japan: if you sell the country to Japan, they will own it, whether you like it or not. And people who own things do what they want with them. That's how it works.

I walked into my bedroom and changed my clothes. On the bedside table, I saw the pictures from my daughter's birthday that I had been sorting when all this started. The pictures that didn't look like her, that didn't fit the reality anymore. I listened to the tinny laughter from the television in the other room. I used to think things were basically all right. But they're not all right.

I walked into my daughter's room. I looked at her crib, and her covers with the elephants sewn on it. I thought of the way she slept, so trustingly, lying on her back, her arms thrown over her head. I thought of the way she trusted me to make her world for her now. And I thought of the world that she would grow into. And as I started to make her bed, I felt uneasy in my heart.

Transcript of: March 15 (99)

INT: All right, Pete, I think that about does it for us. Unless you have anything else.

SUBJ: No. I'm done.

INT: I understand you resigned from the Special Services.

SUBJ: That's right.

INT: And you made a written recommendation to Chief Olson that the Asian liaison program be changed. You said the connection with the Japan–America Amity Foundation should be severed?

SUBJ: Yes.

INT: Why is that?

SUBJ: If the department wants specially trained officers, we should pay to train them. I just think it's healthier.

INT: Healthier?

SUBJ: Yes. It's time for us to take control of our country again. It's time for us to start paying our own way.

INT: Have you had a response from the Chief?

SUBJ: Not yet. I'm still waiting.

If you don't want Japan to buy it, don't sell it

– Akio Morita

AFTERWORD

'People deny reality. They fight against real feelings caused by real circumstances. They build mental worlds of shoulds, oughts, and might-have-beens. Real changes begin with real appraisal and acceptance of what it is. Then realistic action is possible.'

These are the words of David Reynolds, an American exponent of Japanese Morita psychotherapy. He is speaking of personal behavior, but his comments are applicable to the economic behavior of nations, as well.

Sooner or later, the United States must come to grips with the fact that Japan has become the leading industrial nation in the world. The Japanese have the longest lifespan. They have the highest employment, the highest literacy, the smallest gap between rich and poor. Their manufactured products have the highest quality. They have the best food. The fact is that a country the size of Montana, with half our population, will soon have an economy equal to ours.

But they haven't succeeded by doing things our way. Japan is not a Western industrial state; it is organized quite differently. And the Japanese have invented a new kind of trade – adversarial trade, trade like war, trade intended to wipe out the competition – which America has failed to understand for several decades. The United States keeps insisting the Japanese do things our way. But increasingly, their response is to ask, why should *we* change? We're doing better than you are. And indeed they are.

What should the American response be? It is absurd to blame Japan for successful behavior, or to suggest that they slow down. The Japanese consider such American reactions childish whining, and they are right. It is more appropriate for the United States to wake up, to see Japan clearly, and to act realistically.

In the end, that will mean major changes in the United States, but it is inevitably the task of the weaker partner to adjust to the demands of a relationship. And the United States is now without question the weaker partner in any economic discussion with Japan.

A century ago, when Admiral Perry's American fleet opened the nation, Japan was a feudal society. The Japanese realized they had to change, and they did. Starting in the 1860s, they brought in thousands of Western specialists to advise them on how to change their government and their industries. The entire society underwent a revolution. There was a second convulsion, equally dramatic, after World War II.

But in both cases, the Japanese faced the challenge squarely, and met it. They didn't say, let the Americans buy our land and our institutions and hope they will teach us to do things better. Not at all. The Japanese invited thousands of experts to visit – and then sent them home again. We would do well to take the same approach. The Japanese are not our saviors. They are our competitors. We should not forget it.

The Andromeda Strain

for
A.C.D., M.D.
who first proposed
the problem

The survival value of human intelligence has never been satisfactorily demonstrated.

JEREMY STONE

Increasing vision is increasingly expensive.

R. A. JANEK

ANDROMEDA STRAIN

THIS FILE IS CLASSIFIED TOP SECRET

Examination by unauthorized persons
is a criminal offense punishable
by fines and imprisonment up to
20 years and $20,000.

DO NOT ACCEPT FROM COURIER
IF SEAL IS BROKEN

The courier is required by law
to demand your card 7592. He
is not permitted to relinquish
this file without such proof of
identity.

MACHINE SCORE REVIEW BELOW

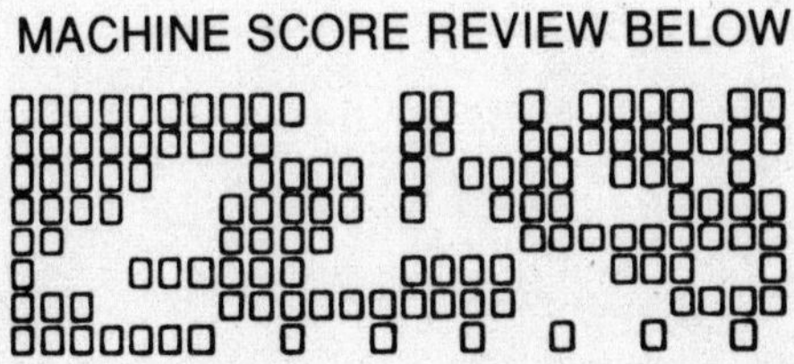

ACKNOWLEDGMENTS

This book recounts the five-day history of a major American scientific crisis.

As in most crises, the events surrounding the Andromeda Strain were a compound of foresight and foolishness, innocence and ignorance. Nearly everyone involved had moments of great brilliance, and moments of unaccountable stupidity. It is therefore impossible to write about the events without offending some of the participants.

However, I think it is important that the story be told. This country supports the largest scientific establishment in the history of mankind. New discoveries are constantly being made, and many of these discoveries have important political or social overtones. In the near future, we can expect more crises on the pattern of Andromeda. Thus I believe it is useful for the public to be made aware of the way in which scientific crises arise, and are dealt with.

In researching and recounting the history of the Andromeda Strain, I received the generous help of many people who felt as I did, and who encouraged me to tell the story accurately and in detail.

My particular thanks must go to Major General Willis A. Haverford, United States Army; Lieutenant Everett J. Sloane, United States Navy (Ret.); Captain L. S. Waterhouse, United States Air Force (Vandenberg Special Projects Division); Colonel Henley Jackson and Colonel Stanley Friedrich, both of Wright Patterson; and Murray Charles of the Pentagon Press Division.

For their help in elucidating the background of the Wildfire Project, I must thank Roger White, National Aeronautics and Space Administration (Houston MSC); John Roble, NASA Kennedy Complex 13; Peter J. Mason, NASA Intelligence (Arlington Hall); Dr. Francis Martin, University of California (Berkeley) and the President's Science Advisory Council; Dr. Max Byrd, USIA; Kenneth Vorhees, White House Press Corps; and Professor Jonathan Percy of the University of Chicago (Genetics Department)

For their review of relevant chapters of the manuscript, and for their technical corrections and suggestions, I wish to thank Christian P. Lewis, Goddard Space Flight Center; Herbert Stanch, Avco, Inc.; James P. Baker, Jet Propulsion Laboratory; Carlos N. Sandos, California Institute of Technology; Dr. Brian Stack, University of Michigan; Edgar Blalock, Hudson Institute; Professor Linus Kjelling, the RAND Corporation; Dr. Eldredge Benson, National Institutes of Health.

Lastly, I wish to thank the participants in the Wildfire Project and the investigation of the so-called Andromeda Strain. All agreed to see me and, with many, my interviews lasted over a period of days. Furthermore, I was able to draw upon the transcripts of their debriefing, which are stored in Arlington Hall (Substation Seven) and which amounted to more than fifteen thousand pages of typewritten manuscript. This material, stored in twenty volumes, represents the full story of the events at Flatrock, Nevada, as told by each of the participants, and I was thus able to utilize their separate viewpoints in preparing a composite account.

This is a rather technical narrative, centering on complex issues of science. Wherever possible, I have explained the scientific questions, problems, and techniques. I have avoided the temptation to simplify both the issues and the answers, and if the reader must occasionally struggle through an arid passage of technical detail, I apologize.

I have also tried to retain the tension and excitement of events in these five days, for there is an inherent drama in the story of Andromeda, and if it is a chronicle of stupid, deadly blunders, it is also a chronicle of heroism and intelligence.

M.C.
Cambridge, Massachusetts
January 1969

day 1
CONTACT

1 The Country of Lost Borders

A man with binoculars. That is how it began: with a man standing by the side of the road, on a crest overlooking a small Arizona town, on a winter night.

Lieutenant Roger Shawn must have found the binoculars difficult. The metal would be cold, and he would be clumsy in his fur parka and heavy gloves. His breath, hissing out into the moonlit air, would have fogged the lenses. He would be forced to pause to wipe them frequently, using a stubby gloved finger.

He could not have known the futility of this action. Binoculars were worthless to see into that town and uncover its secrets. He would have been astonished to learn that the men who finally succeeded used instruments a million times more powerful than binoculars.

There is something sad, foolish, and human in the image of Shawn leaning against a boulder, propping his arms on it, and holding the binoculars to his eyes. Though cumbersome, the binoculars would at least feel comfortable and familiar in his hands. It would be one of the last familiar sensations before his death.

We can imagine, and try to reconstruct, what happened from that point on.

Lieutenant Shawn swept over the town slowly and methodically. He could see it was not large, just a half-dozen wooden buildings, set out along a single main street. It was very quiet: no lights, no activity, no sound carried by the gentle wind.

He shifted his attention from the town to the surrounding hills. They were low, dusty, and blunted, with scrubby vegetation and an occasional withered yucca tree crusted in snow. Beyond the hills were more hills, and then the flat expanse of the Mojave Desert, trackless and vast. The Indians called it the Country of Lost Borders.

Lieutenant Shawn found himself shivering in the wind. It was February, the coldest month, and it was after ten. He walked back up the road toward the Ford Econovan, with the large rotating antenna on top. The motor was idling softly; it was the only sound he could hear. He opened the rear doors and climbed into the back, shutting the doors behind him.

He was enveloped in deep-red light: a night light, so that he would not be blinded when he stepped outside. In the red light the banks of instruments and electronic equipment glowed greenly.

Private Lewis Crane, the electronics technician, was there, also wearing a parka. He was hunched over a map, making calculations with occasional reference to the instruments before him.

Shawn asked Crane if he were certain they had arrived at the place, and Crane confirmed that they had. Both men were tired: they had driven all day from Vandenberg, in search of the latest Scoop satellite. Neither knew much about the Scoops, except that they were a series of secret capsules intended to analyze the upper atmosphere and then return. Shawn and Crane had the job of finding the capsules once they had landed.

In order to facilitate recovery, the satellites were fitted with electronic beepers that began to transmit signals when they came down to an altitude of five miles.

That was why the van had so much radio-directional equipment. In essence, it was performing its own triangulation. In Army parlance it was known as single-unit triangulation, and it was highly effective, though slow. The procedure was simple enough: the van stopped and fixed its position, recording the strength and direction of the radio beam from the satellite. Once this was done, it would be driven in the most likely direction of the satellite for a distance of twenty miles. Then it would stop and take new coordinates. In this way, a series of triangulation points could be mapped, and the van could proceed to the satellite by a zigzag path, stopping every twenty miles to correct any error. The method was slower than using two vans, but it was safer – the Army felt that two vans in an area might arouse suspicion.

For six hours, the van had been closing on the Scoop satellite. Now they were almost there.

Crane tapped the map with a pencil in a nervous way and announced the name of the town at the foot of the hill: Piedmont, Arizona. Population forty-eight; both men laughed over that, though they were both inwardly concerned. The Vandenberg ESA, or Estimated Site of Arrival, had been twelve miles north of Piedmont. Vandenberg computed this site on the basis of radar observations and 1410 computer trajectory projections. The estimates were not usually wrong by more than a few hundred yards.

Yet there was no denying the radio-directional equipment, which located the satellite beeper directly in the center of town. Shawn suggested that someone from the town might have seen it coming down

– it would be glowing with the heat – and might have retrieved it, bringing it into Piedmont.

This was reasonable, except that a native of Piedmont who happened upon an American satellite fresh from space would have told someone – reporters, police, NASA, the Army, *someone.*

But they had heard nothing.

Shawn climbed back down from the van, with Crane scrambling after him, shivering as the cold air struck him. Together, the two men looked out over the town.

It was peaceful, but completely dark. Shawn noticed that the gas station and the motel both had their lights doused. Yet they represented the only gas station and motel for miles.

And then Shawn noticed the birds.

In the light of the full moon he could see them, big birds, gliding in slow circles over the buildings, passing like black shadows across the face of the moon. He wondered why he hadn't noticed them before, and asked Crane what he made of them.

Crane said he didn't make anything of them. As a joke, he added, 'Maybe they're buzzards.'

'That's what they look like, all right,' Shawn said.

Crane laughed nervously, his breath hissing out into the night. 'But why should there be buzzards here? They only come when something is dead.'

Shawn lit a cigarette, cupping his hands around the lighter, protecting the flame from the wind. He said nothing, but looked down at the buildings, the outline of the little town. Then he scanned the town once more with binoculars, but saw no signs of life or movement.

At length, he lowered the binoculars and dropped his cigarette onto the crisp snow, where it sputtered and died.

He turned to Crane and said, 'We'd better go down and have a look.'

2 Vandenberg

Three hundred miles away, in the large, square, windowless room that served as Mission Control for Project Scoop, Lieutenant Edgar Comroe sat with his feet on his desk and a stack of scientific-journal articles before him. Comroe was serving as control officer for the night; it was a duty he filled once a month, directing the evening operations of the skeleton crew of twelve. Tonight, the crew was monitoring the progress and reports of the van coded Caper One, now making its way across the Arizona desert.

Comroe disliked this job. The room was gray and lighted with fluorescent lights; the tone was sparsely utilitarian and Comroe found it unpleasant. He never came to Mission Control except during a launch, when the atmosphere was different. Then the room was filled with busy technicians, each at work on a single complex task, each tense with the peculiar cold anticipation that precedes any spacecraft launch.

But nights were dull. Nothing ever happened at night. Comroe took advantage of the time and used it to catch up on reading. By profession he was a cardiovascular physiologist, with special interest in stresses induced at high-G accelerations.

Tonight, Comroe was reviewing a journal article titled 'Stoichiometrics of Oxygen-Carrying Capacity and Diffusion Gradients with Increased Arterial Gas Tensions.' He found it slow reading, and only moderately interesting. Thus he was willing to be interrupted when the overhead loudspeaker, which carried the voice transmissions from the van of Shawn and Crane, clicked on.

Shawn said, 'This is Caper One to Vandal Deca. Caper One to Vandal Deca. Are you reading. Over.'

Comroe, feeling amused, replied that he was indeed reading.

'We are about to enter the town of Piedmont and recover the satellite.'

'Very good, Caper One. Leave your radio open.'

'Roger.'

This was a regulation of the recovery technique, as outlined in the Systems Rules Manual of Project Scoop. The SRM was a thick gray paperback that sat at one corner of Comroe's desk, where he could refer to it easily. Comroe knew that conversation between van and base was taped, and later became part of the permanent project file, but he had never understood any good reason for this. In fact, it had always seemed to him a straightforward proposition: the van went out, got the capsule, and came back.

He shrugged and returned to his paper on gas tensions, only half listening to Shawn's voice as it said, 'We are now inside the town. We have just passed a gas station and a motel. All quiet here. There is no sign of life. The signals from the satellite are stronger. There is a church half a block ahead. There are no lights or activity of any kind.'

Comroe put his journal down. The strained quality of Shawn's voice was unmistakable. Normally Comroe would have been amused at the thought of two grown men made jittery by entering a small, sleepy desert town. But he knew Shawn personally, and he knew that Shawn, whatever other virtues he might have, utterly lacked an imagination. Shawn could fall asleep in a horror movie. He was that kind of man.

Comroe began to listen.

Over the crackling static, he heard the rumbling of the van engine. And he heard the two men in the van talking quietly.

Shawn: 'Pretty quiet around here.'

Crane: 'Yes sir.'

There was a pause.

Crane: 'Sir?'

Shawn: 'Yes?'

Crane: 'Did you see that?'

Shawn: 'See what?'

Crane: 'Back there, on the sidewalk. It looked like a body.'

Shawn: 'You're imagining things.'

Another pause, and then Comroe heard the van come to a halt, brakes squealing.

Shawn: 'Jesus.'

Crane: 'It's another one, sir.'

Shawn: 'Looks dead.'

Crane: 'Shall I –'

Shawn: 'No. Stay in the van.'

His voice became louder, more formal, as he ran through the call. 'This is Caper One to Vandal Deca. Over.'

Comroe picked up the microphone. 'Reading you. What's happened?'

Shawn, his voice tight, said, 'Sir, we see bodies. Lots of them. They appear to be dead.'

'Are you certain, Caper One?'

'For Christ's sake,' Shawn said. 'Of course we're certain.'

Comroe said mildly, 'Proceed to the capsule, Caper One.'

As he did so, he looked around the room. The twelve other men in the skeleton crew were staring at him, their eyes blank, unseeing. They were listening to the transmission.

The van rumbled to life again.

Comroe swung his feet off the desk and punched the red 'Security' button on his console. That button automatically isolated the Mission Control room. No one would be allowed in or out without Comroe's permission.

Then he picked up the telephone and said, 'Get me Major Manchek. M-A-N-C-H-E-K. This is a stat call. I'll hold.'

Manchek was the chief duty officer for the month, the man directly responsible for all Scoop activities during February.

While he waited, he cradled the phone in his shoulder and lit a cigarette. Over the loudspeaker, Shawn could be heard to say, 'Do they look dead to you, Crane?'

Crane: 'Yes sir. Kind of peaceful, but dead.'

Shawn: 'Somehow they don't really look dead. There's something missing. Something funny . . . But they're all over. Must be dozens of them.'

Crane: 'Like they dropped in their tracks. Stumbled and fallen down dead.'

Shawn: 'All over the streets, on the sidewalks . . .'

Another silence, then Crane: 'Sir!'

Shawn: 'Jesus.'

Crane: 'You see him? The man in the white robe, walking across the street –'

Shawn: 'I see him.'

Crane: 'He's just stepping over them like –'

Shawn: 'He's coming toward us.'

Crane: 'Sir, look, I think we should get out of here, if you don't mind my –'

The next sound was a high-pitched scream, and a crunching noise. Transmission ended at this point, and Vandenberg Scoop Mission Control was not able to raise the two men again.

3 Crisis

Gladstone, upon hearing of the death of 'Chinese' Gordon in Egypt, was reported to have muttered irritably that his general might have chosen a more propitious time to die: Gordon's death threw the Gladstone government into turmoil and crisis. An aide suggested that the circumstances were unique and unpredictable, to which Gladstone crossly answered: 'All crises are the same.'

He meant political crises, of course. There were no scientific crises in 1885, and indeed none for nearly forty years afterward. Since then there have been eight of major importance; two have received wide publicity. It is interesting that both the publicized crises – atomic energy and space capability – have concerned chemistry and physics, not biology.

This is to be expected. Physics was the first of the natural sciences to become fully modern and highly mathematical. Chemistry followed in the wake of physics, but biology, the retarded child, lagged far behind. Even in the time of Newton and Galileo, men knew more about the moon and other heavenly bodies than they did about their own.

It was not until the late 1940's that this situation changed. The postwar period ushered in a new era of biologic research, spurred by the discovery of antibiotics. Suddenly there was both enthusiasm and money for biology, and a torrent of discoveries poured forth: tranquilizers, steroid hormones, immunochemistry, the genetic code. By 1953 the first kidney was transplanted and by 1958 the first birth-control pills were tested. It was not long before biology was the fastest-growing field in all science; it was doubling its knowledge every ten years. Farsighted researchers talked seriously of changing genes, controlling evolution, regulating the mind – ideas that had been wild speculation ten years before.

And yet there had never been a biologic crisis. The Andromeda Strain provided the first.

According to Lewis Bornheim, a crisis is a situation in which a previously tolerable set of circumstances is suddenly, by the addition of another factor, rendered wholly intolerable. Whether the additional factor is political, economic, or scientific hardly matters: the death of a national hero, the instability of prices, or a technological discovery can all set events in motion. In this sense, Gladstone was right: all crises are the same.

The noted scholar Alfred Pockran, in his study of crises (*Culture, Crisis and Change*), has made several interesting points. First, he observes that every crisis has its beginnings long before the actual onset. Thus Einstein published his theories of relativity in 1905–15, forty years before his work culminated in the end of a war, the start of an age, and the beginnings of a crisis.

Similarly, in the early twentieth century, American, German, and Russian scientists were all interested in space travel, but only the Germans recognized the military potential of rockets. And after the war, when the German rocket installation at Peenemünde was cannibalized by the Soviets and Americans, it was only the Russians who made immediate, vigorous moves toward developing space capabilities. The Americans were content to tinker playfully with rockets – and ten years later, this resulted in an American scientific crisis involving Sputnik, American education, the ICBM, and the missile gap.

Pockran also observes that a crisis is compounded of individuals and personalities, which are unique:

> It is as difficult to imagine Alexander at the Rubicon, and Eisenhower at Waterloo, as it is difficult to imagine Darwin writing to Roosevelt about the potential for an atomic bomb. A crisis is made by men, who enter into the crisis with their own prejudices, propensities, and predispositions. A crisis is the sum of intuition and blind spots, a blend of facts noted and facts ignored.
>
> Yet underlying the uniqueness of each crisis is a disturbing sameness. A characteristic of all crises is their predictability, in retrospect. They seem to have a certain inevitability, they seem predestined. This is not true of all crises, but it is true of sufficiently many to make the most hardened historian cynical and misanthropic.

In the light of Pockran's arguments, it is interesting to consider the background and personalities involved in the Andromeda Strain. At the time of Andromeda, there had never been a crisis of biological science, and the first Americans faced with the facts were not disposed to think in terms of one. Shawn and Crane were capable but not thoughtful men, and Edgar Comroe, the night officer at Vandenberg, though a scientist, was not prepared to consider anything beyond the immediate irritation of a quiet evening ruined by an inexplicable problem.

According to protocol, Comroe called his superior officer, Major Arthur Manchek, and here the story takes a different turn. For Manchek was both prepared and disposed to consider a crisis of the most major proportions.

But he was not prepared to acknowledge it.

*

Major Manchek, his face still creased with sleep, sat on the edge of Comroe's desk and listened to the replay of the tape from the van.

When it was finished, he said, 'Strangest damned thing I ever heard,' and played it over again. While he did so, he carefully filled his pipe with tobacco, lit it, and tamped it down.

Arthur Manchek was an engineer, a quiet heavyset man plagued by labile hypertension, which threatened to end further promotions as an Army officer. He had been advised on many occasions to lose weight, but had been unable to do so. He was therefore considering abandoning the Army for a career as a scientist in private industry, where people did not care what your weight or blood pressure was.

Manchek had come to Vandenberg from Wright Patterson in Ohio, where he had been in charge of experiments in spacecraft landing methods. His job had been to develop a capsule shape that could touch down with equal safety on either land or sea. Manchek had succeeded in developing three new shapes that were promising; his success led to a promotion and transfer to Vandenberg.

Here he did administrative work, and hated it. People bored Manchek; the mechanics of manipulation and the vagaries of subordinate personality held no fascination for him. He often wished he were back at the wind tunnels of Wright Patterson.

Particularly on nights when he was called out of bed by some damnfool problem.

Tonight he felt irritable, and under stress. His reaction to this was characteristic: he became slow. He moved slowly, he thought slowly, he proceeded with a dull and plodding deliberation. It was the secret of his success. Whenever people around him became excited, Manchek seemed to grow more disinterested, until he appeared about to fall asleep. It was a trick he had for remaining totally objective and clear-headed.

Now he sighed and puffed on his pipe as the tape spun out for the second time.

'No communications breakdown, I take it?'

Comroe shook his head. 'We checked all systems at this end. We are still monitoring the frequency.' He turned on the radio, and hissing static filled the room. 'You know about the audio screen?'

'Vaguely,' Manchek said, suppressing a yawn. In fact, the audio screen was a system he had developed three years before. In simplest terms, it was a computerized way to find a needle in a haystack – a machine program that listened to apparently garbled, random sound and picked out certain irregularities. For example, the hubbub of conversation at an embassy cocktail party could be recorded and fed through the computer, which would pick out a single voice and separate it from the rest.

It had several intelligence applications.

'Well,' Comroe said, 'after the transmission ended, we got nothing but the static you hear now. We put it through the audio screen, to see if the computer could pick up a pattern. And we ran it through the oscilloscope in the corner.'

Across the room, the green face of the scope displayed a jagged dancing white line – the summated sound of static.

'Then,' Comroe said, 'we cut in the computer. Like so.'

He punched a button on his desk console. The oscilloscope line changed character abruptly. It suddenly became quieter, more regular, with a pattern of beating, thumping impulses.

'I see,' Manchek said. He had, in fact, already identified the pattern and assessed its meaning. His mind was drifting elsewhere, considering other possibilities, wider ramifications.

'Here's the audio,' Comroe said. He pressed another button and the audio version of the signal filled the room. It was a steady mechanical grinding with a repetitive metallic click.

Manchek nodded. 'An engine. With a knock.'

'Yes sir. We believe the van radio is still broadcasting, and that the engine is still running. That's what we're hearing now, with the static screened away.'

'All right,' Manchek said.

His pipe went out. He sucked on it for a moment, then lit it again, removed it from his mouth, and plucked a bit of tobacco from his tongue.

'We need evidence,' he said, almost to himself. He was considering categories of evidence, and possible findings, contingencies . . .

'Evidence of what?' Comroe said.

Manchek ignored the question. 'Have we got a Scavenger on the base?'

'I'm not sure, sir. If we don't, we can get one from Edwards.'

'Then do it.' Manchek stood up. He had made his decision, and now he felt tired again. An evening of telephone calls faced him, an evening of irritable operators and bad connections and puzzled voices at the other end.

'We'll want a flyby over that town,' he said. 'And a complete scan. All canisters to come directly. Alert the labs.'

He also ordered Comroe to bring in the technicians, especially

Jaggers. Manchek disliked Jaggers, who was effete and precious. But Manchek also knew that Jaggers was good, and tonight he needed a good man.

At 11:07 p.m., Samuel 'Gunner' Wilson was moving at 645 miles per hour over the Mojave Desert. Up ahead in the moonlight, he saw the twin lead jets, their afterburners glowing angrily in the night sky. The planes had a heavy, pregnant look: phosphorus bombs were slung beneath the wings and belly.

Wilson's plane was different, sleek and long and black. It was a Scavenger, one of seven in the world.

The Scavenger was the operational version of the X-18. It was an intermediate-range reconnaissance jet aircraft fully equipped for day or night intelligence flights. It was fitted with two side-slung 16mm cameras, one for the visible spectrum, and one for low-frequency radiation. In addition it had a center-mount Homans infrared multispex camera as well as the usual electronic and radio-detection gear. All films and plates were, of course, processed automatically in the air, and were ready for viewing as soon as the aircraft returned to base.

All this technology made the Scavenger almost impossibly sensitive. It could map the outlines of a city in blackout, and could follow the movements of individual trucks and cars at eight thousand feet. It could detect a submarine to a depth of two hundred feet. It could locate harbor mines by wave-motion deformities and it could obtain a precise photograph of a factory from the residual heat of the building four hours after it had shut down.

So the Scavenger was the ideal instrument to fly over Piedmont, Arizona, in the dead of night.

Wilson carefully checked his equipment, his hands fluttering over the controls, touching each button and lever, watching the blinking green lights that indicated that all systems were in order.

His earphones crackled. The lead plane said lazily, 'Coming up on the town, Gunner. You see it?'

He leaned forward in the cramped cockpit. He was low, only five hundred feet above ground, and for a moment he could see nothing but a blur of sand, snow, and yucca trees. Then, up ahead, buildings in the moonlight.

'Roger. I see it.'

'Okay, Gunner. Give us room.'

He dropped back, putting half a mile between himself and the other two planes. They were going into the P-square formation, for direct visualization of target by phosphorus flare. Direct visualization was not really necessary; Scavenger could function without it. But Vandenberg seemed insistent that they gather all possible information about the town.

The lead planes spread, moving wide until they were parallel to the main street of the town.

'Gunner? Ready to roll?'

Wilson placed his fingers delicately over the camera buttons. Four fingers: as if playing the piano.

'Ready.'

'We're going in now.'

The two planes swooped low, dipping gracefully toward the town. They were now very wide and seemingly inches above the ground as they began to release the bombs. As each struck the ground, a blazing white-hot sphere went up, bathing the town in an unearthly, glaring light and reflecting off the metal underbellies of the planes.

The jets climbed, their run finished, but Gunner did not see them. His entire attention, his mind and his body, was focused on the town.

'All yours, Gunner.'

Wilson did not answer. He dropped his nose, cracked down his flaps, and felt a shudder as the plane sank sickeningly, like a stone, toward the ground. Below him, the area around the town was lighted for hundreds of yards in every direction. He pressed the camera buttons and felt, rather than heard, the vibrating whir of the cameras.

For a long moment he continued to fall, and then he shoved the stick forward, and the plane seemed to catch in the air, to grab, and lift and climb. He had a fleeting glimpse of the main street. He saw bodies, bodies everywhere, spreadeagled, lying in the streets, across cars . . .

'Jesus,' he said.

And then he was up, still climbing, bringing the plane around in a slow arc, preparing for the descent into his second run and trying not to think of what he had seen. One of the first rules of air reconnaissance was 'Ignore the scenery'; analysis and evaluation were not the job of the pilot. That was left to the experts, and pilots who forgot this, who became too interested in what they were photographing, got into trouble. Usually they crashed.

As the plane came down into a flat second run, he tried not to look at the ground. But he did, and again saw the bodies. The phosphorus flares were burning low, the lighting was darker, more sinister and subdued. But the bodies were still there: he had not been imagining it.

'Jesus,' he said again. 'Sweet Jesus.'

The sign on the door said DATA PROSSEX EPSILON, and underneath, in red lettering, ADMISSION BY CLEARANCE CARD ONLY. Inside was a comfortable sort of briefing room: screen on one wall, a dozen steel-tubing and leather chairs facing it, and a projector in the back.

When Manchek and Comroe entered the room, Jaggers was already waiting for them, standing at the front of the room by the screen. Jaggers was a short man with a springy step and an eager, rather hopeful face. Though not well liked on the base, he was nonetheless the acknowledged master of reconnaissance interpretation. He had the sort of mind that delighted in small and puzzling details, and was well suited to his job.

Jaggers rubbed his hands as Manchek and Comroe sat down. 'Well then,' he said. 'Might as well get right to it. I think we have something to interest you tonight.' He nodded to the projectionist in the back. 'First picture.'

The room lights darkened. There was a mechanical click, and the screen lighted to show an aerial view of a small desert town.

'This is an unusual shot,' Jaggers said. 'From our files. Taken two months ago from Janos 12, our recon satellite. Orbiting at an altitude of one hundred and eighty-seven miles, as you know. The technical quality here is quite good. Can't read the license plates on the cars yet, but we're working on it. Perhaps by next year.'

Manchek shifted in his chair, but said nothing.

'You can see the town here,' Jaggers said. 'Piedmont, Arizona. Population forty-eight, and not much to look at, even from one hundred and eighty-seven miles. Here's the general store; the gas station – notice how clearly you can read GULF – and the post office; the motel. Everything else you see is private residences. Church over here. Well: next picture.'

Another click. This was dark, with a reddish tint, and was clearly an overview of the town in white and dark red. The outlines of the buildings were very dark.

'We begin here with the Scavenger IR plates. These are infrared films, as you know, which produce a picture on the basis of heat instead of light. Anything warm appears white on the picture; anything cold is black. Now then. You can see here that the buildings are dark – they are colder than the ground. As night comes on, the buildings give up their heat more rapidly.'

'What are those white spots?' Comroe said. There were forty or fifty white areas on the film.

'Those,' Jaggers said, 'are bodies. Some inside houses, some in the street. By count, they number fifty. In the case of some of them, such as this one here, you can make out the four limbs and head clearly. This body is lying flat. In the street.'

He lit a cigarette and pointed to a white rectangle. 'As nearly as we can tell, this is an automobile. Notice it's got a bright white spot at one end. This means the motor is still running, still generating heat.'

'The van,' Comroe said. Manchek nodded.

'The question now arises,' Jaggers said, 'are all these people dead? We cannot be certain about that. The bodies appear to be of different temperatures. Forty-seven are rather cold, indicating death some time ago. Three are warmer. Two of those are in this car, here.'

'Our men,' Comroe said. 'And the third?'

'The third is rather puzzling. You see him here, apparently standing or lying curled in the street. Observe that he is quite white, and therefore quite warm. Our temperature scans indicate that he is about ninety-five degrees, which is a little on the cool side, but probably attributable to peripheral vasoconstriction in the night desert air. Drops his skin temperature. Next slide.'

The third film flicked onto the screen.

Manchek frowned at the spot. 'It's moved.'

'Exactly. This film was made on the second passage. The spot has moved approximately twenty yards. Next picture.'

A third film.

'Moved again!'

'Yes. An additional five or ten yards.'

'So one person down there is alive?'

'That,' Jaggers said, 'is the presumptive conclusion.'

Manchek cleared his throat. 'Does that mean it's what you think?'

'Yes sir. It is what we think.'

'There's a man down there, walking among the corpses?'

Jaggers shrugged and tapped the screen. 'It is difficult to account for the data in any other manner, and –'

At that moment, a private entered the room with three circular metal canisters under his arm.

'Sir, we have films of the direct visualization by P-square.'

'Run them,' Manchek said.

The film was threaded into a projector. A moment later, Lieutenant

Wilson was ushered into the room. Jaggers said, 'I haven't reviewed these films yet. Perhaps the pilot should narrate.'

Manchek nodded and looked at Wilson, who got up and walked to the front of the room, wiping his hands nervously on his pants. He stood alongside the screen and faced his audience, beginning in a flat monotone: 'Sir, my flybys were made between 11:08 and 11:13 p.m. this evening. There were two, a start from the east and a return from the west, done at an average speed of two hundred and fourteen miles per hour, at a median altitude by corrected altimeter of eight hundred feet and an –'

'Just a minute, son,' Manchek said, raising his hand. 'This isn't a grilling. Just tell it naturally.'

Wilson nodded and swallowed. The room lights went down and the projector whirred to life. The screen showed the town bathed in glaring white light as the plane came down over it.

'This is my first pass,' Wilson said. 'East to west, at 11:08. We're looking from the left-wing camera which is running at ninety-six frames per second. As you can see, my altitude is falling rapidly. Straight ahead is the main street of the target . . .'

He stopped. The bodies were clearly visible. And the van, stopped in the street, its rooftop antenna still turning slow revolutions. As the plane continued its run, approaching the van, they could see the driver collapsed over the steering wheel.

'Excellent definition,' Jaggers said. 'That fine-grain film really gives resolution when you need –'

'Wilson,' Manchek said, 'was telling us about his run.'

'Yes sir,' Wilson said, clearing his throat. He stared at the screen. 'At this time I am right over target, where I observed the casualties you see here. My estimate at that time was seventy-five, sir.'

His voice was quiet and tense. There was a break in the film, some numbers, and the image came on again.

'Now I am coming back for my second run,' Wilson said. 'The flares are already burning low but you can see –'

'Stop the film,' Manchek said.

The projectionist froze the film at a single frame. It showed the long, straight main street of the town, and the bodies.

'Go back.'

The film was run backward, the jet seeming to pull away from the street.

'There! Stop it now.'

The frame was frozen. Manchek got up and walked close to the screen, peering off to one side.

'Look at this,' he said, pointing to a figure. It was a man in knee-length white robes, standing and looking up at the plane. He was an old man, with a withered face. His eyes were wide.

'What do you make of this?' Manchek said to Jaggers.

Jaggers moved close. He frowned. 'Run it forward a bit.'

The film advanced. They could clearly see the man turn his head, roll his eyes, following the plane as it passed over him.

'Now backward,' Jaggers said.

The film was run back. Jaggers smiled bleakly. 'The man looks alive to me, sir.'

'Yes,' Manchek said crisply. 'He certainly does.'

And with that, he walked out of the room. As he left, he paused and announced that he was declaring a state of emergency; that everyone on the base was confined to quarters until further notice; that there would be no outside calls or communication; and that what they had seen in this room was confidential.

Outside in the hallway, he headed for Mission Control. Comroe followed him.

'I want you to call General Wheeler,' Manchek said. 'Tell him I have declared an SOE without proper authorization, and ask him to come down immediately.' Technically no one but the commander had the right to declare a state of emergency.

Comroe said, 'Wouldn't you rather tell him yourself?'

'I've got other things to do,' Manchek said.

4 Alert

When Arthur Manchek stepped into the small soundproofed booth and sat down before the telephone, he knew exactly what he was going to do – but he was not very sure why he was doing it.

As one of the senior Scoop officers, he had received a briefing nearly a year before on Project Wildfire. It had been given, Manchek remembered, by a short little man with a dry, precise way of speaking. He was a university professor and he had outlined the project. Manchek had forgotten the details, except that there was a laboratory somewhere, and a team of five scientists who could be alerted to man the laboratory. The function of the team was investigation of possible extraterrestrial life forms introduced on American spacecraft returning to earth.

Manchek had not been told who the five men were; he knew only that a special Defense Department trunk line existed for calling them out. In order to hook into the line, one had only to dial the binary of some number. He reached into his pocket and withdrew his wallet, then fumbled for a moment until he found the card he had been given by the professor:

IN CASE OF FIRE
Notify Division 87
Emergencies Only

He stared at the card and wondered what exactly would happen if he dialed the binary of 87. He tried to imagine the sequence of events: Who would he talk to? Would someone call him back? Would there be an inquiry, a referral to higher authority?

He rubbed his eyes and stared at the card, and finally he shrugged. One way or the other, he would find out.

He tore a sheet of paper from the pad in front of him, next to the telephone, and wrote:

2^0 2^1 2^2 2^3 2^4 2^5 2^6 2^7

This was the basis of the binary system: base two raised to some power. Two to the zero power was one; two to the first was two; two squared was four; and so on. Manchek quickly wrote another line beneath:

2^0	2^1	2^2	2^3	2^4	2^5	2^6	2^7
1	2	4	8	16	32	64	128

Then he began to add up the numbers to get a total of 87. He circled these numbers:

2^0	2^1	2^2	2^3	2^4	2^5	2^6	2^7
(1)	(2)	(4)	8	(16)	32	(64)	128 = 87

And then he drew in the binary code. Binary numbers were designed for computers which utilize an on-off, yes-no kind of language. A mathematician once joked that binary numbers were the way people who have only two fingers count. In essence, binary numbers translated normal numbers – which require nine digits, and decimal places – to a system that depended on only two digits, one and zero.

2^0	2^1	2^2	2^3	2^4	2^5	2^6	2^7
(1)	(2)	(4)	8	(16)	32	(64)	128
1	1	1	0	1	0	1	0

Manchek looked at the number he had just written, and inserted the dashes: 1-110-1010. A perfectly reasonable telephone number.

Manchek picked up the telephone and dialed.

The time was exactly twelve midnight.

day 2
PIEDMONT

5 The Early Hours

The machinery was there. The cables, the codes, the teleprinters had all been waiting dormant for two years. It only required Manchek's call to set the machinery in motion.

When he finished dialing, he heard a series of mechanical clicks, and then a low hum, which meant, he knew, that the call was being fed into one of the scrambled trunk lines. After a moment, the humming stopped and a voice said, 'This is a recording. State your name and your message and hang up.'

'Major Arthur Manchek, Vandenberg Air Force Base, Scoop Mission Control. I believe it is necessary to call up a Wildfire Alert. I have confirmatory visual data at this post, which has just been closed for security reasons.'

As he spoke it occurred to him that it was all rather improbable. Even the tape recorder would disbelieve him. He continued to hold the telephone in his hand, somehow expecting an answer.

But there was none, only a click as the connection was automatically broken. The line was dead; he hung up and sighed. It was all very unsatisfying.

Manchek expected to be called back within a few minutes by Washington; he expected to receive many calls in the next few hours, and so remained at the phone. Yet he received no calls, for he did not know that the process he had initiated was automatic. Once mobilized, the Wildfire Alert would proceed ahead, and not be recalled for at least twelve hours.

Within ten minutes of Manchek's call, the following message clattered across the scrambled maximum-security cabler units of the nation.

■■■■■■■■■UNIT■■■■■■■■■

TOP SECRET

CODE FOLLOWS
AS
CBW 9/9/234/435/6778/90
PULG COORDINATES DELTA 8997

MESSAGE FOLLOWS
AS
WILDFIRE ALERT HAS BEEN CALLED.
REPEAT WILDFIRE ALERT HAS BEEN
CALLED. COORDINATES TO READ
NASA/AMC/NSC COMB DEC.
TIME OF COMMAND TO READ
LL-59-07 ON DATE.

FURTHER NOTATIONS
AS
PRESS BLACKFACE
POTENTIAL DIRECTIVE 7-L2
ALERT STATUS UNTIL FURTHER NOTICE

END MESSAGE

■■■■■■■■■■■

DISENGAGE

This was an automatic cable. Everything about it, including the announcement of a press blackout and a possible directive 7-12, was automatic, and followed from Manchek's call.

Five minutes later, there was a second cable which named the men on the Wildfire team:

■■■■■■■■■ UNIT ■■■■■■■■■

TOP SECRET

CODE FOLLOWS
AS
CBW 9/9/234/435/6778/900

MESSAGE FOLLOWS
AS
THE FOLLOWING MALE AMERICAN
CITIZENS ARE BEING PLACED
ON ZED KAPPA STATUS. PREVIOUS

TOP SECRET CLEARANCE HAS BEEN
CONFIRMED. THE NAMES ARE+

STONE, JEREMY ■■81
LEAVITT, PETER ■■04
BARTON, CHARLES ■L51
CHRISTIANSENKRIKECANCEL THIS LINE CANCEL THIS LINE
CAN TO READ AS
KIRKE, CHRISTIAN ■142
HALL, MARK ■L77

ACCORD THESE MEN ZED KAPPA
STATUS UNTIL FURTHER NOTICE

END MESSAGE END MESSAGE

In theory, this cable was also quite routine; its purpose was to name the five members who were being given Zed Kappa status, the code for 'OK' status. Unfortunately, however, the machine misprinted one of the names, and failed to reread the entire message. (Normally, when one of the printout units of a secret trunk line miswrote part of a message, the entire message was rewritten, or else it was reread by the computer to certify its corrected form.)

The message was thus open to doubt. In Washington and elsewhere, a computer expert was called in to confirm the accuracy of the message, by what is called 'reverse tracing.' The Washington expert expressed grave concern about the validity of the message since the machine was printing out other minor mistakes, such as 'L' when it meant 'I.'

The upshot of all this was that the first two names on the list were accorded status, while the rest were not, pending confirmation.

Allison Stone was tired. At her home in the hills overlooking the Stanford campus, she and her husband, the chairman of the Stanford bacteriology department, had held a party for fifteen couples, and everyone had stayed late. Mrs. Stone was annoyed: she had been raised in official Washington, where one's second cup of coffee, offered pointedly without cognac, was accepted as a signal to go home. Unfortunately, she thought, academics did not follow the rules. She had served the second cup of coffee hours ago, and everybody was still there.

Shortly before one a.m., the doorbell rang. Answering it, she was surprised to see two military men standing side by side in the night. They seemed awkward and nervous to her, and she assumed they were lost; people often got lost driving through these residential areas at night.

'May I help you?'

'I'm sorry to disturb you, ma'am,' one said politely. 'But is this the residence of Dr. Jeremy Stone?'

'Yes,' she said, frowning slightly. 'It is.'

She looked beyond the two men, to the driveway. A blue military sedan was parked there. Another man was standing by the car; he seemed to be holding something in his hand.

'Does that man have a gun?' she said.

'Ma'am,' the man said, 'we must see Dr. Stone at once, please.'

It all seemed strange to her, and she found herself frightened. She looked across the lawn and saw a fourth man, moving up to the house and looking into the window. In the pale light streaming out onto the lawn, she could distinctly see the rifle in his hands.

'What's going on?'

'Ma'am, we don't want to disturb your party. Please call Dr. Stone to the door.'

'I don't know if –'

'Otherwise, we will have to go get him,' the man said.

She hesitated a moment, then said, 'Wait here.'

She stepped back and started to close the door, but one man had already slipped into the hall. He stood near the door, erect and very polite, with his hat in his hand. 'I'll just wait here, ma'am,' he said, and smiled at her.

She walked back to the party, trying to show nothing to the guests. Everyone was still talking and laughing; the room was noisy and dense with smoke. She found Jeremy in a corner, in the midst of some argument about riots. She touched his shoulder, and he disengaged himself from the group.

'I know this sounds funny,' she said, 'but there is some kind of Army man in the hall, and another outside, and two others with guns out on the lawn. They say they want to see you.'

For a moment, Stone looked surprised, and then he nodded. 'I'll take care of it,' he said. His attitude annoyed her; he seemed almost to be expecting it.

'Well, if you knew about this, you might have told –'

'I didn't,' he said. 'I'll explain later.'

He walked out to the hallway, where the officer was still waiting. She followed her husband.

Stone said, 'I am Dr. Stone.'

'Captain Morton,' the man said. He did not offer to shake hands. 'There's a fire, sir.'

'All right,' Stone said. He looked down at his dinner jacket. 'Do I have time to change?'

'I'm afraid not, sir.'

To her astonishment, Allison saw her husband nod quietly. 'All right.'

He turned to her and said, 'I've got to leave.' His face was blank and expressionless, and it seemed to her like a nightmare, his face like that, while he spoke. She was confused, and afraid.

'When will you be back?'

'I'm not sure. A week or two. Maybe longer.'

She tried to keep her voice low, but she couldn't help it, she was upset. 'What is it?' she said. 'Are you under arrest?'

'No,' he said, with a slight smile. 'It's nothing like that. Make my apologies to everyone, will you?'

'But the guns –'

'Mrs. Stone,' the military man said, 'it's our job to protect your husband. From now on, nothing must be allowed to happen to him.'

'That's right,' Stone said. 'You see, I'm suddenly an important person.' He smiled again, an odd, crooked smile, and gave her a kiss.

And then, almost before she knew what was happening, he was walking out the door, with Captain Morton on one side of him and the other man on the other. The man with the rifle wordlessly fell into place behind them; the man by the car saluted and opened the door.

Then the car lights came on, and the doors slammed shut, and the car backed down the drive and drove off into the night. She was still standing by the door when one of her guests came up behind her and said, 'Allison, are you all right?'

And she turned, and found she was able to smile and say, 'Yes, it's nothing. Jeremy had to leave. The lab called him: another one of his late-night experiments going wrong.'

The guest nodded and said, 'Shame. It's a delightful party.'

In the car, Stone sat back and stared at the men. He recalled that their faces were blank and expressionless. He said, 'What have you got for me?'

'Got, sir?'

'Yes, dammit. What did they give you for me? They must have given you something.'

'Oh. Yes sir.'

He was handed a slim file. Stenciled on the brown cardboard cover was PROJECT SUMMARY: SCOOP.

'Nothing else?' Stone said.

'No sir.'

Stone sighed. He had never heard of Project Scoop before; the file would have to be read carefully. But it was too dark in the car to read; there would be time for that later, on the airplane. He found himself thinking back over the last five years, back to the rather odd symposium on Long Island, and the rather odd little speaker from England who had, in his own way, begun it all.

In the summer of 1962, J. J. Merrick, the English biophysicist, presented a paper to the Tenth Biological Symposium at Cold Spring Harbor, Long Island. The paper was entitled 'Frequencies of Biologic Contact According to Speciation Probabilities.' Merrick was a rebellious, unorthodox scientist whose reputation for clear thinking was not enhanced by his recent divorce or the presence of the handsome blond secretary he had brought with him to the symposium. Following the presentation of his paper, there was little serious discussion of Merrick's ideas, which were summarized at the end of the paper.

> I must conclude that the first contact with extraterrestrial life will be determined by the known probabilities of speciation. It is an undeniable fact that complex organisms are rare on earth, while simple organisms flourish in abundance. There are millions of species of bacteria, and thousands of species of insects. There are only a few species of primates, and only four of great apes. There is but one species of man.
>
> With this frequency of speciations goes a corresponding frequency in numbers. Simple creatures are much more common than complex organisms. There are three billion men on the earth, and that seems a great many until we consider that ten or even one hundred times that number of bacteria can be contained within a large flask.
>
> All available evidence on the origin of life points to an evolutionary progression from simple to complex life forms. This is true on earth. It is probably true throughout the universe. Shapley, Merrow, and others have calculated the number of viable planetary systems in the near universe. My own calculations, indicated earlier in the paper, consider the relative abundance of different organisms throughout the universe.

My aim has been to determine the probability of contact between man and another life form. That probability is as follows:

FORM	*PROBABILITY*
Unicellular organisms or less (naked genetic information)	.7840
Multicellular organisms, simple	.1940
Multicellular organisms, complex but lacking coordinated central nervous system	.0140
Multicellular oganisms with integrated organ systems including nervous system	.0078
Multicellular organisms with complex nervous system capable of handling 7+ data (human capability)	.0002
	1.0000

These considerations lead me to believe that the first human interaction with extraterrestrial life will consist of contact with organisms similar to, if not identical to, earth bacteria or viruses. The consequences of such contact are disturbing when one recalls that 3 per cent of all earth bacteria are capable of exerting some deleterious effect upon man.

Later, Merrick himself considered the possibility that the first contact would consist of a plague brought back from the moon by the first men to go there. This idea was received with amusement by the assembled scientists.

One of the few who took it seriously was Jeremy Stone. At the age of thirty-six, Stone was perhaps the most famous person attending the symposium that year. He was professor of bacteriology at Stanford, a post he had held since he was thirty, and he had just won the Nobel Prize.

The list of Stone's achievements – disregarding the particular series of experiments that led to the Nobel Prize – is astonishing. In 1955, he was the first to use the technique of multiplicative counts for bacterial colonies. In 1957, he developed a method for liquid-pure suspension. In 1960, Stone presented a radical new theory of operon activity in *E. coli* and *S. tabuli,* and developed evidence for the physical nature of the inducer and repressor substances. His 1958 paper on linear viral transformations opened broad new lines of scientific inquiry, particularly among the

Pasteur Institute group in Paris, which subsequently won the Nobel Prize in 1966.

In 1961, Stone himself won the Nobel Prize. The award was given for work on bacterial mutant reversion that he had done in his spare time as a law student at Michigan, when he was twenty-six.

Perhaps the most significant thing about Stone was that he had done Nobel-caliber work as a law student, for it demonstrated the depth and range of his interests. A friend once said of him: 'Jeremy knows everything, and is fascinated by the rest.' Already he was being compared to Einstein and to Bohr as a scientist with a conscience, an overview, an appreciation of the significance of events.

Physically, Stone was a thin, balding man with a prodigious memory that catalogued scientific facts and blue jokes with equal facility. But his most outstanding characteristic was a sense of impatience, the feeling he conveyed to everyone around him that they were wasting his time. He had a bad habit of interrupting speakers and finishing conversations, a habit he tried to control with only limited success. His imperious manner, when added to the fact that he had won the Nobel Prize at an early age, as well as the scandals of his private life – he was four times married, twice to the wives of colleagues – did nothing to increase his popularity.

Yet it was Stone who, in the early 1960's, moved forward in government circles as one of the spokesmen for the new scientific establishment. He himself regarded this role with tolerant amusement – 'a vacuum eager to be filled with hot gas,' he once said – but in fact his influence was considerable.

By the early 1960's America had reluctantly come to realize that it possessed, as a nation, the most potent scientific complex in the history of the world. Eighty per cent of all scientific discoveries in the preceding three decades had been made by Americans. The United States had 75 per cent of the world's computers, and 90 per cent of the world's lasers. The United States had three and a half times as many scientists as the Soviet Union and spent three and a half times as much money on research; the U.S. had four times as many scientists as the European Economic Community and spent seven times as much on research. Most of this money came, directly or indirectly, from Congress, and Congress felt a great need for men to advise them on how to spend it.

During the 1950's, all the great advisers had been physicists: Teller and Oppenheimer and Bruckman and Weidner. But ten years later, with more money for biology and more concern for it, a new group emerged, led by DeBakey in Houston, Farmer in Boston, Heggerman in New York, and Stone in California.

Stone's prominence was attributable to many factors: the prestige of the Nobel Prize; his political contacts; his most recent wife, the daughter of Senator Thomas Wayne of Indiana; his legal training. All this combined to assure Stone's repeated appearance before confused Senate subcommittees – and gave him the power of any trusted adviser.

It was this same power that he used so successfully to implement the research and construction leading to Wildfire.

Stone was intrigued by Merrick's ideas, which paralleled certain concepts of his own. He explained these in a short paper entitled 'Sterilization of Spacecraft,' printed in *Science* and later reprinted in the British journal *Nature.* The argument stated that bacterial contamination was a two-edged sword, and that man must protect against both edges.

Previous to Stone's paper, most discussion of contamination dealt with the hazards to other planets of satellites and probes inadvertently carrying earth organisms. This problem was considered early in the American space effort; by 1959, NASA had set strict regulations for sterilization of earth-origin probes.

The object of these regulations was to prevent contamination of other worlds. Clearly, if a probe were being sent to Mars or Venus to search for new life forms, it would defeat the purpose of the experiment for the probe to carry earth bacteria with it.

Stone considered the reverse situation. He stated that it was equally possible for extraterrestrial organisms to contaminate the earth via space probes. He noted that spacecraft that burned up in reentry presented no problem, but 'live' returns – manned flights, and probes such as the Scoop satellites – were another matter entirely. Here, he said, the question of contamination was very great.

His paper created a brief flurry of interest but, as he later said, 'nothing very spectacular.' Therefore, in 1963 he began an informal seminar group that met twice monthly in Room 410, on the top floor of the Stanford Medical School biochemistry wing, for lunch and discussion of the contamination problem. It was this group of five men – Stone and John Black of Stanford, Samuel Holden and Terence Lisset of Cal Med, and Andrew Weiss of Berkeley biophysics – that eventually formed the early nucleus of the Wildfire Project. They presented a petition to the President in 1965, in a letter consciously patterned after the Einstein letter to Roosevelt, in 1940, concerning the atomic bomb.

Stanford University
Palo Alto, Calif.

June 10, 1965

The President of the United States
The White House
1600 Pennsylvania Avenue
Washington, D.C.

Dear Mr. President:

Recent theoretical considerations suggest that sterilization procedures of returning space probes may be inadequate to guarantee sterile reentry to this planet's atmosphere. The consequence of this is the potential introduction of virulent organisms into the present terrestrial ecologic framework.

It is our belief that sterilization for reentry probes and manned capsules can never be wholly satisfactory. Our calculations suggest that even if capsules received sterilizing procedures in space, the probability of contamination would still remain one in ten thousand, and perhaps much more. These estimates are based upon organized life as we know it; other forms of life may be entirely resistant to our sterilizing methods.

We therefore urge the establishment of a facility designed to deal with an extraterrestrial life form, should one inadvertently be introduced to the earth. The purpose of this facility would be two-fold: to limit dissemination of the life form, and to provide laboratories for its investigation and analysis, with a view to protecting earth life forms from its influence.

We recommend that such a facility be located in an uninhabited region of the United States; that it be constructed underground; that it incorporate all known isolation techniques; and that it be equipped with a nuclear device for self-destruction in the eventuality of an emergency. So far as we know, no form of life can survive the two million degrees of heat which accompany an atomic nuclear detonation.

Yours very truly,

Jeremy Stone
John Black
Samuel Holden
Terence Lisset
Andrew Weiss

Response to the letter was gratifyingly prompt. Twenty-four hours later, Stone received a call from one of the President's advisers, and the following day he flew to Washington to confer with the President and members of the National Security Council. Two weeks after that, he flew to Houston to discuss further plans with NASA officials.

Although Stone recalls one or two cracks about 'the goddam penitentiary for bugs,' most scientists he talked with regarded the project favorably. Within a month, Stone's informal team was hardened into an official committee to study problems of contamination and draw up recommendations.

This committee was put on the Defense Department's Advance Research Projects List and funded through the Defense Department. At that time, the ARPL was heavily invested in chemistry and physics – ion sprays, reversal duplication, pimeson substrates – but there was growing interest in biologic problems. Thus one ARPL group was concerned with electronic pacing of brain function (a euphemism for mind control; a second had prepared a study of biosynergics, the future possible combinations of man and machines implanted inside the body; still another was evaluating Project Ozma, the seach for extraterrestrial life conducted in 1961-4. A fourth group was engaged in preliminary design of a machine that would carry out all human functions and would be self-duplicating.

All these projects were highly theoretical, and all were staffed by prestigious scientists. Admission to the ARPL was a mark of considerable status, and it ensured future funds for implementation and development.

Therefore, when Stone's committee submitted an early draft of the Life Analysis Protocol, which detailed the way any living thing could be studied, the Defense Department responded with an outright appropriation of $22,000,000 for the construction of a special isolated laboratory. (This rather large sum was felt to be justified since the project had application to other studies already under way. In 1965, the whole field of sterility and contamination was one of major importance. For example, NASA was building a Lunar Receiving Laboratory, a high-security facility for Apollo astronauts returning from the moon and possibly carrying bacteria or viruses harmful to man. Every astronaut returning from the moon would be quarantined in the LRL for three weeks, until decontamination was complete. Further, the problems of 'clean rooms' of industry, where dust and bacteria were kept at a minimum, and the 'sterile chambers' under study at Bethesda, were also major. Aseptic environments, 'life islands,' and sterile support systems seemed to have great future significance, and Stone's appropriation was considered a good investment in all these fields.

Once money was funded, construction proceeded rapidly. The eventual result, the Wildfire Laboratory, was built in 1966 in Flatrock, Nevada. Design was awarded to the naval architects of the Electric Boat Division of General Dynamics, since GD had considerable experience designing living quarters on atomic submarines, where men had to live and work for prolonged periods.

The plan consisted of a conical underground structure with five floors. Each floor was circular, with a central service core of wiring, plumbing, and elevators. Each floor was more sterile than the one above; the first floor was nonsterile, the second moderately sterile, the third stringently sterile, and so on. Passage from one floor to another was not free; personnel had to undergo decontamination and quarantine procedures in passing either up or down.

Once the laboratory was finished, it only remained to select the Wildfire Alert team, the group of scientists who would study any new organism. After a number of studies of team composition, five men were selected, including Jeremy Stone himself. These five were prepared to mobilize immediately in the event of a biologic emergency.

Barely two years after his letter to the President, Stone was satisfied that 'this country has the capability to deal with an unknown biologic agent.' He professed himself pleased with the response of Washington and the speed with which his ideas had been implemented. But privately, he admitted to friends that it had been almost too easy, that Washington had agreed to his plans almost too readily.

Stone could not have known the reasons behind Washington's eagerness, or the very real concern many government offcials had for the problem. For Stone knew nothing, until the night he left the party and drove off in the blue military sedan, of Project Scoop.

'It was the fastest thing we could arrange, sir,' the Army man said.

Stone stepped onto the airplane with a sense of absurdity. It was a Boeing 727, completely empty, the seats stretching back in long unbroken rows.

'Sit first class, if you like,' the Army man said, with a slight smile. 'It doesn't matter.' A moment later he was gone. He was not replaced by a stewardess but by a stern MP with a pistol on his hip who stood by the door as the engines started, whining softly in the night.

Stone sat back with the Scoop file in front of him and began to read.

It made fascinating reading; he went through it quickly, so quickly that the MP thought his passenger must be merely glancing at the file. But Stone was reading every word.

Scoop was the brainchild of Major General Thomas Sparks, head of the Army Medical Corps, Chemical and Biological Warfare Division. Sparks was responsible for the research of the CBW installations at Fort Detrick, Maryland, Harley, Indiana, and Dugway, Utah. Stone had met him once or twice, and remembered him as being mild-mannered and bespectacled. Not the sort of man to be expected in the job he held.

Reading on, Stone learned that Project Scoop was contracted to the Jet Propulsion Laboratory of the California Institute of Technology in Pasadena in 1963. Its avowed aim was the collection of any organisms that might exist in 'near space,' the upper atmosphere of the earth. Technically speaking, it was an Army project, but it was funded through the National Aeronautics and Space Administration, a supposedly civilian organization. In fact, NASA was a government agency with a heavy military commitment; 43 per cent of its contractual work was classified in 1963.

In theory, JPL was designing a satellite to enter the fringes of space and collect organisms and dust for study. This was considered a project of pure science – almost curiosity – and was thus accepted by all the scientists working on the study.

In fact, the true aims were quite different.

The true aims of Scoop were to find new life forms that might benefit the Fort Detrick program. In essence, it was a study to discover new biological weapons of war.

Detrick was a rambling structure in Maryland dedicated to the discovery of chemical-and-biological-warfare weapons. Covering 1,300 acres, with a physical plant valued at $100,000,000, it ranked as one of the largest research facilities of any kind in the United States. Only 15 per cent of its findings were published in open scientific journals; the rest were classified, as were the reports from Harley and Dugway. Harley was a maximum-security installation that dealt largely with viruses. In the previous ten years, a number of new viruses had been developed there, ranging from the variety coded Carrie Nation (which produces diarrhea) to the variety coded Arnold (which causes clonic seizures and death). The Dugway Proving Ground in Utah was larger than the state of Rhode Island and was used principally to test poison gases such as Tabun, Sklar, and Kuff-11.

Few Americans, Stone knew, were aware of the magnitude of U.S. research into chemical and biological warfare. The total government expenditure in CBW exceeded half a billion dollars a year. Much of this was distributed to academic centers such as Johns Hopkins, Pennsylvania, and the University of Chicago, where studies of weapons systems were contracted under vague terms. Sometimes, of course, the terms were not so vague. The Johns Hopkins program was devised to evaluate 'studies of actual or potential injuries and illnesses, studies on diseases of potential biological-warfare significance, and evaluation of certain chemical and immunological responses to certain toxoids and vaccines.'

In the past eight years, none of the results from Johns Hopkins had been published openly. Those from other universities, such as Chicago and UCLA, had occasionally been published, but these were considered within the military establishment to be 'trial balloons' – examples of ongoing research intended to intimidate foreign observers. A classic was the paper by Tendron and five others entitled 'Researches into a Toxin Which Rapidly Uncouples Oxidative Phosphorylation Through Cutaneous Absorption.'

The paper described, but did not identify, a poison that would kill a person in less than a minute and was absorbed through the skin. It was recognized that this was a relatively minor achievement compared to other toxins that had been devised in recent years.

With so much money and effort going into CBW, one might think that new and more virulent weapons would be continuously perfected. However, this was not the case from 1961 to 1965; the conclusion of the Senate Preparedness Subcommittee in 1961 was that 'conventional research has been less than satisfactory' and that 'new avenues and approaches of inquiry' should be opened within the field.

That was precisely what Major General Thomas Sparks intended to do, with Project Scoop.

In final form, Scoop was a program to orbit seventeen satellites around the earth, collecting organisms and bringing them back to the surface. Stone read the summaries of each previous flight.

Scoop I was a gold-plated satellite, cone-shaped, weighing thirty-seven pounds fully equipped. It was launched from Vandenberg Air Force Base in Purisima, California, on March 12, 1966. Vandenberg is used for west-to-east orbits, as opposed to Cape Kennedy, which launches east-to-west; Vandenberg had the additional advantage of maintaining better secrecy than Kennedy.

Scoop I orbited for six days before being brought down. It landed.

successfully in a swamp near Athens, Georgia. Unfortunately, it was found to contain only standard earth organisms.

Scoop II burned up in reentry, as a result of instrumentation failure. Scoop III also burned up, though it had a new type of plastic-and-tungsten-laminate heat shield.

Scoops IV and V were recovered intact from the Indian Ocean and the Appalachian foothills, but neither contained radically new organisms; those collected were harmless variants of *S. albus,* a common contaminant of normal human skin. These failures led to a further increase in sterilization procedures prior to launch.

Scoop VI was launched on New Year's Day, 1967. It incorporated all the latest refinements from earlier attempts. High hopes rode with the revised satellite, which returned eleven days later, landing near Bombay, India. Unknown to anyone, the 34th Airborne, then stationed in Evreux, France, just outside Paris, was dispatched to recover the capsule. The 34th was on alert whenever a spaceflight went up, according to the procedures of Operation Scrub, a plan first devised to protect Mercury and Gemini capsules should one be forced to land in Soviet Russia or Eastern Bloc countries. Scrub was the primary reason for keeping a single paratroop division in Western Europe in the first half of the 1960's.

Scoop VI was recovered uneventfully. It was found to contain a previously unknown form of unicellular organism, coccobacillary in shape, gram-negative, coagulase, and triokinase-positive. However, it proved generally benevolent to all living things with the exception of domestic female chickens, which it made moderately ill for a four-day period.

Among the Detrick staff, hope dimmed for the successful recovery of a pathogen from the Scoop program. Nonetheless, Scoop VII was launched soon after Scoop VI. The exact date is classified but it is believed to be February 5, 1967. Scoop VII immediately went into stable orbit with an apogee of 317 miles and a perigee of 224 miles. It remained in orbit for two and a half days. At that time, the satellite abruptly left stable orbit for unknown reasons, and it was decided to bring it down by radio command.

The anticipated landing site was a desolate area in northeastern Arizona.

Midway through the flight, his reading was interrupted by an officer who brought him a telephone and then stepped a respectful distance away while Stone talked.

'Yes?' Stone said, feeling odd. He was not accustomed to talking on the telephone in the middle of an airplane trip.

'General Marcus here,' a tired voice said. Stone did not know General Marcus. 'I just wanted to inform you that all members of the team have been called in, with the exception of Professor Kirke.'

'What happened?'

'Professor Kirke is in the hospital,' General Marcus said. 'You'll get further details when you touch down.'

The conversation ended; Stone gave the telephone back to the officer. He thought for a minute about the other men on the team, and wondered at their reactions as they were called out of bed.

There was Leavitt, of course. He would respond quickly. Leavitt was a clinical microbiologist, a man experienced in the treatment of infectious disease. Leavitt had seen enough plagues and epidemics in his day to know the importance of quick action. Besides, there was his ingrained pessimism, which never deserted him. (Leavitt had once said, 'At my wedding, all I could think of was how much alimony she'd cost me.') He was an irritable, grumbling, heavyset man with a morose face and sad eyes, which seemed to peer ahead into a bleak and miserable future; but he was also thoughtful, imaginative, and not afraid to think daringly.

Then there was the pathologist, Burton, in Houston. Stone had never liked Burton very well, though he acknowledged his scientific talent. Burton and Stone were different: where Stone was organized, Burton was sloppy; where Stone was controlled, Burton was impulsive; where Stone was confident, Burton was nervous, jumpy, petulant. Colleagues referred to Burton as 'the Stumbler,' partly because of his tendency to trip over his untied shoelaces and baggy trouser cuffs and partly because of his talent for tumbling by error into one important discovery after another.

And then Kirke, the anthropologist from Yale, who apparently was not going to be able to come. If the report was true, Stone knew he was going to miss him. Kirke was an ill-informed and rather foppish man who possessed, as if by accident, a superbly logical brain. He was capable of grasping the essentials of a problem and manipulating them to get the necessary result; though he could not balance his own checkbook, mathematicians often came to him for help in resolving highly abstract problems.

Stone was going to miss that kind of brain. Certainly the fifth man would be no help. Stone frowned as he thought about Mark Hall. Hall had been a compromise candidate for the team; Stone would have preferred a physician with experience in metabolic disease, and the choice of a surgeon instead had been made with the greatest reluctance. There had been great pressure from Defense and the AEC to accept Hall, since those groups believed in the Odd Man Hypothesis; in the end, Stone and the others had given in.

Stone did not know Hall well; he wondered what he would say when he was informed of the alert. Stone could not have known of the great delay in notifying members of the team. He did not know, for instance, that Burton, the pathologist, was not called until five a.m., or that Peter Leavitt, the microbiologist, was not called until six thirty, the time he arrived at the hospital.

And Hall was not called until five minutes past seven.

It was, Mark Hall said later, 'a horrifying experience. In an instant, I was taken from the most familiar of worlds and plunged into the most unfamiliar.' At six forty-five, Hall was in the washroom adjacent to OR 7, scrubbing for his first case of the day. He was in the midst of a routine he had carried out daily for several years; he was relaxed and joking with the resident, scrubbing with him.

When he finished, he went into the operating room, holding his arms before him, and the instrument nurse handed him a towel, to wipe his hands dry. Also in the room was another resident, who was prepping the body for surgery – applying iodine and alcohol solutions – and a circulating nurse. They all exchanged greetings.

At the hospital, Hall was known as a swift, quick-tempered, and unpredictable surgeon. He operated with speed, working nearly twice as fast as other surgeons. When things went smoothly, he laughed and joked as he worked, kidding his assistants, the nurses, the anesthetist. But if things did not go well, if they became slow and difficult, Hall could turn blackly irritable.

Like most surgeons, he was insistent upon routine. Everything had to be done in a certain order, in a certain way. If not, he became upset.

Because the others in the operating room knew this, they looked up toward the overhead viewing gallery with apprehension when Leavitt appeared. Leavitt clicked on the intercom that connected the upstairs room to the operating room below and said, 'Hello, Mark.'

Hall had been draping the patient, placing green sterile cloths over every part of the body except for the abdomen. He looked up with surprise. 'Hello, Peter,' he said.

'Sorry to disturb you,' Leavitt said. 'But this is an emergency.'

'Have to wait,' Hall said. 'I'm starting a procedure.'

He finished draping and called for the skin knife. He palpated the abdomen, feeling for the landmarks to begin his incision.

'It can't wait,' Leavitt said.

Hall paused. He set down the scalpel and looked up. There was a long silence.

'What the hell do you mean, it can't wait?'

Leavitt remained calm. 'You'll have to break scrub. This is an emergency.'

'Look, Peter, I've got a patient here. Anesthetized. Ready to go. I can't just walk –'

'Kelly will take over for you.'

Kelly was one of the staff surgeons.

'Kelly?'

'He's scrubbing now,' Leavitt said. 'It's all arranged. I'll expect to meet you in the surgeon's change room. In about thirty seconds.'

And then he was gone.

Hall glared at everyone in the room. No one moved, or spoke. After a moment, he stripped off his gloves and stomped out of the room, swearing once, very loudly.

Hall viewed his own association with Wildfire as tenuous at best. In 1966 he had been approached by Leavitt, the chief of bacteriology of the hospital, who had explained in a sketchy way the purpose of the project. Hall found it all rather amusing and had agreed to join the team, if his services ever became necessary; privately, he was confident that nothing would ever come of Wildfire.

Leavitt had offered to give Hall the files on Wildfire and to keep him up to date on the project. At first, Hall politely took the files, but it soon became clear that he was not bothering to read them, and so Leavitt stopped giving them to him. If anything, this pleased Hall, who preferred not to have his desk cluttered.

A year before, Leavitt had asked him whether he wasn't curious about something that he had agreed to join and that might at some future time prove dangerous.

Hall had said, 'No.'

Now, in the doctors' room, Hall regretted those words. The doctors' room was a small place, lined on all four walls with lockers; there were no windows. A large coffeemaker sat in the center of the room, with a stack of paper cups alongside. Leavitt was pouring himself a cup, his solemn, basset-hound face looking mournful.

'This is going to be awful coffee,' he said. 'You can't get a decent cup anywhere in a hospital. Hurry and change.'

Hall said, 'Do you mind telling me first why –'

'I mind, I mind,' Leavitt said. 'Change: there's a car waiting outside and we're already late. Perhaps too late.'

He had a gruffly melodramatic way of speaking that had always annoyed Hall.

There was a loud slurp as Leavitt sipped the coffee. 'Just as I suspected,' he said. 'How can you tolerate it? Hurry, please.'

Hall unlocked his locker and kicked it open. He leaned against the door and stripped away the black plastic shoe covers that were worn in the operating room to prevent buildup of static charges. 'Next, I suppose you're going to tell me this has to do with that damned project.'

'Exactly,' Leavitt said. 'Now try to hurry. The car is waiting to take us to the airport, and the morning traffic is bad.'

Hall changed quickly, not thinking, his mind momentarily stunned. Somehow he had never thought it possible. He dressed and walked out with Leavitt toward the hospital entrance. Outside, in the sunshine, he could see the olive U.S. Army sedan pulled up to the curb, its light flashing. And he had a sudden, horrible realization that Leavitt was not kidding, that nobody was kidding, and that some kind of awful nightmare was coming true.

For his own part, Peter Leavitt was irritated with Hall. In general, Leavitt had little patience with practicing physicians. Though he had an M.D. degree, Leavitt had never practiced, preferring to devote his time to research. His field was clinical microbiology and epidemiology, and his specialty was parasitology. He had done parasitic research all over the world; his work had led to the discovery of the Brazilian tapeworm, *Taenia renzi,* which he had characterized in a paper in 1953.

As he grew older, however, Leavitt had stopped traveling. Public health, he was fond of saying, was a young man's game; when you got your fifth case of intestinal amebiasis, it was time to quit. Leavitt got his fifth case in Rhodesia in 1955. He was dreadfully sick for three months and lost forty pounds. Afterward, he resigned his job in the public health service. He was offered the post of chief of microbiology at the hospital, and he had taken it, with the understanding that he would be able to devote a good portion of his time to research.

Within the hospital he was known as a superb clinical bacteriologist, but his real interest remained parasites. In the period from 1955 to 1964 he published a series of elegant metabolic studies on *Ascaris* and *Necator* that were highly regarded by other workers in the field.

Leavitt's reputation had made him a natural choice for Wildfire, and it was through Leavitt that Hall had been asked to join. Leavitt knew the reasons behind Hall's selection, though Hall did not.

When Leavitt had asked him to join, Hall had demanded to know why. 'I'm just a surgeon,' he had said.

'Yes,' Leavitt said. 'But you know electrolytes.'

'So?'

'That may be important. Blood chemistries, pH, acidity and alkalinity, the whole thing. That may be vital, when the time comes.'

'But there are a lot of electrolyte people,' Hall had pointed out. 'Many of them better than me.'

'Yes,' Leavitt had said. 'But they're all married.'

'So what?'

'We need a single man.'

'Why?'

'It's necessary that one member of the team be unmarried.'

'That's crazy,' Hall had said.

'Maybe,' Leavitt had said. 'Maybe not.'

They left the hospital and walked up to the Army sedan. A young officer was waiting stiffly, and saluted as they came up.

'Dr. Hall?'

'Yes.'

'May I see your card, please?'

Hall gave him the little plastic card with his picture on it. He had been carrying the card in his wallet for more than a year; it was a rather strange card – with just a name, a picture, and a thumbprint, nothing more. Nothing to indicate that it was an official card.

The officer glanced at it, then at Hall, and back to the card. He handed it back.

'Very good, sir.'

He opened the rear door of the sedan. Hall got in and Leavitt followed, shielding his eyes from the flashing red light on the car top. Hall noticed it.

'Something wrong?'

'No. Just never liked flashing lights. Reminds me of my days as an ambulance driver, during the war.' Leavitt settled back and the car started off. 'Now then,' he said. 'When we reach the airfield, you will be given a file to read during the trip.'

'What trip?'

'You'll be taking an F-104,' Leavitt said.

'Where?'

'Nevada. Try to read the file on the way. Once we arrive, things will be very busy.'

'And the others in the team?'

Leavitt glanced at his watch. 'Kirke has appendicitis and is in the hospital. The others have already begun work. Right now, they are in a helicopter, over Piedmont, Arizona.'

'Never heard of it,' Hall said.

'Nobody has,' Leavitt said, 'until now.'

6 Piedmont

At 9:59 a.m. on the same morning, a K-4 jet helicopter lifted off the concrete of Vandenberg's maximum-security hangar MSH-9 and headed east, toward Arizona.

The decision to lift off from an MSH was made by Major Manchek, who was concerned about the attention the suits might draw. Because inside the helicopter were three men, a pilot and two scientists, and all three wore clear plastic inflatable suits, making them look like obese men from Mars, or, as one of the hangar maintenance men put it, 'like balloons from the Macy's parade.'

As the helicopter climbed into the clear morning sky, the two passengers in the belly looked at each other. One was Jeremy Stone, the other Charles Burton. Both men had arrived at Vandenberg just a few hours before – Stone from Stanford and Burton from Baylor University in Houston.

Burton was fifty-four, a pathologist. He held a professorship at Baylor Medical School and served as a consultant to the NASA Manned Spaceflight Center in Houston. Earlier he had done research at the National Institutes in Bethesda. His field had been the effects of bacteria on human tissues.

It is one of the peculiarities of scientific development that such a vital field was virtually untouched when Burton came to it. Though men had known germs caused disease since Henle's hypothesis of 1840, by the middle of the twentieth century there was still nothing known about why or how bacteria did their damage. The specific mechanisms were unknown.

Burton began, like so many others in his day, with *Diplococcus pneumoniae,* the agent causing pneumonia. There was great interest in pneumococcus before the advent of penicillin in the forties; after that, both interest and research money evaporated. Burton shifted to *Staphylococcus aureus,* a common skin pathogen responsible for 'pimples' and 'boils.' At the time he began his work, his fellow researchers laughed at him; staphylococcus, like pneumococcus, was highly sensitive to penicillin. They doubted Burton would ever get enough money to carry on his work.

For five years, they were right. The money was scarce, and Burton often had to go begging to foundations and philanthropists. Yet he persisted, patiently elucidating the coats of the cell wall that caused a reaction in host tissue and helping to discover the half-dozen toxins secreted by the bacteria to break down tissue, spread infection, and destroy red cells.

Suddenly, in the 1950's, the first penicillin-resistant strains of staph appeared. The new strains were virulent, and produced bizarre deaths, often by brain abscess. Almost overnight Burton found his work had assumed major importance; dozens of labs around the country were changing over to study staph; it was a 'hot field.' In a single year, Burton watched his grant appropriations jump from $6,000 a year to $300,000. Soon afterward, he was made a professor of pathology.

Looking back, Burton felt no great pride in his accomplishment; it was, he knew, a matter of luck, of being in the right place and doing the right work when the time came.

He wondered what would come of being here, in this helicopter, now.

Sitting across from him, Jeremy Stone tried to conceal his distaste for Burton's appearance. Beneath the plastic suit Burton wore a dirty plaid sport shirt with a stain on the left breast pocket; his trousers were creased and frayed and even his hair, Stone felt, was unruly and untidy.

He stared out the window, forcing himself to think of other matters. 'Fifty people,' he said, shaking his head. 'Dead within eight hours of the landing of Scoop VII. The question is one of spread.'

'Presumably airborne,' Burton said.

'Yes. Presumably.'

'Everyone seems to have died in the immediate vicinity of the town,' Burton said. 'Are there reports of deaths farther out?'

Stone shook his head. 'I'm having the Army people look into it. They're working with the highway patrol. So far, no deaths have turned up outside.'

'Wind?'

'A stroke of luck,' Stone said. 'Last night the wind was fairly brisk, nine miles an hour to the south and steady. But around midnight, it died. Pretty unusual for this time of year, they tell me.'

'But fortunate for us.'

'Yes.' Stone nodded. 'We're fortunate in another way as well. There is no important area of habitation for a radius of nearly one hundred and twelve miles. Outside that, of course, there is Las Vegas to the north, San Bernardino to the west, and Phoenix to the east. Not nice, if the bug gets to any of them.'

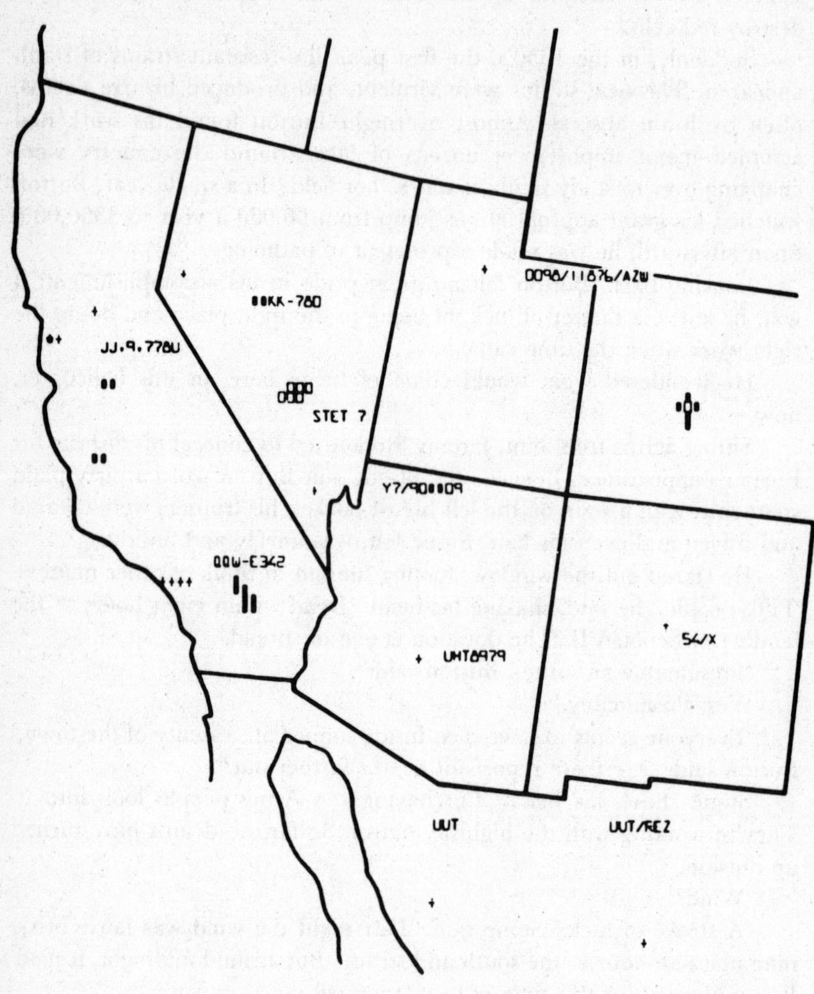

A NOTE ON THE OUTPUT MAPS: these three maps are intended as examples of the staging of computerbase output mapping. The first map is relatively standard, with the addition of computer coordinates around population centers and other important areas.

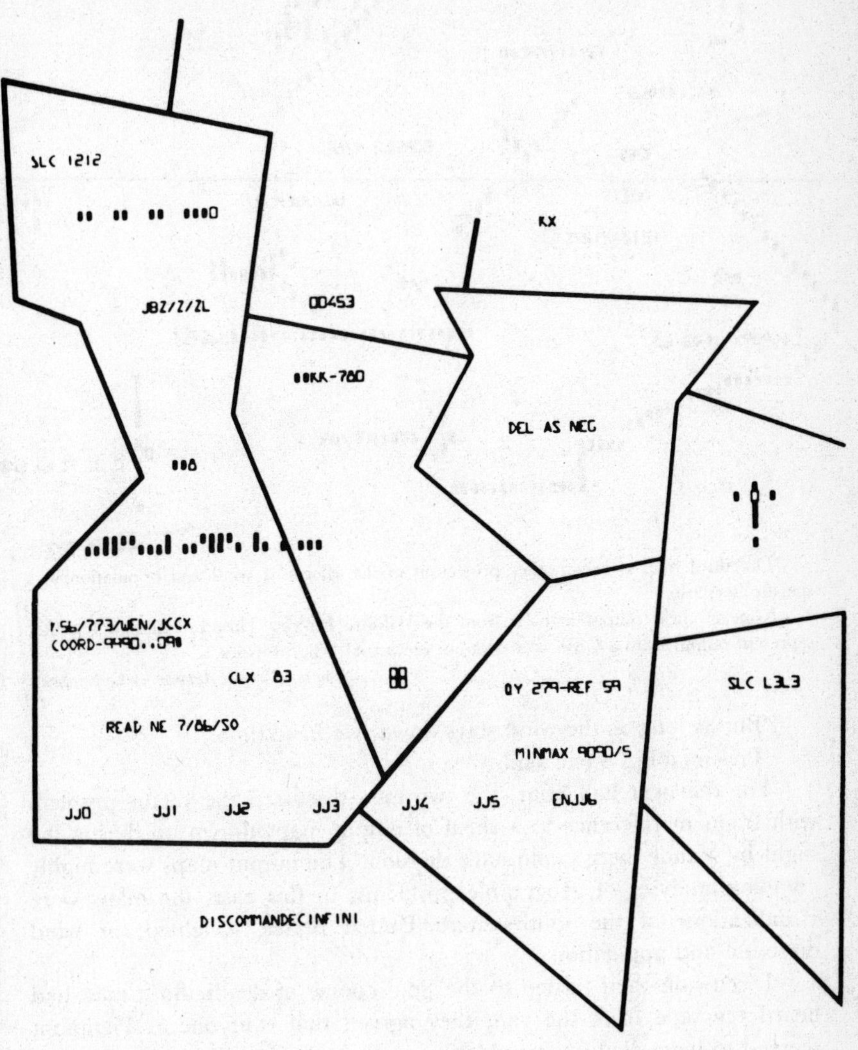

The second map has been weighted to account for wind and population factors, and is consequently distorted.

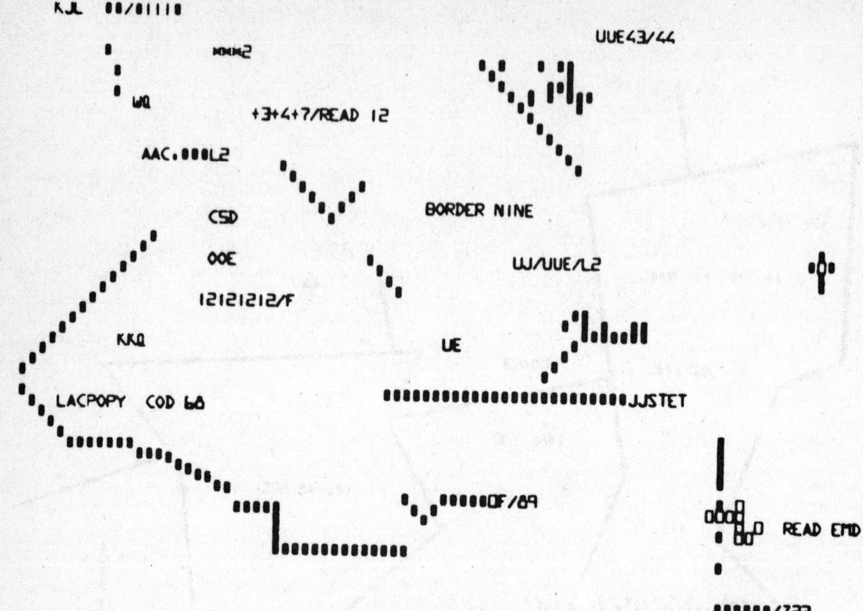

The third map is a computer projection of the effects of wind and population in a specific 'scenario.'

None of these output maps is from the Wildfire Project. They are similar, but they represent output from a CBW scenario, not the actual Wildfire work.

(courtesy General Autonomics Corporation)

'But as long as the wind stays down, we have time.'

'Presumably,' Stone said.

For the next half hour, the two men discussed the vector problem with frequent reference to a sheaf of output maps drawn up during the night by Vandenberg's computer division. The output maps were highly complex analyses of geographic problems; in this case, the maps were visualizations of the southwestern United States, weighted for wind direction and population.

Discussion then turned to the time course of death. Both men had heard the tape from the van; they agreed that everyone at Piedmont seemed to have died quite suddenly.

'Even if you slit a man's throat with a razor,' Burton said, 'you won't get death that rapidly. Cutting both carotids and jugulars still allows ten to forty seconds before unconsciousness, and nearly a minute before death.'

'At Piedmont, it seems to have occurred in a second or two.'

Burton shrugged. 'Trauma,' he suggested. 'A blow to the head.'

'Yes. Or a nerve gas.'

'Certainly possible.'

'It's that, or something very much like it,' Stone said. 'If it was an enzymatic block of some kind – like arsenic or strychnine – we'd expect fifteen or thirty seconds, perhaps longer. But a block of nervous transmission, or a block of the neuromuscular junction, or cortical poisoning – that could be very swift. It could be instantaneous.'

'If it is a fast-acting gas,' Burton said, 'it must have high diffusibility across the lungs –'

'Or the skin,' Stone said. 'Mucous membranes, anything. Any porous surface.'

Burton touched the plastic of his suit. 'If this gas is so highly diffusible . . .'

Stone gave a slight smile. 'We'll find out, soon enough.'

Over the intercom, the helicopter pilot said, 'Piedmont approaching, gentlemen. Please advise.'

Stone said, 'Circle once and give us a look at it.'

The helicopter banked steeply. The two men looked out and saw the town below them. The buzzards had landed during the night, and were thickly clustered around the bodies.

'I was afraid of that,' Stone said.

'They may represent a vector for infectious spread,' Burton said. 'Eat the meat of infected people, and carry the organisms away with them.'

Stone nodded, staring out the window.

'What do we do?'

'Gas them,' Stone said. He flicked on the intercom to the pilot. 'Have you got the canisters?'

'Yes sir.'

'Circle again, and blanket the town.'

'Yes sir.'

The helicopter tilted, and swung back. Soon the two men could not see the ground for the clouds of pale-blue gas.

'What is it?'

'Chlorazine,' Stone said. 'Highly effective, in low concentrations, on aviary metabolism. Birds have a high metabolic rate. They are creatures that consist of little more than feathers and muscle; their heartbeats are usually about one-twenty, and many species eat more than their own weight every day.'

'The gas is an uncoupler?'

'Yes. It'll hit them hard.'

The helicopter banked away, then hovered. The gas slowly cleared in the gentle wind, moving off to the south. Soon they could see the ground again. Hundreds of birds lay there; a few flapped their wings spastically, but most were already dead.

Stone frowned as he watched. Somewhere, in the back of his mind, he knew he had forgotten something, or ignored something. Some fact, some vital clue, that the birds provided and he must not overlook.

Over the intercom, the pilot said, 'Your orders, sir?'

'Go to the center of the main street,' Stone said, 'and drop the rope ladder. You are to remain twenty feet above ground. Do not put down. Is that clear?'

'Yes sir.'

'When we have climbed down, you are to lift off to an altitude of five hundred feet.'

'Yes sir.'

'Return when we signal you.'

'Yes sir.'

'And should anything happen to us –'

'I proceed directly to Wildfire,' the pilot said, his voice dry.

'Correct.'

The pilot knew what that meant. He was being paid according to the highest Air Force pay scales: he was drawing regular pay plus hazardous-duty pay, plus non-wartime special-services pay, plus mission-over-hostile-territory pay, plus bonus air time pay. He would receive more than a thousand dollars for this day's work, and his family would receive an additional ten thousand dollars from the short-term life insurance should he not return.

There was a reason for the money: if anything happened to Burton and Stone on the ground, the pilot was ordered to fly directly to the Wildfire installation and hover thirty feet above ground until such time as the Wildfire group had determined the correct way to incinerate him, and his airplane, in midair.

He was being paid to take a risk. He had volunteered for the job. And he knew that high above, circling at twenty thousand feet, was an Air Force jet with air-to-air missiles. It was the job of the jet to shoot down the helicopter should the pilot suffer a last-minute loss of nerve and fail to go directly to Wildfire.

'Don't slip up,' the pilot said. 'Sir.'

The helicopter maneuvered over the main street of the town and hung in midair. There was a rattling sound: the rope ladder being released. Stone stood and pulled on his helmet. He snapped shut the sealer and inflated his clear suit, puffing it up around him. A small bottle of oxygen on his back would provide enough air for two hours of exploration.

He waited until Burton had sealed his suit, and then Stone opened the hatch and stared down at the ground. The helicopter was raising a heavy cloud of dust.

Stone clicked on his radio. 'All set?'

'All set.'

Stone began to climb down the ladder. Burton waited a moment, then followed. He could see nothing in the swirling dust, but finally felt his shoes touch the ground. He released the ladder and looked over. He could barely make out Stone's suit, a dim outline in a gloomy, dusky world.

The ladder pulled away as the helicopter lifted into the sky. The dust cleared. They could see.

'Let's go,' Stone said.

Moving clumsily in their suits, they walked down the main street of Piedmont.

7 'An Unusual Process'

Scarcely twelve hours after the first known human contact with the Andromeda Strain was made at Piedmont, Burton and Stone arrived in the town. Weeks later, in their debriefing sessions, both men recalled the scene vividly, and described it in detail.

The morning sun was still low in the sky; it was cold and cheerless, casting long shadows over the thinly snow-crusted ground. From where they stood, they could look up and down the street at the gray, weathered wooden buildings; but what they noticed first was the silence. Except for a gentle wind that whined softly through the empty houses, it was deathly silent. Bodies lay everywhere, heaped and flung across the ground in attitudes of frozen surprise.

But there was no sound – no reassuring rumble of an automobile engine, no barking dog, no shouting children.

Silence.

The two men looked at each other. They were painfully aware of how much there was to learn, to do. Some catastrophe had struck this town, and they must discover all they could about it. But they had practically no clues, no points of departure.

They knew, in fact, only two things. First, that the trouble apparently began with the landing of Scoop VII. And second, that death had overtaken the people of the town with astonishing rapidity. If it was a disease from the satellite, then it was like no other in the history of medicine.

For a long time the men said nothing, but stood in the street, looking about them, feeling the wind tug at their oversized suits. Finally, Stone said, 'Why are they all outside, in the street? If this was a disease that arrived at night, most of the people would be indoors.'

'Not only that,' Burton said, 'they're mostly wearing pajamas. It was a cold night last night. You'd think they would have stopped to put on a jacket, or a raincoat. Something to keep warm.'

'Maybe they were in a hurry.'

'To do what?' Burton said.

'To see something,' Stone said, with a helpless shrug.

Burton bent over the first body they came to. 'Odd,' he said. 'Look at the way this fellow is clutching his chest. Quite a few of them are doing that.'

Looking at the bodies, Stone saw that the hands of many were pressed to their chests, some flat, some clawing.

'They didn't seem to be in pain,' Stone said. 'Their faces are quite peaceful.'

'Almost astonished, in fact,' Burton nodded. 'These people look cut down, caught in midstride. But clutching their chests.'

'Coronary?' Stone said.

'Doubt it. They should grimace – it's painful. The same with a pulmonary embolus.'

'If it was fast enough, they wouldn't have time.'

'Perhaps. But somehow I think these people died a painless death. Which means they are clutching their chests because –'

'They couldn't breathe,' Stone said.

Burton nodded. 'It's possible we're seeing asphyxiation. Rapid, painless, almost instantaneous asphyxiation. But I doubt it. If a person can't breathe, the first thing he does is loosen his clothing, particularly around the neck and chest. Look at that man there – he's wearing a tie, and he hasn't touched it. And that woman with the tightly buttoned collar.'

Burton was beginning to regain his composure now, after the initial shock of the town. He was beginning to think clearly. They walked up to the van, standing in the middle of the street, its lights still shining weakly. Stone reached in to turn off the lights. He pushed the stiff body of the driver back from the wheel and read the name on the breast pocket of the parka.

'Shawn.'

The man sitting rigidly in the back of the van was a private named Crane. Both men were locked in rigor mortis. Stone nodded to the equipment in the back.

'Will that still work?'

'I think so,' Burton said.

'Then let's find the satellite. That's our first job. We can worry later about –'

He stopped. He was looking at the face of Shawn, who had obviously pitched forward hard onto the steering wheel at the moment of death. There was a large, arc-shaped cut across his face, shattering the bridge of his nose and tearing the skin.

'I don't get it,' Stone said.

'Get what?' Burton said.

'This injury. Look at it.'

'Very clean,' Burton said. 'Remarkably clean, in fact. Practically no bleeding . . .'

Then Burton realized. He started to scratch his head in astonishment, but his hand was stopped by the plastic helmet.

'A cut like that,' he said, 'on the face. Broken capillaries, shattered bone, torn scalp veins – it should bleed like hell.'

'Yes,' Stone said. 'It should. And look at the other bodies. Even where the vultures have chewed at the flesh: no bleeding.'

Burton stared with increasing astonishment. None of the bodies had lost even a drop of blood. He wondered why they had not noticed it before.

'Maybe the mechanism of action of this disease –'

'Yes,' Stone said. 'I think you may be right.' He grunted and dragged Shawn out of the van, working to pull the stiff body from behind the wheel. 'Let's get that damned satellite,' he said. 'This is really beginning to worry me.'

Burton went to the back and pulled Crane out through the rear doors, then climbed in as Stone turned the ignition. The starter turned over sluggishly, and the engine did not catch.

Stone tried to start the van for several seconds, then said, 'I don't understand. The battery is low, but it should still be enough –'

'How's your gas?' Burton said.

There was a pause, and Stone swore loudly. Burton smiled, and crawled out of the back. Together they walked up the street to the gas station, found a bucket, and filled it with gas from the pump after spending several moments trying to decide how it worked. When they had the gas, they returned to the van, filled the tank, and Stone tried again.

The engine caught and held. Stone grinned. 'Let's go.'

Burton scrambled into the back, turned on the electronic equipment, and started the antenna rotating. He heard the faint beeping of the satellite.

'The signal's weak, but still there. Sounds over to the left somewhere.'

Stone put the van in gear. They rumbled off, swerving around the bodies in the street. The beeping grew louder. They continued down the main street, past the gas station and the general store. The beeping suddenly grew faint.

'We've gone too far. Turn around.'

It took a while for Stone to find reverse on the gearshift, and then they doubled back, tracing the intensity of the sound. It was another fifteen minutes before they were able to locate the origin of the beeps to the north, on the outskirts of the town.

Finally, they pulled up before a plain single-story woodframe house. A sign creaked in the wind: Dr. Alan Benedict.

'Might have known,' Stone said. 'They'd take it to the doctor.'

The two men climbed out of the van and went up to the house. The front door was open, banging in the breeze. They entered the living room and found it empty. Turning right, they came to the doctor's office.

Benedict was there, a pudgy, white-haired man. He was seated before his desk, with several textbooks laid open. Along one wall were bottles, syringes, pictures of his family and several others showing men in combat uniforms. One showed a group of grinning soldiers; the scrawled words: 'For Benny, from the boys of 87, Anzio.'

Benedict himself was staring blankly toward a corner of the room, his eyes wide, his face peaceful.

'Well,' Burton said, 'Benedict certainly didn't make it outside –'

And then they saw the satellite.

It was upright, a sleek polished cone three feet high, and its edges had been cracked and seared from the heat of reentry. It had been opened crudely, apparently with the help of a pair of pliers and chisel that lay on the floor next to the capsule.

'The bastard opened it,' Stone said. 'Stupid son of a bitch.'

'How was he to know?'

'He might have asked somebody,' Stone said. He sighed. 'Anyway, he knows now. And so do forty-nine other people.' He bent over the satellite and closed the gaping, triangular hatch. 'You have the container?'

Burton produced the folded plastic bag and opened it out. Together they slipped it over the satellite, then sealed it shut.

'I hope to hell there's something left,' Burton said.

'In a way,' Stone said softly, 'I hope there isn't.'

They turned their attention to Benedict. Stone went over to him and shook him. The man fell rigidly from his chair onto the floor.

Burton noticed the elbows, and suddenly became excited. He leaned over the body. 'Come on,' he said to Stone. 'Help me.'

'Do what?'

'Strip him down.'

'Why?'

'I want to check the lividity.'

'But why?'

'Just wait,' Burton said. He began unbuttoning Benedict's shirt and loosening his trousers. The two men worked silently for some moments, until the doctor's body was naked on the floor.

'There,' Burton said, standing back.

'I'll be damned,' Stone said.

There was no dependent lividity. Normally, after a person died, blood seeped to the lowest points, drawn down by gravity. A person who died in bed had a purple back from accumulated blood. But Benedict, who had died sitting up, had no blood in the tissue of his buttocks or thighs.

Or in his elbows, which had rested on the arms of the chair.

'Quite a peculiar finding,' Burton said. He glanced around the room and found a small autoclave for sterilizing instruments. Opening it, he removed a scalpel. He fitted it with a blade – carefully, so as not to puncture his airtight suit – and then turned back to the body.

'We'll take the most superficial major artery and vein,' he said.

'Which is?'

'The radial. At the wrist.'

Holding the scalpel carefully, Burton drew the blade along the skin of the inner wrist, just behind the thumb. The skin pulled back from the wound, which was completely bloodless. He exposed fat and subcutaneous tissue. There was no bleeding.

'Amazing.'

He cut deeper. There was still no bleeding from the incision. Suddenly, abruptly, he struck a vessel. Crumbling red-black material fell out onto the floor.

'I'll be damned,' Stone said again.

'Clotted solid,' Burton said.

'No wonder the people didn't bleed.'

Burton said, 'Help me turn him over.' Together, they got the corpse onto its back, and Burton made a deep incision into the medial thigh, cutting down to the femoral artery and vein. Again there was no bleeding, and when they reached the artery, as thick as a man's finger, it was clotted into a firm, reddish mass.

'Incredible.'

He began another incision, this time into the chest. He exposed the ribs, then searched Dr. Benedict's office for a very sharp knife. He wanted an osteotome, but could find none. He settled for the chisel that had been used to open the capsule. Using this he broke away several ribs to expose the lungs and the heart. Again there was no bleeding.

Burton took a deep breath, then cut open the heart, slicing into the left ventricle.

The interior was filled with red, spongy material. There was no liquid blood at all.

'Clotted solid,' he said. 'No question.'

'Any idea what can clot people this way?'

'The whole vascular system? Five quarts of blood? No.' Burton sat heavily in the doctor's chair and stared at the body he had just cut open. 'I've never heard of anything like it. There's a thing called disseminated intravascular coagulation, but it's rare and requires all sorts of special circumstances to initiate it.'

'Could a single toxin initiate it?'

'In theory, I suppose. But in fact, there isn't a toxin in the world –'

He stopped.

'Yes,' Stone said. 'I suppose that's right.'

He picked up the satellite designated Scoop VII and carried it outside to the van. When he came back, he said, 'We'd better search the houses.'

'Beginning here?'

'Might as well,' Stone said.

It was Burton who found Mrs. Benedict. She was a pleasant-looking middle-aged lady sitting in a chair with a book on her lap; she seemed about to turn the page. Burton examined her briefly, then heard Stone call to him.

He walked to the other end of the house. Stone was in a small bedroom, bent over the body of a young teen-age boy on the bed. It was obviously his room: psychedelic posters on the walls, model airplanes on a shelf to one side.

The boy lay on his back in bed, eyes open, staring at the ceiling. His mouth was open. In one hand, an empty tube of model-airplane cement was tightly clenched; all over the bed were empty bottles of airplane dope, paint thinner, turps.

Stone stepped back. 'Have a look.'

Burton looked in the mouth, reached a finger in, touched the now-hardened mass. 'Good God,' he said.

Stone was frowning. 'This took time,' he said. 'Regardless of what made him do it, it took time. We've obviously been oversimplifying events here. Everyone did not die instantaneously. Some people died in their homes; some got out into the street. And this kid here . . .'

He shook his head. 'Let's check the other houses.'

On the way out, Burton returned to the doctor's office, stepping around the body of the physician. It gave him a strange feeling to see the wrist and leg sliced open, the chest exposed – but no bleeding. There was something wild and inhuman about that. As if bleeding were a sign of humanity. Well, he thought, perhaps it is. Perhaps the fact that we bleed to death makes us human.

For Stone, Piedmont was a puzzle challenging him to crack its secret. He was convinced that the town could tell him everything about the nature of the disease, its course and effects. It was only a matter of putting together the data in the proper way.

But he had to admit, as they continued their search, that the data were confusing:

A house that contained a man, his wife, and their young daughter, all sitting around the dinner table. They had apparently been relaxed and happy, and none of them had had time to push back their chairs from the table. They remained frozen in attitudes of congeniality, smiling at each other across the plates of now-rotting food, and flies. Stone noticed the flies, which buzzed softly in the room. He would, he thought, have to remember the flies.

An old woman, her hair white, her face creased. She was smiling gently as she swung from a noose tied to a ceiling rafter. The rope creaked as it rubbed against the wood of the rafter.

At her feet was an envelope. In a careful, neat, unhurried hand: 'To whom it may concern.'

Stone opened the letter and read it. 'The day of judgment is at hand. The earth and the waters shall open up and mankind shall be consumed. May God have mercy on my soul and upon those who have shown mercy to me. To hell with the others. Amen.'

Burton listened as the letter was read. 'Crazy old lady,' he said. 'Senile dementia. She saw everyone around her dying, and she went nuts.'

'And killed herself?'

'Yes, I think so.'

'Pretty bizarre way to kill herself, don't you think?'

'That kid also chose a bizarre way,' Burton said.

Stone nodded.

Roy O. Thompson, who lived alone. From his greasy coveralls they assumed he ran the town gas station. Roy had apparently filled his bathtub with water, then knelt down, stuck his head in, and held it there until he died. When they found him his body was rigid, holding himself under the surface of the water; there was no one else around, and no sign of struggle.

'Impossible,' Stone said. 'No one can commit suicide that way.'

Lydia Everett, a seamstress in the town who had quietly gone out to the back yard, sat in a chair, poured gasoline over herself, and struck a match. Next to the remains of her body they found the scorched gasoline can.

William Arnold, a man of sixty sitting stiffy in a chair in the living room, wearing his World War I uniform. He had been a captain in that war, and he had become a captain again, briefly, before he shot himself through the right temple with a Colt .45. There was no blood in the room when they found him; he appeared almost ludicrous, sitting there with a clean, dry hole in his head.

A tape recorder stood alongside him, his left hand resting on the case. Burton looked at Stone questioningly, then turned it on.

A quavering, irritable voice spoke to them.

'You took your sweet time coming, didn't you? Still I am glad you have arrived at last. We are in need of reinforcements. I tell you, it's been one hell of a battle against the Hun. Lost 40 per cent last night, going over the top, and two of our officers are out with the rot. Not going well, not at all. If only Gary Cooper was here. We need men like that, the men who made America strong. I can't tell you how much it means to me, with those giants out there in the flying saucers. Now they're burning us down, and the gas is coming. You can see them die and we don't have gas masks. None at all. But I won't wait for it. I am going to do the proper thing now. I regret that I have but one life to kill for my country.'

The tape ran on, but it was silent.

Burton turned it off. 'Crazy,' he said. 'Stark raving mad.'

Stone nodded.

'Some of them died instantly, and the others . . . went quietly nuts.'

'But we seem to come back to the same basic question. Why? What was the difference?'

'Perhaps there's a graded immunity to this bug,' Burton said. 'Some people are more susceptible than others. Some people are protected, at least for a time.'

'You know,' Stone said, 'there was that report from the flybys, and those films of a man alive down here. One man in white robes.'

'You think he's still alive?'

'Well, I wonder,' Stone said. 'Because if some people survived longer than others – long enough to dictate a taped speech, or to arrange a hanging – then you have to ask yourself if someone maybe didn't survive for a very long time. You have to ask yourself if there isn't someone in this town who is *still* alive.'

It was then that they heard the sound of crying.

At first it seemed like the sound of the wind, it was so high and thin and reedy, but they listened, feeling puzzled at first, and then astonished. The crying persisted, interrupted by little hacking coughs.

They ran outside.

It was faint, and difficult to localize. They ran up the street, and it seemed to grow louder; this spurred them on.

And then, abruptly, the sound stopped.

The two men came to a halt, gasping for breath, chests heaving. They stood in the middle of the hot, deserted street and looked at each other.

'Have we lost our minds?' Burton said.

'No,' Stone said. 'We heard it, all right.'

They waited. It was absolutely quiet for several minutes. Burton looked down the street, at the houses, and the jeep van parked at the other end, in front of Dr. Benedict's house.

The crying began again, very loud now, a frustrated howl.

The two men ran.

It was not far, two houses up on the right side. A man and a woman lay outside, on the sidewalk, fallen and clutching their chests. They ran past them and into the house. The crying was still louder; it filled the empty rooms.

They hurried upstairs, clambering up, and came to the bedroom. A large double bed, unmade. A dresser, a mirror, a closet.

And a small crib.

They leaned over, pulling back the blankets from a small, very red-faced, very unhappy infant. The baby immediately stopped crying long enough to survey their faces, enclosed in the plastic suits.

Then it began to howl again.

'Scared hell out of it,' Burton said. 'Poor thing.'

He picked it up gingerly and rocked it. The baby continued to scream. Its toothless mouth was wide open, its cheeks purple, and the veins stood out on its forehead.

'Probably hungry,' Burton said.

Stone was frowning. 'It's not very old. Can't be more than a couple of months. Is it a he or a she?'

Burton unwrapped the blankets and checked the diapers. 'He. And he needs to be changed. And fed.' He looked around the room. 'There's probably a formula in the kitchen . . .'

'No,' Stone said. 'We don't feed it.'

'Why not?'

'We don't do anything to that child until we get it out of this town. Maybe feeding is part of the disease process; maybe the people who weren't hit so hard or so fast were the ones who hadn't eaten recently. Maybe there's something protective about this baby's diet. Maybe . . .' He stopped. 'But whatever it is, we can't take a chance. We've got to wait and get him into a controlled situation.'

Burton sighed. He knew that Stone was right, but he also knew that the baby hadn't been fed for at least twelve hours. No wonder the kid was crying.

Stone said, 'This is a very important development. It's a major break for us, and we've got to protect it. I think we should go back immediately.'

'We haven't finished our head count.'

Stone shook his head. 'Doesn't matter. We have something much more valuable than anything we could hope to find. We have a survivor.'

The baby stopped crying for a moment, stuck its finger in its mouth, and looked questioningly up at Burton. Then, when he was certain no food was forthcoming, he began to howl again.

'Too bad,' Burton said, 'he can't tell us what happened.'

'I'm hoping he can,' Stone said.

They parked the van in the center of the main street, beneath the hovering helicopter, and signaled for it to descend with the ladder. Burton held the infant, and Stone held the Scoop satellite – strange trophies, Stone thought, from a very strange town. The baby was quiet now; he had finally tired of crying and was sleeping fitfully, awakening at intervals to whimper, then sleep again.

The helicopter descended, spinning up swirls of dust. Burton wrapped the blankets about the baby's face to protect him. The ladder came down and he climbed up, with difficulty.

Stone waited on the ground, standing with the capsule in the wind and dust and thumpy noise from the helicopter.

And, suddenly, he realized that he was not alone on the street. He turned, and saw a man behind him.

He was an old man, with thin gray hair and a wrinkled, worn face.

He wore a long nightgown that was smudged with dirt and yellowed with dust, and his feet were bare. He stumbled and tottered toward Stone. His chest was heaving with exertion beneath the nightgown.

'Who are you?' Stone said. But he knew: the man in the pictures. The one who had been photographed by the airplane.

'You . . .' the man said.

'Who are you?'

'You . . . did it . . .'

'What is your name?'

'Don't hurt me . . . I'm not like the others . . .'

He was shaking with fear as he stared at Stone in his plastic suit. Stone thought, We must look strange to him. Like men from Mars, men from another world.

'Don't hurt me . . .'

'We won't hurt you,' Stone said. 'What is your name?'

'Jackson. Peter Jackson. Sir. Please don't hurt me.' He waved to the bodies in the street. 'I'm not like the others . . .'

'We won't hurt you,' Stone said again.

'You hurt the others . . .'

'No. We didn't.'

'They're dead.'

'We had nothing –'

'You're lying,' he shouted, his eyes wide. 'You're lying to me. You're not human. You're only pretending. You know I'm a sick man. You know you can pretend with me. I'm a sick man. I'm bleeding, I know. I've had this . . . this . . . this . . .'

He faltered, and then doubled over, clutching his stomach and wincing in pain.

'Are you all right?'

The man fell to the ground. He was breathing heavily, his skin pale. There was sweat on his face.

'My stomach,' he gasped. 'It's my stomach.'

And then he vomited. It came up heavy, deep-red, rich with blood.

'Mr. Jackson –'

But the man was not awake. His eyes were closed and he was lying on his back. For a moment, Stone thought he was dead, but then he saw the chest moving, slowly, very slowly, but moving.

Burton came back down.

'Who is he?'

'Our wandering man. Help me get him up.'

'Is he alive?'

'So far.'

'I'll be damned,' Burton said.

They used the power winch to hoist up the unconscious body of Peter Jackson, and then lowered it again to raise the capsule. Then, slowly, Burton and Stone climbed the ladder into the belly of the helicopter.

They did not remove their suits, but instead clipped on a second bottle of oxygen to give them another two hours of breathing time. That would be sufficient to carry them to the Wildfire installation.

The pilot established a radio connection to Vandenberg so that Stone could talk with Major Manchek.

'What have you found?' Manchek said.

'The town is dead. We have good evidence for an unusual process at work.'

'Be careful,' Manchek said. 'This is an open circuit.'

'I am aware of that. Will you order up a 7–12?'

'I'll try. You want it now?'

'Yes, now.'

'Piedmont?'

'Yes.'

'You have the satellite?'

'Yes, we have it.'

'All right,' Manchek said. 'I'll put through the order.'

8 Directive 7–12

Directive 7–12 was a part of the final Wildfire Protocol for action in the event of a biologic emergency. It called for the placement of a limited thermo-nuclear weapon at the site of exposure of terrestrial life to exogenous organisms. The code for the directive was Cautery, since the function of the bomb was to cauterize the infection – to burn it out, and thus prevent its spread.

As a single step in the Wildfire Protocol, Cautery had been agreed upon by the authorities involved – Executive, State, Defense, and AEC – after much debate. The AEC, already unhappy about the assignment of a nuclear device to the Wildfire laboratory, did not wish Cautery to be accepted as a program; State and Defense argued that any aboveground thermonuclear detonation, for whatever purpose, would have serious repercussions internationally.

The President finally agreed to Directive 7–12, but insisted that he retain control over the decision to use a bomb for Cautery. Stone was displeased with this arrangement, but he was forced to accept it; the President had been under considerable pressure to reject the whole idea and had compromised only after much argument. Then, too, there was the Hudson Institute study.

The Hudson Institute had been contracted to study possible consequences of Cautery. Their report indicated that the President would face four circumstances (scenarios) in which he might have to issue the Cautery order. According to degree of seriousness, the scenarios were:

1. *A satellite or manned capsule lands in an unpopulated area of the United States.* The President may cauterize the area with little domestic uproar and small loss of life. The Russians may be privately informed of the reasons for breaking the Moscow Treaty of 1963 forbidding aboveground nuclear testing.

2. *A satellite or manned capsule lands in a major American city.* (The example was Chicago.) The Cautery will require destruction of a large land area and a large population, with great domestic consequences and secondary international consequences.

3. *A satellite or manned capsule lands in a major neutralist urban center.* (New Delhi was the example.) The Cautery will entail American intervention with nuclear weapons to prevent further spread of disease. According to

the scenarios, there were seventeen possible consequences of American-Soviet interaction following the destruction of New Delhi. Twelve led directly to thermonuclear war.

4. *A satellite or manned capsule lands in a major Soviet urban center.* (The example was Stalingrad.) Cautery will require the United States to inform the Soviet Union of what has happened and to advise that the Russians themselves destroy the city. According to the Hudson Institute scenario, there were six possible consequences of American-Russian interaction following this event, and all six led directly to war. It was therefore advised that if a satellite fell within Soviet or Eastern Bloc territory the United States not inform the Russians of what had happened. The basis of this decision was the prediction that a Russian plague would kill between two and five million people, while combined Soviet-American losses from a thermonuclear exchange involving both first- and second-strike capabilities would come to more than two hundred and fifty million persons.

As a result of the Hudson Institute report, the President and his advisers felt that control of Cautery, and responsibility for it, should remain within political, not scientific, hands. The ultimate consequences of the President's decision could not, of course, have been predicted at the time it was made.

Washington came to a decision within an hour of Manchek's report. The reasoning behind the President's decision has never been clear, but the final result was plain enough:

The President elected to postpone calling Directive 7–12 for twenty-four to forty-eight hours. Instead, he called out the National Guard and cordoned off the area around Piedmont for a radius of one hundred miles. And he waited.

9 Flatrock

Mark William Hall, M.D., sat in the tight rear seat of the F-104 fighter and stared over the top of the rubber oxygen mask at the file on his knees. Leavitt had given it to him just before takeoff – a heavy, thick wad of paper bound in gray cardboard. Hall was supposed to read it during the flight, but the F-104 was not made for reading; there was barely enough room in front of him to hold his hands clenched together, let alone open a file and read.

Yet Hall was reading it.

On the cover of the file was stenciled WILDFIRE, and underneath, an ominous note:

> THIS FILE IS CLASSIFIED TOP SECRET.
> Examination by unauthorized persons
> is a criminal offense punishable
> by fines and imprisonment up to
> 20 years and $20,000.

When Leavitt gave him the file, Hall had read the note and whistled.

'Don't you believe it,' Leavitt said.

'Just a scare?'

'Scare, hell,' Leavitt said. 'If the wrong man reads this file, he just disappears.'

'Nice.'

'Read it,' Leavitt said, 'and you'll see why.'

The plane flight had taken an hour and forty minutes, cruising in eerie, perfect silence at 1.8 times the speed of sound. Hall had skimmed through most of the file; reading it, he had found, was impossible. Much of its bulk of 274 pages consisted of cross-references and interservice notations, none of which he could understand. The first page was as bad as any of them:

THIS IS PAGE __1__ OF __274__ PAGES

PROJECT: WILDFIRE
AUTHORITY: NASA/AMC
CLASSIFICATION: TOP SECRET (NTK BASIS)
PRIORITY: NATIONAL (DX)

SUBJECT: Initiation of high-security facility to prevent dispersion of toxic extraterrestrial agents.
CROSSFILE: Project CLEAN, Project ZERO CONTAMINANTS, Project CAUTERY

SUMMARY OF FILE CONTENTS:

By executive order, construction of a facility initiated January 1965. Planning stage March 1965. Consultants Fort Detrick and General Dynamics (EBD) July 1965. Recommendation for multistory facility in isolated location for investigation of possible or probable contaminatory agents. Specifications reviewed August 1965. Approval with revision same date. Final drafts drawn and filed AMC under WILDFIRE (copies Detrick, Hawkins). Choice of site northeast Montana, reviewed August 1965. Choice of site southwest Arizona, reviewed August 1965. Choice of site northwest Nevada, reviewed September 1965. Nevada site approved October 1965.

Construction completed July 1966. Funding NASA, AMC, DEFENSE (unaccountable reserves). Congressional appropriation for maintenance and personnel under same.

Major alterations: millipore filters, see page 74. Self-destruct capacity (nuclear), page 88. Ultraviolet irradiators removed, see page 81. Single Man Hypothesis (Odd Man Hypothesis), page 255.

PERSONNEL SUMMARIES HAVE BEEN ELIMINATED FROM THIS FILE. PERSONNEL MAY BE FOUND IN AMC (WILDFIRE) FILES ONLY.

The second page listed the basic parameters of the system, as laid down by the original Wildfire planning group. This specified the most important concept of the installation, namely that it would consist of roughly similar, descending levels, all underground. Each would be more sterile than the one above.

THIS IS PAGE 2 OF 274 PAGES

PROJECT: WILDFIRE

PRIMARY PARAMETERS

1. THERE ARE TO BE FIVE STAGES:

Stage I: Non-decontaminated, but clean. Approximates sterility of hospital operating room or NASA clean room. No time delay of entrance.

Stage II: Minimal sterilization procedures: hexachlorophene and methitol bath, not requiring total immersion. One-hour delay with clothing change.

Stage III: Moderate sterilization procedures: total-immersion bath, UV irradiation, followed by two-hour delay for preliminary testing. Afebrile infections of UR and GU tracts permitted to pass. Viral symptomatology permitted to pass.

Stage IV: Maximal sterilization procedures: total immersion in four baths of biocaine, monochlorophin, xantholysin, and prophyne with intermediate thirty-minute UV and IR irradiation. All infection halted at this stage on basis of symptomatology or clinical signs. Routine screening of all personnel. Six-hour delay.

Stage V: Redundant sterilization procedures: no further immersions or testing, but destruct clothing x2 per day. Prophylactic antibiotics for forty-eight hours. Daily screen for superinfection, first eight days.

2. EACH STAGE INCLUDES:

1. Resting quarters, individual
2. Recreation quarters, including movie and game room
3. Cafeteria, automatic
4. Library, with main journals transmitted by Xerox or TV from main library Level I.
5. Shelter, a high-security antimicrobial complex with safety in event of level contamination.
6. Laboratories:

a) biochemistry, with all necessary equipment for automatic amino-acid analysis, sequence determination, O/R potentials, lipid and carbohydrate determinations on human, animal, other subjects.

b) pathology, with EM, phase and LM, microtomes and curing rooms. Five full-time technicians each level. One autopsy room. One room for experimental animals.

c) microbiology, with all facilities for growth, nutrient, analytic, immunologic studies. Subsections bacterial, viral, parasitic, other.

d) pharmacology, with material for dose-relation and receptor site specificity studies of known compounds. Pharmacy to include drugs as noted in appendix.

e) main room, experimental animals. 75 genetically pure strains of mice; 27 of rat; 17 of cat; 12 of dog; 8 of primate.

f) nonspecific room for previously unplanned experiments.

7. Surgery: for care and treatment of staff, including operating-room facilities for acute emergencies.

8. Communications: for contact with other levels by audiovisual and other means.

COUNT YOUR PAGES
REPORT ANY MISSING
PAGES AT ONCE
COUNT YOUR PAGES

As Hall continued to read, he found that only on Level I, the topmost floor, would there be a large computer complex for data analysis, but that this computer would serve all other levels on a time-sharing basis. This was considered feasible since, for biologic problems, real time was unimportant in relation to computer time, and multiple problems could be fed and handled at once.

He was leafing through the rest of the file, looking for the part that interested him – the Odd Man Hypothesis – when he came upon a page that was rather unusual.

THIS IS PAGE 255 OF 274 PAGES

BY THE AUTHORITY OF THE DEPARTMENT OF DEFENSE
THIS PAGE FROM A HIGH-SECURITY FILE HAS BEEN DELETED

THE PAGE IS NUMBER: two hundred fifty-five/255

THE FILE IS CODED: Wildfire

THE SUBJECT MATTER
DELETED IS: Odd Man Hypothesis

PLEASE NOTE THAT THIS CONSTITUTES A LEGAL DELETION FROM THE FILE WHICH NEED NOT BE REPORTED BY THE READER.

MACHINE SCORE REVIEW BELOW

255 WILDFIRE 255

Hall was frowning at the page, wondering what it meant, when the pilot said, 'Dr. Hall?'

'Yes.'

'We have just passed the last checkpoint, sir. We will touch down in four minutes.'

'All right.' Hall paused. 'Do you know where, exactly, we are landing?'

'I believe,' said the pilot, 'that it is Flatrock, Nevada.'

'I see,' Hall said.

A few minutes later, the flaps went down, and he heard a whine as the airplane slowed.

Nevada was the ideal site for Wildfire. The Silver State ranks seventh in size, but forty-ninth in population; it is the least-dense state in the Union after Alaska. Particularly when one considers that 85 per cent of the state's 440,000 people live in Las Vegas, Reno, or Carson City, the population density of 1.2 persons per square mile seems well suited for projects such as Wildfire, and indeed many have been located there.

Along with the famous atomic site at Vinton Flats, there is the Ultra-Energy Test Station at Martindale, and the Air Force Medivator Unit near Los Gados. Most of these facilities are in the southern triangle of the state, having been located there in the days before Las Vegas swelled to receive twenty million visitors a year. More recently, government test stations have been located in the northwest corner of Nevada, which is still relatively isolated. Pentagon classified lists include five new installations in that area; the nature of each is unknown.

10 Stage I

Hall landed shortly after noon, the hottest part of the day. The sun beat down from a pale, cloudless sky and the airfield asphalt was soft under his feet as he walked from the airplane to the small quonset hut at the edge of the runway. Feeling his feet sink into the surface, Hall thought that the airfield must have been designed primarily for night use; at night it would be cold, the asphalt solid.

The quonset hut was cooled by two massive, grumbling air conditioners. It was furnished sparsely: a card table in one corner, at which two pilots sat, playing poker and drinking coffee. A guard in the corner was making a telephone call; he had a machine gun slung over his shoulder. He did not look up as Hall entered.

There was a coffee machine near the telephone. Hall went over with his pilot and they each poured a cup. Hall took a sip and said, 'Where's the town, anyway? I didn't see it as we were coming in.'

'Don't know, sir.'

'Have you been here before?'

'No sir. It's not on the standard runs.'

'Well, what exactly does this airfield serve?'

At that moment, Leavitt strode in and beckoned to Hall. The bacteriologist led him through the back of the quonset and then out into the heat again, to a light-blue Falcon sedan parked in the rear. There were no identifying marks of any kind on the car; there was no driver. Leavitt slipped behind the wheel and motioned for Hall to get in.

As Leavitt put the car in gear, Hall said, 'I guess we don't rate any more.'

'Oh yes. We rate. But drivers aren't used out here. In fact, we don't use any more personnel than we have to. The number of wagging tongues is kept to a minimum.'

They set off across desolate, hilly countryside. In the distance were blue mountains, shimmering in the liquid heat of the desert. The road was pock-marked and dusty; it looked as if it hadn't been used for years.

Hall mentioned this.

'Deceptive,' Leavitt said. 'We took great pains about it. We spent nearly five thousand dollars on this road.'

'Why?'

Leavitt shrugged. 'Had to get rid of the tractor treadmarks. A hell of a lot of heavy equipment has moved over these roads, at one time or another. Wouldn't want anyone to wonder why.'

'Speaking of caution,' Hall said after a pause, 'I was reading in the file. Something about an atomic self-destruct device –'

'What about it?'

'It exists?'

'It exists.'

Installation of the device had been a major stumbling block in the early plans for Wildfire. Stone and the others had insisted that they retain control over the detonate/no detonate decision; the AEC and the Executive branch had been reluctant. No atomic device had been put in private hands before. Stone argued that in the event of a leak in the Wildfire lab, there might not be time to consult with Washington and get a Presidential detonate order. It was a long time before the President agreed that this might be true.

'I was reading,' Hall said, 'that this device is somehow connected with the Odd Man Hypothesis.'

'It is.'

'How? The page on Odd Man was taken from my file.'

'I know,' Leavitt said. 'We'll talk about it later.'

The Falcon turned off the potted road onto a dirt track. The sedan raised a heavy cloud of dust, and despite the heat, they were forced to roll up the windows. Hall lit a cigarette.

'That'll be your last,' Leavitt said.

'I know. Let me enjoy it.'

On their right, they passed a sign that said GOVERNMENT PROPERTY KEEP OFF, but there was no fence, no guard, no dogs – just a battered, weatherbeaten sign.

'Great security measures,' Hall said.

'We try not to arouse suspicion. The security is better than it looks.'

They proceeded another mile, bouncing along the dirt rut, and then came over a hill. Suddenly Hall saw a large, fenced circle perhaps a hundred yards in diameter. The fence, he noticed, was ten feet high and sturdy; at intervals it was laced with barbed wire. Inside was a utilitarian wooden building, and a field of corn.

'Corn?' Hall said.

'Rather clever, I think.'

They came to the entrance gate. A man in dungarees and a T-shirt came out and opened it for them; he held a sandwich in one hand and was chewing vigorously as he unlocked the gate. He winked and smiled and waved them through, still chewing. The sign by the gate said:

GOVERNMENT PROPERTY
U.S. DEPARTMENT OF AGRICULTURE
DESERT RECLAMATION TEST STATION

Leavitt drove through the gates and parked by the wooden building. He left the keys on the dashboard and got out. Hall followed him.

'Now what?'

'Inside,' Leavitt said. They entered the building, coming directly into a small room. A man in a Stetson hat, checked sport shirt, and string tie sat at a rickety desk. He was reading a newspaper and, like the man at the gate, eating his lunch. He looked up and smiled pleasantly.

'Howdy,' he said.

'Hello,' Leavitt said.

'Help you folks?'

'Just passing through,' Leavitt said. 'On the way to Rome.'

The man nodded. 'Have you got the time?'

'My watch stopped yesterday,' Leavitt said.

'Durn shame,' the man said.

'It's because of the heat.'

The ritual completed, the man nodded again. And they walked past him, out of the anteroom and down a corridor. The doors had hand-printed labels: 'Seedling Incubation'; 'Moisture Control'; 'Soil Analysis.' A half-dozen people were at work in the building, all of them dressed casually, but all of them apparently busy.

'This is a real agricultural station,' Leavitt said. 'If necessary, that man at the desk could give you a guided tour, explaining the purpose of the station and the experiments that are going on. Mostly they are attempting to develop a strain of corn that can grow in low-moisture, high-alkalinity soil.'

'And the Wildfire installation?'

'Here,' Leavitt said. He opened a door marked 'Storage' and they found themselves staring at a narrow cubicle lined with rakes and hoes and watering hoses.

'Step in,' Leavitt said.

Hall did. Leavitt followed and closed the door behind him. Hall felt the floor sink and they began to descend, rakes and hoses and all.

In a moment, he found himself in a modern, bare room, lighted by banks of cold overhead fluorescent lights. The walls were painted red. The only object in the room was a rectangular, waist-high box that reminded Hall of a podium. It had a glowing green glass top.

'Step up to the analyzer,' Leavitt said. 'Place your hands flat on the glass, palms down.'

Hall did. He felt a faint tingling in his fingers, and then the machine gave a buzz.

'All right. Step back.' Leavitt placed his hands on the box, waited for the buzz, and then said, 'Now we go over here. You mentioned the security arrangements; I'll show them to you before we enter Wildfire.'

He nodded to a door across the room.

'What was that thing?'

'Finger- and palm-print analyzer,' Leavitt said. 'It is fully automatic. Reads a composite of ten thousand dermatographic lines so it can't make a mistake; in its storage banks it has a record of the prints of everyone cleared to enter Wildfire.'

Leavitt pushed through the door.

They were faced with another door, marked SECURITY, which slid back noiselessly. They entered a darkened room in which a single man sat before banks of green dials.

'Hello, John,' Leavitt said to the man. 'How are you?'

'Good, Dr. Leavitt. Saw you come in.'

Leavitt introduced Hall to the security man, who then demonstrated the equipment to Hall. There were, the man explained, two radar scanners located in the hills overlooking the installation; they were well concealed but quite effective. Then closer in, impedence sensors were buried in the ground; they signaled the approach of any animal life weighing more than one hundred pounds. The sensors ringed the base.

'We've never missed anything yet,' the man said. 'And if we do . . .' He shrugged. To Leavitt: 'Going to show him the dogs?'

'Yes,' Leavitt said.

They walked through into an adjoining room. There were nine large cages there, and the room smelled strongly of animals. Hall found himself looking at nine of the largest German shepherds he had ever seen.

They barked at him as he entered, but there was no sound in the room. He watched in astonishment as they opened their mouths and threw their heads forward in a barking motion.

No sound.

'These are Army-trained sentry dogs,' the security man said. 'Bred for viciousness. You wear leather clothes and heavy gloves when you walk them. They've undergone laryngectomies, which is why you can't hear them. Silent and vicious.'

Hall said, 'Have you ever, uh, used them?'

'No,' the security man said. 'Fortunately not.'

They were in a small room with lockers. Hall found one with his name on it.

'We change in here,' Leavitt said. He nodded to a stack of pink uniforms in one corner. 'Put those on, after you have removed everything you are wearing.'

'Hall changed quickly. The uniforms were loose-fitting one piece suits that zipped up the side. When they had changed they proceeded down a passageway.

Suddenly an alarm sounded and a gate in front of them slid closed abruptly. Overhead, a white light began to flash. Hall was confused, and it was only much later that he remembered Leavitt looked away from the flashing light.

'Something's wrong,' Leavitt said. 'Did you remove everything?'

'Yes,' Hall said.

'Rings, watch, everything?'

Hall looked at his hands. He still had his watch on.

'Go back,' Leavitt said. 'Put it in your locker.'

Hall did. When he came back, they started down the corridor a second time. The gate remained open, and there was no alarm.

'Automatic as well?' Hall said.

'Yes,' Leavitt said. 'It picks up any foreign object. When we installed it, we were worried because we knew it would pick up glass eyes, cardiac pacemakers, false teeth – anything at all. But fortunately nobody on the project has these things.'

'Fillings?'

'It is programmed to ignore fillings.'

'How does it work?'

'Some kind of capacitance phenomenon. I don't really understand it,' Leavitt said.

They passed a sign that said:

YOU ARE NOW ENTERING LEVEL I
PROCEED DIRECTLY TO IMMUNIZATION CONTROL

Hall noticed that all the walls were red. He mentioned this to Leavitt.

'Yes,' Leavitt said. 'All levels are painted a different color. Level I is red; II, Yellow; III, white; IV, green; and V, blue.'

'Any particular reason for the choice?'

'It seems,' Leavitt said, 'that the Navy sponsored some studies a few years back on the psychological effects of colored environments. Those studies have been applied here.'

They came to Immunization. A door slid back revealing three glass booths. Leavitt said, 'Just sit down in one of them.'

'I suppose this is automatic, too?'

'Of course.'

Hall entered a booth and closed the door behind him. There was a couch, and a mass of complex equipment. In front of the couch was a television screen, which showed several lighted points.

'Sit down,' said a flat mechanical voice. 'Sit down. Sit down.'

He sat on the couch.

'Observe the screen before you. Place your body on the couch so that all points are obliterated.'

He looked at the screen. He now saw that the points were arranged in the shape of a man:

```
       *
     *   *
  *         *
*   *     *   *
    *     *
    *     *
```

He shifted his body, and one by one the spots disappeared.

'Very good,' said the voice. 'We may now proceed. State your name for the record. Last name first, first name last.'

'Mark Hall,' he said.

'State your name for the record. Last name first, first name last.'

Simultaneously, on the screen appeared the words:

SUBJECT HAS GIVEN UNCODABLE RESPONSE

'Hall, Mark.'

'Thank you for your cooperation,' said the voice. 'Please recite, 'Mary had a little lamb.'

'You're kidding,' Hall said.

There was a pause, and the faint sound of relays and circuits clicking. The screen again showed:

SUBJECT HAS GIVEN UNCODABLE RESPONSE

'Please recite.'

Feeling rather foolish, Hall said, 'Mary had a little lamb, its fleece was white as snow, and everywhere that Mary went, the lamb was sure to go.'

Another pause. Then the voice: 'Thank you for your cooperation.' And the screen said:

ANALYZER CONFIRMS IDENTITY
HALL, MARK

'Please listen closely,' said the mechanical voice. 'You will answer the following questions with a yes or no reply. Make no other response. Have you received a smallpox vaccination within the last twelve months?'

'Yes.'

'Diphtheria?'

'Yes.'

'Typhoid and paratyphoid A and B?'

'Yes.'

'Tetanus toxoid?'

'Yes.'

'Yellow fever?'

'Yes, yes, yes. I had them all.'

'Just answer the question please. Uncooperative subjects waste valuable computer time.'

'Yes,' Hall said, subdued. When he had joined the Wildfire team, he had undergone immunizations for everything imaginable, even plague and cholera, which had to be renewed every six months, and gamma-globulin shots for viral infection.

'Have you ever contracted tuberculosis or other mycobacterial disease, or had a positive skin test for tuberculosis?'

'No.'

'Have you ever contracted syphilis or other spirochetal disease, or had a positive serological test for syphilis?'

'No.'

'Have you contracted within the past year any gram-positive bacterial infection, such as streptococcus, staphylococcus, or pneumococcus?'

'No.'

'Any gram-negative infection, such as gonococcus, meningeococcus, proteus, pseudomonas, salmonella, or shigella?'

'No.'

'Have you contracted any recent or past fungal infection, including blastomycosis, histoplasmosis, or coccidiomycosis, or had a positive skin test for any fungal disease?'

'No.'

'Have you had any recent viral infection, including poliomyelitis, hepatitis, mononucleosis, mumps, measles, varicella, or herpes?'

'No.'

'Any warts?'

'No.'

'Have you any known allergies?'

'Yes, to ragweed pollen.'

On the screen appeared the words:

ROGEEN PALEN

And then after a moment:

UNCODABLE RESPONSE

'Please repeat your response slowly for our memory cells.'

Very distinctly, he said, 'Ragweed pollen.'

On the screen:

RAGWEED POLLEN CODED

'Are you allergic to albumen?' continued the voice.

'No.'

'This ends the formal questions. Please undress and return to the couch, obliterating the points as before.'

He did so. A moment later, an ultraviolet lamp swung out on a long arm and moved close to his body. Next to the lamp was some kind of scanning eye. Watching the screen he could see the computer print of the scan, beginning with his feet.

'This is a scan for fungus,' the voice announced. After several minutes, Hall was ordered to lie on his stomach, and the process was repeated. He was then told to lie on his back once more and align himself with the dots.

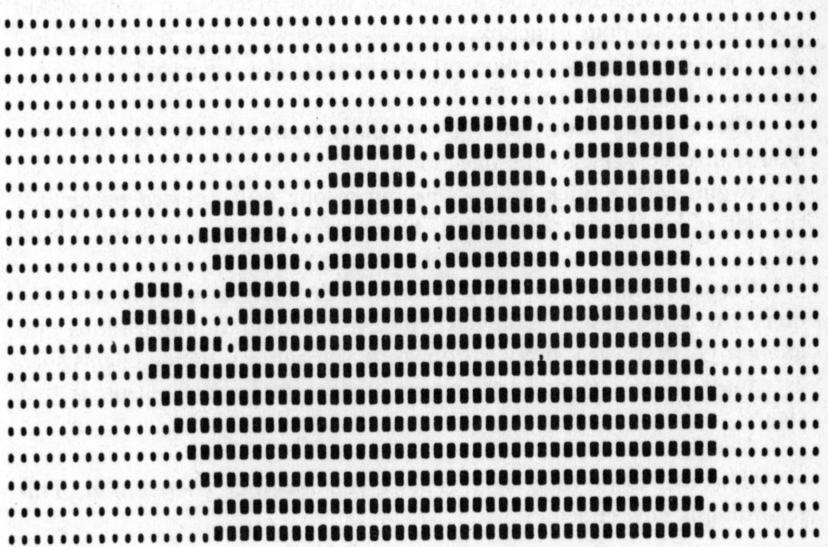

'Physical parameters will now be measured,' the voice said. 'You are requested to lie quietly while the examination is conducted.'

A variety of leads snaked out at him and were attached by mechanical hands to his body. Some he could understand – the half-dozen leads over his chest for an electrocardiogram, and twenty-one on his head for an electroencephalogram. But others were fixed on his stomach, his arms, and his legs.

'Please raise your left hand,' said the voice.

Hall did. From above, a mechanical hand came down, with an electric eye fixed on either side of it. The mechanical hand examined Hall's.

'Place your hand on the board to the left. Do not move. You will feel a slight prick as the intravenous needle is inserted.'

Hall looked over at the screen. It flashed a color image of his hand, with the veins showing in a pattern of green against a blue background. Obviously the machine worked by sensing heat. He was about to protest when he felt a brief sting.

He looked back. The needle was in.

'Now then, just lie quietly. Relax.'

For fifteen seconds, the machinery whirred and clattered. Then the leads were withdrawn. The mechanical hands placed a neat Band-Aid over the intravenous puncture.

'This completes your physical parameters,' the voice said.

'Can I get dressed now?'

'Please sit up with your right shoulder facing the television screen. You will receive pneumatic injections.'

A gun with a thick cable came out of one wall, pressed up against the skin of his shoulder, and fired. There was a hissing sound and a brief pain.

'Now you may dress,' said the voice. 'Be advised that you may feel dizzy for a few hours. You have received booster immunizations and gamma G. If you feel dizzy, sit down. If you suffer systemic effects such as nausea, vomiting, or fever, report at once to Level Control. Is that clear?'

'Yes.'

'The exit is to your right. Thank you for your cooperation. This recording is now ended.'

Hall walked with Leavitt down a long red corridor. His arm ached from the injection.

'That machine,' Hall said. 'You'd better not let the AMA find out about it.'

'We haven't,' Leavitt said.

In fact, the electronic body analyzer had been developed by Sandeman Industries in 1965, under a general government contract to produce body monitors for astronauts in space. It was understood by the government at that time that such a device, though expensive at a cost of $87,000 each, would eventually replace the human physician as a diagnostic instrument. The difficulties, for both doctor and patient, of adjusting to this new machine were recognized by everyone. The government did not plan to release the EBA until 1971, and then only to certain large hospital facilities.

Walking along the corridor, Hall noticed that the walls were slightly curved.

'Where exactly are we?'

'On the perimeter of Level I. To our left are all the laboratories. To the right is nothing but solid rock.'

Several people were walking in the corridor. Everyone wore pink jumpsuits. They all seemed serious and busy.

'Where are the others on the team?' Hall said.

'Right here,' Leavitt said. He opened a door marked CONFERENCE 7, and they entered a room with a large hardwood table. Stone was there, standing stiffly erect and alert, as if he had just taken a cold shower. Alongside him, Burton, the pathologist, somehow appeared sloppy and confused, and there was a kind of tired fright in his eyes.

They all exchanged greetings and sat down. Stone reached into his pocket and removed two keys. One was silver, the other red. The red one had a chain attached to it. He gave it to Hall.

'Put it around your neck,' he said.

Hall looked at it. 'What's this?'

Leavitt said, 'I'm afraid Mark is still unclear about the Odd Man.'

'I thought that he would read it on the plane –'

'His file was edited.'

'I see.' Stone turned to Hall. 'You know nothing about the Odd Man?'

'Nothing,' Hall said, frowning at the key.

'Nobody told you that a major factor in your selection to the team was your single status?'

'What does that have to do –'

'The fact of the matter is,' Stone said, 'that you are the Odd Man. You are the key to all this. Quite literally.'

He took his own key and walked to a corner of the room. He pushed a hidden button and the wood paneling slid away to reveal a burnished metal console. He inserted his key into a lock and twisted it. A green light on the console flashed on; he stepped back. The paneling slid into place.

'At the lowest level of this laboratory is an automatic atomic self-destruct device,' Stone said. 'It is controlled from within the laboratory. I have just inserted my key and armed the mechanism. The device is ready for detonation. The key on this level cannot be removed; it is now locked in place. Your key, on the other hand, can be inserted and removed again. There is a three-minute delay between the time detonation locks in and the time the bomb goes off. That period is to provide you time to think, and perhaps call it all off.'

Hall was still frowning. 'But why me?'

'Because you are single. We had to have one unmarried man.'

Stone opened a briefcase and withdrew a file. He gave it to Hall. 'Read that.'

It was a Wildfire file.

'Page 255,' Stone said.

Hall turned to it.

Project: Wildfire

ALTERATIONS

1. Millipore Filters, insertion into ventilatory system. Initial spec filters unilayer styrilene, with maximal efficiency of 97.4% trapping. Replaced in 1966 when Upjohn developed filters capable of trapping organisms of size up to one micron. Trapping at 90% efficiency per leaf, causing triple-layered membrance to give results of 99.9%. Infective ratio of .1% remainder too low to be harmful. Cost factor of four- or five-layered membrance removing all but .001% considered prohibitive for added gain. Tolerance parameter of 1/1,000 considered sufficient. Installation completed 8/12/66.

2. Atomic Self-Destruct Device, change in detonator close-gap timers. See AEC/Def file 77-12-0918.

3. Atomic Self-Destruct Device, revision of core maintenance schedules for K technicians, see AEC/Warburg file 77-14-0004.

4. Atomic Self-Destruct Device, final command decision change. See AEC/Def file 77-14-0023. SUMMARY APPENDED.

SUMMARY OF ODD MAN HYPOTHESIS: First tested as null hypothesis by Wildfire advisory committee. Grew out of tests conducted by USAF (NORAD) to determine reliability of commanders in making life/death decisions. Tests involved decisions in ten scenario contexts, with prestructured alternatives drawn up by Walter Reed Psychiatric Division, after n-order test analysis by biostatistics unit, NIH, Bethesda.

Test given to SAC pilots and groundcrews, NORAD workers, and others involved in decision-making or positive-action capacity. Ten scenarios drawn up by Hudson Institute; subjects required to make YES/NO decision in each case. Decisions always involved thermonuclear or chembiol destruction of enemy targets.

Data on 7420 subjects tested by H_1H_2 program for multifactorial analysis of variance; later test by ANOVAR program; final discrimination by CLASSIF program. NIH biostat summarizes this program as follows:

It is the object of this program to determine the effectiveness of assigning individuals to distinct groups on the basis of scores which can be quantified. The program produces group contours and probability of classification for individuals as a control of data.
Program prints: mean scores for groups, contour confidence limits, and scores of individual test subjects.

K G Borgrand

K.G. Borgrand, Ph.D. NIH

RESULTS OF ODD MAN STUDY: The study concluded that married individuals performed differently from single individuals on several parameters of the test. Hudson Institute provided mean answers, i.e. theoretical 'right' decisions, made by computer on basis of data given in scenario. Conformance of study groups to these right answers produced an index of effectiveness, a measure of the extent to which correct decisions were made.

Group	Index of Effectiveness
Married males	.343
Married females	.399
Single females	.402
Single males	.824

The data indicate that married men choose the correct decision only once in three times, while single men choose correctly four out of five times. The group of single males was then broken down further, in search of highly accurate subgroups within that classification.

Group	Index of Effectiveness
Single males, total	.824
Military:	
commissioned officer	.655
noncommissioned officer	.624
Technical:	
engineers	.877
ground crews	.901
Service:	
maintenance and utility	.758
Professional:	
scientists	.946

These results concerning the relative skill of decision-making individuals should not be interpreted hastily. Although it would appear that janitors are better decision-makers than generals, the situation is in reality more complex. PRINTED SCORES ARE SUMMATIONS OF TEST AND INDIVIDUAL VARIATIONS. DATA MUST BE INTERPRETED WITH THIS IN MIND. Failure to do so may lead to totally erroneous and dangerous assumptions.

Application of study to Wildfire command personnel conducted at request of AEC at time of implantation of self-destruct nuclear capacity. Test given to all Wildfire personnel; results filed under CLASSIF WILDFIRE: GENERAL PERSONNEL (see ref. 77-14-0023). Special testing for command group.

Name	Index of Effectiveness
Burton	.543
Reynolds	.601
Kirke	.614
Stone	.687
Hall	.899

Results of special testing confirm the Odd Man Hypothesis, that an unmarried male should carry out command decisions involving thermonuclear or chem-biol destruct contexts.

When Hall had finished reading, he said, 'It's crazy.'

'Nonetheless,' Stone said, 'it was the only way we could get the government to put control of the weapon in our hands.'

'You really expect me to put in my key, and fire that thing?'

'I'm afraid you don't understand,' Stone said. 'The detonation mechanism is automatic. Should breakthrough of the organism occur, with contamination of all Level V, detonation will take place within three minutes *unless* you lock in your key, and call it off.'

'Oh,' Hall said, in a quiet voice.

11 Decontamination

A bell rang somewhere on the level; Stone glanced up at the wall clock. It was late. He began the formal briefing, talking rapidly, pacing up and down the room, hands moving constantly.

'As you know,' he said, 'we are on the top level of a five-story underground structure. According to protocol it will take us nearly twenty-four hours to descend through the sterilization and decontamination procedures to the lowest level. Therefore we must begin immediately. The capsule is already on its way.'

He pressed a button on a console at the head of the table, and a television screen glowed to life, showing the cone-shaped satellite in a plastic bag, making its descent. It was being cradled by mechanical hands.

'The central core of this circular building,' Stone said, 'contains elevators and service units – plumbing, wiring, that sort of thing. That is where you see the capsule now. It will be deposited shortly in a maximum-sterilization assembly on the lowest level.'

He went on to explain that he had brought back two other surprises from Piedmont. The screen shifted to show Peter Jackson, lying on a litter, with intravenous lines running into both arms.

'This man apparently survived the night. He was the one walking around when the planes flew over, and he was still alive this morning.'

'What's his status now?'

'Uncertain,' Stone said. 'He is unconscious, and he was vomiting blood earlier today. We've started intravenous dextrose to keep him fed and hydrated until we can get down to the bottom.'

Stone flicked a button and the screen showed the baby. It was howling, strapped down to a tiny bed. An intravenous bottle was running into a vein in the scalp.

'This little fellow also survived last night,' Stone said. 'So we brought him along. We couldn't really leave him, since a Directive 7–12 was being called. The town is now destroyed by a nuclear blast. Besides, he and Jackson are living clues which may help us unravel this mess.'

Then, for the benefit of Hall and Leavitt, the two men disclosed what they had seen and learned at Piedmont. They reviewed the findings of rapid death, the bizarre suicides, the clotted arteries and the lack of bleeding.

Hall listened in astonishment. Leavitt sat shaking his head.

When they were through, Stone said, 'Questions?'

'None that won't keep,' Leavitt said.

'Then let's get started,' Stone said.

They began at a door, which said in plain white letters: TO LEVEL II. It was an innocuous, straightforward, almost mundane sign. Hall had expected something more – perhaps a stern guard with a machine gun, or a sentry to check passes. But there was nothing, and he noticed that no one had badges, or clearance cards of any kind.

He mentioned this to Stone. 'Yes,' Stone said. 'We decided against badges early on. They are easily contaminated and difficult to sterilize; usually they are plastic and high-heat sterilization melts them.'

The four men passed through the door, which clanged shut heavily and sealed with a hissing sound. It was airtight. Hall faced a tiled room, empty except for a hamper marked 'clothing.' He unzipped his jumpsuit and dropped it into the hamper; there was a brief flash of light as it was incinerated.

Then, looking back, he saw that on the door through which he had come was a sign: 'Return to Level I is NOT Possible Through this Access.'

He shrugged. The other men were already moving through the second door, marked simply EXIT. He followed them and stepped into clouds of steam. The odor was peculiar, a faint woodsy smell that he guessed was scented disinfectant. He sat down on a bench and relaxed, allowing the steam to envelop him. It was easy enough to understand the purpose of the steam room; the heat opened the pores, and the steam would be inhaled into the lungs.

The four men waited, saying little, until their bodies were coated with a sheen of moisture, and then walked into the next room.

Leavitt said to Hall, 'What do you think of this?'

'It's like a goddam Roman bath,' Hall said.

The next room contained a shallow tub ('Immerse Feet ONLY') and a shower. ('Do not swallow shower solution. Avoid undue exposure to eyes and mucous membranes.') It was all very intimidating. He tried to guess what the solutions were by smell, but failed; the shower was slippery, though, which meant it was alkaline. He asked Leavitt about this, and Leavitt said the solution was alpha chlorophin at pH 7.7. Leavitt said that whenever possible, acidic and alkaline solutions were alternated.

'When you think about it,' Leavitt said, 'we've faced up to quite a planning problem here. How to disinfect the human body – one of the dirtiest things in the known universe – without killing the person at the same time. Interesting.'

He wandered off. Dripping wet from the shower, Hall looked around for a towel but found none. He entered the next room and blowers turned on from the ceiling in a rush of hot air. From the sides of the room, UV lights clicked on, bathing the room in an intense purple light. He stood there until a buzzer sounded, and the dryers turned off. His skin tingled slightly as he entered the last room, which contained clothing. They were not jumpsuits, but rather like surgical uniforms – light yellow, a loose-fitting top with a V-neck and short sleeves; elastic banded pants; low rubber-soled shoes, quite comfortable, like ballet slippers.

The cloth was soft, some kind of synthetic. He dressed and stepped with the others through a door marked EXIT TO LEVEL II. He entered the elevator and waited as it descended.

Hall emerged to find himself in a corridor. The walls here were painted yellow, not red as they had been on Level I. The people wore yellow uniforms. A nurse by the elevator said, 'The time is 2:47 p.m., gentlemen. You may continue your descent in one hour.'

They went to a small room marked INTERIM CONFINEMENT. It contained a half-dozen couches with plastic disposable covers over them.

Stone said, 'Better relax. Sleep if you can. We'll need all the rest we can get before Level V.' He walked over to Hall. 'How did you find the decontamination procedure?'

'Interesting,' Hall said. 'You could sell it to the Swedes and make a fortune. But somehow I expected something more rigorous.'

'Just wait,' Stone said. 'It gets tougher as you go. Physicals on Levels III and IV. Afterward there will be a brief conference.'

Then Stone lay down on one of the couches and fell instantly asleep. It was a trick he had learned years before, when he had been conducting experiments around the clock. He learned to squeeze in an hour here, two hours there. He found it useful.

The second decontamination procedure was similar to the first. Hall's yellow clothing, though he had worn it just an hour, was incinerated.

'Isn't that rather wasteful?' he asked Burton.

Burton shrugged. 'It's paper.'

'Paper? That cloth?'

Burton shook his head. 'Not cloth. Paper. New process.'

They stepped into the first total-immersion pool. Instructions on the wall told Hall to keep his eyes open under water. Total immersion, he soon discovered, was guaranteed by the simple device of making the connection between the first room and the second an underwater passage. Swimming through, he felt a slight burning of his eyes, but nothing bad.

The second room contained a row of six boxes, glass-walled, looking rather like telephone booths. Hall approached one and saw a sign that said, 'Enter and close both eyes. Hold arms slightly away from body and stand with feet one foot apart. Do not open eyes until buzzer sounds. BLINDNESS MAY RESULT FROM EXPOSURE TO LONG-WAVE RADIATION.'

He followed the directions and felt a kind of cold heat on his body. It lasted perhaps five minutes, and then he heard the buzzer and opened his eyes. His body was dry. He followed the others to a corridor, consisting of four showers. Walking down the corridor, he passed beneath each shower in turn. At the end, he found blowers, which dried him, and then clothing. This time the clothing was white.

They dressed, and took the elevator down to Level III.

There were four nurses waiting for them; one took Hall to an examining room. It turned out to be a two-hour physical examination, given not by a machine but by a blank-faced, thorough young man. Hall was annoyed, and thought to himself that he preferred the machine.

The doctor did everything, including a complete history; birth, education, travel, family history, past hospitalizations and illnesses. And an equally complete physical. Hall became angry; it was all so damned unnecessary. But the doctor shrugged and kept saying, 'It's routine.'

After two hours, he rejoined the others, and proceeded to Level IV.

Four total-immersion baths, three sequences of ultraviolet and infrared light, two of ultrasonic vibrations, and then something quite astonishing at the end. A steel-walled cubicle, with a helmet on a peg. The sign said, 'This is an ultraflash apparatus. To protect head and facial hair, place metal helmet securely on head, then press button below.'

Hall had never heard of ultraflash, and he followed directions, not knowing what to expect. He placed the helmet over his head, then pressed the button.

There was a single, brief, dazzling burst of white light, followed by a wave of heat that filled the cubicle. He felt a moment of pain, so swift he hardly recognized it until it was over. Cautiously, he removed the helmet and looked at his body. His skin was covered with a fine, white ash – and then he realized that the ash was his skin, or had been; the machine had burned away the outer epithelial layers. He proceeded to a shower and washed the ash off. When he finally reached the dressing room, he found green uniforms.

Another physical. This time they wanted samples of everything: sputum, oral epithelium, blood, urine, stool. He submitted passively to the tests, examinations, questions. He was tired, and was beginning to feel disoriented. The repetitions, the new experiences, the colors on the walls, the same bland artificial light . . .

Finally, he was brought back to Stone and the others. Stone said, 'We have six hours on this level – that's protocol, waiting while they do the lab tests on us – so we might as well sleep. Down the corridor are rooms, marked with your names. Further down is the cafeteria. We'll meet there in five hours for a conference. Right?'

Hall found his room, marked with a plastic door tag. He entered, surprised to find it quite large. He had been expecting something the size of a Pullman cubicle, but this was bigger and better-furnished. There was a bed, a chair, a small desk, and a computer console with built-in TV set. He was curious about the computer, but also very tired. He lay down on the bed and fell asleep quickly.

Burton could not sleep. He lay in his bed on Level IV and stared at the ceiling, thinking. He could not get the image of that town out of his mind, or those bodies, lying in the street without bleeding . . .

Burton was not a hematologist, but his work had involved some blood studies. He knew that a variety of bacteria had effects on blood. His own research with staphylococcus, for example, had shown that this organism produced two enzymes that altered blood.

One was the so-called exotoxin, which destroyed skin and dissolved red cells. Another was a coagulase, which coated the bacteria with protein to inhibit destruction by white cells.

So it was possible that bacteria could alter blood. And it could do it many different ways; strep produced an enzyme, streptokinase, that dissolved coagulated plasma. Clostridia and pneumococci produced a variety of hemolysins that destroyed red cells. Malaria and amebae also destroyed red cells, by digesting them as food. Other parasites did the same thing.

So it was possible.

But it didn't help them in finding out how the Scoop organism worked.

Burton tried to recall the sequence for blood clotting. He remembered that it operated like a kind of waterfall: one enzyme was set off, and activated, which acted on a second enzyme, which acted on a third; the third on a fourth; and so on, down through twelve or thirteen steps, until finally blood clotted.

And vaguely he remembered the rest, the details: all the intermediate steps, the necessary enzymes, the metals, ions, local factors. It was horribly complex.

He shook his head and tried to sleep.

Leavitt, the clinical microbiologist, was thinking through the steps in isolation and identification of the causative organism. He had been over it before; he was one of the original founders of the group, one of the men who developed the Life Analysis Protocol. But now, on the verge of putting that plan into effect, he had doubts.

Two years before, sitting around after lunch, talking speculatively, it had all seemed wonderful. It had been an amusing intellectual game then, a kind of abstract test of wits. But now, faced with a real agent that caused real and bizarre death, he wondered whether all their plans would prove to be so effective and so complete as they once thought.

The first steps were simple enough. They would examine the capsule minutely and culture everything onto growth media. They would be hoping like hell to come up with an organism that they could work with, experiment on, and identify.

And after that, attempt to find out how it attacked. There was already the suggestion that it killed by clotting the blood; if that turned out to be the case, they had a good start, but if not, they might waste valuable time following it up.

The example of cholera came to mind. For centuries, men had known that cholera was a fatal disease, and that it caused severe diarrhea, sometimes producing as much as thirty quarts of fluid a day. Men knew this, but they somehow assumed that the lethal effects of the disease were unrelated to the diarrhea; they searched for something else: an antidote, a drug, a way to kill the organism. It was not until modern times that cholera was recognized as a disease that killed through dehydration primarily; if you could replace a victim's water losses rapidly, he would survive the infection without other drugs or treatment.

Cure the symptoms, cure the disease.

But Leavitt wondered about the Scoop organism. Could they cure the disease by treating the blood clotting? Or was the clotting secondary to some more serious disorder?

There was also another concern, a nagging fear that had bothered him since the earliest planning stages of Wildfire. In those early meetings, Leavitt had argued that the Wildfire team might be committing extraterrestrial murder.

Leavitt had pointed out that all men, no matter how scientifically objective, had several built-in biases when discussing life. One was the assumption that complex life was larger than simple life. It was certainly true on the earth. As organisms became more intelligent, they grew larger, passing from the single-celled stage to multicellular creatures, and then to larger animals with differentiated cells working in groups called organs. On earth, the trend had been toward larger and more complex animals.

But this might not be true elsewhere in the universe. In other places, life might progress in the opposite direction – toward smaller and smaller forms. Just as modern human technology had learned to make things smaller, perhaps highly advanced evolutionary pressures led to smaller life forms. There were distinct advantages to smaller forms; less consumption of raw materials, cheaper spaceflight, fewer feeding problems . . .

Perhaps the most intelligent life form on a distant planet was no larger than a flea. Perhaps no larger than a bacterium. In that case, the Wildfire Project might be committed to destroying a highly developed life form, without ever realizing what it was doing.

This concept was not unique to Leavitt. It had been proposed by Merton at Harvard, and by Chalmers at Oxford. Chalmers, a man with a keen sense of humor, had used the example of a man looking down on a microscope slide and seeing the bacteria formed into the words 'Take us to your leader.' Everyone thought Chalmers's idea highly amusing.

Yet Leavitt could not get it out of his mind. Because it just might turn out to be true.

Before he fell asleep, Stone thought about the conference coming up. And the business of the meteorite. He wondered what Nagy would say, or Karp, if they knew about the meteorite.

Probably, he thought, it would drive them insane. Probably it will drive us all insane.

And then he slept.

Delta sector was the designation of three rooms on Level I that contained all communication facilities for the Wildfire installation. All intercom and visual circuits between levels were routed through there, as were cables for telephone and teletype from the outside. The trunk lines to the library and the central storage unit were also regulated by delta sector.

In essence it functioned as a giant switchboard, fully computerized. The three rooms of delta sector were quiet; all that could be heard was the soft hum of spinning tape drums and the muted clicking of relays. Only one person worked here, a single man sitting at a console, surrounded by the blinking lights of the computer.

There was no real reason for the man to be there; he performed no necessary function. The computers were self-regulating, constructed to run check patterns through their circuits every twelve minutes; the computers shut down automatically if there was an abnormal reading.

According to protocol, the man was required to monitor MCN communications, which were signaled by the ringing of a bell on the teleprinter. When the bell rang, he notified the five level command centers that the transmission was received. He was also required to report any computer dysfunction to Level I command, should that unlikely event occur.

day 3
WILDFIRE

12 The Conference

'Time to wake up, sir.'

Mark Hall opened his eyes. The room was lit with a steady, pale fluorescent light. He blinked and rolled over on his stomach.

'Time to wake up, sir.'

It was a beautiful female voice, soft and seductive. He sat up in bed and looked around the room: he was alone.

'Hello?'

'Time to wake up, sir.'

'Who are you?'

'Time to wake up, sir.'

He reached over and pushed a button on the nightstand by his bed. A light went off. He waited for the voice again, but it did not speak.

It was, he thought, a hell of an effective way to wake a man up. As he slipped into his clothes, he wondered how it worked. It was not a simple tape, because it worked as a response of some sort. The message was repeated only when Hall spoke.

To test his theory, he pushed the nightstand button again. The voice said softly, 'Do you wish something, sir?'

'I'd like to know your name, please.'

'Will that be all, sir?'

'Yes, I believe so.'

'Will that be all, sir?'

He waited. The light clicked off. He slipped into his shoes and was about to leave when a male voice said, 'This is the answering-service supervisor, Dr. Hall. I wish you would treat the project more seriously.'

Hall laughed. So the voice responded to comments, and taped his replies. It was a clever system.

'Sorry,' he said, 'I wasn't sure how the thing worked. The voice is quite luscious.'

'The voice,' said the supervisor heavily, 'belongs to Miss Gladys Stevens, who is sixty-three years old. She lives in Omaha and makes her living taping messages for SAC crews and other voice-reminder systems.'

'Oh,' Hall said.

He left the room and walked down the corridor to the cafeteria. As he walked, he began to understand why submarine designers had been called in to plan Wildfire. Without his wristwatch, he had no idea of the time, or even whether it was night or day. He found himself wondering whether the cafeteria would be crowded, wondering whether it was dinner time or breakfast time.

As it turned out, the cafeteria was almost deserted. Leavitt was there; he said the others were in the conference room. He pushed a glass of dark-brown liquid over to Hall and suggested he have breakfast.

'What's this?' Hall said.

'Forty-two-five nutrient. It has everything needed to sustain the average seventy-kilogram man for eighteen hours.'

Hall drank the liquid, which was syrupy and artificially flavored to taste like orange juice. It was a strange sensation, drinking brown orange juice, but not bad after the initial shock. Leavitt explained that it had been developed for the astronauts, and that it contained everything except air-soluble vitamins.

'For that, you need this pill,' he said.

Hall swallowed the pill, then got himself a cup of coffee from a dispenser in the corner. 'Any sugar?'

Leavitt shook his head. 'No sugar anywhere here. Nothing that might provide a bacterial growth medium. From now on, we're all on high-protein diets. We'll make all the sugar we need from the protein breakdown. But we won't be getting any sugar into the gut. Quite the opposite.'

He reached into his pocket.

'Oh, no.'

'Yes,' Leavitt said. He gave him a small capsule, sealed in aluminum foil.

'No,' Hall said.

'Everyone else has them. Broad-spectrum. Stop by your room and insert it before you go into the final decontamination procedures.'

'I don't mind dunking myself in all those foul baths,' Hall said. 'I don't mind being irradiated. But I'll be goddammed –'

'The idea,' Leavitt said, 'is that you be as nearly sterile as possible on Level V. We have sterilized your skin and mucous membranes of the respiratory tract as best we can. But we haven't done a thing about the GI tract yet.'

'Yes,' Hall said, 'but suppositories?'

'You'll get used to it. We're all taking them for the first four days. Not, of course, that they'll do any good,' he said, with the familiar wry, pessimistic look on his face. He stood. 'Let's go to the conference room. Stone wants to talk about Karp.'

'Who?'

'Rudolph Karp.'

Rudolph Karp was a Hungarian-born biochemist who came to the United States from England in 1951. He obtained a position at the University of Michigan and worked steadily and quietly for five years. Then, at the suggestion of colleagues at the Ann Arbor observatory, Karp began to investigate meteorites with the intent of determining whether they harbored life, or showed evidence of having done so in the past. He took the proposal quite seriously and worked with diligence, writing no papers on the subject until the early 1960's, when Calvin and Vaughn and Nagy and others were writing explosive papers on similar subjects.

The arguments and counter-arguments were complex, but boiled down to a simple substrate: whenever a worker would announce that he had found a fossil, or a proteinaceous hydrocarbon, or other indication of life within a meteorite, the critics would claim sloppy lab technique and contamination with earth-origin matter and organisms.

Karp, with his careful, slow techniques, was determined to end the arguments once and for all. He announced that he had taken great pains to avoid contamination: each meterorite he examined had been washed in twelve solutions, including peroxide, iodine, hypertonic saline and dilute acids. It was then exposed to intense ultraviolet light for a period of two days. Finally, it was submerged in a germicidal solution and placed in a germ-free, sterile isolation chamber; further work was done within the chamber.

Karp, upon breaking open his meteorites, was able to isolate bacteria. He found that they were ring-shaped organisms, rather like a tiny undulating inner tube, and he found they could grow and multiply. He claimed that, while they were essentially similar to earthly bacteria in structure, being based upon proteins, carbohydrates, and lipids, they had no cell nucleus and therefore their manner of propagation was a mystery.

Karp presented his information in his usual quiet, unsensational manner, and hoped for a good reception. He did not receive one; instead, he was laughed down by the Seventh Conference of Astrophysics and Geophysics, meeting in London in 1961. He became discouraged and set his work with meteorites aside; the organisms were later destroyed in an accidental laboratory explosion on the night of June 27, 1963.

Karp's experience was almost identical to that of Nagy and the others. Scientists in the 1960's were not willing to entertain notions of life existing in meteorites; all evidence presented was discounted, dismissed, and ignored.

A handful of people in a dozen countries remained intrigued, however. One of them was Jeremy Stone; another was Peter Leavitt. It was Leavitt who, some years before, had formulated the Rule of 48. The Rule of 48 was intended as a humorous reminder to scientists, and referred to the massive literature collected in the late 1940's and the 1950's concerning the human chromosome number.

For years it was stated that men had forty-eight chromosomes in their cells; there were pictures to prove it, and any number of careful studies. In 1953, a group of American researchers announced to the world that the human chromosome number was forty-six. Once more, there were pictures to prove it, and studies to confirm it. But these researchers also went back to reexamine the old pictures, and the old studies – and found only forty-six chromosomes, not forty-eight.

Leavitt's Rule of 48 said simply, 'All Scientists Are Blind.' And Leavitt had invoked his rule when he saw the reception Karp and others received. Leavitt went over the reports and the papers and found no reason to reject the meteorite studies out of hand; many of the experiments were careful, well reasoned, and compelling.

He remembered this when he and the other Wildfire planners drew up the study known as the Vector Three. Along with the Toxic Five, it formed one of the firm theoretical bases for Wildfire.

The Vector Three was a report that considered a crucial question: If a bacterium invaded the earth, causing a new disease, where would that bacterium come from?

After consultation with astronomers and evolutionary theories, the Wildfire group concluded that bacteria could come from three sources.

The first was the most obvious – an organism, from another planet or galaxy, which had the protection to survive the extremes of temperature and vacuum that existed in space. There was no doubt that organisms could survive – there was, for instance, a class of bacteria known as thermophilic that thrived on extreme heat, multiplying enthusiastically in temperatures as high as 70°C. Further, it was known that bacteria had been recovered from Egyptian tombs, where they had been sealed for thousands of years. These bacteria were still viable.

The secret lay in the bacteria's ability to form spores, molding a hard calcific shell around themselves. This shell enabled the organism to survive freezing or boiling, and, if necessary, thousands of years without food. It combined all the advantages of a space suit with those of suspended animation.

There was no doubt that a spore could travel through space. But was another planet or galaxy the most *likely* source of contamination for the earth?

Here, the answer was no. The most likely source was the closest source – the earth itself.

The report suggested that bacteria could have left the surface of the earth eons ago, when life was just beginning to emerge from the oceans and the hot, baked continents. Such bacteria would depart before the fishes, before the primitive mammals, long before the first ape-man. The bacteria would head up into the air, and slowly ascend until they were literally in space. Once there, they might evolve into unusual forms, perhaps even learning to derive energy for life directly from the sun, instead of requiring food as an energy source. These organisms might also be capable of direct conversion of energy to matter.

Leavitt himself suggested the analogy of the upper atmosphere and the depths of the sea as equally inhospitable environments, but equally viable. In the deepest, blackest regions of the oceans, where oxygenation was poor, and where light never reached, life forms were known to exist in abundance. Why not also in the far reaches of the atmosphere? True, oxygen was scarce. True, food hardly existed. But if creatures could live miles beneath the surface, why could they not also live five miles above it?

And if there were organisms out there, and if they had departed from the baking crust of the earth long before the first men appeared, then they would be foreign to man. No immunity, no adaptation, no antibodies would have been developed. They would be primitive aliens to modern man, in the same way that the shark, a primitive fish unchanged for a hundred million years, was alien and dangerous to modern man, invading the oceans for the first time.

The third source of contamination, the third of the vectors, was at the same time the most likely and the most troublesome. This was contemporary earth organisms, taken into space by inadequately sterilized spacecraft. Once in space, the organisms would be exposed to harsh radiation, weightlessness, and other environmental forces that might exert a mutagenic effect, altering the organisms.

So that when they came down, they would be different.

Take up a harmless bacterium – such as the organism that causes pimples, or sore throats – and bring it back in a new form, virulent and unexpected. It might do anything. It might show a preference for the aqueous humor of the inner eye, and invade the eyeball. It might thrive on the acid secretions of the stomach. It might multiply on the small currents of electricity afforded by the human brain itself, drive men mad.

This whole idea of mutated bacteria seemed farfetched and unlikely to the Wildfire people. It is ironic that this should be the case, particularly in view of what happened to the Andromeda Strain. But the Wildfire team staunchly ignored both the evidence of their own experience – that bacteria mutate rapidly and radically – and the evidence of the Biosatellite tests, in which a series of earth forms were sent into space and later recovered.

Biosatellite II contained, among other things, several species of bacteria. It was later reported that the bacteria had reproduced at a rate twenty to thirty times normal. The reasons were still unclear, but the results unequivocal: space could affect reproduction and growth.

And yet no one in Wildfire paid attention to this fact, until it was too late.

Stone reviewed the information quickly, then handed each of them a cardboard file. 'These files,' he said, 'contain a transcript of autoclock records of the entire flight of Scoop VII. Our purpose in reviewing the transcript is to determine, if possible, what happened to the satellite while it was in orbit.'

Hall said, 'Something happened to it?'

Leavitt explained. 'The satellite was scheduled for a six-day orbit, since the probability of collecting organisms is proportional to time in orbit. After launch, it was in stable orbit. Then, on the second day, it went out of orbit.'

Hall nodded.

'Start,' Stone said, 'with the first page.'

Hall opened his file.

AUTOCLOCK TRANSCRIPT
PROJECT: SCOOP VII
LAUNCHDATE:
ABRIDGED VERSION. FULL TRANSCRIPT
STORED VAULTS 179-99, VDBG COMPLEX
EPSILON.

HOURS	MIN	SEC	PROCEDURE
T MINUS TIME			
0002	01	05	Vandenberg Launchpad Block 9, Scoop Mission Control, reports systems check on schedule.

0001	39	52	Scoop MC holds for fuel check reported from Ground Control.
STOP CLOCK			STOP CLOCK. REAL TIME LOSS 12 MINUTES.
0001	39	52	Count resumed. Clock corrected.
0000	41	12	Scoop MC holds 20 seconds for Launchpad Block 9 check. Clock not stopped for built-in hold.
0000	30	00	Gantry removed.
0000	24	00	Final craft systems check.
0000	19	00	Final capsule systems check.
0000	13	00	Final systems checks read as negative.
0000	07	12	Cable decoupling.
0000	01	07	Stat-link decoupling.
0000	00	05	Ignition.
0000	00	04	Launchpad Block 9 clears all systems.
0000	00	00	Core clamps released. Launch.
T PLUS TIME			
0000	00	06	Stable. Speed 6 fps. Smooth EV approach.
0000	00	09	Tracking reported.
0000	00	11	Tracking confirmed.
0000	00	27	Capsule monitors at g 1.9. Equipment check clear.
0000	01	00	Launchpad Block 9 clears rocket and capsule systems for orbit.

'No point in dwelling on this,' Stone said. 'It is the record of a perfect launch. There is nothing here, in fact, nothing for the next ninety-six hours of flight, to indicate any difficulty on board the spacecraft. Now turn to page 10.'

They all turned.

TRACK TRANSCRIPT CONT'D
SCOOP VII
LAUNCHDATE: –
ABRIDGED VERSION

HOURS	MIN	SEC	PROCEDURE
0096	10	12	Orbital check stable as reported by Grand Bahama Station.
0096	34	19	Orbital check stable as reported by Sydney.
0096	47	34	Orbital check stable as reported by Vdbg.
0097	04	12	Orbital check stable but system malfunction reported by Kennedy Station.
0097	05	18	Malfunction confirmed.
0097	07	22	Malfunction confirmed by Grand Bahama. Computer reports orbital instability.
0097	34	54	Sydney reports orbital instability.
0097	39	02	Vandenberg computations indicate orbital decay.
0098	27	14	Vandenberg Scoop Mission Control orders radio reentry.
0099	12	56	Reentry code transmitted.
0099	13	13	Houston reports initiation of reentry. Stabilized flightpath.

'What about voice communication during the critical period?'

'There were linkups between Sydney, Kennedy, and Grand Bahama, all routed through Houston. Houston had the big computer as well. But in this instance, Houston was just helping out; all decisions came from Scoop Mission Control in Vandenberg. We have the voice communication at the back of the file. It's quite revealing.'

TRANSCRIPT OF VOICE COMMUNICATIONS
SCOOP MISSION CONTROL
VANDENBERG AFB
HOURS 0096:59 TO 0097:39

THIS IS A CLASSIFIED TRANSCRIPT.
IT HAS NOT BEEN ABRIDGED OR EDITED.

HOURS	MIN	SEC	COMMUNICATION
0096	59	00	HELLO KENNEDY THIS IS SCOOP MISSION CONTROL. AT THE END OF 96 HOURS OF FLIGHT TIME WE HAVE STABLE ORBITS FROM ALL STATIONS. DO YOU CONFIRM.
0097	00	00	I think we do, Scoop. Our check is going through now. Hold this line open for a few minutes, fellows.
0097	03	31	Hello, Scoop MC. This is Kennedy. We have a stable orbit confirmation for you on the last passby. Sorry about the delay but there is an instrument snag somewhere here.
0097	03	34	KENNEDY PLEASE CLARIFY. IS YOUR SNAG ON THE GROUND OR ALOFT.
0097	03	39	I am sorry we have no tracer yet. We think it is on the ground.
0097	04	12	Hello, Scoop MC. This is Kennedy. We have a preliminary report of system malfunction aboard your spacecraft. Repeat we have a preliminary report of malfunction in the air. Awaiting confirmation.
0097	04	15	KENNEDY PLEASE CLARIFY SYSTEM INVOLVED
0097	04	18	I'm sorry they haven't given me that. I assume they are waiting for final confirmation of the malfunction.
0097	04	21	DOES YOUR ORBITAL CHECK AS STABLE STILL HOLD.
0097	04	22	Vandenberg, we have confirmed your orbital check as stable. Repeat the orbit is stable.
0097	05	18	Ah, Vandenberg, I am afraid we also confirm readings consistent with system malfunction on board your spacecraft. These include the stationary rotor elements and spanner units going to mark twelve. I repeat mark twelve.

HOURS	MIN	SEC	COMMUNICATION
0097	05	30	HAVE YOU RUN CONSISTENCY CHECK ON YOUR COMPUTERS.
0097	05	35	Sorry fellows but our computers check out. We read it as a real malfunction.
0097	05	45	HELLO, HOUSTON. OPEN THE LINE TO SYDNEY, WILL YOU. WE WANT CONFIRMATION OF DATA.
0097	05	51	Scoop Mission Control. This is Sydney Station. We confirm our last reading. There was nothing wrong with the spacecraft on its last passby here.
0097	06	12	OUR COMPUTER CHECK INDICATES NO SYSTEMS MALFUNCTION AND GOOD ORBITAL STABILITY ON SUMMATED DATA. WE QUESTION KENNEDY GROUND INSTRUMENT FAILURE.
0097	06	18	This is Kennedy, Scoop MC. We have run repeat checkouts at this end. Our reading of system malfunction remains. Have you got something from Bahama.
0097	06	23	NEGATIVE, KENNEDY. STANDING BY.
0097	06	36	HOUSTON, THIS IS SCOOP MC. CAN YOUR PROJECTION GROUP GIVE US ANYTHING.
0097	06	46	Scoop, at this time we cannot. Our computers have insufficient data. They still read stable orbit with all systems going.
0097	07	22	Scoop MC, this is Grand Bahama Station. We report passby of your craft Scoop Seven according to schedule. Preliminary radar fixes were normal with question of increased transit time. Please hold for systems telemetry.
0097	07	25	HOLDING, GRAND BAHAMA.
0097	07	29	Scoop MC, we are sorry to say we confirm Kennedy observations. Repeat, we confirm Kennedy observations of systems malfunction. Our data are on the trunk to Houston. Can they be routed to you as well.

HOURS	MIN	SEC	COMMUNICATION
0097	07	34	NO, WE WILL WAIT FOR HOUSTON'S PRINTOUT. THEY HAVE LARGER PREDICTIVE BANKING UNITS.
0097	07	36	Scoop MC, Houston has the Bahama Data. It is going through the Dispar Program. Give us ten seconds.
0097	07	47	Scoop MC, this is Houston. The Dispar Program confirms systems malfunction. Your vehicle is now in unstable orbit with increased transit time of zero point three seconds per unit of arc. We are analyzing orbital parameters at this time. Is there anything further you wish as interpreted data.
0097	07	59	NO, HOUSTON. SOUNDS LIKE YOU'RE DOING BEAUTIFULLY.
0097	08	10	Sorry, Scoop. Bad break.
0097	08	18	GET US THE DECAY RATIOS AS SOON AS POSSIBLE. COMMAND WISHES TO MAKE A DECISION ON INSTRUMENTATION TAKEDOWN WITHIN THE NEXT TWO ORBITS.
0097	08	32	Understand, Scoop. Our condolences here.
0097	11	35	Scoop, Houston Projection Group has confirmed orbital instability and decay ratios are now being passed by the data trunk to your station.
0097	11	44	HOW DO THEY LOOK, HOUSTON.
0097	11	51	Bad.
0097	11	59	NOT UNDERSTOOD. PLEASE REPEAT.
0097	12	07	Bad: B as in broken, A as in awful, D as in dropping.
0097	12	15	HOUSTON, DO YOU HAVE A CAUSATION. THAT SATELLITE HAS BEEN IN EXCELLENT ORBIT FOR NEARLY ONE HUNDRED HOURS. WHAT HAPPENED TO IT.

HOURS	MIN	SEC	COMMUNICATION
0097	12	29	Beats us. We wonder about collision. There is a good wobble component to the new orbit.
0097	12	44	HOUSTON, OUR COMPUTERS ARE WORKING THROUGH THE TRANSMITTED DATA. WE AGREE A COLLISION. HAVE YOU GUYS GOT SOMETHING IN THE NEIGHBORHOOD.
0097	13	01	Air Force Skywatch confirms our report that we have nothing around your baby, Scoop.
0097	13	50	HOUSTON, OUR COMPUTERS ARE READING THIS AS A RANDOM EVENT. PROBABILITIES GREATER THAN ZERO POINT SEVEN NINE.
0097	15	00	We can add nothing. Looks reasonable. Are you going to bring it down.
0097	15	15	WE ARE HOLDING ON THAT DECISION, HOUSTON, WE WILL NOTIFY AS SOON AS IT IS MADE.
0097	17	54	HOUSTON, OUR COMMAND GROUP HAS RAISED THE QUESTION OF WHETHER ***** ******************************
0097	17	59	[reply from Houston deleted]
0097	18	43	[Scoop query to Houston deleted]
0097	19	03	[reply from Houston deleted]
0097	19	11	AGREE, HOUSTON. WE WILL MAKE OUR DECISION AS SOON AS WE HAVE FINAL CONFIRMATION OF ORBITAL SHUTDOWN FROM SYDNEY. IS THIS ACCEPTABLE.
0097	19	50	Perfectly, Scoop. We are standing by.
0097	24	32	HOUSTON, WE ARE REWORKING OUR DATA AND NO LONGER CONSIDER THAT ********* IS LIKELY.
0097	24	39	Roger, Scoop.
0097	29	13	HOUSTON, WE ARE STANDING BY FOR SYDNEY.

HOURS	MIN	SEC	COMMUNICATION
0097	34	54	Scoop Mission Control, this is Sydney Station. We have just followed the passby of your vehicle. Our initial readings confirm a prolonged transit time. It is quite striking at this time.
0097	35	12	THANK YOU, SYDNEY.
0097	35	22	Bit of nasty luck, Scoop. Sorry.
0097	39	02	THIS IS SCOOP MISSION CONTROL TO ALL STATIONS. OUR COMPUTERS HAVE JUST CALCULATED THE ORBITAL DECAY FOR THE VEHICLE AND WE FIND IT TO BE COMING DOWN AS A PLUS FOUR. STANDBY FOR THE FINAL DECISION AS TO WHEN WE WILL BRING IT DOWN.

Hall said, 'What about the deleted passages?'

'Major Manchek at Vandenberg told me,' Stone said, 'that they had to do with the Russian craft in the area. The two stations eventually concluded that the Russians had not, either accidentally or purposely, brought down the Scoop satellite. No one has since suggested differently.'

They nodded.

'It's tempting,' Stone said. 'The Air Force maintains a watchdog facility in Kentucky that tracks all satellites in earth orbit. It has a dual function, both to follow old satellites known to be in orbit and to track new ones. There are twelve satellites in orbit at this time that cannot be accounted for; in other words, they are not ours, and are not the result of announced Soviet launches. It is thought that some of these represent navigation satellites for Soviet submarines. Others are presumed to be spy satellites. But the important thing is that, Russian or not, there are a hell of a lot of satellites up there. As of last Friday, the Air Force reported five hundred and eighty-seven orbiting bodies around the earth. This includes some old, nonfunctioning satellites from the American Explorer series and the Russian Sputnik series. It also includes boosters and final stages – anything in stable orbit large enough to reflect back a radar beam.'

'That's a lot of satellites.'

'Yes, and there are probably many more. The Air Force thinks there is a lot of junk out there – nuts, bolts, scraps of metal – all in more or less stable orbit. No orbit, as you know, is completely stable. Without frequent corrections, any satellite will eventually decay out and spiral down to earth, burning up in the atmosphere. But that may be years, even decades, after the launch. In any event, the Air Force estimates that the total number of individual orbiting objects could be anything up to seventy-five thousand.'

'So a collision with a piece of junk is possible.'

'Yes. Possible.'

'How about a meteor?'

'That is the other possibility, and the one Vandenberg favors. A random event, most likely a meteor.'

'Any showers these days?'

'None, apparently. But that does not rule out a meteor collision.'

Leavitt cleared his throat. 'There is still another possibility.'

Stone frowned. He knew that Leavitt was imaginative, and that this trait was both a strength and a defect. At times, Leavitt could be startling and exciting; at others, merely irritating. 'It's rather farfetched,' Stone said, 'to postulate debris from some extragalactic source other than –'

'I agree,' Leavitt said. 'Hopelessly farfetched. No evidence for it whatever. But I don't think we can afford to ignore the possibility.'

A gong sounded softly. A lush female voice, which Hall now recognized as that of Gladys Stevens of Omaha, said softly, 'You may proceed to the next level, gentlemen.'

13 Level V

Level V was painted a quiet shade of blue, and they all wore blue uniforms. Burton showed Hall around.

'This floor,' he said, 'is like all the others. It's circular. Arranged in a series of concentric circles, actually. We're on the outer perimeter now; this is where we live and work. Cafeteria, sleeping rooms, everything is out here. Just inside is a ring of laboratories. And inside that, sealed off from us, is the central core. That's where the satellite and the two people are now.'

'But they're sealed off from us?'

'Yes.'

'Then how do we get to them?'

'Have you ever used a glove box?' Burton asked.

Hall shook his head.

Burton explained that glove boxes were large clear plastic boxes used to handle sterile materials. The boxes had holes cut in the sides, and gloves attached with an airtight seal. To handle the contents, you slipped your hands into the gloves and reached into the box. But your fingers never touched the material, only the gloves.

'We've gone one step further,' Burton said. 'We have whole rooms that are nothing more than glorified glove boxes. Instead of a glove for your hand, there's a whole plastic suit, for your entire body. You'll see what I mean.'

They walked down the curved corridor to a room marked CENTRAL CONTROL. Leavitt and Stone were there, working quietly. Central Control was a cramped room, stuffed with electronic equipment. One wall was glass, allowing the workers to look into the adjacent room.

Through the glass, Hall saw mechanical hands moving the capsule to a table and setting it down. Hall, who had never seen a capsule before, watched with interest. It was smaller than he had imagined, no more than a yard long; one end was seared and blackened from the heat of reentry.

The mechanical hands, under Stone's direction, opened the little scoop-shaped trough in the side of the capsule to expose the interior.

'There,' Stone said, taking his hands from the controls. The controls looked like a pair of brass knuckles; the operator slipped his own hands into them and moved his hands as he wanted the mechanical hands to move.

'Our next step,' he said, 'is to determine whether there is still anything in the capsule which is biologically active. Suggestions?'

'A rat,' Leavitt said. 'Use a black Norway.'

The black Norway rat was not black at all; the name simply designated a strain of laboratory animal, perhaps the most famous strain in all science. Once, of course, it had been both black and Norwegian; but years of breeding and countless generations had made it white, small, and docile. The biological explosion had created a demand for genetically uniform animals. In the last thirty years more than a thousand strains of 'pure' animals had been evolved artificially. In the case of the black Norwegian, it was now possible for a scientist anywhere in the world to conduct experiments using this animal and be assured that other scientists elsewhere could repeat or enlarge upon his work using virtually identical organisms.

'Follow with a rhesus,' Burton said. 'We will want to get onto primates sooner or later.'

The others nodded. Wildfire was prepared to conduct experiments with monkeys and apes, as well as smaller, cheaper animals. A monkey was exceedingly difficult to work with: the little primates were hostile, quick, intelligent. Among scientists, the New World monkeys, with their prehensile tails, were considered particularly trying. Many a scientist had engaged three or four lab assistants to hold down a monkey while he administered an injection – only to have the prehensile tail whip up, grasp the syringe, and fling it across the room.

The theory behind primate experimentation was that these animals were closer biologically to man. In the 1950's, several laboratories even attempted experiments on gorillas, going to great trouble and expense to work with these seemingly most human of animals. However, by 1960 it had been demonstrated that of the apes, the chimpanzee was biochemically more like man than the gorilla. (On the basis of similarity to man, the choice of laboratory animals is often surprising. For example, the hamster is preferred for immunological and cancer studies, since his responses are so similar to man's, while for studies of the heart and circulation, the pig is considered most like man.)

Stone put his hands back on the controls, moving them gently. Through the glass, they saw the black metal fingers move to the far wall of the adjoining room, where several caged lab animals were kept, separated from the room by hinged airtight doors. The wall reminded Hall oddly of an automat.

The mechanical hands opened one door and removed a rat in its cage, brought it into the room, and set it down next to the capsule.

The rat looked around the room, sniffed the air, and made some stretching movements with its neck. A moment later it flopped over onto its side, kicked once, and was still.

It had happened with astonishing speed. Hall could hardly believe it had happened at all.

'My God,' Stone said. 'What a time course.'

'That will make it difficult,' Leavitt said.

Burton said, 'We can try tracers . . .'

'Yes. We'll have to use tracers on it,' Stone said. 'How fast are our scans?'

'Milliseconds, if necessary.'

'It will be necessary.'

'Try the rhesus,' Burton said. 'You'll want a post on it, anyway.'

Stone directed the mechanical hands back to the wall, opening another door and withdrawing a cage containing a large brown adult rhesus monkey. The monkey screeched as it was lifted and banged against the bars of its cage.

Then it died, after flinging one hand to its chest with a look of startled surprise.

Stone shook his head. 'Well, at least we know it's still biologically active. Whatever killed everyone in Piedmont is still there, and still as potent as ever.' He sighed. 'If potent is the word.'

Leavitt said, 'We'd better start a scan of the capsule.'

'I'll take these dead animals,' Burton said, 'and run the initial vector studies. Then I'll autopsy them.'

Stone worked the mechanical hands once more. He picked up the cages that held the rat and monkey and set them on a rubber conveyor belt at the rear of the room. Then he pressed a button on a control console marked AUTOPSY. The conveyor belt began to move.

Burton left the room, walking down the corridor to the autopsy room, knowing that the conveyor belt, made to carry materials from one lab to another, would have automatically delivered the cages.

Stone said to Hall, 'You're the practicing physician among us. I'm afraid you've got a rather tough job right now.'

'Pediatrician and geriatrist?'

'Exactly. See what you can do about them. They're both in our miscellaneous room, the room we built precisely for unusual circumstances like this. There's a computer linkup there that should help you. The technician will show you how it works.'

14 Miscellaneous

Hall opened the door marked MISCELLANEOUS, thinking to himself that his job was indeed miscellaneous – keeping alive an old man and a tiny infant. Both of them vital to the project, and both of them, no doubt, difficult to manage.

He found himself in another small room similar to the control room he had just left. This one also had a glass window, looking inward to a central room. In the room were two beds, and on the beds, Peter Jackson and the infant. But the incredible thing was the suits: standing upright in the room were four clear plastic inflated suits in the shape of men. From each suit, a tunnel ran back to the wall.

Obviously, one would have to crawl down the tunnel and then stand up inside the suit. Then one could work with the patients inside the room.

The girl who was to be his assistant was working in the room, bent over the computer console. She introduced herself as Karen Anson, and explained the working of the computer.

'This is just one substation of the Wildfire computer on the first level,' she said. 'There are thirty substations throughout the laboratory, all plugging into the computer. Thirty different people can work at once.'

Hall nodded. Time-sharing was a concept he understood. He knew that as many as two hundred people had been able to use the same computer at once; the principle was that computers operated very swiftly – in fractions of a second – while people operated slowly, in seconds or minutes. One person using a computer was inefficient, because it took several minutes to punch in instructions, while the computer sat around idle, waiting. Once instructions were fed in, the computer answered almost instantaneously. This meant that a computer was rarely 'working,' and by permitting a number of people to ask questions of the computer simultaneously, you could keep the machine more continuously in operation.

'If the computer is really backed up,' the technician said, 'there may be a delay of one or two seconds before you get your answer. But usually it's immediate. What we are using here is the MEDCOM program. Do you know it?'

Hall shook his head.

'It's a medical-data analyzer,' she said. 'You feed in information and it will diagnose the patient and tell you what to do next for therapy, or to confirm the diagnosis.'

'Sounds very convenient.'

'It's fast,' she said. 'All our lab studies are done by automated machines. So we can have complex diagnoses in a matter of minutes.'

Hall looked through the glass at the two patients. 'What's been done on them so far?'

'Nothing. At Level I, they were started on intravenous infusions. Plasma for Peter Jackson, dextrose and water for the baby. They both seem well hydrated now, and in no distress. Jackson is still unconscious. He has no pupillary signs but is unresponsive and looks anemic.'

Hall nodded. 'The labs here can do everything?'

'Everything. Even assays for adrenal hormones and things like partial thromboplastin times. Every known medical test is possible.'

'All right. We'd better get started.'

She turned on the computer. 'This is how you order laboratory tests,' she said. 'Use this light pen here, and check off the tests you want. Just touch the pen to the screen.'

She handed him a small penlight, and pushed the START button.

The screen glowed.

```
MEDCOM PROGRAM
LAB/ANALYS
CK/JGG/1223098

BLOOD                              PROTEIN

  COUNTS RBC
           RETIC                           ALB
           PLATES                          GLOB
           WBC                             FIBRIN
           DIFF                            TOTAL
   HEMATOCRIT                              FRACTION
   HEMOGLOBIN
   INDICES MCV                     DIAGNOSTICS
           MCHC
   PROTIME                                 CHOLEST
   PTT                                     CREAT
   SED RATE                                GLUCOSE
                                           PBI
 CHEMISTRY                                 BEI
                                           I
```

BRO
CA
CL
MG
PO4
K
NA
CO2

ENZYMES

AMYLASE
CHOLINESTERASE
LIPASE
PHOSPHATASE, ACID
ALKALINE
LDH
SGOT
SGPT

STEROIDS
ALDO
L7-OH
17-KS
ACTH

VITS
A
ALL B
C
E
K

IBC
NPN
BUN
BILIRU, DIFF
CEPH/FLOC
THYMOL/TURB
BSP

PULMONARY

TVC
TV
IC
IRV
ERV
MBC

URINE

SP GR
PH
PROT
GLUC
KETONE
ALL ELECTROLYTES
ALL STEROIDS
ALL INORGANICS
CATBCHOLS
PORPHYRINS
UROBIL
5-HIAA

Hall stared at the list. He touched the tests he wanted with the penlight; they disappeared from the screen. He ordered fifteen or twenty, then stepped back.

The screen went blank for a moment, and then the following appeared:

TESTS ORDERED WILL REQUIRE FOR EACH
SUBJECT

20 CC WHOLE BLOOD
L0 CC OXALATED BLOOD
L2 CC CITRATED BLOOD
15 CC URINE

The technician said, 'I'll draw the bloods if you want to do physicals. Have you been in one of these rooms before?'

Hall shook his head.

'It's quite simple, really. We crawl through the tunnels into the suits. The tunnel is then sealed off behind us.'

'Oh? Why?'

'In case something happens to one of us. In case the covering of the suit is broken – the integrity of the surface is ruptured, as the protocol says. In that case, bacteria could spread back through the tunnel to the outside.'

'So we're sealed off.'

'Yes. We get air from a separate system – you can see the thin lines coming in over there. But essentially you're isolated from everything, when you're in that suit. I don't think you need worry, though. The only way you might possibly break your suit is to cut it with a scalpel, and the gloves are triple-thickness to prevent just such an occurrence.'

She showed him how to crawl through, and then, imitating her, he stood up inside the plastic suit. He felt like some kind of giant reptile, moving cumbersomely about, dragging his tunnel like a thick tail behind him.

After a moment, there was a hiss: his suit was being sealed off. Then another hiss, and the air turned cold as the special line began to feed air in to him.

The technician gave him his examining instruments. While she drew blood from the child, taking it from a scalp vein, Hall turned his attention to Peter Jackson.

An old man, and pale: anemia. Also thin: first thought, cancer. Second thought, tuberculosis, alcoholism, some other chronic process. And unconscious: he ran through the differential in his mind, from epilepsy to hypoglycemic shock to stroke.

Hall later stated that he felt foolish when the computer provided him with a differential, complete with probabilities of diagnosis. He was not at that time aware of the skill of the computer, the quality of its program.

He checked Jackson's blood pressure. It was low, 85/50. Pulse fast at 110. Temperature 97.8. Respirations 30 and deep.

He went over the body systematically, beginning with the head and working down. When he produced pain – by pressing on the nerve through the supraorbital notch, just below the eyebrow – the man grimaced and moved his arms to push Hall away.

Perhaps he was not unconscious after all. Perhaps just stuporous. Hall shook him.

'Mr. Jackson. Mr. Jackson.'

The man made no response. And then, slowly, he seemed to revive. Hall shouted his name in his ear and shook him hard.

Peter Jackson opened his eyes, just for a moment, and said, 'Go . . . away . . .'

Hall continued to shake him, but Jackson relaxed, going limp, his body slipping back to its unresponsive state. Hall gave up, returning to his physical examination. The lungs were clear and the heart seemed normal. There was some tenseness of the abdomen, and Jackson retched once, bringing up some bloody drooling material. Quickly, Hall did a basolyte test for blood: it was positive. He did a rectal exam and tested the stool. It was also positive for blood.

He turned to the technician, who had drawn all the bloods and was feeding the tubes into the computer analysis apparatus in one corner.

'We've got a GI bleeder here,' he said. 'How soon will the results be back?'

She pointed to a TV screen mounted near the ceiling. 'The lab reports are flashed back as soon as they come in. They are displayed there, and on the console in the other room. The easy ones come back first. We should have hematocrit in two minutes.'

Hall waited. The screen glowed, the letters printing out:

JACKSON, PETER
LABORATORY ANALYSES

TEST	NORMAL	VALUE
HEMATOCRIT	38–54	21

'Half normal,' Hall said. He slapped an oxygen mask on Jackson's face, fixed the straps, and said, 'We'll need at least four units. Plus two of plasma.'

'I'll order them.'

'To start as soon as possible.'

She went to phone the blood bank on Level II and asked them to hurry on the requisition. Meantime, Hall turned his attention to the child.

It had been a long time since he had examined an infant, and he had forgotten how difficult it could be. Every time he tried to look at the eyes, the child shut them tightly. Every time he looked down the throat, the child closed his mouth. Every time he tried to listen to the heart, the child shrieked, obscuring all heart sounds.

Yet he persisted, remembering what Stone had said. These two people, dissimilar though they were, nonetheless represented the only survivors of Piedmont. Somehow they had managed to beat the disease. That was a link between the two, between the shriveled old man vomiting blood and the pink young child, howling and screaming.

At first glance, they were as different as possible; they were at opposite ends of the spectrum, sharing nothing in common.

And yet there must be something in common.

It took Hall half an hour to finish his examination of the child. At the end of that time he was forced to conclude that the infant was, to his exam, perfectly normal. Totally normal. Nothing the least bit unusual about him.

Except that, somehow, he had survived.

15 Main Control

Stone sat with Leavitt in the main control room, looking into the inner room with the capsule. Though cramped, main control was complex and expensive: it had cost $2,000,000, the most costly single room in the Wildfire installation. But it was vital to the functioning of the entire laboratory.

Main control served as the first step in scientific examination of the capsule. Its chief function was detection – the room was geared to detect and isolate microorganisms. According to the Life Analysis Protocol, there were three main steps in the Wildfire program: detection, characterization, and control. First the organism had to be found. Then it had to be studied and understood. Only then could ways be sought to control it.

Main control was set up to find the organism.

Leavitt and Stone sat side by side in front of the banks of controls and dials. Stone operated the mechanical hands, while Leavitt manipulated the microscopic apparatus. Naturally it was impossible to enter the room with the capsule and examine it directly. Robot-controlled microscopes, with viewing screens in the control room, would accomplish this for them.

An early question had been whether to utilize television or some kind of direct visual linkup. Television was cheaper and more easily set up; TV image-intensifiers were already in use for electron microscopes, X-ray machines, and other devices. However, the Wildfire group finally decided that a TV screen was too imprecise for their needs; even a double-scan camera, which transmitted twice as many lines as the usual TV and gave better image resolution, would be insufficient. In the end, the group chose a fiber optics system in which a light image was transmitted directly through a snakelike bundle of glass fibers and then displayed on the viewers. This gave a clear, sharp image.

Stone positioned the capsule and pressed the appropriate controls. A black box moved down from the ceiling and began to scan the capsule surface. The two men watched the viewer screens.

'Start with five power,' Stone said. Leavitt set the controls. They watched as the viewer automatically moved around the capsule, focusing on the surface of the metal. They watched one complete scan, then shifted up to twenty-power magnification. A twenty-power scan took much longer, since the field of view was smaller. They still saw nothing on the surface: no punctures, no indentations, nothing that looked like a small growth of any kind.

'Let's go to one hundred,' Stone said. Leavitt adjusted the controls and sat back. They were beginning what they knew would be a long and tedious search. Probably they would find nothing. Soon they would examine the interior of the capsule; they might find something there. Or they might not. In either case, they would take samples for analysis, plating out the scrapings and swabs onto growth media.

Leavitt glanced from the viewing screens to look into the room. The viewer, suspended from the ceiling by a complex arrangement of rods and wires, was automatically moving in slow circles around the capsule. He looked back to the screens.

There were three screens in main control, and all showed exactly the same field of view. In theory, they could use three viewers projecting onto three screens, and cover the capsule in one third the time. But they did not want to do that – at least, not now. Both men knew that their interest and attention would fatigue as the day wore on. No matter how hard they tried, they could not remain alert all the time. But if two men watched the same image, there was less chance of missing something.

The surface area of the cone-shaped capsule, thirty-seven inches long and a foot in diameter at the base, was just over 650 square inches. Three scans, at five, twenty, and one hundred power, took them slightly more than two hours. At the end of the third scan, Stone said, 'I suppose we ought to proceed with the 440 scan as well.'

'But?'

'I am tempted to go directly to a scan of the interior. If we find nothing, we can come back outside and do a 440.'

'I agree.'

'All right,' Stone said. 'Start with five. On the inside.'

Leavitt worked the controls. This time, it could not be done automatically; the viewer was programmed to follow the contours of any regularly shaped object, such as a cube, a sphere, or a cone. But it could not probe the interior of the capsule without direction. Leavitt set the lenses at five diameters and switched the remote viewer to manual control. Then he directed it down into the scoop opening of the capsule.

Stone, watching the screen, said, 'More light.'

Leavitt made adjustments. Five additional remote lights came down from the ceiling and clicked on, shining into the scoop.

'Better?'

'Fine.'

Watching his own screen, Leavitt began to move the remote viewer. It took several minutes before he could do it smoothly; it was difficult to coordinate, rather like trying to write while you watched in a mirror. But soon he was scanning smoothly.

The five-power scan took twenty minutes. They found nothing except a small indentation the size of a pencil point. At Stone's suggestion, when they began the twenty-power scan they started with the indentation.

Immediately, they saw it: a tiny black fleck of jagged material no larger than a grain of sand. There seemed to be bits of green mixed in with the black.

Neither man reacted, though Leavitt later recalled that he was 'trembling with excitement. I kept thinking, if this is it, if it's really something new, some brand new form of life . . .'

However, all he said was, 'Interesting.'

'We'd better complete the scan at twenty power,' Stone said. He was working to keep his voice calm, but it was clear that he was excited too.

Leavitt wanted to examine the fleck at higher power immediately, but he understood what Stone was saying. They could not afford to jump to conclusions – any conclusions. Their only hope was to be grindingly, interminably thorough. They had to proceed methodically, to assure themselves at every point that they had overlooked nothing.

Otherwise, they could pursue a course of investigation for hours or days, only to find it ended nowhere, that they had made a mistake, misjudged the evidence, and wasted time.

So Leavitt did a complete scan of the interior at twenty power. He paused, once or twice, when they thought they saw other patches of green, and marked down the coordinates so they could find the areas later, under higher magnification. Half an hour passed before Stone announced he was satisfied with the twenty-power scan.

They took a break for caffeine, swallowing two pills with water. The team had agreed earlier that amphetamines should not be used except in times of serious emergency; they were stocked in the Level V pharmacy, but for routine purposes caffeine was preferred.

The aftertaste of the caffeine pill was sour in his mouth as Leavitt clicked in the hundred-power lenses, and began the third scan. As before, they started with the indentation, and the small black fleck they had noted earlier.

It was disappointing: at higher magnification it appeared no different from their earlier views, only larger. They could see, however, that it was an irregular piece of material, dull, looking like rock. And they could see there were definitely flecks of green mined on the jagged surface of the material.

'What do you make of it?' Stone said.

'If that's the object the capsule collided with,' Leavitt said, 'it was either moving with great speed, or else it is very heavy. Because it's not big enough –'

'To knock the satellite out of orbit otherwise. I agree. And yet it did not make a very deep indentation.'

'Suggesting?'

Stone shrugged. 'Suggesting that it was either not responsible for the orbital change, or that it has some elastic properties we don't yet know about.'

'What do you think of the green?'

Stone grinned. 'You won't trap me yet. I am curious, nothing more.'

Leavitt chuckled and continued the scan. Both men now felt elated and inwardly certain of their discovery. They checked the other areas where they had noted green, and confirmed the presence of the patches at higher magnification.

But the other patches looked different from the green on the rock. For one thing, they were larger, and seemed somehow more luminous. For another, the borders of the patches seemed quite regular, and rounded.

'Like small drops of green paint, spattered on the inside of the capsule,' Stone said.

'I hope that's not what it is.'

'We could probe,' Stone said.

'Let's wait for 440.'

Stone agreed. By now they had been scanning the capsule for nearly four hours, but neither man felt tired. They watched closely as the viewing screens blurred for a moment, the lenses shifting. When the screens came back into focus, they were looking at the indentation, and the black fleck with the green areas. At this magnification, the surface irregularities of the rock were striking – it was like a miniature planet, with jagged peaks and sharp valleys. It occurred to Leavitt that this was exactly what they were looking at: a minute, complete planet, with its life forms intact. But he shook his head, dismissing the thought from his mind. Impossible.

Stone said, ' If that's a meteor, it's damned funny-looking.'

'What bothers you?'

'That left border, over there.' Stone pointed to the screen. 'The surface of the stone – if it is stone – is rough everywhere except on that left border, where it is smooth and rather straight.'

'Like an artificial surface?'

Stone sighed. 'If I keep looking at it,' he said, 'I might start to think so. Let's see those other patches of green.'

Leavitt set the coordinates and focused the viewer. A new image appeared on the screens. This time, it was a close-up of one of the green patches. Under high magnification the borders could be seen clearly. They were not smooth, but slightly notched: they looked almost like a gear from the inside of a watch.

'I'll be damned,' Leavitt said.

'It's not paint. That notching is too regular.'

As they watched, it happened: the green spot turned purple for a fraction of a second, less than the blink of an eye. Then it turned green once more.

'Did you see that?'

'I saw it. You didn't change the lighting?'

'No. Didn't touch it.'

A moment later, it happened again: green, a flash of purple, green again.

'Amazing.'

'This may be –'

And then, as they watched, the spot turned purple and remained purple. The notches disappeared; the spot had enlarged slightly, filling in the V-shaped gaps. It was now a complete circle. It became green once more.

'It's growing,' Stone said.

They worked swiftly. The movie cameras were brought down, recording from five angles at ninety-six frames per second. Another time-lapse camera clicked off frames at half-second intervals. Leavitt also brought down two more remote cameras, and set them at different angles from the original camera.

In main control, all three screens displayed different views of the green spot.

'Can we get more power? More magnification?' Stone said.

'No. You remember we decided 440 was the top.'

Stone swore. To obtain higher magnification, they would have to go to a separate room, or else use the electron microscopes. In either case, it would take time.

Leavitt said, 'Shall we start culture and isolation?'

'Yes. Might as well.'

Leavitt turned the viewers back down to twenty power. They could now see that there were four areas of interest – three isolated green patches, and the rock with its indentation. On the control console, he pressed a button marked CULTURE, and a tray at the side of the room slid out, revealing stacks of circular, plastic-covered petri dishes. Inside each dish was a thin layer of growth medium.

The Wildfire project employed almost every known growth medium. The media were jellied compounds containing various nutrients on which bacteria would feed and multiply. Along with the usual laboratory standbys – horse and sheep blood agar, chocolate agar, simplex, Sabouraud's medium – there were thirty diagnostic media, containing various sugars and minerals. Then there were forty-three specialized culture media, including those for growth of tubercule bacilli and unusual fungi, as well as the highly experimental media, designated by numbers: ME-997, ME-423, ME-A12, and so on.

With the tray of media was a batch of sterile swabs. Using the mechanical hands, Stone picked up the swabs singly and touched them to the capsule surface, then to the media. Leavitt punched data into the computer, so that they would know later where each swab had been taken. In this manner, they swabbed the outer surface of the entire capsule, and went to the interior. Very carefully, using high viewer magnification, Stone took scrapings from the green spots and transferred them to the different media.

Finally, he used fine forceps to pick up the rock and move it intact to a clean glass dish.

The whole process took better than two hours. At the end of that time, Leavitt punched through the MAXCULT computer program. This program automatically instructed the machine in the handling of the hundreds of petri dishes they had collected. Some would be stored at room temperature and pressure, with normal earth atmosphere. Others would be subjected to heat and cold; high pressure and vacuum; low oxygen and high oxygen; light and dark. Assigning the plates to the various culture boxes was a job that would take a man days to work out. The computer could do it in seconds.

When the program was running, Stone placed the stacks of petri dishes on the conveyor belt. They watched as the dishes moved off to the culture boxes.

There was nothing further they could do, except wait twenty-four to forty-eight hours, to see what grew out.

'Meantime,' Stone said, 'we can begin analysis of this piece of rock – if it actually is rock. How are you with an EM?'

'Rusty,' Leavitt said. He had not used an electron microscope for nearly a year.

'Then I'll prepare the specimen. We'll also want mass spectometry done. That's all computerized. But before we do that, we ought to go to higher power. What's the highest light magnification we can get in Morphology?'

'A thousand diameters.'

'Then let's do that first. Punch the rock through to Morphology.'

Leavitt looked down at the console and pressed MORPHOLOGY. Stone's mechanical hands placed the glass dish with the rock onto the conveyor belt.

They looked at the wall clock behind them. It showed 1100 hours; they had been working for eleven straight hours.

'So far,' Stone said, 'so good.'

Leavitt grinned, and crossed his fingers.

16 Autopsy

Burton was working in the autopsy room. He was nervous and tense, still bothered by his memories of Piedmont. Weeks later, in reviewing his work and his thoughts on Level V, he regretted his inability to concentrate.

Because in his initial series of experiments, Burton made several mistakes.

According to the protocol, he was required to carry out autopsies on dead animals, but he was also in charge of preliminary vector experiments. In all fairness, Burton was not the man to do this work; Leavitt would have been better suited to it. But it was felt that Leavitt was more useful working on preliminary isolation and identification.

So the vector experiments fell to Burton.

They were reasonably simple and straightforward, designed to answer the question of how the disease was transmitted. Burton began with a series of cages, lined up in a row. Each had a separate air supply; the air supplies could be interconnected in a variety of ways.

Burton placed the corpse of the dead Norway rat, which was contained in an airtight cage, alongside another cage containing a living rat. He punched buttons; air was allowed to pass freely from one cage to the other.

The living rat flopped over and died.

Interesting, he thought. Airborne transmission. He hooked up a second cage with a live rat, but inserted a millipore filter between the living and dead rat cages. This filter had perforations 100 angstroms in diameter – the size of a small virus.

He opened the passage between the two cages. The rat remained alive.

He watched for several moments, until he was satisfied. Whatever it was that transmitted the disease, it was larger than a virus. He changed the filter, replacing it with a larger one, and then another still larger. He continued in this way until the rat died.

The filter had allowed the agent to pass. He checked it: two microns in diameter, roughly the size of a small cell. He thought to himself that he had just learned something very valuable indeed: the size of the infectious agent.

This was important, for in a single simple experiment he had ruled out the possibility that a protein or a chemical molecule of some kind was doing the damage. At Piedmont, he and Stone had been concerned about a gas, perhaps a gas released as waste from the living organism.

Yet, clearly, no gas was responsible. The disease was transmitted by something the size of a cell that was very much bigger than a molecule, or gas droplet.

The next step was equally simple – to determine whether dead animals were potentially infectious.

He took one of the dead rats and pumped the air out of its cage. He waited until the air was fully evacuated. In the pressure fall, the rat ruptured, bursting open. Burton ignored this.

When he was sure all air was removed, he replaced the air with fresh, clean, filtered air. Then he connected the cage to the cage of a living animal.

Nothing happened.

Interesting, he thought. Using a remotely controlled scalpel, he sliced open the dead animal further, to make sure any organisms contained inside the carcass would be released into the atmosphere.

Nothing happened. The live rat scampered about its cage happily.

The results were quite clear: dead animals were not infectious. That was why, he thought, the buzzards could chew at the Piedmont victims and not die. Corpses could not transmit the disease; only the bugs themselves, carried in the air, could do so.

Bugs in the air were deadly.

Bugs in the corpse were harmless.

In a sense, this was predictable. It had to do with theories of accommodation and mutual adaptation between bacteria and man. Burton had long been interested in this problem, and had lectured on it at the Baylor medical school.

Most people, when they thought of bacteria, thought of diseases. Yet the fact was that only 3 per cent of bacteria produced human disease; the rest were either harmless or beneficial. In the human gut, for instance, there were a variety of bacteria that were helpful to the digestive process. Man needed them, and relied upon them.

In fact, man lived in a sea of bacteria. They were everywhere – on his skin, in his ears and mouth, down his lungs, in his stomach. Everything he owned, anything he touched, every breath he breathed, was drenched in bacteria. Bacteria were ubiquitous. Most of the time you weren't aware of it.

And there was a reason. Both man and bacteria had gotten used to each other, had developed a kind of mutual immunity. Each adapted to the other.

And this, in turn, for a very good reason. It was a principle of biology that evolution was directed toward increased reproductive potential. A man easily killed by bacteria was poorly adapted; he didn't live long enough to reproduce.

A bacteria that killed its host was also poorly adapted. Because any parasite that kills its host is a failure. It must die when the host dies. The successful parasites were those that could live off the host without killing him.

And the most successful hosts were those that could tolerate the parasite, or even turn it to advantage, to make it work for the host.

'The best adapted bacteria,' Burton used to say, 'are the ones that cause minor diseases, or none at all. You may carry the same single cell of *Strep. viridians* on your body for sixty or seventy years. During that time, you are growing and reproducing happily; so is the *Strep.* You can carry *Staph. aureus* around, and pay only the price of some acne and pimples. You can carry tuberculosis for many decades; you can carry syphilis for a lifetime. These last are not minor diseases, but they are much less severe than they once were, because both man and organism have adapted.'

It was known, for instance, that syphilis had been a virulent disease four hundred years before, producing huge festering sores all over the body, often killing in weeks. But over the centuries, man and the spirochete had learned to tolerate each other.

Such considerations were not so abstract and academic as they seemed at first. In the early planning of Wildfire, Stone had observed that 40 per cent of all human disease was caused by microorganisms. Burton had countered by noting that only 3 per cent of all microorganisms caused disease. Obviously, while much human misery was attributable to bacteria, the chances of any particular bacteria being dangerous to man were very small. This was because the process of adaptation – of fitting man to bacteria – was complex.

'Most bacteria,' Burton observed, 'simply can't live within a man long enough to harm him. Conditions are, one way or another, unfavorable. The body is too hot or too cold, too acid or too alkaline, there is too much oxygen or not enough. Man's body is as hostile as Antarctica to most bacteria.'

This meant that the chances of an organism from outer space being suited to harm man were very slim. Everyone recognized this, but felt that Wildfire had to be constructed in any event.. Burton certainly agreed, but felt in an odd way that his prophecy had come true.

Clearly, the bug they had found could kill men. But it was not really adapted to men, because it killed and died within the organism. It could not be transmitted from corpse to corpse. It existed for a second or two in its host, and then died with it.

Satisfying intellectually, he thought.

But practically speaking they still had to isolate it, understand it, and find a cure.

Burton already knew something about transmission, and something about the mechanism of death: clotting of the blood. The question remained – How did the organisms get into the body?

Because transmission appeared to be airborne, contact with skin and lungs seemed likely. Possibly the organisms burrowed right through the skin surface. Or they might be inhaled. Or both.

How to determine it?

He considered putting protective suitings around an experimental animal to cover all but the mouth. That was possible, but it would take a long time. He sat and worried about the problem for an hour.

Then he hit upon a more likely approach.

He knew that the organism killed by clotting blood. Very likely it would initiate clotting at the point of entrance into the body. If skin, clotting would start near the surface. If lungs, it would begin in the chest, radiating outward.

This was something he could test. By using radioactively tagged blood proteins, and then following his animals with scintillometer scans, he could determine where in the body the blood first clotted.

He prepared a suitable animal, choosing a rhesus monkey because its anatomy was more human than a rat's. He infused the radioactive tagging substance, a magnesium isotope, into the monkey and calibrated the scanner. After allowing equilibration, he tied the monkey down and positioned the scanner overhead.

He was now ready to begin.

The scanner would print out its results on a series of human block outlines. He set the computer printing program and then exposed the rhesus to air containing the lethal microorganism.

Immediately, the printout began to clatter out from the computer:

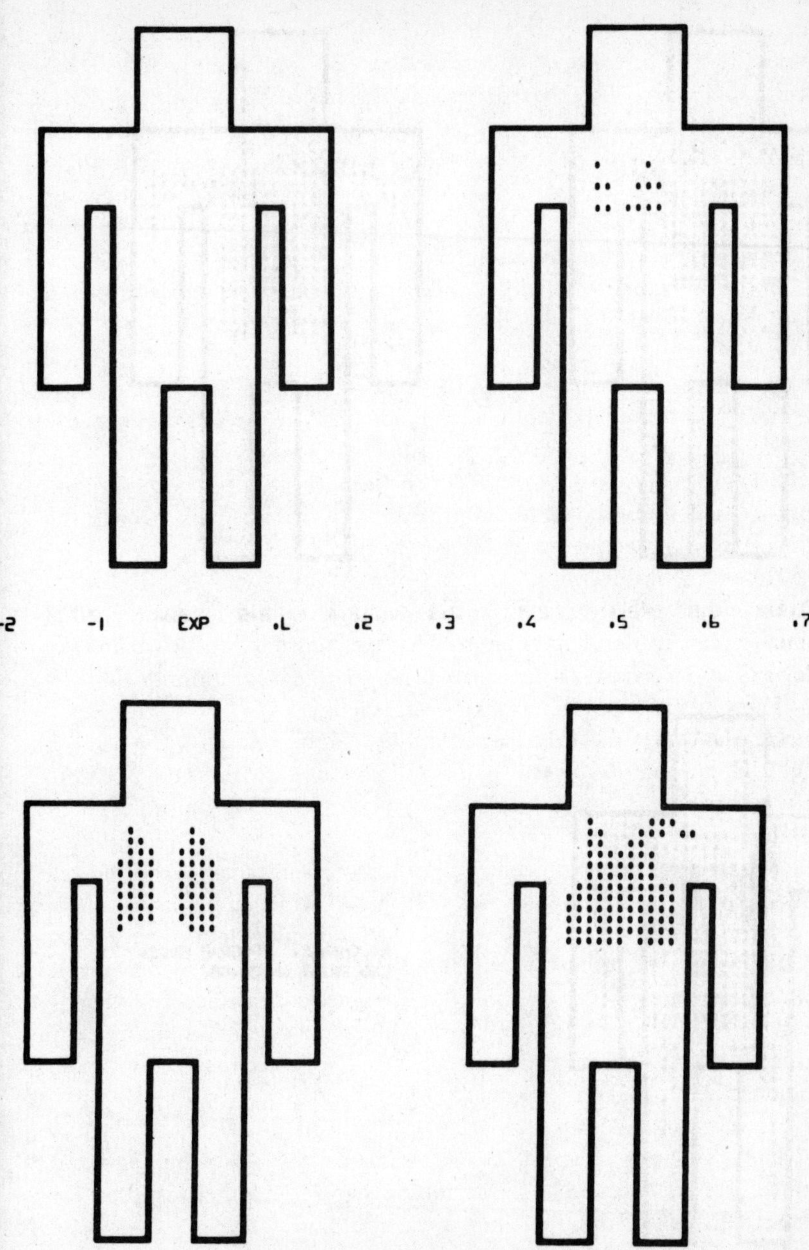
-2 -1 EXP .1 .2 .3 .4 .5 .6 .7
.9 1.0 1.1 1.2 1.3 1.4 1.5 1.6 1.7

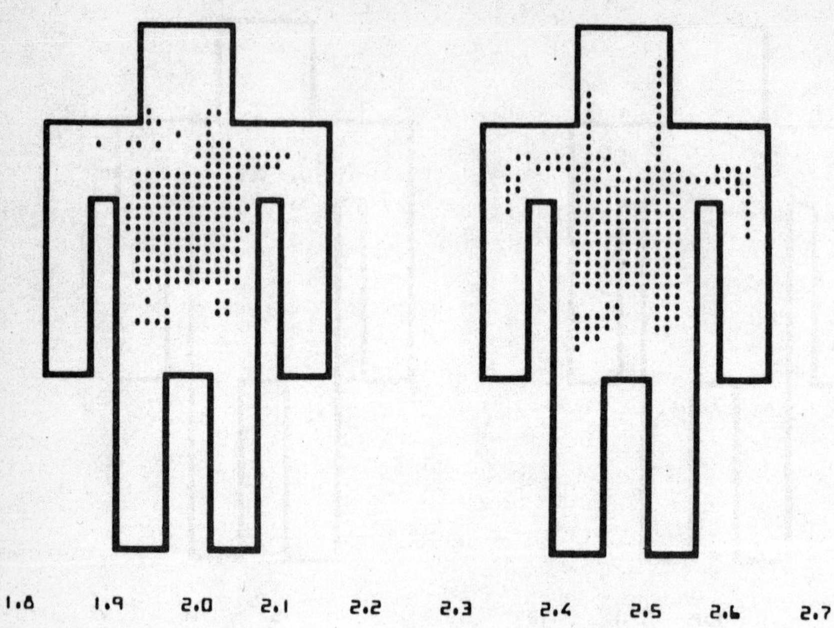
1.8
1.9
2.0
2.1
2.2
2.3
2.4
2.5
2.6
2.7

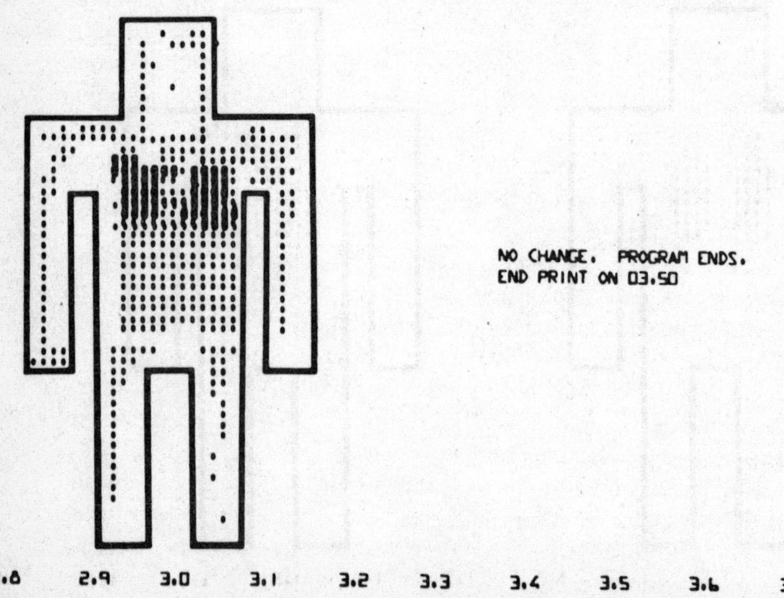
NO CHANGE. PROGRAM ENDS.
END PRINT ON 03.50
2.8
2.9
3.0
3.1
3.2
3.3
3.4
3.5
3.6
3.7

It was all over in three seconds. The graphic printout told him what he needed to know, that clotting began in the lungs and spread outward through the rest of the body.

But there was an additional piece of information gained. Burton later said, 'I had been concerned that perhaps death and clotting did not coincide – or at least did not coincide exactly. It seemed impossible to me that death could occur in three seconds, but it seemed even more unlikely that the total blood volume of the body – five quarts – could solidify in so short a period. I was curious to know whether a single crucial clot might form, in the brain, perhaps, and the rest of the body clot at a slower pace.'

Burton was thinking of the brain even at this early stage of his investigation. In retrospect, it is frustrating that he did not follow this line of inquiry to its logical conclusion. He was prevented from doing this by the evidence of the scans, which told him that clotting began in the lungs and progressed up the carotid arteries to the brain one or two seconds later.

So Burton lost immediate interest in the brain. And his mistake was compounded by his next experiment.

It was a simple test, not part of the regular Wildfire Protocol. Burton knew that death coincided with blood clotting. If clotting could be prevented, could death be avoided?

He took several rats and injected them with heparin, an anticoagulating drug – preventing blood-clot formation. Heparin was a rapid-acting drug widely used in medicine; its actions were thoroughly understood. Burton injected the drug intravenously in varying amounts, ranging from a low-normal dose to a massively excessive dose.

Then he exposed the rats to air containing the lethal organism.

The first rat, with a low dose, died in five seconds. The others followed within a minute. A single rat with a massive dose lived nearly three minutes, but he also succumbed in the end.

Burton was depressed by the results. Although death was delayed, it was not prevented. The method of symptomatic treatment did not work.

He put the dead rats to one side, and then made his crucial mistake.

Burton did not autopsy the anticoagulated rats.

Instead, he turned his attention to the original autopsy specimens, the first black Norway rat and the first rhesus monkey to be exposed to the capsule. He performed a complete autopsy on these animals, but discarded the anticoagulated animals.

It would be forty-eight hours before he realized his error.

The autopsies he performed were careful and good; he did them slowly, reminding himself that he must overlook nothing. He removed the internal organs from the rat and monkey and examined each, removing samples for both the light and electron microscopes.

To gross inspection, the animals had died of total, intravascular coagulation. The arteries, the heart, lungs, kidneys, liver and spleen – all the blood-containing organs – were rock-hard, solid. This was what he had expected.

He carried his tissue slices across the room to prepare frozen sections for microscopic examination. As each section was completed by his technician, he slipped it under the microscope, examined it, and photographed it.

The tissues were normal. Except for the clotted blood, there was nothing unusual about them at all. He knew that these same pieces of tissue would now be sent to the microscopy lab, where another technician would prepare stained sections, using hematoxylin-eosin, periodic acid-Schiff, and Zenker-formalin stains. Sections of nerve would be stained with Nissl and Cajal gold preparations. This process would take an additional twelve to fifteen hours. He could hope, of course, that the stained sections would reveal something more, but he had no reason to believe they would.

Similarly, he was unenthusiastic about the prospects for electron microscopy. The electron microscope was a valuable tool, but occasionally it made things more difficult, not easier. The electron microscope could provide great magnification and clear detail – but only if you knew where to look. It was excellent for examining a single cell, or part of a cell. But first you had to know which cell to examine. And there were billions of cells in a human body.

At the end of ten hours of work, he sat back to consider what he had learned. He drew up a short list:

1. The lethal agent is approximately 1 micron in size. Therefore it is not a gas or molecule, or even a large protein or virus. It is the size of a cell, and may actually be a cell of some sort.

2. The lethal agent is transmitted by air. Dead organisms are not infectious.

3. The lethal agent is inspired by the victim, entering the lungs. There it presumably crosses over into the bloodstream and starts coagulation.

4. The lethal agent causes death through coagulation. This occurs

within seconds, and coincides with total coagulation of the entire body vascular system.

5. Anticoagulant drugs do not prevent this process.

6. No other pathologic abnormalities are known to occur in the dying animal.

Burton looked at his list and shook his head. Anticoagulants might not work, but the fact was that *something* stopped the process. There was a way that it could be done. He knew that.

Because two people had survived.

17 Recovery

At 1147 hours, Mark Hall was bent over the computer, staring at the console that showed the laboratory results from Peter Jackson and the infant. The computer was giving results as they were finished by the automated laboratory equipment; by now, nearly all results were in.

The infant, Hall observed, was normal. The computer did not mince words:

SUBJECT CODED–INFANT– SHOWS ALL LABORATORY VALUES WITHIN NORMAL LIMITS

However, Peter Jackson was another problem entirely. His results were abnormal in several respects.

SUBJECT CODED JACKSON, PETER
LABORATORY VALUES NOT WITHIN NORMAL LIMITS FOLLOW

TEST	NORMAL	VALUE
HEMATOCRIT	38–54	21 INITIAL
		25 REPEAT
		29 REPEAT
		33 REPEAT
		37 REPEAT
BUN	10–20	50
COUNTS RETIC	1	6

BLOOD SMEAR SHOWS MANY IMMATURE ERYTHROCYTE FORMS

TEST	NORMAL	VALUE
PRO TIME	L2	12
BLOOD PH	7.40	7.31
SGOT	40	75
SED RATE	9	29
AMYLASE	70–200	450

Some of the results were easy to understand, others were not. The hematocrit, for example, was rising because Jackson was receiving transfusions of whole blood and packed red cells. The BUN, or blood urea nitrogen, was a test of kidney function and was mildly elevated, probably because of decreased blood flow.

Other analyses were consistent with blood loss. The reticulocyte count was up from 1 to 6 per cent – Jackson had been anemic for some time. He showed immature red-cell forms, which meant that his body was struggling to replace lost blood, and so had to put young, immature red cells into circulation.

The prothrombin time indicated that while Jackson was bleeding from somewhere in his gastrointestinal tract, he had no primary bleeding problem: his blood clotted normally.

The sedimentation rate and SGOT were indices of tissue destruction. Somewhere in Jackson's body, tissues were dying off.

But the pH of the blood was a bit of a puzzle. At 7.31, it was too acid, though not strikingly so. Hall was at a loss to explain this. So was the computer.

SUBJECT CODED JACKSON, PETER
DIAGNOSTIC PROBABILITIES
1. ACUTE AND CHRONIC BLOOD LOSS
ETIOLOGY GASTROINTESTINAL .884
NO OTHER STATISTICALLY SIGNIFICANT
SOURCES.
2. ACIDOSIS
ETIOLOGY UNEXPLAINED
FURTHER DATA REQUIRED
SUGGEST HISTORY

Hall read the printout and shrugged. The computer might suggest he talk to the patient, but that was easier said than done. Jackson was comatose, and if he had ingested anything to make his blood acid, they would not find out until he revived.

On the other hand, perhaps he could test blood gases. He turned to the computer and punched in a request for blood gases.

The computer responded stubbornly.

PATIENT HISTORY PREFERABLE TO LABORATORY ANALYSES

Hall typed in: 'Patient comatose.'

The computer seemed to consider this, and then flashed back:

PATIENT MONITORS NOT COMPATIBLE WITH COMA
EEG SHOWS ALPHA WAVES DIAGNOSTIC OF SLEEP

'I'll be damned,' Hall said. He looked through the window and saw that Jackson was, indeed, stirring sleepily. He crawled down through the tunnel to his plastic suit and leaned over the patient.

'Mr. Jackson, wake up . . .'

Slowly, he opened his eyes and stared at Hall. He blinked, not believing.

'Don't be frightened,' Hall said quietly. 'You're sick, and we have been taking care of you. Do you feel better?'

Jackson swallowed, and nodded. He seemed afraid to speak. But the pallor of his skin was gone; his cheeks had a slight pinkish tinge; his fingernails were no longer gray.

'How do you feel now?'

'Okay . . . Who are you?'

'I am Dr. Hall. I have been taking care of you. You were bleeding very badly. We had to give you a transfusion.'

He nodded, accepting this quite calmly. Somehow, his manner rung a bell for Hall, who said, 'Has this happened to you before?'

'Yes,' he said. 'Twice.'

'How did it happen before?'

'I don't know where I am,' he said, looking around the room. 'Is this a hospital? Why are you wearing that thing?'

'No, this isn't a hospital. It is a special laboratory in Nevada.'

'Nevada?' He closed his eyes and shook his head. 'But I'm in Arizona . . .'

'Not now. We brought you here, so we could help you.'

'How come that suit?'

'We brought you from Piedmont. There was a disease in Piedmont. You are now in an isolation chamber.'

'You mean I'm contagious?'

'Well, we don't know for sure. But we must –'

'Listen,' he said, suddenly trying to get up, 'this place gives me the creeps. I'm getting out of here. I don't like it here.'

He struggled in the bed, trying to move against the straps. Hall pushed him back gently.

'Just relax, Mr. Jackson. Everything will be all right, but you must relax. You've been a sick man.'

Slowly, Jackson lay back. Then: 'I want a cigarette.'

'I'm afraid you can't have one.'

'What the hell, I want one.'

'I'm sorry, smoking is not allowed –'

'Look here, young fella, when you've lived as long as I have you'll know what you can do and what you can't do. They told me before. None of that Mexican food, no liquor, no butts. I tried it for a spell. You know how that makes a body feel? Terrible, just terrible.'

'Who told you?'

'The doctors.'

'What doctors?'

'Those doctors in Phoenix. Big fancy hospital, all that shiny equipment and all those shiny white uniforms. Real fancy hospital. I wouldn't have gone there, except for my sister. She insisted. She lives in Phoenix, you know, with that husband of hers, George. Stupid ninny. I didn't want no fancy hospital, I just wanted to rest up, is all. But she insisted, so I went.'

'When was this?'

'Last year. June it was, or July.'

'Why did you go to the hospital?'

'Why does anybody go to the hospital? I was sick, dammit.'

'What was your problem?'

'This damn stomach of mine, same as always.'

'Bleeding?'

'Christ, bleeding. Ever time I hiccoughed I came up with blood. Never knew a body had so much blood in it.'

'Bleeding in your stomach?'

'Yeah. Like I said, I had it before. All these needles stuck in you' – he nodded to the intravenous lines – 'and all the blood going into you. Phoenix last year, and then Tucson the year before that. Now, Tucson was a right nice place. Right nice. Had me a pretty little nurse and all.' Abruptly, he closed his mouth. 'How old are you, son, anyhow? You don't seem old enough to be a doctor.'

'I'm a surgeon,' Hall said.

'Surgeon! Oh no you don't. They kept trying to get me to do it, and I kept saying, Not on your sweet life. No indeedy. Not taking it out of me.'

'You've had an ulcer for two years?'

'A bit more. The pains started out of the clear blue. Thought I had a touch of indigestion, you know, until the bleeding started up.'

A two-year history, Hall thought. Definitely ulcer, not cancer.

'And you went to the hospital?'

'Yep. Fixed me up fine. Warned me off spicy foods and hard stuff and cigarettes. And I tried, sonny, I sure did. But it wasn't no good. A man gets used to his pleasures.'

'So in a year, you were back in the hospital.'

'Yeah. Big old place in Phoenix, with that stupid ninny George and my sister visiting me every day. He's book-learning fool, you know. Lawyer. Talks real big, but he hasn't got the sense God gave a grasshopper's behind.'

'And they wanted to operate in Phoenix?'

'Sure they did. No offense, sonny, but any doctor'll operate on you, give him half a chance. It's the way they think. I just told them I'd gone this far with my old stomach, and I reckoned I'd finish the stretch with it.'

'When did you leave the hospital?'

'Must have been early August sometime. First week, or thereabouts.'

'And when did you start smoking and drinking and eating the wrong foods?'

'Now don't lecture me, sonny,' Jackson said. 'I've been living for sixty-nine years, eating all the wrong foods and doing all the wrong things. I like it that way, and if I can't keep it up, well then the hell with it.'

'But you must have had pain,' Hall said, frowning.

'Oh, sure, it kicked up some. Specially if I didn't eat. But I found a way to fix that.'

'Yes?'

'Sure. They gave me this milk stuff at the hospital, and wanted me to keep on with it. Hundred times a day, in little sips. Milk stuff. Tasted like chalk. But I found a better thing.'

'What was that?'

'Aspirin,' Jackson said.

'Aspirin?'

'Sure. Works real nice.'

'How much aspirin did you take?'

'Fair bit, toward the end. I was doing a bottle a day. You know them bottles it comes in?'

Hall nodded. No wonder the man was acid. Aspirin was acetylsalicylic acid, and if it was taken in sufficient quantities, it would acidify you. Aspirin was a gastric irritant, and it could exacerbate bleeding.

'Didn't anybody tell you aspirin would make the bleeding worse?' he asked.

'Sure,' Jackson said. 'They told me. But I didn't mind none. Because it stopped the pains, see. That, plus a little squeeze.'

'Squeeze?'

'Red-eye. You know.'

Hall shook his head. He didn't know.

'Sterno. Pink lady. You take it, see, and put it in cloth, and squeeze it out . . .'

Hall sighed. 'You were drinking Sterno,' he said.

'Well, only when I couldn't get nothing else. Aspirin and squeeze, see, really kills that pain.'

'Sterno isn't only alcohol. It's methanol, too.'

'Doesn't hurt you, does it?' Jackson asked, in a voice suddenly concerned.

'As a matter of fact, it does. It can make you go blind, and it can even kill you.'

'Well, hell, it made me feel better, so I took it,' Jackson said.

'Did this aspirin and squeeze have any effect on you? On your breathing?'

'Well, now you mention it, I was a tad short of breath. But what the hell, I don't need much breath at my age.'

Jackson yawned and closed his eyes.

'You're awful full of questions, boy. I want to sleep now.'

Hall looked at him, and decided the man was right. It would be best to proceed slowly, at least for a time. He crawled back down the tunnel and out to the main room. He turned to his assistant:

'Our friend Mr. Jackson has a two-year history of ulcer. We'd better keep the blood going in for another couple of units, then we can stop and see what's happening. Drop an NG tube and start icewater lavage.'

A gong rang, echoing softly through the room.

'What's that?'

'The twelve-hour mark. It means we have to change our clothing. And it means you have a conference.'

'I do? Where?'

'The CR off the dining room.'

Hall nodded, and left.

In delta sector, the computers hummed and clicked softly, as Captain Arthur Morris punched through a new program on the console. Captain Morris was a programmer; he had been sent to delta sector by the command on Level I because no MCN messages had been received for nine hours. It was possible, of course, that there had been no priority transmissions; but it was also unlikely.

And if there had been unreceived MCN messages, then the computers were not functioning properly. Captain Morris watched as the computer ran its usual internal check program, which read out as all circuits functioning.

Unsatisfied, he punched in the CHECKLIM program, a more rigorous testing of the circuit banks. It required 0.03 seconds for the machine to come back with its answer: a row of five green lights blinked on the console. He walked over to the teleprinter and watched as it typed:

MACHINE FUNCTION ON ALL CIRCUITS
WITHIN RATIONAL INDICES

He looked and nodded, satisfied. He could not have known, as he stood before the teleprinter, that there was indeed a fault, but that it was purely mechanical, not electronic, and hence could not be tested on the check programs. The fault lay within the teleprinter box itself. There a sliver of paper from the edge of the roll had peeled away and, curling upward, had lodged between the bell and striker, preventing the bell from ringing. It was for this reason that no MCN transmissions had been recorded.

Neither machine nor man was able to catch the error.

18 The Noon Conference

According to protocol, the team met every twelve hours for a brief conference, at which results were summarized and new directions planned. In order to save time the conferences were held in a small room off the cafeteria; they could eat and talk at the same time.

Hall was the last to arrive. He slipped into a chair behind his lunch – two glasses of liquid and three pills of different colors – just as Stone said, 'We'll hear from Burton first.'

Burton shuffled to his feet and in a slow, hesitant voice outlined his experiments and his results. He noted first that he had determined the size of the lethal agent to be one micron.

Stone and Leavitt looked at each other. The green flecks they had seen were much larger than that; clearly, infection could be spread by a mere fraction of the green fleck.

Burton next explained his experiments concerning airborne transmission, and coagulation beginning at the lungs. He finished with his attempts at anticoagulation therapy.

'What about the autopsies?' Stone said. 'What did they show?'

'Nothing we don't already know. The blood is clotted throughout. No other demonstrable abnormalities at the lightmicroscope level.'

'And clotting is initiated at the lungs?'

'Yes. Presumably the organisms cross over to the bloodstream there – or they may release a toxic substance, which crosses over. We may have an answer when the stained sections are finished. In particular, we will be looking for damage to blood vessels, since this releases tissue thromboplastin, and stimulates clotting at the site of damage.'

Stone nodded and turned to Hall, who told of the tests carried out on his two patients. He explained that the infant was normal to all tests and that Jackson had a bleeding ulcer, for which he was receiving transfusions.

'He's revived,' Hall said. 'I talked with him briefly.'

Everyone sat up.

'Mr. Jackson is a cranky old goat of sixty-nine who has a two-year history of ulcer. He's bled out twice before: two years ago, and again last year. Each time he was warned to change his habits; each time he went back to his old ways, and began bleeding again. At the time of the Piedmont contact, he was treating his problems with his own regimen: a bottle of aspirin a day, and some Sterno on top of it. He says this left him a little short of breath.'

'And made him acidotic as hell,' Burton said.

'Exactly.'

Methanol, when broken down by the body, was converted to formaldehyde and formic acid. In combination with aspirin, it meant Jackson was consuming great quantities of acid. The body had to maintain its acid-base balance within fairly narrow limits or death would occur. One way to keep the balance was to breathe rapidly, and blow off carbon dioxide, decreasing carbonic acid in the body.

Stone said, 'Could this acid have protected him from the organism?'

Hall shrugged. 'Impossible to say.'

Leavitt said, 'What about the infant? Was it anemic?'

'No,' Hall said. 'But on the other hand, we don't know for sure that it was protected by the same mechanism. It might have something entirely different.'

'How about the acid-base balance of the child?'

'Normal,' Hall said. 'Perfectly normal. At least it is now.'

There was a moment of silence. Finally Stone said, 'Well, you have some good leads here. The problem remains to discover what, if anything, that child and that old man have in common. Perhaps, as you suggest, there is nothing in common. But for a start, we have to assume that they were protected in the same way, by the same mechanism.'

Hall nodded.

Burton said to Stone, 'And what have you found in the capsule?'

'We'd better show you,' Stone said.

'Show us what?'

'Something we believe may represent the organism,' Stone said.

The door said MORPHOLOGY. Inside, the room was partioned into a place for the experimenters to stand, and a glass-walled isolation chamber further in. Gloves were provided so the men could reach into the chamber and move instruments about.

Stone pointed to the glass dish, and the small fleck of black inside it.

'We think this is our "meteor," ' he said. 'We have found something apparently alive on its surface. There were also other areas within the capsule that may represent life. We've brought the meteor in here to have a look at it under the light microscope.'

Reaching through with the gloves, Stone set the glass dish into an opening in a large chrome box, then withdrew his hands.

'The box,' he said, 'is simply a light microscope fitted with the usual image intensifiers and resolution scanners. We can go up to a thousand diameters with it, projected on the screen here.'

Leavitt adjusted dials while Hall and the others stared at the viewer screen.

'Ten power,' Leavitt said.

On the screen, Hall saw that the rock was jagged, blackish, dull. Stone pointed out green flecks.

'One hundred power.'

The green flecks were larger now, very clear.

'We think that's our organism. We have observed it growing; it turns purple, apparently at the point of mitotic division.'

'Spectrum shift?'

'Of some kind.'

'One thousand power,' Leavitt said.

The screen was filled with a single green spot, nestled down in the jagged hollows of the rock. Hall noticed the surface of the green, which was smooth and glistening, almost oily.

'You think that's a single bacterial colony?'

'We can't be sure it's a colony in the conventional sense,' Stone said. 'Until we heard Burton's experiments, we didn't think it was a colony at all. We thought it might be a single organism. But obviously the single units have to be a micron or less in size; this is much too big. Therefore it is probably a larger structure – perhaps a colony, perhaps something else.'

As they watched, the spot turned purple, and green again.

'It's dividing now,' Stone said. 'Excellent.'

Leavitt switched on the cameras.

'Now watch closely.'

The spot turned purple and held the color. It seemed to expand slightly, and for a moment, the surface broke into fragments, hexagonal in shape, like a tile floor.

'Did you see that?'

'It seemed to break up.'

'Into six-sided figures.'

'I wonder,' Stone said, 'whether those figures represent single units.'

'Or whether they are regular geometric shapes all the time, or just during division?'

'We'll know more,' Stone said, 'after the EM.' He turned to Burton. 'Have you finished your autopsies?'

'Yes.'

'Can you work the spectrometer?'

'I think so.'

'Then do that. It's computerized, anyway. We'll want an analysis of samples of both the rock and the green organism.'

'You'll get me a piece?'

'Yes.' Stone said to Leavitt: 'Can you handle the AA analyzer?'

'Yes.'

'Same tests on that.'

'And a fractionation?'

'I think so,' Stone said. 'But you'll have to do that by hand.'

Leavitt nodded; Stone turned back to the isolation chamber and removed a glass dish from the light microscope. He set it to one side, beneath a small device that looked like a miniature scaffolding. This was the microsurgical unit.

Microsurgery was a relatively new skill in biology – the ability to perform delicate operations on a single cell. Using microsurgical techniques, it was possible to remove the nucleus from a cell, or part of the cytoplasm, as neatly and cleanly as a surgeon performed an amputation.

The device was constructed to scale down human hand movements into fine, precise miniature motions. A series of gears and servomechanisms carried out the reduction; the movement of a thumb was translated into a shift of a knife blade millionths of an inch.

Using a high magnification viewer, Stone began to chip away delicately at the black rock, until he had two tiny fragments. He set them aside in separate glass dishes and proceeded to scrape away two small fragments from the green area.

Immediately, the green turned purple, and expanded.

'It doesn't like you,' Leavitt said, and laughed.

Stone frowned. 'Interesting. Do you suppose that's a nonspecific growth response, or a trophic response to injury and irradiation?'

'I think,' Leavitt said, 'that it doesn't like to be poked at.'

'We must investigate further,' Stone said.

19 Crash

For Arthur Manchek, there was a certain kind of horror in the telephone conversation. He received it at home, having just finished dinner and sat down in the living room to read the newspapers. He hadn't seen a newspaper in the last two days, he had been so busy with the Piedmont business.

When the phone rang, he assumed that it must be for his wife, but a moment later she came in and said, 'It's for you. The base.'

He had an uneasy feeling as he picked up the receiver. 'Major Manchek speaking.'

'Major, this is Colonel Burns at Unit Eight.' Unit Eight was the processing and clearing unit of the base. Personnel checked in and out through Unit Eight, and calls were transmitted through it.

'Yes, Colonel?'

'Sir, we have you down for notification of certain contingencies.' His voice was guarded; he was choosing his words carefully on the open line. 'I'm informing you now of an RTM crash forty-two minutes ago in Big Head, Utah.'

Manchek frowned. Why was he being informed of a routine training-mission crash? It was hardly his province.

'What was it?'

'Phantom, sir. En route San Francisco to Topeka.'

'I see,' Manchek said, though he did not see at all.

'Sir, Goddard wanted you to be informed in this instance so that you could join the post team.'

'Goddard? Why Goddard?' For a moment, as he sat there in the living room, staring at the newspaper headline absently – NEW BERLIN CRISIS FEARED – he thought that the colonel meant Lewis Goddard, chief of the codes section of Vandenberg. Then he realized he meant Goddard Spaceflight Center, outside Washington. Among other things, Goddard acted as collating center for certain special projects that fell between the province of Houston and the governmental agencies in Washington.

'Sir,' Colonel Burns said, 'the Phantom drifted off its flight plan forty minutes out of San Francisco and passed through Area WF.'

Manchek felt himself slowing down. A kind of sleepiness came over him. 'Area WF?'

'That is correct, sir.'

'When?'

'Twenty minutes before the crash.'

'At what altitude?'

'Twenty-three thousand feet, sir.'

'When does the post team leave?'

'Half an hour, sir, from the base.'

'All right,' Manchek said. 'I'll be there.'

He hung up and stared at the phone lazily. He felt tired; he wished he could go to bed. Area WF was the designation for the cordoned-off radius around Piedmont, Arizona.

They should have dropped the bomb, he thought. They should have dropped it two days ago.

At the time of the decision to delay Directive 7-12, Manchek had been uneasy. But officially he could not express an opinion, and he had waited in vain for the Wildfire team, now located in the underground laboratory, to complain to Washington. He knew Wildfire had been notified; he had seen the cable that went to all security units; it was quite explicit.

Yet for some reason Wildfire had not complained. Indeed, they had paid no attention to it whatever.

Very odd.

And now there was a crash. He lit his pipe and sucked on it, considering the possibilities. Overwhelming was the likelihood that some green trainee had daydreamed, gone off his flight plan, panicked, and lost control of the plane. It had happened before, hundreds of times. The post team, a group of specialists who went out to the site of the wreckage to investigate all crashes, usually returned a verdict of 'Agnogenic Systems Failure.' It was military doubletalk for crash of unknown cause; it did not distinguish between mechanical failure and pilot failure, but it was known that most systems failures were pilot failures. A man could not afford to daydream when he was running a complex machine at two thousand miles an hour. The proof lay in the statistics: though only 9 per cent of flights occurred after the pilot had taken a leave or weekend pass, these flights accounted for 27 per cent of casualties.

Manchek's pipe went out. He stood, dropping the newspaper, and went into the kitchen to tell his wife he was leaving.

'This is movie country,' somebody said, looking at the sandstone cliffs, the brilliant reddish hues, against the deepening blue of the sky. And it was true, many movies had been filmed in this area of Utah. But Manchek could not think of movies now. As he sat in the back of the limousine moving away from the Utah airport, he considered what he had been told.

During the flight from Vandenberg to southern Utah, the post team had heard transcripts of the flight transmission between the Phantom and Topeka Central. For the most part it was dull, except for the final moments before the pilot crashed.

The pilot had said: 'Something is wrong.'

And then, a moment later, 'My rubber air hose is dissolving. It must be the vibration. It's just disintegrating to dust.'

Perhaps ten seconds after that, a weak, fading voice said, 'Everything made of rubber in the cockpit is dissolving.'

There were no further transmissions.

Manchek kept hearing that brief communication, in his mind, over and over. Each time, it sounded more bizarre and terrifying.

He looked out the window at the cliffs. The sun was setting now, and only the tops of the cliffs were lighted by fading reddish sunlight; the valleys lay in darkness. He looked ahead at the other limousine, raising a small dust cloud as it carried the rest of the team to the crash site.

'I used to love westerns,' somebody said. 'They were all shot out here. Beautiful country.'

Manchek frowned. It was astonishing to him how people could spend so much time on irrelevancies. Or perhaps it was just denial, the unwillingness to face reality.

The reality was cold enough: the Phantom had strayed into Area WF, going quite deep for a matter of six minutes before the pilot realized the error and pulled north again. However, once in WF, the plane had begun to lose stability. And it had finally crashed.

He said, 'Has Wildfire been informed?'

A member of the group, a psychiatrist with a crew cut – all post teams had at least one psychiatrist – said, 'You mean the germ people?'

'Yes.'

'They've been told,' somebody else said. 'It went out on the scrambler an hour ago.'

Then, thought Manchek, there would certainly be a reaction from Wildfire. They could not afford to ignore this.

Unless they weren't reading their cables. It had never occurred to him before, but perhaps it was possible – they weren't reading the cables. They were so absorbed in their work, they just weren't bothering.

'There's the wreck,' somebody said. 'Up ahead.'

Each time Manchek saw a wreck, he was astonished. Somehow, one never got used to the idea of the sprawl, the mess – the destructive force of a large metal object striking the earth at thousands of miles an hour. He always expected a neat, tight little clump of metal, but it was never that way.

The wreckage of the Phantom was scattered over two square miles of desert. Standing next to the charred remnants of the left wing, he could barely see the others, on the horizon, near the right wing. Everywhere he looked, there were bits of twisted metal, blackened, paint peeling. He saw one with a small portion of a sign still intact, the stenciled letters clear: DO NOT. The rest was gone.

It was impossible to make anything of the remnants. The fuselage, the cockpit, the canopy were all shattered into a million fragments, and the fires had disfigured everything.

As the sun faded, he found himself standing near the remains of the tail section, where the metal still radiated heat from the smoldering fire. Half-buried in the sand he saw a bit of bone; he picked it up and realized with horror that it was human. Long, and broken, and charred at one end, it had obviously come from an arm or a leg. But it was oddly clean – there was no flesh remaining, only smooth bone.

Darkness descended, and the post team took out their flashlights, the half-dozen men moving among smoking metal, flashing their yellow beams of light about.

It was late in the evening when a biochemist whose name he did not know came up to talk with him.

'You know,' the biochemist said, 'it's funny. That transcript about the rubber in the cockpit dissolving.'

'How do you mean?'

'Well, no rubber was used in this airplane. It was all a synthetic plastic compound. Newly developed by Ancro; they're quite proud of it. It's polymer that has some of the same characteristics as human tissue. Very flexible, lots of applications.'

Manchek said, 'Do you think vibrations could have caused the disintegration?'

'No,' the man said. 'There are thousands of Phantoms flying around the world. They all have this plastic. None of them has ever had this trouble.'

'Meaning?'

'Meaning that I don't know what the hell is going on,' the biochemist said.

20 Routine

Slowly, the Wildfire installation settled into a routine, a rhythm of work in the underground chambers of a laboratory where there was no night or day, morning or afternoon. The men slept when they were tired, awoke when they were refreshed, and carried on their work in a number of different areas.

Most of this work was to lead nowhere. They knew that, and accepted it in advance. As Stone was fond of saying, scientific research was much like prospecting: you went out and you hunted, armed with your maps and your instruments, but in the end your preparations did not matter, or even your intuition. You needed your luck, and whatever benefits accrued to the diligent, through sheer, grinding hard work.

Burton stood in the room that housed the spectrometer along with several other pieces of equipment for radioactivity assays, ratio-density photometry, thermocoupling analysis, and preparation for X-ray crystallography.

The spectrometer employed in Level V was the standard Whittington model K-5. Essentially it consisted of a vaporizer, a prism, and a recording screen. The material to be tested was set in the vaporizer and burned. The light from its burning then passed through the prism, where it was broken down to a spectrum that was projected onto a recording screen. Since different elements gave off different wavelengths of light as they burned, it was possible to analyze the chemical makeup of a substance by analyzing the spectrum of light produced.

In theory it was simple, but in practice the reading of spectrometrograms was complex and difficult. No one in the Wildfire laboratory was trained to do it well. Thus results were fed directly into a computer, which performed the analysis. Because of the sensitivity of the computer, rough percentage compositions could also be determined.

Burton placed the first chip, from the black rock, onto the vaporizer and pressed the button. There was a single bright burst of intensely hot light; he turned away, avoiding the brightness, and then put the second chip onto the lamp. Already, he knew, the computer was analyzing the light from the first chip.

He repeated the process with the green fleck, and then checked the time. The computer was now scanning the self-developing photographic plates, which were ready for viewing in seconds. But the scan itself would take two hours – the electric eye was very slow.

Once the scan was completed, the computer would analyze results and print the data within five seconds.

The wall clock told him it was now 1500 hours – three in the afternoon. He suddenly realized he was tired. He punched in instructions to the computer to wake him when analysis was finished. Then he went off to bed.

In another room, Leavitt was carefully feeding similar chips into a different machine, an amino-acid analyzer. As he did so, he smiled slightly to himself, for he could remember how it had been in the old days, before AA analysis was automatic.

In the early fifties, the analysis of amino acids in a protein might take weeks, or even months. Sometimes it took years. Now it took hours – or at the very most, a day – and it was fully automatic.

Amino acids were the building blocks of proteins. There were twenty-four known amino acids, each composed of a half-dozen molecules of carbon, hydrogen, oxygen, and nitrogen. Proteins were made by stringing these amino acids together in a line, like a freight train. The order of stringing determined the nature of the protein – whether it was insulin, hemoglobin, or growth hormone. All proteins were composed of the same freight cars, the same units. Some proteins had more of one kind of car than another, or in a different order. But that was the only difference. The same amino acids, the same freight cars, existed in human proteins and flea proteins.

That fact had taken approximately twenty years to discover.

But what controlled the order of amino acids in the protein? The answer turned out to be DNA, the genetic-coding substance, which acted like a switching manager in a freightyard.

That particular fact had taken another twenty years to discover.

But then once the amino acids were strung together, they began to twist and coil upon themselves; the analogy became closer to a snake than a train. The manner of coiling was determined by the order of acids, and was quite specific: a protein had to be coiled in a certain way, and no other, or it failed to function.

Another ten years.

Rather odd, Leavitt thought. Hundreds of laboratories, thousands of workers throughout the world, all bent on discovering such essentially simple facts. It had all taken years and years, decades of patient effort.

And now there was this machine. The machine would not, of course, give the precise order of amino acids. But it would give a rough percentage composition: so much valine, so much arginine, so much cystine and proline and leucine. And that, in turn, would give a great deal of information.

Yet it was a shot in the dark, this machine. Because they had no reason to believe that either the rock or the green organism was composed even partially of proteins. True, every living thing on earth had at least some proteins – but that didn't mean life elsewhere had to have it.

For a moment, he tried to imagine life without proteins. It was almost impossible: on earth, proteins were part of the cell wall, and comprised all the enzymes known to man. And life without enzymes? Was that possible?

He recalled the remark of George Thompson, the British biochemist, who had called enzymes 'the matchmakers of life.' It was true; enzymes acted as catalysts for all chemical reactions, by providing a surface for two molecules to come together and react upon. There were hundreds of thousands, perhaps millions, of enzymes, each existing solely to aid a single chemical reaction. Without enzymes, there could be no chemical reactions.

Without chemical reactions, there could be no life.

Or could there?

It was a long-standing problem. Early in planning Wildfire, the question had been posed: How do you study a form of life totally unlike any you know? How would you even know it was alive?

This was not an academic matter. Biology, as George Wald had said, was a unique science because it could not define its subject matter. Nobody had a definition for life. Nobody knew what it was, really. The old definitions – an organism that showed ingestion, excretion, metabolism, reproduction, and so on – were worthless. One could always find exceptions.

The group had finally concluded that energy conversion was the hallmark of life. All living organisms in some way took in energy – as food, or sunlight – and converted it to another form of energy, and put it to use. (Viruses were the exception to this rule, but the group was prepared to define viruses as nonliving.)

For the next meeting, Leavitt was asked to prepare a rebuttal to the definition. He pondered it for a week, and returned with three objects: a swatch of black cloth, a watch, and a piece of granite. He set them down before the group and said, 'Gentlemen, I give you three living things.'

He then challenged the team to prove that they were not living. He placed the black cloth in the sunlight; it became warm. This, he announced, was an example of energy conversion – radiant energy to heat.

It was objected that this was merely passive energy absorption, not conversion. It was also objected that the conversion, if it could be called that, was not purposeful. It served no function.

'How do you know it is not purposeful?' Leavitt had demanded.

They then turned to the watch. Leavitt pointed to the radium dial, which glowed in the dark. Decay was taking place, and light was being produced.

The men argued that this was merely release of potential energy held in unstable electron levels. But there was growing confusion; Leavitt was making his point.

Finally, they came to the granite. 'This is alive,' Leavitt said. 'It is living, breathing, walking, and talking. Only we cannot see it, because it is happening too slowly. Rock has a lifespan of three billion years. We have a lifespan of sixty or seventy years. We cannot see what is happening to this rock for the same reason that we cannot make out the tune on a record being played at the rate of one revolution every century. And the rock, for its part, is not even aware of our existence because we are alive for only a brief instant of its lifespan. To it, we are like flashes in the dark.'

He held up his watch.

His point was clear enough, and they revised their thinking in one important respect. They conceded that it was possible that they might not be able to analyze certain life forms. It was possible that they might not be able to make the slightest headway, the least beginning, in such an analysis.

But Leavitt's concerns extended beyond this, to the general problem of action in uncertainty. He recalled reading Talbert Gregson's 'Planning the Unplanned' with close attention, poring over the complex mathematical models the author had devised to analyze the problem. It was Gregson's conviction that:

> All decisions involving uncertainty fall within two distinct categories – those with contingencies, and those without. The latter are distinctly more difficult to deal with.
>
> Most decisions, and nearly all human interaction, can be incorporated into a contingencies model. For example, a President may start a war, a man may sell his business, or divorce his wife. Such an action will produce a

reaction; the number of reactions is infinite but the number of *probable* reactions is manageably small. Before making a decision, an individual can predict various reactions, and he can assess his original, or primary-mode, decision more effectively.

But there is also a category which cannot be analyzed by contingencies. This category involves events and situations which are *absolutely* unpredictable, not merely disasters of all sorts, but those also including rare moments of discovery and insight, such as those which produced the laser, or penicillin. Because these moments are unpredictable, they cannot be planned for in any logical manner. The mathematics are wholly unsatisfactory.

We may only take comfort in the fact that such situations, for ill or for good, are exceedingly rare.

Jeremy Stone, working with infinite patience, took a flake of the green material and dropped it into molten plastic. The plastic was the size and shape of a medicine capsule. He waited until the flake was firmly imbedded, and poured more plastic over it. He then transferred the plastic pill to the curing room.

Stone envied the others their mechanized routines. The preparation of samples for electron microscopy was still a delicate task requiring skilled human hands; the preparation of a good sample was as demanding a craft as that ever practiced by an artisan – and took almost as long to learn. Stone had worked for five years before he became proficient at it.

The plastic was cured in a special high-speed processing unit, but it would still take five hours to harden to proper consistency. The curing room would maintain a constant temperature of 61° C. with a relative humidity of 10 per cent.

Once the plastic was hardened, he would scrape it away, and then flake off a small bit of green with a microtome. This would go into the electron microscope. The flake would have to be of the right thickness and size, a small round shaving 1,500 angstroms in depth, no more.

Only then could he look at the green stuff, whatever it was, at sixty thousand diameters magnification.

That, he thought, would be interesting.

In general, Stone believed the work was going well. They were making fine progress, moving forward in several promising lines of inquiry. But most important, they had time. There was no rush, no panic, no need to fear.

The bomb had been dropped on Piedmont. That would destroy airborne organisms, and neutralize the source of infection. Wildfire was the only place that any further infection could spread from, and Wildfire was specifically designed to prevent that. Should isolation be broken in the lab, the areas that were contaminated would automatically seal off. Within a half-second, sliding airtight doors would close, producing a new configuration for the lab.

This was necessary because past experience in other laboratories working in so-called axenic, or germ-free, atmospheres indicated that contamination occurred in 15 per cent of cases. The reasons were usually structural – a seal burst, a glove tore, a seam split – but the contamination occurred, nonetheless.

At Wildfire, they were prepared for that eventuality. But if it did not happen, and the odds were it would not, then they could work safely here for an indefinite period. They could spend a month, even a year, working on the organism. There was no problem, no problem at all.

Hall walked through the corridor, looking at the atomic-detonator substations. He was trying to memorize their positions. There were five on the floor, positioned at intervals along the central corridor. Each was the same: small silver boxes no larger than a cigarette packet. Each had a lock for the key, a green light that was burning, and a dark-red light.

Burton had explained the mechanism earlier. 'There are sensors in all the duct systems and in all the labs. They monitor the air in the rooms by a variety of chemical, electronic, and straight bioassay devices. The bioassay is just a mouse whose heartbeat is being monitored. If anything goes wrong with the sensors, the lab automatically seals off. If the whole floor is contaminated, it will seal off, and the atomic device will cut in. When that happens, the green light will go out, and the red light will begin to blink. That signals the start of the three-minute interval. Unless you lock in your key, the bomb will go off at the end of three minutes.'

'And I have to do it myself?'

Burton nodded. 'The key is steel. It is conductive. The lock has a system which measures the capacitance of the person holding the key. It responds to general body size, particularly weight, and also the salt content of sweat. It's quite specific, actually, for you.'

'So I'm really the only one?'

'You really are. And you only have one key. But there's a complicating problem. The blueprints weren't followed exactly; we only discovered the error after the lab was finished and the device installed. But there is an error: we are short three detonator substations. There are only five, instead of eight.'

'Meaning?'

'Meaning that if the floor starts to contaminate, you must rush to locate yourself at a substation. Otherwise there is a chance you could be sealed off in a sector without a substation. And then, in the event of a malfunction of the bacteriologic sensors, a false positive malfunction, the laboratory could be destroyed needlessly.'

'That seems a rather serious error in planning.'

'It turns out,' Burton said, 'that three new substations were going to be added next month. But that won't help us now. Just keep the problem in mind, and everything'll be all right.'

Leavitt awoke quickly, rolling out of bed and starting to dress. He was excited: he had just had an idea. A fascinating thing, wild, crazy, but fascinating as hell.

It had come from his dream.

He had been dreaming of a house, and then of a city – a huge, complex, interconnecting city around the house. A man lived in the house, with his family; the man lived and worked and commuted within the city, moving about, acting, reacting.

And then, in the dream, the city was suddenly eliminated, leaving only the house. How different things were then! A single house, standing alone, without the things it needed – water, plumbing, electricity, streets. And a family, cut off from the supermarkets, schools, drugstores. And the husband, whose work was in the city, interrelated to others in the city, suddenly stranded.

The house became a different organism altogether. And from that to the Wildfire organism was but a single step, a single leap of the imagination . . .

He would have to discuss it with Stone. Stone would laugh, as usual – Stone always laughed – but he would also pay attention. Leavitt knew that, in a sense, he operated as the idea man for the team. The man who would always provide the most improbable, mind-stretching theories.

Well, Stone would at least be interested.

He glanced at the clock. 2200 hours. Getting on toward midnight. He hurried to dress.

He took out a new paper suit and slipped his feet in. The paper was cool against his bare flesh.

And then suddenly it was warm. A strange sensation. He finished dressing, stood, and zipped up the one-piece suit. As he left, he looked once again at the clock.

2210.

Oh, Christ, he thought.

It had happened again. And this time, for ten minutes. What had gone on? He couldn't remember. But it was ten minutes gone, disappeared, while he had dressed – an action that shouldn't have taken more than thirty seconds.

He sat down again on the bed, trying to remember, but he could not. Ten minutes gone.

It was terrifying. Because it was happening again, though he had hoped it would not. It hadn't happened for months, but now, with the excitement, the odd hours, the break in his normal hospital schedule, it was starting once more.

For a moment, he considered telling the others, then shook his head. He'd be all right. It wouldn't happen again. He was going to be just fine.

He stood. He had been on his way to see Stone, to talk to Stone about something. Something important and exciting.

He paused.

He couldn't remember.

The idea, the image, the excitement was gone. Vanished, erased from his mind.

He knew then that he should tell Stone, admit the whole thing. But he knew what Stone would say and do if he found out. And he knew what it would mean to his future, to the rest of his life, once the Wildfire Project was finished. Everything would change, if people knew. He couldn't ever be normal again – he would have to quit his job, do other things, make endless adjustments. He couldn't even drive a car.

No, he thought. He would not say anything. And he would be all right: as long as he didn't look at blinking lights.

Jeremy Stone was tired, but knew he was not ready for sleep. He paced up and down the corridors of the laboratory, thinking about the birds at Piedmont. He ran over everything they had done: how they had seen the birds, how they had gassed them with chlorazine, and how the birds had died. He went over it in his mind, again and again.

Because he was missing something. And that something was bothering him.

At the time, while he had been inside Piedmont itself, it had bothered him. Then he had forgotten, but his nagging doubts had been revived at the noon conference, while Hall was discussing the patients.

Something Hall had said, some fact he had mentioned, was related, in some off way, to the birds. But what was it? What was the exact thought, the precise words, that had triggered the association?

Stone shook his head. He simply couldn't dig it out. The clues, the connection, the keys were all there, but he couldn't bring them to the surface.

He pressed his hands to his head, squeezing against the bones, and he damned his brain for being so stubborn.

Like many intelligent men, Stone took a rather suspicious attitude toward his own brain, which he saw as a precise and skilled but temperamental machine. He was never surprised when the machine failed to perform, though he feared those moments, and hated them. In his blackest hours, Stone doubted the utility of all thought, and all intelligence. There were times when he envied the laboratory rats he worked with; their brains were so simple. Certainly they did not have the intelligence to destroy themselves; that was a peculiar invention of man.

He often argued that human intelligence was more trouble than it was worth. It was more destructive than creative, more confusing than revealing, more discouraging than satisfying, more spiteful than charitable.

There were times when he saw man, with his giant brain, as equivalent to the dinosaurs. Every schoolboy knew that dinosaurs had outgrown themselves, had become too large and ponderous to be viable. No one ever thought to consider whether the human brain, the most complex structure in the known universe, making fantastic demands on the human body in terms of nourishment and blood, was not analogous. Perhaps the human brain had become a kind of dinosaur for man and perhaps, in the end, would prove his downfall.

Already, the brain consumed one quarter of the body's blood supply. A fourth of all blood pumped from the heart went to the brain, an organ accounting for only a small percentage of body mass. If brains grew larger, and better, then perhaps they would consume more – perhaps so much that, like an infection, they would overrun their hosts and kill the bodies that transported them.

Or perhaps, in their infinite cleverness, they would find a way to destroy themselves and each other. There were times when, as he sat at State Department or Defense Department meetings, and looked around the table, he saw nothing more than a dozen gray, convoluted brains sitting on the table. No flesh and blood, no hands, no eyes, no fingers. No mouths, no sex organs – all these were superfluous.

Just brains. Sitting around, trying to decide how to outwit other brains, at other conference tables.

Idiotic.

He shook his head, thinking that he was becoming like Leavitt, conjuring up wild and improbable schemes.

Yet, there was a sort of logical consequence to Stone's ideas. If you really feared and hated your brain, you would attempt to destroy it. Destroy your own, and destroy others.

'I'm tired,' he said aloud, and looked at the wall clock. It was 2340 hours – almost time for the midnight conference.

21 The Midnight Conference

They met again, in the same room, in the same way. Stone glanced at the others and saw they were tired; no one, including himself, was getting enough sleep.

'We're going at this too hard,' he said. 'We don't need to work around the clock, and we shouldn't do so. Tired men will make mistakes, mistakes in thinking and mistakes in action. We'll start to drop things, to screw things up, to work sloppily. And we'll make wrong assumptions, draw incorrect inferences. That mustn't happen.'

The team agreed to get at least six hours sleep in each twenty-four-hour period. That seemed reasonable, since there was no problem on the surface; the infection at Piedmont had been halted by the atomic bomb.

Their belief might never have been altered had not Leavitt suggested that they file for a code name. Leavitt stated that they had an organism and that it required a code. The others agreed.

In a corner of the room stood the scrambler typewriter. It had been clattering all day long, typing out material sent in from the outside. It was a two-way machine; material transmitted had to be typed in lowercase letters, while received material was printed out in capitals.

No one had really bothered to look at the input since their arrival on Level V. They were all too busy; besides, most of the input had been routine military dispatches that were sent to Wildfire but did not concern it. This was because Wildfire was one of the Cooler Circuit substations, known facetiously as the Top Twenty. These substations were linked to the basement of the White House and were the twenty most important strategic locations in the country. Other substations included Vandenberg, Kennedy, NORAD, Patterson, Detrick, and Virginia Key.

Stone went to the typewriter and printed out his message. The message was directed by computer to Central Codes, a station that handled the coding of all projects subsumed under the system of Cooler.

The transmission was as follows:

open line to transmit
UNDERSTAND TRANSMIT STATE ORIGIN
stone project wildfire
STATE DESTINATION
central codes

UNDERSTAND CENTRAL CODES
message follows
SEND
have isolated extraterrestrial organism secondary to return of
scoop seven wish coding for organism
end message
TRANSMITTED

There followed a long pause. The scrambler teleprinter hummed and clicked, but printed nothing. Then the typewriter began to spit out a message on a long roll of paper.

MESSAGE FROM CENTRAL CODES FOLLOWS
UNDERSTAND ISOLATION OF NEW ORGANISM PLEASE
CHARACTERIZE
END MESSAGE

Stone frowned. 'But we don't know enough.' However, the teleprinter was impatient:

TRANSMIT REPLY TO CENTRAL CODES

After a moment, Stone typed back:

message to central codes follows
cannot characterize at this time but suggest
tentative classification as bacterial strain
end message

MESSAGE FROM CENTRAL CODES FOLLOWS

UNDERSTAND REQUEST FOR BACTERIAL CLASSIFICATION
OPENING NEW CATEGORY CLASSIFICATION ACCORDING TO
ICDA STANDARD REFERENCE
CODE FOR YOUR ORGANISM WILL BE ANDROMEDA
CODE WILL READ OUT ANDROMEDA STRAIN
FILED UNDER ICDA LISTINGS AS 053.9 [UNSPECIFIED ORGANISM]
FURTHER FILING AS E866 [AIRCRAFT ACCIDENT]
THIS FILING REPRESENTS CLOSEST FIT TO
ESTABLISHED CATEGORIES

Stone smiled. 'It seems we don't fit the established categories.'
He typed back:

understand coding as andromeda strain
accepted
end message
TRANSMITTED

'Well,' Stone said, 'that's that.'

Burton had been looking over the sheaves of paper behind the teleprinter. The teleprinter wrote its messages out on a long roll of paper, which fell into a box. There were dozens of yards of paper that no one had looked at.

Silently, he read a single message, tore it from the rest of the strip, and handed it to Stone.

1134/443/KK/Y-U/9
INFORMATION STATUS
TRANSMIT TO ALL STATIONS
CLASSIFICATION TOP SECRET

REQUEST FOR DIRECTIVE 7-12 RECEIVED TODAY BY
EXEC AND NSC-COBRA
ORIGIN VANDENBERG/WILDFIRE
CORROBORATION NASA/AMC
AUTHORITY PRIMARY MANCHEK, ARTHUR, MAJOR USA
IN CLOSED SESSION THIS DIRECTIVE HAS NOT
BEEN ACTED UPON
FINAL DECISION HAS BEEN POSTPONED TWENTY
FOUR TO FORTY EIGHT HOURS
RECONSIDERATION AT THAT TIME
ALTERNATIVE TROOP DEPLOYMENT ACCORDING TO
DIRECTIVE 7-11 NOW IN EFFECT
NO NOTIFICATION
END MESSAGE

TRANSMIT ALL STATIONS
CLASSIFICATION TOP SECRET
END TRANSMISSION

The team stared at the message in disbelief. No one said anything for a long time. Finally, Stone ran his fingers along the upper corner of the sheet and said in a low voice, 'This was a 443. That makes it an MCN transmission. It should have rung the bell down here.'

'There's no bell on this teleprinter,' Leavitt said. 'Only on Level I, at sector five. But they're supposed to notify us whenever –'

'Get sector five on the intercom,' Stone said.

Ten minutes later, the horrified Sergeant Morris had connected Stone to Robertson, the head of the President's Science Advisory Committee, who was in Houston.

Stone spoke for several minutes with Robertson, who expressed initial surprise that he hadn't heard from Wildfire earlier. There then followed a heated discussion of the President's decision not to call a Directive 7–12.

'The President doesn't trust scientists,' Robertson said. 'He doesn't feel comfortable with them.'

'It's your job to make him comfortable,' Stone said, 'and you haven't been doing it.'

'Jeremy –'

'There are only two sources of contamination,' Stone said. 'Piedmont, and this installation. We're adequately protected here, but Piedmont –'

'Jeremy, I agree the bomb should have been dropped.'

'Then work on him. Stay on his back. Get him to call a 7–12 as soon as possible. It may already be too late.'

Robertson said he would, and would call back. Before he hung up, he said, 'By the way, any thoughts about the Phantom?'

'The what?'

'The Phantom that crashed in Utah.'

There was a moment of confusion before the Wildfire group understood that they had missed still another important teleprinter message.

'Routine training mission. The jet strayed over the closed zone, though. That's the puzzle.'

'Any other information?'

'The pilot said something about his air hose dissolving. Vibration, or something. His last communication was pretty bizarre.'

'Like he was crazy?' Stone asked.

'Like that,' Robertson said.

'Is there a team at the wreck site now?'

'Yes, we're waiting for information from them. It could come at any time.'

'Pass it along,' Stone said. And then he stopped. 'If a 7–11 was ordered, instead of a 7-12,' he said, 'then you have troops in the area around Piedmont.'

'National Guard, yes.'

'That's pretty damned stupid,' Stone said.

'Look, Jeremy, I agree –'

'When the first one dies,' Stone said, 'I want to know when, and how. And most especially, *where.* The wind there is from the east predominantly. If you start losing men west of Piedmont –'

'I'll call, Jeremy,' Robertson said.

The conversation ended, and the team shuffled out of the conference room. Hall remained behind a moment, going through some of the rolls in the box, noting the messages. The majority were unintelligible to him, a weird set of nonsense messages and codes. After a time he gave up; he did so before he came upon the reprinted news item concerning the peculiar death of Officer Martin Willis, of the Arizona highway patrol.

day 4
SPREAD

22 The Analysis

With the new pressures of time, the results of spectrometry and amino-acid analysis, previously of peripheral interest, suddenly became matters of major concern. It was hoped that these analyses would tell, in a rough way, how foreign the Andromeda organism was to earth life forms.

It was thus with interest that Leavitt and Burton looked over the computer printout, a column of figures written on green paper:

MASS SPECTROMETRY DATA OUTPUT
PRINT
PERCENTAGE OUTPUT SAMPLE 1 – BLACK OBJECT UNIDENTIFIED ORIGIN –

H	HE								
21.07	0								
L1	BE	B	C	N	O	F			
0	0	0	54.90	0	18.00	0			
NA	MG	AL	SI	P	S	CL			
0	0	0	00.20	–	01.01	0			
K	CA	SC	TI	V	CR	MN	FE	CO	NI
0	0	0	–	–	–	–	–	–	–
CU	ZN	GA	GE	AS	SE	BR			
–	–	0	0	0	00.34	0			

ALL HEAVIER METALS SHOW ZERO CONTENT

SAMPLE 2 – GREEN OBJECT UNIDENTIFIED ORIGIN –

H	HE					
27.00	0					
L1	BE	B	C	N	O	F
0	0	0	45.00	05.00	23.00	0

ALL HEAVIER METALS SHOW ZERO CONTENT

END PRINT

END PROGRAM

–STOP–

What all this meant was simple enough. The black rock contained hydrogen, carbon, and oxygen, with significant amounts of sulfur, silicon, and selenium, and with trace quantities of several other elements.

The green spot, on the other hand, contained hydrogen, carbon, nitrogen, and oxygen. Nothing else at all. The two men found it peculiar that the rock and the green spot should be so similar in chemical makeup. And it was peculiar that the green spot should contain nitrogen, while the rock contained none at all.

The conclusion was obvious: the 'black rock' was not rock at all, but some kind of material similar to earthly organic life. It was something akin to plastic.

And the green spot, presumably alive, was composed of elements in roughly the same proportion as earth life. On earth, these same four elements – hydrogen, carbon, nitrogen, and oxygen – accounted for 99 per cent of all the elements in life organisms.

The men were encouraged by these results, which suggested similarity between the green spot and life on earth. Their hopes were, however, short-lived as they turned to the amino-acid analysis:

AMINO ACID ANALYSIS DATA OUTPUT
PRINT
SAMPLE 1 – BLACK OBJECT UNIDENTIFIED ORIGIN –
SAMPLE 2 – GREEN OBJECT UNIDENTIFIED ORIGIN –

	SAMPLE 1	SAMPLE 2
NEUTRAL AMINO ACIDS		
GLYCINE	00.00	00.00
ALANINE	00.00	00.00
VALINE	00.00	00.00
ISOLEUCINE	00.00	00.00
SERINE	00.00	00.00
THREONINE	00.00	00.00
LEUCINE	00.00	00.00
AROMATIC AMINO ACIDS		
PHENYLALANINE	00.00	00.00
TYROSINE	00.00	00.00
TRYPTOPHAN	00.00	00.00
SULFURIC AMINO ACIDS		
CYSTINE	00.00	00.00
CYSTEINE	00.00	00.00
METHIONINE	00.00	00.00

	SAMPLE 1	SAMPLE 2
SECONDARY AMINO ACIDS		
PROLINE	00.00	00.00
HYDROXYPROLINE	00.00	00.00
DICARBOXYLIC AMINO ACIDS		
ASPARTIC ACID	00.00	00.00
GLUTAMIC ACID	00.00	00.00
BASIC AMINO ACIDS		
HISTIDINE	00.00	00.00
ARGININE	00.00	00.00
LYSINE	00.00	00.00
HYDROXYLYSINE	00.00	00.00
TOTAL AMINO ACID CONTENT	00.00	00.00

END PRINT
END PROGRAM

–STOP–

'Christ,' Leavitt said, staring at the printed sheet. 'Will you look at that.'

'No amino acids,' Burton said. 'No proteins.'

'Life without proteins,' Leavitt said. He shook his head; it seemed as if his worst fears were realized.

On earth, organisms had evolved by learning to carry out biochemical reactions in a small space, with the help of protein enzymes. Biochemists were now learning to duplicate these reactions, but only by isolating a single reaction from all others.

Living cells were different. There, within a small area, reactions were carried out that provided energy, growth, and movement. There was no separation, and man could not duplicate this any more than a man could prepare a complete dinner from appetizers to dessert by mixing together the ingredients for everything into a single large dish, cooking it, and hoping to separate the apple pie from the cheese dip later on.

Cells could keep the hundreds of separate reactions straight, using enzymes. Each enzyme was like a single worker in a kitchen, doing just one thing. Thus a baker could not make a steak, any more than a steak griller could use his equipment to prepare appetizers.

But enzymes had a further use. They made possible chemical

reactions that otherwise would not occur. A biochemist could duplicate the reactions by using great heat, or great pressure, or strong acids. But the human body, or the individual cell, could not tolerate such extremes of environment. Enzymes, the matchmakers of life, helped chemical reactions to go forward at body temperature and atmospheric pressure.

Enzymes were essential to life on earth. But if another form of life had learned to do without them, it must have evolved in a wholly different way.

Therefore, they were dealing with an entirely alien organism.

And this in turn meant that analysis and neutralization would take much, much longer.

In the room marked MORPHOLOGY, Jeremy Stone removed the small plastic capsule in which the green fleck had been imbedded. He set the now-hard capsule into a vise, fixing it firmly, and then took a dental drill to it, shaving away the plastic until he exposed bare green material.

This was a delicate process, requiring many minutes of concentrated work. At the end of that time, he had shaved the plastic in such a way that he had a pyramid of plastic, with the green fleck at the peak of the pyramid.

He unscrewed the vise and lifted the plastic out. He took it to the microtome, a knife with a revolving blade that cut very thin slices of plastic and imbedded green tissue. These slices were round; they fell from the plastic block into a dish of water. The thickness of the slice could be measured by looking at the light as it reflected off the slices – if the light was faint silver, the slice was too thick. If, on the other hand, it was a rainbow of colors, then it was the right thickness, just a few molecules in depth.

That was how thick they wanted a slice of tissue to be for the electron microscope.

When Stone had a suitable piece of tissue, he lifted it carefully with forceps and set it onto a small round copper grid. This in turn was inserted into a metal button. Finally, the button was set into the electron microscope, and the microscope sealed shut.

The electron microscope used by Wildfire was the BVJ model JJ-42. It was a high-intensity model with an image resolution attachment. In principle, the electron microscope was simple enough: it worked exactly like a light microscope, but instead of focusing light rays, it focused an electron beam. Light is focused by lenses of curved glass. Electrons are focused by magnetic fields.

In many respects, the EM was not a great deal different from television, and in fact, the image was displayed on a television screen, a coated surface that glowed when electrons struck it. The great advantage of the electron microscope was that it could magnify objects far more than the light microscope. The reason for this had to do with quantum mechanics and the waveform theory of radiation. The best simple explanation had come from the electron microscopist Sidney Polton, also a racing enthusiast.

'Assume,' Polton said, 'that you have a road, with a sharp corner. Now assume that you have two automobiles, a sports car and a large truck. When the truck tries to go around the corner, it slips off the road; but the sports car manages it easily. Why? The sports car is lighter, and smaller, and faster; it is better suited to tight, sharp curves. On large, gentle curves, the automobiles will perform equally well, but on sharp curves, the sports car will do better.

'In the same way, an electron microscope will 'hold the road' better than a light microscope. All objects are made of corners, and edges. The electron wavelength is smaller than the quantum of light. It cuts the corners closer, follows the road better, and outlines it more precisely. With a light microscope – like a truck – you can follow only a large road. In microscopic terms this means only a large object, with large edges and gentle curves: cells, and nuclei. But an electron microscope can follow all the minor routes, the byroads, and can outline very small structures within the cell – micochondria, ribosomes, membranes, reticula.'

In actual practice there were several drawbacks to the electron microscope, which counterbalanced its great powers of magnification. For one thing, because it used electrons instead of light, the inside of the microscope had to be a vacuum. This meant it was impossible to examine living creatures.

But the most serious drawback had to do with the sections of specimen. These were extremely thin, making it difficult to get a good three-dimensional concept of the object under study.

Again, Polton had a simple analogy. 'Let us say you cut an automobile in half down the middle. In that case, you could guess the complete, 'whole' structure. But if you cut a very thin slice from the automobile, and if you cut it on a strange angle, it could be more difficult. In your slice, you might have only a bit of bumper, and rubber tire, and glass. From such a slice, it would be hard to guess the shape and function of the full structure.'

Stone was aware of all the drawbacks as he fitted the metal button into the EM, sealed it shut, and started the vacuum pump. He knew the drawbacks and he ignored them, because he had no choice. Limited as it was, the electron microscope was their only available high-power tool.

He turned down the room lights and clicked on the beam. He adjusted several dials to focus the beam. In a moment, the image came into focus, green and black on the screen.

It was incredible.

Jeremy Stone found himself staring at a single unit of the organism. It was a perfect, six-sided hexagon, and it interlocked with other hexagons on each side. The interior of the hexagon was divided into wedges, each meeting at the precise center of the structure. The overall appearance was accurate, with a kind of mathematical precision he did not associate with life on earth.

It looked like a crystal.

He smiled: Leavitt would be pleased: Leavitt liked spectacular, mind-stretching things. Leavitt had also frequently considered the possi-

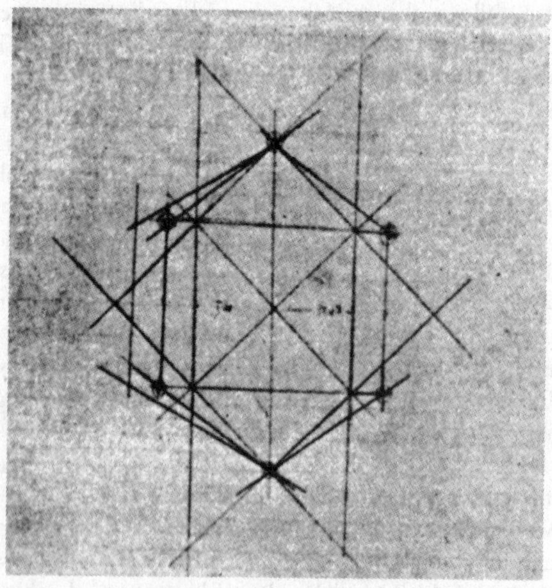

Early sketch by Jeremy Stone of hexagonal Andromeda configuration.

Photo courtesy Project Wildfire

bility that life might be based upon crystals of some kind, that it might be ordered in some regular pattern.

He decided to call Leavitt in.

As soon as he arrived, Leavitt said, 'Well, there's our answer.'

'Answer to what?'

'To how this organism functions. I've seen the results of spectrometry and amino-acid analysis.'

'And?'

'The organism is made of hydrogen, carbon, oxygen, and nitrogen. But it has no amino acids at all. None. Which means that it has no proteins as we know them, and no enzymes. I was wondering how it could survive without protein-based organization. Now I know.'

'The crystalline structure.'

'Looks like it,' Leavitt said, peering at the screen. 'In three dimensions, it's probably a hexagonal slab, like a piece of tile. Eight-sided, with each face a hexagon. And on the inside, those wedge-shaped compartments leading to the center.'

'They would serve to separate biochemical functions quite well.'

'Yes,' Leavitt said. He frowned.

'Something the matter?'

Leavitt was thinking, remembering something he had forgotten. A dream, about a house and a city. He thought for a moment and it began to come back to him. A house and a city. The way the house worked alone, and the way it worked in a city.

It all came back.

'You know,' he said, 'it's interesting, the way this one unit interlocks with the others around it.'

'You're wondering if we're seeing part of a higher organism?'

'Exactly. Is this unit self-sufficient, like a bacterium, or is it just a block from a larger organ, or a larger organism? After all, if you saw a single liver cell, could you guess what kind of an organ it came from? No. And what good would one brain cell be without the rest of the brain?'

Stone stared at the screen for a long time. 'A rather unusual pair of analogies. Because the liver can regenerate, can grow back, but the brain cannot.'

Leavitt smiled. 'The Messenger Theory.'

'One wonders,' Stone said.

The Messenger Theory had come from John R. Samuels, a communications engineer. Speaking before the Fifth Annual Conference on

Astronautics and Communication, he had reviewed some theories about the way in which an alien culture might choose to contact other cultures. He argued that the most advanced concepts in communications in earth technology were inadequate, and that advanced cultures would find better methods.

'Let us say a culture wishes to scan the universe,' he said.

'Let us say they wish to have a sort of 'coming-out party' on a galactic scale – to formally announce their existence. They wish to spew out information, clues to their existence, in every direction. What is the best way to do this? Radio? Hardly – radio is too slow, too expensive, and it decays too rapidly. Strong signals weaken within a few billion miles. TV is even worse. Light rays are fantastically expensive to generate. Even if one learned a way to detonate whole stars, to explode a sun as a kind of signal, it would be costly.

'Besides expense, all these methods suffer the traditional drawback to any radiation, namely decreasing strength with distance. A light bulb may be unbearably bright at ten feet; it may be powerful at a thousand feet; it may be visible at ten miles. But at a million miles, it is completely obscure, because radiant energy decreases according to the fourth power of the radius. A simple, unbeatable law of physics.

'So you do not use physics to carry your signal. You use biology. You create a communications system that does not diminish with distance, but rather remains as powerful a million miles away as it was at the source.

'In short, you devise an organism to carry your message. The organism would be self-replicating, cheap, and could be produced in fantastic numbers. For a few dollars, you could produce trillions of them, and send them off in all directions into space. They would be tough, hardy bugs, able to withstand the rigors of space, and they would grow and duplicate and divide. Within a few years, there would be countless numbers of these in the galaxy, speeding in all directions, waiting to contact life.

'And when they did? Each single organism would carry the potential to develop into a full organ, or a full organism. They would, upon contacting life, begin to grow into a complete communicating mechanism. It is like spewing out a billion brain cells, each capable of regrowing a complete brain under the proper circumstances. The newly grown brain would then speak to the new culture – informing it of the presence of the other, and announcing ways in which contact might be made.'

Samuels's theory of the Messenger Bug was considered amusing by practical scientists, but it could not be discounted now.

'Do you suppose,' Stone said, 'that it is already developing into some kind of organ of communication?'

'Perhaps the cultures will tell us more,' Leavitt said.

'Or X-ray crystallography,' Stone said. 'I'll order it now.'

Level V had facilities for X-ray crystallography, though there had been much heated discussion during Wildfire planning as to whether such facilities were necessary. X-ray crystallography represented the most advanced, complex, and expensive method of structural analysis in modern biology. It was a little like electron microscopy, but one step further along the line. It was more sensitive, and could probe deeper – but only at great cost in terms of time, equipment, and personnel.

The biologist R. A. Janek has said that 'increasing vision is increasingly expensive.' He meant by this that any machine to enable men to see finer or fainter details increased in cost faster than it increased in resolving power. This hard fact of research was discovered first by the astronomers, who learned painfully that construction of a two-hundred-inch telescope mirror was far more difficult and expensive than construction of a one-hundred-inch mirror.

In biology this was equally true. A light microscope, for example, was a small device easily carried by a technician in one hand. It could outline a cell, and for this ability a scientist paid about $1,000.

An electron microscope could outline small structures within the cell. The EM was a large console and cost up to $100,000.

In contrast, X-ray crystallography could outline individual molecules. It came as close to photographing atoms as science could manage. But the device was the size of a large automobile, filled an entire room, required specially trained operators, and demanded a computer for interpretation of results.

This was because X-ray crystallography did not produce a direct visual picture of the object being studied. It was not, in this sense, a microscope, and it operated differently from either the light or electron microscope.

It produced a diffraction pattern instead of an image. This appeared as a pattern of geometric dots, in itself rather mysterious, on a photographic plate. By using a computer, the pattern of dots could be analyzed and the structure deduced.

It was a relatively new science, retaining an old-fashioned name. Crystals were seldom used any more; the term 'X-ray crystallography' dated from the days when crystals were chosen as test objects. Crystals had regular structures and thus the pattern of dots resulting from a beam of X rays shot at a crystal were easier to analyze. But in recent years the X rays had been shot at irregular objects of varying sorts. The X rays were bounced off at different angles. A computer could 'read' the photographic plate and measure the angles, and from this work back to the shape of the object that had caused such a reflection.

The computer at Wildfire performed the endless and tedious calculations. All this, if done by manual human calculation, would take years, perhaps centuries. But the computer could do it in seconds.

'How are you feeling, Mr. Jackson?' Hall asked.

The old man blinked his eyes and looked at Hall, in his plastic suit.

'All right. Not the best, but all right.'

He gave a wry grin.

'Up to talking a little?'

'About what?'

'Piedmont.'

'What about it?'

'That night,' Hall said. 'The night it all happened.'

'Well, I tell you. I've lived in Piedmont all my life. Traveled a bit – been to LA, and even up to Frisco. Went as far east as St. Louis, which was far enough for me. But Piedmont, that's where I've lived. And I have to tell you –'

'The night it all happened,' Hall repeated.

He stopped, and turned his head away. 'I don't want to think about it,' he said.

'You have to think about it.'

'No.'

He continued to look away for a moment, and then turned back to Hall. 'They all died, did they?'

'Not all. One other survived.' He nodded to the crib next to Jackson.

Jackson peered over at the bundle of blankets. 'Who's that?'

'A baby.'

'Baby? Must be the Ritter child. Jamie Ritter. Real young, is it?'

'About two months.'

'Yep. That's him. A real little heller. Just like the old man. Old Ritter likes to kick up a storm, and his kid's the same way. Squalling morning, noon, and night. Family couldn't keep the windas open, on account of the squalling.'

'Is there anything else unusual about Jamie?'

'Nope. Healthy as a water buffalo, except he squalls. I remember he was squalling like the dickens that night.'

Hall said, 'What night?'

'The night Charley Thomas brought the damned thing in. We all seen it, of course. It came down like one of them shooting stars, all glowing, and landed just to the north. Everybody was excited, and Charley Thomas went off to get it. Came back about twenty minutes later with the thing in the back of his Ford station wagon. Brand-new wagon. He's real proud of it.'

'Then what happened?'

'Well, we all gathered around, looking at it. Reckoned it must be one of those space things. Annie figured it was from Mars, but you know how Annie is. Lets her mind carry her off, at times. The rest of us, we didn't feel it was no Martian thing, we just figured it was something sent up from Cape Canaveral. You know, that place in Florida where they shoot the rockets?'

'Yes. Go on.'

'So, once we figured that out good and proper, we didn't know what to do. Nothing like that ever happened in Piedmont, you know. I mean, once we had that tourist with the gun, shot up the Comanche Chief motel, but that was back in '48 and besides, he was just a GI had a little too much to drink, and there were exterminating circumstances. His gal run out on him while he was in Germany or some damn place. Nobody gave him a bad time; we understood how it was. But nothing happened since, really. Quiet town. That's why we like it, I reckon.'

'What did you do with the capsule?'

'Well, we didn't know what to do with it. Al, he said open 'er up, but we didn't figure that was right, especially since it might have some scientific stuff inside, so we thought awhile. And then Charley, who got it in the first place, Charley says, let's give it to Doc. That's Doc Benedict. He's the town doctor. Actually, he takes care of everybody around, even the Indians. But he's a good fella anyhow, and he's been to lots of schools. Got these degrees on the walls? Well, we figured Doc Benedict would know what to do with the thing. So we brought it to him.'

'And then?'

'Old Doc Benedict, he's not so old actually, he looks 'er over real careful, like it was his patient, and then he allows as how it might be a thing from space, and it might be one of ours, or it might be one of theirs. And he says he'll take care of it, and maybe make a few phone calls, and let everybody know in a few hours. See, Doc always played poker

Monday nights with Charley and Al and Herb Johnstone, over at Herb's place, and we figured that he'd spread the word around then. Besides, it was getting on suppertime and most of us were a bit hungry, so we all kind of left it with Doc.'

'When was that?'

'Bout seven-thirty or so.'

'What did Benedict do with the satellite?'

'Took it inside his house. None of us saw it again. It was about eight, eight-thirty that it all started up, you see. I was over at the gas station, having a chat with Al, who was working the pump that night. Chilly night, but I wanted a chat to take my mind off the pain. And to get some soda from the machine, to wash down the aspirin with. Also, I was thirsty, squeeze makes you right thirsty, you know.'

'You'd been drinking Sterno that day?'

'Bout six o'clock I had some, yes.'

'How did you feel?'

'Well, when I was with Al, I felt good. Little dizzy, and my stomach was paining me, but I felt good. And Al and me were sitting inside the office, you know, talking, and suddenly he shouts, "Oh God, my head!" He ups and runs outside, and falls down. Right there in the street, not a word from him.

'Well, I didn't know what to make of it. I figured he had a heart attack or a shock, but he was pretty young for that, so I went after him. Only he was dead. Then . . . they all started coming out. I believe Mrs. Langdon, the Widow Langdon, was next. After that, I don't recall, there was so many of them. Just pouring outside, it seemed like. And they just grab their chests and fall, like they slipped. Only they wouldn't get up afterward. And never a word from any of them.'

'What did you think?'

'I didn't know what to think, it was so damned peculiar. I was scared, I don't mind telling you, but I tried to stay calm. I couldn't, naturally. My old heart was thumping, and I was wheezin' and gaspin'. I was scared. I thought everybody was dead. Then I heard the baby crying, so I knew not *everybody* could be dead. And then I saw the General.'

'The General?'

'Oh, we just called him that. He wasn't no general, just been in the war, and liked to be remembered. Older'n me, he is. Nice fella, Peter Arnold. Steady as a rock all his life. and he's standing by the porch, all got up in his military clothes. It's dark, but there's a moon, and he sees me in the street and he says, "That you, Peter?" We both got the same name, see. And I says, "Yes it is." And he says, "What the hell's happening? Japs coming in?" And I think that's a mighty peculiar thing for him to be saying. And he says, "I think it must be the Japs, come to kill us all." And I say, "Peter, you gone loco?" And he says he don't feel too good and he goes inside. Course, he must have gone loco, 'cause he shot himself. But others went loco, too. It was the disease.'

'How do you know?'

'People don't burn themselves, or drown themselves, if they got sense, do they? All them in that town were good, normal folks until that night. Then they just seemed to go crazy.'

'What did you do?'

'I thought to myself, Peter, you're dreaming. You had too much to drink. So I went home and got into bed, and figured I'd be better in the morning. Only about ten o'clock, I hear a noise, and it's a car, so I go outside to see who it is. It's some kind of car, you know, one of those vans. Two fellers inside. I go up to them, and damn but they don't fall over dead. Scariest thing you ever saw. But it's funny.'

'What's funny?'

'That was the only other car to come through all night. Normally, there's lots of cars.'

'There was another car?'

'Yep. Willis, the highway patrol. He came through about fifteen, thirty seconds before it all started. Didn't stop, though; sometimes he doesn't. Depends if he's late on his schedule; he's got a regular patrol, you know, he has to stick to.'

Jackson sighed and let his head fall back against the pillow. 'Now,' he said, 'if you don't mind, I'm going to get me some sleep. I'm all talked out.'

He closed his eyes. Hall crawled back down the tunnel, out of the unit, and sat in the room looking through the glass at Jackson, and the baby in the crib alongside. He stayed there, just looking, for a long time.

23 Topeka

The room was huge, the size of a football field. It was furnished sparsely, just a few tables scattered about. Inside the room, voices echoed as the technicians called to each other, positioning the pieces of wreckage. The post team was reconstructing the wreck in this room, placing the clumps of twisted metal from the Phantom in the same positions as they had been found on the sand.

Only then would the intensive examination begin.

Major Manchek, tired, bleary-eyed, clutching his coffee cup, stood in a corner and watched. To him, there was something surrealistic about the scene: a dozen men in a long, whitewashed room in Topeka, rebuilding a crash.

One of the biophysicists came up to him, holding a clear plastic bag. He waved the contents under Manchek's nose.

'Just got it back from the lab,' he said.

'What is it?'

'You'll never guess.' The man's eyes gleamed in excitement.

All right, Manchek thought irritably, I'll never guess.

'What is it?'

'A depolymerized polymer,' the biochemist said, smacking his lips with satisfaction. 'Just back from the lab.'

'What kind of polymer?'

A polymer was a repeating molecule, built up from thousands of the same units, like a stack of dominos. Most plastics, nylon, rayon, plant cellulose, and even glycogen in the human body were polymers.

'A polymer of the plastic used on the air hose of the Phantom jet. The face mask to the pilot. We thought as much.'

Manchek frowned. He looked slowly at the crumbly black powder in the bag. 'Plastic?'

'Yes. A polymer, depolymerized. It was broken down. Now that's no vibration effect. It's a biochemical effect, purely organic.'

Slowly, Manchek began to understand. 'You mean something tore the plastic apart?'

'Yes, you could say that,' the biochemist replied. 'It's a simplification, of course, but –'

'What tore it apart?'

The biochemist shrugged. 'Chemical reaction of some sort. Acid could do it, or intense heat, or . . .'

'Or?'

'A microorganism, I suppose. If one existed that could eat plastic. If you know what I mean.'

'I think,' Manchek said, 'that I know what you mean.'

He left the room and went to the cable transmitter, located in another part of the building. He wrote out his message to the Wildfire group, and gave it to the technician to transmit. While he waited, he said, 'Has there been any reply yet?'

'Reply, sir?' the technician asked.

'From Wildfire,' Manchek said. It was incredible to him that no one had acted upon the news of the Phantom crash. It was so obviously linked . . .

'Wildfire, sir?' the technician asked.

Manchek rubbed his eyes. He was tired: he would have to remember to keep his big mouth shut.

'Forget it,' he said.

After his conversation with Peter Jackson, Hall went to see Burton. Burton was in the autopsy room, going over his slides from the day before.

Hall said, 'Find anything?'

Burton stepped away from the microscope and sighed. 'No. Nothing.'

'I keep wondering,' Hall said, 'about the insanity. Talking with Jackson reminded me of it. A large number of people in that town went insane – or at least became bizarre and suicidal – during the evening. Many of those people were old.'

Burton frowned. 'So?'

'Old people,' Hall said, 'are like Jackson. They have lots wrong with them. Their bodies are breaking down in a variety of ways. The lungs are bad. The hearts are bad. The livers are shot. The vessels are sclerotic.'

'And this alters the disease process?'

'Perhaps. I keep wondering, What makes a person become rapidly insane?'

Burton shook his head.

'And there's something else,' Hall said. 'Jackson recalls hearing one victim say, just before he died, "Oh God, my head." '

Burton stared away into space. 'Just before death?'

'Just before.'

'You're thinking of hemorrhage?'

Hall nodded. 'It makes sense,' he said. 'At least to check.'

If the Andromeda Strain produced hemorrhage inside the brain for any reason, then it might produce rapid, unusual mental aberrations.

'But we already know the organism acts by clotting –'

'Yes,' Hall said, 'in most people. Not all. Some survive, and some go mad.'

Burton nodded. He suddenly became excited. Suppose that the organism acted by causing damage to blood vessels. This damage would initiate clotting. Anytime the wall of a blood vessel was torn, or cut, or burned, then the clotting sequence would begin. First platelets would clump around the injury, protecting it, preventing blood loss. Then red cells would accumulate. Then a fibrin mesh would bind all the elements together. And finally, the clot would become hard and firm.

That was the normal sequence.

But if the damage was extensive, if it began at the lungs and worked its way . . .

'I'm wondering,' Hall said, 'if our organism attacks vessel walls. If so, it would initiate clotting. But if clotting were prevented in certain persons, then the organism might eat away and cause hemorrhage in those persons.'

'And insanity,' Burton said, hunting through his slides. He found three of the brain, and checked them.

No question.

The pathology was striking. Within the internal layer of cerebral vessels were small deposits of green. Burton had no doubt that, under higher magnification, they would turn out to be hexagonal in shape.

Quickly, he checked the other slides, for vessels in lung, liver, and spleen. In several instances he found green spots in the vessel walls, but never in the profusion he found for cerebral vessels.

Obviously the Andromeda Strain showed a predilection for cerebral vasculature. It was impossible to say why, but it was known that the cerebral vessels are peculiar in several respects. For instance, under circumstances in which normal body vessels dilate or contract – such as extreme cold, or exercise – the brain vasculature does not change, but maintains a steady, constant blood supply to the brain.

In exercise, the blood supply to muscle might increase five to twenty times. But the brain always has a steady flow: whether its owner is taking an exam or a nap, chopping wood or watching TV. The brain receives the same amount of blood every minute, hour, day.

The scientists did not know why this should be, or how, precisely, the cerebral vessels regulate themselves. But the phenomenon is known to exist, and cerebral vessels are regarded as a special case among the body's arteries and veins. Clearly, something is different about them.

And now there was an example of an organism that destroyed them preferentially.

But as Burton thought about it, the action of Andromeda did not seem so unusual. For example, syphilis causes an inflammation of the aorta, a very specific, peculiar reaction. Schistosomiasis, a parasitic infection, shows a preference for bladder, intestine, or colonic vessels – depending on the species. So such specificity was not impossible.

'But there's another problem,' he said. 'In most people, the organism begins clotting at the lungs. We know that. Presumably vessel destruction begins there as well. What is different about –'

He stopped.

He remembered the rats he had anticoagulated. The ones who had died anyway, but had no autopsies.

'My God,' he said.

He drew out one of the rats from cold storage and cut it open. It bled. Quickly he incised the head, exposing the brain. There he found a large hemorrhage over the gray surface of the brain.

'You've got it,' Hall said.

'If the animal is normal, it dies from coagulation, beginning at the lungs. But if coagulation is prevented, then the organism erodes through the vessels of the brain, and hemorrhage occurs.'

'And insanity.'

'Yes.' Burton was now very excited. 'And coagulation could be prevented by any blood disorder. Or too little vitamin K. Malabsorption syndrome. Poor liver function. Impaired protein synthesis. Any of a dozen things.'

'All more likely to be found in an old person,' Hall said.

'Did Jackson have any of those things?'

Hall took a long time to answer, then finally said, 'No. He has liver disease, but not significantly.'

Burton sighed. 'Then we're back were we started.'

'Not quite. Because Jackson and the baby both survived. They didn't hemorrhage – as far as we know – they survived untouched. Completely untouched.'

'Meaning?'

'Meaning that they somehow prevented the primary process, which is invasion of the organism into the vessel walls of the body. The Andromeda organism didn't get to the lungs, or the brain. It didn't get anywhere.'

'But why?'

'We'll know that,' Hall said, 'when we know why a sixty-nine-year-old Sterno drinker with an ulcer is like a two-month-old baby.'

'They seem pretty much opposites,' Burton said.

'They do, don't they?' Hall said. It would be hours before he realized Burton had given him the answer to the puzzle – but an answer that was worthless.

24 Evaluation

Sir Winston Churchill once said that 'true genius resides in the capacity for evaluation of uncertain, hazardous, and conflicting information.' Yet it is a peculiarity of the Wildfire team that, despite the individual brilliance of team members, the group grossly misjudged their information at several points.

One is reminded of Montaigne's acerbic comment: 'Men under stress are fools, and fool themselves.' Certainly the Wildfire team was under severe stress, but they were also prepared to make mistakes. They had even predicted that this would occur.

What they did not anticipate was the magnitude, the staggering dimensions of their error. They did not expect that their ultimate error would be a compound of a dozen small clues that were missed, a handful of crucial facts that were dismissed.

The team had a blind spot, which Stone later expressed this way: 'We were problem-oriented. Everything we did and thought was directed toward finding a solution, a cure to Andromeda. And, of course, we were fixed on the events that had occurred at Piedmont. We felt that if we did not find a solution, no solution would be forthcoming, and the whole world would ultimately wind up like Piedmont. We were very slow to think otherwise.'

The error began to take on major proportions with the cultures.

Stone and Leavitt had taken thousands of cultures from the original capsule. These had been incubated in a wide variety of atmospheric, temperature, and pressure conditions. The results of this could only be analyzed by computer.

Using the GROWTH/TRANSMATRIX program, the computer did not print out results from all possible growth combinations. Instead, it printed out only significant positive and negative results. It did this after first weighing each petri dish, and examining any growth with its photoelectric eye.

When Stone and Leavitt went to examine the results, they found several striking trends. Their first conclusion was that growth media did not matter at all – the organism grew equally well on sugar, blood, chocolate, plain agar, or sheer glass.

However, the gases in which the plates were incubated were crucial, as was the light.

Ultraviolet light stimulated growth under all circumstances. Total darkness, and to a lesser extent infrared light, inhibited growth.

Oxygen inhibited growth in all circumstances, but carbon dioxide stimulated growth. Nitrogen had no effect.

Thus, best growth was achieved in 100 per cent carbon dioxide, lighted by ultraviolet radiation. Poorest growth occurred in pure oxygen, incubated in total darkness.

'What do you make of it?' Stone said.

'It looks like a pure conversion system,' Leavitt said.

'I wonder,' Stone said.

He punched through the coordinates of a closed-growth system. Closed-growth systems studied bacterial metabolism by measuring intake of gases and nutrients, and output of waste products. They were completely sealed and self-contained. A plant in such a system, for example, would consume carbon dioxide and give off water and oxygen.

But when they looked at the Andromeda Strain, they found something remarkable. The organism had no excretions. If incubated with carbon dioxide and ultraviolet light, it grew steadily until all carbon dioxide had been consumed. Then growth stopped. There was no excretion of any kind of gas or waste product at all.

No waste.

'Clearly efficient,' Stone said.

'You'd expect that,' Leavitt said.

This was an organism highly suited to its environment. It consumed everything, wasted nothing. It was perfect for the barren existence of space.

He thought about this for a moment, and then it hit him. It hit Leavitt at the same time.

'Good Christ.'

Leavitt was already reaching for the phone. 'Get Robertson,' he said. 'Get him immediately.'

'Incredible,' Stone said softly. 'No waste. It doesn't require growth media. It can grow in the presence of carbon, oxygen, and sunlight. Period.'

'I hope we're not too late,' Leavitt said, watching the computer console screen impatiently.

Stone nodded. 'If this organism is really converting matter to energy, and energy to matter – directly – then it's functioning like a little reactor.'

'And an atomic detonation . . .'

'Incredible,' Stone said. 'Just incredible.'

```
000000000000000000000000000000000000000000000000000000000000000000000000000000000000000000000000
000000000000000000000000000000......................00000000000000000000000000000000000000000000
000000000000000000000000000.............................0000000000000000000000000000000000000000
00000000000000000000000..................112211.............000000000000000000000000000000000000
000000000000000000000...................112332111.............0000000000000000000000000000000000
0000000000000000000......................11223211...............00000000000000000000000000000000
000000000000000000..........................11221................0000000000000000000000000000000
0000000000000000..............................11...................00000000000000000000000000000
000000000000000....................................................00000000000000000000000000000
000000000000000.....................................................0000000000000000000000000000
000000000000000......................................................000000000000000000000000000
000000000000000................11.....................................000000000000000000000000000
000000000000000..............112221..................................000000000000000000000000000
000000000000000............11234432221...............................000000000000000000000000000
000000000000000...........1223456776543221...........................000000000000000000000000000
0000000000000000..........1223456788776543211.......................0000000000000000000000000000
0000000000000000..........12334567899876543221......................0000000000000000000000000000
00000000000000000........1123445567889987654321.....................0000000000000000000000000000
00000000000000000.........1234556788987654321......................00000000000000000000000000000
000000000000000000...........1123567767854221...................00000000000000000000000000000000
00000000000000000000.........11234564321.......................000000000000000000000000000000000
00000000000000000000000.......123221.........................00000000000000000000000000000000000
0000000000000000000000000.......1221......................00000000000000000000000000000000000000
00000000000000000000000000000..11.....................000000000000000000000000000000000000000000
0000000000000000000000000000000000...............00000000000000000000000000000000000000000000000
000000000000000000000000000000000000000000000000000000000000000000000000000000000000000000000000
```

CULTURE DESIG - 779.223,187.
ANDROMEDA
MEDIA DESIG - 779
ATMOSPHERE DESIG - 223
LUMIN DESIG - L87 UV/HI
FINAL SCANNER PRINT

An example of a scanner printout from the photoelectric eye that examined all growth media. Within the circular petri dish the computer has noted the presence of two separate colonies. The colonies are 'read' in two-millimeter-square segments, and graded by density on a scale from one to nine.

The screen came to life; they saw Robertson, looking tired, smoking a cigarette.

'Jeremy, you've got to give me time. I haven't been able to get through to –'

'Listen,' Stone said, 'I want you to make sure Directive 7–12 is not carried out. It is imperative: no atomic device must be detonated around the organisms. That's the last thing in the world, literally, that we want to do.'

He explained briefly what he had found.

Robertson whistled. 'We'd just provide a fantastically rich growth medium.'

'That's right,' Stone said.

The problem of a rich growth medium was a peculiarly distressing one to the Wildfire team. It was known, for example, that checks and balances exist in the normal environment. These manage to dampen the exuberant growth of bacteria.

The mathematics of uncontrolled growth are frightening. A single cell of the bacterium *E. coli* would, under ideal circumstances, divide every twenty minutes. That is not particularly disturbing until you think about it, but the fact is that bacteria multiply geometrically: one becomes two, two become four, four become eight, and so on. In this way, it can be shown that in a single day, one cell of *E. coli* could produce a supercolony equal in size and weight to the entire planet earth.

This never happens, for a perfectly simple reason: growth cannot continue indefinitely under 'ideal circumstances.' Food runs out. Oxygen runs out. Local conditions within the colony change, and check the growth of organisms.

On the other hand, if you had an organism that was capable of directly converting matter to energy, and if you provided it with a huge rich source of energy, like an atomic blast . . .

'I'll pass along your recommendation to the President,' Robertson said. 'He'll be pleased to know he made the right decision on the 7–12.'

'You can congratulate him on his scientific insight,' Stone said, 'for me.'

Robertson was scratching his head. 'I've got some more data on the Phantom crash. It was over the area west of Piedmont at twenty-three thousand feet. The post team has found evidence of the disintegration the pilot spoke of, but the material that was destroyed was a plastic of some kind. It was depolymerized.'

'What does the post team make of that?'

'They don't know what the hell to make of it,' Robertson admitted.

'And there's something else. They found a few pieces of bone that have been identified as human. A bit of humerus and tibia. Notable because they are clean – almost polished.'

'Flesh burned away?'

'Doesn't look that way,' Robertson said.

Stone frowned at Leavitt.

'What *does* it look like?'

'It looks like clean, polished bone,' Robertson said. 'They say it's weird as hell. And there's something else. We checked into the National Guard around Piedmont. The 112th is stationed in a hundred-mile radius, and it turns out they've been running patrols into the area for a distance of fifty miles. They've had as many as one hundred men west of Piedmont. No deaths.'

'None? You're quite sure?'

'Absolutely.'

'Were there men on the ground in the area the Phantom flew over?'

'Yes. Twelve men. They reported the plane to the base, in fact.'

Leavitt said, 'Sounds like the plane crash is a fluke.'

Stone nodded. To Robertson: 'I'm inclined to agree with Peter. In the absence of fatalities on the ground . . .'

'Maybe it's only in the upper air.'

'Maybe. But we know at least this much: we know how Andromeda kills. It does so by coagulation. Not disintegration, or bone-cleaning, or any other damned thing. By coagulation.'

'All right,' Robertson said, 'let's forget the plane for the time being.'

It was on that note that the meeting ended.

Stone said, 'I think we'd better check our cultured organisms for biologic potency.'

'Run some of them against a rat?'

Stone nodded. 'Make sure it's still virulent. Still the same.'

Leavitt agreed. They had to be careful the organism didn't mutate, didn't change to something radically different in its effects.

As they were about to start, the Level V monitor clicked on and said, 'Dr. Leavitt. Dr. Leavitt.'

Leavitt answered. On the computer screen was a pleasant young man in a white lab coat.

'Yes?'

'Dr. Leavitt, we have gotten our electroencephalograms back from the computer center. I'm sure it's all a mistake, but . . .'

His voice trailed off.

'Yes?' Leavitt said. 'Is something wrong?'

'Well, sir, yours were read as grade four, atypical, probably benign. But we would like to run another set.'

Stone said, 'It must be a mistake.'

'Yes,' Leavitt said. 'It must be.'

'Undoubtedly, sir,' the man said. 'But we would like another set of waves to be certain.'

'I'm rather busy now,' Leavitt said.

Stone broke in, talking directly to the technician. 'Dr. Leavitt will get a repeat EEG when he has the chance.'

'Very good, sir,' the technician said.

When the screen was blank, Stone said, 'There are times when this damned routine gets on anybody's nerves.'

Leavitt said, 'Yes.'

They were about to begin biologic testing of the various culture media when the computer flashed that preliminary reports from X-ray crystallography were prepared. Stone and Leavitt left the room to check the results, delaying the biologic tests of media. This was a most unfortunate decision, for had they examined the media, they would have seen that their thinking had already gone astray, and that they were on the wrong track.

25 Willis

X-ray crystallography analysis showed that the Andromeda organism was not composed of component parts, as a normal cell was composed of nucleus, mitochondria, and ribosomes. Andromeda had no subunits, no smaller particules. Instead, a single substance seemed to form the walls and interior. This substance produced a characteristic precession photograph, or scatter pattern of X rays.

Looking at the results, Stone said, 'A series of six-sided rings.'

'And nothing else,' Leavitt said. 'How the hell does it operate?'

The two men were at a loss to explain how so simple an organism could utilize energy for growth.

'A rather common ring structure,' Leavitt said. 'A phenolic group, nothing more. It should be reasonably inert.'

'Yet it can convert energy to matter.'

Leavitt scratched his head. He thought back to the city analogy, and the brain-cell analogy. The molecule was simple in its building blocks. It possessed no remarkable powers, taken as single units. Yet collectively, it had great powers.

'Perhaps there is a critical level,' he suggested. 'A structural complexity that makes possible what is not possible in a similar but simple structure.'

'The old chimp-brain argument,' Stone said.

Leavitt nodded. As nearly as anyone could determine, the chimp brain was as complex as the human brain. There were minor differences in structure, but the major difference was size – the human brain was larger, with more cells, more interconnections.

And that, in some subtle way, made the human brain different. (Thomas Waldren, the neurophysiologist, once jokingly noted that the major difference between the chimp and human brain was that 'we can use the chimp as an experimental animal, and not the reverse.')

Stone and Leavitt puzzled over the problem for several minutes until they came to the Fourier electron-density scans. Here, the probability of finding electrons was mapped for the structure on a chart that resembled a topological map.

They noticed something odd. The structure was present but the Fourier mapping was inconstant.

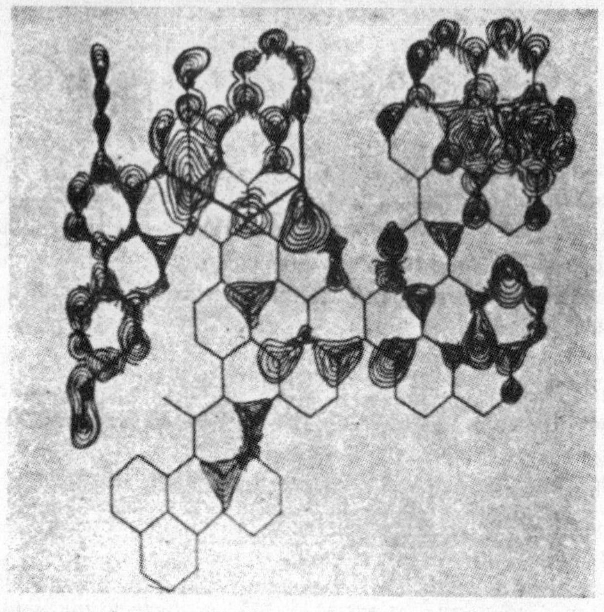

Electron-density mapping of Andromeda structure as derived from micrographic studies. It was this mapping which disclosed activity variations within an otherwise uniform structure.
Photo courtesy Project Wildfire

'It almost looks,' Stone said, 'as if part of the structure is switched off in some way.'

'It's not uniform after all,' Leavitt said.

Stone sighed, looking at the map. 'I wish to hell,' he said, 'that we'd brought a physical chemist along on the team.'

Unspoken was the added comment, 'instead of Hall.'

Tired, Hall rubbed his eyes and sipped the coffee, wishing he could have sugar. He was alone in the cafeteria, which was silent except for the muted ticking of the teleprinter in the corner.

After a time he got up and went over to the teleprinter, examining the rolls of paper that had come from it. Most of the information was meaningless to him.

But then he saw one item which had come from the DEATHMATCH program. DEATHMATCH was a news-scanning computer program that recorded all significant deaths according to whatever criterion the computer was fed. In this case, the computer was alerted to pick up all deaths in the Arizona-Nevada-California area, and to print them back.

The item he read might have gone unnoticed, were it not for Hall's conversation with Jackson. At the time, it had seemed like a pointless conversation to Hall, productive of little and consuming a great deal of time.

But now, he wondered.

```
PRINT PROGRAM
DEATHMATCH
DEATHMATCH/998
SCALE 7,Y,0. X,4,0
PRINT AS
ITEM FROM ASSOCIATED PRESS VERBATIM 778-778

BRUSH RIDGE, ARIZ. – – – ,: An Arizona highway patrol officer was
allegedly involved in the death today of five persons in a highway diner.
Miss Sally Conover, waitress at the Dine-eze diner on Route 15, ten miles
south of Flagstaff, was the sole survivor of the incident.

    Miss Conover told investigators that at 2:40 a.m., Officer Martin Willis
entered the diner and ordered coffee and donut. Officer Willis had
frequently visited the diner in the past. After eating, he stated that he had
a severe headache and that 'his ulcer was acting up.' Miss Conover gave
him two aspirin and a tablespoon of bicarbonate of soda. According to her
statement, Officer Willis then looked suspiciously at the other people in
the diner and whispered, 'They're after me.'

    Before the waitress could reply, Willis took out his revolver and shot
the other customers in the diner, moving methodically from one to the
next, shooting each in the forehead. Then, he allegedly turned to Miss
Conover and, smiling, said 'I love you, Shirley Temple,' placed the barrel
in his mouth, and fired the last bullet.

    Miss Conover was released by police here after questioning. The
names of the deceased customers are not known at this time.

END ITEM VERBATIM
END PRINT
END PROGRAM

TERMINATE
```

Hall remembered that Officer Willis had gone through Piedmont earlier in the evening – just a few minutes before the disease broke out. He had gone through without stopping.

And had gone mad later on.

Connection?

He wondered. There might be. Certainly, he could see many similarities: Willis had an ulcer, had taken aspirin, and had, eventually, committed suicide.

That didn't prove anything, of course. It might be a wholly unrelated series of events. But it was certainly worth checking.

He punched a button on the computer console. The TV screen lighted and a girl at a switchboard, with a headset pressing down her hair, smiled at him.

'I want the chief medical officer for the Arizona highway patrol. The western sector, if there is one.'

'Yes sir,' she said briskly.

A few moments later, the screen came back on. It was the operator. 'We have a Dr. Smithson who is the medical officer for the Arizona highway patrol west of Flagstaff. He has no television monitor but you can speak to him on audio.'

'Fine,' Hall said.

There was a crackling, and a mechanical hum. Hall watched the screen, but the girl had shut down her own audio and was busy answering another call from elsewhere in the Wildfire station. While he watched her, he heard a deep, drawling voice ask tentatively, 'Anyone there?'

'Hello, Doctor,' Hall said. 'This is Dr. Mark Hall, in . . . Phoenix. I'm calling for some information about one of your patrolmen, Officer Willis.'

'The girl said it was some government thing,' Smithson drawled. 'That right?'

'That is correct. We require –'

'Dr. Hall,' Smithson said, still drawling, 'perhaps you'd identify yourself and your agency.'

It occurred to Hall that there was probably a legal problem involved in Officer Willis's death. Smithson might be worried about that.

Hall said, 'I am not at liberty to tell you exactly what it is –'

'Well, look here, Doctor. I don't give out information over the phone, and especially I don't when the feller at the other end won't tell me what it's all about.'

Hall took a deep breath. 'Dr. Smithson, I must ask you –'

'Ask all you want. I'm sorry, I simply won't –'

At that moment, a bell sounded on the line, and a flat mechanical voice said:

'Attention please. This is a recording. Computer monitors have analyzed cable properties of this communication and have determined that the communication is being recorded by the outside party. All parties should be informed that the penalty for outside recording of a classified government communication is a minimum of five years' prison sentence. If the recording is continued this connection will automatically be broken. This is a recording. Thank you.'

There was a long silence. Hall could imagine the surprise Smithson was feeling; he felt it himself.

'What the hell kind of a place are you calling from, anyhow?' Smithson said, finally.

'Turn it off,' Hall said.

There was a pause, a click, then: 'All right. It's off.'

'I am calling from a classified government installation,' Hall said.

'Well, look here, mister –'

'Let me be perfectly plain, Hall said. 'This is a matter of considerable importance and it concerns Officer Willis. No doubt there's a court inquiry pending on him, and no doubt you'll be involved. We may be able to demonstrate that Officer Willis was not responsible for his actions, that he was suffering from a purely medical problem. But we can't do that unless you tell us what you know about his medical status. And if you don't tell us, Dr. Smithson, and tell us damned fast, we can have you locked away for twelve years for obstructing an official government inquiry. I don't care whether you believe that or not. I'm telling you, and you'd better believe it.'

There was a very long pause, and finally the drawl: 'No need to get excited, Doctor. Naturally, now that I understand the situation –'

'Did Willis have an ulcer?'

'Ulcer? No. That was just what he said, or was reported to have said. He never had an ulcer that I know of.'

'Did he have any medical problem?'

'Diabetes,' Smithson said.

'Diabetes?'

'Yeah. And he was pretty casual about it. We diagnosed him five, six years ago, at the age of thirty. Had a pretty severe case. We put him on insulin, fifty units a day, but he was casual, like I said. Showed up in the hospital once or twice in coma, because he wouldn't take his insulin. Said he hated the needles. We almost put him off the force, because we were afraid to let him drive a car – thought he'd go into acidosis at the wheel and conk out. We scared him plenty and he promised to go straight. That was three years ago, and as far as I know, he took his insulin regularly from then on.'

'You're sure of that?'

'Well, I think so. But the waitress at that restaurant, Sally Conover, told one of our investigators that she figured Willis had been drinking, because she could smell liquor on his breath. And I know for a fact that Willis never touched a drop in his life. He was one of these real religious fellows. Never smoked and never drank. Always led a clean life. That was why his diabetes bothered him so: he felt he didn't deserve it.'

Hall relaxed in his chair. He was getting near now, coming closer. The answer was within reach; the final answer, the key to it all.

'One last question,' Hall said. 'Did Willis go through Piedmont on the night of his death?'

'Yes. He radioed in. He was a little behind schedule, but he passed through. Why? Is it something about the government tests being held there?'

'No,' Hall said, but he was sure Smithson didn't believe him.

'Well, listen, we're stuck here with a bad case, and if you have any information which would –'

'We will be in touch,' Hall promised him, and clicked off.

The girl at the switchboard came back on.

'Is your call completed, Dr. Hall?'

'Yes. But I need information.'

'What kind of information?'

'I want to know if I have the authority to arrest someone.'

'I will check, sir. What is the charge?'

'No charge. Just to hold someone.'

There was a moment while she looked over at her computer console.

'Dr. Hall, you may authorize an official Army interview with anyone involved in project business. This interview may last up to forty-eight hours.'

'All right,' Hall said. 'Arrange it.'

'Yes sir. Who is the person?'

'Dr. Smithson,' Hall said.

The girl nodded and the screen went blank. Hall felt sorry for Smithson, but not very sorry; the man would have a few hours of sweating, but nothing more serious than that. And it was essential to halt rumors about Piedmont.

He sat back in his chair and thought about what he had learned. He was excited, and felt on the verge of an important discovery.

Three people:

A diabetic in acidosis, from failure to take insulin.

An old man who drank Sterno and took aspirin, also in acidosis.

A young infant.

One had survived for hours, the other two had survived longer, apparently permanently. One had gone mad, the other two had not. Somehow, they were all interrelated.

In a very simple way.

Acidosis. Rapid breathing. Carbon-dioxide content. Oxygen saturation. Dizziness. Fatigue. Somehow they were all logically coordinated. And they held the key to beating Andromeda.

At that moment, the emergency bell sounded, ringing in a high-pitched, urgent way as the bright-yellow light began to flash.

He jumped up and left the room.

26 The Seal

In the corridor, he saw the flashing sign that indicated the source of the trouble: AUTOPSY. Hall could guess the problem – somehow the seals had been broken, and contamination had occurred. That would sound the alarm.

As he ran down the corridor, a quiet, soothing voice on the loudspeakers said, 'Seal has been broken in Autopsy. Seal has been broken in Autopsy. This is an emergency.'

His lab technician came out of the lab and saw him. 'What is it?'

'Burton, I think. Infection spread.'

'Is he all right?'

'Doubt it,' Hall said, running. She ran with him.

Leavitt came out of the MORPHOLOGY room and joined them, sprinting down the corridor, around the gentle curves. Hall thought to himself that Leavitt was moving quite well, for an older man, when suddenly Leavitt stopped.

He stood riveted to the ground. And stared straight forward at the flashing sign, and the light above it, blinking on and off.

Hall looked back. 'Come on,' he said.

Then the technician: 'Dr. Hall, he's in trouble.'

Leavitt was not moving. He stood, eyes open, but otherwise he might have been asleep. His arms hung loosely at his sides.

'Dr. Hall.'

Hall stopped, and went back.

'Peter, boy, come on, we need your –'

He said nothing more, for Leavitt was not listening. He was staring straight forward at the blinking light. When Hall passed his hand in front of his face, he did not react. And then Hall remembered the other blinking lights, the lights Leavitt had turned away from, had joked off with stories.

'The son of a bitch,' Hall said. 'Now, of all times.'

'What is it?' the technician said.

A small dribble of spittle was coming from the corner of Leavitt's mouth. Hall quickly stepped behind him and said to the technician, 'Get in front of him and cover his eyes. Don't let him look at the blinking light.'

'Why?'

'Because it's blinking three times a second,' Hall said.

'You mean –'

'He'll go any minute now.'

Leavitt went.

With frightening speed, his knees gave way and he collapsed to the floor. He lay on his back and his whole body began to vibrate. It began with his hands and feet, then involved his entire arms and legs, and finally his whole body. He clenched his teeth and gave a gasping, loud cry. His head hammered against the floor; Hall slipped his foot beneath the back of Leavitt's head and let him bang against his toes. It was better than having him hit the hard floor.

'Don't try to open his mouth,' Hall said. 'You can't do it. He's clenched tight.'

As they watched, a yellow stain began to spread at Leavitt's waist.

'He may go into status,' Hall said. 'Go to the pharmacy and get me a hundred milligrams of phenobarb. Now. In a syringe. We'll get him onto Dilantin later, if we have to.'

Leavitt was crying, through his clenched teeth, like an animal. His body rapped like a tense rod against the floor.

A few moments later, the technician came back with the syringe. Hall waited until Leavitt relaxed, until his body stopped its seizures, and then he injected the barbiturate.

'Stay with him,' he said to the girl. 'If he has another seizure, just do what I did – put your foot under his head. I think he'll be all right. Don't try to move him.'

And Hall ran down to the autopsy lab.

For several seconds, he tried to open the door to the lab, and then he realized it had been sealed off. The lab was contaminated. He went on to main control, and found Stone looking at Burton through the closed-circuit TV monitors.

Burton was terrified. His face was white and he was breathing in rapid, shallow gasps, and he could not speak. He looked exactly like what he was: a man waiting for death to strike him.

Stone was trying to reassure him. 'Just take it easy, boy. Take it easy. You'll be okay. Just take it easy.'

'I'm scared,' Burton said. 'Oh Christ, I'm scared . . .'

'Just take it easy,' Stone said in a soft voice. 'We know that Andromeda doesn't do well in oxygen. We're pumping pure oxygen through your lab now. For the moment, that should hold you.'

Stone turned to Hall. 'You took your time getting here. Where's Leavitt?'

'He fitted,' Hall said.

'What?'

'Your lights flash at three per second, and he had a seizure.'

'*What?*'

'Petit mal. It went on to a grand-mal attack: tonic clonic seizure, urinary incontinence, the whole bit. I got him onto phenobarb and came as soon as I could.'

'Leavitt has epilepsy?'

'That's right.'

Stone said, 'He must not have known. He must not have realized.'

And then Stone remembered the request for a repeat electroencephalogram.

'Oh,' Hall said, 'he knew, all right. He was avoiding flashing lights, which will bring on an attack. I'm sure he knew. I'm sure he has attacks where he suddenly doesn't know what happened to him, where he just loses a few minutes from his life and can't remember what went on.'

'Is he all right?'

'We'll keep him sedated.'

Stone said, 'We've got pure oxygen running into Burton. That should help him, until we know something more.' Stone flicked off the microphone button connecting voice transmission to Burton. 'Actually, it will take several minutes to hook in, but I've told him we've already started. He's sealed off in there, so the infection is stopped at that point. The rest of the base is okay, at least.'

Hall said, 'How did it happen? The contamination.'

'Seal must have broken,' Stone said. In a lower voice, he added, 'We knew it would, sooner or later. All isolation units break down after a certain time.'

Hall said, 'You think it was just a random event?'

'Yes,' Stone said. 'Just an accident. So many seals, so much rubber, of such-and-such a thickness. They'd all break, given time. Burton happened to be there when one went.'

Hall didn't see it so simply. He looked in at Burton, who was breathing rapidly, his chest heaving in terror.

Hall said, 'How long has it been?'

Stone looked up at the stop-clocks. The stop-clocks were special timing clocks that automatically cut in during emergencies. The stop-clocks were now timing the period since the seal broke.

'Four minutes.'

Hall said, 'Burton's still alive.'

'Yes, thank God.' And then Stone frowned. He realized the point.

'Why,' Hall said, '*is he still alive*?'

'The oxygen . . .'

'You said yourself the oxygen isn't running yet. What's protecting Burton?'

At that moment, Burton said over the intercom, 'Listen. I want you to try something for me.'

Stone flicked on the microphone. 'What?'

'Kalocin,' Burton said.

'No.' Stone's reaction was immediate.

'Dammit, it's my life.'

'No,' Stone said.

Hall said, 'Maybe we should try –'

'Absolutely not. We don't dare. Not even once.'

Kalocin was perhaps the best-kept American secret of the last decade. Kalocin was a drug developed by Jensen Pharmaceuticals in the spring of 1965, an experimental chemical designated UJ-44759W, or K-9 in the short abbreviation. It had been found as a result of routine screening tests employed by Jensen for all new compounds.

Like most pharmaceutical companies. Jensen tested all new drugs with a scatter approach, running the compounds through a standard battery of tests designed to pick up any significant biologic activity. These tests were run on laboratory animals – rats, dogs, and monkeys. There were twenty-four tests in all.

Jensen found something rather peculiar about K-9. It inhibited growth. An infant animal given the drug never attained full adult size.

This discovery prompted further tests, which produced even more intriguing results. The drug, Jensen learned, inhibited metaplasia, the shift of normal body cells to a new and bizarre form, a precursor to cancer. Jensen became excited, and put the drug through intensive programs of study.

By September 1965, there could be no doubt: Kalocin stopped cancer. Through an unknown mechanism, it inhibited the reproduction of the virus responsible for myelogenous leukemia. Animals taking the drug did not develop the disease, and animals already demonstrating the disease showed a marked regression as a result of the drug.

The excitement at Jensen could not be contained. It was soon recognized that the drug was a broad-spectrum antiviral agent. It killed the virus of polio, rabies, leukemia, and the common wart. And, oddly enough, Kalocin also killed bacteria.

And fungi.

And parasites.

Somehow, the drug acted to destroy all organisms built on a unicellular structure, or less. It had no effect on organ systems – groups of cells organized into larger units. The drug was perfectly selective in this respect.

In fact, Kalocin was the universal antibiotic. It killed everything, even the minor germs that caused the common cold. Naturally, there were side effects – the normal bacteria in the intestines were destroyed, so that all users of the drug experienced massive diarrhea – but that seemed a small price to pay for a cancer cure.

In December 1965, knowledge of the drug was privately circulated among government agencies and important health officials. And then for the first time, opposition to the drug arose. Many men, including Jeremy Stone, argued that the drug should be suppressed.

But the arguments for suppression seemed theoretical, and Jensen, sensing billions of dollars at hand, fought hard for a clinical test. Eventually the government, the HEW, the FDA, and others agreed with Jensen and sanctioned further clinical testing over the protests of Stone and others.

In February 1966, a pilot clinical trial was undertaken. It involved twenty patients with incurable cancer, and twenty normal volunteers from the Alabama state penitentiary. All forty subjects took the drug daily for one month. Results were as expected: normal subjects experienced unpleasant side effects, but nothing serious. Cancer patients showed striking remission of symptoms consistent with cure.

On March 1, 1966, the forty men were taken off the drug. Within six hours, they were all dead.

It was what Stone had predicted from the start. He had pointed out that mankind had, over centuries of exposure, developed a carefully regulated immunity to most organisms. On his skin, in the air, in his lungs, gut, and even bloodstream were hundreds of different viruses and bacteria. They were potentially deadly, but man had adapted to them over the years, and only a few could still cause disease.

All this represented a carefully balanced state of affairs. If you introduced a new drug that killed *all* bacteria, you upset the balance and undid the evolutionary work of centuries. And you opened the way to superinfection, the problem of new organisms, bearing new diseases.

Stone was right: the forty volunteers each had died of obscure and horrible diseases no one had ever seen before. One man experienced swelling of his body, from head to foot, a hot, bloated swelling until he suffocated from pulmonary edema. Another man fell prey to an organism that ate away his stomach in a matter of hours. A third was hit by a virus that dissolved his brain to a jelly.

And so it went.

Jensen reluctantly took the drug out of further study. The government, sensing that Stone had somehow understood what was happening, agreed to his earlier proposals, and viciously suppressed all knowledge and experimentation with the drug Kalocin.

And that was where the matter had rested for two years.

Now Burton wanted to be given the drug.

'No,' Stone said. 'Not a chance. It might cure you for a while, but you'd never survive later, when you were taken off.'

'That's easy for you to say, from where you are.'

'It's not easy for me to say. Believe me, it's not.' He put his hand over the microphone again. To Hall: 'We know that oxygen inhibits growth of the Andromeda Strain. That's what we'll give Burton. It will be good for him – make him a little giddy, a little relaxed, and slow his breathing down. Poor fellow is scared to death.'

Hall nodded. Somehow, Stone's phrase stuck in his mind: scared to death. He thought about it, and then began to see that Stone had hit upon something important. That phrase was a clue. It was the answer.

He started to walk away.

'Where are you going?'

'I've got some thinking to do.'

'About what?'

'About being scared to death.'

27 Scared to Death

Hall walked back to his lab and stared through the glass at the old man and the infant. He looked at the two of them and tried to think, but his brain was running in frantic circles. He found it difficult to think logically, and his earlier sensation of being on the verge of a discovery was lost.

For several minutes, he stared at the old man while brief images passed before him: Burton dying, his hand clutched to his chest. Los Angeles in panic, bodies everywhere, cars going haywire, out of control . . .

It was then that he realized that he, too, was scared. Scared to death. The words came back to him.

Scared to death.

Somehow, that was the answer.

Slowly, forcing his brain to be methodical, he went over it again.

A cop with diabetes. A cop who didn't take his insulin and had a habit of going into ketoacidosis.

An old man who drank Sterno, which gave him methanolism, and acidosis.

A baby, who did . . . what? What gave him acidosis?

Hall shook his head. Always, he came back to the baby, who was normal, not acidotic. He sighed.

Take it from the beginning, he told himself. Be logical. If a man has metabolic acidosis – any kind of acidosis – what does he do?

He has too much acid in his body. He can die from too much acid, just as if he had injected hydrochloric acid into his veins.

Too much acid meant death.

But the body could compensate. By breathing rapidly. Because in that manner, the lungs blew off carbon dioxide, and the body's supply of carbonic acid, which was what carbon dioxide formed in the blood, decreased.

A way to get rid of acid.

Rapid breathing.

And Andromeda? What happened to the organism, when you were acidotic and breathing fast?

Perhaps fast breathing kept the organism from getting into your lungs long enough to penetrate to blood vessels. Maybe that was the answer.

But as soon as he thought of it, he shook his head. No: something else. Some simple, direct fact. Something they had always known, but somehow never recognized.

The organism attacked through the lungs.

It entered the bloodstream.

It localized in the walls of arteries and veins, particularly of the brain.

It produced damage.

This led to coagulation. Which was dispersed throughout the body, or else led to bleeding, insanity, and death.

But in order to produce such rapid, severe damage, it would take many organisms. Millions upon millions, collecting in the arteries and veins. Probably you did not breathe in so many.

So they must multiply in the bloodstream.

At a great rate. A fantastic rate.

And if you were acidotic? Did that halt multiplication?

Perhaps.

Again, he shook his head. Because a person with acidosis like Willis or Jackson was one thing. But what about the baby?

The baby was normal. If it breathed rapidly, it would become alkalotic – basic, too little acid – not acidotic. The baby would go to the opposite extreme.

Hall looked through the glass, and as he did, the baby awoke. Almost immediately it began to scream, its face turning purple, the little eyes wrinkling, the mouth, toothless and smooth-gummed, shrieking.

Scared to death.

And then the birds, with the fast metabolic rate, the fast heart rates, the fast breathing rates. The birds, who did everything fast. They, too, survived.

Breathing fast?

Was it as simple as that?

He shook his head. It couldn't be.

He sat down and rubbed his eyes. He had a headache, and he felt tired. He kept thinking of Burton, who might die at any minute. Burton, sitting there in the sealed room.

Hall felt the tension was unbearable. He suddenly felt an overwhelming urge to escape it, to get away from everything.

The TV screen clicked on. His technician appeared and said, 'Dr. Hall, we have Dr. Leavitt in the infirmary.'

And Hall found himself saying, 'I'll be right there.'

*

He knew he was acting strangely. There was no reason to see Leavitt. Leavitt was all right, perfectly fine, in no danger. In going to see him, Hall knew that he was trying to forget the other, more immediate problems. As he entered the infirmary, he felt guilty.

His technician said, 'He's sleeping.'

'Post-ictal,' Hall said. Persons after a seizure usually slept.

'Shall we start Dilantin?'

'No. Wait and see. Perhaps we can hold him on phenobarb.'

He began a slow and meticulous examination of Leavitt. His technician watched him and said, 'You're tired.'

'Yes,' said Hall. 'It's past my bedtime.'

On a normal day, he would now be driving home on the expressway. So would Leavitt: going home to his family in Pacific Palisades. The Santa Monica Expressway.

He saw it vividly for a moment, the long lines of cars creeping slowly forward.

And the signs by the side of the road. Speed limit 65 maximum, 40 minimum. They always seemed like a cruel joke at rush hour.

Maximum and minimum.

Cars that drove slowly were a menace. You had to keep traffic moving at a fairly constant rate, little difference between the fastest and the slowest, and you had to . . .

He stopped.

'I've been an idiot,' he said.

And he turned to the computer.

In later weeks, Hall referred to it as his 'highway diagnosis.' The principle of it was so simple, so clear and obvious, he was surprised none of them had thought of it before.

He was excited as he punched in instructions for the GROWTH program into the computer; he had to punch in the directions three times; his fingers kept making mistakes.

At last the program was set. On the display screen, he saw what he wanted: growth of Andromeda as a function of pH, of acidity-alkalinity.

The results were quite clear.

The Andromeda Strain grew within a narrow range. If the medium for growth was too acid, the organism would not multiply. If it was too basic, it would not multiply. Only within the range of pH 7.39 to 7.42 would it grow well.

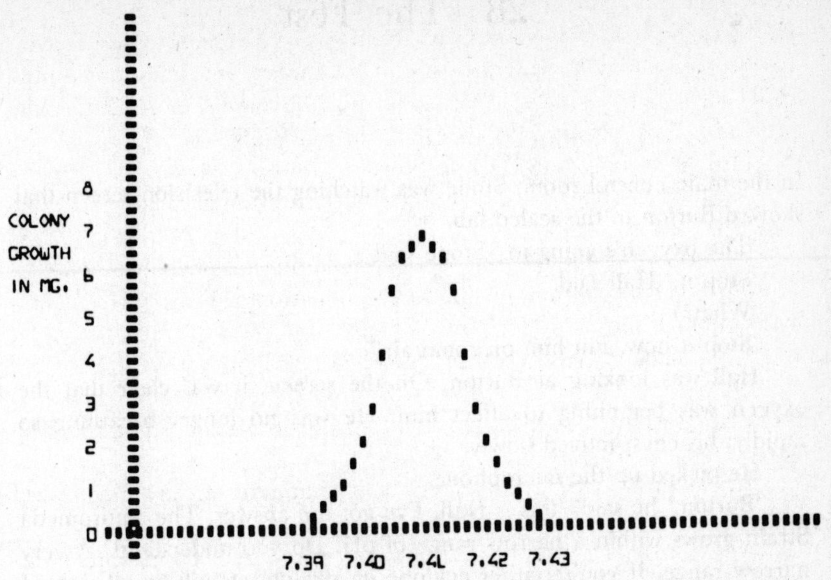

ACIDITY OF MEDIUM AS LOG H – ION CONCENTRATION

CORRECTED FOR SKEW
MEANS, MODES, S.D. FOUND
IN CORREL/PRINT
MM –76
CALL COORDINATES
0,Y,88,Z,09.

REVIEW CHECK

END PRINT

He stared at the graph for a moment, then ran for the door. On his way out he grinned at his assistant and said, 'It's all over. Our troubles are finished.'

He could not have been more wrong.

28 The Test

In the main control room, Stone was watching the television screen that showed Burton in the sealed lab.

'The oxygen's going in,' Stone said.

'Stop it,' Hall said.

'What?'

'Stop it now. Put him on room air.'

Hall was looking at Burton. On the screen, it was clear that the oxygen was beginning to affect him. He was no longer breathing so rapidly; his chest moved slowly.

He picked up the microphone.

'Burton,' he said, 'this is Hall. I've got the answer. The Andromeda Strain grows within a narrow range of pH. Do you understand? A very narrow range. If you're either acidotic or alkalotic, you'll be all right. I want you to go into respiratory alkalosis. I want you to breathe as fast as you can.'

Burton said, 'But this is pure oxygen. I'll hyperventilate and pass out. I'm a little dizzy now.'

'No. We're switching back to air. Now start breathing as fast as you can.'

Hall turned back to Stone. 'Give him a higher carbon-dioxide atmosphere.'

'But the organism flourishes in carbon dioxide!'

'I know, but not at an unfavorable pH of the blood. You see, that's the problem: air doesn't matter, but blood does. We have to establish an unfavorable acid balance for Burton's blood.'

Stone suddenly understood. 'The child,' he said, 'It screamed.'

'Yes.'

'And the old fellow with the aspirin hyperventilated.'

'Yes. And drank Sterno besides.'

'And both of them shot their acid-base balance to hell,' Stone said.

'Yes,' Hall said. 'My trouble was, I was hung up on the acidosis. I didn't understand how the baby could become acidotic. The answer, of course, was that it didn't. It became basic – too little acid. But that was all right – you could go either way, too much acid or too little – as long as you got out of the growth range of Andromeda.'

He turned back to Burton. 'All right now,' he said. 'Keep breathing rapidly. Don't stop. Keep your lungs going and blow off your carbon dioxide. How do you feel?'

'Okay,' Burton panted. 'Scared . . . but . . . okay.'

'Good.'

'Listen,' Stone said, 'we can't keep Burton that way forever. Sooner or later –'

'Yes,' Hall said. 'We'll alkalinize his blood.'

To Burton: 'Look around the lab. Do you see anything we could use to raise your blood pH?'

Burton looked. 'No, not really.'

'Bicarbonate of soda? Ascorbic acid? Vinegar?'

Burton searched frantically among the bottles and reagents on the lab shelf, and finally shook his head. 'Nothing here that will work.'

Hall hardly heard him. He had been counting Burton's respirations; they were up to thirty-five a minute, deep and full. That would hold him for a time, but sooner or later he would become exhausted – breathing was hard work – or pass out.

He looked around the lab from his vantage point. And it was while doing this that he noticed the rat. A black Norway, sitting calmly in its cage in a corner of the room, watching Burton.

He stopped.

'That rat . . .'

It was breathing slowly and easily. Stone saw the rat and said, 'What the hell . . . '

And then, as they watched, the lights began to flash again, and the computer console blinked on:

EARLY DEGENERATIVE CHANGE IN GASKET V-112-6886

'Christ,' Stone said.

'Where does that gasket lead?'

'It's one of the core gaskets; it connects all the labs. The main seal is –'

The computer came back on.

DEGENERATIVE CHANGE IN GASKETS A-009-5478
V-430-0030
N-966-6656

They looked at the screen in astonishment. 'Something is wrong,' Stone said. 'Very wrong.'

In rapid succession the computer flashed the number of nine more gaskets that were breaking down.

'I don't understand . . .'

And then Hall said, 'The child. Of course!'

'The child?'

'And that damned airplane. It all fits.'

'What are you talking about?' Stone said.

'The child was normal,' Hall said. 'It could cry, and disrupt its acid-base balance. Well and good. That would prevent the Andromeda Strain from getting into its bloodstream, and multiplying, and killing it.'

'Yes, yes,' Stone said. 'You've told me all that.'

'*But what happens when the child stops crying?*'

Stone stared at him. He said nothing.

'I mean,' Hall said, 'that sooner or later, that kid had to stop crying. It couldn't cry forever. Sooner or later it would stop, and its acid-base balance would return to normal. Then it would be vulnerable to Andromeda.'

'True.'

'But it didn't die.'

'Perhaps some rapid form of immunity –'

'No. Impossible. There are only two explanations. When the child stopped crying, either the organism was no longer there – had been blown away, cleared from the air – or else the organism –'

'Changed,' Stone said. 'Mutated.'

'Yes. Mutated to a noninfectious form. And perhaps it is still mutating. Now it is no longer directly harmful to man, but it eats rubber gaskets.'

'The airplane.'

Hall nodded. 'National guardsmen could be on the ground, and not be harmed. But the pilot had his aircraft destroyed because the plastic was dissolved before his eyes.'

'So Burton is now exposed to a harmless organism. That's why the rat is alive.'

'That's why Burton is alive,' Hall said. 'The rapid breathing isn't necessary. He's only alive because Andromeda changed.'

'It may change again,' Stone said. 'and if most mutations occur at times of multiplication, when the organism is growing most rapidly –'

The sirens went off, and the computer flashed a message in red.

GASKET INTEGRITY ZERO. LEVEL V CONTAMINATED AND SEALED.

Stone turned to Hall. 'Quick,' he said, 'get out of here. There's no substation in this lab. You have to go to the next sector.'

For a moment, Hall did not understand. He continued to sit in his seat, and then, when the realization hit him, he scrambled for the door and hurried outside to the corridor. As he did so he heard a hissing sound, and a thump as a massive steel plate slid out from a wall and closed off the corridor.

Stone saw it and swore. 'That does it,' he said. 'We're trapped here. And if that bomb goes off, it'll spread the organism all over the surface. There will be a thousand mutations, each killing in a different way. We'll never be rid of it.'

Over the loudspeaker, a flat mechanical voice was saying, 'The level is closed. The level is closed. This is an emergency. The level is closed.'

There was a moment of silence, and then a scratching sound as a new recording came on, and Miss Gladys Stevens of Omaha, Nebraska, said quietly, 'There are now three minutes to atomic self-destruct.'

29 Three Minutes

A new rising and falling siren came on, and all the clocks snapped their hands back to 1200 hours, and the second hands began to sweep out the time. The stop-clocks all glowed red, with a green line on the dial to indicate when detonation would occur.

And the mechanical voice repeated calmly, 'There are now three minutes to self-destruct.'

'Automatic,' Stone said quietly. 'The system cuts in when the level is contaminated. We can't let it happen.'

Hall was holding the key in his hand. 'There's no way to get to a substation?'

'Not on this level. Each sector is sealed from every other.'

'But there *are* substations, on the other levels?'

'Yes . . .'

'How do I get up?'

'You can't. All the conventional routes are sealed.'

'What about the central core?' The central core communicated with all levels.

Stone shrugged. 'The safeguards . . .'

Hall remembered talking to Burton earlier about the central-core safeguards. In theory, once inside the central core you could go straight to the top. But in practice, there were ligamine sensors located around the core to prevent this. Originally intended to prevent escape of lab animals that might break free into the core, the sensors released ligamine, a curare derivative that was water-soluble, in the form of a gas. There were also automatic guns that fired ligamine darts.

The mechanical voice said, 'There are now two minutes forty-five seconds to self-destruct.'

Hall was already moving back into the lab and staring through the glass into the inner work area; beyond that was the central core.

Hall said, 'What are my chances?'

'They don't exist,' Stone explained.

Hall bent over and crawled through a tunnel into a plastic suit. He waited until it had sealed behind him, and then he picked up a knife and cut away the tunnel, like a tail. He breathed in the air of the lab, which was cool and fresh, and laced with Andromeda organisms.

Nothing happened.

Back in the lab, Stone watched him through the glass. Hall saw his lips move, but heard nothing; then a moment later the speakers cut in and he heard Stone say, '– best that we could devise.'

'What was?'

'The defense system.'

'Thanks very much,' Hall said, moving toward the rubber gasket. It was circular and rather small, leading into the central core.

'There's only one chance,' Stone said. 'The doses are low. They're calculated for a ten-kilogram animal, like a large monkey, and you weigh seventy kilograms or so. You can stand a fairly heavy dose before –'

'Before I stop breathing,' Hall said. The victims of curare suffocate to death, their chest muscles and diaphragms paralyzed. Hall was certain it was an unpleasant way to die.

'Wish me luck,' he said.

'There are now two minutes thirty seconds to self-destruct,' Gladys Stevens said.

Hall slammed the gasket with his fist, and it crumbled in a dusty cloud. He moved out into the central core.

It was silent. He was away from the sirens and flashing lights of the level, and into a cold, metallic, echoing space. The central core was perhaps thirty feet wide, painted a utilitarian gray; the core itself, a cylindrical shaft of cables and machinery, lay before him. On the walls he could see the rungs of a ladder leading upward to Level IV.

'I have you on the TV monitor,' Stone's voice said. 'Start up the ladder. The gas will begin any moment.'

A new recorded voice broke in. 'The central core has been contaminated,' it said. 'Authorized maintenance personnel are advised to clear the area immediately.'

'Go!' Stone said.

Hall climbed. As he went up the circular wall, he looked back and saw pale clouds of white smoke blanketing the floor.

'That's the gas,' Stone said. 'Keep going.'

Hall climbed quickly, hand over hand, moving up the rungs. He was breathing hard, partly from the exertion, partly from emotion.

'The sensors have you,' Stone said. His voice was dull.

Stone was sitting in the Level V laboratory, watching on the consoles as the computer electric eyes picked up Hall and outlined his body moving up the wall. To Stone he seemed painfully vulnerable. Stone glanced over at a third screen, which showed the ligamine ejectors pivoting on their wall brackets, the slim barrels coming around to take aim.

'Go!'

On the screen, Hall's body was outlined in red on a vivid green background. As Stone watched, a crosshair was superimposed over the body, centering on the neck. The computer was programmed to choose a region of high blood flow; for most animals, the neck was better than the back.

Hall, climbing up the core wall, was aware only of the distance and his fatigue. He felt strangely and totally exhausted, as if he had been climbing for hours. Then he realized that the gas was beginning to affect him.

'The sensors have picked you up,' Stone said. 'But you have only ten more yards.'

Hall glanced back and saw one of the sensor units. It was aimed directly at him. As he watched, it fired, a small puff of bluish smoke spurting from the barrel. There was a whistling sound, and then something struck the wall next to him, and fell to the ground.

'Missed that time. Keep going.'

Another dart slammed into the wall near his neck. He tried to hurry, tried to move faster. Above, he could see the door with the plain white markings LEVEL IV. Stone was right; less than ten yards to go.

A third dart, and then a fourth. He still was untouched. For an ironic moment he felt irritation: the damned computers weren't worth anything, they couldn't even hit a simple target . . .

The next dart caught him in the shoulder, stinging as it entered his flesh, and then there was a second wave of burning pain as the liquid was injected. Hall swore.

Stone watched it all on the monitor. The screen blandly recorded STRIKE and then proceeded to rerun a tape of the sequence, showing the dart moving through the air, and hitting Hall's shoulder. It showed it three times in succession.

The voice said, 'There are now two minutes to self-destruct.'

'It's a low dose,' Stone said to Hall. 'Keep going.'

Hall continued to climb. He felt sluggish, like a four-hundred-pound man, but he continued to climb. He reached the next door just as a dart slammed into the wall near his cheekbone.

'Nasty.'

'Go! Go!'

The door had a seal and handle. He tugged at the handle while still another dart struck the wall.

'That's it, that's it, you're going to make it,' Stone said.

'There are now ninety seconds to self-destruct,' the voice said.

The handle spun. With a hiss of air the door came open. He moved into an inner chamber just as a dart struck his leg with a brief, searing wave of heat. And suddenly, instantly, he was a thousand pounds heavier. He moved in slow motion as he reached for the door and pulled it shut behind him.

'You're in an airlock,' Stone said. 'Turn the next door handle.'

Hall moved toward the inner door. It was several miles away, an infinite trip, a distance beyond hope. His feet were encased in lead; his legs were granite. He felt sleepy and achingly tired as he took one step, and then another, and another.

'There are now sixty seconds to self-destruct.'

Time was passing swiftly. He could not understand it; everything was so fast, and he was so slow.

The handle. He closed his fingers around it, as if in a dream. He turned the handle.

'Fight the drug. You can do it,' Stone said.

What happened next was difficult to recall. He saw the handle turn, and the door open; he was dimly aware of a girl, a technician, standing in the hallway as he staggered through. She watched him with frightened eyes as he took a single clumsy step forward.

'Help me,' he said.

She hesitated; her eyes got wider, and then she ran down the corridor away from him.

He watched her stupidly, and fell to the ground. The substation was only a few feet away, a glittering, polished metal plate on the wall.

'Forty-five seconds to self-destruct,' the voice said, and then he was angry because the voice was female, and seductive, and recorded, because someone had planned it this way, had written out a series of inexorable statements, like a script, which was now being followed by the computers, together with all the polished, perfect machinery of the laboratory. It was as if this was his fate, planned from the beginning.

And he was angry.

Later, Hall could not remember how he managed to crawl the final distance; nor could he remember how he was able to get to his knees and reach up with the key. He did remember twisting it in the lock, and watching as the green light came on again.

'Self-destruct has been canceled,' the voice announced, as if it were quite normal.

Hall slid to the floor, heavy, exhausted, and watched as blackness closed in around him.

day 5
RESOLUTION

30 The Last Day

A voice from very far away said, 'He's fighting it.'

'Is he?'

'Yes. Look.'

And then, a moment later, Hall coughed as something was pulled from his throat, and he coughed again, gasped for air, and opened his eyes.

A concerned female face looked down at him. 'You okay? It wears off quickly.'

Hall tried to answer her but could not. He lay very still on his back, and felt himself breathe. It was a little stiff at first, but soon became much easier, his ribs going in and out without effort. He turned his head and said, 'How long?'

'About forty seconds,' the girl said, 'as nearly as we can figure. Forty seconds without breathing. You were a little blue when we found you, but we got you intubated right away, and onto a respirator.'

'When was that?'

'Twelve, fifteen minutes ago. Ligamine is short-acting, but even so, we were worried about you . . . How are you feeling?'

'Okay.'

He looked around the room. He was in the infirmary on Level IV. On the far wall was a television monitor, which showed Stone's face.

'Hello,' Hall said.

Stone grinned. 'Congratulations.'

'I take it the bomb didn't?'

'The bomb didn't,' Stone said.

'That's good,' Hall said, and closed his eyes. He slept for more than an hour, and when he awoke the television screen was blank. A nurse told him that Dr. Stone was talking to Vandenberg.

'What's happening?'

'According to predictions, the organism is over Los Angeles now.'

'And?'

The nurse shrugged. 'Nothing. It seems to have no effect at all.'

'None whatsoever,' Stone said, much later. 'It has apparently mutated to a benign form. We're still waiting for a bizarre report of death or disease, but it's been six hours now, and it gets less likely with every minute. We suspect that ultimately it will migrate back out of the atmosphere, since there's too much oxygen down here. But of course if the bomb had gone off in Wildfire . . .'

Hall said, 'How much time was left?'

'When you turned the key? About thirty-four seconds.'

Hall smiled. 'Plenty of time. Hardly even exciting.'

'Perhaps from where you were,' Stone said. 'But down on Level V, it was very exciting indeed. I neglected to tell you that in order to improve the subterranean detonation characteristics of the atomic device, all air is evacuated from Level V, beginning thirty seconds before explosion.'

'Oh,' Hall said.

'But things are now under control,' Stone said. 'We have the organism, and can continue to study it. We've already begun to characterize a variety of mutant forms. It's a rather astonishing organism in its versatility.' He smiled. 'I think we can be fairly confident that the organism will move into the upper atmosphere without causing further difficulty on the surface, so there's no problem there. And as for us down here, we understand what's happening now, in terms of the mutations. That's the important thing. That we understand.'

'Understand,' Hall repeated.

'Yes,' Stone said. 'We have to understand.'

EPILOGUE

Officially, the loss of Andros V, the manned spacecraft that burned up as it reentered the atmosphere, was explained on the basis of mechanical failure. The tungsten-and-plastic-laminate heat shield was said to have eroded away under the thermal stress of returning to the atmosphere, and an investigation was ordered by NASA into production methods for the heat shield.

In Congress, and in the press, there was clamor for safer spacecraft. As a result of governmental and public pressure, NASA elected to postpone future manned flights for an indefinite period. This decision was announced by Jack Marriott, 'the voice of Andros,' in a press conference at the Manned Spaceflight Center in Houston. A partial transcript of the conference follows:

Q: Jack, when does this postponement go into effect?
A: Immediately. Right as I talk to you, we are shutting down.
Q: How long do you anticipate this delay will last?
A: I'm afraid that's impossible to say.
Q: Could it be a matter of months?
A: It could.
Q: Jack, could it be as long as a year?
A: It's just impossible for me to say. We must wait for the findings of the investigative committee.
Q: Does this postponement have anything to do with the Russian decision to curtail their space program after the crash of Zond 19?
A: You'd have to ask the Russians about that.
Q: I see that Jeremy Stone is on the list of the investigative committee. How did you happen to include a bacteriologist?
A: Professor Stone has served on many scientific advisory councils in the past. We value his opinion on a broad range of subjects.
Q: What will this delay do to the Mars-landing target date?
A: It will certainly set the scheduling back.
Q: Jack, how far?
A: I'll tell you frankly, it's something that all of us here would like to know. We regard the failure of Andros V as a scientific error, a breakdown in systems technology, and not as a specifically

human error. The scientists are going over the problem now, and we'll have to wait for their findings. The decision is really out of our hands.

Q: Jack, would you repeat that?
A: The decision is out of our hands.

Binary

This book was written before it became too embarrassing for the Republican Party to hold its 1972 convention in San Diego, and I preferred not to follow the convention to Miami Beach.

John Lange

BINARY: any system composed of two interacting elements. As in binary stars, binary numbers, binary gases, etc.

Chemical agents lend themselves to covert use in sabotage against which it is exceedingly difficult to visualize any really effective defence . . . I will not dwell upon this use of CBW because, as one pursues the possibilities of such covert uses, one discovers that the scenarios resemble that in which the components of a nuclear weapon are smuggled into New York City and assembled in the basement of the Empire State Building.

In other words, once the possibility is recognized to exist, about all that one can do is worry about it.

Dr Ivan L. Bennett, Jr testifying before the Subcommittee on National Security Policy and Scientific Developments, November 20, 1969

PROLOGUE
BETA SCENARIO

The facts are these:

1. On August 22nd, 1972, seven men flew into Salt Lake International Airport, Salt Lake City, Utah. The men came from Las Vegas, Chicago, Dallas, and New York. All seven men have been identified; they all have connexions with organized crime. Thus far four have been picked up for questioning and their testimony provides the major portion of this report.

Each man was first contacted in his home city by an anonymous telephone call. They were each paid a thousand dollars in cash to do an unspecified job. All they knew in advance was that the job would take forty-eight hours, and that they must bring heavy boots and dark, warm clothing. Each was given an assumed name which he was to use for the duration of the job.

The men arrived in Salt Lake between noon and four PM local time. They were met separately. When all had arrived, they were transported in a 1968 white Plymouth sedan outside the city.

The trip out from Salt Lake was made in total silence. After an hour of travel they arrived in Ramrock, Utah, a town of 407 persons located in the north-central region of the state.

2. The men remained in Ramrock until nightfall, staying in a one-storey wood frame house previously rented by an unknown party. While in the house, the seven men wore surgical rubber gloves so that no fingerprints could be recovered. The men changed into their dark heavy clothing in the house, and received instructions on their job from the leader, a man identified only as 'Jones'. Jones is described as a heavyset muscular man with a broken nose and greying hair. Positive identification has not yet been made of this person.

3. Jones told the assembled men that they were going to steal a quantity of insecticide from a train. He told them that he had not personally planned the theft, that it had been worked out by someone else. They believed this when they heard the plans. Although not formally educated, these men had a well-developed sense of personality and they all agree

that Jones, who was described by one as a 'drill-sergeant type', lacked the acumen to formulate the plans.

4. The plans were remarkable for their detail. For example, the men were told that the train would be travelling at 35 mph, according to Department of Transportation regulations covering shipment of dangerous cargo. The men were told the timetable the train would follow from its point of origin in Dugway Proving Grounds, Utah, through the state. The men were told of the existence of impedance trip sensors in the rails, and were instructed in relay timing mechanisms involved. They were told that the insecticide would be stored in 500-pound canisters of two varieties – one kind painted yellow, the other black. They were told that they must steal one yellow canister and one black canister. Two yellows or two blacks would not do.

Equally important is what the men were *not* told. They were not told that the train would be guarded. This is an important point. It means either that plans were drawn up for the robbery one month before – when there were no guards on the trains – or else that the presence of the guards was known by the planners, who elected not to inform the men. This point is still in debate.

The men were also not told why they were stealing the insecticide in the first place. Significantly, none of them asked. Apparently it was a matter of total indifference to them.

5. They remained in the wood frame house in Ramrock until 8 PM. Then each man was issued a machine gun and a pistol. The machine guns were of the usual variety, that is, war surplus equipment sold with plugged barrels. Some other party had simply machined new barrels and replaced the original plugged barrels (cf Memorandum 245/779: Abuses of War Surplus Weaponry). The men then climbed aboard a Land Rover which was stored in the garage of the house. It had apparently been there waiting for some weeks, because it was dusty. They drove off into the desert to meet the train.

6. They arrived at an unnamed site in northeast Utah shortly after 2 AM. They carried out their preparations quickly and efficiently in the light of a full moon.

One man was sent down the tracks until he found the impedance trip sensor. He blocked the mechanism of this sensor by attaching an electronic override device. Thus no one knew for six hours that the train had been stopped farther up the tracks; it was assumed that the trip sensor had broken down.

Meanwhile four other men walked across the sand towards a half-dozen cattle grazing nearby. The robbery site was minimal rangeland and had been chosen specifically because of this. The men shot the steer nearest the tracks. The other cattle ran off at the sound of the shot.

The men looped ropes around the dead steer and dragged it across the railroad tracks. The animal was doused with gasoline and a timing device was attached to it.

Then all seven men climbed aboard the Land Rover and rode it to a nearby hiding place behind some low dunes. They waited approximately fifteen minutes before the train appeared in the distance. The men were surprised to see that it was a government train consisting of three flatcars lettered US GOVERNMENT PROPERTY on the sides. They were also surprised to see an armoured caboose at the end of the train.

7. The engine slowed, apparently as the engineer sighted the obstacle across the tracks. When the train stopped, the timing device caused the dead steer to burst into flames. At that moment six of the men ran forward, intending to remove the canisters. There was some scattered firing from the armoured caboose. One man ran up to it, stuck his machine gun into an armoured port, and delivered a burst of fire to the interior. All five soldiers (and one physician) inside the caboose were killed. The engineer was also killed a few moments later.

8. The men unloaded two canisters from the train, one black and one yellow. Each was marked with lettering so vivid that the men remembered it well; stencilled warnings to the effect that the canisters contained highly dangerous chemicals.

They carried the canisters across the desert to a flat location nearby. They set them down 100 yards apart and burned a red flare near each.

9. Two or three minutes passed, and then two helicopters appeared over the horizon. The helicopters landed in tandem alongside the flares. They were commercial helicopters of a nondescript nature. The only unusual aspect was that each had been fitted with a nylon web sling to hold a canister. The men loaded the canisters onto the slings. The helicopters lifted off again into the night.

10. The men returned to the Land Rover and drove back to Salt Lake

City, arriving at 6 AM on the morning of August 23rd, 1972. Over the next eighteen hours they flew out of the city to their points of origin. None had any knowledge of what happened to the canisters. None had any knowledge of the true contents of the canisters.

It is clear from the foregoing that these seven underworld figures were engaged in an activity closely approximating the RAND Corporation 'Analog Scenario' sequence called CBW Beta. These scenarios were prepared in the fall of 1965 for the Department of Defence (Command and Control). They considered the options and ramifications of theft of thermonuclear bomb components and chem/biol agents.

Beta Scenario treated the possibility that a relatively small number of men, either criminal figures or political extremists, might steal these materials for blackmail, sabotage, or terrorist purposes. The consequences of theft were considered uniformly disastrous. Therefore the scenario outlined ways to prevent this occurrence.

The chief preventive mechanism was deemed secrecy in transport schedules and methods. That is, the thieves would not know where, or when, the material was being shipped. As a result of the Beta Scenario conclusions, timetables for shipment were established by a closed-code computer mechanism operating from a table of random numbers. That mechanism was regarded as foolproof and unbreakable.

However, it is obvious that these seven men received instructions derived from breaking the timetable. It is not known how the timetable was broken, enabling the men to easily, almost effortlessly, steal one half-ton of the most potent nerve gas in the world.

HOUR 12

LOS ANGELES

5 AM PDT

The grey government sedan was waiting in a deserted corner of Los Angeles International Airport. Seen from the air, it cast a long shadow across the concrete runway in the pale morning light. He watched the sedan as his helicopter descended and landed a short distance from the car.

The driver came running up, bent over beneath the spinning blades, and opened the door. A gust of warm, dry August air swirled into the interior of the helicopter.

'Mr Graves?'

'That's right.'

'Come with me please.'

Graves got out, carrying his briefcase, and walked to the car. He climbed into the back seat and they drove off away from the runway towards the freeway.

'Do you know where we're going?' Graves asked.

The driver consulted a clipboard. 'One-oh-one-three-one Washington, Culver City, I have.'

'I think that's right.' Graves settled back in the seat. California numbering: he'd never get used to it. It was as bad as a zip code. He opened his early edition of *The New York Times* and tried to read it. He had tried on the helicopter but had found it impossible to concentrate. He assumed that was because of the noise. And the distractions: when they passed over San Clemente, halfway between Los Angeles and San Diego, he had been craning his neck, peering out the window like an ordinary tourist. The President was there now, had been for the last week.

He looked at the headlines: trouble in the UN, arguments in the German parliament about the mark, Britain and France squabbling . . . He put the paper aside and stared out the window at Los Angeles, flat and bleak in the early morning light.

'Good trip, sir?' the driver asked. It was perfectly said – no inflection, no prying, just detached polite interest. The driver didn't know who Graves was. He didn't know where he had come from. He didn't know what his business was. All the driver knew was that Graves was important enough to have a government helicopter fly him in and a government sedan pick him up.

'Fine, thanks.' Graves smiled, staring out the window. In fact the trip had been horrible. Phelps had called him just an hour before and asked him to come up and give a briefing on Wright. That was the way Phelps worked – everything was a crisis, there were no routine activities. It was typical that Phelps hadn't bothered to let Graves know beforehand that he was even in Los Angeles.

Although on reflection, Graves knew he should have expected that. With the Republican Convention in San Diego, all the activity of the country had shifted from Washington to the West Coast. The President was in the Western White House in San Clemente; the Convention was eighty miles to the south; and Phelps – what would Phelps do? Obviously, relocate discreetly in the nearest large city, which was Los Angeles. As Graves considered it, Los Angeles became the inevitable choice.

Phelps needed the telephone lines for data transmission. It was as simple as that. LA was the third largest city in America, and it would have plenty of telephone lines that the Department of State (Intelligence Division) could take over on short notice. It was inevitable.

'Here we are, sir,' the driver said, pulling over to the kerb. He got out and opened the door for Graves. 'Am I to wait for you, sir?'

'Yes, I think so.'

'Very good, sir.'

Graves paused and looked up at the building. It was a rather ordinary four-storey office building in an area of Los Angeles that seemed almost a slum. The building, not particularly new, was outstandingly ugly. And the paint was flaking away from the facade.

Graves walked up the steps and entered the lobby. As he went through the doors he looked at his watch. It was exactly 5 AM. Phelps was waiting for him in the deserted lobby. Phelps wore a lightweight glen-plaid suit and a worried expression. He shook hands with Graves and said, 'How was your flight?' His voice echoed slightly in the lobby.

'Fine,' Graves said.

They walked to the elevators, passing the ground-floor offices, which seemed mostly devoted to a bank.

'Like this place?' Phelps said.

'Not much.'

'It was the best we could find on short notice,' he said.

A guard with a sign-in book stood in front of the elevators. Graves let Phelps sign first; then he took the pen and wrote his name, his authorization, and the time. He saw that Decker and Venn were already there.

They got into the elevator and pressed the button for the third floor. 'Decker and Venn are already here,' Phelps said.

'I saw.'

Phelps nodded and smiled, as much as he ever smiled. 'I keep forgetting about you and your powers of observation.'

'I keep forgetting about you, too,' Graves said.

Phelps ignored the remark. 'I've planned two meetings for today,' he said. 'You've got the briefing in an hour – Wilson, Peckham, and a couple of others. But I think you should hear about Sigma Station first.'

'All right,' Graves said. He didn't know what the hell Phelps was talking about, but he wasn't going to give him the satisfaction of asking.

They got off at the third floor and walked past some peeling posters of Milan and Tahiti and through a small typing pool, the desks now deserted, the typewriters neatly covered.

'What is this place?' Graves said.

'Travel agency,' Phelps said. 'They went out of business but they had a lot of –'

'Telephone lines.'

'Yes. We took over the floor.'

'How long you planning to stay?' Graves asked. There was an edge to his voice that he didn't bother to conceal. Phelps knew how he felt about the Department.

'Just through the Convention,' Phelps said, with elaborate innocence. 'What did you think?'

'I thought it might be permanent.'

'Good Lord, no. Why would we do a thing like that?'

'I can't imagine,' Graves said.

Past the typing pool they came to a section of private offices. The walls were painted an institutional beige. It reminded Graves of a prison, or a hospital. No wonder the travel agency went out of business, he thought.

'I know how you feel,' Phelps said.

'Do you?' Graves asked.

'Yes. You're . . . ambivalent about the section.'

'I'm ambivalent about the domestic activities.'

'We all are,' Phelps said. He said it easily, in the smooth, oil-on-the-waters manner that he had perfected. And his father before him. Phelps' father had been an under-secretary of state during the Roosevelt administration. Phelps himself was a product of the Dalton School, Andover, Yale, and Harvard Law School. If he sat still, ivy would sprout from his ears. But he never sat still.

'How do you find San Diego?' he asked, walking along with his maddeningly springy step.

'Boring and hot.'

Phelps sighed. 'Don't blame me. *I* didn't choose it.'

Graves did not reply. They continued down a corridor and came upon a guard, who nodded to Phelps. 'Good morning, Mr Phelps.' And to Graves: 'Good morning, sir.' Phelps flashed his pink card; so did Graves. The guard allowed them to pass farther down the corridor past a large banner that read FIRST CLASS SERVICE ON COACH.

'You've got a guard already,' Graves said.

'There's a lot of expensive equipment to look after,' Phelps said. They made a right turn and entered a conference room.

There were just four of them: Graves; Phelps, looking springy and alert as he greeted everyone; Decker, who was thin and dark, intense-looking; and Venn, who was nearly fifty, greying, sloppy in his dress. Graves had never met Decker or Venn before, but he knew they were both scientists. They were too academic and too uncomfortable to be anything else.

Phelps ran the meeting. 'This is John Graves, who is the world's foremost expert on John Wright.' He smiled slightly. 'Mr Graves has plenty of background, so you can speak as technically as you want. Decker, why don't you begin.'

Decker cleared his throat and opened a briefcase in front of him, removing a sheaf of computer printout. He slipped through the green pages as he spoke. 'I've been working in Special Projects Division for the last six months,' he said. 'I was assigned to establish redundancy programmes on certain limited-access files so that we could check call-up locations to these data banks, which are mostly located in Arlington Hall in Washington.'

He paused and glanced at Graves to see if the information was making sense. Graves nodded.

'The problem is basically one of access-line proliferation. A data bank is just a collection of information stored on magnetic tape drums. It can be anywhere in the country. To get information out of it, you need to hook into the main computer with an access substation. That can also be anywhere in the country. Every major data bank has a large number of access substations. For limited or special-purpose access – stations that need to draw out information once or twice a week, let's say – we employ commercial telephone lines; we don't have our own lines. To tie in to a peripheral computer substation, you telephone a call number and hook your phone up to the computer terminal. That's it. As long as you have a half-duplex or full-duplex telephone line, you're in business.'

Graves nodded. 'How is the call number coded?'

'We'll come to that,' Decker said, looking at Venn. 'For now, we'll concentrate on the system. Some of the major data banks, like the ones held by Defence, may have five hundred or a thousand access lines. A year ago, Wilkens' congressional committee started to worry about unauthorized tapping into those access lines. In theory, a bright boy who knew computers could tap into the system and call out any information he wanted from the data banks. He could get all sorts of classified information.'

Decker sighed. 'So I was hired to install redundancy checks on the system. Echo checks, bit additions, that sort of thing. My job was to make sure we could verify which stations drew out information from the data banks, and what information they drew. I finished that work a month ago.'

Graves glanced at Phelps. Phelps was watching them all intently, pretending he was following the discussion. Graves knew that it was over Phelps' head.

'Just before I finished,' Decker said, 'we discovered that an unauthorized station was tapping into the system. We called it Sigma Station, but we were unable to characterize it. By that I mean that we knew Sigma was drawing information, but we didn't know where, or how.'

He flipped to a green sheet of computer printout and pushed it across the table to Graves. 'Sigma is the underlined station. You can see that on this particular day, July 21st, 1972, it tapped into the system at ten oh four PM Eastern time and maintained the contact for seven minutes; then it broke out. We determined that Sigma was tapping in at around ten o'clock two or three nights a week. But that was all we knew.'

Decker turned to Venn, who said, 'I came into the picture at this point. I'd been at Bell Labs working on telephone tracer mechanisms. The telephone company has a problem with unauthorized calls – calls verbally charged to a phone number, calls charged to a wrong credit card number, that kind of thing. I was working on a computer tracing system. Defence asked me to look at the Sigma Station problem.'

'One ought to say,' Phelps said, 'that the data bank being tapped by Sigma was a Defence bank.'

'Yes,' Venn said. 'It was a Defence bank. With two or three taps a week at about ten PM. That was all I knew when I began. However, I made some simple assumptions. First, you've got to have a computer terminal in order to tap the system. That is, once you've called the number that links you to the computer, you must use a teletypewriting or CRT apparatus compatible with the Defence system.'

'Are those terminals common?'

'No,' Venn said. 'They are quite advanced and fairly uncommon. I started with a list of them.'

Graves nodded.

'Then I considered the timing. Ten PM Eastern time is seven PM in California, where most of these sophisticated terminals in defence industry applications are located. If an employee were illegally using a terminal to tap into Defence, he couldn't do it during office hours. On the other hand, it requires an extraordinary access to get into an East Coast terminal location at ten at night – or into a Midwest location at eight or nine. Therefore Sigma was probably on the West Coast.'

'So you checked the West Coast terminals?'

'Yes. Because in order to hook into the Defence system, you'd have to unhook from your existing system. What corporation, R&D group, or production unit had a terminal that was unhooked at seven PM Western time twice a week? Answer: None. New question: What group had its terminals repaired twice a week? Repairing would entail unhooking. Answer: The Southern California Association of Insurance Underwriters, a company based in San Diego.'

Graves said, 'So you investigated the repairman and you found –'

'We found our man,' Venn said, looking slightly annoyed with Graves. 'His name is Timothy Drew. He has been doing repair work on the SC Association computers for about six weeks. It turns out nobody authorized those repairs; he just showed up and –'

'But you haven't picked him up.'

Phelps coughed. 'No, actually. We haven't picked him up yet because he's –'

'Disappeared,' Graves said.

'That's right,' Phelps said. 'How did you know?'

'Tim Drew is a friend of John Wright. He's had dinner with him several times a week for the last month or so.' As he spoke, Graves had a mental image of Drew – early thirties, blond-looking, muscular. Graves had run a check on him some weeks back and had discovered only that Drew was an ex-Army lieutenant, discharged one year before. A clean record in computer work, nothing good, nothing bad.

'We weren't able to find him,' Venn said, 'but we're still looking. We thought –'

Graves said, 'There's only one thing I want to know. What information did Drew tap from the classified files?'

There was a long silence around the table. Finally Decker said, 'We don't know.'

'You don't know?' Graves lit a cigarette. 'But that's the most important question –'

'Let me explain,' Decker said. 'Drew was an ex-Army officer with knowledge of computer systems. He knew that he couldn't call in on any old number. The call-in numbers are changed at irregular intervals, roughly once a week. But the possible permutations of the call-in number aren't great. With trial and error, he might have found it.'

'You know he found the number,' Graves said, 'because you know he tapped in. The question is, what did he tap *out* from the system?'

'Well, once he was hooked up, he still had a problem. You need subroutine codes to extract various kinds of information, and –'

'How often are the codes changed?'

'Not very often.'

Graves found himself getting impatient. 'How often are the codes changed?'

'About once a year.'

Graves sighed. 'So Drew might have used his old codes to get what he wanted?'

'Yes.'

'Then we want to know what codes he knew. What sort of work did Drew do when he was in the Army?'

'He did topological work. Surface configurations, shipment routings, that sort of thing.'

Graves glanced at Phelps. 'Can we be more specific?'

'I'm afraid not,' Phelps said. 'Defence is unwilling to release Drew's work record to us. Defence is a little defensive, you might say, about the fact that this tap occurred in the first place.'

There was a long silence. Graves stared at the men around the table. There were times, he thought, when working for the government was an exercise in total stupidity. Finally he said, 'How can you get Defence to release the information?'

'I'm not sure we can,' Phelps said. 'But one of the reasons you're being briefed is that we were hoping you might be able to shed light on the situation.'

'I might?'

'Yes. Drew was working for Wright, after all.'

Before Graves could answer, the telephone rang. Phelps answered it, and said, 'Yes, thank you,' and hung up. He looked at Graves. 'Do you have any thoughts about this?'

'None,' Graves said.

'None at all?'

'None at all.'

'Well,' Phelps said, 'perhaps something will occur to you in the next hour.' He gave Graves a heavily disapproving look, then stood up and turned to Decker and Venn. 'Thank you, gentlemen,' he said. And to Graves: 'Let's go.'

HOUR 11

LOS ANGELES

6 AM PDT

Another conference room, another group. This room was decorated entirely in Tahiti posters; it occurred to Graves that whoever had owned the travel agency before it went bankrupt was a Tahiti-nut. Perhaps he was himself Tahitian. Graves began to wonder why the Tahitian owner had gone out of business. Too much time away from the office, basking in the sun? Discrimination against him by Angelenos? Some rare disease carried by coconuts which had made him an invalid?

'Gentlemen,' Phelps said, and cleared his throat. Graves was snapped back to the present. He looked around the room. There were, he saw, a number of high-ranking Washington people. They all looked tired and disgruntled. Phelps had brought them out to California on a red-eye flight, let them sleep a few hours, then dragged them up for a meeting with . . . John Graves?

'John Graves,' Phelps said, 'has come up from San Diego this morning to brief you on John Wright. Mr. Graves has been in charge of Wright's surveillance in New York and San Diego for the past three months.' Phelps nodded to Graves, and Graves stood.

'We have some footage which is quite revealing,' Graves said. 'I thought we'd begin with that, if we can screen it . . .'

The men in the room looked confused. Even Phelps, who never lost his aplomb, seemed uncertain. Graves settled it by tearing down several Tahitian posters from the wall, clearing a blank white space. He was embarrassed for a moment – the tearing noise sounded somehow indiscreet with all these Washington guns, and the whole business emphasized the makeshift nature of the surroundings.

Phelps seemed to sense it, too. 'You must excuse us,' he said, 'but these are temporary quarters for the duration of the Republican Convention.'

Graves stepped to one side as the room lights dimmed. A black-and-white image was projected on the wall. It showed a dapper, rather handsome man standing at a podium. For a moment there was no sound, and then it came on abruptly. The voice was sharp, vigorous, and slightly petulant.

'– can a person do in the twentieth century? The question is not rhetorical, my friends. Each and every one of us is powerless in the face of giant corporations, giant institutions, giant government. Do you think automobiles are badly made? Do you think your electricity bill is too high? Do you disagree with the nation's foreign policy? Well, there's nothing much you can do about it. No matter what you think, or I think, the wheels continue to spin of their own inertia.'

The film image of John Wright paused to take a drink of water. 'Perhaps you think that a few people have power – high government officials, high corporate executives, wealthy individuals. But that also is untrue. Everyone is locked into a system which he has inherited and is powerless to change. We are all trapped, my friends. That is the meaning of the twentieth century. It is the century of impotence.'

Wright's voice dropped lower, became more ominous. His face was grim. 'Impotence,' he repeated. 'Inability to act. Inability to be effective. This is what we must change. And with the help of God, we shall.'

There was some applause on the sound track before the film ran out of the camera and the room lights came back on. Graves lit a cigarette and flipped through the pages of his own file on Wright before speaking.

'I showed you that film for psychological, not political, reasons,' he said, 'because it summarizes most of what we know about John Wright's mental state. The speech was given last year before the annual conference of the Americans for a Better Nation, an extremist group which Wright started and still leads. You've probably never heard of it. It's small, and has no significance whatsoever in national politics. Over the last few years, Wright has poured 1.7 million dollars into the organization. The money apparently doesn't matter to him. But the lack of impact – the impotence – matters a great deal.'

He paused and glanced around the faces at the table. They seemed to be paying attention, but just barely. Two were doodling on the pads before them. 'John Wright,' he said, 'is now forty-nine years old. He is the son of Edmund Wright, of the Wright steel family. He is an only child. His father was a crude, domineering man and an alcoholic. John grew up in his shadow, a very strange child. He was a good student and learned quite a lot of mathematics, even made a minor reputation for himself in that field. On the other hand, he was an inveterate gambler, horse racer, and womanizer.'

The assembled men began to fidget. Graves nodded to the projectionist, who began flashing up slides. The first showed Edmund Wright glaring into the camera. 'Edmund Wright died of cirrhosis in 1955. John Wright changed completely when that happened. He moved to New York from Pittsburgh and became a kind of local celebrity. He was married four times to well-known actresses; all the marriages ended in divorce. The last divorce, from Sarah Layne, occurred in 1967 and coincided with a six-month nervous breakdown for Wright. He was hospitalized in McClain General outside Atlanta for paranoid ideation and feelings of impotence. Apparently he had been impotent with his last wife.'

A picture of Sarah Layne flashed up. The men all stirred uncomfortably as they stared at the image: handsome, but haughty and undeniably challenging.

'Wright left the hospital against doctors' advice and plunged into the political organization he formed: Americans for a Better Nation. For the next four years he gave speeches and wrote pamphlets. In 1968 he worked hard to influence the national elections on every level – mostly without success. He fell into a depression after that.

'Recently, his interest in politics dropped sharply. He seems to have withdrawn from any kind of public life; he no longer holds large parties and no longer participates in the social life of New York. According to all information, he has been intensely studying a variety of subjects that are rather ominous. These include sociology, radiation theory, physics, and some aspects of biology. He has interviewed experts in several different areas –' Graves flipped the pages of his file '– including cancer experts, civil engineers, horticulture specialists, and aerosol spray-can designers. He –'

'Aerosol spray-can designers?' someone asked.

'That is correct.'

There was some head scratching among those present.

'He also became interested in the meteorology of the Southwest.'

The men were listening now and looking very puzzled. All the doodling had stopped.

'Wright was listed as a Potential Surveillance Subject at the end of 1968, after he had engaged in some questionable activities to influence the national election. As a PSS he did nothing out of the ordinary until six months ago. Then two things happened.

'First, Wright began to transfer large amounts of money from various accounts in this country and in Switzerland. As you know, we keep an eye on private capital transfers in excess of $300,000. Wright was moving much more than that. Secondly, he began to be seen with known underworld figures. The pattern of behaviour suggested a courtship, and we became very concerned at that point.'

The slides changed again several times in rapid succession, showing smooth-faced businessmen. 'Robert "Trigger" Cannino. Sal Martucci.

Benny Flick. Gerald "Tiny" Margolin. These are some of the men he saw during that period.'

The slides now showed Wright in restaurants, at taxi stands, and in Central Park with these men.

'Active surveillance began in June 1972, when Wright left New York for San Diego. He was clearly making plans for the Republican Convention, but their nature was not clear, and he was giving himself much too much time. I ran the surveillance from the start. During the surveillance period his contacts with organized crime have substantially decreased. He has been seeing only one person consistently – this man.'

The screen showed a bald, glowering face.

'Eddie "The Key" Trasker, fifty-three, a resident of Las Vegas who lives mostly in San Diego. He is reputed to be the power behind the Teamsters, and his influence over all forms of interstate transportation is enormous. Wright has seen him nearly every week, often during the early hours of the morning.

'He has also come in contact with this man, Timothy Drew, an ex-Army officer with a background in computers. The meaning of that association was unclear to me until this morning. Drew clearly represents Sigma Station; Drew tapped out classified Defence information for Wright. We do not know what kind of information, or why it was stolen.'

Graves sat down and looked at the faces. Phelps said, 'Questions, gentlemen?'

McPherson, from the President's staff, cleared his throat. 'I gather from Mr Graves' excellent but rather psychologically oriented presentation that we have no damned idea what Wright is up to. Is that substantially correct?'

'Yes, it is,' Graves said.

'Well then,' McPherson said, 'I'm afraid we can do nothing. Wright has acted suspicously and is quite probably deranged. Neither is a crime in this country.'

'I disagree,' Corey said, sitting back in his chair. Corey was Defence liaison; a heavyset man with thick eyebrows that joined over his nose. 'I think we have plenty of reason to apprehend Wright at this time.'

'Plenty of reason,' McPherson said, 'but no evidence, no charges . . .'

Whitlock, from the Justice Department, straightened his tie and said, 'I'm sure we all agree this is an unpleasant sort of meeting. Mr Wright is a private citizen and he is entitled to do as he pleases so long as he does not commit a crime. I've seen and heard nothing that suggests a crime has been or will be committed, and –'

'What about the underworld contacts?' Corey said.

Whitlock smiled. 'What about them?'

'I think that's very suggestive –'

'But he has broken no law,' Whitlock said. 'And until he does . . .' He shrugged.

Corey frowned, pushing his eyebrows into a black, ominous V. 'An interrogation would be useful, even without a criminal act,' he said. 'I think we have a basis for interrogation here – Wright's association with Timothy Drew, who has stolen classified information, probably for Wright. Can't we pick him up on that?'

'I feel we should,' Phelps said, speaking for the first time.

Graves spun around to look at Phelps.

'I disagree,' McPherson said.

Whitlock made some notes on the pad in front of him. Finally he said, 'Perhaps an interrogation is the safest route. I think we need to know what was tapped out by Sigma Station. Mr Corey?'

'Pick him up.'

'Mr Phelps?'

'Pick him up.'

'Mr McPherson?'

'Opposed.'

Whitlock spread his hands. Graves said nothing. The meeting was over.

'If there are no further questions,' Phelps said, 'we can adjourn.'

'You didn't like that, did you?' Phelps said, as they walked back through the travel agency.

'No,' Graves said. 'I didn't.'

'Still,' Phelps said. 'I think it's best. Arrest him today, on suspicion of conspiracy to commit grand larceny involving classified information.'

'Isn't it robbery?'

Phelps sighed patiently. 'Robbery and larceny are different crimes.'

Graves said, 'How long can I wait?'

'A few hours. Play with him if you want, but pick him up by evening. I want to get to the bottom of this.'

Graves couldn't make the arrest himself. He'd need federal marshals. 'You'll notify the marshals in San Diego?'

'They're waiting for your call,' Phelps said, and smiled. As much as he ever did.

Graves had fifteen minutes before he had to return to the airport. As he walked out of the travel agency, he heard a room filled with mechanical chatter. Curious, he paused and opened the door. He found that one office had been converted into a temporary hardware room. It had once been somebody's office, but now there were six teletypes and computer consoles installed there. He was reminded that the State Department (Intelligence Division) and the NSA had more computers than any other organizations in the world.

The room was empty at this hour. He glanced at the teletypes, noting their colour. When he first started working at State in the early sixties, rooms like this had contained five red teletypes and one blue teletype. The red machines recorded information from overseas stations and embassies; the blue was for domestic data. Now, four of the machines were blue and only two were red.

There had been a shift in orientation for State Intelligence. Nobody cared any longer about the movements of an eighth assistant deputy minister in the Yugoslav government. They were much more interested in the number five man in the Black Panther Party, or the number three man in the John Birch Society, or the number six man in Americans for a Better Nation.

He sat down at a computer console, stared at the blank TV screen, and began typing in Wright's call numbers. The screen glowed and printed out the categories of stored information:

WRIGHT, JOHN HENSEN
001 FILE SUMMARY
002 PERSONAL APPEARANCE, COMPLETE
003 PHOTOS
004 PERSONAL HISTORY, COMPLETE
005 RECENT ACTIVITIES (2 WEEK UPDATE)
006 FINANCIAL HISTORY, COMPLETE
007 POLITICAL HISTORY, COMPLETE
008 MISCELLANEOUS
009 CROSS REFERENCES LISTING, COMPLETE

Graves stared at the categories with some distaste. It was disturbing that the government should have so much information on a private individual – particularly one who had committed no criminal act at any time.

Then on an impulse he pushed the 'Wipe' button and the screen went blank. He typed in 'Graves, John Norman', followed by his own call-up number. He sat back and watched the numbers print out on the screen:

GRAVES, JOHN NORMAN 445798054
INTELLIGENCE, DEPT STATE/INVESTIGATIONS (DOM)
TELEPHONE: 808-415-7800 X 4305
FILE CONTENTS CANNOT BE DISPLAYED ON THIS
CONSOLE WITHOUT AUTHORIZATION VQ

He hesitated, then punched 'Auth: VQ'

AUTHORIZATION VQ RECORDED
STATE NAME

After another hesitation, he punched 'Phelps, Richard D'.

RECORD CALL-UP NAME AS PHELPS, RICHARD D. FILE CONTENTS CANNOT BE DISPLAYED ON THIS CONSOLE TO THE ABOVENAMED PERSON. CALL-UP PERSON IS ADVISED TO ACQUIRE NTK AUTHORIZATION FROM DEPARTMENT HEAD.

Graves smiled. So even Phelps couldn't call up Graves' file without a special need-to-know authorization. Who *could* call it up? Feeling whimsical, he typed out 'This is the President of the United States.'

The screen glowed:

RECORD CALL-UP AS PRESIDENTOFTHEUNITEDSTATES IS THIS A CODE NAME
STATE GIVEN NAME

Graves sighed. Computers just didn't show any respect. He pressed the 'Wipe' button and returned to the question of Wright.

He didn't really know what he was looking for. Graves had supplied most of the computerized file contents himself. But perhaps someone else had added to it. He pushed the 008 sequence calling up miscellaneous information. That category had been empty two weeks ago. Now it contained an academic history of Wright's work in mathematics, prepared by 'S. Vessen, State/Anal/412'. Whoever that was. He had a moment of pleasure at the thought that State's analysis people were abbreviated 'anal'. It was fitting.

He turned to the information itself:

HX ACADEMIC – JOHN WRIGHT (BIBLIO FOLLOWS: 008/02)

WRIGHT STUDIED MATHEMATICS AT PRINCETON UNDER REIMANN. FROM THE START HIS INTEREST, LIKE THAT OF HIS TEACHER, WAS HEAVILY STATISTICAL AND PROBABILISTIC. HIS FIRST PAPER CONCERNED STOCK MARKET FLUCTUATIONS. THIS WAS WRITTEN IN 1942, BEFORE HIGH SPEED DIGITAL COMPUTERS WERE

AVAILABLE. HOWEVER, WITHOUT SUCH TOOLS WRIGHT DECIDED THAT THE STOCK MARKET WAS TOTALLY RANDOM IN ITS BEHAVIOUR. (THAT IS, THE CHANCE THAT A GIVEN STOCK WOULD GO UP OR DOWN ON ANY DAY BORE NO RELATIONSHIP TO WHAT IT HAD DONE THE PREVIOUS DAY.) THIS FACT WAS FINALLY CONFIRMED BEYOND ALL DOUBT IN 1961.

WRIGHT WAS ALSO INTERESTED IN SPORTS AND GAMBLING. IN 1944 HE WROTE AN AMUSING SHORT ARTICLE 'ON BEING DUE'. IN IT HE ARGUED CORRECTLY THAT THE ORDINARY NOTION THAT A MAN IS 'DUE FOR A HIT' IF HE HAS BEEN RECENTLY UNSUCCESSFUL AT BAT IS TOTALLY FALLACIOUS. EACH TIME AT BAT IS A SEPARATE EVENT.

HE WAS ALSO INTERESTED IN HISTORICAL CONTEXTS: THE FACT THAT JOHN ADAMS, JAMES MONROE, AND THOMAS JEFFERSON ALL DIED ON JULY 4th, AND SO ON. HE WROTE A PAPER ON ASSIGNING CAUSATION TO HISTORICAL AND POLITICAL EVENTS. IN THIS WORK HE WAS STRONGLY INFLUENCED BY THEORETICAL PHYSICISTS.

HE SHOWED THAT YOU CAN NEVER DETERMINE 'THE CHIEF REASON' FOR THE AMERICAN CIVIL WAR, NAPOLEON'S DEFEAT AT WATERLOO, THE FALL OF THE ROMAN EMPIRE, OR ANY OTHER HISTORICAL EVENT. THE CHIEF REASON CANNOT BE KNOWN IN ANY PRECISE SENSE. FOR ANY EVENT THERE ARE HUNDREDS OR THOUSANDS OF CONTRIBUTING CAUSES, AND NO WAY TO ASSIGN PRIORITIES TO THESE CAUSES. HISTORIANS HAVE ATTACKED THE WRIGHT THESIS VIGOROUSLY SINCE IT TENDS TO PUT THEM OUT OF A JOB. HE WAS, HOWEVER, MATHEMATICALLY CORRECT BEYOND DOUBT.

FINALLY WRIGHT TURNED TO THE GENERAL THEORY OF INTERACTIONS. FOR SIMPLICITY HE STUDIED TWO-COMPONENT INTERACTIONS LEADING TO A SINGLE EVENT OR OUTCOME. HE BECAME QUITE KNOWLEDGEABLE IN THIS AREA.

SUMMARY: WRIGHT IS A TALENTED MATHEMATICIAN WHOSE PERSONAL INTERESTS FALL IN THE AREA OF PROBABILITY AND STATISTICS AS THEY APPLY TO HUMAN ACTIVITIES SUCH AS SPORTS, GAMBLING, AND THE INTERPRETATION OF HISTORY. HIS DEVELOPMENT AS A MATHEMATICIAN DISPOSED HIM TO BE INTERESTED IN TWO-COMPONENT INTERACTIONS LEADING TO A SINGLE EVENT OR OUTCOME.

Graves stared at the screen. The notion of two-component interactions fascinated him. It seemed to have all sorts of connotations. He punched buttons and looked at the bibliography, which was not revealing. He looked at the abstracts of articles written by Wright. They were equally unrevealing. Then he saw that a final study was available: Apparently S. Vessen had applied a statistical analysis of his own to Wright's work.

S. VESSEN: ANALYSIS OF WORD FREQUENCIES IN PAPERS OF JOHN WRIGHT.
THE FOLLOWING WORDS APPEAR MORE FREQUENTLY THAN EXPECTED ACCORDING TO RATIOS OF TOTAL WORDAGE FOR MATHEMATICAL TREATISES

PROBABILITY
COINCIDENCE
GAUSSIAN
INSTABILITY
INTERACTION
TWO-COMPONENT
IMPOTENCE

Graves frowned, staring at the last word. Then he pressed the 'Wipe' button a final time and hurried to catch his plane.

[illegible] have all sorts of [illegible] [illegible] which you [illegible] [illegible] of [illegible] [illegible]. Then [illegible] that [illegible] [illegible] [illegible] Wright's work.

[illegible] ANALYSIS OF [illegible] [illegible] OF
JOHN WRIGHT.
THE FOLLOWING WORDS APPEAR MORE FREQUENTLY [illegible]
[illegible] TO THE [illegible]
[illegible]

[illegible]
COINCIDENCE
GAUSSIAN
[illegible]
[illegible]
[illegible]
[illegible]

[illegible] at the [illegible] the phrase [illegible] [illegible]

HOUR 10
EN ROUTE TO
SAN DIEGO
7 AM PDT

The aircraft banked steeply over the oil fields of Long Beach and headed south towards San Diego. Graves stared out the window, thinking of Wright's file. Then he thought about his own. He wondered what it looked like, the information displayed on the unblinking cathode-ray screen in sharp white easy-to-read block letters. He wondered how accurate it was, how fair, how honest, how kind.

Graves was thirty-six years old. He had worked for the government fifteen years – nearly half his life. That fact implied a dedication which had never been there; from the start his career in government had been a kind of accident.

In college Graves had studied subjects that interested him, whether they were practical or not. On the surface they seemed highly impractical: Russian literature and mathematics. He was drafted immediately after college and did push-ups for five weeks before somebody in the Army discovered what he knew. Then he was sent to the language school in Monterey, where he remained forty-eight hours – just long enough to be tested – before being flown to Washington.

That was in 1957, and the Cold War was grim. Washington needed Russian translators desperately. There were fears of a land war in Europe, fears of grand conquistadorial campaigns conducted by World Communism, meaning those two friendly allies, Russia and China. At the time the fears had seemed compelling and logical.

Graves worked for two years in the Army as a Slavic translator, and after his discharge joined the State Department in the same capacity. The pay was good and the work was interesting; he had the feeling of being useful, of doing necessary and even important work. In 1959 he married a girl on Senator Westlake's staff. They had a daughter in 1961. They got divorced two years later. He had a kidney stone and spent five days in the hospital. He met a nice girl, almost married her, but didn't. He bought a new car. He moved to a new apartment.

In retrospect, these seemed to be the signposts, the significant shifts and alterations in his life. The years went by: he wore his hair a little longer, but the hair was thinner, exposing more of his temples. His trousers got tight, then flared, and now were baggy again, as they had been in the fifties. There were cyclic changes in himself and his world – but he was still working for the government.

State no longer wanted Russian translators. The big push was for Chinese and Japanese translators. Graves transferred into Intelligence, a division of State that was highly mathematical, heavily computerized. He worked in the foreign division for five years, doing a lot of code breaking. At that time the foreign embassies were all utilizing computer-generated codes of various kinds, and it was challenging work – even if the messages usually turned out to be requests for funds to refurbish the ballroom on the second floor, or to hire additional kitchen help. Graves was interested in the codes, not in the content.

In 1970 he was moved to the domestic end. It seemed a minor change at the time, and a change he welcomed. He was ready to do something different. It was a long time before he realized just how different it was.

During his fifteen years in the government, slowly and imperceptibly his enemy had shifted from the Big Bear, the Russkies, the Reds, the ChiComs – to his fellow Americans. That was his job now, and he hated it. It was tapping telephone transmissions and competing with other agencies; it was value judgements and it was very, very political.

Nothing was clean and direct any more. And Graves didn't like it. Not any more.

Graves had been planning to quit State for a long time, ever since his domestic work had become distasteful. But he hadn't quit.

What kept him was partly inertia and partly the fear that he might be unable to teach Slavic or mathematics. At least, that was what he told himself. He was reluctant to admit the real reason, even to himself.

The fact was that he took a genuine pleasure in his work. The pleasure was abstract, the pleasure of a compulsive jigsaw puzzle worker who will fit the pieces together without caring what the puzzle really means. It was a game he loved to play, even if it was fundamentally nasty.

He also liked the notion of an opponent. In the foreign division he had been up against institutions – embassies, foreign press corps, political groups of various kinds. In the domestic division, it was most often a single individual.

Graves had long ago discovered his skill at poker, backgammon, and chess – games which required a combination of mathematical insight, memory, and psychological daring. To him the ideal was chess – one man pitted against another man, each trying to calculate the intentions of the other in a game of enormous complexity with many alternatives.

That was why he had agreed to leave Washington in order to follow the activities of John Wright. In the realm of puzzles and games, nothing was more challenging than John Wright.

He and Wright were well matched: the same intelligence, the same mathematical background, the same fondness for games, particularly chess and poker.

But now after three months, Phelps was rolling him up. Wright would be arrested; the game would be called off. Graves sighed, trying to tell himself that this did not represent a personal defeat. Yet it was; he knew it.

With a low whine the plane began its descent towards San Diego, skimming in over the roofs of the highest buildings. Graves didn't much like San Diego. It was a utilitarian town dominated by the needs of the Navy, which ran it with a firm, conservative hand. Even its sins were dreary: the downtown area was filled with bars, pool halls, and porno movie houses which advertised 'Beaver films – direct from Frisco!' as if San Francisco were six thousand miles away and not just an hour up the coast. Fresh-faced sailors wandered all over the downtown area looking for something to do. They never seemed to understand that there was nothing to do. Except, possibly, to get drunk.

Despite the early hour San Diego was hot, and Graves was grateful for the car's air conditioning. Lewis drove away from the airport, glancing occasionally at Graves. 'The marshals checked in with us an hour ago.'

'So you know?'

'Everybody knows. They're just waiting for you to say the word.'

As they left the airport they passed beneath a banner stretched across the road: WELCOME REPUBLICANS. Graves smiled. 'I'm going to hold off for a while,' he said. 'At least until this afternoon.'

Lewis nodded and said nothing. Graves liked that about him, his silence. He was young and enthusiastic – characteristics Graves severely lacked – but he knew when to keep his mouth shut. 'We'll go directly to his apartment,' he said.

'All right,' Lewis said. He didn't ask why.

'What time did Wright quit last night?'

'Nine. Lights out at nine.'

'Rather early.' Graves frowned. It was rare for Wright to go to bed before midnight.

'Duly noted on the time-clock sheets,' Lewis said. 'I checked them myself this morning.'

'Has he ever done that before? Gone to bed at nine?'

'July fifth. He had the flu then, you remember.'

'But he's not sick now,' Graves said, and tugged at his ear. It was a nervous habit he had. And he was very nervous now.

There were a lot of cops stationed on the road from the airport to the city. Graves commented on it.

'You haven't heard?' Lewis said.

'Heard what?'

'The President's coming in today.'

'No,' Graves said. 'When was that decided? This is only the second day. I'm surprised he'd show before he's nominated.'

'Everybody's surprised. Apparently he intends to address the Convention delegates before the balloting.'

'Oh?'

'Yeah.' Lewis smiled. 'It's also apparently true that there are some squabbles in the rules committee and the platform committee. He's going to straighten that out.'

'Ah.' It was making more sense. The President was a practical politician. He'd sacrifice the drama of a grand entrance if he had to get a political job done earlier.

'We just got the word a couple of hours ago,' Lewis said. 'Same with the police. They're furious. The Chief has been making statements about how hard it is to provide security . . .' He gestured at all the waiting cops. They were stationed every thirty yards or so along the road. 'I guess he managed.'

'Looks like it. What time is he due?'

'Around noon, I think.'

They drove on in silence for a while, leaving the coast road and heading into the centre of town. Graves noticed that Broadway had been dressed up, its honkytonk glitter subdued a little. But there were a lot of tough-looking girls around.

Lewis commented on it. 'The City Fathers are going crazy,' he said. 'About *that.*' He jerked his thumb towards one spectacularly constructed girl in a tightly clinging pants suit.

'I thought it wasn't allowed.' Traditionally San Diego was free of hookers despite the large sailor population. Tijuana was just twenty mi[illegible]way; those services were usually provided across the border.

'Nothing they can do about it,' Lewis said. 'Just in the last few hours they've all been coming in. Every damned hooker for a thousand miles is here. All the girls from Vegas and Reno and Tahoe. It's the Convention.'

'But the City Fathers don't like it.'

'The City Fathers hate it,' Lewis said, and grinned. It was a youthful grin, the grin of a person who still found sin amusing, risqué, fun.

Graves could no longer find the fun in prostitution. Why not? he wondered. Was it age – or was it striking some uncomfortable chord in himself?

But he didn't pursue the thought. Lewis turned left, going up into the hilly section of town towards Wright's apartment.

HOUR 9
SAN DIEGO
8 AM PDT

Lewis slowed as they approached a dry cleaning van advertising 24 HOUR SERVICE AT NO ADDITIONAL CHARGE and PLANT ON PREMISES.

'You want to talk to 702?' Lewis said.

'Yeah, for a minute,' Graves said.

Lewis pulled over. Graves got out. The driver in the van wound down his window.

'I hear you're rolling it up,' the driver said.

'That's right,' Graves said.

'When?'

'Later today.'

'What's proto until then?' Proto was slang for protocol.

'Business as usual,' Graves said. 'Where's 703?'

'Off duty today.' The driver shrugged.

'Call them in. I want them to pick up the girl this morning.'

'Oh?'

'Yeah.'

'Anything else?'

'Yeah. You got some coffee in there?'

'Sure. Two cups?'

Graves looked into the sedan at Lewis. 'You want coffee?'

Lewis shook his head.

'Just one,' Graves said. 'Black with four sugars.'

The driver sighed and looked into the interior of the dry cleaning van. 'Give the boss his usual,' he shouted. A moment later a styrofoam cup was passed out to Graves.

'You're going to catch diabetes,' the driver said.

'This is breakfast,' Graves said, and walked back to his car. In the background he heard the van driver saying, '702 to 703. Over. 702 to 703. Over.'

Graves got in the car, slammed the door. To Lewis: 'Let's go.'

'The apartment?'

'The apartment.'

Wright had taken a fashionable apartment in the hilly north-central section of San Diego, not far from the Cortez Hotel. His building looked out over the city and the harbour. At this hour people were leaving the apartment house, standing in front and waiting until the doorman brought their cars around from the underground garage. Graves had had some trouble getting used to that when he first came here. He was accustomed to the East, where people in cities walked to work or took public transportation. In California, everybody drove. Everybody.

Wright himself was an exception. He had a driver and a limousine. But then, Wright was always an exception, he thought.

Wright usually came out about 8:20. His girl for the night – one of five or six he saw with some frequency – preceded him by ten or fifteen minutes.

'There she is,' Lewis said.

Graves nodded. It was odd how you could tell Wright's girls. Even from across the street they could be spotted instantly. Yet there was no particular physical type, no particular details of dress. They weren't professionals. But there was a certain quality about them, something blatantly erotic. They were the girls a man would choose if he wanted to be reassured. Graves watched this one, who wore a simple white dress and had very long legs, as she climbed into a Datsun sportscar and drove off.

'701 to 703,' he said, speaking into the intercom mounted on the dash.

There was a crackle of static. '703 here. I thought we could sleep in today.'

Graves ignored the complaint. 'Red Datsun sportscar, convertible, California licence ZVW 348. Got it?'

'Got it. Out.'

A moment later, a Ford station wagon drove past them, and the driver gave them the high sign briefly. That was 703.

Graves slumped down in his seat, thinking. They had not bothered to interrogate Wright's girls in recent weeks. When they began, they had had dozens of interviews with the girls. Sometimes they had been straight interrogations; more often they were casually arranged meetings. In both cases the information was monotonously the same. John Wright was a nice and kind and generous and charming man. He was also nervous and definitely conservative. He sweated a lot, preferred the missionary style, kept the room dark, and always remained a little aloof.

Hardly valuable intelligence insight.

'Why do you want this one?' Lewis asked. And then he said, 'Here comes the limo.'

A black Lincoln limousine pulled up in front of the apartment building. The chauffeur, George Marks, got out, buttoned his uniform jacket, and stood by the door of the passenger side.

Graves had never picked George up for questioning. It had seemed too risky. Now he wondered if that had been a mistake. But he could think of a hundred possible mistakes he had made, especially today. Especially when Wright was being arrested.

'Why are they going to arrest Wright?' Lewis asked. He hadn't got an answer on his previous question, so he was trying another.

Graves lit a cigarette. 'Phelps is nervous.'

'But this computer-tapping business isn't enough –'

'Phelps is running scared just now. There's talk of closing down his division of Intelligence. In fact, the new Secretary is thinking of closing down all State Intelligence work.'

Lewis raised his eyebrows. 'Where'd you hear that?'

Graves smiled. 'I'm in Intelligence myself.'

Lewis glanced at him a moment, then looked back out the window. A man emerged from the apartment building – stocky, neatly dressed, moving purposefully.

'There's Wright,' Lewis said and started the engine of his car.

Graves had watched John Wright get into his limousine every morning for sixty-six days. He knew the routine well: George opened the door and tipped his cap; Wright nodded to him, bent over at the waist, and slipped quickly into the back seat. George closed the door, paused to tug at his leather gloves, and walked around to the driver's side. In the back seat Wright stared straight ahead or opened his newspaper to read.

But this time John Wright stared across the street directly at Graves. And he continued to stare until the limousine moved off in the hot San Diego morning.

Lewis was now very good at following in San Diego traffic; he kept pace three cars back. After a time Lewis said, 'He was looking at you.'

'He certainly was.'

'Do you think he's on to us?'

'Impossible,' Graves said. He thought of the closet in his apartment. He had five distinctly different suits in that closet, and he rotated them on different days. He thought of the three sedans and the four delivery trucks that the Department used for surveillance work. Different manufacturers, different colours, and a new licence plate every week. He had never parked in the same place, never waited for Wright in the same way. He had never presented Wright with a recognizable pattern.

'Impossible,' he said again.

And then Graves thought of himself. If he were Wright, would he discover that he was being followed? Even with all the precautions, the safeguards, the changes? He liked to think that he would.

And if he would, why not Wright?

'He's deviating,' Lewis said, nodding at the limousine. Graves saw that it was true. Normally on Wednesday mornings Wright went to Balboa Park, where he walked in the gardens, fed the pigeons, and relaxed. But he wasn't doing that today.

He was going downtown.

'Where's our other car?' Graves said.

Lewis picked up the car radio receiver. '701 to 702. Where are you?'

There was a hiss of static. '701, we're at Third and B, going downtown.'

Lewis glanced at Graves, who nodded.

'Very good, 702,' Lewis said, and clicked off.

The second car, the dry cleaning van, was running in advance of the limousine. That was standard procedure – one car tailing from the front, one from behind. In cities on really big jobs, they sometimes used four cars, working all around the suspect. But Graves didn't want a four-car tail, and in any case Phelps would never have approved the expense.

The limousine went down Third to Avenue A, then turned left going west.

'702, you have him?'

'We still have him.'

Lewis followed the limousine as it went crosstown on A and stopped, pulling up in front of a warehouse. Lewis pulled to the kerb half a block behind. They watched as Wright got out and went inside.

Graves lit a cigarette, and they waited. But after only a minute or so, Wright reappeared and got back into his car. The limousine started off.

'Wonder what that was about?' Lewis said.

As they passed the warehouse, Graves read the lettering. He was surprised to find it wasn't a warehouse at all.

BURNS BROS PLASTICS
VACUUM MOULDING
Containers of all sorts

'Damned if I know,' Graves said. He made a note of the name and address in his notebook and then looked up at the street. The limousine was going north now. It went two blocks and turned left, then left again. It pulled up in front of another warehouse.

'It seems he's doing some shopping,' Lewis said.

'He's in the wrong part of town.'

'I'll drive past,' Lewis said, and continued smoothly past the warehouse and the parked limousine. Graves looked out of the corner of his eye. He saw George, the chauffeur, lighting a cigarette. He saw the large glass windows of the warehouse, which was also a salesroom of some kind. Inside he saw Wright standing at the counter receiving a package. In the window were displayed various shining pieces of laboratory equipment.

SANDERSON SCIENTIFIC EQUIPMENT AND SUPPLY
Serving Hospitals and Laboratories
Since 1953

Graves had to smile. Only in California would a date like 1953 seem proof of ageless service to the consumer. 'We'll wait for him here,' he said, and Lewis pulled over at the end of the block and cut the engine.

Graves checked his watch. It was 8:39. A moment later the limousine sped past them while he was making a note of the scientific supply company and its address. Lewis followed a short distance behind.

The limo again went uptown and pulled over in front of a machine shop. Wright got out and was met at the door by a man carrying a small paper bag. Wright shook hands with the man, who was dressed in dungarees and a blue work shirt. Then Wright opened the paper bag to look inside. He removed one small, shiny metal object, nodded, exchanged a few more words with the man, and got back into his car.

The limousine drove off.

As they passed the machine shop, Graves noted the address and the name. He stared at his list. 'A plastics manufacturer, a scientific supply house, and now a machine shop.'

'He isn't buying presents for his girls,' Lewis said, and laughed.

'Did you check out that purchase last week?' The week before, Wright had also visited several small industrial manufacturers.

'Yeah,' Lewis said. 'It was two twelve-foot lengths of flexible hosing. Very unusual.'

'What's unusual about that?'

'It was stainless steel.'

'Meaning?'

Lewis shrugged. 'The guy I talked to said that nobody bought flexible stainless steel hosing any more. People use either plastic or something like aluminium. Stainless is only used for piping very corrosive materials.'

'Such as?'

'Concentrated dyes, corrosive gases, that kind of thing. The guy said it was pretty uncommon. Most highly corrosive stuff is pumped through glass piping. But of course, glass isn't flexible.'

'And Wright bought two lengths of flexible steel?'

'Right. Twelve-foot lengths. At eighty-three dollars a foot.'

Graves nodded and watched the car. 'He's buying a lot of specialized equipment. Why?'

'You mean, why is he doing it?'

'No,' Graves said. 'I mean, why is he doing it himself, in person?'

'I don't follow you. Why shouldn't he do it himself?'

'Because he's too smart for that,' Graves said.

The limousine went uptown twenty blocks and pulled over in front of another building. The sign said HARRELSON GARMENTS AND CUSTOM GOODS. They watched Wright get out of the limo and go inside.

'I'll be goddamned,' Graves said.

'What is it?' Lewis said.

'Harrelson was in the papers a year ago. They made rubber suits and whips and things like that; there was a minor scandal.'

Lewis shook his head: 'It really is true, then.'

'What?'

'About your memory.'

Graves shook his head. He'd been through all this before. 'I don't have a photographic memory,' he said. 'I have a better than average memory, that's all.'

'Are you trying to convince me?'

'No, just telling you.'

'You sound sore.'

'You better understand,' Graves said, 'that I don't have any special powers. None at all. I just plod along, doing a job.'

'Here he comes,' Lewis said. He pointed to Wright emerging from the store with an armful of packages wrapped in brown paper. George, the chauffeur, jumped out and came around to help carry the packages. Wright indicated that they were to go into the trunk of the car. George locked them there, then came around, shut Wright's door, and drove off.

'I'd like to know what was in those packages,' Graves said, making notes in his book.

'Bet you anything it's kinky rubber clothing,' Lewis said.

'What will you bet?'

At that, Lewis laughed. He knew you didn't bet with Graves. Nobody bet with Graves. He might deny special skills until he was blue in the face, but the fact was that Graves was the best gambler, bettor, poker player that any of them had ever seen.

They followed the car for another five minutes. Then it pulled up in front of a sporting goods store. Wright again got out. He said something to George, who nodded and went across the street to a coffee shop. The car was left alone. It could not be seen easily from either the sports store or the coffee shop.

'Looks like we have our chance,' Graves said. 'Pull over.'

As Lewis pulled the sedan over, Graves opened the glove compartment and took out a large, circular key ring. On it were keys to Wright's apartment in New York, his apartment in San Diego, his limousine, his Alfa sportscar, his summer house in Southampton, his winter house in Jamaica. And several others as well. They were all neatly tagged.

Lewis said, 'Isn't this a little risky –'

'We're going to arrest him today,' Graves said. 'It doesn't matter now.' He got out of the car, feeling the heat of the morning air. He walked forward to the limousine. It took just a moment to insert his key in the trunk and open it. He raised the trunk lid partway and looked at the brown paper packages. There were three, closed with strips of tape. He opened a corner of one and peered inside.

The package contained black rubber belts, about six inches wide, formed into loops of varying diameters. He closed the package and squeezed the others. They all seemed to contain belts.

Frowning, he shut the trunk. And then, because he was in a gambling mood, he walked into the sporting goods store. As he went through the door he glanced back at Lewis. Lewis looked horrified.

The store was large and spacious; he did not see Wright immediately. Walking among the aisles of equipment, he finally spotted him in the water sports department. Wright was gesturing with his hands, forming a shape in the air.

Graves walked over and stood beside him at the counter. To do so gave Graves an immediate burst of excitement. He had never been so close to his subject before. Wright was smaller than he had thought – several inches shorter than Graves himself. And much finer-boned. A delicate man in an English-cut suit, dapper as Phelps, but without the vanity that made Phelps unbearable.

The salesman said, 'I'll be right with you, sir,' and Graves nodded.

Wright glanced over at him and smiled vaguely. There was no recognition in the glance. None at all: Graves was sure of it. They were just two customers at the same counter.

Graves bent over, peering down at the glass case, which contained depth gauges and underwater watches. He could see Wright's face reflected in the glass surface.

'Is this the one you mean, sir?' the salesman asked.

Graves glanced up and saw the salesman holding a small air tank, painted yellow.

'That's the one,' Wright said.

'Now, do you understand about this tank?' the salesman said. 'It's not the standard seventy-two cubic foot model. This one only has twenty-five minutes of air at –'

'That's the one I want.' Wright said it quietly, but his voice cut the salesman off. Graves was impressed by the understated authority in the voice – and presumably in the man.

'Yes, sir. How many was that?'

'Three.'

'I think we have three in the storeroom,' the salesman said. He turned to Graves: 'Was there anything in particular?'

It seemed to Graves that the salesman was much less deferential to him than he was to Wright. But perhaps he was being paranoid.

'I need a depth gauge,' Graves said.

'They're all down there,' the salesman said, pointing to the case. 'Be with you in a minute. Three, was it, sir? I'll get them.'

The salesman walked off.

After a moment Graves said, 'I don't know anything about this.'

There was a short, ambiguous pause. Finally Wright said, 'Diving?'

'Yes. It's a present for my son.'

'He does a lot of diving?' Wright was being formal, polite, barely interested.

Wait until I put the handcuffs on, Graves thought. 'Oh, he's a nut about it, but he doesn't really get much chance. Twice a year during school vacations we go down to Mexico. That's really all.'

Wright said, 'That one there is a good one.' He pointed to a gauge in the case.

Graves nodded. 'I really don't know anything about this,' he repeated.

'You don't dive yourself?'

'No,' Graves said. 'It always seemed too dangerous to me.'

'There's a certain thrill in danger, though.'

'Not for me. Not at my age.'

'You prefer golf?'

'Poker,' Graves said, and looked directly at Wright for the first time.

Wright smiled. 'Poker can be very challenging,' he said. 'But it's like any other game. If you get too good, you're limited in your opponents.'

'Yes, I've found that.'

'You're good?' There was just the slightest taunt in the voice, the slightest goading.

'Yes, I'm good,' Graves found himself saying.

For a moment the two men exchanged a level, appraising look. Wright broke it; he looked down at the counter. 'Still,' he said, 'I admire the young, with their exuberance in physical sports. It raises the stakes. You can be hurt, you can be injured. You can even be killed.'

'But when you're young, you don't think of that. It doesn't matter.'

'Oh,' Wright said, 'I think it always matters. Dying always matters.'

The salesman came back. 'You're in luck, Mr Johnson,' he said cheerfully. 'You got the last three tanks. Shall I have them put in your car?'

'That will be fine,' Wright said, smiling.

'You must be out of your mind,' Lewis said. They were back in the car, following the limousine.

'Not at all.'

'I suppose you went up and talked to him.'

'As a matter of fact, I did.'

Lewis smiled. 'I know you've been doing this a long time, but still . . .'

'Look,' Graves said, 'we're picking him up later today.'

'But you're teasing him, playing a game . . .'

'Of course,' Graves said.

The limousine went up Avenue D and pulled to a stop in front of a large hotel. A man came out, bent over the limo, and talked to Wright in the back seat. The conversation lasted several minutes. Finally the man turned and went inside. The limousine pulled away from the kerb.

Graves snatched up the microphone. '701 to 702.'

'702 here.'

'He's all yours from now on. Stick to him. Out.'

Lewis looked stunned. 'What the –'

Graves pointed to the figure of the man going back into the hotel. 'Follow that man and see where he goes. His name is Timothy Drew.'

Hour 8

SAN DIEGO

9 AM PDT

'Hold out your hands.'

Peters held out his hands and waited while the supervisor ran the Geiger counter over them. It made a soft clicking sound in the cavernous warehouse garage.

'Stand still.'

He stood and watched as the counter probe was passed over his chest, his abdomen, his legs. It was a little like being frisked.

'Turn around.'

He turned. He heard the counter clicking as it was passed down his spine to his feet.

'Okay. Next.'

Peters stepped aside, and the driver moved forward. As the driver was being checked by the Geiger counter, the dispatcher said to Peters, 'First run?'

'Yes,' Peters said.

'Ever done a DC before?'

Peters pointed to the counter. 'Not like this.'

'What've you done, explosives?'

'Yes.'

'This is easier than explosives or flammables,' the dispatcher said. 'We've got a regulation for two men in the cab, and another for staying under forty-five miles an hour. That's it. We can take all the roads, all the tunnels and bridges. Much easier than explosives.'

Peters nodded. 'What exactly is it?'

The dispatcher consulted his clipboard. 'Mostly hospital supplies. Cases of intravenous saline, twelve quarts to the case, thirty cases in all. Cases of penicillin G, forty-eight ampoules to the case, fifteen cases in all. And two rad cartridges.'

'Rad cartridges?'

'Two bars of plutonium-238 oxide. That's a radioactive isotope. One thousand grammes each – they're packed in lead cylinders.'

'That's our dangerous cargo?' Peters asked.

'You bet,' the dispatcher said.

The driver finished his check and came over to join them. 'What was that all about?'

'Insurance,' the dispatcher said. 'You have to be cleared before exposure to the cargo, in order for our coverage to be effective. We should also do a blood test, but we don't bother.' He turned to Peters. 'Reeves, this is your rider, Peters. Peters, Reeves.'

Reeves shook hands with Peters. As he did so he gave him a slightly surprised look, as if something were mildly wrong.

The dispatcher nodded across the warehouse. 'Truck's over there,' he said. 'Have a good trip.'

Peters blinked in the sun and put on his sunglasses. Beside him, Reeves sighed. 'Bright day,' he said.

'Sure is.'

'You new at this?'

'Yeah.'

'What'd you do before?'

'Aeroplane tail assembly. Lockheed, in Palmdale.'

'Tail assembly, huh?' Reeves said, and laughed loudly.

'They laid me off.'

Reeves stopped laughing and nodded sympathetically. 'Rough,' he said. And then after a moment, 'Laid off the tail assembly.' And he chuckled some more.

Peters smiled. He felt confident about Reeves, who was fat and sloppy and casual – and fifteen years his senior. There wouldn't be any difficulty.

'Well,' Reeves said, 'since you're new at this, you might as well learn the ropes.' He reached into his pocket and withdrew a plastic bottle of yellow pills. He handed it to Peters.

'What's this?' Peters asked.

'Dex. Go ahead, take one. Feel terrific.'

Peters shook a pill into his hand and paused. Reeves took one, then reached into his leather jacket and produced a flask.

'Wash it down with this,' he said. 'Vodka. No smell.' He handed Peters the flask.

Peters dropped the pill from his hand, letting it roll down between the seats. He pretended to swig from the flask, then returned it to Reeves.

'You'll learn,' the driver said, and smiled.

Peters nodded and leaned forward slightly in his seat. That way he could see out the side-view mirror and keep an eye on the black Ford sedan that had been following them for the past fifteen minutes.

Ten minutes later they were on the San Diego Freeway, moving down the far right lane. They passed a green and silver sign: HACKLEY RD EXIT 1 MILE. Peters shifted in his seat. Reeves was talking about his children.

'They're good kids,' he was saying, 'but they don't show proper respect. All this screaming about the President, all this revolution talk, it makes me want to –'

'We get off at the next exit,' Peters said.

'No,' Reeves said, 'we don't stop for another –' He broke off.

Peters had taken the pistol from the pocket of his leather jacket.

'Hackley Road,' Peters said quietly. 'Turn off the ramp and go half a mile east. You'll see a small dirt road. Turn right onto that.'

'I'll be goddamned,' the driver said.

They came to Hackley Road and turned off on the exit ramp. They drove east. Peters glanced in the side mirror and saw that the Ford sedan was still following.

'I should have known,' Reeves said.

'How's that?'

'I should have known something was wrong when I shook hands. It's your hands.'

'What about them?'

'They're as soft as a baby's ass,' Reeves said. 'You never worked in your life.'

'Turn right, up here,' Peters said.

It went smoothly. Reeves pulled the truck onto the dirt road and stopped in a clump of eucalyptus trees. Peters made Reeves get out and lie on his stomach on the ground, with his hands over his head.

Reeves said nothing for a long time. Finally he said, 'You going to shoot me?'

'Not if you stay quiet,' Peters said.

The Ford sedan drew up behind the truck and three men, all wearing children's Halloween masks, jumped out. A driver remained at the wheel. Nobody spoke as the men opened the back of the truck, climbed up on the hydraulic tailgate, and went into the cargo area.

'Nice and easy,' Peters said, standing near Reeves with the gun. 'Nice and easy.'

Reeves did not move.

The men emerged from the truck carrying two small, extremely heavy boxes. Peters could see the triple-blade radiation symbol on the boxes. The men closed the truck and started to load the boxes into the car. One of them came over and expertly tied and gagged Reeves with adhesive tape.

Then, speaking for the first time, the man said, 'Let's go.'

Peters was confused. 'I thought you were going to take –'

'Let's go.'

Peters went with the man, who wore a Donald Duck mask, and got into the car. The sedan backed out of the road and drove off.

The men all left their masks on. One of them said, 'What's the time?'

'Nine thirty-two.'

'Perfect.'

Peters was given a mask of his own, a witch's mask with day-glo pink cheeks and wild eyes. He pulled it on and said, 'I thought we were taking the penicillin too.'

'The plan was changed,' somebody said.

'But if we just take the capsules –'

'The plan was changed this morning. We were told to take only the capsules.'

Peters frowned and said nothing. He felt the change in plan was a terrible mistake. By stealing the penicillin they would have confused the issue; it might have taken the truckers several days to discover the theft of the radiation capsules. But now they'd find only the capsules gone . . . It was too obvious, too simple. Why had the change been made?

'Time?'

'Nine thirty-six.'

The driver nodded and pulled over to the side of the road. The men sat quietly, not removing their masks. Peters looked at the backs of their necks, noticing the length of their hair, the condition of their collars, the way they were dressed. Several minutes passed.

'Time?'

'Nine forty.'

The driver put the car in gear. He drove down the road through gently rolling farm country. the morning air was still cool.

'There it is.'

Up ahead was another dirt road turnoff, with another truck pulled off the road and another man standing over the driver.

'Remember, we want twenty pounds of it.'

The black sedan pulled up behind the truck. Peters was given the spool of inch-wide adhesive tape; he quickly tied and gagged the driver. Meanwhile the others opened the truck and removed several small packages. They were wrapped in clear plastic and looked like bread dough: a whitish, puttylike substance. The men carried two packages each, bringing them around to the trunk of the sedan, setting them in carefully, then going back for more.

Peters gave a mask to the man standing over the driver with the gun. The gunman did not speak. Then Peters went around to the trunk of the sedan and began counting the plastic packages. When there were twenty, he placed them in a suitcase, locked the case, and closed the trunk.

The men climbed back into the sedan and drove off.

'Time?'

'Nine fifty-one.'

'Beautiful.'

The black sedan drove back to the San Diego Freeway and stopped at the on-ramp for Hackley Road. Peters got out. So did the other gunman. Peters went around to the trunk and removed the suitcase with the plastic packages. The other gunman placed the two radiation capsules into the blue canvas gym bag.

He stood with Peters until the sedan had pulled onto the freeway and disappeared. Then, his back to the road, he took off his mask. Peters took off his mask as well. The other man removed a paper American flag from the bag. With Peters' help, he taped the flag onto the side of the suitcase.

Then Peters removed his black-haired wig and his moustache. The other man removed his blond wig and peeled away a reddish, new-looking scar on the side of his cheek.

The two men looked at each other and laughed.

'Well done, brother,' Peters said, and clapped him on the back.

They waited five minutes, and then another black sedan, very dusty, pulled up. An older man leaned out and said, 'Give you boys a lift?'

Peters said, 'We're going to Phoenix.' As he said it, he glanced at his brother, who was frowning.

'Hell of a long way,' the old man said. 'Anyhow, you want to go south. This is the north ramp.'

'We're just resting a minute.'

The man looked at them as if they were peculiar, shrugged, and drove onto the ramp. His car rattled as he gathered speed, and then he was gone. They were left by the roadside.

His brother lit a cigarette.

'You know,' his brother said, 'this is going to create a hell of a mess.'

'That was the idea.'

'When are you leaving?'

'Four.'

'That's cutting it awfully close. I'm getting out at three.'

'To Vegas?'

His brother nodded. 'You?'

'Chicago.'

'You better hope nothing delays that plane on the ground.'

'There's another flight at four thirty. I'm booked on that one as well.'

His brother nodded.

Down the road they saw a car approach. It was black and white, a sedan. they couldn't see it clearly, but as it came closer they saw the configuration better. A police car.

'Shit,' Peters said.

His brother lit another cigarette. 'What if he wants to look in the suitcase? What if he –'

'We haven't done anything wrong,' Peters said. He glanced at his watch. It was almost ten o'clock. Where the hell was the pickup?

The police car came closer.

'I don't like this at all,' his brother said.

'We haven't done anything wrong,' Peters said again.

The police car approached them and put on its blinker.

'The bastard's pulling over.'

But the car did not pull over. Instead, it drove onto the ramp and merged with traffic. The cop hardly glanced at them.

They sighed.

'What time is it?'

'I have ten, on the nose.'

In the distance a car got off the far ramp and made a U turn under the freeway. It was a Cadillac convertible with a woman driving. She came around and started up the ramp, going back the way she had come. She stopped when she saw them.

'I took the wrong turnoff. Can I give you fellows a lift?'

'We're going to Phoenix,' Peters said.

'No kidding,' the woman said. 'That's my home town.'

'No kidding,' Peters said. 'Which part?'

'The right part,' she said.

The two men exchanged glances, then got into the car, placing the suitcase in the back seat. The woman said, 'Sorry I'm late,' and drove off. Nothing else was said.

HOUR 7

SAN DIEGO

10 AM PDT

The voice crackled over the telephone line. 'Fucking around with the computers,' Phelps said, 'is not my idea of a joke.'

Graves sat in the hotel phone booth and stared across the lobby at Lewis and a marshal. Lewis was gesturing to Graves to get off the phone. 'It wasn't intended as a joke.'

'How was it intended?' Phelps said, his voice heavy with sarcasm.

'It was intended as an attempt to recall my own file.'

'You're not supposed to do that.'

'There are a lot of things I'm not supposed to do.'

'And you seem bent on doing all of them,' Phelps said. 'Have you picked up Wright yet?'

'No.'

'You've certainly had time; it's ten –'

'I want to play him a little. Besides, I have somebody else.'

'Oh?'

'Timothy Drew.'

'Where?'

'Upstairs. We've got him in a hotel on Third.'

'We've been looking for him for forty-eight hours,' Phelps said. 'And I mean looking *hard*. How did you find him?'

'Wright led us to him,' Graves said. That was the only thing that bothered Graves. It was too much like a setup, as if Wright were giving him Drew.

'How convenient,' Phelps said. 'When are you going to arrest him?'

'He's already arrested. The federal marshals are up there with him.'

'I mean Wright.'

'Later in the day,' Graves said.

'You and your goddamned poker games,' Phelps said. 'I want you to call me in an hour.'

'All right.'

'Stop agreeing with me. Just do it.' And he hung up.

Graves left the phone booth. Lewis came over with his notebook open. They headed for the elevator.

'What've you got?' Graves said.

'It's pretty strange,' Lewis said. 'At Sanderson's today, Wright bought a Model 477 scintillation counter. Retail price, two hundred forty-seven dollars.'

'A scintillation counter?'

'Yeah. It's apparently a kind of high-grade Geiger counter. Reads radiation.'

'Does it have any other uses?'

'Nobody knows of any.'

'What else?'

'The machine shop ground three fittings for him to custom specifications. All high-grade stainless steel. Two of them are on-off pressure valves with special handles. The third is a T coupling which brings together two hoses into a common outlet.'

'What's special about the valve handles?'

'The handles have a series of perforations, presumably so the valves can be turned on and off by some sort of machine.'

'Any information about what kind of machine would be used to turn the valves on and off?'

Lewis shook his head. 'But they said the handles are spring-loaded. A moderate pressure will snap them from full shut to the full open position.'

'Now that's really interesting,' Graves said. 'You mean there are no intermediate positions for the valves?'

'Yes. It's either full shut or full open.'

The elevator came. Graves pressed the button for the sixth floor.

'When did Wright order these custom fittings?'

'Last week. Rush order.'

'Really interesting,' Graves said. 'What about the plastics store?'

Lewis scratched his head. 'Three weeks ago Wright ordered two pressure-moulded plastic tanks from them. Long tanks roughly a foot in diameter and eight feet long. Specified as triple-laminate things able to withstand pressures up to five hundred pounds per square inch. The shop was surprised to get the order.'

'Why?'

'Well, the guy said nobody orders tanks like that in plastic. It's too dangerous. All high-pressure tanks are metal and seamless. There's no advantage to plastic, even in weight. Plastic tanks, if they're triple-thickness, are heavier than metal.'

'Wright wouldn't order something that had no advantage.'

'Well,' Lewis said, 'the guy thought Wright was a pretty strange customer. Not only did he want these plastic tanks, but he wanted them made out of allacron.'

'Which is?'

'A very tough resilient plastic, but highly combustible. It burns like a bastard, so it isn't used much.'

'Have the tanks been finished?'

'They were delivered a week ago to a private airfield hangar in El Cajon, about twelve miles from here.'

'You have the address?'

'Yeah. I tried to call; no telephone there.'

Graves frowned. He was more convinced than ever that Wright was playing with him, leading him on a chase, daring him to put the puzzle together.

Two high-pressure tanks of combustible plastic.

Special steel fittings, including a T nozzle.

Two steel hoses, flexible.

All that made a kind of sense. You had two tanks, and two hoses that joined in a T nozzle, so that the contents of the two tanks – liquid or gas, presumably – would come together at the T nozzle and then be expelled as a mixture.

That was easy to visualize.

But what was the point? And what was the point of the skin-diving tanks, and the rubber strips, and the Geiger counter?

The elevator stopped at the sixth floor. They both got out and walked to Drew's room.

'Where is Wright now?'

'I just checked with 702. He's in that apartment on Alameda.'

'The one he rented last week?'

'Right.'

The newly rented apartment was also a puzzle. Wright had apparently leased it on the spur of the moment. It seemed to coincide with nothing, except with the fact that one girl had been seen leaving his old apartment near the Cortez hotel three mornings in a row. This was unusual enough to suggest that Wright was going to set her up as his mistress.

'702 talked to the doorman. Wright told the doorman they'd be moving furniture into the apartment later in the day.'

'Hmmm.' That seemed totally unreasonable to Graves. Wright wouldn't spend time supervising domestic arrangements for a girl. It was beneath him.

Stopping in the hallway, Lewis said, 'Does all this make sense to you?'

'No,' Graves said. 'Not yet. But I except to get some help.'

Without knocking he opened the door and entered Drew's room.

Timothy Drew sat in an overstuffed chair and said, 'I want to see my lawyer.' His voice was calm. The fact of his arrest, and the presence of two federal marshals standing by the doors with their hands resting on the butts of their revolvers, did not seem to disturb him at all.

Graves' eyes swept the living-room. It was an expensive hotel suite, furnished in a heavily elegant style. Altogether, not bad for a man one year out of the Army. He sat down in a chair opposite Drew.

'I want to see my lawyer,' Drew repeated. His eyes flicked once to Graves, then went back to the cops, as if he had decided Graves was unimportant.

'You'll have that opportunity,' Graves said.

Drew's eyes snapped back, fixed on him.

'In due time,' Graves added.

'I want to do it now.'

'We're in a hurry,' Graves said. His voice was not hurried at all. 'We'd prefer to have a statement from you now.'

'I have nothing to say.'

Graves shrugged, and lit a cigarette. He never took his eyes off Drew. This was going to be a kind of chess game, he knew, and it was a game he could win if he kept his temper.

'I want to see my lawyer,' Drew repeated.

Graves did not reply. He just stared. That was the simplest form of pressure, and he wanted to see if it would work.

'Listen,' Drew said, 'who are you guys, anyway? You haven't got the right to push me around. You haven't got a warrant –'

'Did you show him the warrant?' Graves said.

'Yeah, we showed him the warrant,' one of the marshals said.

'Show him again.'

The marshal snapped open the warrant in front of Drew, then took it away.

'Signed by a federal district court judge at nine thirty this morning,' Graves said. 'All in order, all perfectly legal. You're arrested on a charge of conspiracy to steal classified information. It carries a mandatory twenty-year prison sentence if you're convicted. Parole is not granted for such charges. Do you know what that means?'

'I want to see my lawyer.'

'I'm trying to help you,' Graves said quietly. 'Keep your mouth shut and listen: You were observed tampering with the computer terminals at Southern California Underwriters. You tapped into classified data banks at known times which coincide with your access to the terminals in question. We have traced back the lines. Furthermore, you utilized certain codes known to you but outdated. This gives you away. It's quite straightforward. You'll get out of prison when you're about fifty.'

Graves stood up. 'Now think carefully, Mr Drew. Is it worth it?'

Drew's face went blank, neutral, composed. 'I want to see my lawyer.'

Graves sighed and walked around the living-room, looking idly at details. He glanced into the bedroom and saw a packed suitcase next to the bed. He looked back at Drew. 'Planning a trip?'

'I want to see my lawyer.'

Graves walked into the bedroom and opened the suitcase. The bottom half was filled with lightweight clothing, bathing trunks, sports clothes.

The top was packed with money, neat stacks of twenty-dollar bills held tight in paper sleeves. Fresh from the bank. He counted the stacks: it came to roughly twenty thousand dollars.

In a corner of the bedroom draped over a chair was a sports coat. He found a ticket for the noon plane to Acapulco in the pocket. A first-class ticket, one-way.

He returned to the living-room. Drew watched him, wary now.

'Planning a trip, Mr Drew?'

'I want to see my lawyer.'

'That's a lot of money in there, Mr Drew.'

'I have nothing to say.'

'From your ticket, it looks like you were planning to stay down there. Not come back.'

Drew shook his head. He did not speak. He was sweating, but still in control; he showed no sign of cracking.

'Can you account for all that money?'

'No comment. I want to see –'

'All right,' Graves said. He sighed and turned to the marshals. 'Okay, lock him up.'

The marshals grabbed Drew roughly, each taking an arm. For the first time Drew became excited: 'What's going on?'

Graves found the reaction interesting. Was Drew afraid of jail? Was he homosexual? Did he need drugs? Graves decided to play on the jail fear. 'We don't have many options, Mr Drew. I know it's not pleasant, but we've got to put you in jail. You know, there's a lot of paperwork, and sometimes people get lost. Inadvertently deprived of their rights. I mean, people have spent a day or two in jail, and their papers get mixed up. So they don't get any food, or water, or anything. But you see, nobody knows you're there. For a while.'

'Where are you taking me?' Drew's voice was strained now, very tense.

'Downtown. We'll be talking to you again in a day or so, when you're more . . . relaxed.'

'*Downtown San Diego?*'

'Yes,' Graves said. And he suddenly realized that Drew wasn't afraid of jail at all. He didn't want to stay in the city. That was what he was afraid of.

'You can't do that!'

'Just watch it happen,' Graves said, lighting a cigarette.

'I've got to leave,' Drew said. He was now openly agitated. 'I have to leave. I have to leave.'

'Why?'

'It's my sister. She's sick, in Mexico. That's why I have the money, I need it –'

'You don't have a sister,' Graves said. 'You have one brother two years older than you, who sells insurance in Portland, Oregon. Your father is still alive and lives in Michigan. Your mother died two years ago of a heart attack.'

Drew's body sagged.

'Put him down,' Graves said to the marshals. They dropped him back into the chair. 'Now listen to me,' Graves said. 'You aren't going anywhere without giving us some help.'

Drew stared at him. 'I want a cigarette.'

Graves gave him one.

'What time is it now?' Drew asked dully.

'Ten thirty.' Graves lit the cigarette for him and watched as Drew sat back and inhaled.

'Listen,' Drew said, 'I have to catch that plane at noon.'

'Why is that?' Graves said.

'I don't know,' Drew said. 'I swear to God I don't know.'

'What do you know?'

'I know I have to get out of San Diego today, because . . . something is going to happen.'

'How do you know this?'

'John told me.'

'John Wright?'

'Yes.'

'What did he say?'

'He said that the binary would go off today. In San Diego.'

'And what is the binary?'

'I don't know.' He sucked on the cigarette.

'Mr Drew, you're going to have to do better –'

'I swear to you, I don't know.'

Graves paused. He let Drew sweat, and let him smoke. Finally he said, 'How is the binary related to the information you tapped from the data banks?'

'I can't be sure. The information was in two areas. One was easy to get, the other was hard. First, John wanted supply routings. I spent a couple of days learning how to plug into the subroutines to release the information. I kept getting "no authorization" printouts, but finally I managed to plug in.'

'And extract what?'

'Supply routings for different things.'

'Things?'

'Well, John gave me the codes for what he wanted. Don't ask me where he got those codes. One of the codes was for a thing called "Binary 75 slash 76". I got a supply routing for that.'

'And you have no idea what the code represents?'

'None. Except that it's obviously Defence Department material, transported by rail.'

'How do you know that?'

'From the routings themselves. You can't be sure what's being transported, but you can tell the method air, rail, other surface vehicle, truck convoy. You can tell the method.'

'What else can you tell?'

'You can tell the C and C ratings.'

'What's that?'

'Command and control provides a rating for all material transportation. The ratings are in grades: grades one through seven. One is pretty safe, or pretty inexpensive. Like clothing, or spare auto parts – that sort of thing. Seven is very expensive or very dangerous.'

'What was Binary 75 slash 76?'

'It was grade seven.'

'What did you think Binary 75 slash 76 represented?'

Drew puffed on his cigarette. He did not answer for a long time. Finally he said, 'I thought it was radioactive materials.'

'Meaning?'

'I don't know. Components for a bomb, maybe. I don't know.'

Graves almost immediately rejected that explanation, although it fitted with the scintillation counter.

'What else could it be?'

'You asked me what I thought it was. I told you.'

'You think Wright planned to make an atomic bomb?'

'I think he planned to steal the components. Maybe he already has.'

'And do what with them?'

'I don't know. But it's going to happen today.'

Graves sat back. Drew put out his cigarette. Graves offered him another.

'What does a code like "binary" mean?'

'It could be just a random code,' Drew said. 'But they usually have some specific meaning. That's why I thought it was atomic components.'

'Binary . . .'

'Meaning a twin system,' Drew said. 'Something with two active parts, two units. Nuclear bombs are like that. You have two sections of uranium, neither of which will explode by itself. But you bring them together, and you reach critical mass, start a chain reaction.' He snapped his fingers. 'Bingo.'

By now Graves was convinced that Drew believed this explanation. Graves did not. Whatever Wright planned, it had nothing to do with atomic bombs. That didn't fit with the tanks and hoses and nozzles, all of which pointed to some gas or liquid apparatus.

'He's insane,' Drew said suddenly. 'That's the trouble. He's crazy. He's convinced that everybody is out to get him, and he's convinced that the government is being turned over to the wrong elements, and he's convinced that only he can set things right.'

'You mentioned that there was something else you had to tap from the data banks. What was it?'

'That was strange,' Drew said. 'I'd already tapped the Defence routings. My job was over. Then John asked me to tap into the State data banks.'

'State?'

'State Department. I said I couldn't. He told me to try, and gave me some more codes. I don't know where he got those either, but they worked.'

'What was the information he wanted?'

'File summary on one person,' Drew said. 'A man who worked in State Department Intelligence named Graves.'

'I see,' Graves said. 'Did you obtain the information?'

'Eventually.'

'And you gave it to Wright?'

'Yes. He wasn't interested in it, I don't think, except for one part. The psychological test scores.'

'Do you remember anything else?'

'No. Only that John was very interested in the psychological tests.' He puffed on the cigarette. 'I remember he said when he saw it, "Well, this is the final cog in the machine", and laughed.'

'What did he mean by that?'

'Damned if I know,' Drew said.

[illegible] said I [illegible]
some name today. I don't know what [illegible]
[illegible]

[illegible] was the information he wanted?

The company on one project. [illegible]
[illegible] Intelligence [illegible]

[illegible]

[illegible]

Yes. He wasn't interested in [illegible] except for [illegible]
[illegible]

[illegible]

[illegible]
He pulled [illegible]. I remember he [illegible]
[illegible] and [illegible]

[illegible]

[illegible] said.

HOUR 6
SAN DIEGO
11 AM PDT

As they left Drew's room, Lewis said, 'By the way, they're still holding the girl.'

'The girl?' Graves was distracted, thinking about what Drew had said.

'The girl we picked up this morning.'

'Oh yes. Where is she?'

'They've got her downstairs. In the grand ballroom.'

Graves nodded and checked his watch. They'd held the girl for several hours already. 'I'd better see her now,' he said. 'What's her name?'

Lewis consulted his notes. 'Cynthia Lembeck.'

'How does she seem?'

Lewis shrugged. 'Nervous.'

Anyone would be nervous, Graves thought, who had to spend much time in the hotel's grand ballroom. It was a cavernous space with ornate walls and ceiling, but for some reason all the tables and chairs had been removed. The ballroom was empty except for a girl sitting in a fold-up chair near one wall, and a marshal standing nearby.

Graves went over to her.

Seen close, she was darkly tanned, conventionally pretty, and older than he had expected – in her late twenties or early thirties.

'Miss Lembeck?'

'Oh,' she said in surprise. 'It's you.'

That stopped him. Stopped him cold. 'You recognize me?'

'Well, just your face. I've seen your picture.'

'Where?'

'John's apartment.'

'I see.'

'Are you a friend of his?'

'Not exactly,' Graves said. 'I work for the government.'

'Something to do with the Convention?'

'Not exactly.' He switched into a straightforward interrogation mode. 'How long have you known Mr Wright, Miss Lembeck?'

'About a month.'

'How did you meet him?'

'Through friends.' She glanced from Graves to the marshal. 'Have I done something wrong?'

'No, no. We just want to ask you some questions. What can you tell us about Mr Wright?'

'He's very nice,' she said. 'We're engaged.'

'Oh?' That was a surprise.

'Yes. He bought me an apartment, just last week.'

'I see.'

'It's very nice. At least, it will be.'

The girl was not very bright, but she had a sweet sexiness that was unmistakable. Still, he couldn't imagine Wright marrying her. In the past he had married well-known women, celebrities.

'There's nothing there now,' the girl said. 'They're moving furniture in today.'

'You must be excited.'

'Oh, I am. John's excited, too. But he has so much on his mind.'

'How do you mean?'

'Well, business things. He's very interested in politics, you know.'

'No, I didn't know that.'

'You didn't?' she seemed puzzled. 'I thought – well, anyway, he is. And this morning, we had the news on the television, and they announced that the President was coming into town. Well, he got very upset, and started making telephone calls. A lot of them.'

'What sort of calls?'

'I don't know. They were long distance.'

'Did you hear any of them?'

'No.'

'Are you sure?'

'Well, I heard him ask the operator for area code 801. That's Washington, isn't it?'

'Yes,' Graves said. He knew that it wasn't but he could check it later.

'He was very upset. And then later, he mentioned China. He doesn't like the President about China, you know.' She sighed. 'He thinks it's very wrong.'

'I see. You say you've seen my picture –'

'Only last night,' she said. 'That was the first time. I thought you were related to him or something. Because he has your picture up all over the place.'

'This happened last night?'

'Yes. But he was strange last night, anyway. Nervous.'

'I see. What about?'

'I don't know. He's worried about business things. He said something about a shipment he's expecting.'

'What else was strange, last night?'

She hesitated, apparently embarrassed.

'Go on,' Graves said gently.

'Well, it was different last night. He was very . . . vigorous. He did it three times.'

'I see,' Graves said.

Outside the ballroom Lewis was in a phone booth, checking the area code. He came out and fell into step with Graves. 'Eight oh one,' he said, 'is Utah.'

'Any particular place?'

'No. The whole state is one area code.'

'Shit,' Graves said. 'I wish we had a tap on his phone.'

'Well, we did our best to get it,' Lewis reminded him.

'Yeah,' Graves said. He sighed. 'I never thought I'd hear myself complaining because we hadn't tapped a phone.'

'Things are different now,' Lewis said.

'They sure are.'

They went outside into the bright hot morning sun and climbed into the car. Lewis started the engine.

'Where to?'

'Miss Lembeck's new apartment. The one Wright just rented.'

'Okay,' Lewis said.

When they arrived at the apartment building, they saw Wright's limousine parked in front. Behind the wheel George was reading a newspaper.

'Are we fully set up across the street?' Graves said.

'We should be,' Lewis said.

Graves nodded. 'Wait here. I'll go see what they've found.'

The day before, they had set up a surveillance unit in the apartment building facing Wright's. Graves rode to the nineteenth floor, got out, and walked to Room 1905. He knocked once.

'Who is it?'

'Graves.'

The door was opened for him. He entered the room. It was small and bare except for equipment clustered around the windows. There were two sets of binoculars on tripods and three sets of cameras; four chairs; a directional microphone, also on a tripod; recording equipment; film canisters; heaped ashtrays. And a television set.

On the TV Walter Cronkite was saying, '– are trying to get a vote from the Alabama delegation, which is apparently still in caucus.' In the background a booming, echoing mechanical voice was saying, 'Alabama . . . Alabama . . . Alabama . . .'

Graves ignored the TV. 'What've you got?' he asked.

One of the three men in the room stepped away from the binoculars. 'Have a look,' he said.

Graves looked.

From this vantage point he could see directly into one window of Wright's apartment on the nineteenth floor of the opposite building. There were no drapes on the window, which made it easy to see in. The room was bare except for four peculiar wooden structures standing in the centre of the floor.

'They had drapes on that window too,' the man said, 'but they took them off half an hour ago.'

'From all the windows?'

'No. Just this one.'

Graves frowned. Why? Did they know they were being observed? Did they want to make it easier? Because that was what they had done. He could see Wright striding around the room, directing two other people. Wright was working in shirtsleeves.

'The window's open,' Graves said. 'It must be hot as hell in there.'

'That's right,' the man said. 'The window has been open ever since Wright showed up. An hour ago.'

'What're those wooden things on the floor?'

'Sawhorses,' the man said. 'We figure they had paperhangers in there. Paperhangers use sawhorses. But there's something funny going on.'

'How do you mean?'

'Well, look at the sawhorses closely. They have indentations cut in them.'

Graves looked. He could see a broadly curved, U-shaped cut in each sawhorse.

'Why?'

'Beats me. They just cut them a while back.'

'You mean, specially?'

'That's right. They've been doing a lot of unusual things in there. Every so often Wright sticks his hand out the window, and he's got this whirling thing, like a kid's whirling top . . . He sticks his hand out there for a minute, then pulls it back.'

Graves looked away from the window. 'Describe it exactly.'

'It has four arms,' the man said, 'and at the end of each is a cup, to catch the wind. Sort of a weathervane. But there isn't much wind today.'

'Anemometer,' Graves said.

'A what?'

'It measures wind velocity.' Why should Wright want to know the wind velocity outside the window of his girl friend's apartment?

'Why does he care about that?' the man said.

Graves shook his head and turned back to the window, examining the sawhorses through the binoculars. Each sawhorse with its single indentation in the crossbar.

Four sawhorses.

Two tanks. Of course! The crossbars would have indentations so that the tank wouldn't roll off. 'You seen any tanks in there?'

'Nothing like that,' the man said. 'All we've seen is a lot of mechanical equipment.'

'What kind of mechanical equipment?' Graves peered through the binoculars. He didn't see any equipment at all.

'It looks like pumps and stuff,' the man said. 'It was right in the middle of the floor.' He glanced through the binoculars, then shook his head. 'They must have moved it to another room. They had some electronic equipment, too.'

'What kind?'

'Looked like a hi-fi, maybe.'

Graves thought of several nasty remarks, but said nothing. A hi-fi, for Christ's sake.

'That guy in there must be pretty weird,' the man said.

Graves turned on him. 'He is not weird. He is a brilliant and a dedicated man. He is engaged in a complicated plot and he is daring –' He broke off. The man was staring. 'He's not weird,' Graves finished, and returned to the binoculars.

As he watched, John Wright stepped to the window and extended his hand. He held an anemometer; the cups spun lazily. After a moment Wright withdrew the instrument and returned to directing the other men in the room.

Graves turned away from the window and made some calls.

'Department of Defence.'

'Public Information, please.'

'Just a minute, please.' There was a clicking.

'Public Information, Miss Conover speaking.'

'I'd like to talk to Lieutenant Morrison, please.'

'One minute, please.' More clicking.

'Lieutenant Morrison's office.'

'John Graves calling for Lieutenant Morrison.'

'Just a minute, I'll see if he's in.' Still more clicking.

'Morrison here. What is it?' As usual, Morrison sounded harried.

'Pete, this is John Graves at State. I'm in San Diego, and I need some information.'

'Shoot.'

'Pete, I need to know what a code word represents. The code word is Binary 75 slash 76.'

Morrison coughed in surprise. 'Where'd you hear that?'

'Pete, just tell me what it means.'

'Jesus, this is an open line.'

'I know it's an open line. Tell me what it means.'

'Where are you calling from?'

'San Diego.'

'Jesus, you must be out of your mind.'

'I need the information, Pete. And I need it now.'

'Look,' Morrison said, 'if you don't mind me saying so, this is pretty irregular. You've just popped a –' He broke off again. 'Honestly,' he said, in his most honest, public-information officer's voice, 'I'd have to obtain clearances and confirmation of need-to-know from your department, and then I'd have to pass it on to the Army, and then –'

'Okay, fine. Do it.'

'You have to supply the clearances.'

'I haven't got time.'

'You're asking me on an open line to define a hot new weapons system and break its code and you haven't got –'

'Look,' Graves said. 'If I call Phelps, can he call you and requisition this information?'

'*Verbal* requisition?' Morrison seemed shocked. 'This is pretty heavy stuff for a verbal. You sure you don't want specifications on the ABM sites while you're at it, and maybe Polaris submarine coordinates? Any other minor details?'

Graves suppressed his anger. Morrison was such a bureaucratic ass. 'I need the information,' he repeated. 'I need it now.'

'Sounds like this may be a matter for Defence to look into,' Morrison said. 'We'd be curious to know how you got that coding in the first place. Why don't you forward us a complete report along with a requisition AB-212; that's the green form. I may be able to release the data to you in a day or so, and –'

Graves hung up.

'This is Graves.'

'I know who it is,' Phelps said. 'What do you have to say for yourself?'

'Binary 75 slash 76,' Graves said. 'It's a coding – I need to know what it means.'

'Binary 75 slash 76,' Phelps said. There was a long pause; faintly, Graves could hear him writing it down. Finally he said, 'Are you going to tell me where you came across it?'

'It's what Drew tapped from the system,' Graves said.

'Oh,' Phelps said.

'But Drew doesn't know what it means, either.'

'How did he happen to tap in?'

'Wright told him to.'

'Well, did you ask Wright why?'

'No.'

'Why not?'

'I haven't picked him up yet,' Graves said.

'You haven't picked him up yet.'

'That's right.'

'What are you waiting for, a divine edict?'

'I thought I already had that,' Graves said. 'But the situation is complicated. You see, Wright asked for more information from the data banks.'

'More information?'

'About a State Department Intelligence officer named John Graves. He pulled my file.'

'Don't be an ass,' Phelps said. 'Pick him up immediately. He's on to you, that's clear.'

'Not only is he on to me,' Graves said, 'he's showing me a puzzle and daring me to work it out.'

'This is not a fucking poker game,' Phelps said. 'We can convict Wright on the basis of evidence we already have, and –'

'You can't touch him,' Graves said. 'When he cools down, Drew won't testify against him. You haven't got a prayer of making a case against Wright. Our only chance is to wait – and to get me my own file contents.'

'You're joking.'

'I'm not.'

'It's out of the question.'

'I want to know what he knows.'

'About yourself?'

'Yes. Especially psychological test scores.'

'Out of the question. Unheard of.'

'You've got to do this for me,' Graves said. 'You've got to get me that file.'

'I can't requisition it,' Phelps said, 'without higher authority. You know that. You're much better off picking Wright up.'

'Not yet.'

'I have to go to lunch,' Phelps said. 'Call me later. I think you're acting like a fool.'

And Phelps hung up.

'State Department.' A singsong voice.

'Office of the Secretary, please.'

'Thank you.' Lilting.

'Secretary of State, can we help you?'

'Mr Burnett, please.' Burnett was one of the Secretary's advisers. Although young, he had worked himself up from a speech writer to a close and influential position. Graves knew him slightly.

'Mr Burnett has gone to lunch and is not back yet. He is expected shortly.'

'Did he leave a number?'

'No, I'm sorry – just a moment, he's coming through the door. Whom shall I say is calling?'

'John Graves. State Intelligence.'

'One moment please, Mr Graves.'

There was a very long wait, and a humming sound as Graves was put on 'hold'. Then a click.

'Burnett here.'

'Tom, this is John Graves calling.'

'How are you, John? It's been a long time. When was it? Senator Evans' party, I think. You had a very cute –'

'Listen, Tom. I have a problem. I need your help.'

'I'll do what I can.' Said very smoothly, in the manner that all those people adopted sooner or later. No promises, but very smooth.

Graves paused. 'I need my file.'

'Your file?'

'Yes. My Department file.'

'I don't think – just a minute – no, please hold that, I'll call him right back – John?'

'I'm here.'

'I'll have to call him right back. Yes, in a few minutes. Absolutely. Five minutes, tell him five minutes. John?'

'I'm here,' Graves said again.

'Now what was it? Your file?'

'Yes. I need my own file.'

'I've never heard of anyone *needing* their own file,' Burnett chuckled. 'Curiosity, yes, but –'

'Tom. Stop being polite. This is Department business and it's very important.'

'Perhaps you could stop by the office and –'

'I can't stop by the office. I'm not in Washington. I'm in San Diego.'

'Oh?' There was hesitation now, the smoothness gone. 'San Diego?'

'I'm doing an SS here. A guy named John Wright. I need my own –'

'Who?'

'John Wright.'

'Well why didn't you say so before? I'll get it to you right away. The Secretary has directed everyone to cooperate fully with the San Diego operation.'

Graves sighed. That was refreshing. He had an enormous sense of relief. What was that joke? It felt so good when he stopped.

'Let's see,' Burnett said. 'I'll have to get an authorization. I can do that with the Undersecretary; I don't have to bother the boss. Then we have to get it to you. You don't have access to a photoprinter?'

'No.'

'Well, let's see . . . I don't know what sort of facilities are available in San Diego. Look. There's one sure bet. The police department. They have a printer for sure. I can transmit the file contents to you over that. But it'll take time to do the whole thing.'

'I don't want the whole thing. I just want the psychological test scores.'

'You do?'

'That's right,' Graves said.

'Well,' Burnett said, 'I can have that for you right away. They'll transmit in fifteen or twenty minutes. Okay?'

'Okay,' Graves said. 'And thanks.'

'For Christ's sake, don't mention it,' Burnett said. Graves hung up.

Downstairs in the car, Lewis said, 'You look like you've gargled with Drāno.'

'I have,' Graves said. He got into the car. 'We're going to the police station.'

Lewis pulled out into traffic. 'Anything interesting happening upstairs?'

'They've found that Wright is preoccupied with weather today.'

'Weather?'

'Yes.'

'I don't get it,' Lewis said.

'Neither do I,' Graves said.

HOUR 5

SAN DIEGO

12 NOON PDT

'You're very quiet,' Lewis said, as they drove to the police headquarters.

Graves nodded. 'I was thinking of an old story. It's back in the soft-data section of Wright's file. You know about the Murdock killing?'

Lewis shook his head.

'It happened in New York five years ago. Wright was married to a girl named Sarah Layne, and when it broke up, she started seeing a man named Murdock. A Texas oil man. Big spender, big ladies' man.'

Lewis nodded.

'Well, Murdock got an anonymous tip that he would be killed. Got it about seven in the morning. He believed it, so he called his chauffeur and had him go over the car carefully. The chauffeur found a bomb, and notified Murdock. Murdock went down to the garage to see the bomb and had his chauffeur remove it. The chauffeur carried it away. And Murdock, who was an oilman and interested in explosives, leaned into the engine compartment to examine how the bomb had been wired in. And thirty seconds after the first bomb was removed, a second one exploded. Murdock was killed instantly.'

'Nice.'

'Wright was questioned but never charged. There was nothing to point to him. that's the story. But whoever did it knew a lot about Murdock.'

'You think that's the way Wright operates?'

'I know it is.'

Lewis was silent for a moment. 'Why are we going to the police station?'

'To find out how much Wright knows about me,' Graves said.

The spinning drum produced the transmitted image with almost painful slowness. It made a loud, distracting, clanking sound. neverthless, when the first sheet came off the drum Graves grabbed it up eagerly and read with intense concentration – ignoring the clanking, the room, the cops all around, Lewis, everything.

The first sheet was printed out in block letters, as Wright's file had been:

PSYCHOLOGICAL TESTING: JOHN NORMAN GRAVES (STATE INT: DOM)
REASON FOR TEST: FIVE YEAR SURVEY
AUTHORIZATION FOR TEST: D/STATE 784-334-404
SPECIAL CONSIDERATIONS: QUERY SUITABILITY FOR DOMESTIC WORK

TEST SCORES AND RESULTS:

1. RORSCHACH INK BLOT

A. TEST SCORES: OF CHIEF INTEREST IS THE USE OF COLOUR AS RESPONSE DETERMINANT. THIS IS CONFUSING. ON THE ONE HAND, SUBJECT USES COLOUR AS A MAJOR FACTOR IN DETERMINING WHAT HE SEES IN THE FORM. THIS SUGGESTS EMOTIONAL VOLATILITY AND IMPULSIVENESS. ON THE OTHER HAND, HE IS RESPECTFUL OF THE FORMS OF THE COLOUR, SUGGESTING CAUTION AND PERHAPS OVER COMPLIANCE.

B. DYNAMIC CONTENT: THERE IS A HEAVY EMPHASIS ON THEMES OF MASCULINE AGGRESSION. WAR, ANIMALS FIGHTING, WEAPONS, AND BLOOD RECUR OFTEN. A SENSE OF COMPETITION AND STRUGGLE IS USUALLY PRESENT. THERE IS A REMARKABLE LACK OF GUILT EXPRESSED IN ASSOCIATION WITH THESE THEMES. SUBJECT IS APPARENTLY COMFORTABLE IN SITUATIONS OF TENSION AND COMPETITION.

C. PATTERNS OF THOUGHT ORGANIZATION: NO MAJOR INSIGHTS HERE EXCEPT A STRONG SENSE OF EXCITEMENT RELATING TO ALL COMPETITIVE THEMES AND SUBJECTS.

D. TEST BEHAVIOUR: SUBJECT CLEARLY REGARDS THIS TESTING SITUATION AS ONE IN WHICH HE MUST PROVE HIMSELF. IN LINE WITH HIS COMPETITIVE IMPULSES, HE DEFINITELY PLAYS OFF THE TESTER IN A RATHER UNUSUAL MANNER. HE DOES NOT TRY TO PLEASE THE TESTER OR WIN HIS APPROVAL. NOR DOES HE EVIDENCE HESITANCY OR UNCERTAINTY ABOUT HIS CHOSEN ANSWERS. INSTEAD, HE UTILIZES THE TESTER AS A SOURCE OF INSIDE INFORMATION ABOUT THE TEST ITSELF. HE ATTEMPTS TO MANIPULATE THE TESTER. ONE HAS THE SENSE THAT HE BRINGS ALL POSSIBLE RESOURCES TO ANY TEST SITUATION – AND HE REGARDS THE TESTER AS ONE AVAILABLE RESOURCE. THIS IS NOT STRICTLY FAIR, OF COURSE. BUT THERE IS A CERTAIN AMORAL QUALITY ABOUT THE SUBJECT IN COMPETITIVE SITUATIONS. ONE FEELS HE WILL DO ANYTHING TO WIN.

2. THEMATIC APPERCEPTION TEST (TAT)

COMPETITION, THE NEED FOR ACTION, THE EXCITEMENT OF STRESS, AND THE HORROR OF FAILURE IN COMPETITIVE ACTIVITY WERE FREQUENT THEMES. IN CERTAIN INSTANCES THERE WAS A SENSE OF IMMORTALITY ACHIEVED BY VIGOROUS COMPETITION: THE SUBJECT TALKED ABOUT ONE PICTURE AS SHOWING A MAN WHO HAD 'CHEATED DEATH'. IT IS WORTH INDICATING THAT IN MOST AREAS THE SUBJECT HAS A STRONGLY DEVELOPED SENSE OF CONVENTIONAL MORALS, PERHAPS EVEN AN OVERRESTRICTED SENSE. HOWEVER,

'Where's the next page?' Graves said impatiently.

'Coming off now,' Lewis said, and pulled it from the machine. He handed it to Graves.

IN COMPETITIVE SITUATIONS THESE MORALITIES ARE ABANDONED, AND IF THERE IS A CONFLICT – SUCH AS TWO MEN COMPETING FOR THE FAVOURS OF ONE WOMAN – THE SUBJECT WILL CHEERFULLY PROPOSE CHEATING IN ORDER TO WIN THE DAY. PSYCHOGENETICALLY IT IS CLEAR THE SUBJECT IS COMPETING WITH HIS FATHER IN A CLASSIC OEDIPAL SITUATION. STORIES ABOUT THE FATHER EMPHASIZE THE DEMANDING, UNCOMPROMISING, AND COMPETITIVE QUALITY OF THE FATHER-FIGURE AND THE DIFFICULTY OF WINNING APPROVAL. IT IS LIKELY THAT THE SUBJECT LIVES IN A WORLD PEOPLED BY HIS FATHER, AGAINST WHOM HE MUST CONSTANTLY STRIVE AND COMPETE.

FAILURE IS ABHORRENT TO THE SUBJECT. HE USUALLY DOES NOT ALLOW THAT IT MIGHT OCCUR. PHYSICALLY HE EQUATES FAILURE WITH CASTRATION. THE FEAR OF FAILURE IS SO GREAT THAT THE SUBJECT MAY BE IMPULSIVE. QUICKNESS OF RESPONSE IS IMPORTANT TO HIM, AND A SOURCE OF PRIDE.

3. ABBREVIATED WAIS IQ TEST

RAPIDITY OF RESPONSE WAS A MAJOR FACTOR HERE IN PRODUCING AN INITIAL TEST SCORE OF 121. THE SUBJECT FELT COMPELLED TO FINISH EACH SECTION IN LESS THAN THE ALLOTTED TIME. TESTER'S IMPRESSION IS THAT THE SUBJECT HAS A TEST SCORE AT LEAST 10 POINTS HIGHER THAN THAT. THIS IS CONFIRMED BY PAST IQ TESTS, WHICH HAVE SCORED THE SUBJECT IN THE 130-140 RANGE. THE SUBJECT'S WILLINGNESS TO DAMAGE HIS OWN PERFORMANCE BY OVERLY FAST REACTION SHOULD BE NOTED.

4. CRONBERG DIAGNOSTIC PERSONALITY QUESTIONNAIRE

SUBJECT SCORES HIGHLY IN MANIC SCALES WITH SOME CONSISTENT EVIDENCE OF PARANOIA. THIS MAY WELL RELATE TO HIS COMPETITIVE DRIVES.

5. SUMMARY

'Is there another sheet?' Graves asked.

'It's coming, it's coming,' Lewis said. He smiled. 'You're really devouring this, aren't you?'

'I think it's important.'

'Don't you know it all already? It's about you.'

'No,' Graves said. 'It's what somebody else thinks of me. There's a difference.'

Lewis shrugged. The third and final sheet came from the printer. Graves read it.

IN SUMMARY WE CAN SAY THAT JOHN GRAVES IS A HIGHLY INTELLIGENT, IMAGINATIVE, AND CONVENTIONALLY MORAL MAN WITH AN ASTOUNDINGLY STRONG COMPETITIVE DRIVE. HIS NEED TO COMPETE IS ALMOST HIS MOST OUTSTANDING TRAIT. IT SEEMS TO OVERWHELM EVERY OTHER ASPECT OF HIS PERSONALITY. IT IS HIGHLY DEVELOPED, AND RUTHLESS IN THE EXTREME. THERE IS NO QUESTION THAT HE IS A GOOD BETTOR, GAMBLER, POKER AND CHESS PLAYER – TO NAME HOBBIES HE PROFESSES TO LIKE.

IF THERE ARE ANY DEFECTS OR HIDDEN FLAWS IN HIS BEHAVIOUR, THEY ARE HIS IMPULSIVENESS AND HIS DESIRE TO FINISH A TEST SITUATION RAPIDLY. HE FREQUENTLY PERFORMS BELOW HIS MAXIMUM LEVEL BECAUSE OF A DESIRE FOR SPEED. HE OFTEN FEELS THAT A PROBLEM IS SOLVED WHEN IT IS ONLY HALF FINISHED, OR TWO-THIRDS FINISHED. THIS SITUATION MUST BE GUARDED AGAINST BY HAVING A LESS BRILLIANT BUT MORE THOROUGH PERSON CHECKING HIS WORK AT INTERVALS.

Graves stared at the last page. 'Is that all?'

Lewis nodded at the photoprinter, which had turned itself off, the roller no longer spinning. 'Looks like it.'

'I'll be damned,' Graves said. He folded the sheets carefully, put them in his pocket, and left the police station.

The radio crackled. '701, this is 702. We are following the limo east on Route Five.'

Graves picked up the microphone. 'Who's in the limo?'

'Only the subject, 701. And the chauffeur.'

'Nobody else?'

'No, 701.'

'When did they leave the apartment?'

'About five minutes ago.'

'All right, 702. Out.'

Graves looked at Lewis. 'Where now?' Lewis asked. 'Route Five, east,' Graves said. 'And step on it.'

The White Grumman Gulf Stream jet landed gracefully and taxied to a stop near a small hangar. The side door went down and two men climbed off. Several workmen in coveralls boarded the plane. After a moment they began unloading two large cardboard boxes.

Standing near the end of the runway of the small private field in El Cajon, Graves squinted through binoculars. The heat made everything shimmer; San Diego was hot, but El Cajon, twelve miles inland, was much hotter. 'Can you make it out?' Graves asked.

Beside him Lewis leaned against the roof of the sedan to steady his arms as he held the binoculars. He pulled his elbows up quickly. 'Ouch,' he said. He held the binoculars freehand. 'I don't know what they are,' he said. 'But I know what they look like. They look like mattress boxes.'

Graves lowered his glasses. 'That's what they look like to me. Where did this flight originate?'

'Salt Lake. A private airfield.'

'Mattresses from Utah? Did the plane make intermediate stops?'

Lewis shook his head. 'I don't know. But it certainly wouldn't have to stop: it's got a cruising range of just under four thousand miles.'

While they watched, they heard the tinny sound of the car radio saying, 'The President is due to arrive at any moment. The delegates are tense with anticipation. No one yet knows what he intends –'

Graves reached in and clicked it off.

Meanwhile, the workmen carried the two mattress-sized boxes into a green hangar.

'He rented that hangar last week,' Lewis said. 'Moved a lot of equipment in.'

'What kind of equipment?'

'Nobody's had a look yet.'

Graves bit his lip. That was an opportunity they'd missed. Several days ago somebody should have been in that hangar at midnight, taking pictures.

'Do you want to move in on him now?' Lewis asked.

Graves shook his head. 'He's got five or six workmen there. There's two of us, and two in 702. None of us have guns.' He sighed. 'Besides, what if they really are mattresses?'

'They can't be.'

Graves didn't think it possible either. But he wasn't willing to take a chance. He found himself worrying about Wright's new apartment in San Diego. Perhaps this was all a diversion, a feint to get him away from the apartment while something important was done there. He had no confidence in the men sitting across the street, observing and filming. Like every organization in the world, the State Department hired mundane men to carry out mundane jobs. Stationary surveillance was the most mundane. If the men weren't dull when they started, they soon became that way.

'We'll wait,' he said.

The mattresses were taken into the hangar, and the limousine was driven inside. The doors were closed.

'Time?'

'Twelve forty-one,' Lewis said.

A minute passed, and then something remarkable happened. The men came out of the hangar and walked over to the aeroplane. They stood alongside it, ostensibly checking it over but actually doing nothing at all; just waiting.

Wright was not among them.

'I don't get it,' Graves said. 'Where's Wright?'

'He must still be inside.'

Their sedan was parked more than 200 yards from the hangar. But the wind was blowing in their direction, and they heard a faint mechanical sound. A kind of thumping or chugging.

Lewis opened the trunk and took out a directional microphone. It looked like a miniature radar antenna – a dish two feet in diameter, with a central barrel protruding. He put on earphones and tuned in the microphone.

'What are you getting?'

Lewis shifted the direction of the mike slightly. It was quite sensitive, but had to be aimed precisely.

'Wind.'

'Can you get that noi –'

'Here.'

He gave Graves the earphones. Graves listened. With the microphone aimed directly, the mechanical sound was clear. It consisted of a low hum with an intermittent pulsing thump.

'Sounds like a pump to me,' he said. He listened to the sound for several seconds more. 'What do you make of it?'

'A pump,' Lewis said, glancing at his watch. 'It's been going five minutes now.'

Graves turned from the hangar to the aeroplane and the men who were clustered around it. They had broken up into small groups of two and three, talking quietly, occasionally glancing at the hangar. George, the chauffeur, was among them. Several of the workmen asked George questions. George kept shaking his head.

Graves set down his binoculars. Why would you clear everybody out of the hangar? He could think of only one reason: Wright didn't want them to see what was going on. But as he thought about it, he saw a second reason: that Wright was engaged in something very dangerous and wanted the others a safe distance away.

Dangerous how? Radiation? Explosives? What?

'Ten minutes now,' Lewis said.

Graves scratched his head. He lit a cigarette and stared at the others by the aeroplane. It didn't make sense, he thought. Whatever Wright intended, it didn't make sense. If he didn't want the workmen around, he could easily have timed it so that they would be out to lunch. Instead he'd aroused their curiosity. They'd talk about this episode for days, maybe weeks afterwards.

Apparently Wright didn't care about that. Why not? And then as he watched, the workmen began walking back to the hangar. He had seen no signal, but they all moved at once.

Lewis took off the earphones. 'Fifteen minutes,' he said. 'The pump's stopped.'

Graves checked his watch. It was a few minutes before 1 PM. He was beginning to feel tired. It had been a long day already, starting with the call from Phelps at 4 AM and the trip to Los Angeles.

He lit another cigarette and watched the hangar. And then things began to happen very fast. The limousine drove out and off towards the entrance to the airfield. And a second vehicle emerged from the hangar.

A moving van. It followed the limousine.

Graves got onto the intercom.'702, this is 701. You got them?'

'Got them, 701.'

'Stay with them. If they split up, follow the limousine; forget the van.'

'Right, 701. Are you with us?'

'No,' Graves said. 'We're staying here.' He clicked off the microphone and said to Lewis, 'I want to look inside that hangar.'

HOUR 4
EL CAJON
1 PM PDT

It took them three minutes to get to the hangar, and by that time it was deserted except for an elderly man who was cleaning up with a long broom. There were one or two workmen out by the jet, but they paid no attention as Graves and Lewis went into the hangar.

The old man waved and leaned on his broom. 'You looking for Mr Johnson?'

'Yes,' Graves said.

'Just missed him,' the old man said. 'Left a couple minutes ago.'

'Damn,' Graves said. 'You know where he went?'

'No idea,' the old man said. 'He's a strange one. I guess rich people get that way.' He pointed to a corner of the room. 'I mean, look at that,' he said. There were several boxes stacked in the corner. 'Now what am I supposed to do with that? Oh, bring in plenty of it, says Mr Johnson. And then he doesn't touch it.'

Graves looked at the boxes. 'What's in them?'

'Detergent,' the old man said. 'Gallon jugs of detergent. He wanted ten of them. Don't ask me why – he didn't touch them.'

'When did he ask for them?' Graves said. He walked over and opened one of the cardboard boxes. Inside was a jug marked KEN-ALL 7588 INDUSTRIAL DETERGENT.

'Last week. Wanted to be sure he had them.'

'What's this stuff normally used for?'

The old man shrugged and continued sweeping. 'This is an airfield,' he said. 'We use a lot of it to get grease off parts. That stuff will cut anything. Axle grease, anything, cuts it right off.'

Graves nodded.

Across the hangar Lewis was bent over. 'Have a look at this,' he said. He pointed to a small plastic bag on the concrete floor.

'Dozens of those around,' the old man said. 'All over the floor when I came in.'

Graves picked up the bag, sniffed it, touched the inside surface. There was some kind of milky, oily stuff inside.

'He's been getting this place ready for a week,' the old man said. 'Bring in equipment, take out equipment, new stuff, old stuff. Damnedest thing you ever saw. For instance, he has this washing machine –'

'Washing machine?'

'Sure. It's still here.' He pointed to the corner. 'You're probably too young to remember those things.'

Graves walked over to it. It was an old-fashioned hand-operated tub washing machine with two rollers mounted above for a wringer. The rollers were operated with a crank. Beyond the rollers was a long, flat tray of highly polished metal.

Graves looked at the manufacturer's label: WESTINGHOUSE. The year was 1931.

'Now what,' asked the old man, 'does Mr Johnson want with an old washing machine? Huh?'

Graves began to feel nervous. For the first time all day, he felt that Wright was too far ahead of him, that the clues were too subtle, that the game was beyond him. A washing machine?

Lewis touched the roller assembly. 'I guess you could squeeze out a thin strip of anything on that machine,' he said, 'assuming it had the right consistency. A putty kind of consistency.'

Plastic bags on the floor, boxes of industrial detergent in the corner – ordered but unused – and a washing machine. Then he remembered.

'Where's the pump?'

'I don't know,' Lewis said. 'But it doesn't matter. Look over here.' He pointed to some equipment near the washing machine. A canvas tarp was draped over it; he pulled it away.

'Spray gun and four cans of paint.' He bent over. 'Black, yellow, white, red.'

'He was using the pump to spray paint?'

'That'd be my guess,' Lewis said.

Graves looked around the room. 'What'd he spray it onto?'

'Whatever it was, he took it with him. Wait a minute.' Lewis was again bent over. 'Have a look at this.'

He moved another tarp to reveal a full rubber diving wet suit, a full face mask that covered eyes, nose, and mouth, and a small air tank – one of the three that Graves had seen Wright purchase earlier in the day.

There were also several black rubber loops of different sizes.

'Just one suit?'

'Looks like it,' Lewis said. He moved the suit with his foot, spreading it flat on the floor. 'Wright's size?'

'Roughly. But these black loops . . .'

'I counted six,' Lewis said. 'Four little ones, one big one, and one medium.'

'What the hell did he use them for?'

The old man came over and stood by them, staring down at the rubber suit. 'You ask me,' he said, 'he's just a crazy man. Rich people get that way.' He sighed. 'Ten gallons of detergent. Now what am I going to do with that?'

Graves was tense in the car going back to San Diego. Lewis asked him what he was thinking about and he said, 'My psychological tests.'

'Did they surprise you?'

'In a way.' He didn't bother to explain.

Graves felt the same way about his tests that he did whenever somebody sent him a photograph of himself. The question in his mind was, Is that the way you see me? Really? It was surprising. There was nothing new, no great discovery – but the quality, the emphasis, could be unsettling.

It was no news to him that he was competitive. He'd spent enough late nights playing poker with killers – and Washington had plenty of lethal poker players, blood players who got into nothing but twenty-dollar-ante games – to know that he was fiercely competitive. He liked to win and he hated to lose. That was nothing new.

The idea of his impulsiveness was not new, either. He had recognized it in himself. But the notion that this impulsiveness could be destructive – could get in his way – that was new. He had never considered it before.

There was a second problem relating to the psychological tests: How had he managed to get them in the first place? Burnett had been reluctant until Graves mentioned something about Wright. Then Burnett couldn't move fast enough.

Why?

The car radio buzzed. Lewis answered it. '701 here.'

'701, this is Central. Do you have Mr Graves there?'

'He's with me,' Lewis said, and handed the mike to Graves.

'Graves speaking.'

'We have a Washington call for you. Hold on please.'

There was a clicking, an electronic tone, and more clicking.

'Listen, you son of a bitch, I want your information.' Graves recognized the voice as Morrison at Defence.

'What information?' He glanced at Lewis and lit a cigarette.

'Look, god damn it, we had a shipment stolen last night.'

'Did you?' Graves kept his voice calm, but his heart was thumping wildly.

'Yes we did, and now somebody's got themselves a half-ton of ZV gas in binary aerosol cylinders, and we want to know who.'

'You certainly ought to be concerned,' Graves said, 'but this is an open line.'

'Screw the open –'

'You say it was ZV gas?' Graves said.

'You're fucking right.'

'Isn't that nerve gas?'

'You get your –'

'I'll tell you what,' Graves said. 'You fill out requisition form KL-915 and send it over to us, and maybe we can get you the information by the end of the week.'

When he hung up, he began to feel better. The pieces were beginning to fall together. Wright was no longer so far ahead.

'Was he serious?' Lewis asked.

'Completely,' Graves said.

'Half a ton of nerve gas was stolen?'

'Right,' Graves said.

The radio buzzed again. Graves answered it.

'Where are you? This is Phelps.'

'I know who it is. I'm going west on Route Five from El Cajon.'

'Do you have Wright with you?'

'No.'

'You've made a terrible mistake,' Phelps said. 'Binary 75 slash 76 is –'

'I know what it is,' Graves said.

'I doubt that,' Phelps said. 'I'm at the Westgate Plaza Hotel, Room 1012. How fast can you get here?'

'Fifteen minutes.'

'Be here in ten,' Phelps said. 'I have somebody you better meet.'

'Is it Wright?' Graves asked.

But Phelps had already hung up.

The Westgate Plaza was one of the three greatest hotels in the world, if you believed *Esquire* magazine. If you didn't, it was a pretentious modern dump decorated with a lot of phoney statuary in the lobby and downstairs lounge. Walking past statues of winged Mercury and Diana hunting, Graves took the elevator to Room 1012.

Phelps answered the door and said, 'The poker game is over. I just ordered them to arrest Wright.'

Graves said, 'May I come in?' He was not really concerned. He knew the limousine and the furniture van were still en route back to the city. There was time to countermand the order.

'Come in,' Phelps said. As Graves entered, he said, 'This is Dr Nordmann from UCSD.'

Graves had never seen Nordmann before, though he knew who he was. He was a biologist on the faculty of the University of California at San Diego, and he was on the President's Advisory Council on something or other. And he was a strongly vocal opponent of chemical and biological weapons. He had been influential in getting Nixon to disavow biologicals in November 1970. He was reportedly still pushing for a similar disavowal on chemicals.

Nordmann was a tall and ungainly man with a sour expression. Graves wondered if it was permanent, or special for the occasion. Nordmann shook hands and said with some distaste, 'Are you in State Intelligence too?'

'Yes,' Graves said. 'But we're not all the same.'

Phelps gave him a sharp look.

'Well, I'm not very clear on the reason for this briefing,' Nordmann said. 'But I brought the film.'

'Good,' Phelps said. 'There's a projector in the bedroom.'

As they went into the bedroom, they passed the TV. Graves paused to watch: it was a demonstration in the Convention hall – a 'spontaneous' demonstration for the President, who stood on the podium smiling, waving his arms, giving the V sign with both hands.

'There's very little time,' Phelps said. Graves went into the bedroom.

Drapes and shades had been drawn and it was quite dark. Graves sat on the bed. Phelps took a chair. Nordmann stood in front of the small projection screen, which was mounted above the bedroom dresser. He said to Phelps, 'Where should I begin?'

'Just give us necessary background for the film.'

Nordmann nodded, looking sourer than ever. Distantly in the background they could hear the chanting of the delegates on the living-room TV: 'We want the President; we want the President . . .'

'You will be seeing,' Nordmann said, 'the final product of more than half a century of research in chemical warfare. The official date for the start of chemical war is April 22nd, 1915, when the Germans launched an attack with chlorine gas. It was a primitive business – you sat in your trench, opened a canister of gas, and hoped the wind would blow it towards the enemy. If it didn't you were in trouble.

'A lot of improvements – if that's the word – came in the course of the First World War. Gas bombs, and better agents. Mustard gas, nitrogen mustard, and lewisite. All oily liquids that burn and blister your skin. They could kill you, too, but not very efficiently.'

Nordmann paused. 'Second World War: a new advance, again from the Germans. Remember, the Germans were the best chemists in the world for most of the twentieth century. In 1936 they synthesized a complex organophosphorous ester called tabun. It was a nerve gas. It would kill anybody who breathed enough of it. All later developments – sarin, soman, GB, VX, and ZV – are just refinements within this basic class of chemical compounds.

'It's called nerve gas,' Nordmann said, 'because it kills by interfering with transmission of nerve impulses. Nerves work electrically, but the impulses jump from nerve cell to nerve cell – across gaps called synapses – by chemical means. Nerve gases such as tabun, sarin, and ZV interfere with that jumping process. The result is difficulty in breathing, respiratory paralysis, and death. Now let's talk about potency.'

Graves lit a cigarette and glanced at Phelps. Phelps was smiling, nodding his head as Nordmann talked. Faintly from the TV they heard: 'He's our man, he's our man, he's our man . . .' And loud cheers.

'Tabun and sarin,' Nordmann said, 'or the American gas GB, must be inhaled to kill. Therefore gas masks provide an adequate defence. These gases are also relatively weak. They're not produced any more. But there is another family of gases, like VX, which can kill by absorption through the skin as well as by inhalation. The smallest fraction of an ounce is lethal. Am I clear?'

'You're clear,' Graves said.

'VX is terribly powerful,' Nordmann said. 'The lethal dose is estimated to be between two and ten milligrammes, or a few thousandths of an ounce. But powerful as that is, it's nothing compared to ZV. ZV, like VX, is an oil. It's sticky, it clings to things, it hangs around the environment. But a tenth of a milligramme is a lethal dose. In other words, it's about a hundred times as powerful as VX. We're now talking about extraordinary potency.'

Phelps was still smiling, still nodding. Graves felt very cold.

'It is so potent that it has never been manufactured as a single gas. Instead, it's a binary – that is, it's produced as two separate gases, each harmless by itself. But when they mix, they're deadly. The gases are designated Binary 75 and Binary 76 respectively. They're generally stored in yellow and black tanks. The film you are going to see is a French Army training film showing the effects of ZV on a condemned prisoner.'

Phelps got up and turned on the projector.

On the screen they saw a man in denim clothing standing in an enclosed room. The man was looking around nervously.

'This subject,' Nordmann said, 'is going to be exposed to the LD500 dose of the gas, that is, five tenths of a milligramme. It is a fully lethal dose.'

Faintly from the other room they heard, 'My fellow Americans, it is with great pleasure that I –'

At the bottom of the screen appeared the words GAS 75 INTRODUCED. The prisoner did not react. Moments later: GAS 76 INTRODUCED. The prisoner responded instantly. He placed his hand on his chest, coughed, and wiped his nose.

'– join you in this great tradition, this reaffirmation of the democratic process –'

On the screen: EARLY STAGES – RUNNING NOSE, CHEST TIGHTNESS, DIMNESS OF VISION

'– and I must urge you to follow the vision of our great land, to seek the promise, to fulfil the expectations. Let me make one thing perfectly clear –'

'Will somebody shut that door?' Graves said.

On the screen the prisoner appeared in close-up. His nose was running profusely; the liquid dripped down to his shirt. His eyes were hard black dots.

PINPOINT PUPILS

A full-body shot showed the man bent over in evident pain.

MIDDLE STAGES – CRAMPS AND NAUSEA

The prisoner vomited explosively, and the caption stated unnecessarily, VOMITING.

Very faint now from the living-room they heard the sound of prolonged applause.

On the screen the prisoner was clearly confused and in great pain. A dark stain appeared on his trousers.

INVOLUNTARY URINATION

The man staggered and leaned against the wall. His legs and arms twitched and jerked spastically.

STAGGERING

The prisoner looked around briefly, but his face was contorted in agony. He lost his balance and fell, twitching and jerking, to the floor. The camera panned down to follow him. From the other room the applause continued.

DROWSINESS

The man was not really awake. He lifted his head from the floor in short jerks and finally flopped down, not moving.

COMA

The camera remained on the man. His chest was still moving slightly. Then it stopped.

CESSATION OF BREATHING

A moment later.

DEATH

The screen faded to dark. And the last letters appeared. TIME FROM INTRODUCTION OF BINARY GAS TO DEATH: 1.7 MINUTES.

The film ran out. The screen was white. Phelps turned the room lights back on.

'Jesus Christ,' Graves said. He lit a cigarette and noticed that his hands were shaking.

'As I said, that man received five times the minimum lethal dose,' Nordmann said quietly. 'Had he got less, he would still have died – more slowly.'

'How much more slowly?'

'From tests on animals, it may take as long as an hour or two.'

'That same progression?'

'The very same.'

'Jesus Christ,' Graves said again.

He walked back into the living-room, which seemed glaringly bright. Through the windows he could look out over the downtown area of the city. He stood with his back to the television and listened to the familiar voice saying, 'My fellow Americans, and my fellow Republicans, we have come to a momentous time for our nation. We face great problems, and we face great challenges. We must act now to –'

The set abruptly clicked off. Graves turned and saw that Phelps had done it. 'I hope you understand now,' Phelps said. 'Wright has half a ton of that gas. In the San Diego area there are a million people. Plus some very distinguished visitors. We can't afford cat-and-mouse games any longer.'

'I agree,' Graves said, staring out at the street below. There were no trees. He wondered why they hadn't put any trees in downtown San Diego. Trees made a difference.

Behind him Phelps picked up the telephone and dialled a number. He said, 'Phelps here. I want 702.' There was a pause.

Nordmann came over to stand by Graves and look down at the street. 'You know,' he said, 'I told the Army four years ago if they kept transporting this crap all around, it was only a matter of time before somebody –'

'You have?' Phelps said into the phone. His voice was excited. 'Where?'

Graves turned. Phelps was nodding, his head bobbing up and down like a mechanical bird.

'Yes, yes . . . yes . . . good work. We'll be there in five minutes.' He hung up and turned to Graves. '702 followed the limousine back to Wright's old apartment house. The van split off and went somewhere else, but the limo went back to Avenue B.'

'And?'

'They arrested John Wright as he stepped from his car.'

Graves nodded and tried to feel the same excitement that Phelps so clearly showed. But he still had a nagging sense of defeat, as if he had cheated at the game – or had quit too early.

'Come on,' Phelps said. 'You can introduce him to me.'

At the apartment house two men were standing up facing the wall, guarded by the men from car 702. Phelps and Graves hurried over.

One of the men was George, the chauffeur. He was muttering something under his breath. Wright was beside him, neatly dressed in his English-cut suit.

Graves said, 'You can let them turn around now.' He glanced at Phelps, who had a look of total triumph on his face.

George turned and looked at Graves uncomprehendingly. Then Wright turned, and it was Graves who stared.

'This isn't John Wright,' he said.

'What do you mean?' Phelps demanded.

'I've never seen this man before,' Graves said. 'He isn't Wright.'

'We checked the wallet,' one of the 702 men said. 'He has his identification –'

'I don't give a damn about identification,' Graves said. 'This man isn't John Wright.'

The man in the English suit smirked slightly.

'Who the hell is he?' Phelps said.

'That,' Graves said, 'is the least important question we have to answer.'

And he ran for his car.

HOUR 3
SAN DIEGO
2 PM PDT

'Take it easy,' Phelps said, grabbing the door handle. Graves took the turn from B onto Third very fast, tyres squealing. 'For Christ's sake.'

'You said it yourself,' Graves said. 'A million people.'

'But we have him, we know the plot, we know how it's going together –'

'We may not be able to stop it,' Graves said.

'Not stop it? What are you talking about?'

Graves raced down Third, weaving among the traffic. He ran the light at Laurel. Phelps made a gurgling noise.

'Wright has been ahead of us all along,' Graves said. 'He must have switched clothes in the airfield hangar and sent somebody else back to San Diego in the limousine. He himself went with the furniture van.'

'Well, if you know where he is now –'

'I know where he is,' Graves said. 'But it may be too late to stop him.'

'How can it be too late?' Phelps said.

Graves didn't answer. With a squeal of tyres he continued uptown, then turned down the wrong way on Alameda Street. Cars honked at him; he pulled over to the kerb on the wrong side, facing the wrong way, in front of a fire hydrant.

Phelps didn't complain. He didn't have time. Graves was already out of the car and running for the building opposite Wright's new apartment house. In front of Wright's building was the furniture van

.

All the men in the room were clustered around the cameras and binoculars at the window. Graves burst in and said, 'Is Wright there?'

'I don't know,' one of the men said. 'We heard he was arrested, but somebody in there sure looks like –'

'Let me see.'

Graves bent over a pair of binoculars. It took only a moment to confirm his worst fears. Wright was there, donning another rubber wet suit. He was pulling rubber loops onto his ankles, his wrists, his waist, and his neck. Of course! Those strips – six strips – protected the seams of his suit from gas. As he watched, Wright put on a full face mask and twisted the valve on the small yellow air tank. The other men in the room cleared out.

'What's he doing?' Phelps said, watching through another pair of binoculars.

Graves looked around Wright's room. The four sawhorses were still in position. Across them lay two cylinders, each about eight feet long. One was painted black, the other yellow. There were stencilled letters on their sides. As he watched, Wright began connecting hoses from each of the tanks to a central T valve, which joined the hoses into a common outlet. Then he turned his attention to other equipment in the room.

'Well, that's it.'

Phelps said, 'Let's go get him.'

'You're joking,' Graves said.

'Not at all,' Phelps said. 'We know he's there, we've seen him connect up the hoses so that he can –'

Phelps broke off and stared at Graves.

'Exactly,' Graves said.

'But this is terrible!'

'It's not terrible, it's just a fact,' Graves said. 'There's no way we can break into that room fast enough to get control before he turns on the valves and releases the gas.'

'If we go in shooting –'

'You risk puncturing the tanks.'

'Well we can't just sit here and watch.' Phelps said.

Graves lit a cigarette. 'At the moment there isn't much else we *can* do.'

Phelps set down his binoculars. His face was twisted; the earlier look of triumph was completely gone. 'Do you have another cigarette?' he said.

Graves gave him one and then went to the phone.

'Morrison here.'

'This is Graves. We've found your tanks.'

'Listen, you better tell us –'

'They're on Alameda Street in San Diego.'

'*San Diego!*'

'I want you to get me some people from the Navy chemical corps. I don't care where you find them or what you do to get them, just have them here in an hour. Make sure some of them have gas-protective clothing. And make sure at least one of them knows a hell of a lot about this binary gas.'

Graves gave him the address and hung up. He glanced over at Phelps, who was sitting in a corner.

'Has somebody notified the President?'

'Who?'

'The President of the United States,' Graves said.

'I assume so.'

'Let's not assume,' Graves said. 'Use the other phone.' And he pointed to a phone near Phelps.

Graves started to dial another call.

'I don't know how to get him,' Phelps said, in a plaintive voice.

'Use the prestige of your office,' Graves said, and turned away.

'Dr Nordmann's office.'

'This is Mr Graves from the State Department. I want to speak to Dr Nordmann.'

'Dr Nordmann had a luncheon conference and is not back yet.'

'When do you expect him?'

'Well, not for several hours. He has a faculty meeting at two thirty to discuss PhD candidates, and –'

'Find him,' Graves said, 'and tell him to call me. Tell him it's about Binary 75 slash 76. Here's my number.' He gave it to the secretary.

When he hung up, one of the men at the window said, 'Look what he's doing now.' Graves peered through the binoculars. He saw that Wright had removed his rubber suit and was now attaching wires to the floor of the room, to the ceiling, to the walls. He plugged the wires into a central metal box the size of a shoe box.

'What the hell is that box?' Graves said.

In a corner of the room, Phelps was saying, 'Yes, that's right . . . That's what I'm telling you, yes . . . a half-ton of nerve gas . . . Of course it's not a joke . . .'

Graves saw Wright attach two small mechanical devices to the valves of the two tanks. Then he ran more wires back to the box. Finally he stacked a second metal unit on top of the original box and connected still more wires.

Then Wright looked at his watch.

'Well, *somebody* better get through to him,' Phelps was saying. 'Yes, I'm sure it's hard . . .'

'What time is it?' Graves said.

'Two forty.'

'The gas is called ZV,' Phelps was saying. 'An Army shipment was stolen in Utah during the early hours this morning. He's probably already been informed . . . Well, god damn it, I don't care if *you* don't know anything about it. He does . . . Yes, it's here . . .'

One of the men at the window said, 'He must be insane.'

'Of course,' Graves said. 'You'd have to be insane to wipe out a million people and one whole political party. But the fact is that we've really been lucky.'

'Lucky?'

'Just see that he gets the *message*,' Phelps said.

'Sure,' Graves said. 'Those Army shipments have been going on for years. They're sitting ducks. Anybody with a little money, a little intelligence, and a screw loose somewhere could arrange for a steal. Look: Richard Speck knocked off eight nurses, but he was an incompetent. Charles Whitman was an expert rifleman, and on that basis could knock off seventeen people. John Wright is highly intelligent and very wealthy. He's going to go for a million people and one American President. And thanks to the US Army, he has a chance of succeeding.'

'I don't see how you can blame the Army.'

'You don't?' Graves asked. He watched the other apartment through the binoculars. His eyes felt the strain; his vision blurred intermittently, and he swore. Wright appeared to be fooling with the two metal boxes in the centre of the floor. He had been adjusting them for a long time.

Graves wasn't sure what it all meant. It was a control or alarm system of some kind, though – that much was clear. And if it was a control system, it required power. Power. As Graves watched, he had an idea – one possible way to beat the system that Wright was so carefully setting up. A chance, a slim chance . . .

'Do it,' he whispered, watching Wright. 'Do it, do it . . .'

'Do what?' Phelps asked. He was off the telephone now.

Graves did not answer. Wright had finished with the boxes. He turned some dials, made some final adjustments. Then he took the main plug in his hand.

'He's going to do it,' Graves said.

And he plugged it into the wall socket. Very plainly, very clearly, he plugged it into the wall.

'He's done it.'

'Done what?' Phelps said, angry now.

'He's connected his device to the apartment electricity.'

'So?'

'That's a mistake,' Graves said. 'He should have used a battery unit.'

'Why?'

'Because we can turn off the electricity in that apartment,' Graves said. 'Remotely.'

'Oh,' Phelps said. And then he smiled. 'That's good thinking.'

Graves said nothing. His mind raced forward in exhilarating high gear. For the first time all day, he felt that he was not only keeping abreast of Wright but actually moving a few steps ahead. It was a marvellous feeling.

'Time?'

'Two fifty-one.'

And then, as he watched, Wright did something very peculiar. He placed a small white box alongside the two other metal boxes. And he closed the windows to the apartment. Then he taped the joints and seams of the windows shut.

Then he left.

'What the hell does all that mean?' somebody asked.

'I don't know,' Graves said. 'But I know how we can find out.'

HOUR 2
SAN DIEGO
3 PM PTD

Wright emerged from the apartment house lobby wearing a grey suit. He carried a raincoat over his shoulder. Graves was waiting for him, along with two federal marshals carrying drawn guns.

Wright did not look surprised. He smiled and said, 'Did your son like his gift, Mr Graves?'

Before Graves could reply, one of the marshals had spun Wright around, saying gruffly, 'Up against the wall hands wide stand still and you won't get hurt.'

'Gentlemen,' Wright said in an offended voice. He looked at Graves over his shoulder. 'I don't think any of this is necessary. Mr Graves knows what he is looking for.'

'Yes, I do,' Graves said. He had already noticed the raincoat. Nobody carried a raincoat in San Diego in August. It was as out of place as a Bible in a whore-house. 'But I want to know what time it leaves.'

'There's only one possible flight today,' Wright said. 'Connexions in Miami. Leaves San Diego at four thirty.'

The marshal took Wright's shoulder wallet and handed it to Graves. The ticket was inside: San Diego to Los Angeles to Miami to Montego Bay, Jamaica. The ticket was made out to Mr. A. Johnson.

'May I turn around now?' Wright asked.

'Shut up,' the marshal said.

'Let him turn around,' Graves said.

Wright turned, rubbing the grit of the wall from his hands. He smiled at Graves. 'Your move.' In the smile and the slight nod of the head, Graves got a chilling sense of the profound insanity of the man. The eyes gave it away.

Wright's eyes were genuinely amused: a clever chess player teasing an inferior opponent. But this wasn't chess, not really. Not with stakes like these.

Death in 1.7 minutes, Graves thought, and he had a mental image of the prisoner twisting and writhing on the floor, liquid running from his nose in a continuous stream, vomit spewing out.

Graves realized then that he had mistaken his opponent for too long.

Wright was insane. He was capable of anything. It produced a churning sensation in Graves' stomach.

'Take him inside,' Graves said to the marshal. 'I want to talk to him.'

The three of them sat in the lobby of the apartment building. It was the kind of lobby that aspired to look like the grossest Miami Beach hotels; there were plastic palms in plastic pots and fake Louis XIV furniture which, apparently out of fear that someone would want to steal it, was bolted to the imitation marble floor. Under other circumstances the artificiality of the surroundings would have annoyed Graves, but now it somehow seemed appropriate. By implication the room suggested that falsehoods were acceptable, even preferable, to the truth.

Graves sat in a chair facing Wright. The marshal sat diagonally facing both of them and the only exit. The marshal held his gun loosely in his lap.

Wright looked at the marshal and the position of the gun. 'That's what it's all about,' he said, and smiled again. That insane smile.

'How do you mean?' Graves said.

Wright sighed patiently. 'Do I confuse you?'

'Of course. That was your intention.'

'I doubt that I've confused you much,' Wright said. 'You've really done very well, Mr Graves. May I call you John?'

The condescending tone was unmistakable, but Graves merely shrugged. He glanced at his watch: 3:05.

'Very well, indeed,' Wright continued. 'For the last month or so, John, I've had the feeling that you were a worthy adversary. I can't tell you how reassuring that was.'

'Reassuring?'

'I prefer to do things well,' he said. He took a slim cigar from a gunmetal case and lit it. 'I mean elegantly, with a certain finesse. In a situation like this, one needs a proper opponent. I was immensely reassured that my opponent was you, John.' Wright sighed. 'Of course, I have another opponent as well,' he said. 'One totally lacking in finesse, elegance, and grace. The sad thing is, he thinks he's a statesman.'

'You mean the President?'

'I prefer to think of him,' Wright said, 'as that man who rode the bench for so many years. Why did he ride the bench? Did you ever think of that? The answer is simple enough – because he wasn't a good player. He was inept. He was incompetent. He was a bumbling fool.'

'You feel strongly about him.'

'I feel strongly about his *policies.*'

'China?'

'Ten years ago,' Wright said, 'if I asked you the name of the American President most likely to institute wage and price controls, welfare reform, and diplomatic relations with Communist China, would you have ever thought of this man? It's *insane,* what he's doing.'

'What about what you're doing?'

'Somebody has to stop him,' Wright said. 'It's as simple as that.'

'I wouldn't call nerve gas a democratic method.' Graves stared at him. 'What are those metal boxes in the centre of the floor upstairs?'

Wright smiled. 'Enough politics, eh?' He puffed on his cigar, billowing light smoke. 'Very well. Down to business.' A thought seemed to occur to him. 'But if I tell you, how will you know it's the truth?'

'That's my job.'

'True, true. There are actually three boxes, as I'm sure you observed from your surveillance station across the street. I had to get an extension cord in order to place the boxes in clear view of the window.'

'Very thoughtful.'

'I felt you'd appreciate it,' Wright said. 'The first box is a timer. It controls a rather intricate set of staging sequences for the equipment in the room.'

Graves took out a cigarette. His hands shook slightly as he lit it. He hoped Wright wouldn't notice – but that, of course, was wishful thinking. Wright would notice.

But Wright didn't comment on it. 'The second box,' he said, 'is an impedance and vibration sensor. There are contact points located around the room. On the door, on the floor, on the walls. Any excessive vibration – for example, a man walking on the floor of the room – will set off the gas. It's a commercial unit. I bought it last week.' He smiled then. 'A friend made the purchase, so that you wouldn't be aware of it.'

'The third box?'

'The third box is the little white unit alongside the other boxes. It's a battery. We wouldn't want to be dependent on electricity in the apartment, after all. You could turn that off remotely.'

Graves had a sinking feeling, and it must have showed, because Wright laughed. 'Oh, you were planning to do that, were you?' He shook his head. 'Too simple. Much too simple. I wouldn't make a mistake like *that.*'

'What's the voltage of the batteries?' Graves snapped, trying to regain control of the situation.

'A very intelligent question,' Wright said. 'I am tempted to lie, but I won't. It is a twelve-volt unit.'

'Amperage?'

'I haven't the faintest idea.'

'That doesn't concern you?'

'The amperage is adequate.'

'Adequate for what?'

Wright smiled. 'Really,' he said, 'you don't expect me to hand you everything on a silver platter.'

'Actually, I do.'

'Then you're being naïve. How do you expect to extract information from me?' He glanced at his watch. 'There is not a lot of time, and although I am sure you could torture me inventively, you couldn't get me to talk. Not fast enough.'

'Why did you close the apartment windows?'

Wright smiled. 'Fascinating. I was wondering if you'd catch that. I taped them, too.'

'Yes, you did.'

'I closed the windows,' Wright said, 'because the mechanism in that room anticipates some action you will take.'

'Some action I will take?'

'Yes.'

'You're being cryptic.'

'I can afford to be cryptic.'

'What's the point of the scintillation counter?'

'An interesting problem, but not so interesting as the explosives.'

Graves tried to keep his face blank, but it didn't work.

'Ah,' Wright said. 'You don't know about the explosives? There was a robbery of twenty pounds of plastic explosive – Compound C, I believe it's called – earlier today, on the freeway. A hijacked truck. I'm surprised you haven't already been informed.'

Graves was beginning to sweat. He resisted the impulse to wipe his forehead. He sat back in his chair and tried to be calm.

'You seem nervous,' Wright said.

'Concerned.'

'There is no need to be nervous,' Wright said. 'I can assure you right now, it is impossible for you to get into that room alive. I don't advise you to try.'

'You seem quite nonchalant.'

'Oh, I am.' He turned the cigar in his mouth, removed it, stared at the burning tip.

'We can hold you, of course.'

'You mean, prevent me from leaving San Diego?'

'Yes.'

'I'd expect that.'

'You don't care?'

'Not particularly.'

'But you'll die,' Graves said.

'A great many people will die, in fact,' Wright said, and his eyes glowed with a sudden mad intensity. 'You may have noticed that weather conditions are perfect. There is an inversion layer over the city. Any released gases will be blown west – across the city – and will be trapped there. Do you know much about meteorology?'

'A little.'

'You know,' Wright said, 'it's a funny thing about chemical agents. The military makes them, but they don't have much military use. By their very nature, they work best in high population density situations. And that means civilian populations. That's where you get the most bangs for your buck, so to speak.'

His eyes literally sparkled as he talked. 'But the irony goes even farther,' he said. 'Modern city life improves the effectiveness of these weapons. You can imagine a city like San Diego as existing with a giant plastic dome over it. That's the inversion layer. It blankets the area, holds in all the automobile fumes and exhaust gases that make city air so obnoxious. That inversion layer will hold any released gas – or, in the case of ZV, oil droplet suspension.'

Graves snapped his fingers. 'The detergent!'

'Yes,' Wright said. 'Good for you. The detergent was ordered in case I had an accident in the hangar. Have to cut that oil somehow. Detergent was the best way. But,' he said, 'I didn't have an accident. Nothing went wrong.'

At that moment Phelps stuck his head in the door. 'Nordmann's here.'

'All right,' Graves said.

Wright looked appreciative. 'Good move,' he said. 'Nordmann's an excellent man. In fact, it was one of his articles – detailed, scholarly, and complete – that suggested to me the possibility of stealing some gas in the first place.'

Again there was that glow in Wright's eyes. Graves found himself getting angry. He stood up abruptly. 'Don't let him go anywhere,' he said to the marshal.

'I wouldn't think of it, until I've finished my cigar,' Wright said.

Graves left the lobby.

Nordmann was outside, standing on the sidewalk with Phelps. They were both looking up, talking.

Graves said, 'The gas is up there. Is there any antidote?'

'To ZV? Nothing very good.'

'But there is an antidote?'

'There's a sort of theoretical antidote. If a person has a mild exposure, it may be possible to inject chemicals to block the effects of the gas.'

'Can you get those chemicals?'

'Yes, but not in sufficient quantities to protect very many –'

'Get as much as you can,' Graves said. 'Do it immediately.' He turned to Phelps. 'Notify the San Diego police. Evacuate this block and cordon it off. Cordon off the blocks on both sides as well. And I mean a cordon – nobody in and nobody out.' He paused. 'What happened with the President?'

'He's leaving within the hour.'

'For sure?'

'I assume so.'

'Better check again.'

Phelps nodded towards the lobby. 'Is he talking?'

'He's saying what he wants to say,' Graves said.

'My God, he's a cool customer.'

'What did you expect?' Graves said, and went back inside.

When he returned, he found the marshal smoking one of Wright's slim cigars. Graves shot him a look; the marshal quickly stubbed it out.

'Waste of a good cigar,' Wright said. 'Why can't we all be friends?'

Graves sat down. 'What did you paint in the hangar?'

'Paint?'

'Yes. We found a spray gun and several cans of paint.'

'Oh, that.'

'What did you paint?'

'I don't believe I'll answer that.'

'What did you paint?'

'You show a certain redundancy of mind,' Wright said. 'It's tiresome, and disappointing. I expected you to be more clever.' He was silent a moment. 'I will tell you one thing,' he said.

'What's that?' Graves resented the eagerness that he heard in his own voice.

'I have devised a multiple staging system. Actually, several interlocking systems. If one fails or is thwarted, another takes over. It's quite beyond you, I can assure you of that. However, I will tell you I am dependent on one external system, which is fortunately quite reliable.'

'What's that?'

'You,' Wright said. 'Everything has been designed especially for you, so to speak.'

Wright's calmness was infuriating. Graves bit his lip, trying to control his anger.

'What time is it?' Wright asked.

'Three forty,' the marshal said.

'Thank you. Do you have any other questions, John?'

'One or two,' Graves said. His anger was so intense that it clouded his judgement. He fought the feeling.

'I can see you're upset,' Wright said. 'And you haven't asked me some rather obvious questions. One is, when will the gas go off?'

Graves stared at him, almost shaking with fury.

'The answer,' Wright said, 'is five PM exactly. The gas will go off then. It will begin to drift in a predictable way and will have blanketed the city with good saturation by about five thirty, the peak of the rush hour: maximum number of people on the streets, and so on. Now, it seems to me there was something else I wanted to tell you . . .'

Graves wanted to beat the man to a pulp. He wanted to smash his face, to shatter his nose, his teeth . . . He had a brief image of himself standing over Wright, pounding him.

'Damn,' Wright said, 'it was just on the tip of my tongue. Well, no matter. It couldn't have been that important.' He sighed. 'I think,' he said, 'this concludes the questions for today. I have nothing else to say.'

Graves stared at him for a moment. 'You don't leave us much choice.'

Wright smiled. 'I believe you call it "softening up"; is that right?'

'More or less.'

'An interesting notion,' Wright said, 'but now I must leave.'

And with astonishing speed he jumped from his chair and raced for the door. The marshal crouched down and held his gun stiffly.

'Don't!' Graves shouted, and knocked the pistol away. The marshal looked stunned. 'Don't shoot him!'

Wright was out the door. A second marshal stood outside. He wore a look of surprise as Wright slammed him in the groin with one knee. He doubled over. Wright sprinted for the stairs to the basement.

'He's going for the garage,' Graves said. He pushed the other marshal towards the door to the basement and then ran outside.

Phelps was directing a half-dozen marshals and policemen to cordon off the area.

'Wright's escaped!' Graves shouted. He ran down the street, looking for the underground garage exit.

'Where?'

'The garage.'

'Can he get out?'

The marshals and police all drew their guns. A single shot echoed inside the garage.

'How did this happen?' Phelps demanded.

Graves looked at the marshals and the cops standing by the ramp from the garage. 'Don't shoot him,' he said. 'Whatever happens, don't shoot him.'

There was a long silence. Nothing further was heard from inside the garage.

'I demand to know what happened,' Phelps said.

Graves listened.

Nothing.

The cops looked at each other.

'Hey,' a cop shouted, from the garage. 'He went out the other exit!'

Graves instantly realized that he had made a mistake. Wright was too smart to think he could escape from the garage of this building; he would have another plan. Graves started to run. So did the police.

'Where'd he go?'

'Next building. Other block.'

Graves sprinted down the ramp into the garage and towards the other garage exit. He ran up a short flight of stairs through an open door and came out into an alley. The alley connected with the opposite block. He ran down it, the cops following, their footsteps echoing.

They saw no one.

'Where'd he go?'

Graves held up his hand. Everyone paused. They heard the sound of an engine. It was coming from the garage of a building on the adjacent block.

'Where's the exit from that garage?'

Graves ran forward. The exit must be on the street. They came out into the next street – deserted, heavily cordoned off at each end, with a police car crosswise blocking the road, cops standing around.

The sound of a racing engine. They saw a ramp.

'Don't sh – '

Wright's Alfa came up the ramp, moving very fast. The cops and marshals scrambled out of the way. They fired as they ran.

Graves felt sick.

But the Alfa was still going. It made a twisting righthand turn, slamming into a parked car. There were more gunshots. The side windows shattered into great spiderwebs, but somehow the car continued, gears grinding as it raced down the street.

Wright had planned it well, Graves thought. He would have made his escape by sneaking through the buildings if it hadn't been for the roadblock. He didn't expect that; Graves himself had ordered it on the spur of the moment.

The Alfa roared down the street.

'He wasn't expecting the roadblock,' Graves said. 'He didn't count on that.'

'Whose side are you on?' Phelps demanded.

At the end of the street four policemen waited by the parked patrol car. As the Alfa bore down on them, they dropped to their knees, holding their guns stiff-armed before them.

'Don't shoot!' Graves screamed.

The cops began to fire. The tyres on the Alfa exploded. The front windshield shattered. The car wobbled, flipped on its side, and slammed into a parked car. The horn began to blare.

Graves ran over to the Alfa and tried to open the door. It was jammed shut. He looked in through the shattered windscreen and saw Wright's face, a bloody pulp, the features indistinguishable. As he watched, a tiny stream of blood spurted rhythmically from Wright's neck. Then it became a seeping red stain across his collar.

He turned away from the car.

'Is he dead?' Phelps said, running up.

'Yes,' Graves said. 'He's dead.'

'How can we turn off that fucking horn?' Phelps said.

Graves stared at him and walked away.

HOUR 1
SAN DIEGO
4 PM PDT

His sense of shock was profound. Of all the alternatives, of all the possibilities and options, he had never expected this. He had never expected Wright to die.

Graves walked back up the street slowly, trying to gather his thoughts. What did he do next?

Nordmann came up to him. 'That's a damned shame,' he said.

'You bet it is,' Graves said.

Nordmann looked at the crowd clustered around the wrecked car. 'One thing, though,' he said.

'What's that?'

'It proves he could make a mistake.'

'It was a big one,' Graves said.

'Yes,' Nordmann said, in a calm, logical voice. 'But it *was* a mistake.'

Graves nodded and walked back towards the surveillance building. He thought about what Nordmann had said. The more he thought about it, the more encouraged he was. Because Nordmann was right.

Wright had erred. And that was encouraging.

One of the aides came running out of the building, waving Wright's ticket. 'Mr Graves,' he said. 'There's something very strange going on. We just checked this ticket. He cancelled that reservation yesterday.'

Protect me from fools, Graves thought. 'Of course he did.'

'Of course?'

'Look,' Graves said. 'He planned to let us catch him, and he planned his escape. But he couldn't get far if we knew his real aeroplane reservation, could he?'

'Well, I guess not . . .'

'Keep checking the airlines. Check Los Angeles, too. You'll find he had a reservation somewhere.'

Phelps came over. 'The sniffer's arrived.'

'Has it? Good.' Graves walked across the street to Wright's apartment building. Phelps trailed behind him in silence.

Finally Phelps said, 'I hope you know what you're doing.'

Graves didn't answer. Because the fact was that he didn't know what he was doing. He knew only in a general way what Wright intended. Wright had made Graves a part of the total mechanism, and therefore

Graves would have to cancel himself out – inactivate himself – by not doing what was expected of him.

In order to do that, he had to decipher as many elements of the total staging mechanism as possible. Only then could he determine how he was intended to participate in the staging sequence that controlled the final release of the gas.

The sniffer was the first step in deciphering the sequence.

Graves stood outside the door to Wright's apartment. Next to him Lewis held a gunlike instrument in his hand. The gun was attached to a shoulder pack with a dial. Lewis pointed the instrument at the door and ran it along the cracks and seams.

Behind them at the far end of the hallway, six people, including Phelps, stood and watched. Graves wanted everyone away from the door so that they wouldn't accidentally trip the vibration sensors. He didn't know how sensitively they were tuned, but he wasn't taking any chances.

After a moment Lewis turned away with the instrument. 'Wow,' he said.

'You get a reading?'

'Yeah,' he said. 'High nitrogen and oxygen content, trace phosphorus.'

'Meaning?'

'Plastic explosive, very near.'

'Near the door?'

'Probably just on the other side,' he said.

Graves said, 'Is there any chance you're wrong?'

'The sniffer is never wrong,' he said. 'You've got oxide of nitrogen fumes, and that's explosives. You can count on it.'

'All right,' Graves said. He walked away from the door. He had to trust the sniffer. It had been developed for use in Vietnam and had been adapted for customs operations, smuggling, and so on. It was incredibly sensitive and incredibly accurate. If the sniffer said plastic explosive was behind the door, he had to believe it. He walked back to Phelps at the end of the hallway.

'Well?'

'There's explosive on the other side of the door.'

'Nice,' Phelps said. 'What do we do now?'

'Try to get a better look inside the apartment,' Graves said. He glanced at his watch.

'It's four ten,' Phelps said. 'When did your friend say it would go off?'

'Five,' Graves said.

'I hope you know what you're doing,' Phelps said again.

Graves sighed. He wondered if he could ever explain to Phelps that that wasn't the problem. The problem was figuring out what Wright expected him to do – and then *not* doing it.

Across the street in the surveillance room looking down on Wright's apartment, he talked to Nordmann. Nordmann had brought a cardboard box full of medical supplies – syringes, needles, bottles of liquid. He was frowning down at it. 'This is the best I could manage on short notice,' he said.

'Will it work?' Graves said.

'It's the standard therapy,' Nordmann said. 'But we haven't got much. This quantity will treat two or three people for exposure, that's all.'

'Then let's make sure it doesn't come to that.'

Nordmann smiled slightly. 'It better not,' he said. 'Because you need somebody alive and well to administer it.'

'Is it hard to administer?'

'Tricky,' Nordmann said. 'There are two different chemicals, atropine and parladoxime. They have to be balanced.'

Graves sighed. 'So the antidote is a binary, too.'

'In a sense. The two chemicals treat different effects of the gas. One treats the peripheral nervous system, the other the central. The chemicals are dangerous in themselves, which makes it all much harder.'

'Fighting fire with fire?'

'In a sense,' Nordmann said.

The two men stood staring out the window at the apartment opposite. Phelps was in a corner using a walkie-talkie. 'You in position?'

A response crackled back. 'In position, sir.'

'Very good.' Phelps clicked off the walkie-talkie. 'We've got two cops stationed outside the door to that apartment,' he said.

'Fine,' Graves said. 'Just so they don't get too close to the door.'

'I have them ten feet away.'

'That should be fine.'

In the hallway outside Wright's apartment, officers Martin and Jencks of the San Diego Police Department stared at the closed door and leaned against the wall.

'You understand any of this?' Jencks said.

'Nope,' Martin said.

'But they said not to get too close to the door.'

'That's right.'

'You know why?'

'I don't know nothing,' Martin said. He took out a cigarette. 'You got a match?'

'Maybe we shouldn't smoke . . .'

'Who's going to know?' Martin said.

Jencks gave him a match.

Graves stood with Nordmann in the surveillance room across the street.

'Wright booby-trapped the apartment?'

'Elaborately,' Graves said. 'He told me some of it. I'm sure he didn't tell me everything.'

'And it goes off at five?'

'Yes.'

'Forty-five minutes from now,' Nordmann said. 'Is the Navy sending people with protective suits? Because protected people could just walk right in.'

'Nobody can walk right in,' Graves said. 'He's wired the room with explosive. That's why we've got the guards over there.'

Nordmann grimaced. 'Explosive?'

'Twenty pounds of it.'

The TV in the corner of the room showed the Convention. A monotonous voice was saying, 'Mr Chairman . . . Mr Chairman, we request the floor . . . Mr Chairman . . .' There was the loud banging of a gavel.

'Turn that damned thing off,' Graves said. Someone turned it off.

At the window two men grunted as they lifted a huge lens onto a heavy-duty tripod. It was screwed into place and adjusted. 'Ready, Mr Graves.'

'Thank you.' Graves went to the window.

'What's that?' Nordmann said.

'A fifteen-hundred-millimeter telephoto,' Graves said. 'It's the best look we can get.'

He peered through the giant lens. The view was so enormously magnified that at first he didn't know what he was looking at. Using a fine-knurled knob, he moved the lens and saw he was focused on a crack in the floor. He moved across the floor to the boxes. He shifted the lens upward, examining each box in detail.

'Take a look at this,' he said, stepping away.

Nordmann squinted through the lens. 'Three stacked boxes,' he said. 'I can't make out much . . .'

'Neither can I.' Graves folded his arms across his chest and stared out the window. He tried to think logically, but he was having trouble; Wright's death had unnerved him, whether he wanted to admit it or not.

And the system seemed so complicated. Staging sequences, timers, vibration sensors, explosives . . . His head ached. How the hell would he unravel it?

'Let's work it backward,' Nordmann said. 'What's the most important element in the system?'

'The gas.'

'How is it controlled?'

'There are spring-loaded valve mechanisms. They can be tripped by a solenoid.'

'And they presumably have a timer of some kind.'

'Presumably.'

'Battery-powered or line-powered?'

'Well, he's plugged one of the boxes into the wall. But the valve mechanisms are probably battery-powered.'

Nordmann nodded. 'That makes sense,' he said. 'He wouldn't have the most important elements dependent on an external system. So what did he plug into the wall?'

'I don't know.'

'Vibration sensors?'

'Maybe,' Graves said. He looked at his watch. It was 4:20. He would have to move soon. What had Wright expected him to do? The psychological report was folded up in his pocket. He took it out and looked at the last few lines.

IF THERE ARE ANY DEFECTS OR HIDDEN FLAWS IN HIS BEHAVIOUR, THEY ARE HIS IMPULSIVENESS AND HIS DESIRE TO FINISH A TEST SITUATION RAPIDLY.

Well, he didn't have much choice now. He was going to have to make a move, and soon.

'You know,' Nordmann said thoughtfully, 'most of the equipment in that room is defensive. It's designed to keep people out of there until the gas is ready to be released. But I suspect some of those defences are meant to be penetrated.'

'I agree,' Graves said. 'And in any case, we have to start penetrating.'

'Wall current first?' Nordmann asked.

Graves nodded. He glanced at Phelps, who was sitting in a corner of the room literally chewing his nails. Graves sent Lewis across the street to disconnect power to the apartment. Four minutes later, the power was off. Graves watched through the big telephoto lens. He saw a single yellow pilot light in the vibration sensor box go out.

'Well,' Nordmann said, 'that's a start. We've killed part of the system.'

'Have we?' Graves said. He watched through the telephoto as the solenoid mechanism tripped open the tank valves, then a moment later tripped them shut.

The apartment became filled with whitish gas.

'What's happening?' Phelps said, very agitated.

'Quick,' Graves said. 'Those cops. Tell the cops.'

'What cops?' Phelps said.

Officer Martin finished his cigarette and ground it out on the floor. His heel squeaked.

'Sssh,' Jencks said, suddenly tense.

'What is it?'

'Sssssh. Listen.'

The two men listened in silence. There was a hissing.

'You hear that?' Jencks said.

'Yeah. It's coming from the room.'

'Are you sure?'

Martin moved closer to the door. 'I think so –'

'Maybe you shouldn't –'

Martin began to cough. His nose ran. 'Shit,' he said. 'What is this?' He coughed again.

Jencks went forward to help him. Then Jencks felt the stinging in his nostrils, and the liquid began to pour over his shirt. He didn't know a nose could run that way. His eyes ached and stung; he felt dizzy. 'What the hell . . .' He had a coughing fit.

The walkie-talkie crackled. 'This is Phelps,' a voice said. 'Over.'

Martin took a step towards the walkie-talkie and fell to the floor. Now he could see the faint wispy whiteness seeping through the door.

'This is Phelps. Over.'

Jencks was coughing loudly and groaning.

Martin stretched out his hand towards the walkie-talkie. He was weak. His arm trembled. Then, without warning, he vomited and lost consciousness.

'I'm not getting an answer,' Phelps said.

Graves and Nordmann exchanged glances, then looked back out the window at the opposite apartment. The room now had a faint milky haze.

'Are they dead?' Phelps said.

'Probably.'

'How can you just stand there?'

'Because,' Graves said, 'it was just a short burst. The valves are turned off again.'

Phelps looked puzzled.

'It wasn't a full release,' Graves said. 'It's just a partial release, to fill the room with gas. That's why Wright carefully closed the windows. Now we *really* can't get in there.'

'You sound so appreciative,' Phelps said.

'I'm not. But we understand now what Wright meant by a complex staging sequence.'

'God damn it, this is not a jigsaw puzzle! Two cops have died and –'

'We're all right,' Nordmann said quietly, 'until five PM.'

'And what do you intend to do between now and then?' Phelps demanded angrily. 'I'm going to call the Navy,' he said. 'Their men were supposed to be here an hour ago. It's four thirty now.'

Graves stared at the gas-filled apartment. He had a brief mental image of the two cops staggering drunkenly in the hallway. He pushed it away; he could consider it later.

Beside him Nordmann said, 'It's really quite clever.'

Graves said, 'How thick is the gas in that room?'

'Hard to say,' Nordmann said. 'The normal colour of the gas is white. I don't think the density is very great. Why?'

'If you shot me full of those antidotes, could I survive the atmosphere in that room?'

'I don't know.'

'Would I have a chance?'

'A chance? Of course. But even if you could survive, how would you get in? You said yourself it's wired with explosives. You can't go in the front door.'

'I wasn't thinking of the door,' Graves said. 'I was thinking of the window.'

'The window?' Nordmann frowned. 'I don't know . . .'

Graves looked down at the street below, where an ambulance had pulled alongside the wrecked Alfa. A half-dozen cops and orderlies were trying to open the door, but it was still jammed shut. 'Damn,' he said. 'I wish he were still alive.'

'It probably wouldn't matter,' Nordmann said absently. He was staring across at the other building.

Graves said, 'How good are my chances with the antidote?'

'Four thirty-five,' somebody said.

'Maybe one in two,' Nordmann said. 'At best.'

'All right. Let's do it.'

'Are you sure?'

'What choice do I have?'

Nordmann considered this, then nodded. 'Sit down,' he said. 'I'll fix a syringe.'

He quickly filled a syringe with two solutions, one pale yellow, the other clear.

Graves sat and watched him. 'How do I take it?'

'Intravenously.'

'You mean, in the vein?'

'Yes.'

'I can't possibly shoot into my veins.'

'You can,' Nordmann said, 'if I tape on an IV line. Roll up your sleeve.'

Graves rolled up his sleeve, and Nordmann tied a rubber tourniquet around his arm. He slapped the veins to make them stand out. Then he turned back to the syringe. 'I hope I've got this mixture right,' he said. He tapped the bubbles of air out of the syringe.

'So do I,' Graves said.

Nordmann attached the syringe to a piece of flexible plastic tubing. At the end of the tubing was a needle. 'I'll put the needle into your vein,' he said, 'and tape the syringe to your arm. Just before you enter the room, you can inject the contents.'

Graves felt the coldness of alcohol on his forearm, and then the prick of the needle.

'Don't move,' Nordmann said. 'Let me tape it down.' He removed the tourniquet, applied the tape, and stepped back. 'Done.'

Graves looked at the equipment taped to his arm. 'You sure this will work?'

'I told you the odds,' Nordmann said.

Graves stood up. 'Okay,' he said. 'Time?'

'Four thirty-nine.'

'Let's go,' he said, and ran for the elevator.

They came to the street and ran outside. By his side Nordmann was puffing, red in the face. Graves felt no strain at all; he was tense and full of energy. 'Rope,' he shouted to a cop. 'We need rope.'

The cop went off to get some.

'Hurry!'

The cop hurried.

Graves looked at Nordmann. 'Listen,' he said. 'I just had a thought. The gas leaked out of the nineteenth floor and killed those two cops. Right?'

'Right.'

'What's to prevent us from getting knocked off in the elevator as we go up to the twentieth floor?'

'Nothing,' Nordmann said. 'It's a risk we have to take. If enough gas has leaked back into the building, we may die on our way up.'

'Is that all you have to say?'

Nordmann shrugged. 'That's the situation.'

Two burly cops came over. One had a coil of white nylon rope over his shoulder. 'Come with us,' Graves said. And he ran with Nordmann into the apartment building.

The elevator creaked up slowly. Graves fidgeted. Nordmann seemed very calm. The two cops looked at each other, obviously not understanding what was going on. They stared suspiciously at the syringe taped to Graves' arm.

They passed the tenth floor.

'Listen,' Graves said. 'I had another thought. ZV is an oil, right?'

'Yes.'

'Well, when I get into that room, all the surfaces will be coated with oil. And deadly. Right?'

'Probably not,' Nordmann said. 'It takes time for the droplets to settle. If the room is cleared of gas fast enough, the surfaces should be safe.'

'You sure?'

'I'm not sure about anything.'

They passed the fifteenth floor. Graves resisted the impulse to hold his breath. He looked at Nordmann. Nordmann crossed his fingers.

Seventeenth floor. Eighteenth floor. Nineteenth floor. Graves waited for the gas to hit him, but nothing happened. They came to the twentieth, and the doors opened.

'We made it,' he said.

'So far,' Nordmann said.

They hurried down the corridor.

'Time?'

'Four forty-two,' one of the cops said.

They came to Apartment 2011, the one directly above Wright's. The building had been evacuated and the door was locked. The two policemen threw themselves at the door. It didn't move. They tried again without success.

Nordmann went hurrying down the hallway and returned with a fire axe. He swung once at the door. The axe barely bit into the wood.

'Let me do that,' one of the cops said, and swung hard near the lock.

'Knock it down, knock it down,' Graves said.

It took time. There was no easy crash and splintering; the wood was new and strong and thick. Finally the cop managed to bash a hole large enough to admit his hand. He reached in and turned the lock. The door swung open, and they came into an apartment that was all chintz and doilies and heavy furniture.

Graves went directly to the window and flung it open. He looked out and down, feeling the hot, gusty August wind. He was sweating hard.

One of the cops tied the nylon rope around his waist.

'Tell me what I do,' Graves said to Nordmann, and pointed to the syringe.

'Okay,' Nordmann said. 'You press that syringe to give yourself an injection of the antidote. You can push the plunger this far –' he touched the side of the syringe '– and be safe. More than that, and you will suffer effects similar to the gas itself. Clear?'

'Christ,' Graves said.

The cop cinched the rope tight around his waist.

'Remember,' Nordmann said, 'that you're counteracting the effects of the gas and you must pay out antidote in relation to your exposure to the toxin. Clear?'

'What happens if I undershoot?'

'That's worse than overshooting. It's better to give yourself too much than too little. But not too much too much.'

'When do I begin to inject?'

'Just before your exposure to the gas. If you're exposed before injecting, you'll have only five or ten seconds of clear consciousness. So do it before.'

'Four forty-five,' one of the cops said.

Graves swung one leg over the window ledge.

'You afraid of heights?' Nordmann asked.

'Terrified,' Graves said.

'Good luck,' Nordmann said as Graves crawled completely over the sill and hung there for a moment with his hands.

'We've got you,' one of the cops said.

Graves let go and began his descent down the face of the building.

He tried to balance himself against the stone wall. It was remarkable how dirty the outside of an apartment building could be. His fingers scraped over a crust of dirt and grime and pigeon droppings. He tried not to look down, but once he lost his balance and twisted upside-down, so that he was descending head first. He stared straight at the ground.

The people were minute below him. He was vaguely aware of the hot wind whistling in his ears; it was the only sound he heard. He seemed completely isolated, completely alone. He reached for the stones of the apartment wall with tense fingers. He slowly pulled himself around until he was upright again.

His descent continued more slowly. He checked his watch. It was 4:47. Plenty of time, plenty of time . . . .

He was now just above Wright's window. He could see the interior of the apartment clearly – the two tanks, yellow and black, the connecting hoses, the equipment, the snaking cables and electrical lines.

'Okay,' Nordmann shouted. 'Inject yourself!'

Graves hung dangling and twisting on the rope, nineteen floors above the street, and tried to grab his own forearm. He was clumsy; his breath came in hissing gasps; the rope was tight around his ribs. Finally he got the syringe and pushed the plunger partway down.

'Go!' Nordmann shouted.

Graves kicked away from the wall, swinging out into space, and came back with his legs stiffly extended. The glass smashed under his feet, and he was swung smoothly, almost easily, into the apartment.

He dropped to the floor, coughed, and got to his feet. Immediately the acrid piercing sting of the gas invaded his nostrils and brought tears to his eyes. He felt light-headed. *The antidote isn't working,* he thought, and fell to his knees. He was gasping for breath. He looked up at the equipment, the tanks above him.

He was very dizzy. He injected more antidote. And then suddenly he was all right. His mouth was dry and he was still light-headed, but he was all right. He got to his feet and moved towards the tanks. At every moment he expected to hear the ominous hiss and sizzle of the releasing gas, but it never came. He stood in the centre of the room, with the wires and cords all across the floor at his feet and the white gas drifting gently out the broken window.

He disengaged the first valve mechanism, unhooking the solenoid trip wire. Then the other mechanism. And then he sighed.

It was done.

The mechanism could not release the gas; the tanks were isolated. He relaxed, blinked his aching eyes, swallowed dryly, and checked his watch. 4:49. It hadn't even been close.

'Graves!'

That was Nordmann, shouting to him from the floor above. Graves went to the window and looked up.

'You all right?'

Graves tried to talk, but a hoarse, dry croak came out. He nodded and waved instead.

'Can't talk?'

Graves shook his head.

'That's the effect of the antidote,' Nordmann said. 'You'll be okay. We want to come down. Can you open that door for us?'

Graves nodded.

'Okay. We'll come down.'

Graves opened all the other windows in the apartment, then went back to the centre of the room and crouched over the three metal boxes. One was a timer; one was a battery; the third, when he turned it over, was a hollow shell, empty inside. He stared at it and shook his head. Another diversion – but it didn't matter now.

He went to the door and looked closely at the vibration sensors. They were just rubber suction cups from a toy bow-and-arrow set, with some wires attached. Totally phoney. He sighed.

Nordmann called from the other side of the door. 'Graves? You there?'

Graves let him in. He had a glimpse of two San Diego cops sprawled on the floor in the hallway as Nordmann came into the room. 'Gas is dissipated now, but those poor bastards got it full. How do you feel?'

Graves nodded, smiled.

'Dry mouth?'

Graves nodded.

'You'll be all right. Just don't inject any more of that stuff. You uncouple the tanks?'

Graves pointed.

'Well,' Nordmann said. 'That's it, then.' He looked around the room. 'Quite an elaborate setup.'

With a *pluck!* Graves pulled one of the rubber suction 'vibration sensors' off the wall and showed it to Nordmann.

'I'll be damned,' Nordmann said. 'Phoney as a four-dollar bill. But he really kept us guessing.'

Phelps came into the room. 'What's going on here?'

'The tanks have been uncoupled,' Nordmann said. 'There's no danger any more.'

'Good work,' Phelps said. He said it to Nordmann. Graves was angry about that, but he made no gesture. There was no sense in giving Phelps the satisfaction.

Phelps left. Somebody brought Graves a glass of water. Graves sipped it and wandered around the room, looking at the equipment, touching it idly.

'Well, anyway,' Nordmann said. 'Congratulations.'

Graves shrugged.

'You're not accepting congratulations?'

Graves finished the water, tried his voice. 'I'm not sure they're in order yet.'

'Why? Surely it's clear –'

'The double whammy,' Graves said. 'Wright is a master of it.'

'That may be,' Nordmann said, 'but –'

'Then where's the second punch?' Graves said. He continued to wander around the room. When he came to the scintillation counter, he clicked it on. The machine chattered loudly like an angry insect.

'Damn,' Nordmann said. 'Everybody out!'

Graves laughed and shook his head. Everybody left the room quickly. Phelps was outside in the corridor, talking with policemen who were removing the two dead bodies. 'What is it now?' Phelps asked.

'A second punch,' Nordmann said. 'Radiation in that room.'

Phelps smiled in total triumph. 'We're prepared for that,' he said. He picked up a walkie-talkie. 'We have a radiation hazard on the nineteenth floor,' he said. 'Get the shielding up here.'

Graves and Nordmann exchanged glances.

'Oh,' Phelps said, 'I'm not a complete fool.'

'Nobody ever suggested you were a *complete* fool,' Nordmann said.

It took two minutes for the policeman to arrive. He entered the room with the lead cases, which were carried on small, rolling dollies. He also had a pair of long tongs. He emerged a moment later. 'All clear,' he said. 'Two bars of some isotope. Shielded now.'

Phelps smiled. 'As soon as we heard about the explosive,' he said, 'I checked truck hijackings. There were two today: one for the explosive and another for the isotope.'

'Good work,' Graves said. He said it to Nordmann.

Phelps looked pained.

Graves and Nordmann went back into the room. Nordmann said, 'Satisfied now?'

'Almost.'

Nordmann laughed. 'You're a hard man to satisfy.'

'It's not me,' Graves said. 'It's *him.*'

Nordmann looked around the room. 'Well,' he said, 'I don't know what you expect to find here . . .'

'Neither do I.'

'You seem so certain.'

'I'm not certain. I'm just worried.'

Nordmann raised an eyebrow. 'A *triple* whammy?'

'Maybe.'

'I think you're giving him too much credit.'

'Maybe.'

Graves continued to prowl around the room.

'Well,' Nordmann said, 'in the meantime I think we'd better move these tanks apart. Just in case. I'll be happier when they're separated by a distance of several miles.'

'Okay,' Graves said. He was hardly paying attention, looking at the equipment in the room. 'You know,' he said, 'I can't get over the feeling that it's been too simple.'

'Too simple? It's been complicated as hell.' Nordmann put his arm over Graves' shoulder. 'I think you're tired,' he said gently.

Across the room Lewis said, 'It's five o'clock, gentlemen.' Everyone, including the cops, laughed. One or two of the men in the room clapped.

On the floor the timer wheel clicked once. There was a loud metallic snap.

The battery light blinked on.

The twin solenoids clicked to the 'open' position.

And nothing happened, because the solenoids had been disengaged from the tanks.

'Well,' Nordmann said, 'I can't imagine that there's anything else.'

'I guess not,' Graves said.

He and Nordmann left the apartment and walked down the corridor towards the elevators.

HOUR O
SAN DIEGO:
5 PM PDT

At 5:02 Graves pressed the button for the elevator. The light didn't go on. He looked up at the floor numbers, one of which should have been lighted; they were all dark.

'That's funny,' he said.

Nordmann frowned. 'Maybe they went on the blink.'

'Why?' Graves asked.

'Maybe when we cut the power to the apartment –'

'But they worked before.'

'Yes, that's true. They did.'

'Why should they break down now?'

At that moment a cop came up the stairs, panting heavily. 'Damned elevators are broken down,' he said. 'We checked the circuit breakers in the basement. There was a timer wired in to knock out the elevators exactly at five.'

'At five?' Graves asked. He looked at Nordmann.

Nordmann shrugged. 'Probably just a little irritant he threw in.'

'An irritant? But that doesn't make sense.'

'It's plenty irritating to me,' Nordmann said. 'I don't want to walk down nineteen flights of stairs.'

'Of course,' Graves said. 'But why do it now?'

'I don't get you.'

'Well, if Wright wanted to make things difficult, he would have knocked out the elevators at four PM. And that would have made things very difficult for us. It might even have delayed us until the gas went off.'

'True.'

'But why wait until five? By then we've either beaten his system or we haven't.'

'Listen,' Nordmann said, 'I think you're tired. You've been worrying about Wright for so long –'

'I am not tired,' Graves said, shaking off Nordmann's arm. 'Wright was a logical man, and there is logic in this move.'

'There are no more moves,' Nordmann said. 'We've won.'

'Yes,' Graves said. 'That's exactly what we're supposed to think.'

And he turned and walked back to the apartment.

'John,' Nordmann said, running to catch up with him. 'John, listen –'

'You listen,' Graves said. 'What's the point of knocking out the elevators after five?'

'It has no point. It's a foolish irritation.'

'Wrong,' Graves said. 'It has one important point. It traps everybody on the nineteenth floor. And it traps the tanks as well.'

'That's true,' Nordmann said. 'But it hardly matters. We've disarmed the mechanism.'

'Have we?'

'Oh, for Christ's sake, of course we have. You did it yourself. You know it's disarmed.'

'But what if it's not?'

'How can it not be?'

At that, Graves sighed. 'I don't know,' he admitted. He reentered the apartment.

HE OFTEN FEELS THAT A PROBLEM IS SOLVED WHEN IT IS ONLY HALF FINISHED, OR TWO-THIRDS FINISHED.

Graves remembered the psychological report as he paced the apartment, talking out loud. Nordmann watched him and listened. In the background, cops were disassembling the tank mechanisms.

'All right,' Graves said. 'Let's think it through. Wright designed a mechanism.'

'Yes.'

'And the mechanism had a purpose.'

'Yes, to dump nerve gas over the city at five PM.'

Graves nodded. 'And we have thwarted that.'

'Yes,' Nordmann said.

'Did he have any other purpose?'

'Well, I don't know. You could answer that better than anyone. Somebody mentioned something about disagreeing with the President over China –'

'No, no,' Graves said. 'Let's forget about motivation. Let's consider only the intent of his system. Did he intend to do anything besides dump the nerve gas?'

'Raise hell, create panic . . .' Nordmann shrugged.

Graves was silent, frowning at the room. 'I mean,' he said, 'did Wright intend his elaborate mechanism to do anything besides dump the gas?'

'No,' Nordmann said.

'I agree,' Graves said.

There was a long pause. Graves considered everything he knew, from every angle. He could make no sense of it, but he somehow felt certain that pieces were missing. Vital pieces . . .

'He knew about you,' Graves said suddenly.

'What?'

'He knew about you. He knew that I had called you in.'

'So what?'

'Why should he care?'

'He didn't care.'

Graves began to see. It was coming into focus. 'Because,' he said, 'Wright knew about you. He knew your position, and he knew your expertise. He must have known that you could provide an antidote to the binary gas.

'If he knew you could provide an antidote, then he also knew his protection – filling this room with gas – would not work. We'd break in. He knew that.'

'Are you sure?'

'Yes, I'm sure. And he didn't care.'

'Perhaps he was bluffing,' Nordmann said.

'It's too important for a bluff. He must have had another part of his system to cover that eventuality. He must have planned it so that if we did break in, he'd still manage to win.'

Nordmann considered it all very carefully. At length he sighed and shook his head. 'I'm sorry, John,' he said, 'I think you're entirely wrong about this. You're making hypothetical sand castles in the air –'

'No!' Graves snapped his fingers. 'No, I'm not. Because there was a second purpose to his system.'

'What second purpose?'

'Wright was going to Jamaica, or *somewhere*, correct?'

'Correct.'

'And he was not suicidal, correct?'

'Correct. He expected to get there.'

'All right. Then that establishes the need for a second purpose. His mechanism had to do *two* things.'

'What two things?'

'Look,' Graves said. He spoke as rapidly as he could, but he was hardly able to keep pace with his racing mind. 'Wright planned all this and planned it carefully. If he succeeded, a million people would die, including the President. A major political party would be wiped out.

There would be national panic of incredible proportions. And for some reason, he wanted that.'

'He was insane, yes . . .'

'But not suicidal. He planned an escape. And the question is, what about afterwards?'

'Afterwards?'

'Sure. Wright is on some beach sunning himself and gloating as he reads the headlines. But for how long?'

'Damn,' Nordmann said, nodding.

Phelps was also listening. 'I don't follow you,' he said.

'You never do,' Graves snapped. 'But the point is this. Sooner or later, Navy men in protective suits would enter San Diego. They would determine that people died of nerve gas. They would search for the source. They would find this apartment. They would enter it. They would find the tanks. They would put the pieces together.'

'And they would come after Wright,' Nordmann said.

'Exactly,' Graves said.

'Wherever he went, he wouldn't be safe. He would be a mass murderer and he would have left a very clear trail behind him.' He gestured at all the equipment. 'Would he really leave such a clear trail for others to follow?'

'It must be true,' Nordmann said, getting excited. 'He had to have two purposes – first to discharge the gas, and second to obliterate the evidence.'

'Obliterate the evidence *how*?' Phelps asked.

Graves leaned on a tank. He turned to Nordmann. 'How long would it take this cylinder of gas to discharge?'

Nordmann shrugged. 'Ten or fifteen minutes.' Then he said, 'I see. You want to know exactly.'

'Yes,' Graves said.

'Why exactly?' Phelps asked.

Graves ignored him.

Nordmann said, 'Normal Army pressure tanks are usually stabilized at five hundred pounds per square inch. So these tanks . . . Anybody got a tape measure?' He looked around the room. One of the cops had a tape. Nordmann measured the tank. 'Thirty-seven inches in circumference,' he said. 'Eight feet long, that's ninety-six inches, with a radius of . . .' He wrote on a small pad, doing rapid calculations.

Phelps said to Graves, 'Why do you need it exactly?'

'Because,' Graves said, 'Wright didn't care if we broke into this room.

He had another contingency plan to cover that. And we need to know when it will take effect.'

Phelps looked totally confused.

'A radius of six inches,' Nordmann was saying. 'And a length of ninety-six inches gives a volume . . . well, figure for a cylinder . . . at five hundred psi . . . let me check the nozzles . . .'

He wandered off. Graves said to a cop, 'What time is it?'

'Five oh seven, Mr Graves.'

Nordmann finished his calculations and turned to Graves. 'At normal discharge rates, it would take these tanks sixteen minutes to empty.'

'That's it, then,' Graves said. 'At five sixteen, a bomb will go off in this room, destroying everything. We've got to find it.'

Everyone paused. They stared at him.

Phelps said, 'A bomb?'

'Of course. That's why he knocked out the elevators – to trap us here. In case we managed to disengage the mechanism, he wanted us here when the bomb went off, releasing the gas and eliminating the evidence.'

Phelps said, 'But there's no evidence of a bomb –'

'Remember the sniffer?' Nordmann asked.

Phelps frowned.

'The sniffer,' Graves said, 'picked up oxides of nitrogen. Plastic explosive.'

'Yes . . .'

'Okay,' Graves said. 'Where is that explosive now?'

Phelps looked around the room. 'I don't see it anywhere,' he said.

'But the sniffer detected it.'

'Yes . . .'

'There must be a bomb,' Graves said. 'And it must be in plain sight.'

'Five oh eight,' a cop said.

'We better get these tanks out,' Nordmann said. 'We don't want them damaged by the bomb.'

'Right,' Graves said. 'And let's get the sniffer in here. It'll help us find it.'

The sniffer had been taken to the other building. Phelps turned on the walkie-talkie and talked to Lewis. Lewis said he would bring it as soon as he could, but it would take time to climb nineteen flights. Phelps told him to hurry and added a string of expletives.

Meanwhile Nordmann supervised the removal of the tanks to the hallway. The cops carried them, four men to a cylinder, grunting under the weight. Graves searched the room – scanning the wall surfaces, the door, the window ledges for any irregularity, any discontinuity that would suggest the location of explosive. Plastic explosive, Compound C, could be shaped and moulded into a variety of forms. That was its advantage.

It could be anywhere.

Nordmann stuck his head into the room. 'Maybe you should get out of here,' he said. 'We can let the room blow if the tanks are far enough away. No sense in risking anything.'

'I'll stay until we find it,' Graves said. He walked to the window and looked out. He saw Lewis running across the street with the sniffer on his shoulder.

'Five ten,' Phelps said.

It would take Lewis at least two minutes to scramble up all those stairs. Graves stared out the window, wondering what was happening to Wright. Had they managed to cut his body out of the wrecked car yet?

Odd, he thought, how the game continues.

'Lewis is coming,' Phelps said.

'I saw.'

'How much explosive is supposed to be in this room?'

'Twenty pounds.'

'Christ.'

Graves continued to stare out the window. Where would Wright hide twenty pounds of explosive? What would be the supremely logical hiding place? Nothing less would satisfy Wright, he was sure of that.

He shifted his position at the window, careful to avoid the jagged splinters of glass around the sill. As he did so, he looked down at his shirt. There was printing on the shirt; some of the lettering from the tanks had come off on his arms and chest when he had leaned on them.

' **IMƎHƆ** ,' it said, and then faintly, ' **TOИ OD** .'

He looked at his watch. 5:12.

'Where the hell is Lewis?'

Lewis appeared, running down the corridor red-faced and out of breath. 'Sorry,' he said. 'Came as fast as I could.' He turned on his sniffer and walked around the room, pointing the gunlike wand, staring at the dial on the shoulder unit.

Graves and Nordmann watched him.

Lewis began with the door, then turned to the walls. He checked carefully from baseboard to ceiling. In a slow, methodical way he went entirely around the room. Finally he stopped.

5:13.

'You get a reading?'

'No,' Lewis said, checking the machine. 'Nothing.'

'Maybe it's in another room,' Nordmann said.

'I doubt it,' Graves said.

'Let's check it,' Lewis said. He disappeared into the bathroom, worked through it and through the adjoining bedroom of the apartment. He came back a moment later. 'Maybe the machine's broken.'

'How can we test it?'

'Give it a smell of some kind.'

'Like what?'

'Anything strong. Cologne, perfume, food . . .'

Graves went to the refrigerator, but it was empty. When he came back he saw Nordmann strike a match, blow it out, and hold the smoking tip in front of the sniffer wand.

'Off the dial,' Lewis said. 'It works all right. Reading sulphur and carbon, minor phosphorous. It works.'

'Then why isn't it picking up explosive in this room?'

Graves sighed. 'Maybe I was wrong,' he said. 'Maybe there isn't any explosive. Maybe it's over, after all.'

'There's certainly nothing in here,' Lewis said.

One of the cops came in to Nordmann. 'We're going to carry the tanks down the stairs now,' he said. 'We –'

'Take them one at a time,' Nordmann said. 'I want those tanks well separated from now on.'

'Okay,' the cop said and went back to the hallway.

Graves stared at Lewis. 'Look,' he said, 'there was a lot of information Wright gave us that hasn't paid off. The washing machine, the spray paint . . .'

As he spoke he wandered restlessly around the apartment, from the living-room into the empty bedroom, then into the bathroom. He looked at himself in the bathroom mirror.

'We'll probably never know,' Lewis said. 'Maybe they were all false clues designed to throw us.'

'And those plastic tanks,' Graves said. 'We've completely forgotten the fact that –'

He stopped. He stared at himself in the mirror. The lettering from the tanks that had come off on his shirt was clear now. It was reversed in the mirror.

DO NOT

CHEMI

'My God,' he said. 'Of course!' He went running back into the living-room.

'What is it?' Nordmann said.

'What? What?'

'The tanks!' Graves said, going out to the hallway. The first tank was already being carried down the stairs. The second still lay on the hallway floor. It was the black tank, with yellow and white stencilling.

5:15.

Graves bent over the tank and rubbed the lettering. It streaked on his finger.

'Go to the window,' Graves said to a cop. 'Use the bullhorn and clear the street below. Do you understand? Get everybody the hell away from the street.'

The cop looked confused.

'Go!'

The cop ran.

Graves pushed at the surface of the tank in front of him. His finger left a minute indentation. 'That's where your plastic explosive is,' he said. 'It's wrapped around the tanks in thin strips – strips pressed through the rollers of an old washing machine. There must be a timer . . .'

He ran his fingers quickly along the surface, feeling for lumps and irregularities. He couldn't find it, but he was in a hurry.

'Christ,' Lewis said, pointing his sniffer. 'This is it. Plastic explosive.'

'The timer, the timer . . .'

'It's after five fifteen,' Nordmann said.

'Get those cops in the stairway away from that tank,' Graves said. 'Tell them to drop it and run.'

His fingers raced along the surface, back and forth. But it was eight feet of tank – too much surface to cover easily. It was probably a small timer, too. Perhaps miniaturized, perhaps the size of a thumbnail.

'Damn!'

'I get it,' Lewis said. 'That was why he wanted inflammable plastic for the tanks. It'll explode and burn without leaving a –'

'Coming up on five sixteen,' Nordmann said, looking at his watch.

Where was the timer?

'I can't find it,' Graves said. 'Come on.' He picked up the tank by the nozzle and began dragging it back into the apartment. 'Help me,' he said.

There were three of them, but the 500-pound tank was bulky. As they entered the apartment, the cop at the window was on the bullhorn saying, 'Clear the area, clear the area.'

Graves had a quick glimpse out the window and saw that people were running. He helped lift the tank up to the sill.

'Listen,' Nordmann said, 'are you sure you should –'

'No choice,' Graves said. 'We've got to get the tanks separated.'

'Five sixteen,' somebody said.

They pushed the tank out the window.

The huge cylinder fell slowly, almost lazily, but picked up speed as it went. It was halfway to the street when it exploded in a violent ball of red and black flame. Graves and Nordmann, who had been looking out the window, were knocked back inside.

A moment later there was a second explosion inside the building. The walls shook. The men looked at each other. Everyone was pale.

'Jesus,' Nordmann said.

'I knew it,' Graves said. 'We had to get that separation.'

Even so, he was thinking, there might be some mixture of the gases. And just a few droplets could kill . . .

'We better get everybody out of here,' he said. They walked back towards the stairwell. Acrid stinging smoke billowed up towards them. Graves said, 'Did the cops carrying that thing get away?'

Nobody seemed to know.

The smoke coming from the stairs was so harsh that they were unable to descend. They returned to the apartment and to the windows looking down on the street. A heavy cloud of grey smoke was clearing. On the pavement there were globs of burning plastic, and smoke rising. In the distance they heard the sound of sirens and fire trucks.

Graves reached in his pocket for a cigarette, brought one out, and dropped it from his shaking hand. He took out another and lit it. He went to the window and looked down at the street. The fire trucks were coming. He watched them turn the corner and move past the police barricades.

Directly beneath him the pieces of molten plastic continued to burn on the pavement.

He turned to Nordmann. 'Is he dead?'

'Who?'

'Wright.'

'Yes,' Nordmann said quietly. 'He's dead.'

Graves watched as the fire trucks pulled up and sprayed the burning plastic with long hoses. The water formed reflecting puddles, gleaming red from the firelight and the San Diego sunset. He watched the harsh, streaming water for another moment, and then turned away from the window.

'Let's go down,' Nordmann said.

'Yes,' Graves said. 'Let's.

EPILOGUE
BETA SCENARIO REVISIONS

By a complicated mechanism, John Wright, an ordinary American citizen, arranged to disperse one half-ton of ZV nerve gas over the city of San Diego at 5 PM August 23rd, 1972. This event was to coincide with the political events occurring in that city at that time.

The plan was halted by intervention of the Defence Department, with some minor assistance by State Department personnel, particularly Mr R. Phelps.

The Department of Defence is to be congratulated on its successful efforts in this matter.

Three weeks later, the Secretary of Defence ordered a contingency study based upon reevaluation of RAND Scenario Beta (theft of CBW or nuclear components).

The contingency study advised the following:

1. *Destruction of all unnecessary chemical stockpiles.* This includes all chemical agents stored aboveground (as in Rocky Mountain Arsenal, etc). This includes all chemical agents combined with outmoded delivery systems (as in 12,000 Bolt rockets evacuated to ocean in 1969). This includes all redundant chemical agents (as in all gas GB stockpiles, now outmoded by VX, ZV).

2. *Severe limitation of transport of chemical agents.* This includes all chemical agents, in whatever quantities. The necessity for any transportation must be verified by direct order from the Secretary of Defence himself.

3. *Severe restriction of total stockpiling locations.* Chemical agents are now stored in twenty-two locations in the continental United States. The contingency study concluded that there was no rationale for maintaining more than four (± one) stockpile locations.

4. *Severe regulations governing transport of chemicals.* No quantity of chemical agent, however small, should travel with less than two platoons (eighty men) who are trained to deal with subversive attempts and also with accidents during shipment.

5. *Severe regulations governing data bank access.* Classified information should be unavailable over any temporary line system. No multidrop lines should be utilized. Codings should be changed no less than every forty-eight hours. Permutations on each code should be no fewer than 2^5.

The report of the Beta Scenario contingency study was evaluated by the Secretary of Defence and the Joint Chiefs of Staff on November 10th, 1972. The evaluation committee consisted of R. Gottlieb (RAND); K. Villadsen (Defence Systems Review); P. Lazarus (Defence C/C); L. M. Rich (State); A. Epstein (JCS); R. Dozier (Advanced Research PL); R. Phelps (State Intelligence). It was the unanimous conclusion of those present at the meeting that none of the recommendations needed to be acted upon at that time. A review committee was suggested for further evaluation of the report. Members of the review committee will be appointed in the near future.

In the meantime, present regulations and operating methods remain in effect.